THE
TIME
PATROL

THE TIME PATROL

Poul Anderson

A Tom Doherty Associates Book
New York

This is a work of fiction. All the characters and events portrayed in this book are fictitious, and any resemblance to real people or events is purely coincidental.

THE TIME PATROL

Copyright © 1991 by Poul Anderson.
"The Year of the Ransom" Copyright © 1988 by Byron Preiss Visual Publications; Copyright © 1988 by Poul Anderson.

Reprinted by arrangement with Walker and Company.

A Tor Book
Published by Tom Doherty Associates, Inc.
49 West 24th Street
New York, N.Y. 10010

Library of Congress Cataloging-in-Publication Data

Anderson, Poul.
      The time patrol / Poul Anderson.
           p.   cm.
     ISBN 0-312-85231-2
     I. Title.
    PS3551.N378T6 1991
    813'.54—dc20   91-21597
                                       CIP

First edition: October 1991

Printed in the United States of America

0 9 8 7 6 5 4 3 2 1

CONTENTS

Time Patrol

1

"THE work is, you understand, somewhat unusual," said Mr. Gordon. "And confidential. I trust you can keep a secret?"

"Normally," said Manse Everard. "Depends on what the secret is, of course."

Mr. Gordon smiled. It was a curious smile, a closed curve of his lips which was not quite like any Everard had seen before. He spoke easy colloquial General American, and wore an undistinguished business suit, but there was a foreignness over him which was more than dark complexion, beardless cheeks, and the incongruity of Mongolian eyes above a thin Caucasian nose. It was hard to place.

"We're not spies, if that's what you're thinking," he said.

Everard grinned. "Sorry. Please don't think I've gone as hysterical as the rest of the country. I've never had access to confidential data anyway. But your ad mentioned overseas operations, and the way things are—I'd like to keep my passport, you understand."

He was a big man, with blocky shoulders and a slightly battered face under crew-cut brown hair. His papers lay before him: Army discharge, the record of work in several places as a mechanical engineer. Mr. Gordon had seemed barely to glance at them.

The office was ordinary, a desk and a couple of chairs, a filing cabinet, and a door leading off in the rear. A window opened on the banging traffic of New York, six stories down.

"Independent spirit," said the man behind the desk. "I like that. So many of them come cringing in, as if they'd be grateful for a kick. Of course, with your background you aren't desperate yet. You can still get work, even in . . . ah, I believe the current term is a rolling readjustment."

"I was interested," said Everard. "I've worked abroad, as you can see, and would like to travel again. But frankly, I still don't have the faintest idea what your outfit does."

"We do a good many things," said Mr. Gordon. "Let me see . . . you've been in combat. France and Germany." Everard blinked; his papers had included a record of medals, but he'd have sworn the man hadn't had time to read them. "Um . . . would you mind grasping those knobs on the arms of your chair? Thank you. Now, how do you react to physical danger?"

Everard bristled. "Look here—"

Mr. Gordon's eyes flicked to an instrument on his desk: it was merely a box with an indicator needle and a couple of dials. "Never mind. What are your views on internationalism?"

"Say, now—"

"Communism? Fascism? Women? Your personal ambitions? . . . That's all. You don't have to answer."

"What the devil is this, anyway?" snapped Everard.

"A bit of psychological testing. Forget it. I've no interest in your opinions except as they reflect basic emotional orientation." Mr. Gordon leaned back, making a bridge of his fingers. "Very promising so far. Now, here's the set up. We're doing work which is, as I've told you, highly confidential. We . . . ah . . . we're planning to spring a surprise on our competitors." He chuckled. "Go ahead and report me to the FBI if you wish. We've already been investigated and have a clean bill of health. You'll find that we really do carry on worldwide financial and engineering operations. But there's another aspect of the job, and that's the one we want men for. I'll pay you one hundred dollars to go in the back room and take a set of tests. It'll last about three hours. If you don't pass, that's the end of it. If you do, we'll sign you on, tell you the facts, and start you training. Are you game?"

Everard hesitated. He had a feeling of being rushed. There was more to this enterprise than an office and one bland stranger. Still. . . .

Decision. "I'll sign on *after* you've told me what it's all about."

"As you wish," shrugged Mr. Gordon. "Suit yourself. The tests will say whether you're going to or not, you know. We use some very advanced techniques."

That, at least, was entirely true. Everard knew a little something about modern psychology: encephalographs, association tests, the Minnesota profile. He did not recognize any of the hooded machines that hummed and blinked around him. The questions which the assistant—a white-skinned, completely hairless man of indeterminate age, with a heavy accent and no facial expression—fired at him seemed irrelevant to anything. And what was the metal cap he was supposed to wear on his head? Into what did the wires from it lead?

He stole glances at the meter faces, but the letters and numerals were like nothing he had seen before. Not English, French, Russian, Greek, Chinese, anything belonging to A.D. 1954. Perhaps he was already beginning to realize the truth, even then.

A curious self-knowledge grew in him as the tests proceeded. Manson Emmert Everard, age thirty, onetime lieutenant in the U.S. Army Engineers; design and production experience in America, Sweden, Arabia; still a bachelor, though with increasingly wistful thoughts about his married friends; no current girl, no close ties of any kind; a bit of a bibliophile; a dogged poker player; fondness for sailboats and horses and rifles; a camper and fisherman on his vacations. He had known it all, of course, but only as isolated shards of fact. It was peculiar, this sudden sensing of himself as an integrated organism, this realization that each characteristic was a single inevitable facet of an overall pattern.

He came out exhausted and wringing wet. Mr. Gordon offered him a cigarette and swept eyes rapidly over a series of coded sheets which the assistant gave him. Now and then he muttered a phrase: ". . . Zeth-20 cortical . . . undifferentiated evaluation here . . . psychic reaction to antitoxin . . . weakness in central coordination. . . ." He had slipped into an accent, a lilt and a treatment of vowels which were like nothing Everard had heard in a long experience of the ways in which the English language can be mangled.

It was half an hour before he looked up again. Everard was getting restless, a faint anger stirring at this cavalier treatment, but interest kept him sitting quietly. Mr. Gordon flashed improbably white teeth in a broad, satisfied grin. "Ah. At last. Do you know, I've had to reject twenty-four candidates already? But you'll do. You'll definitely do."

"Do for what?" Everard leaned forward, conscious of his pulse picking up.

"The Patrol. You're going to be a kind of policeman."

"Yeah? Where?"

"Everywhere. And everywhen. Brace yourself, this is going to be a shock.

"You see, our company, while legitimate enough, is only a front and a source of funds. Our real business is patrolling time."

2

The Academy was in the American West. It was also in the Oligocene period, a warm age of forests and grasslands when man's ratty ancestors scuttled away from the tread of giant mammals. It had been built a thousand years ago; it would be maintained for half a million—long enough to graduate as many as the Time Patrol would require—and then be carefully demolished so that no trace would remain. Later the glaciers would come, and there would be men, and in the year 19352 A.D. (the 7841st year of the Morennian Triumph), these men would find a way to travel through time and return to the Oligocene to establish the Academy.

It was a complex of long, low buildings, smooth curves and shifting colors, spreading over a greensward between enormous ancient trees. Beyond it, hills and woods rolled off to a great brown river, and at night you could sometimes hear the bellowing of titanotheres or the distant squall of a sabertooth.

Everard stepped out of the time shuttle—a big, featureless metal box—with a dryness in his throat. It felt like his first day in the Army, twelve years ago—or fifteen to twenty million years in the future, if you preferred—lonely and helpless, and wishing desperately for some honorable way to go home. It was a small comfort to see the other shuttles, discharging a total of fifty-odd young men and women. The recruits moved slowly together, forming an awkward clump. They didn't speak at first, but stood staring at each other. Everard recognized a Hoover collar and a bowler; the styles of dress and hairdo moved up through 1954 and on. Where was she from, the girl with the iridescent, close-fitting culottes and the green lipstick and the fantastically waved yellow hair? No . . . when?

A man of about twenty-five happened to stand beside him: obviously British, from the threadbare tweeds and the long, thin face. He seemed to be hiding a truculent bitterness under his mannered exterior. "Hello," said Everard. "Might as well get acquainted." He gave his name and origin.

"Charles Whitcomb, London, 1947," said the other shyly. "I was just demobbed—R.A.F.—and this looked like a good chance. Now I wonder."

"It may be," said Everard, thinking of the salary. Fifteen thousand a year to start with! How did they figure years, though? Must be in terms of one's actual duration-sense.

A man strolled in their direction. He was a slender young fellow in a skin-tight gray uniform with a deep-blue cloak which seemed to twinkle, as if it had stars sewn in. His face was pleasant, smiling, and he spoke genially with a neutral accent: "Hello, there! Welcome to the Academy. I take it you all know English?" Everard noticed a man in the shabby remnants of a German uniform, and a Hindu, and others who were probably from several foreign countries.

"We'll use English, then, till you've all learned Temporal." The man lounged easily, hands on his hips. "My name is Dard Kelm. I was born in—let me see—9573 Christian reckoning, but I've made a specialty of your period. Which, by the way, extends from 1850 to 2000, though you're all from some in-between years. I'm your official wailing wall, if something goes wrong.

"This place is run along different lines from what you've probably been expecting. We don't turn out men en masse, so the elaborate discipline of a classroom or an army is not required. Each of you will have individual as well as general instruction. We don't need to punish failure in studies, because the preliminary tests have guaranteed there won't be any and made the chance of failure on the job small. Each of you has a high maturity rating in terms of your particular cultures. However, the variation in aptitudes means that if we're to develop each individual to the fullest, there must be personal guidance.

"There's little formality here beyond normal courtesy. You'll have chances for recreation as well as study. We never expect more of you than you can give. I might add that the hunting and fishing are still pretty good even in this neighborhood, and if you fly just a few hundred miles they're fantastic.

"Now, if there aren't any questions, please follow me and I'll get you settled."

Dard Kelm demonstrated the gadgets in a typical room. They were the sort you would have expected by, say, A.D. 2000: unobtrusive furniture readily adjusted to a perfect fit, refresher cabinets, screens which could draw on a huge library of recorded sight and sound for entertainment. Nothing too advanced, as yet. Each cadet had his own room in the "dormitory" building; meals were in a central refectory, but arrangements could be made for private parties. Everard felt the tension easing within him.

A welcoming banquet was held. The courses were familiar but the silent machines which rolled up to serve them were not. There was wine, beer, an ample supply of tobacco. Maybe something had been slipped into the food, for Everard felt as euphoric as the others. He ended up beating out boogie on a piano while half a dozen people made the air hideous with attempts at song.

Only Charles Whitcomb held back, sipping a moody glass over in a corner by himself. Dard Kelm was tactful and did not try to force him into joining.

Everard decided he was going to like it. But the work and the organization and the purpose were still shadows.

"Time travel was discovered at a period when the Chorite Heresiarchy was breaking up," said Kelm, in the lecture hall. "You'll study the details later; for now, take my word that it was a turbulent age, when commercial and genetic rivalry was a tooth-and-claw matter between giant combines; anything went, and the various governments were pawns in a galactic game. The time effect was the by-product of a search for a means of instantaneous transportation, which some of you will realize requires infinitely discontinuous functions for its mathematical description . . . as does travel into the past. I won't go into the theory of it—you'll get some of that in the physics classes—but merely state that it involves the concept of infinite-valued relationships in a continuum of 4N dimensions, where N is the total number of particles in the universe.

"Naturally, the group which discovered this, the Nine, were aware of the possibilities. Not only commercial—trading, mining, and other enterprises you can readily imagine—but the chance of striking a deathblow at their enemies. You see, time is variable; the past can be changed—"

"Question!" It was the girl from 1972, Elizabeth Gray, who was a rising young physicist in her own period.

"Yes?" said Kelm politely.

"I think you're describing a logically impossible situation. I'll grant the possibility of time travel, seeing that we're here, but an event cannot both *have* happened and *not* happened. That's self-contradictory."

"Only if you insist on a logic which is not Aleph-sub-Aleph-valued," said Kelm "What happens is like this: suppose I went back in time and prevented your father from meeting your mother. You would never have been born. That portion of universal history would read differently; it would always have been different, though I would retain memory of the 'original' state of affairs."

"Well, how about doing the same to yourself?" asked Elizabeth. "Would you cease existing?"

"No, because I would belong to the section of history prior to my own intervention. Let's apply it to you. If you went back to, I would guess, 1946, and worked to prevent your parents' marriage in 1947, you would still have existed in that year; you would not go out of existence just because you had influenced events. The same would apply even if you had only been in 1946 one microsecond before shooting the man who would otherwise have become your father."

"But then I'd exist without—without an origin!" she protested. "I'd have life, and memories, and . . . everything . . . though *nothing* had produced them."

Kelm shrugged. "What of it? You insist that the causal law, or strictly speaking the conversation-of-energy law, involve only continuous functions. Actually, discontinuity is entirely possible."

He laughed and leaned on the lectern. "Of course, there are impossibilities," he said. "You could not be your own mother, for instance, because of sheer genetics. If you went back and married your former father, the children would be different, none of them you, because each would have only half your chromosomes."

Clearing his throat: "Let's not stray from the subject. You'll learn the details in other classes. I'm only giving you a general background. To continue: the Nine saw the possibility of going back in time and preventing their enemies from ever having gotten started, even from ever being born. But then the Danellians appeared."

For the first time, his casual, half-humorous air dropped, and he stood there as a man in the presence of the unknowable. He spoke quietly: "The Danellians are part of the future—our future, more than a million years ahead of me. Man has evolved into something . . . impossible to describe. You'll probably never meet a Danellian. If you ever should, it will be . . . rather a shock. They aren't malignant—nor benevolent—they are as far beyond anything we can know or feel as we are beyond those insectivores who are going to be our ancestors. It isn't good to meet that sort of thing face to face.

"They were simply concerned with protecting their own existence. Time travel was old when they emerged, there had been uncountable opportunities for the foolish and the greedy and the mad to go back and turn history inside out. They did not wish to forbid the travel—it was part of the complex which had led to them—but they had to regulate it. The Nine were prevented from carrying out their schemes. And the Patrol was set up to police the time lanes.

"Your work will be mostly within your own eras, unless you graduate to unattached status. You will live, on the whole, ordinary lives, family and friends as usual; the secret part of those lives will have the satisfactions of good pay, protection, occasional vacations in some very interesting places, supremely worthwhile work. But you will always be on call. Sometimes you will help time travelers who have gotten into difficulties, one way or another. Sometimes you will work on missions, the apprehension of would-be political or military or economic conquistadors. Sometimes the Patrol will accept damage as done, and work instead to set up counteracting influences in later periods which will swing history back to the desired track.

"I wish all of you luck."

The first part of instruction was physical and psychological. Everard had never realized how his own life had crippled him, in body and mind; he was only half the man he could be. It came hard, but in the end it was a joy to feel the utterly controlled power of muscles, the emotions which had grown deeper for being disciplined, the swiftness and precision of conscious thought.

Somewhere along the line he was thoroughly conditioned against revealing anything about the Patrol, even hinting at its existence, to any unauthorized person. It was simply impossible for him to do so, under any influence; as impossible as jumping to the moon. He also learned the ins and outs of his twentieth-century public *persona*.

Temporal, the artificial language with which Patrolmen from all ages could communicate without being understood by strangers, was a miracle of logically organized expressiveness.

He thought he knew something about combat, but he had to learn the tricks and the weapons of fifty thousand years, all the way from a Bronze Age rapier to a cyclic blast which could annihilate a continent. Returned to his own era, he would be given a limited arsenal, but he might be called into other periods and overt anachronism was rarely permissible.

There was the study of history, science, arts and philosophies, fine details of dialect and mannerism. These last were only for the 1850–1975 period; if he had occasion to go elsewhere he would pick up special instruction from a hypnotic conditioner. It was such machines that made it possible to complete his training in three months.

He learned the organization of the Patrol. Up "ahead" lay the mystery which was Danellian civilization, but there was little direct contact with it. The Patrol was set up in semimilitary fashion, with ranks, though without special formalities. History was divided into milieus, with a head office located in a major city for a selected twenty-year period (disguised by some ostensible activity such as commerce) and various branch offices. For his time, there were three milieus: the Western world, headquarters in London; Russia, in Moscow; Asia, in Peiping; each in the easygoing years 1890–1910, when concealment was less difficult than in later decades, when there were smaller offices such as Gordon's. An ordinary attached agent lived as usual in his own time, often with an authentic job. Communication between years was by tiny robot shuttles or by courier, with automatic shunts to keep such messages from piling up at one instant.

The entire organization was so vast that he could not really appreciate the fact. He had entered something new and exciting, that was all he truly grasped with all layers of consciousness . . . as yet.

He found his instructors friendly, ready to gab. The grizzled veteran who taught him to handle spaceships had fought in the Martian war of 3890. "You boys catch on fairly quick," he said. "It's hell, though, teaching pre-industrial people. We've quit even trying to give them more than the rudiments. Had a Roman here once—Caesar's time—fairly bright boy, too, but he never got it through his head that a machine can't be treated like a horse. As for the Babylonians, time travel just wasn't in their world-picture. We had to give them a battle-of-the-gods routine."

"What routine are you giving us?" asked Whitcomb.

The spaceman regarded him narrowly. "The truth," he said at last. "As much of it as you can take."

"How did you get into this job?"

"Oh . . . I was shot up off Jupiter. Not much left of me. They picked me up, built me a new body—since none of my people were alive, and I was presumed dead, there didn't seem much point in going back home. No fun living under the Guidance Corps. So I took this position here. Good company, easy living, and furloughs in a lot of eras." The spaceman grinned. "Wait till you've been to the decadent stage of the Third Matriarchy! You don't know what fun is."

Everard said nothing. He was too captured by the spectacle of Earth, rolling enormous against the stars.

He made friends with his fellow cadets. They were a congenial bunch—naturally, with the same type being picked for Patrollers, bold and intelligent minds. There were a couple of romances. No *Portrait of Jenny* stuff; marriage was entirely possible, with the couple picking some year in which to set up housekeeping. He himself liked the girls, but kept his head.

Oddly, it was the silent and morose Whitcomb with whom he struck up the closest friendship. There was something appealing about the Englishman; he was so cultured, such a thoroughly good fellow, and still somehow lost.

They were out riding one day, on horses whose remote ancestors scampered before their gigantic descendants. Everard had a rifle, in the hope of bagging a shovel-tusker he had seen. Both wore Academy uniform, light grays which were cool and silky under the hot yellow sun.

"I wonder we're allowed to hunt," remarked the American. "Suppose I shoot a sabertooth—in Asia, I suppose—which was originally slated to eat one of those prehuman insectivores. Won't that change the whole future?"

"No," said Whitcomb. He had progressed faster in studying the theory of time travel. "You see, it's rather as if the continuum were a mesh of tough rubber bands. It isn't easy to distort it; the tendency is always for it to snap back to its, uh, 'former' shape. One individual insectivore doesn't matter, it's the total genetic pool of their species which led to man.

"Likewise, if I killed a sheep in the Middle Ages, I wouldn't wipe out all its later descendants, maybe all the sheep there were by 1940. Rather, those would still be there, unchanged down to their very genes in spite of a different ancestry, because over so long a period of time all the sheep, or men, are descendants of *all* the earlier sheep or men. Compensation, don't you see; somewhere along the line, some other ancestor supplies the genes you thought you had eliminated.

"In the same way . . . oh, suppose I went back and prevented Booth from killing Lincoln. Unless I took very elaborate precautions, it would probably happen that someone else did the shooting and Booth got blamed anyway.

"That resilience of time is the reason travel is permitted at all. If you want to change things, you have to go about it just right and work very hard, usually."

His mouth twisted. "Indoctrination! We're told again and again that if *we* interfere, there's going to be punishment for us. I'm not allowed to go back and shoot that ruddy bastard Hitler in his cradle. I'm supposed to let him grow up as he did, and start the war, and kill my girl."

Everard rode quietly for a while. The only noise was the squeak of saddle leather and the rustle of long grass. "Oh," he said at last. "I'm sorry. Want to talk about it?"

"Yes. I do. But there isn't much. She was in the W.A.A.F.—Mary Nelson—we were going to get married after the war. She was in London in '44. November seventeenth, I'll never forget that date. The V-bombs got her. She'd gone over to a neighbor's house in Streatham—was on furlough, you see, staying with her mother. That house was blown up; her own home wasn't scratched."

Whitcomb's cheeks were bloodless. He stared emptily before him. "It's going to be jolly hard not to . . . not to go back, just a few years, and see her at the very least. Only see her again. . . . No! I don't dare."

Everard laid a hand on the man's shoulder, awkwardly, and they rode on in silence.

The class moved ahead, each at his own pace, but there was enough compensation so that all graduated together: a brief ceremony followed by a huge party and many maudlin arrangements for later reunions. Then each went back to the same year he had come from: the same hour.

Everard accepted Gordon's congratulations, got a list of contemporary agents (several of them holding jobs in places like military intelligence), and returned to his apartment. Later he might find work arranged for him in some sensitive listening post, but his present assignment—for income-tax purposes, "special consultant to Engineering Studies Co."—was only to read a dozen papers a day for the indications of time travel he had been taught to spot, and hold himself ready for a call.

As it happened, he made his own first job.

3

It was a peculiar feeling to read the headlines and know, more or less, what was coming next. It took the edge off, but added a sadness, for this was a tragic era. He could sympathize with Whitcomb's desire to go back and change history.

Only, of course, one man was too limited. He could not change it for the better, except by some freak; most likely he would bungle everything. Go back and kill Hitler and the Japanese and Soviet leaders—maybe someone shrewder would take their place. Maybe atomic energy would lie fallow, and the glorious flowering of the Venusian Renaissance never happen. The devil we know. . . .

He looked out of his window. Lights flamed against a hectic sky; the street crawled with automobiles and a hurrying, faceless crowd; he could not see the towers of Manhattan from here, but he knew they reared arrogant toward the clouds. And it was all one swirl on a river that swept from the peaceful prehuman landscape where he had been to the unimaginable Danellian future. How many billions and trillions of human creatures lived, laughed, wept, worked, hoped, and died in its currents!

Well. . . . He sighed, stoked his pipe, and turned back. A long walk had not made him less restless; his mind and body were impatient for something to do. But it was late and. . . . He went over to the bookshelf, picked out a volume more or less at random, and started to read. It was a collection of Victorian and Edwardian stories.

A passing reference struck him. Something about a tragedy at Addleton and the singular contents of an ancient British barrow. Nothing more. Hm. Time travel? He smiled to himself.

Still. . . .

No, he thought. *This is crazy.*

It wouldn't do any harm to check up, though. The incident was mentioned as occurring in the year 1894, in England. He could get out back files of the

London *Times*. Nothing else to do. . . . Probably that was why he was stuck with his dull newspaper assignment: so that his mind, grown nervous from boredom, would prowl into every conceivable corner.

He was on the steps of the public library as it opened.

The account was there, dated June 25, 1894, and several days following. Addleton was a village in Kent, distinguished chiefly by a Jacobean estate belonging to Lord Wyndham and a barrow of unknown age. The nobleman, an enthusiastic amateur archaeologist, had been excavating it, together with one James Rotherhithe, an expert from the British Museum who happened to be a relative. Lord Wyndham had uncovered a rather meager burial chamber: a few artifacts nearly rusted and rotted away, bones of men and horses. There was also a chest in surprisingly good condition, containing ingots of an unknown metal presumed to be a lead or silver alloy. He fell deathly ill, with symptoms of a peculiarly lethal poisoning; Rotherhithe, who had barely looked into the casket, was not affected, and circumstantial evidence suggested that he had slipped the nobleman a dose of some obscure Asiatic concoction. Scotland Yard arrested the man when Lord Wyndham died, on the twenty-fifth. Rotherhithe's family engaged the services of a well-known private detective, who was able to show, by most ingenious reasoning, followed by tests on animals, that the accused was innocent and that a "deadly emanation" from the chest was responsible. Box and contents had been thrown into the English Channel. Congratulations all around. Fade-out to happy ending.

Everard sat quietly in the long, hushed room. The story didn't tell enough. But it was highly suggestive, to say the least.

Then why hadn't the Victorian office of the Patrol investigated? Or had they? Probably. They wouldn't advertise their results, of course.

Still, he'd better send a memorandum.

Returning to his apartment, he took one of the little message shuttles given him, laid a report in it, and set the control studs for the London office, June 25, 1894. When he pushed the final button the box vanished with a small whoosh of air rushing in where it had been.

It returned in a few minutes. Everard opened it and took out a sheet of foolscap covered with neat typing—yes, the typewriter had been invented by then, of course. He scanned it with the swiftness he had learned.

"Dear Sir:
"In reply to yrs. of September 6, 1954, beg to acknowledge receipt and would commend your diligence. The affair has only just begun at this end, and we are much occupied at present with preventing assassination of Her Majesty, as well as with the Balkan Question, the deplorable opium trade with China, &c. While we can, of course, settle current business and then return to this,

it is well to avoid *curiosa* such as being in two places at once, which might be noticed. Would therefore much appreciate it if you and some qualified British agent would come to our assistance. Unless we hear otherwise, we shall expect you at 14-B, Old Osborne Road, on June 26, 1894, at 12 midnight. Believe me, Sir, yr. humble & obt. svt.,

J. Mainwethering"

There followed a note of the spatio-temporal coordinates, incongruous under all that floridness.

Everard called up Gordon, got an okay, and arranged to pick up a time hopper at the "company's" warehouse. Then he shot a note to Charlie Whitcomb in 1947, got a one-word reply—"Surely"—and went off to get his machine.

It was reminiscent of a motorcycle without wheels or kickstand. There were two saddles and an antigravity propulsion unit. Everard set the dials for Whitcomb's era, touched the main button, and found himself in another warehouse.

London, 1947. He sat for a moment, reflecting that at this instant he himself, seven years younger, was attending college back in the States. Then Whitcomb shouldered past the watchman and took his hand. "Good to see you again, old chap," he said. His haggard face lit up in the curiously charming smile which Everard had come to know. "And so Victoria, eh?"

"Reckon so. Jump on." Everard reset. This time he would emerge in an office. A very private inner office.

It blinked into existence around him. There was an unexpectedly heavy effect to the oak furniture, the thick carpet, the flaring gas mantles. Electric lights were available, but Dalhousie & Roberts was a solid, conservative import house. Mainwethering himself got out of a chair and came to greet them: a large and pompous man with bushy side whiskers and a monocle. But he had also an air of strength, and an Oxford accent so cultivated that Everard could hardly understand it.

"Good evening, gentlemen. Pleasant journey, I trust? Oh, yes . . . sorry . . . you gentlemen are new to the business, eh, what? Always a bit disconcerting at first. I remember how shocked I was on a visit to the twenty-first century. Not British at all. . . . Only a *res naturae,* though, only another facet of an always surprising universe, eh? You must excuse my lack of hospitality, but we really are frightfully busy. Fanatic German up in 1917 learned the time-travel secret from an unwary anthropologist, stole a machine, has come to London to assassinate Her Majesty. We're having the devil's own time finding him."

"Will you?" asked Whitcomb.

"Oh, yes. But deuced hard work, gentlemen, especially when we must operate secretly. I'd like to engage a private inquiry agent, but the only worthwhile one is entirely too clever. He operates on the principle that when one has eliminated the impossible, whatever remains, however improbable, must be the truth. And time trafficking may not be too improbable for him."

"I'll bet he's the same man who's working on the Addleton case, or will be tomorrow," said Everard. "That isn't important; we know he'll prove Rotherhithe's innocence. What matters is the strong probability that there's been hanky-panky going on back in ancient British times."

"Saxon, you mean," corrected Whitcomb, who had checked on the data himself. "Good many people confuse British and Saxons."

"Almost as many as confuse Saxons and Jutes," said Mainwethering blandly. "Kent was invaded from Jutland, I understand . . . Ah. Hm. Clothes here, gentlemen. And funds. And papers, all prepared for you. I sometimes think you field agents don't appreciate how much work we have to do in the offices for even the smallest operation. Haw! Pardon. Have you a plan of campaign?"

"Yes." Everard began stripping off his twentieth-century garments. "I think so. We both know enough about the Victorian era to get by. I'll have to remain American, though . . . yes, I see you put that in my papers."

Mainwethering looked mournful. "If the barrow incident has gotten into a famous piece of literature as you say, we will be getting a hundred memoranda about it. Yours happened to come first. Two others have arrived since, from 1923 and 1960. Dear me, how I wish I were allowed a robot secretary!"

Everard struggled with the awkward suit. It fitted him well enough, his measurements were on file in this office, but he hadn't appreciated the relative comfort of his own fashions before. Damn that waistcoat! "Look here," he said, "this business may be quite harmless. In fact, since we're here now, it must have *been* harmless. Eh?"

"As of now," said Mainwethering. "But consider. You two gentlemen go back to Jutish times and find the marauder. But you fail. Perhaps he shoots you before you can shoot him; perhaps he waylays those we send after you. Then he goes on to establish an industrial revolution or whatever he's after. History changes. You, being back there before the change-point, still exist . . . if only as cadavers . . . but we up here have never been. This conversation never took place. As Horace puts it—"

"Never mind!" Whitcomb laughed. "We'll investigate the barrow first, in this year, then pop back here and decide what's next." He bent over and began transferring equipment from a twentieth-century suitcase to a Gladstonian monstrosity of flowered cloth. A couple of guns, some physical and chemical apparatus which his own age had not invented, a tiny radio with which to call up the office in case of trouble.

Mainwethering consulted his Bradshaw. "You can get the 8:23 out of Charing Cross tomorrow morning," he said. "Allow half an hour to get from here to the station."

"Okay." Everard and Whitcomb remounted their hopper and vanished. Mainwethering sighed, yawned, left instructions with his clerk, and went home. At 7:45 A.M. the clerk was there when the hopper materialized.

4

This was the first moment that the reality of time travel struck home to Everard. He had known it with the top of his mind, been duly impressed, but it was, for his emotions, merely exotic. Now, clopping through a London he did not know in a hansom cab (not a tourist-trap anachronism, but a working machine, dusty and battered), smelling an air which held more smoke than a twentieth-century city but no gasoline fumes, seeing the crowds which milled past—gentlemen in bowlers and top hats, sooty navvies, long-skirted women, and not actors but real, talking, perspiring, laughing and somber human beings off on real business—it hit him with full force that he was *here*. At this moment his mother had not been born, his grandparents were young couples just getting settled to harness, Grover Cleveland was President of the United States and Victoria was Queen of England, Kipling was writing and the last Indian uprisings in America yet to come. . . . It was like a blow on the head.

Whitcomb took it more calmly, but his eyes were never still as he watched this day of England's glory. "I begin to understand," he murmured. "They never have agreed whether this was a period of unnatural, stuffy convention and thinly veneered brutality, or the last flower of Western civilization before it started going to seed. Just seeing these people makes me realize; it was everything they have said about it, good and bad, because it wasn't a simple thing happening to everyone, but millions of individual lives."

"Sure," said Everard. "That must be true of every age."

The train was almost familiar, not very different from the carriages of British railways anno 1954, which gave Whitcomb occasion for sardonic remarks about inviolable traditions. In a couple of hours it let them off at a sleepy village station among carefully tended flower gardens, where they engaged a buggy to drive them to the Wyndham estate.

A polite constable admitted them after a few questions. They were passing themselves off as archaeologists, Everard from America and Whitcomb from

Australia, who had been quite anxious to meet Lord Wyndham and were shocked by his tragic end. Mainwethering, who seemed to have tentacles everywhere, had supplied them with letters of introduction from a well-known authority at the British Museum. The inspector from Scotland Yard agreed to let them look at the barrow—"The case is solved, gentlemen, there are no more clues, even if my colleague does not agree, hah, hah!" The private agent smiled sourly and watched them with a narrow eye as they approached the mound; he was tall, thin, hawkfaced, and accompanied by a burly, mustached fellow with a limp who seemed a kind of amaneunsis.

The barrow was long and high, covered with grass save where a raw scar showed excavation to the funeral chamber. This had been lined with rough-hewn timbers but had long ago collapsed; fragments of what had been wood still lay on the dirt. "The newspapers mentioned something about a metal casket," said Everard. "I wonder if we might have a look at it too?"

The inspector nodded agreeably and led them off to an outbuilding where the major finds were laid forth on a table. Except for the box, they were only fragments of corroded metal and crumbled bone.

"Hm," said Whitcomb. His gaze was thoughtful on the sleek, bare face of the small chest. It shimmered bluely, some time-proof alloy yet to be discovered. "Most unusual. Not primitive at all. You'd almost think it had been machined, eh?"

Everard approached it warily. He had a pretty good idea of what was inside, and all the caution about such matters natural to a citizen of the *soi-distant* Atomic Age. Pulling a counter out of his bag, he aimed it at the box. Its needle wavered, not much but. . . .

"Interesting item there," said the inspector. "May I ask what it is?"

"An experimental electroscope," lied Everard. Carefully, he threw back the lid and held the counter above the box.

God! There was enough radioactivity inside to kill a man in a day! He had just a glimpse of heavy, dull-shining ingots before he slammed the lid down again. "Be careful with that stuff," he said shakily. Praise heaven, whoever carried that devil's load had come from an age when they knew how to block off radiation!

The private detective had come up behind them, noiselessly. A hunter's look grew on his keen face. "So you recognized the contents, sir?" he asked, quietly.

"Yes. I think so." Everard remembered that Becquerel would not discover radioactivity for almost two years; even X rays were still more than a year in the future. He had to be cautious. "That is . . . in Indian territory I've heard stories about an ore like this which is poisonous—"

"*Most* interesting." The detective began to stuff a big-bowled pipe. "Like mercury vapor, what?"

"So Rotherhithe placed that box in the grave, did he?" muttered the inspector.

"Don't be ridiculous!" snapped the detective. "I have three lines of conclusive proof that Rotherhithe is entirely innocent. What puzzled me was the actual cause of his lordship's death. But if, as this gentleman says, there happened to be a deadly poison buried in that mound . . . to discourage grave-robbers? I wonder, though, how the old Saxons came by an American mineral. Perhaps there is something to these theories about early Phoenician voyages across the Atlantic. I have done a little research on a notion of mine that there are Chaldean elements in the Cymric language, and this seems to bear me out."

Everard felt guilty about what he was doing to the science of archaeology. Oh, well, this box was going to be dumped in the Channel and forgotten. He and Whitcomb made an excuse to leave as soon as possible.

On the way back to London, when they were safely alone in their compartment, the Englishman took out a moldering fragment of wood. "Slipped this into my pocket at the barrow," he said. "It'll help us date the thing. Hand me that radiocarbon counter, will you?" He popped the wood into the device, turned some knobs, and read off the answer. "One thousand, four hundred and thirty years, plus or minus about ten. The mound went up around . . . um . . . A.D. 464, then, when the Jutes were just getting established in Kent."

"If those ingots are still that hellish after so long," murmured Everard, "I wonder what they were like originally? Hard to see how you could have that much activity with such a long half-life, but then, up in the future they can do things with the atom my period hasn't dreamed of."

Turning in their report to Mainwethering, they spent a day sight-seeing while he sent messages across time and activated the great machine of the Patrol. Everard was interested in Victorian London, almost captivated in spite of the grime and poverty. Whitcomb got a faraway look in his eyes. "I'd like to have lived here," he said.

"Yeah? With their medicine and dentistry?"

"And no bombs falling." Whitcomb's answer held a defiance.

Mainwethering had arrangements made when they returned to his office. Puffing a cigar, he strode up and down, pudgy hands clasped behind his tailcoat, and rattled off the story.

"Metal been identified with high probability. Isotopic fuel from around the thirtieth century. Checkup reveals that a merchant from the Ing Empire was visiting year 2987 to barter his raw materials for their synthrope, secret of

which had been lost in the Interregnum. Naturally, he took precautions, tried
to pass himself off as a trader from the Saturnian System, but nevertheless
disappeared. So did his time shuttle. Presumably someone in 2987 found out
what he was and murdered him for his machine. Patrol notified, but no trace
of machine. Finally recovered from fifth-century England by two Patrolmen
named, haw! Everard and Whitcomb."

"If we've already succeeded, why bother?" The American grinned.

Mainwethering looked shocked. "But my dear fellow! You have not already
succeeded. The job is yet to do, in terms of your and my duration-sense. And
please do not take success for granted merely because history records it. Time
is not rigid; man has free will. If you fail, history will change and will not ever
have recorded your success; I will not have told you about it. That is
undoubtedly what happened, if I may use the term 'happened,' in the few
cases where the Patrol has a record of failure. Those cases are still being
worked on, and if success is achieved at last, history will be changed and there
will 'always' have been success. *Tempus non nascitur, fit,* if I may indulge in
a slight parody."

"All right, all right, I was only joking," said Everard. "Let's get going.
Tempus fugit." He added an extra "g" with malice aforethought, and
Mainwethering winced.

It turned out that even the Patrol knew little about the dark period when the
Romans had left Britain, the Romano-British civilization was crumbling, and
the English were moving in. It had never seemed an important one. The office
at London, A.D. 1000, sent up what material it had, together with suits of
clothes that would get by. Everard and Whitcomb spent an hour unconscious
under the hypnotic educators, to emerge with fluency in Latin and in several
Saxon and Jutish dialects, and with a fair knowledge of the mores.

The clothes were awkward: trousers, shirts, and coats of rough wool, leather
cloaks, an interminable collection of thongs and laces. Long flaxen wigs
covered modern haircuts; a clean shave would pass unnoticed, even in the fifth
century. Whitcomb carried an ax, Everard a sword, both made to measure of
high-carbon steel, but put more reliance on the little twenty-sixth-century
sonic stun guns stuck under their coats. Armor had not been included, but the
time hopper had a pair of motorcycle crash helmets in one saddlebag: these
would not attract much attention in an age of homemade equipment, and were
a good deal stronger and more comfortable than the real thing. They also
stowed away a picnic lunch and some earthenware jugs full of good Victorian
ale.

"Excellent." Mainwethering pulled a watch out of his pocket and consulted
it. "I shall expect you back here at . . . shall we say four o'clock? I will have

some armed guards on hand, in case you have a prisoner along, and we can go out to tea afterward." He shook their hands. "Good hunting!"

Everard swung onto the time hopper, set the controls for A.D. 464 at Addleton Barrow, a summer midnight, and threw the switch.

5

There was a full moon. Under it, the land lay big and lonely, with a darkness of forest blocking out the horizon. Somewhere a wolf howled. The mound was there yet; they had come late.

Rising on the antigravity unit, they peered across a dense, shadowy wood. A thorp lay about a mile from the barrow, one hall of hewn timber and a cluster of smaller buildings around a courtyard. In the drenching moonlight, it was very quiet.

"Cultivated fields," observed Whitcomb. His voice was hushed in the stillness. "The Jutes and Saxons were mostly yeomen, you know, who came here looking for land. Imagine the Britons were pretty well cleared out of this area some years ago."

"We've got to find out about that burial," said Everard. "Shall we go back and locate the moment the grave was made? No, it might be safer to inquire now, at a later date when whatever excitement there was has died down. Say tomorrow morning."

Whitcomb nodded, and Everard brought the hopper down into the concealment of a thicket and jumped up five hours. The sun was blinding in the northeast, dew glistened on the long grass, and the birds were making an unholy racket. Dismounting, the agents sent the hopper shooting up at fantastic velocity, to hover ten miles aboveground and come to them when called on a midget radio unit built into their helmets.

They approached the thorp openly, whacking off the savage-looking dogs which came snarling at them with the flat of sword and ax. Entering the courtyard, they found it unpaved but richly carpeted with mud and manure. A couple of naked, tow-headed children gaped at them from a hut of earth and wattles. A girl who was sitting outside milking a scrubby little cow let out a small shriek; a thick-built, low-browed farmhand swilling the pigs grabbed for a spear. Wrinkling his nose, Everard wished that some of the "Noble Nordic" enthusiasts of his century could visit this one.

A gray-bearded man with an ax in his hand appeared in the hall entrance. Like everyone else of this period, he was several inches shorter than the twentieth-century average. He studied them warily before wishing them good morning.

Everard smiled politely. "I hight Uffa Hundingsson, and my brother is Knubbi," he said. "We are merchants from Jutland, come hither to trade at Canterbury." (He gave it the present name, Cant-wara-byrig.) "Wandering from the place where our ship is beached, we lost our way, and after fumbling about all night found your home."

"I hight Wulfnoth, son of Aelfred," said the yeoman. "Enter and break your fast with us."

The hall was big and dim and smoky, full of a chattering crowd: Wulfnoth's children, their spouses and children, dependent carls and *their* wives and children and grandchildren. Breakfast consisted of great wooden trenchers of half-cooked pork, washed down by horns of thin sour beer. It was not hard to get a conversation going; these people were as gossipy as isolated yokels anywhere. The trouble was with inventing plausible accounts of what was going on in Jutland. Once or twice, Wulfnoth, who was no fool, caught them in some mistake, but Everard said firmly: "You have heard a falsehood. News takes strange forms when it crosses the sea." He was surprised to learn how much contact there still was with the old countries. But the talk of weather and crops was not very different from the kind he knew in the twentieth-century Middle West.

Only later was he able to slip in a question about the barrow. Wulfnoth frowned, and his plump, toothless wife hastily made a protective sign toward a rude wooden idol. "It is not good to speak of such things," muttered the Jute. "I would the wizard had not been buried on my land. But he was close to my father, who died last year and would hear of naught else."

"Wizard?" Whitcomb pricked up his ears. "What tale is this?"

"Well, you may as well know," grumbled Wulfnoth. "He was a stranger hight Stane, who appeared in Canterbury some six years ago. He must have been from far away, for he spoke not the English or British tongues, but King Hengist guested him and eftsoons he learned. He gave the king strange but goodly gifts, and was a crafty redesman, on whom the king came more and more to lean. None dared cross him, for he had a wand which threw thunderbolts and had been seen to cleave rocks and once, in battle with the Britons, burn men down. There are those who thought he was Woden, but that cannot be since he died."

"Ah, so." Everard felt a tingle of eagerness. "And what did he whilst yet he lived?"

"Oh . . . he gave the king wise redes, as I have said. It was his thought that we of Kent should cease thrusting back the Britons and calling in ever more of our kinsmen from the old country; rather, we should make peace with the natives. He thought that with our strength and their Roman learning, we could together shape a mighty realm. He may have been right, though I for one see little use in all these books and baths, to say naught of that weird cross-god they have. . . . Well, anyhow, he was slain by unknowns three years ago, and buried here with sacrifices and such of his possessions as his foes had not reaved. We give him an offering twice a year, and I must say his ghost has not made trouble for us. But still am I somewhat uneasy about it."

"Three years, eh?" breathed Whitcomb. "I see. . . . ."

It took a good hour to break away, and Wulfnoth insisted on sending a boy along to guide them to the river. Everard, who didn't feel like walking that far, grinned and called down the hopper. As he and Whitcomb mounted it, he said gravely to the bulging-eyed lad: "Know that thou hast guested Woden and Thunor, who will hereafter guard thy folk from harm." Then he jumped three years back in time.

"Now comes the rough part," he said, peering out of the thicket at the nighted thorp. The mound was not there now, the wizard Stane was still alive. "It's easy enough to put on a magic show for a kid, but we've got to extract this character from the middle of a big, tough town where he's the king's right-hand man. *And* he has a blast-ray."

"Apparently we succeeded—or will succeed," said Whitcomb.

"Nope. It's not irrevocable, you know. If we fail, Wulfnoth will be telling us a different story three years from now, probably that Stane is there—he may kill us twice! And England, pulled out of the Dark Ages into a neoclassical culture, won't evolve into anything you'd recognize by 1894. . . . I wonder what Stane's game is."

He lifted the hopper and sent it through the sky toward Canterbury. A night wind whistled darkly past his face. Presently the town loomed near, and he grounded in a copse. The moon was white on the half-ruined Roman walls of ancient Durovernum, dappled black on the newer earth and wood of the Jutish repairs. Nobody would get in after sunset.

Again the hopper brought them to daytime—near noon—and was sent skywards. His breakfast, two hours ago and three years in the future, felt soggy as Everard led the way onto a crumbling Roman road and toward the city. There was a goodly traffic, mostly farmers driving creaky oxcarts of produce in to market. A pair of vicious-looking guards halted them at the gate and demanded their business. This time they were the agents of a trader on Thanet who had sent them to interview various artisans here. The hoodlums looked surly till Whitcomb slipped them a couple of Roman coins; then the spears went down and they were waved past.

The city brawled and bustled around them, though again it was the ripe smell which impressed Everard most. Among the jostling Jutes, he spotted an occasional Romano-Briton, disdainfully picking a way through the muck and pulling his shabby tunic clear of contact with these savages. It would have been funny if it weren't pathetic.

There was an extraordinarily dirty inn filling the moss-grown ruins of what had been a rich man's town house. Everard and Whitcomb found that their money was of high value here where trade was principally in kind. By standing a few rounds of drinks, they got all the information they wanted. King Hengist's hall was near the middle of town . . . not really a hall, an old building which had been deplorably prettied up under the direction of that outlander Stane . . . not that our good and doughty king is any pantywaist, don't get me wrong, stranger . . . why, only last month . . . oh, yes, Stane! He lived in the house right next to it. Strange fellow, some said he was a god . . . he certainly had an eye for the girls . . . Yes, they said he was behind all this peace-talk with the Britons. More and more of those slickers coming in every day, it's getting so an honest man can't let a little blood without. . . . Of course, Stane is very wise, I wouldn't say anything against him, understand, after all, he can throw lightning. . . .

"So what do we do?" asked Whitcomb, back in their own room. "Go on in and arrest him?"

"No, I doubt if that's possible," said Everard cautiously. "I've got a sort of a plan, but it depends on guessing what he really intends. Let's see if we can't get an audience." As he got off the straw tick which served for a bed, he was scratching. "Damn! What this period needs isn't literacy but flea powder!"

The house had been carefully renovated, its white, porticoed facade almost painfully clean against the grubbiness around it. Two guards lounged on the stairs, and snapped to alertness as the agents approached. Everard fed them money and a story about being a visitor who had news that would surely interest the great wizard. "Tell him, 'Man from tomorrow.' 'Tis a password. Got it?"

"It makes not sense," complained the guard.

"Passwords need not make sense," said Everard with hauteur.

The Jute clanked off, shaking his head dolefully. All these newfangled notions!

"Are you sure this is wise?" asked Whitcomb. "He'll be on the alert now, you know."

"I also know a VIP isn't going to waste time on just any stranger. This business is urgent, man! So far, he hasn't accomplished anything permanent, not even enough to become a lasting legend. But if Hengist should make a genuine union with the Britons. . . ."

The guard returned, grunted something, and led them up the stairs and across the peristyle. Beyond was the atrium, a good-sized room where modern bearskin rugs jarred with chipped marble and faded mosaics. A man stood waiting before a rude wooden couch. As they entered, he raised his hand, and Everard saw the slim barrel of a thirtieth-century blast-ray.

"Keep your hands in sight and well away from your sides," said the man gently. "Otherwise I shall belike have to smite you with a thunderbolt."

Whitcomb sucked in a sharp, dismayed breath, but Everard had been rather expecting this. Even so, there was a cold knot in his stomach.

The wizard Stane was a small man, dressed in a fine embroidered tunic which must have come from some British villa. His body was lithe, his head large, with a face of rather engaging ugliness under a shock of black hair. A grin of tension bent his lips.

"Search them, Eadgar," he ordered. "Take out aught they may bear in their clothing."

The Jute's frisking was clumsy, but he found the stunners and tossed them to the floor. "Thou mayst go," said Stane.

"Is there no danger from them, my lord?" asked the soldier.

Stane grinned wider. "With this in my hand? Nay, go." Eadgar shambled out. *At least we still have sword and ax,* thought Everard. *But they're not much use with that thing looking at us.*

"So you come from tomorrow," murmured Stane. A sudden film of sweat glistened on his forehead. "I wondered about that. Speak you the later English tongue?"

Whitcomb opened his mouth, but Everard, improvising with his life at wager, beat him to the draw. "What tongue mean you?"

"Thus-wise." Stane broke into an English which had a peculiar accent but was recognizable to twentieth-century ears: "Ih want know where an' when y're from, what y'r 'tentions sir, an' all else. Gimme d' facts 'r Ih'll burn y' doon."

Everard shook his head. "Nay," he answered in Jutish. "I understand you not." Whitcomb threw him a glance and then subsided, ready to follow the American's lead. Everard's mind raced; under the brassiness of desperation, he knew that death waited for his first mistake. "In our day we talked thus. . . ." And he reeled off a paragraph of Mexican-Spanish chatter, garbling it as much as he dared.

"So . . . a Latin tongue!" Stane's eyes glittered. The blaster shook in his hand. "*When* be you from?"

"The twentieth century after Christ, and our land hight Lyonesse. It lies across the western ocean—"

"America!" It was a gasp. "Was it ever called America?"

"No. I wot not what you speak of."

Stane shuddered uncontrollably. Mastering himself: "Know you the Roman tongue?"

Everard nodded.

Stane laughed nervously. "Then let us speak that. If you know how sick I am of this local hog language. . . ." His Latin was a little broken, obviously he had picked it up in this century, but fluent enough. He waved the blaster. "Pardon my discourtesy. But I have to be careful."

"Naturally," said Everard. "Ah . . . my name is Mencius, and my friend is Iuvenalis. We came from the future, as you have guessed; we are historians, and time travel has just been invented."

"Properly speaking, I am Rozher Schtein, from the year 2987. Have you . . . heard of me?"

"Who else?" said Everard. "We came back looking for this mysterious Stane who seemed to be one of the crucial figures of history. We suspected he might have been a time traveler, *peregrinator temporis,* that is. Now we know."

"Three years," Schtein began pacing feverishly, the blaster swinging in his hand; but he was too far off for a sudden leap. "Three years I have been here. If you knew how often I have lain awake, wondering if I would succeed. . . . Tell me, is your world united?"

"The world and the planets," said Everard. "They have been for a long time." Inwardly, he shivered. His life hung on his ability to guess what Schtein's plans were.

"And you are a free people?"

"We are. That is to say, the Emperor presides, but the Senate makes the laws and it is elected by the people."

There was an almost holy look on the gnomish face, transfiguring it. "As I dreamed," whispered Schtein. "Thank you."

"So you came back from your period to . . . create history?"

"No," said Schtein. "To change it."

Words tumbled out of him, as if he had wished to speak and dared not for many years: "I was a historian too. By chance I met a man who claimed to be a merchant from the Saturnian moons, but since I had lived there once, I saw through the fraud. Investigating, I learned the truth. He was a time traveler from the very far future.

"You must understand, the age I lived in was a terrible one, and as a psychographic historian I realized that the war, poverty, and tyranny which cursed us were not due to any innate evil in man, but to simple cause and effect. Machine technology had risen in a world divided against itself, and war grew to be an ever larger and more destructive enterprise. There had been periods of peace, even fairly long ones; but the disease was too deep-rooted, conflict was a part of our very civilization. My family had been wiped out in a Venusian raid, I had nothing to lose. I took the time machine after . . . disposing . . . of its owner.

"The great mistake, I thought, had been made back in the Dark Ages. Rome had united a vast empire in peace, and out of peace justice can always arise. But Rome exhausted herself in the effort, and was now falling apart. The barbarians coming in were vigorous, they could do much, but they were quickly corrupted.

"But here is England. It has been isolated from the rotting fabric of Roman society. The Germanics are entering, filthy oafs but strong and willing to learn. In my history, they simply wiped out British civilization and then, being intellectually helpless, were swallowed up by the new—and evil—civilization called Western. I want to see something better happen.

"It hasn't been easy. You would be surprised how hard it is to survive in a different age until you know your way around, even if you have modern weapons and interesting gifts for the king. But I have Hengist's respect now, and increasingly more of the confidence of the Britons. I can unite the two people in a mutual war on the Picts. England will be one kingdom, with Saxon strength and Roman learning, powerful enough to stand off all invaders. Christianity is inevitable, of course, but I will see to it that it is the right kind of Christianity, one which will educate and civilize men without shackling their minds.

"Eventually England will be in a position to start taking over on the Continent. Finally, one world. I will stay here long enough to get the anti-Pictish union started, then vanish with a promise to return later. If I reappear at, say, fifty-year intervals for the next several centuries, I will be a legend, a god, who can make sure they stay on the right track."

"I have read much about St. Stanius," said Everard slowly.

"And I won!" cried Schtein. "I gave peace to the world." Tears were on his cheeks.

Everard moved closer. Schtein pointed the blast-ray at his belly, not yet quite trusting him. Everard circled casually, and Schtein swiveled to keep him covered. But the man was too agitated by the seeming proof of his own success to remember Whitcomb. Everard threw a look over his shoulder at the Englishman.

Whitcomb hurled his ax. Everard dove for the floor. Schtein screamed, and the blast-ray sizzled. The ax had cloven his shoulder. Whitcomb sprang, getting a grip on his gun hand. Schtein howled, struggling to force the blaster around. Everard jumped up to help. There was a moment of confusion.

Then the blaster went off again and Schtein was suddenly a dead weight in their arms. Blood drenched their coats from the hideous opening in his chest.

The two guards came running in. Everard snatched his stunner off the floor and thumbed the ratchet up to full intensity. A flung spear grazed his arm. He fired twice, and the burly forms crashed. They'd be out for hours.

Crouching a moment, Everard listened. A feminine scream sounded from the inner chambers, but no one was entering at the door. "I guess we've carried it off," he panted.

"Yes." Whitcomb looked dully at the corpse sprawled before him. It seemed pathetically small.

"I didn't mean for him to die," said Everard. "But time is . . . tough. It was written, I suppose."

"Better this way than a Patrol court and the exile planet," said Whitcomb.

"Technically, at least, he was a thief and a murderer," said Everard. "But it was a great dream he had."

"And we upset it."

"History might have upset it. Probably would have. One man just isn't powerful enough, or wise enough. I think most human misery is due to well-meaning fanatics like him."

"So we just fold our hands and take what comes."

"Think of all your friends, up in 1947. They'd never even have existed."

Whitcomb took off his cloak and tried to wipe the blood from his clothes.

"Let's get going," said Everard. He trotted through the rear portal. A frightened concubine watched him with large eyes.

He had to blast the lock off an inner door. The room beyond held an Ing-model time shuttle, a few boxes with weapons and supplies, some books. Everard loaded it all into the machine except the fuel chest. That had to be left, so that up in the future he would learn of this and come back to stop the man who would be God.

"Suppose you take this to the warehouse in 1894," he said. "I'll ride our hopper back and meet you at the office."

Whitcomb gave him a long stare. The man's face was drawn. Even as Everard watched him, it stiffened with resolution.

"All right, old chap," said the Englishman. He smiled, almost wistfully, and clasped Everard's hand. "So long. Good luck."

Everard stared after him as he entered the great steel cylinder. That was an odd thing to say, when they'd be having tea up in 1894 in a couple of hours.

Worry nagged him as he went out of the building and mingled with the crowd. Charlie was a peculiar cuss. Well. . . .

No one interfered with him as he left the city and entered the thicket beyond. He called the time hopper back down and, in spite of the need for haste lest someone come to see what kind of bird had landed, cracked a jug of ale. He needed it badly. Then he took a last look at Old England and jumped up to 1894.

Mainwethering and his guards were there as promised. The officer looked alarmed at the sight of one man arriving with blood clotting across his garments, but Everard gave him a reassuring report.

It took a while to wash up, change clothes, and deliver a full account to the secretary. By then, Whitcomb should have arrived in a hansom, but there was no sign of him. Mainwethering called the warehouse on the radio, and turned back with a frown. "He hasn't come yet," he said. "Could something have gone wrong?"

"Hardly. Those machines are foolproof." Everard gnawed his lip. "I don't know what the matter is. Maybe he misunderstood and went up to 1947 instead."

An exchange of notes revealed that Whitcomb had not reported in at that end either. Everard and Mainwethering went out for their tea. There was still no trace of Whitcomb when they got back.

"I had best inform the field agency," said Mainwethering. "Eh, what? They should be able to find him."

"No. Wait." Everard stood for a moment, thinking. The idea had been germinating in him for some time. It was dreadful.

"Have you a notion?"

"Yes. Sort of." Everard began shucking his Victorian suit. His hands trembled. "Get my twentieth-century clothes, will you? I may be able to find him by myself."

"The Patrol will want a preliminary report of your idea and intentions," reminded Mainwethering.

"To hell with the Patrol," said Everard.

6

London, 1944. The early winter night had fallen, and a thin cold wind blew down streets which were gulfs of darkness. Somewhere came the *crump* of an explosion, and a fire was burning, great red banners flapping above the roofs.

Everard left his hopper on the sidewalk—nobody was out when the V-bombs were falling—and groped slowly through the murk. November seventeenth; his trained memory had called up the date for him. Mary Nelson had died this day.

He found a public phone booth on the corner and looked in the directory.

There were a lot of Nelsons, but only one Mary listed for the Streatham area. That would be the mother, of course. He had to guess that the daughter would have the same first name. Nor did he know the time at which the bomb had struck, but there were ways to learn that.

Fire and thunder roared at him as he came out. He flung himself on his belly while glass whistled where he had been. November seventeenth, 1944. The younger Manse Everard, lieutenant in the United States Army Engineers, was somewhere across the Channel, near the German guns. He couldn't recall exactly where, just then, and did not stop to make the effort. It didn't matter. He knew he was going to survive *that* danger.

The new blaze was a-dance behind him as he ran for his machine. He jumped aboard and took off into the air. High above London, he saw only a vast darkness spotted with flame. *Walpurgisnacht,* and all hell let loose on earth!

He remembered Streatham well, a dreary stretch of brick inhabited by little clerks and greengrocers and mechanics, the very petite bourgeoisie who had stood up and fought the power which conquered Europe to a standstill. There had been a girl living there, back in 1943. . . . Eventually she married someone else.

Skimming low, he tried to find the address. A volcano erupted not far off. His mount staggered in the air, he almost lost his seat. Hurrying toward the place, he saw a house tumbled and smashed and flaming. It was only three blocks from the Nelson home. He was too late.

No! He checked the time—just ten-thirty—and jumped back two hours. It was still night, but the slain house stood solid in the gloom. For a second he wanted to warn those inside. But no. All over the world, people were dying. He was not Schtein, to take history on his shoulders.

He grinned wryly, dismounted, and walked through the gate. He was not a damned Danellian either. He knocked on the door, and it opened. A middle-aged woman looked at him through the murk, and he realized it was odd to see an American in civilian clothes here.

"Excuse me," he said. "Do you know Miss Mary Nelson?"

"Why, yes." Hesitation. "She lives nearby. She's coming over soon. Are you a friend?"

Everard nodded. "She sent me here with a message for you, Mrs. . . . ah. . . ."

"Enderby."

"Oh, yes, Mrs. Enderby. I'm terribly forgetful. Look, Miss Nelson wanted me to say she's very sorry but she can't come. However, she wants you and your entire family over at ten-thirty."

"All of us, sir? But the children—"

"By all means, the children too. Every one of you. She has a very special surprise arranged, something she can only show you then. All of you have to be there."

"Well, . . . all right, sir, if she says so."

"All of you at ten-thirty, without fail. I'll see you then, Mrs. Enderby." Everard nodded and walked back to the street.

He had done what he could. Next was the Nelson house. He rode his hopper three blocks down, parked it in the gloom of an alley, and walked up to the house. He was guilty too now, as guilty as Schtein. He wondered what the exile planet was like.

There was no sign of the Ing shuttle, and it was too big to conceal. So Charlie hadn't arrived yet. He'd have to play by ear till then.

As he knocked on the door, he wondered what his saving of the Enderby family would mean. Those children would grow up, have children of their own: quite insignificant middle-class Englishmen, no doubt, but somewhere in the centuries to come an important man would be born or fail to be born. Of course, time was not very flexible. Except in rare cases, the precise ancestry didn't matter, only the broad pool of human genes and human society did. Still, this might be one of those rare cases.

A young woman opened the door for him. She was a pretty little girl, not spectacular but nice looking in her trim uniform. "Miss Nelson?"

"Yes?"

"My name is Everard. I'm a friend of Charlie Whitcomb. May I come in? I have a rather surprising bit of news for you."

"I was about to go out," she said apologetically.

"No, you weren't." Wrong line; she was stiffening with indignation. "Sorry. Please, may I explain?"

She led him into a drab and cluttered parlor. "Won't you sit down, Mr. Everard? Please don't talk too loudly. The family are all asleep. They get up early."

Everard made himself comfortable. Mary perched on the edge of the sofa, watching him with large eyes. He wondered if Wulfnoth and Eadgar were among her ancestors. Yes . . . undoubtedly they were, after all these centuries. Maybe Schtein was too.

"Are you in the Air Force?" she asked. "Is that how you met Charlie?"

"No. I'm in Intelligence, which is the reason for this mufti. May I ask when you last saw him?"

"Oh, weeks ago. He's stationed in France just now. I hope this war will soon be over. So silly of them to keep on when they must know they're finished, isn't it?" She cocked her head curiously. "But what is this news you have?"

"I'll come to it in a moment." He began to ramble as much as he dared, talking of conditions across the Channel. It was strange to sit conversing with a ghost. And his conditioning prevented him from telling the truth. He wanted to, but when he tried his tongue froze up on him.

". . . and what it costs to get a bottle of red-ink ordinaire—"

"Please," she interrupted impatiently. "Would you mind coming to the point? I do have an engagement for tonight."

"Oh, sorry. Very sorry, I'm sure. You see, it's this way—"

A knock at the door saved him. "Excuse me," she murmured, and went out past the blackout drapes to open it. Everard padded after her.

She stepped back with a small shriek. *"Charlie!"*

Whitcomb pressed her to him, heedless of the blood still wet on his Jutish clothes. Everard came into the hall. The Englishman stared with a kind of horror. "You. . . ."

He snatched for his stunner, but Everard's was already out. "Don't be a fool," said the American. "I'm your friend. I want to help you. What crazy scheme did you have, anyway?"

"I . . . keep her here . . . keep her from going to—"

"And do you think *they* haven't got means of spotting you?" Everard slipped into Temporal, the only possible language in Mary's frightened presence. "When I left Mainwethering, he was getting damn suspicious. Unless we do this right, every unit of the Patrol is going to be alerted. The error will be rectified, probably by killing her. You'll go to exile."

"I. . . ." Whitcomb gulped. His face was a mask of fear. "You . . . would you let her go ahead and die?"

"No. But this has to be done more carefully."

"We'll escape . . . find some period away from everything . . . go back to the dinosaur age, if we must."

Mary slipped free of him. Her mouth was pulled open, ready to scream. "Shut up!" said Everard to her. "Your life is in danger, and we're trying to save you. If you don't trust me, trust Charlie."

Turning back to the man, he went on in Temporal: "Look, fellow, there isn't any place or any time you can hide in. Mary Nelson died tonight. That's history. She wasn't around in 1947. That's history. I've already got myself in Dutch: the family she was going to visit will be out of their home when the bomb hits it. If you try to run away with her, you'll be found. It's pure luck that a Patrol unit hasn't already arrived."

Whitcomb fought for steadiness. "Suppose I jump up to 1948 with her. How do you know she hasn't suddenly reappeared in 1948? Maybe that's history too."

"Man, you *can't*. Try it. Go on, tell her you're going to hop her four years into the future."

Whitcomb groaned. "A giveaway—and I'm conditioned—"

"Yeh. You have barely enough latitude to appear this way before her, but talking to her, you'll have to lie out of it because you can't help yourself. Anyway, how would you explain her? If she stays Mary Nelson, she's a deserter from the W.A.A.F. If she takes another name, where's her birth certificate, her school record, her ration book, any of those bits of paper these twentieth-century governments worship so devoutly? It's hopeless, son."

"Then what can we do?"

"Face the Patrol and slug it out. Wait here a minute." There was a cold calm over Everard, no time to be afraid or to wonder at his own behavior.

Returning to the street, he located his hopper and set it to emerge five years in the future, at high noon in Piccadilly Circus. He slapped down the main switch, saw the machine vanish, and went back inside. Mary was in Whitcomb's arms, shuddering and weeping. The poor, damned babes in the woods!

"Okay." Everard led them back to the parlor and sat down with his gun ready. "Now we wait some more."

It didn't take long. A hopper appeared, with two men in Patrol gray aboard. There were weapons in their hands. Everard cut them down with a low-powered stun beam. "Help me to tie 'em up, Charlie," he said.

Mary huddled voiceless in a corner.

When the men awoke, Everard stood over them with a bleak smile. "What are we charged with, boys?" he asked in Temporal.

"I think you know," said one of the prisoners calmly. "The main office had us trace you. Checking up next week, we found that you had evacuated a family scheduled to be bombed. Whitcomb's record suggested you had then come here, to help him save this woman who was supposed to die tonight. Better let us go or it will be worse for you."

"I have not changed history," said Everard. "The Danellians are still up there, aren't they?"

"Yes, of course, but—"

"How did you know the Enderby family was supposed to die?"

"Their house was struck, and they said they had only left it because—"

"Ah, but the point is they did leave it. That's written. Now it's you who wants to change the past."

"But this woman here—"

"Are you sure there wasn't a Mary Nelson who, let us say, settled in London in 1850 and died of old age about 1900?"

The lean face grinned. "You're trying hard, aren't you? It won't work. You can't fight the entire Patrol."

"Can't I, though? I can leave you here to be found by the Enderbys. I've set my hopper to emerge in public at an instant known only to myself. What's that going to do to history?"

"The Patrol will take corrective measures . . . as you did back in the fifth century."

"Perhaps! I can make it a lot easier for them, though, if they'll hear my appeal. I want a Danellian."

"What?"

"You heard me," said Everard. "If necessary, I'll mount that hopper of yours and ride a million years up. I'll point out to them personally how much simpler it'll be if they give us a break."

That will not be necessary.

Everard spun around with a gasp. The stunner fell from his hand.

He could not look at the shape which blazed before his eyes. There was a dry sobbing in his throat as he backed away.

Your appeal has been considered, said the soundless voice. *It was known and weighed ages before you were born. But you were still a necessary link in the chain of time. If you had failed tonight, there would not be mercy.*

To us, it was a matter of record that one Charles and Mary Whitcomb lived in Victoria's England. It was also a matter of record that Mary Nelson died with the family she was visiting in 1944, and that Charles Whitcomb had lived a bachelor and finally been killed on active duty with the Patrol. The discrepancy was noted, and as even the smallest paradox is a dangerous weakness in the space-time fabric, it had to be rectified by eliminating one or the other fact from ever having existed. You have decided which it will be.

Everard knew, somewhere in his shaking brain, that the Patrolmen were suddenly free. He knew that his hopper had been . . . was being . . . would be snatched invisibly away the instant it materialized. He knew that history now read: W.A.A.F. Mary Nelson missing, presumed killed by bomb near the home of the Enderby family, who had all been at her house when their own was destroyed; Charles Whitcomb disappearing in 1947, presumed accidentally drowned. He knew that Mary was given the truth, conditioned against ever revealing it, and sent back with Charlie to 1850. He knew they would make their middle-class way through life, never feeling quite at home in Victoria's reign, that Charlie would often have wistful thoughts of what he had been in the Patrol . . . and then turn to his wife and children and decide it had not been such a great sacrifice after all.

That much he knew, and then the Danellian was gone. As the whirling darkness in his head subsided and he looked with clearing eyes at the two Patrolmen, he did not know what his own destiny was.

"Come on," said the first man. "Let's get out of here before somebody wakes up. We'll give you a lift back to your year. 1954, isn't it?"

"And then what?" asked Everard.

The Patrolman shrugged. Under his casual manner lay the shock which had seized him in the Danellian's presence. "Report to your sector chief. You've shown yourself obviously unfit for steady work."

"So . . . just cashiered, huh?"

"You needn't be so dramatic. Did you think this case was the only one of its kind in a million years of Patrol work? There's a regular procedure for it.

"You'll want more training, of course. Your type of personality goes best with Unattached status—any age, any place, wherever and whenever you may be needed. I think you'll like it."

Everard climbed weakly aboard the hopper. And when he got off again, a decade had passed.

Brave to Be a King

1

ON an evening in mid-twentieth-century New York, Manse Everard had changed into a threadbare lounging outfit and was mixing himself a drink. The doorbell interrupted. He swore at it. A tiring several days lay behind him and he wanted no other company than the lost narratives of Dr. Watson.

Well, maybe this character could be gotten rid of. He slippered across his apartment and opened the door, his expression mutinous. "Hello," he said coldly.

And then, all at once, it was as if he were aboard some early spaceship which had just entered free fall; he stood weightless and helpless in a blaze of stars.

"Oh," he said. "I didn't know. . . . Come in."

Cynthia Denison paused a moment, looking past him to the bar. He had hung two crossed spears and a horse-plumed helmet from the Achaean Bronze Age over it. They were dark and shining and incredibly beautiful. She tried to speak with steadiness, but failed. "Could I have a drink, Manse? Right away?"

"Of course." He clamped his mouth shut and helped her off with her coat. She closed the door and sat down on a Swedish modern couch as clean and functional as the Homeric weapons. Her hands fumbled with her purse, getting out cigarettes. For a time she did not look at him, nor he at her.

"Do you still drink Irish on the rocks?" he asked. His words seemed to come from far away, and his body was awkward among bottles and glasses, forgetting how the Time Patrol had trained it.

"Yes," she said. "So you do remember." Her lighter snapped, unexpectedly loud in the room.

"It's been just a few months," he said, for lack of other phrases.

"Entropic time. Regular, untampered-with, twenty-four-hours-to-the-day time." She blew a cloud of smoke and stared at it. "Not much more than that for me. I've been in now almost continuously since my, my wedding. Just eight and a half months of my personal, biological, lifeline time since Keith and I. . . . But how long has it been for you, Manse? How many years have you rung up, in how many different epochs, since you were Keith's best man?"

She had always had a rather high and thin voice. It was the only flaw he had ever found in her, unless you counted her being so small—barely five feet. So she could never put much expression into her tones. But he could hear that she was staving off a scream.

He gave her a drink. "Down the hatch," he said. "All of it." She obeyed, strangling a little. He got her a refill and completed his own Scotch and soda. Then he drew up a chair and took pipe and tobacco from the depths of his moth-eaten smoking jacket. His hands still shook, but so faintly he didn't think she would notice. It had been wise of her not to blurt whatever news she carried; they both needed a chance to get back their control.

Now he even dared to look straight at her. She hadn't changed. Her figure was almost perfect in a delicate way, as the black dress emphasized. Sunlight-colored hair fell to her shoulders; the eyes were blue and enormous, under arched brows, in a tip-tilted face with the lips always just a little parted. She hadn't enough makeup for him to tell for sure if she had cried lately. But she looked very near to it.

Everard became busy filling his pipe. "Okay, Cyn," he said. "Want to tell me?"

She shivered. Finally she got out: "Keith. He's disappeared."

"Huh?" Everard sat up straight. "On a mission?"

"Yes. Where else? Ancient Iran. He went back there and never returned. That was a week ago." She set her glass down on the couch arm and twisted her fingers together. "The Patrol searched, of course. I just heard the results today. They can't find him. They can't even find out what happened to him."

"Judas," whispered Everard.

"Keith always . . . always thought of you as his best friend," she said frantically. "You wouldn't believe how often he spoke of you. Honestly,

Manse, I know we've neglected you, but you never seemed to be in and. . . ."

"Of course," he said. "How childish do you think I am? I was busy. And after all, you two were newly married."

After I introduced you, that night beneath Mauna Loa and the moon. The Time Patrol doesn't bother with snobbishness. A youngster like Cynthia Cunningham, a mere clerk fresh out of the Academy and Attached to her own century, is quite free to see a ranking veteran . . . like myself, for instance . . . as often as they both wish, off duty. There is no reason why he should not use his skill at disguise to take her waltzing in Strauss's Vienna or to the theater in Shakespeare's London—as well as exploring funny little bars in Tom Lehrer's New York or playing tag in the sun and surf of Hawaii a thousand years before the canoe men arrived. And a fellow member of the Patrol is equally free to join them both. And later to marry her. Sure.

Everard got his pipe going. When his face was screened with smoke, he said: "Begin at the beginning. I've been out of touch with you for—two or three years of my own lifeline time—so I'm not certain precisely what Keith was working on."

"That long?" she asked wonderingly. "You never even spent your furloughs in this decade? We did want you to come visit us."

"Quit apologizing!" he snapped. "I could have dropped in if I'd wished." The elfin face looked as if he had slapped it. He backed up, appalled. "I'm sorry. Naturally I wanted to. But as I said . . . we Unattached agents are so damned busy, hopping around in all space-time like fleas on a griddle. . . . Oh, hell." He tried to smile. "You know me, Cyn, tactless, but it doesn't mean anything. I originated a chimaera legend all by myself, back in Classic Greece. I was known as the *dilaiopod*, a curious monster with two left feet, both in its mouth."

She returned a dutiful quirk of lips and picked up her cigarette from the ashtray. "I'm still just a clerk in Engineering Studies," she said. "But it puts me in close contact with all the other offices in this entire milieu, including headquarters. So I know exactly what's been done about Keith . . . and it isn't enough! They're just abandoning him! Manse, if you won't help Keith is dead!"

She stopped, shakily. To give them both a little more time, Everard reviewed the career of Keith Denison.

Born Cambridge, Mass., 1927, to a moderately wealthy family, Ph.D. in archaeology with a distinguished thesis at the age of twenty-three, after having also taken a collegiate boxing championship and crossed the Atlantic in a thirty-foot ketch. Drafted in 1950, served in Korea with a bravery which would have earned him some fame in a more popular war. Yet you had to know him quite a while before you learned any of this. He spoke, with a gift of dry humor, about impersonal things, until there was work to be done. Then, without needless fuss, he did it. *Sure,* thought Everard, *the best man got the girl. Keith could've made Unattached easily, if he'd cared to. But he had roots here that I didn't. More stable, I guess.*

Discharged and at loose ends in 1952, Denison was contacted by a Patrol agent and recruited. He had accepted the fact of time travel more readily than most. His mind was supple and, after all, he was an archaeologist. Once trained, he found a happy coincidence of his own interests and the needs of the Patrol; he became a Specialist, East Indo-European Protohistory, and in many ways a more important man than Everard.

For the Unattached officer might rove up and down the time lanes, rescuing the distressed and arresting the lawbreaker and keeping the fabric of human destiny secure. But how could he tell what he was doing without a record? Ages before the first hieroglyphics there had been wars and wanderings, discoveries and achievements, whose consequences reached through all the continuum. The Patrol had to know them. Charting their course was a job for the Specialist ratings.

Besides all of which, Keith was a friend of mine.

Everard took the pipe from his mouth. "Okay, Cynthia," he said. "Tell me what did happen."

2

The little voice was almost dry now, so rigidly had she harnessed herself. "He was tracing the migrations of the different Aryan clans. They're very obscure, you know. You have to start at a point when the history is known for certain, and work backward. So on this last job, Keith was going to Iran in the year 558 B.C. That was near the close of the Median period, he said. He'd make inquiries among the people, learn their own traditions, and then afterward check back at a still earlier point, and so on. . . . But you must know all about this, Manse. You helped him once, before we met. He often spoke about that."

"Oh, I just went along in case of trouble," shrugged Everard. "He was studying the prehistoric trek of a certain band from the Don over the Hindu Kush. We told their chief we were passing hunters, claimed hospitality, and accompanied the wagon train for a few weeks. It was fun."

He remembered steppes and enormous skies, a windy gallop after antelope and a feast by campfires and a certain girl whose hair had held the bittersweet of woodsmoke. For a while he wished he could have lived and died as one of those tribesmen.

"Keith went back alone this time," continued Cynthia. "They're always so shorthanded in his branch, in the entire Patrol, I suppose. So many thousands of years to watch and so few man-lifetimes to do it with. He'd gone alone before. I was always afraid to let him, but he said . . . dressed as a wandering shepherd with nothing worth stealing . . . he'd be safer in the Iranian highlands than crossing Broadway. Only this time he wasn't!"

"I take it, then," said Everard quickly, "he left—a week ago, did you say?—intending to get his information, report it to the clearinghouse of his specialty, and come back to the same day here as he'd left you." *Because only a blind buckethead would let more of your lifespan pass without being there himself.* "But he didn't."

"Yes." She lit another cigarette from the butt of the first. "I got worried right away. I asked the boss about it. He obliged me by querying himself a week ahead—today—and got the answer that Keith had not returned. The information clearinghouse said he never came to them. So we checked with Records in milieu headquarters. Their answer was . . . was . . . Keith never did come back and no trace of him was ever found."

Everard nodded with great care. "Then, of course, the search was ordered which MHQ has a record of."

Mutable time made for a lot of paradoxes, he reflected for the thousandth occasion.

In the case of a missing man, you were not required to search for him just because a record somewhere said you had done so. But how else would you stand a chance of finding him? You *might* possibly go back and thereby change events so that you did find him after all—in which case the report you filed would "always" have recorded your success, and you alone would know the "former" truth.

It could get very messed up. No wonder the Patrol was fussy, even about small changes which would not affect the main pattern.

"Our office notified the boys in the Old Iranian milieu, who sent a party to investigate the spot," foretold Everard. "They only knew the approximate site at which Keith had intended to materialize, didn't they? I mean, since he couldn't know exactly where he'd be able to hide the scooter, he didn't file precise coordinates." Cynthia nodded. "But what I don't understand is, why didn't they find the machine afterward? Whatever happened to Keith, the scooter would still be somewhere around, in some cave or whatever. The Patrol has detectors. They should have been able to track down the scooter, at least, and then work backwards from it to locate Keith."

She drew on her cigarette with a violence that caved in her cheeks. "They tried," she said. "But I'm told it's a wild, rugged ccuntry, hard to search. Nothing turned up. They couldn't find a trace. They might have, if they'd looked very, very hard—made a mile-by-mile, hour-by-hour search. But they didn't dare. You see, that particular milieu is critical. Mr. Gordon showed me the analysis. I couldn't follow all those symbols, but he said it was a very dangerous century to tamper with."

Everard closed one large hand on the bowl of his pipe. Its warmth was somehow comforting. Critical eras gave him the willies.

"I see," he said. "They couldn't search as thoroughly as they wanted, because it might disturb too many of the local yokels, which might make them act differently when the big crisis came. Uh-huh. But how about making inquiries in disguise, among the people?"

"Several Patrol experts did. They tried that for weeks. Persian time. And the natives never even gave them a hint. Those tribes are so wild and suspicious . . . maybe they feared our agents were spies from the Median king, I understand they didn't like his rule. . . . No. The Patrol couldn't find a trace. And anyhow, there's no reason to think the pattern was affected. They believe Keith was murdered and his scooter vanished somehow. And what difference—" Cynthia sprang to her feet. Suddenly she yelled—"What difference does one more skeleton in one more gully make?"

Everard rose too, she came into his arms, and he let her have it out. For himself, he had never thought it would be this bad. He had stopped remembering her, except maybe ten times a day, but now she came to him and the forgetting would have to be done all over again.

"Can't they go back locally?" she pleaded. "Can't somebody hop back a week from now, just to tell him not to go, is that so much to ask? What kind of monsters made that law against it?"

"Ordinary men did," said Everard. "If we once started doubling back to tinker with our personal pasts, we'd soon get so tangled up that none of us would exist."

"But in a million years or more—there must be exceptions!"

Everard didn't answer. He knew that there were. He knew also that Keith Denison's case wouldn't be one of them. The Patrol was not staffed by saints, but its people dared not corrupt their own law for their own ends. You took your losses like any other corps, and raised a glass to the memory of your dead, and you did not travel back to look upon them again while they had lived.

Presently Cynthia left him, returned to her drink and tossed it down. The yellow locks swirled past her face as she did. "I'm sorry," she said. She got out a handkerchief and wiped her eyes. "I didn't mean to bawl."

"It's okay."

She stared at the floor. "You could try to help Keith. The regular agents have given up, but you could try."

It was an appeal from which he had no recourse. "I could," he told her. "I might not succeed. The existing records show that, if I tried, I failed. And any alteration of space-time is frowned on, even a trivial one like this."

"It isn't trivial to Keith," she said.

"You know, Cyn," he murmured, "you're one of the few women that ever lived who'd have phrased it that way. Most would have said, It isn't trivial to me."

Her eyes captured his, and for a moment she stood very quiet. Then, whispering:

"I'm sorry. Manse. I didn't realize. . . . I thought, what with all the time that's gone past for you, you would have—"

"What are you talking about?" he defended himself.

"Can't the Patrol psychs do anything for you?" she asked. Her head drooped again. "I mean, if they can condition us so we just simply can't tell anyone unauthorized that time travel exists . . . I should think it would also be possible to, to condition a person out of—"

"Skip it," said Everard roughly.

He gnawed his pipestem a while. "Okay," he said at last. "I've an idea or two of my own that may not have been tried. If Keith can be rescued in any way, you'll get him back before tomorrow noon."

"Could you time-hop me up to that moment, Manse?" She was beginning to tremble.

"I could," he said, "but I won't. One way or another, you'll need to be rested tomorrow. I'll take you home now and see that you swallow a sleepy pill. And then I'll come back here and think about the situation." He twisted his mouth into a sort of grin. "Cut out that shimmy, huh? I told you I had to think."

"Manse. . . ." Her hands closed about his.

He knew a sudden hope for which he cursed himself.

3

In the fall of the year 542 B.C., a solitary man came down out of the mountains and into the valley of the Kur. He rode a handsome chestnut gelding, bigger even than most cavalry horses, which might elsewhere have been an invitation to bandits; but the Great King had given so much law to his dominions that it was said a virgin with a sack of gold could walk unmolested across all Persia.

It was one reason Manse Everard had chosen to hop to this date, sixteen years after Keith Denison's destination.

Another motive was to arrive long after any excitement which the time traveler had conceivably produced in 558 had died away. Whatever the truth about Keith's fate, it might be more approachable from the rear; at least, straightforward methods had failed.

Finally, according to the Achaemenid Milieu office, autumn 542 happened to be the first season of relative tranquility since the disappearance. The years 558–553 had been tense ones when the Persian king of Anshan, Kuru-sh (he whom the future knew as Koresh and Cyrus), was more and more at odds with his Median overlord Astyages. Then came three years when Cyrus revolted, civil war racked the empire, and the Persians finally overcame their northerly neighbors. But Cyrus was scarcely victorious before he must face counter-uprisings, as well as Turanian incursions; he spent four years putting down that trouble and extending his rule eastward. This alarmed his fellow monarchs; Babylon, Egypt, Lydia, and Sparta formed a coalition to destroy him, with King Croesus of Lydia leading an invasion in 546. The Lydians were broken and annexed, but they revolted and had to be broken all over again; the troublesome Greek colonies of Ionia, Caria, and Lycia must be settled with; and while his generals did all this in the west, Cyrus himself must war in the east, forcing back the savage horsemen who would otherwise burn his cities.

Now there was a breathing spell. Cilicia would yield without a fight, seeing that Persia's other conquests were governed with a humanity and a tolerance of local custom such as the world had not known before. Cyrus would leave the eastern marches to his nobles, and devote himself to consolidating what he had won. Not until 539 would the war with Babylon be taken up again and Mesopotamia acquired. And then Cyrus would have another time of peace, until the wild men grew too strong beyond the Aral Sea and the King rode forth against them to his death.

Manse Everard entered Pasargadae as if into a springtime of hope.

Not that any actual era lends itself to such flowery metaphors. He jogged through miles where peasants bent with sickles, loading creaky unpainted oxcarts, and dust smoked off the stubble fields into his eyes. Ragged children sucked their thumbs outside windowless mud huts and stared at him. A chicken squawked back and forth on the highway until the galloping royal messenger who had alarmed it was past and the chicken dead. A squad of lancers trotting by were costumed picturesquely enough, baggy pants and scaly armor, spiked or plumed helmets, gaily striped cloaks; but they were also dusty, sweaty, and swapping foul jokes. Behind adobe walls the aristocrats possessed large houses with very beautiful gardens, but an economy like this would not support many such estates. Pasargadae was ninety percent an

Oriental town of twisted slimy streets between faceless hovels, greasy headcloths and dingy robes, screaming merchants in the bazaars, beggars displaying their sores, traders leading strings of battered camels and over-loaded donkeys, dogs raiding offal heaps, tavern music like a cat in a washing machine, men who windmilled their arms and screamed curses—whatever started this yarn about the inscrutable East?

"Alms, lord. Alms, for the love of Light! Alms, and Mithras will smile upon you! . . ."

"Behold sir! By my father's beard I swear that never was there finer work from a more skilled hand than this bridle which I offer to you, most fortunate of men, for the ridiculous sum of . . ."

"This way, master, this way, only four houses down to the finest sarai in all Persia—no, in all the world. Our pallets are stuffed with swan's down, my father serves wine fit for a Devi, my mother cooks a pilau whose fame has spread to the ends of the earth, and my sisters are three moons of delight available for a mere. . . ."

Everard ignored the childish runners who clamored at his sides. One of them tugged his ankle, he swore and kicked, and the boy grinned without shame. The man hoped to avoid staying at an inn; the Persians were cleaner than most folk in this age, but there would still be insect life.

He tried not to feel defenseless. Ordinarily a Patrolman could have an ace in the hole: say, a thirtieth-century stun pistol beneath his coat and a midget radio to call the hidden space-time antigravity scooter to him. But not when he might be frisked. Everard wore a Greek outfit: tunic and sandals and long wool cloak, sword at waist, helmet and shield hung at the horse's crupper, and that was it; only the steel was anachronistic. He could turn to no local branch office if he got into trouble, for this relatively poor and turbulent transition epoch attracted no Temporal commerce; the nearest Patrol unit was milieu HQ in Persepolis, a generation futureward.

The streets widened as he pushed on, bazaars thinned out and houses grew larger. At last he emerged in a square enclosed by four mansions. He could see pruned trees above their outer walls. Guards, lean lightly armed youths, squatted beneath on their heels because standing at attention had not yet been invented. They rose, nocking wary arrows, as Everard approached. He might simply have crossed the plaza, but he veered and hailed a fellow who looked like a captain.

"Greetings, sir, may the sun fall bright upon you." The Persian which he had learned in an hour under hypno flowed readily off his tongue. "I seek hospitality from some great man who may care to hear my poor tales of foreign travel."

"May your days be many," said the guard. Everard remembered that he must not offer baksheesh: these Persians of Cyrus's own clans were a proud hardy folk, hunters, herdsmen, and warriors. All spoke with the dignified politeness common to their type throughout history. "I serve Croesus the Lydian, servant of the Great King. He will not refuse his roof to—"

"Meander from Athens," supplied Everard. It was an alias which would explain his large bones, light complexion, and short hair. He had, though, been forced to stick a realistic Van Dyke effect on his chin. Herodotus was not the first Greek globetrotter, so an Athenian would not be inconveniently outré. At the same time, half a century before Marathon, Europeans were still uncommon enough here to excite interest.

A slave was called, who got hold of the majordomo, who sent another slave, who invited the stranger through the gate. The garden beyond was as cool and green as hoped; there was no fear that anything would be stolen from his baggage in this household; the food and drink should be good; and Croesus himself would certainly interview the guest at length. *We're playing in luck, lad,* Everard assured himself, and accepted a hot bath, fragrant oils, fresh clothing, dates and wine brought to his austerely furnished room, a couch and a pleasant view. He only missed a cigar.

Of attainable things, that is.

To be sure, if Keith had unamendably died. . . .

"Hell and purple frogs," muttered Everard. "Cut that out, will you?"

4

After sunset it grew chilly. Lamps were lit with much ceremony, fire being sacred, and braziers were blown up. A slave prostrated himself to announce that dinner was served. Everard accompanied him down a long hall where vigorous murals showed the Sun and the Bull of Mithras, past a couple of spearmen, and into a small chamber brightly lit, sweet with incense and lavish with carpeting. Two couches were drawn up in the Hellenic manner at a table covered with un-Hellenic dishes of silver and gold; slave waiters hovered in the background and Chinese-sounding music twanged from an inner door.

Croesus of Lydia nodded graciously. He had been handsome once, with regular features, but seemed to have aged a lot in the few years since his wealth and power were proverbial. Grizzled of beard and with long hair, he was dressed in a Grecian chlamys but wore rouge in the Persian manner. "Rejoice, Meander of Athens," he said in Greek, and lifted his face.

Everard kissed his cheek as indicated. It was nice of Croesus thus to imply

that Meander's rank was but little inferior to his own, even if Croesus had been
eating garlic. "Rejoice, master. I thank you for your kindness."

"This solitary meal was not to demean you," said the ex-king. "I only
thought. . . ." He hesitated. "I have always considered myself near kin to
the Greeks, and we could talk seriously—"

"My lord honors me beyond my worth." They went through various rituals
and finally got to the food. Everard spun out a prepared yarn about his travels;
now and then Croesus would ask a disconcertingly sharp question, but a
Patrolman soon learned how to evade that kind.

"Indeed times are changing, you are fortunate in coming at the very dawn
of a new age," said Croesus. "Never has the world known a more glorious
King than," etc., etc., doubtless for the benefit of any retainers who doubled
as royal spies. Though it happened to be true.

"The very gods have favored our King," went on Croesus. "Had I known
how they sheltered him—for truth, I mean, not for the mere fable which I
believed it was—I should never have dared oppose myself to him. For it
cannot be doubted, he is a Chosen One."

Everard maintained his Greek character by watering the wine and wishing
he had picked some less temperate nationality. "What is that tale, lord?" he
asked. "I knew only that the Great King was the son of Cambyses, who held
this province as a vassal of Median Astyages. Is there more?"

Croesus leaned forward. In the uncertain light, his eyes held a curious bright
look, a Dionysian blend of terror and enthusiasm which Everard's age had long
forgotten. "Hear, and bring the account to your countrymen," he said.
"Astyages wed his daughter Mandane to Cambyses, for he knew that the
Persians were restless under his own heavy yoke and he wished to tie their
leaders to his house. But Cambyses became ill and weak. If he died and his
infant son Cyrus succeeded in Anshan, there would be a troublesome regency
of Persian nobles not bound to Astyages. Dreams also warned the Median king
that Cyrus would be the death of his dominion.

"Thereafter Astyages ordered his kinsman, the King's Eye Aurvagaush
[Croesus rendered the name Harpagus, as he Hellenized all local names], to do
away with the prince. Harpagus took the child despite Queen Mandane's
protests; Cambyses lay too sick to help her, nor could Persia in any case revolt
without preparation. But Harpagus could not bring himself to the deed. He
exchanged the prince for the stillborn child of a herdsman in the mountains,
whom he swore to secrecy. The dead baby was wrapped in royal clothes and
left on a hillside; presently officials of the Median court were summoned to
witness that it had been exposed, and buried it. Our lord Cyrus grew up as a
herdsman.

"Cambyses lived for twenty years more without begetting other sons, not strong enough in his own person to avenge the firstborn. But at last he was plainly dying, with no successor whom the Persians would feel obliged to obey. Again Astyages feared trouble. At this time Cyrus came forth, his identity being made known through various signs. Astyages, regretting what had gone before, welcomed him and confirmed him as Cambyses's heir.

"Cyrus remained a vassal for five years, but found the tyranny of the Medes ever more odious. Harpagus in Ecbatana had also a dreadful thing to avenge: as punishment for his disobedience in the matter of Cyrus, Astyages made Harpagus eat his own son. So Harpagus conspired with certain Median nobles. They chose Cyrus as their leader, Persia revolted, and after three years of war Cyrus made himself the master of the two peoples. Since then, of course, he has added many others. When ever did the gods show their will more plainly?"

Everard lay quiet on the couch for a little. He heard autumn leaves rustle dryly in the garden, under a cold wind.

"This is true, and no fanciful gossip?" he asked.

"I have confirmed it often enough since I joined the Persian court. The King himself has vouched for it to me, as well as Harpagus and others who were directly concerned."

The Lydian could not be lying if he cited his ruler's testimony: the upper-class Persians were fanatics about truthfulness. And yet Everard had heard nothing so incredible in all his Patrol career. For it was the story which Herodotus recorded—with a few modifications to be found in the *Shah Nameh*—and anybody could spot that as a typical hero myth. Essentially the same yarn had been told about Moses, Romulus, Sigurd, a hundred great men. There was no reason to believe it held any fact, no reason to doubt that Cyrus had been raised in a perfectly normal manner at his father's house, had succeeded by plain right of birth and revolted for the usual reasons.

Only, this tall tale was sworn to by eyewitnesses!

There was a mystery here. It brought Everard back to his purpose. After appropriate marveling remarks, he led the conversation until he could say: "I have heard rumors that sixteen years ago a stranger entered Pasargadae, clad as a poor shepherd but in truth a mage who did miracles. He may have died here. Does my gracious host know anything of it?"

He waited then, tensed. He was playing a hunch, that Keith Denison had not been murdered by some hillbilly, fallen off a cliff and broken his neck, or come to grief in any such way. Because in that case, the scooter should still have been around when the Patrol searched. They might have gridded the area too loosely to find Denison himself, but how could their detectors miss a time hopper?

So, Everard thought, something more complicated had happened. And if Keith survived at all, he would have come down here to civilization.

"Sixteen years ago?" Croesus tugged his beard. "I was not here then. And surely in any case the land would have been full of portents, for that was when Cyrus left the mountains and took his rightful crown of Anshan. No, Meander, I know nothing of it."

"I have been anxious to find this person," said Everard, "because an oracle," etc., etc.

"You can inquire among the servants and townspeople," suggested Croesus. "I will ask at court on your behalf. You will stay here awhile, will you not? Perhaps the King himself will wish to see you; he is always interested in foreigners."

The conversation broke up soon after. Croesus explained with a rather sour smile that the Persians believed in early to bed, early to rise, and he must be at the royal palace by dawn. A slave conducted Everard back to his room, where he found a good-looking girl waiting with an expectant smile. He hesitated a moment, remembering a time twenty-four hundred years hence. But—the hell with that. A man had to take whatever the gods offered him, and they were a miserly lot.

5

It was not long after sunrise when a troop reined up in the plaza and shouted for Meander the Athenian. Everard left his breakfast to go out and stare up a gray stallion into the hard, hairy hawk-face of a captain of those guards called the Immortals. The men made a backdrop of restless horses, cloaks and plumes blowing, metal jingling and leather squeaking, the young sun ablaze on polished mail.

"You are summoned by the Chiliarch," rapped the officer. The title he actually used was Persian: commander of the guard and grand vizier of the empire.

Everard stood for a moment, weighing the situation. His muscles tightened. This was not a very cordial invitation. But he could scarcely plead a previous engagement.

"I hear and obey," he said. "Let me but fetch a small gift from my baggage, in token of the honor paid me."

"The Chiliarch said you were to come at once. Here is a horse."

An archer sentry offered cupped hands, but Everard pulled himself into the saddle without help, a trick it was useful to know in eras before stirrups were introduced. The captain nodded a harsh approval, whirled his mount, and led at a gallop off the plaza and up a wide avenue lined with sphinxes and the homes of the great. This was not as heavily trafficked as the bazaar streets, but there were enough riders, chariots, litters, and pedestrians scrambling out of the way. The Immortals stopped for no man. They roared through palace gates flung open before them. Gravel spurted under hoofs; they tore around a lawn where fountains sparkled, and clanged to a stop outside the west wing.

The palace, gaudily painted brick, stood on a wide platform with several lesser buildings. The captain himself sprang down, gestured curtly, and strode up a marble staircase. Everard followed, hemmed in by warriors who had taken the light battle axes from their saddlebows for his benefit. The party went among household slaves, robed and turbaned and flat on their faces, through a red and yellow colonnade, down a mosaic hall whose beauty Everard was in no mood to appreciate, and so past a squad of guards into a room where slender columns upheld a peacock dome and the fragrance of late-blooming roses entered through arched windows.

There the Immortals made obeisance. *What's good enough for them is good enough for you, son,* thought Everard, and kissed the Persian carpet. The man on the couch nodded. "Rise and attend," he said. "Fetch a cushion for the Greek." The soldiers took their stance by him. A Nubian bustled forth with a pillow, which he laid on the floor beneath his master's seat. Everard sat down on it, cross-legged. His mouth felt dry.

The Chiliarch, whom he remembered Croesus identifying as Harpagus, leaned forward. Against the tiger skin on the couch and the gorgeous red robe on his own gaunt frame, the Mede showed as an aging man, his shoulder-length hair the color of iron and his dark craggy-nosed face sunken into a mesh of wrinkles. But shrewd eyes considered the newcomer.

"Well," he said, his Persian having the rough accent of a North Iranian, "so you are the man from Athens. The noble Croesus spoke of your advent this morning and mentioned some inquiries you were making. Since the safety of the state may be involved, I would know just what it is you seek." He stroked his beard with a jewel-flashing hand and smiled frostily. "It may even be, if your search is harmless, that I can help it."

He had been careful not to employ the usual formulas of greeting, to offer refreshment, or otherwise give Meander the quasi-sacred status of guest. This was an interrogation. "Lord, what is it you wish to know?" asked Everard. He could well imagine, and it was a troublous anticipation.

"You sought a mage in shepherd guise, who entered Pasargadae sixteen summers ago and did miracles." The voice was ugly with tension. "Why is this and what more have you heard of such matters? Do not pause to invent a lie—speak!"

"Great lord," said Everard, "the oracle at Delphi told me I should mend my fortunes if I learned the fate of a herdsman who entered the Persian capital in, er, the third year of the first tyranny of Pisistratus. More than that I have never known. My lord is aware how dark are the oracular sayings."

"Hm, hm." Fear touched the lean countenance and Harpagus drew the sign of the cross, which was a Mithraic sun-symbol. Then, roughly: "What have you discovered so far?"

"Nothing, great lord. No one could tell—"

"You lie!" snarled Harpagus. "All Greeks are liars. Have a care, for you touch on unholy matters. Who else have you spoken to?"

Everard saw a nervous tic lift the Chiliarch's mouth. His own stomach was a cold jump in him. He had stumbled on something which Harpagus had thought safely buried, something so big that the risk of a clash with Croesus, who was duty bound to protect a guest, became nothing. And the most reliable gag ever invented was a snickersnee . . . after rack and pincers had extracted precisely what the stranger knew. . . . *But what the blue hell do I know?*

"None, my lord," he husked. "None but the oracle, and the Sun God whose voice the oracle is, and who sent me here, has heard of this before last night."

Harpagus sucked in a sharp breath, taken aback by the invocation. But then, almost visibly squaring his shoulders: "We have only your word, the word of a Greek, that you were told by an oracle—that you did not spy out state secrets. Or even if the God did indeed send you here, it may as well have been to destroy you for your sins. We shall ask further about this." He nodded at the captain. "Take him below. In the King's name."

The King!

It blazed upon Everard. He jumped to his feet.

"Yes, the King!" he shouted. "The God told me . . . there would be a sign . . . and then I should bear his word to the Persian King!"

"Seize him!" yelled Harpagus.

The guardsmen whirled to obey. Everard sprang back, yelling for King Cyrus as loudly as he could. Let them arrest him. Word would be carried to the throne and. . . . Two men hemmed him against the wall, their axes raised. Others pressed behind them. Over their helmets, he saw Harpagus leap up on the couch.

"Take him out and behead him!" ordered the Mede.

"My lord," protested the captain, "he called upon the King."

"To cast a spell! I know him now, the son of Zohak and agent of Ahriman! Kill him!"

"No, wait," cried Everard, "wait, can you not see, it is this traitor who would keep me from telling the King. . . . Let go, you sod!"

A hand closed on his right arm. He had been prepared to sit a few hours in jail, till the big boss heard of the affair and bailed him out, but matters were a bit more urgent after all. He threw a left hook which ended in a squelching of nose. The guardsman staggered back. Everard plucked the ax from his hand, spun about, and parried the blow of the warrior on his left.

The Immortals attacked. Everard's ax clanged against metal, darted in and smashed a knuckle. He outreached most of these people. But he hadn't a cellophane snowball's chance in hell of standing them off. A blow whistled toward his head. He ducked behind a column; chips flew. An opening—he stiff-armed one man, hopped over the clashing mail-clad form as it fell, and got onto open floor under the dome. Harpagus scuttled up, drawing a saber from beneath his robe; the old bastard was brave enough. Everard twirled to meet him, so that the Chiliarch was between him and the guards. Ax and sword rattled together. Everard tried to close in . . . a clinch would keep the Persians from throwing their weapons at him, but they were circling to get at his rear. Judas, this might be the end of one more Patrolman. . . .

"Halt! Fall on your faces! The King comes!"

Three times it was blared. The guardsmen froze in their tracks, stared at the gigantic scarlet-robed person who stood bellowing in the doorway, and hit the rug. Harpagus dropped his sword. Everard almost brained him; then, remembering, and hearing the hurried tramp of warriors in the hall, he let go his own weapon. For a moment, he and the Chiliarch panted into each other's faces.

"So . . . he got word . . . and came . . . at once," gasped Everard.

The Mede crouched like a cat and hissed back: "Have a care, then! I will be watching you. If you poison his mind there will be poison for you, or a dagger. . . ."

"The King! The King!" bellowed the herald.

Everard joined Harpagus on the floor.

A band of Immortals trotted into the room and made an alley to the couch. A chamberlain dashed to throw a special tapestry over it. Then Cyrus himself entered, robe billowing around long muscular strides. A few courtiers followed, leathery men privileged to bear arms in the royal presence, and a slave MC wringing his hands in their wake at not having been given time to spread a carpet or summon musicians.

The King's voice rang through the silence: "What is this? Where is the stranger who called on me?"

Everard risked a peek. Cyrus was tall, broad of shoulder and slim of body, older-looking than Croesus's account suggested—he was forty-seven years old, Everard knew with a shudder—but kept supple by sixteen years of war and the chase. He had a narrow dark countenance with hazel eyes, a sword scar on the left cheekbone, a straight nose and full lips. His black hair, faintly grizzled, was brushed back and his beard trimmed more closely than was Persian custom. He was dressed as plainly as his status allowed.

"Where is the stranger whom the slave ran to tell me of?"

"I am he, Great King," said Everard.

"Arise. Declare your name."

Everard stood up and murmured: "Hi, Keith."

6

Vines rioted about a marble pergola. They almost hid the archers who ringed it. Keith Denison slumped on a bench, stared at leaf shadows dappled onto the floor, and said wryly, "At least we can keep our talk private. The English language hasn't been invented yet."

After a moment he continued, with a rusty accent: "Sometimes I've thought that was the hardest thing to take about this situation, never having a minute to myself. The best I can do is throw everybody out of the room I'm in; but they stick around just beyond the door, under the windows, guarding, listening. I hope their dear loyal souls fry."

"Privacy hasn't been invented yet either," Everard reminded him. "And VIPs like you never did have much, in all history."

Denison raised a tired visage. "I keep wanting to ask how Cynthia is," he said, "but of course for her it has been—will be—not so long. A week, perhaps. Did you by any chance bring some cigarettes?"

"Left 'em in the scooter," said Everard. "I figured I'd have trouble enough without explaining that away. I never expected to find you running this whole shebang."

"I didn't myself." Denison shrugged. "It was the damnedest fantastic thing. The time paradoxes—"

"So what did happen?"

Denison rubbed his eyes and sighed. "I got myself caught in the local gears. You know, sometimes everything that went before seems unreal to me, like a dream. Were there ever such things as Christendom, contrapuntal music, or the Bill of Rights? Not to mention all the people I knew. You yourself don't belong here, Manse, I keep expecting to wake up. . . . Well, let me think back.

"Do you know what the situation was? The Medes and the Persians are pretty near kin, racially and culturally, but the Medes were top dog then, and they'd picked up a lot of habits from the Assyrians which didn't sit so well in the Persian viewpoint. We're ranchers and freehold farmers, mostly, and of course it isn't right that we should be vassals—" Denison blinked. "Hey, there I go again! What do I mean 'we'? Anyhow, Persia was restless. King Astyages of Media had ordered the murder of little Prince Cyrus twenty years before, but now he regretted it, because Cyrus's father was dying and the dispute over succession could touch off a civil war.

"Well, I appeared in the mountains. I had to scout a little bit in both space and time—hopping through a few days and several miles—to find a good hiding place for my scooter. That's why the Patrol couldn't locate it afterward . . . part of the reason. You see, I did finally park it in a cave and set out on foot, but right away I came to grief. A Median army was bound through that region to discourage the Persians from making trouble. One of their scouts saw me emerge, checked my back trail—first thing I knew, I'd been seized and their officer was grilling me about what that gadget was I had in the cave. His men took me for a magician of some kind and were in considerable awe, but more afraid of showing fear than they were of me. Naturally, the word ran like a brushfire through the ranks and across the countryside. Soon all the area knew that a stranger had appeared under remarkable circumstances.

"Their general was Harpagus himself, as smart and tough-minded a devil as the world has ever seen. He thought I could be used. He ordered me to make my brazen horse perform, but I wasn't allowed to mount it. However, I did get a chance to kick it into time-drive. That's why the search party didn't find the thing. It was only a few hours in this century, then it probably went clear back to the Beginning."

"Good work," said Everard.

"Oh, I knew the orders forbidding that degree of anachronism." Denison's lips twisted. "But I also expected the Patrol to rescue me. If I'd known they wouldn't, I'm not so sure I'd have stayed a good self-sacrificing Patrolman. I might have hung on to my scooter, and played Harpagus's game till a chance came to escape on my own."

Everard looked at him a moment, somberly. Keith had changed, he thought: not just in age, but the years among aliens had marked him more deeply than he knew. "If you risked altering the future," he said, "you risked Cynthia's existence."

"Yes. Yes, true. I remember thinking of that .   . at the time. . . . How long ago it seems!"

Denison leaned forward, elbows on knees, staring into the pergola screen. His words continued, flat. "Harpagus spit rivets, of course. I thought for a while he was going to kill me. I was carried off, trussed up like butcher's meat. But as I told you, there were already rumors about me, which were losing nothing in repetition. Harpagus saw a still better chance. He gave me a choice, string along with him or have my throat cut. What else could I do? It wasn't even a matter of hazarding an alteration; I soon saw I was playing a role which history had *already* written.

"You see, Harpagus bribed a herdsman to support his tale, and produced me as Cyrus, son of Cambyses."

Everard nodded, unsurprised. "What's in it for him?" he asked.

"At the time, he only wanted to bolster the Median rule. A king in Anshan under his thumb would have to be loyal to Astyages, and thereby help keep all the Persians in line. I was rushed along, too bewildered to do more than follow his lead, still hoping minute by minute for a Patrol hopper to appear and get me out of the mess. The truth fetish of all these Iranian aristocrats helped us a lot—few of them suspected I perjured myself in swearing I was Cyrus, though I imagine Astyages quietly ignored the discrepancies. And he put Harpagus in his place by punishing him in an especially gruesome way for not having done away with Cyrus as ordered—even if Cyrus turned out to be useful now—and of course the double irony was that Harpagus really had followed orders, two decades before!

"As for me, in the course of five years I got more and more sickened by Astyages myself. Now, looking back, I see he wasn't really such a hound from hell, just a typical Oriental monarch of the ancient world, but that's kind of hard to appreciate when you're forced to watch a man being racked.

"So Harpagus, wanting revenge, engineered a revolt, and I accepted the leadership of it which he offered me." Denison grinned crookedly. "After all, I was Cyrus the Great, with a destiny to play out. We had a rough time at first, the Medes clobbered us again and again, but you know, Manse, I found myself enjoying it. Not like that wretched twentieth-century business of sitting in a foxhole wondering if the enemy barrage will ever let up. Oh, war is miserable enough here, especially if you're a buck private when disease breaks out, as it always does. But when you fight, by God, you fight, with your own hands! And I even found a talent for that sort of thing. We've pulled some gorgeous stunts." Everard watched life flow back into him: "Like the time the Lydian cavalry had us outnumbered. We sent our baggage camels in the van, with the infantry behind and horse last. Croesus's nags got a whiff of the camels and stampeded. For all I know, they're running yet. We mopped him up!"

He jarred to silence, stared awhile into Everard's eyes, and bit his lip. "Sorry. I keep forgetting. Now and then, I remember I was not a killer at home—after a battle, when I see the dead scattered around, and worst of all the wounded. But I couldn't help it, Manse! I've had to fight! First there was the revolt. If I hadn't played along with Harpagus, how long do you think I'd have lasted, personally? And then there's been the realm itself. I didn't ask the Lydians to invade us, or the eastern barbarians. Have you ever seen a town sacked by Turanians, Manse? It's them or us, and when *we* conquer somebody we don't march them off in chains, they keep their own lands and customs and. . . . For Mithras's sake, Manse, could I do anything else?"

Everard sat listening to the garden rustle under a breeze. At last: "No. I understand. I hope it hasn't been too lonesome."

"I got used to it," said Denison carefully. "Harpagus is an acquired taste, but interesting. Croesus turned out to be a very decent fellow. Kobad the Mage has some original thoughts, and he's the only man alive who dares beat me at chess. And there's the feasting, and hunting, and women. . . ." He gave the other a defiant look. "Yeah. What else would you have me do?"

"Nothing," said Everard. "Sixteen years is a long time."

"Cassandane, my chief wife, is worth a lot of the trouble I've had. Though Cynthia—God in heaven, Manse!" Denison stood up and laid hands on Everard's shoulders. The fingers closed with bruising strength; they had held ax, bow, and bridle for a decade and a half. The King of the Persians shouted aloud:

"How are you going to get me out of here?"

7

Everard rose too, walked to the floor's edge and stared through lacy stonework, thumbs hooked in his belt and head lowered.

"I don't see how," he answered.

Denison smote a fist into one palm. "I've been afraid of that. Year by year I've grown more afraid that if the Patrol ever finds me it'll. . . . You've got to help."

"I tell you, I can't!" Everard's voice cracked. He did not turn around. "Think it over. You must have done so already. You're not some lousy little barbarian chief whose career won't make a jot of difference a hundred years from now. You're Cyrus, the founder of the Persian Empire, a key figure in a key milieu. If Cyrus goes, so does the whole future! There won't have been any twentieth century with Cynthia in it."

"Are you certain?" pleaded the man at his back.

"I boned up on the facts before hopping here," said Everard through clenched jaws. "Stop kidding yourself. We're prejudiced against the Persians because at one time they were the enemies of Greece, and we happen to get some of the more conspicuous features of our own culture from Hellenic sources. But the Persians are at least as important!

"You've watched it happen. Sure, they're pretty brutal by your standards:

the whole era is, including the Greeks. And they're not democratic, but you can't blame them for not making a European invention outside their whole mental horizon. What counts is this:

"Persia was the first conquering power which made an effort to respect and conciliate the people it took over; which obeyed its own laws; which pacified enough territory to open steady contact with the Far East; which created a viable world religion, Zoroastrianism, not limited to any one race or locality. Maybe you don't know how much Christian belief and ritual is of Mithraic origin, but believe me, it's plenty. Not to mention Judaism, which you, Cyrus the Great, are personally going to rescue. Remember? You'll take over Babylon and allow those Jews who've kept their identity to return home; without you, they'd be swallowed up and lost in the general ruck as the ten other tribes already have been.

"Even when it gets decadent, the Persian Empire will be a matrix for civilization. What were most of Alexander's conquests but just taking over Persian territory? And that spread Hellenism through the known world! And there'll be Persian successor states: Pontus, Parthia, the Persia of Firduzi and Omar and Hafiz, the Iran we know and the Iran of a future beyond the twentieth century. . . ."

Everard turned on his heel. "If you quit," he said, "I can imagine them still building ziggurats and reading entrails—and running through the woods up in Europe, with America underdiscovered—three thousand years from now!"

Denison sagged. "Yeah," he answered. "I thought so."

He paced awhile, hands behind his back. The dark face looked older each minute. "Thirteen more years," he murmured, almost to himself. "In thirteen years I'll fall in battle against the nomads. I don't know exactly how. One way or another, circumstances will force me to it. Why not? They've forced me into everything else I've done, willy-nilly . . . In spite of everything I can do to train him, I know my own son Cambyses will turn out to be a sadistic incompetent and it will take Darius to save the empire—God!" He covered his face with a flowing sleeve. "Excuse me. I do despise self-pity, but I can't help this."

Everard sat down, avoiding the sight. He heard how the breath rattled in Denison's lungs.

Finally the King poured wine into two chalices, joined Everard on the bench and said in a dry tone: "Sorry. I'm okay now. And I haven't given up yet."

"I can refer your problem to headquarters," said Everard with a touch of sarcasm.

Denison echoed it: "Thanks, little chum. I remember their attitude well enough. We're expendable. They'll interdict the entire lifetime of Cyrus to visitors, just so I won't be tempted, and send me a nice message. They will point out that I'm the absolute monarch of a civilized people, with palaces, slaves, vintages, chefs, entertainers, concubines, and hunting grounds at my disposal in unlimited quantities, so what am I complaining about? No, Manse, this is something you and I will have to work out between us."

Everard clenched his fists till he felt the nails bite into the palms. "You're putting me in a hell of a spot, Keith," he said.

"I'm only asking you to think on the problem—and Ahriman damn you, you will!" Again the fingers closed on his flesh, and the conqueror of the East snapped forth a command. The old Keith would never have taken that tone, thought Everard, anger flickering up; and he thought:

If you don't come home, and Cynthia is told that you never will. . . . She could come back and join you; one more foreign girl in the King's harem won't affect history. But if I reported to headquarters before seeing her, reported the problem as insoluble, which it doubtless is in fact . . . why, then the reign of Cyrus would be interdicted and she could not join you.

"I've been over this ground before, with myself," said Denison more calmly. "I know the implications as well as you do. But look, I can show you the cave where my machine rested for those few hours. You could go back to the moment I appeared there and warn me."

"No," said Everard. "That's out. Two reasons. First, the regulation against that sort of thing, which is a sensible one. They might make an exception under different circumstances, but there's a second reason too: you are Cyrus. They're not going to wipe out an entire future for one man's sake."

Would I do it for one woman's? I'm not sure. I hope not . . . Cynthia wouldn't have to know the facts. It would be kinder if she didn't. I could use my Unattached authority to keep the truth secret from lower echelons and tell her nothing except that Keith had irrevocably died under circumstances which forced us to shut off this period to time traffic. She'd grieve awhile, of course, but she's too healthy to mourn forever. . . . Sure, it's a lousy trick. But wouldn't it be kinder in the long run than letting her come back here, to servile status, and share her man with at least the dozen princesses that politics forces him to be married to? Wouldn't it be better for her to make a clean break and a fresh start, among her own people?

"Uh-huh," said Denison. "I mentioned that idea only to dispose of it. But there must be some other way. Look, Manse, sixteen years ago a situation existed from which everything else has followed, not through human caprice but through the sheer logic of events. Suppose I had not showed up? Mightn't Harpagus have found a different pseudo-Cyrus? The exact identity of the King doesn't matter. Another Cyrus would have acted differently from me in a million day-to-day details. Naturally. But if he wasn't a hopeless moron or maniac, if he was a reasonably able and decent person—give me credit for being that much—then his career would have been the same as mine in all the important ways, the ways that got into the history books. You know that as well as I do. Except at the crucial points, time always reverts to its own shape. The small differences damp out in days or years, negative feedback. It's only at key instants that a positive feedback can be set up and the effects multiply with passing time instead of disappearing. You know that!"

"Sure," said Everard. "But judging from your own account, your appearance in the cave *was* crucial. It was that which put the idea in Harpagus's head. Without it, well, I can imagine a decadent Median Empire falling apart, maybe falling prey to Lydia, or to the Turanians, because the Persians wouldn't have had the kind of royal divine-right-by-birth leadership they needed. . . . No. I wouldn't come near that moment in the cave without authorization from anyone less than a Danellian."

Denison looked at him over a raised chalice, lowered it and kept on looking. His face congealed into a stranger's. He said at last, very softly:

"You don't want me to come back, do you?"

Everard leaped off the bench. He dropped his own cup; it rang on the floor and wine ran from it like blood.

"Shut up!" he yelled.

Denison nodded. "I am the King," he said. "If I raise my finger, those guards will hack you in pieces."

"That's a hell of a way to get my help," growled Everard.

Denison's body jerked. He sat motionless for a while, before he got out: "I'm sorry. You don't realize what a shock. . . . Oh, yes, yes, it hasn't been a bad life. It's had more color in it than most, and this business of being quasi-divine grows on you. I suppose that's why I'll take the field beyond the Jaxartes, thirteen years from now: because I can't do anything else, with all those young lion eyes on me. Hell, I may even think it was worth it."

His expression writhed smilewards. "Some of my girls have been absolute knockouts. And there's always Cassandane. I made her my chief wife because in a dark way she reminds me of Cynthia. I think. It's hard to tell, after all this time. The twentieth century isn't real to me. And there's more actual satisfaction in a good horse than a sports car . . . and I know my work here is valuable, which isn't a knowledge granted to many. . . . Yeh. I'm sorry I barked at you. I know you'd help if you dared. Since you don't, and I don't blame you, you needn't regret it for my sake."

"Cut that out!" groaned Everard.

It felt as if there were gears in his brain, spinning against emptiness. Overhead he saw a painted roof, where a youth killed a bull, and the Bull was the Sun and the Man. Beyond columns and vines trod guards in dragon-skin mailcoats, their bows strung, their faces like carved wood. The harem wing of the palace could be glimpsed, where a hundred or a thousand young women counted themselves fortunate to await the King's occasional pleasure. Beyond the city walls lay harvest fields where peasants readied sacrifice to an Earth Mother who was old in this land when the Aryans came, and that was in a dark predawn past. High over the walls floated the mountains, haunted by wolf, lion, boar, and demon. It was too alien a place. Everard had thought himself hardened to otherness, but now he wanted suddenly to run and hide, up to his own century and his own people and a forgetting.

He said in a careful voice, "Let me consult a few associates. We can check the whole period in detail. There might be some kind of switch point where . . . I'm not competent to handle this alone, Keith. Let me go back upstairs and get some advice. If we work out anything we'll return to . . . this very night."

"Where's your scooter?" asked Denison.

Everard waved a hand. "Up in the hills."

Denison stroked his beard. "You aren't telling me more than that, eh? Well, it's wise. I'm not sure I'd trust myself, if I knew where a time machine could be gotten."

"I don't mean that!" shouted Everard.

"Oh, never mind. Let's not fight about it." Denison sighed. "Sure, go on home and see what you can do. Want an escort?"

"Better not. It isn't necessary, is it?"

"No. We've made this area safer than Central Park."

"That isn't saying much." Everard held out his hand. "Just get me back my horse. I'd hate to lose him: special Patrol animal, trained to time hop." His gaze closed with the other man's. "I'll return. In person. Whatever the decision is."

"Sure, Manse," said Denison.

They walked out together, to go through the various formalities of notifying guardsmen and gatekeepers. Denison indicated a palace bedchamber where he said he would be every night for a week, as a rendezvous. And then at last Everard kissed the King's feet, and when the royal presence had departed he got aboard his horse and jogged slowly out through the palace gates.

He felt empty inside. There was really nothing to be done; and he had promised to come back himself and pass that sentence upon the King.

8

Late that day he was in the hills, where cedars gloomed above cold, brawling brooks and the side road onto which he had turned became a rutted upward track. Though arid enough, the Iran of this age still had a few such forests. The horse plodded beneath him, worn down. He should find some herdsman's house and request lodging, simply to spare the creature. But no, there would be a full moon; he could walk if he must and reach the scooter before sunrise. He didn't think he could sleep.

A place of long sere grass and ripe berries did invite him to rest, though. He had food in the saddlebags, a wineskin, and a stomach unfilled since dawn. He clucked encouragingly to the horse and turned.

Something caught his eye. Far down the road, level sunlight glowed off a dust cloud. It grew bigger even as he watched. Several riders, he guessed, coming in one devil of a hurry. King's messengers? But why, into this section? Uneasiness tickled his nerves. He put on his helmet cap, buckled the helmet itself above, hung shield on arm and loosened the short sword in its sheath. Doubtless the party would just hurrah on past him, but. . . .

Now he could see that there were eight men. They had good horseflesh beneath them, and the rearmost led a string of remounts. Nevertheless the animals were pretty jaded; sweat had made streaks down their dusty flanks and manes were plastered to necks. It must have been a long gallop. The riders were decently clad in the usual full white pants, shirt, boots, cloak, and tall brimless hat: not courtiers or professional soldiers, but not bandits either. They were armed with swords, bows, and lariats.

Suddenly Everard recognized the greybeard at their head. It exploded in him: Harpagus!

And through whirling haze he could also see—even for ancient Iranians, the followers were a tough-looking crew.

"Oh-oh," said Everard, half aloud. "School's out."

His mind clicked over. There wasn't time to be afraid, only to think. Harpagus had no other obvious motive for hightailing into the hills than to catch the Greek Meander. Surely, in a court riddled with spies and blabber-mouths, Harpagus would have learned within an hour that the King spoke to the stranger as an equal in some unknown tongue and let him go back northward. It would take the Chiliarch a while longer to manufacture some excuse for leaving the palace, round up his personal bully boys, and give chase. Why? Because "Cyrus" had once appeared in these uplands, riding some device which Harpagus had coveted. No fool, the Mede must never have been satisfied with the evasive yarn Keith had handed him. It would seem reasonable that one day another mage from the King's home country must appear; and this time Harpagus would not let the engine go from him so easily.

Everard paused no longer. They were only a hundred yards away. He could see the Chiliarch's eyes glitter beneath shaggy brows. He spurred his horse, off the road and across the meadow.

"Stop!" yelled a remembered voice behind him. "Stop, Greek!"

Everard got an exhausted trot out of his mount. The cedars threw long shadows across him.

"Stop or we shoot! . . . halt! . . . shoot, then! Not to kill! Get the steed!"

At the forest edge, Everard slipped from his saddle. He heard an angry whirr and a score of thumps. The horse screamed. Everard cast a glance behind; the poor beast was on its knees. By God, somebody would pay for this! But he was one man and they were eight. He hurried under the trees. A shaft smote a trunk by his left shoulder, burying itself.

He ran, crouched, zigzag in a chilly sweet-smelling twilight. Now and then a low branch whipped across his face. He could have used more underbrush, there were some Algonquian stunts for a hunted man to try, but at least the soft floor was noiseless under his sandals. The Persians were lost to sight. Almost instinctively, they had tried to ride after him. Cracking and crashing and loud obscenities ripped the air to show how well that had worked.

They'd come on foot in a minute. He cocked his head. A faint rush of water. . . . He moved in its direction, up a steep boulder-strewn slope. His hunters were not helpless urbanites, he thought. At least some of them were sure to be mountaineers, with eyes to read the dimmest signs of his passage. He had to break the trail; then he could hole up until Harpagus must return to court duties. The breath grew harsh in his throat. Behind him voices snapped forth, a note of decision, but he couldn't make out what was said. Too far. And the blood pounded so loudly in his ears.

If Harpagus had fired on the King's guest, then Harpagus surely did not intend that that guest should ever report it to the King. Capture, torture till he revealed where the machine lay and how to operate it, and a final mercy of cold steel were the program. *Judas,* thought Everard through the clamor in his veins, *I've mucked this operation up till it's a manual of how not to be a Patrolman. And the first item is, don't think so hard about a certain girl who isn't yours that you neglect elementary precautions.*

He came out on the edge of a high, wet bank. A brook roiled valleyward below him. They'd see he had come this far, but it would be a toss-up which way he splashed in the streambed . . . which should it be, anyhow? . . . the mud was cold and slippery on his skin as he scrambled down. Better go upstream. That would bring him closer to his scooter, and Harpagus might assume it more likely he'd try to double back to the King.

Stones bruised his feet and the water numbed them. The trees made a wall above either bank, so that he was roofed by a narrow strip of sky whose blue deepened momentarily. High up there floated an eagle. The air grew colder. But he had one piece of luck: the brook twisted like a snake in delirium and

60 THE TIME PATROL

he had quickly slipped and stumbled his way from sight of his entry point. *I'll go on a mile or so,* he thought, *and maybe there'll be an overhanging branch I can grab so I won't leave an outgoing trail.* Slow minutes passed.

So I get to the scooter, he thought, *and go upstairs and ask my chiefs for help. I know damn well they aren't going to give me any. Why not sacrifice one man to insure their own existence and everything they care about? Therefore Keith is stuck here, with thirteen years to go till the barbarians cut him down. But Cynthia will still be young in thirteen years, and after so long a nightmare of exile and knowing her man's time to die, she'd be cut off, an alien in an interdicted era, alone in the frightened court of mad Cambyses II. . . . No, I've got to keep the truth from her, keep her at home, thinking Keith is dead. He'd want it that way himself. And after a year or two she'd be happy again; I could teach her to be happy.*

He had stopped noticing how the rocks smashed at his thinly shod feet, how his body pitched and staggered or how noisy the water was. But then he came around a bend and saw the Persians.

There were two of them, wading downstream. Evidently his capture meant enough to overcome their religious prejudice against defiling a river. Two more walked above, threading between the trees on either bank. One of the latter was Harpagus. Their long swords hissed from the scabbards.

"Stop!" called the Chiliarch. "Halt, Greek! Yield!"

Everard stood death-still. The water purled about his ankles. The pair who splashed to meet him were unreal down here in a well of shadow, their faces blotted out so that he saw only white clothes and a shimmer along curved blades. It hit him in the belly: the pursuers had seen his trail down into the brook. So they split up, half in each direction, running faster on solid ground than he could move in the bed. Having gone beyond his possible range, they started working their way back, more slowly when they were bound to the stream's course but quite certain of their quarry.

"Take him alive," reminded Harpagus. "Hamstring him if you must, but take him alive."

Everard snarled and turned toward that bank. "Okay, buster, you asked for it," he said in English. The two men in the water yelled and began to run. One tripped and went on his face. The man opposite tobogganed down the slope on his backside.

The mud was slippery. Everard chopped the lower edge of his shield into it and toiled up. Harpagus moved coolly to await him. As he came near, the old noble's blade whirred, striking from above. Everard rolled his head and caught the blow on his helmet, which bonged. The edge slid down a cheekpiece and cut his right shoulder, but not badly. He felt only a sting and then was too busy to feel anything.

He didn't expect to win out. But he would make them kill him, and pay for the privilege.

He came onto grass and raised his shield just in time to protect his eyes. Harpagus probed for the knees. Everard beat that aside with his own short sword. The Median saber whistled. But at close quarters a lightly armed Asian hadn't a chance against the hoplite, as history was to prove a couple of generations hence. *By God,* thought Everard, *if only I had cuirass and greaves, I might be able to take all four of 'em!* He used his big shield with skill, put it in front of every blow and thrust, and always worked near to get beneath the longer blade and into Harpagus's defenseless guts.

The Chiliarch grinned tautly through tangled gray whiskers and skipped away. A play for time, of course. It succeeded. The other three men climbed the bank, shouted and rushed. It was a disorderly attack. Superb fighters as individuals, the Persians had never developed the mass discipline of Europe, on which they would break themselves at Marathon and Gaugamela. But four against unarmored one was impossible odds.

Everard got his back to a tree bole. The first man came in recklessly, sword clashing on the Greek shield. Everard's blade darted from behind the bronze oblong. There was a soft, somehow heavy resistance. He knew that feeling from other days, pulled his weapon out and stepped quickly aside. The Persian sat down, spilling out his life. He groaned once, saw he was a dead man, and raised his face toward the sky.

His mates were already at Everard, one to a side. Overhanging boughs made lassos useless; they would have to do battle. The Patrolman held off the left-hand blade with his shield. That exposed his right ribs, but since his opponents were ordered not to kill he could afford it. The right-hand man slashed at Everard's ankles. Everard sprang in the air and the sword hissed under his feet. The left-hand attacked, stabbed low. Everard sensed a dull shock and saw steel in his calf. He jerked free. A sunset ray came between bunched needles and touched the blood, making it an impossibly brilliant red. Everard felt that leg buckle under him.

"So, so," cried Harpagus, hovering ten feet away. "Chop him!"

Everard growled above his shield rim: "A task your jackal leader has no courage to attempt for himself, after I drove him back with his tail between his legs!"

It was calculated. The attack on him stopped a bare instant. He reeled forward. "If you Persians must be the dogs of a Mede," he croaked, "can you not choose a Mede who is a man, rather than this creature which betrayed its king and now runs from a single Greek?"

Even this far west and this long ago, an Oriental could not lose face in such a manner. Not that Harpagus had ever been a coward; Everard knew how unfair his taunts were. But the Chiliarch spat a curse and dashed at him. Everard had a moment's glimpse of eyes wild in a sunken hook-nosed face. He lumbered lopsidedly forward. The two Persians hesitated for a second more. That was long enough for Everard and Harpagus to meet. The Median blade rose and fell, bounced off Greek helmet and shield, snaked sideways for another leg cut. A loose white tunic flapped before Everard's gaze. He hunched shoulders and drove his sword in.

He withdrew it with the cruel professional twist which assures a mortal wound, pivoted on his right heel, and caught a blow on his shield. For a minute he and one Persian traded fury. At the edge of an eye, he saw the other circling about to get behind him. Well, he thought in a remote way, he had killed the one man dangerous to Cynthia. . . .

"Hold! Halt!"

The call was a weak flutter in the air, less loud than the mountain stream, but the warriors stepped back and lowered their weapons. Even the dying Persian took his eyes from heaven.

Harpagus struggled to sit up, in a puddle of his own blood. His skin was turned gray. "No . . . hold," he whispered. "Wait. There is a purpose here. Mithras would not have struck me down unless. . . ."

He beckoned, a somehow lordly gesture. Everard dropped his sword, limped over and knelt by Harpagus. The Mede sank bank into his arms.

"You are from the King's homeland," he rasped in the bloody beard. "Do not deny that. But know . . . Aurvagaush the son of Khshayavarsha . . . is no traitor." The thin form stiffened itself, imperious, as if ordering death to wait upon its pleasure. "I knew there were powers—of heaven, of hell, I know not which to this day—powers behind the King's advent. I used them, I used him, not for myself, but because I had sworn loyalty to my own king, Astyages, and he needed a . . . a Cyrus . . . lest the realm be torn asunder. Afterward, by his cruelty, Astyages forfeited my oath. But I was still a Mede. I saw in Cyrus the only hope—the best hope—of Media. For he has been a good king to us also—we are honored in his domains second only to the Persians. . . . Do you understand, you from the King's home?" Dim eyes rolled about, trying to see into Everard's but without enough control. "I wanted to capture you—to force your engine and its use from you, and then to kill you . . . yes . . . but not for my own gain. It was for the realm's. I feared you would take the King home, as I know he has longed to go. And what would become of us? Be merciful, as you too must hope for mercy."

"I shall," said Everard. "The King will remain."

"It is well," sighed Harpagus. "I believe you speak the truth . . . I dare not believe otherwise . . . Then I have atoned?" he asked in a thin anxious voice. "For the murder I did at my old king's behest—that I laid a helpless infant upon the mountainside and watched him die—have I atoned, King's countryman? For it was that prince's death . . . which brought the land close to ruin . . . but I found another Cyrus! I saved us! Have I atoned?"

"You have," said Everard, and wondered how much absolution it lay in his power to give.

Harpagus closed his eyes. "Then leave me," he said, like the fading echo of a command.

Everard laid him upon the earth and hobbled away. The two Persians knelt by their master, performing certain rites. The third man returned to his own contemplations. Everard sat down under a tree, tore a strip from his cloak and bandaged his hurts. The leg cut would need attention. Somehow he must get to the scooter. That wouldn't be fun, but he could manage it and then a Patrol doctor could repair him in a few hours with a medical science future to his home era. He'd go to some branch office in an obscure milieu, because there'd be too many questions in the twentieth century.

And he couldn't afford that. If his superiors knew what he planned, they would probably forbid it.

The answer had come to him not as a blinding revelation, but as a tired consciousness of knowledge which he might well have had subconsciously for a long time. He leaned back, getting his breath. The other four Persians arrived and were told what had happened. All of them ignored Everard, except for glances where terror struggled with pride, and made furtive signs against evil. The lifted their dead chief and their dying companion and bore them into the forest. Darkness thickened. Somewhere an owl hooted.

9

The Great King sat up in bed. He had heard a noise beyond the curtains.

Cassandane, the Queen, stirred invisibly. One slim hand touched his face. "What is it, sun of my heaven?" she asked.

"I do not know." He fumbled for the sword which lay always beneath his pillow. "Nothing."

Her palm slipped down over his breast. "No, it is much," she whispered, suddenly shaken. "Your heart goes like a war drum."

"Stay there." He trod out past the drapes.

Moonlight streamed from a deep-purple sky through an arched window to the floor. It glanced almost blindingly off a bronze mirror. The air was cold upon bare skin.

A thing of dark metal, whose rider gripped two handlebars and touched tiny controls on a panel, drifted like another shadow. It landed on the carpet without a sound and the rider got off. He was a burly man in Grecian tunic and helmet. "Keith," he breathed.

"Manse!" Denison stepped into the moonlight. "You came!"

"Tell me more," snorted Everard sarcastically. "Think anybody will hear us? I don't believe I was noticed. Materialized directly over the roof and floated slowly down on antigrav."

"There are guards just outside the door," said Denison, "but they won't come in unless I strike that gong, or yell."

"Good. Put on some clothes."

Denison dropped his sword. He stood rigid for an instant, then it blazed from him: "You've got a way out?"

"Maybe. Maybe." Everard looked away from the other man, drummed fingers on his machine's control panel. "Look, Keith," he said at last, "I've an idea which might or might not work. I'll need your help to carry it out. If it does work, you can go home. The front office will accept a *fait accompli* and wink at any broken regulations. But if it fails, you'll have to come back to this very night and live out your life as Cyrus. Can you do that?"

Denison shivered with more than chill. Very low: "I think so."

"I'm stronger than you are," said Everard roughly, "and I'll have the only weapons. If necessary, I'll shanghai you back here. Please don't make me."

Denison drew a long breath. "I won't."

"Then let's hope the Norns cooperate. Come on, get dressed. I'll explain as we go. Kiss this year good-bye, and trust it isn't 'So long'—because if my notion pans out, neither you nor anyone else will ever see it again."

Denison, who had half turned to the garments thrown in a corner for a slave to replace before dawn, stopped. "What?" he said.

"We're going to try rewriting history," said Everard. "Or maybe to restore the history which was there in the first place. I don't know. Come on, hop to it!"

"But—"

"Quick, man, quick! D'you realize I came back to the same day as I left you, that at this moment I'm crawling through the mountains with one leg stabbed open, just to save you that extra time? Get moving!"

Decision closed upon Denison. His face was in darkness, but he spoke very low and clear: "I've got one personal good-bye to say."

"What?"

"Cassandane. She's been my wife here for, God, for fourteen years! She's borne me three children, and nursed me through two fevers and a hundred fits of despair, and once when the Medes were at our gates she led the women of Pasargadae out to rally us and we won. . . . Give me five minutes, Manse."

"All right, all right. Though it'll take more than that to send a eunuch to her room and—"

"She's here."

Denison vanished behind the bed curtains.

Everard stood for a moment as if struck. *You expected me to come tonight,* he thought, *and you hoped I'd be able to take you back to Cynthia. So you sent for Cassandane.*

And then, when his fingertips had begun to hurt from the tightness of his grip on the sword hilt: *Oh, shut up, Everard, you smug self-righteous whelp.*

Presently Denison came back. He did not speak as he put on his clothes and mounted the rear seat on the scooter. Everard space-hopped, an instantaneous jump; the room vanished and moonlight flooded the hills far below. A cold gust searched around the men in the sky.

"Now for Ecbatana." Everard turned on his dashlight and adjusted controls according to notes scribbled on the pilot pad.

"Ec—Oh, you mean Hagmatan? The old Median capital?" Denison sounded astonished. "But it's only a summer residence now."

"I mean Ecbatana thirty-six years ago," said Everard.

"Huh?"

"Look, all the scientific historians in the future are convinced that the story of Cyrus's childhood as told by Herodotus and the Persians is pure fable. Well, maybe they were right all along. Maybe your experiences here have been only one of those little quirks in space-time which the Patrol tries to eliminate."

"I see," said Denison slowly.

"You were at Astyages's court pretty often when you were his vassal, I suppose. Okay, you guide me. We want the old guy himself, preferably alone at night."

"Sixteen years was a long time," said Denison.

"Hm?"

"If you're trying to change the past anyway, why use me at this point? Come get me when I'd been Cyrus only one year, long enough to be familiar with Ecbatana but—"

"Sorry, no. I don't dare. We're steering close enough to the wind as is. Lord knows what a secondary loop in the world lines could lead to. Even if we got away with it, the Patrol would send us both to the exile planet for taking that kind of chance."

"Well . . . yes. I see your point."

"Also," said Everard, "you're not a suicidal type. Would you actually want the you of this instant never to have existed? Think for a minute precisely what that implies."

He completed his settings. The man behind him shuddered. "Mithras!" said Denison. "You're right. Let's not talk about it."

"Here goes, then." Everard threw the main switch.

He hung over a walled city on an unfamiliar plain. Though this was also a moonlit night, the city was only a black huddle to his eyes. He reached into the saddlebags. "Here," he said. "Let's put on these costumes. I had the boys in the Middle Mohenjodaro office fix 'em up to my specs. Their situation is such that they often need this type of disguise for themselves."

Air whistled darkly as the hopper slanted earthward. Denison reached an arm past Everard to point. "That's the palace. The royal bedchamber is over on the east side. . . ."

It was a heavier, less graceful building than its Persian successor in Pasargadae. Everard glimpsed a pair of winged bulls, white in an autmnal garden, left over from the Assyrians. He saw that the windows before him were too narrow for entrance, swore, and aimed at the nearest doorway. A pair of mounted sentries looked up, saw what was coming, and shrieked. Their horses reared, throwing them. Everard's machine splintered the door. One more miracle wasn't going to affect history, especially when such things were believed in as devoutly as vitamin pills at home, and possibly with more reason. Lamps guided him down a corridor where slaves and guards squalled their terror. At the royal bedroom he drew his sword and knocked with the pommel. "Take over, Keith," he said. "You know the Median version of Aryan."

"Open, Astyages!" roared Denison. "Open to the messengers of Ahuramazda!"

Somewhat to Everard's surprise, the man within obeyed. Astyages was as brave as most of his people. But when the king—a thickset, hardfaced person in early middle age—saw two beings, luminously robed, halos around their heads and fountaining wings of light on their backs, seated on an iron throne in midair, he fell prostrate.

Everard heard Denison thunder in the best tent-meeting style, using a dialect he could barely follow:

"O infamous vessel of iniquity, heaven's anger is upon you! Do you believe that your least thought, though it skulk in the darkness which begot it, was ever hidden from the Day's Eye? Do you believe that almighty Ahuramazda would permit a deed so foul as you plot. . . ."

Everard didn't listen. He strayed into his own thoughts: Harpagus was probably somewhere in this very city, full of his youth and unridden as yet by guilt. Now he would never bear that burden. He would never lay a child upon the mountain and lean on his spear as it cried and shivered and finally became still. He would revolt in the future, for his own reasons, and become the

Chiliarch of Cyrus, but he would not die in his enemy's arms in a haunted forest; and a certain Persian, whose name Everard did not know, would also be spared a Greek sword and a slow falling into emptiness.

Yet the memory of two men whom I killed is printed on my brain cells; there is a thin white scar on my leg; Keith Denison is forty-seven years old and has learned to think like a king.

". . . Know, Astyages, that this child Cyrus is favored of heaven. And heaven is merciful: you have been warned that if you stain your soul with his innocent blood, the sin can never be washed away. Leave Cyrus to grow up in Anshan, or burn forever with Ahriman! Mithras has spoken!"

Astyages groveled, beating his head on the floor.

"Let's go," said Denison in English.

Everard hopped to Persian hills, thirty-six years futureward. Moonlight fell upon cedars near a road and a stream. It was cold, and a wolf howled.

He landed the scooter, got off and began to remove his costume. Denison's bearded face came out of the mask, with strangeness written upon it. "I wonder," he said. His voice was nearly lost in the silence under the mountains. "I wonder if we didn't throw too much of a scare into Astyages. History does record that he gave Cyrus a three-year fight when the Persians revolted."

"We can always go back to the outbreak of the war and provide a vision encouraging him to resist," said Everard, struggling to be matter-of-fact; for there were ghosts around him. "But I don't believe that'll be necessary. He'll keep hands off the prince, but when a vassal rebels, well, he'll be mad enough to discount what by then will seem like a dream. Also, his own nobles, Median vested interests, would hardly allow him to give in. But let's check up. Doesn't the King lead a procession at the winter solstice festival?"

"Yeah. Let's go. Quickly."

And the sunlight burned around them, high above Pasargadae. They left their machine hidden and walked down on foot, two travelers among many streaming in to celebrate the Birthday of Mithras. On the way, they inquired what had happened, explaining that they had been long abroad. The answers satisfied them, even in small details which Denison's memories recorded but the chronicles hadn't mentioned.

At last they stood under a frosty-blue sky, among thousands of people, and salaamed when Cyrus the Great King rode past with his chief courtiers Kobad, Croesus, and Harpagus, and the pride and pomp and priesthood of Persia followed.

"He's younger than I was," whispered Denison. "He would be, I guess. And a little smaller . . . different face entirely, isn't it? . . . but he'll do."

"Want to stay for the fun?" asked Everard.

Denison drew his cloak around him. The air was bitter. "No," he said. "Let's go back. It's been a long time. Even if it never happened."

"Uh-huh." Everard seemed more grim than a victorious rescuer should be. "It never happened."

10

Keith Denison left the elevator of a building in New York. He was vaguely surprised that he had not remembered what it looked like. He couldn't even recall his apartment number, but had to check with the directory. Details, details. He tried to stop trembling.

Cynthia opened the door as he reached it. "Keith," she said, almost wonderingly.

He could find no other words than: "Manse warned you about me, didn't he? He said he would."

"Yes. It doesn't matter. I didn't realize your looks would have changed that much. But it doesn't matter. Oh, my darling!"

She drew him inside, closed the door and crept into his arms.

He looked around the place. He had forgotten how cramped it was. And he had never liked her taste in decoration, though he had yielded to her.

The habit of giving in to a woman, even of asking her opinion, was one he'd have to learn all over again. It wouldn't be easy.

She raised a wet face for his kiss. Was *that* how she looked? But he didn't remember—he didn't. After all that time, he had only remembered she was little and blond. He had lived with her a few months; Cassandane had called him her morning star and given him three children and waited to do his will for fourteen years.

"Oh, Keith, welcome home," said the high small voice.

Home! he thought. *God!*

Gibraltar Falls

THE Time Patrol base would only remain for the hundred-odd years of inflow. During that while, few people other than scientists and maintenance crew would stay there for long at a stretch. Thus it was small, a lodge and a couple of service buildings, nearly lost in the land.

Five and a half million years before he was born, Tom Nomura found that southern end of Iberia still more steep than he remembered it. Hills climbed sharply northward until they became low mountains walling the sky, riven by canyons where shadows lay blue. It was dry country, rained on violently but briefly in winter, its streams shrunken to runnels or nothing as its grass burnt yellow in summer. Trees and shrubs grew far apart, thorn, mimosa, acacia, pine, aloe; around the water holes palm, fern, orchid.

Withal, it was rich in life. Hawks and vultures were always at hover in cloudless heaven. Grazing herds mingled their millions together; among their scores of kinds were zebra-striped ponies, primitive rhinoceros, okapi-like ancestors of the giraffe, sometimes mastodon—thinly red-haired, hugely tusked—or peculiar elephants. Among the predators and scavengers were sabertooths, early forms of the big cats, hyenas, and scuttering ground apes which occasionally walked on their hind legs. Ant heaps lifted six feet into the air. Marmots whistled.

It smelled of hay, scorch, baked dung and warm flesh. When wind awoke, it boomed, pushed, threw dust and heat into the face. Often the earth resounded to hoofbeats, birds clamored or beasts trumpeted. At night a sudden chill struck down, and the stars were so many that one didn't much notice the alienness of their constellations.

Thus had things been until lately. And as yet there was no great change. But now had begun a hundred years of thunder. When that was done, nothing would ever be the same again.

Manse Everard regarded Tom Nomura and Feliz a Rach for a squinting moment before he smiled and said, "No, thanks, I'll just poke around here today. You go have fun."

Did an eyelid of the big, bent-nosed, slightly grizzled man droop a little in Nomura's direction? The latter couldn't be sure. They were from the same milieu, indeed the same country. That Everard had been recruited in New York, A.D. 1954, and Nomura in San Francisco, 1972, ought to make scant difference. The upheavals of that generation were bubble pops against what had happened before and what would happen after. However, Nomura was fresh out of the Academy, a bare twenty-five years of lifespan behind him. Everard hadn't told how much time his own farings through the world's duration added up to; and given the longevity treatment the Patrol offered its people, it was impossible to guess. Nomura suspected the Unattached agent had seen enough existence to have become more foreign to him than Feliz—who was born two millenniums past either of them.

"Very well, let's start," she said. Curt though it was, Nomura thought her voice made music of the Temporal language.

They stepped from the veranda and walked across the yard. A couple of other corpsmen hailed them, with a pleasure directed at her. Nomura agreed. She was young and tall, the curve-nosed strength of her features softened by large green eyes, large mobile mouth, hair that shone auburn in spite of being hacked off at the ears. The usual gray coverall and stout boots could not hide her figure or the suppleness of her stride. Nomura knew he himself wasn't bad-looking—a stocky but limber frame, high-cheeked regular features, tawny skin—but she made him feel drab.

Also inside, he thought. *How does a new-minted Patrolman—not even slated for police duty, a mere naturalist—how does he tell an aristocrat of the First Matriarchy that he's fallen in love with her?*

The rumbling which always filled the air, these miles from the cataracts, sounded to him like a chorus. Was it imagination, or did he really sense an endless shudder through the ground, up into his bones?

Feliz opened a shed. Several hoppers stood inside, vaguely resembling wheelless two-seater motorcycles, propelled by antigravity and capable of leaping across several thousand years. (They and their present riders had been transported hither in heavy-duty shuttles.) Hers was loaded with recording gear. He had failed to convince her it was overburdened and knew she'd never forgive him if he finked on her. His invitation to Everard—the ranking officer in hand, though here-now simply on vacation—to join them today had been made in a slight hope that the latter would see that load and order her to let her assistant carry part of it.

She sprang to the saddle. "Come on!" she said. "The morning's getting old."

He mounted his vehicle and touched controls. Both glided outside and aloft. At eagle height, they leveled off and bore south, where the River Ocean poured into the Middle of the World.

Banks of upflung mist always edged that horizon, argent smoking off into azure. As one drew near afoot, they loomed topplingly overhead. Farther on, the universe swirled gray, shaken by the roar, bitter on human lips, while water flowed off rock and gouged through mud. So thick was the cold salt fog that it was unsafe to breathe for more than a few minutes.

From well above, the sight was yet more awesome. There one could see the end of a geological epoch. For a million and a half years the Mediterranean basin had lain a desert. Now the Gates of Hercules stood open and the Atlantic was coming through.

The wind of his passage around him, Nomura peered west across unrestful, many-hued and intricately foam-streaked immensity. He could see the currents run, sucked toward the new-made gap between Europe and Africa. There they clashed together and recoiled, a white and green chaos whose violence toned from earth to heaven and back, crumbled cliffs, overwhelmed valleys, blanketed the shore in spume for miles inland. From them came a stream, snow-colored in its fury, with flashes of livid emerald, to stand in an eight-mile wall between the continents and bellow. Spray roiled aloft, dimming the torrent after torrent wherein the sea crashed onward.

Rainbows wheeled through the clouds it made. This far aloft, the noise was no more than a monstrous millstone grinding. Nomura could clearly hear Feliz's voice out of his receiver, as she stopped her vehicle and lifted an arm. "Hold. I want a few more takes before we go on."

"Haven't you enough?" he asked.

Her words softened. "How can we get enough of a miracle?"

His heart jumped. *She's not a she-soldier, born to lord it over a ruck of underlings. In spite of her early life and ways, she isn't. She feels the dread, the beauty, yes, the sense of God at work—*

A wry grin at himself: *She'd better!*

After all, her task was to make a full-sensory record of the whole thing, from its beginning until that day when, a hundred years hence, the basin was full and the sea lapped calm where Odysseus would sail. It would take months of her lifespan. (*And mine, please, mine.*) Everybody in the corps wanted to experience this stupendousness; the hope of adventure was practically required for recruitment. But it wasn't feasible for many to come so far downstairs, crowding into so narrow a time-slot. Most would have to do it vicariously. Their chiefs would not have picked someone who was not a considerable artist, to live it on their behalf and pass it on to them.

Nomura remembered his astonishment when he was assigned to assist her. Short-handed as it was, could the Patrol afford artists?

Well, after he answered a cryptic advertisement and took several puzzling tests and learned about intertemporal traffic, he had wondered if police and rescue work were possible and been told that, usually, they were. He could see the need for administrative and clerical personnel, resident agents, historiographers, anthropologists, and, yes, natural scientists like himself. In the weeks they had been working together, Feliz convinced him that a few artists were at least as vital. Man does not live by bread alone, nor guns, paperwork, theses, naked practicalities.

She restowed her apparatus. "Come," she ordered. As she flashed eastward ahead of him, her hair caught a sunbeam and shone as if molten. He trudged mute in her wake.

The Mediterranean floor lay ten thousand feet below sea level. The inflow took most of that drop within a fifty-mile strait. Its volume amounted to ten thousand cubic miles a year, a hundred Victoria Falls or a thousand Niagaras.

Thus the statistics. The reality was a roar of white water, spray-shrouded, earth-sundering, mountain-shaking. Men could see, hear, feel, smell, taste the thing; they could not imagine it.

When the channel widened, the flow grew smoother, until it ran green and black. Then mists diminished and islands appeared, like ships which cast up huge bow waves; and life could again grow or go clear to the shore. Yet most of those islands would be eroded away before the century was out, and much of that life would perish in weather turned strange. For this event would move the planet from its Miocene to its Pliocene epoch.

And as he flitted onward, Nomura did not hear less noise, but more. Though the stream itself was quieter here, it moved toward a bass clamor which grew and grew till heaven was one brazen bell. He recognized a headland whose worn-down remnant would someday bear the name Gibraltar. Not far beyond, a cataract twenty miles wide made almost half the total plunge.

With terrifying ease, the waters slipped over that brink. They were glass-green against the darkling cliffs and umber grass of the continents. Light flamed off their heights. At their bottom another cloud bank rolled white in never-ending winds. Beyond reached a blue sheet, a lake whence rivers hewed canyons, out and out across the alkaline sparkle, dust devils, and mirage shimmers of the furnace land which they would make into a sea.

It boomed, it brawled, it querned.

Again Feliz poised her flyer. Nomura drew alongside. They were high; the air whittered chilly around them.

"Today," she told him, "I want to try for an impression of the sheer size. I'll move in close to the top, recording as I go, and then down."

"Not too close," he warned.

She bridled. "I'll judge that."

"Uh, I . . . I'm not trying to boss you or anything." *I'd better not. I, a plebe and a male.* "As a favor, please—" Nomura flinched at his own clumsy speech. "—be careful, will you? I mean, you're important to me."

Her smile burst upon him. She leaned hard against her safety harness to catch his hand. "Thank you, Tom." After a moment, turned grave: "Men like you make me understand what is wrong in the age I come from."

She had often spoken kindly to him: most times, in fact. Had she been a strident militant, no amount of comeliness would have kept him awake nights. He wondered if perhaps he had begun loving her when first he noticed how conscientiously she strove to regard him as her equal. It was not easy for her, she being almost as new in the Patrol as he—no easier than it was for men from other areas to believe, down inside where it counted, that she had the same capabilities they did and that it was right she use herself to the full.

She couldn't stay solemn. "Come on!" she shouted. "Hurry! That straight dropoff won't last another twenty years!"

Her machine darted. He slapped down the face screen of his helmet and plunged after, bearing the tapes and power cells and other auxiliary items. *Be careful,* he pleaded, *oh, be careful, my darling.*

She had gotten well ahead. He saw her like a comet, a dragonfly, everything vivid and swift, limned athwart yonder mile-high precipice of sea. The noise grew in him till there was nothing else, his skull was full of its doomsday.

Yards from the waters, she rode her hopper chasmward. Her head was buried in a dial-studded box, her hands at work on its settings; she steered with her knees. Salt spray began to fog Nomura's screen. He activated the self-cleaner. Turbulence clawed at him; his carrier lurched. His eardrums, guarded against sound but not changing pressure, stabbed with pain.

He had come quite near Feliz when her vehicle went crazy. He saw it spin, saw it strike the green immensity, saw it and her engulfed. He could not hear himself scream through the thunder.

He rammed the speed switch, swooped after her. Was it blind instinct which sent him whirling away again, inches before the torrent grabbed him too? She was gone from sight. There was only the water wall, clouds below and unpitying blue calm above, the noise that took him in its jaws to shake him apart, the cold, the damp, the salt on his mouth that tasted like tears.

He fled for help.

Noonday glowered outside. The land looked bleached, lay moveless and lifeless except for a carrion bird. The distant falls alone had voice.

A knock on the door of his room brought Nomura off the bed, onto his feet. Through an immediately rackety pulse he croaked, "Come in. Do."

Everard entered. In spite of air conditioning, sweat spotted his garments. He gnawed a fireless pipe and his shoulders slumped.

"What's the word?" Nomura begged of him.

"As I feared. Nothing. She never returned home."

Nomura sank into a chair and stared before him. "You're certain?"

Everard sat down on the bed, which creaked beneath his weight. "Yeah. The message capsule just arrived. In answer to my inquiry, et cetera, Agent Feliz a Rach has not reported back to her home milieu base from the Gibraltar assignment, and they have no further record of her."

"Not in *any* era?"

"The way agents move around in time and space, nobody keeps dossiers, except maybe the Danellians."

"Ask them!"

"Do you imagine they'd reply?" Everard snapped—they, the supermen of the remote future who were the founders and ultimate masters of the Patrol. One big fist clenched on his knee. "And don't tell me we ordinary mortals could keep closer tabs if we wanted to. Have you checked your personal future, son? We don't want to, and that's that."

The roughness left him. He shifted the pipe about in his grip and said most gently, "If we live long enough, we outlive those we've cared for. The common fate of man; nothing unique to our corps. But I'm sorry you had to strike it so young."

"Never mind me!" Nomura exclaimed. "What of her?"

"Yes . . . I've been thinking about your account. My guess is, the airflow patterns are worse than tricky around that fall. What should've been expected, no doubt. Overloaded, her hopper was less controllable than usual. An air pocket, a flaw, whatever it was, something like that grabbed her without warning and tossed her into the stream."

Nomura's fingers writhed against each other. "And I was supposed to look after her."

Everard shook his head. "Don't punish yourself worse. You were simply her assistant. She should have been more careful."

"But—God damn it, we can rescue her still, and you won't allow us to?" Nomura half screamed.

"Stop," Everard warned. "Stop right there."

Never say it: that several Patrolmen could ride backward in time, lay hold on her with tractor beams and haul her free of the abyss. Or that I could tell her and my earlier self to beware. It did not happen, therefore it will not happen.

It must *not happen.*

For the past becomes in fact mutable, as soon as we on our machines have transformed it into our present. And if ever a mortal takes himself that power, where can the changing end? We start by saving a glad girl; we go on to save Lincoln, but somebody else tries to save the Confederate States—No, none less than God can be trusted with time. The Patrol exists to guard what is real. Its men may no more violate that faith than they may violate their own mothers.

"I'm sorry," Nomura mumbled.

"It's okay, Tom."

"No, I . . . I thought . . . when I saw her vanish, my first thought was that we could make up a party, ride back to that very instant and snatch her clear—"

"A natural thought in a new man. Old habits of the mind die hard. The fact is, we did not. It'd scarcely have been authorized anyway. Too dangerous. We can ill afford to lose more. Certainly we can't when the record shows that our rescue attempt would be foredoomed if we made it."

"Is there no way to get around that?"

Everard sighed. "I can't think of any. Make your peace with fate, Tom." He hesitated. "Can I . . . can we do anything for you?"

"No." It came harsh out of Nomura's throat. "Except leave me be for a while."

"Sure." Everard rose. "You weren't the only person who thought a lot of her," he reminded, and left.

When the door had closed behind him, the sound of the falls seemed to wax, grinding, grinding. Nomura stared at emptiness. The sun passed its apex and began to slide very slowly toward night.

I should have gone after her myself, at once.

And risked my life.

Why not follow her into death, then?

No. That's senseless. Two deaths do not make a life. I couldn't have saved her. I didn't have the equipment or—The sane thing was to fetch help.

Only the help was denied—whether by man or by fate hardly matters, does it?—and so she went down. The stream hurled her into the gulf, she had a moment's terror before it smashed the awareness out of her, then at the bottom it crushed her, plucked her apart, strewed the pieces of her bones across the floor of a sea that I, a youngster, will sail upon one holiday, unknowing that there is a Time Patrol or ever was a Feliz. Oh, God, I want my dust down with hers, five and a half million years from this hour!

A remote cannonade went through the air, a tremor through earth and floor. An undercut bank must have crumbled into the torrent. It was the kind of scene she would have loved to capture.

"Would have?" Nomura yelled and surged from the chair. The ground still vibrated beneath him.

"She will!"

He ought to have consulted Everard, but feared—perhaps mistakenly, in his grief and his inexperience—that he would be refused permission and sent upstairs at once.

He ought to have rested for several days, but feared that his manner would betray him. A stimulant pill must serve in place of nature.

He ought to have checked out a tractor unit, not smuggled it into the locker on his vehicle.

When he took the hopper forth, a Patrolman who saw asked where he was bound. "For a ride," Nomura answered. The other nodded sympathetically. He might not suspect that a love had been lost, but the loss of a comrade was bad enough. Nomura was careful to get well over the northern horizon before he swung toward the seafall.

Right and left, it reached farther than he could see. Here, more than halfway down that cliff of green glass, the very curve of the planet hid its ends from him. Then as he entered the spume clouds, whiteness enfolded him, roiling and stinging.

His face shield stayed clear, but vision was ragged, upward along immensity. The helmet warded his hearing but could not stave off the storm which rattled his teeth and heart and skeleton. Winds whirled and smote, the carrier staggered, he must fight for every inch of control.

And to find the exact second—

Back and forth he leaped across time, reset the verniers, reflicked the main switch, glimpsed himself vague in the mists, and peered through them toward heaven; over and over, until abruptly he was *then.*

Twin gleams far above . . . He saw the one strike and go under, go down, while the other darted around until soon it ran away. Its rider had not seen him, where he lurked in the chill salt mists. His presence was not on any damned record.

He darted forward. Yet patience was upon him. He could cruise for a long piece of lifespan if need be, seeking the trice which would be his. The fear of death, even the knowing that she might be dead when he found her, were like half-remembered dreams. The elemental powers had taken him. He was a will that flew.

He hovered within a yard of the water. Gusts tried to cast him into its grip, as they had done to her. He was ready for them, danced free, returned to peer—returned through time as well as space, so that a score of him searched along the fall in that span of seconds when Feliz might be alive.

He paid his other selves no heed. They were merely stages he had gone through or must still go through.

THERE!

The dim dark shape tumbled past him, beneath the flood, on its way to destruction. He spun a control. A tractor beam locked onto the other machine. His reeled and went after it, unable to pull such a mass free of such a might.

The tide nearly had him when help came. Two vehicles, three, four, all straining together, they hauled Feliz's loose. She sagged horribly limp in her saddle harness. He didn't go to her at once. First he went back those few blinks in time, and back, to be her rescuer and his own.

When finally they were alone among fogs and furies, she freed and in his arms, he would have burnt a hole through the sky to get ashore where he could care for her. But she stirred, her eyes blinked open, after a minute she smiled at him. Then he wept.

Beside them, the ocean roared onward.

The sunset to which Nomura had leaped ahead was not on anybody's record either. It turned the land golden. The falls must be afire with it. Their song resounded beneath the evening star.

Feliz propped pillows against headboard, sat straighter in the bed where she was resting, and told Everard: "If you lay charges against him, that he broke regulations or whatever male stupidity you are thinking of, I'll also quit your bloody Patrol."

"Oh, no." The big man lifted a palm as if to fend off attack. "Please. You misunderstand. I only meant to say, we're in a slightly awkward position."

"How?" Nomura demanded, from the chair in which he sat and held Feliz's hand. "I wasn't under any orders not to attempt this, was I? All right, agents are supposed to safeguard their own lives if possible, as being valuable to the corps. Well, doesn't it follow that the salvaging of a life is worthwhile too?"

"Yes. Sure." Everard paced the floor. It thudded beneath his boots, above the drumbeat of the flood. "Nobody quarrels with success, even in a much tighter organization than ours. In fact, Tom, the initiative you showed today makes your future prospects look good, believe me." A grin went lopsided around his pipestem. "As for an old soldier like myself, it'll be forgiven that I was too ready to give up." A flick of somberness: "I've seen so many lost beyond hope."

He stopped in his treading, confronted them both, and stated: "But we cannot have loose ends. The fact is, her unit does not list Feliz a Rach as returning, ever."

Their clasps tightened on each other.

Everard gave him and her a smile—haunted, nevertheless a smile—before he continued: "Don't get scared, though. Tom, earlier you wondered why we, we ordinary humans at least, don't keep closer track of our people. Now do you see the reason?

"Feliz a Rach never checked back into her original base. She may have visited her former home, of course, but we don't ask officially what agents do on their furloughs." He drew breath. "As for the rest of her career, if she should want to transfer to a different headquarters and adopt a different name, why, any officer of sufficient rank could approve that. Me, for example.

"We operate loose in the Patrol. We dare not do otherwise."

Nomura understood, and shivered.

Feliz recalled him to the ordinary world. "But who might I become?" she wondered.

He pounced on the cue. "Well," he said, half in laughter and half in thunder, "how about Mrs. Thomas Nomura?"

The Only Game in Town

1

JOHN Sandoval did not belong to his name. Nor did it seem right that he should stand in slacks and aloha shirt before an apartment window opening on mid-twentieth-century Manhattan. Everard was used to anachronism, but the dark hooked face confronting him always seemed to want war paint, a horse, and a gun sighted on some pale thief.

"Okay," he said. "The Chinese discovered America. Interesting, but why does the fact need my services?"

"I wish to hell I knew," Sandoval answered.

His stocky form turned about on the polar bear rug, which Bjarni Herjulfsson had once given to Everard, until he was staring outward. Towers were sharp against a clear sky; the noise of traffic was muted by height. His hands clasped and unclasped behind his back.

"I was ordered to co-opt an Unattached agent, go back with him and take whatever measures seemed indicated," he went on after a while. "I knew you best, so. . . ." His voice trailed off.

"But shouldn't you get an Indian like yourself?" asked Everard. "I'd seem rather out of place in thirteenth-century America."

"So much the better. Make it impressive, mysterious. . . . It won't be too tough a job, really."

"Of course not," said Everard. "Whatever the job actually is."

He took pipe and tobacco pouch from his disreputable smoking jacket and stuffed the bowl in quick, nervous jabs. One of the hardest lessons he had had to learn, when first recruited into the Time Patrol, was that every important task does not require a vast organization. That was the characteristic twentieth-century approach; but earlier cultures, like Athenian Hellas and Kamakura Japan—and later civilizations too, here and there in history—had concentrated on the development of individual excellence. A single graduate of the Patrol Academy (equipped, to be sure, with tools and weapons of the future) could be the equivalent of a brigade.

But it was a matter of necessity as well as aesthetics. There were all too few people to watch over all too many thousands of years.

"I get the impression," said Everard slowly, "that this is not a simple rectification of extratemporal interference."

"Right," said Sandoval in a harsh voice. "When I reported what I'd found, the Yuan milieu office made a thorough investigation. No time travelers are involved. Kublai Khan thought this up entirely by himself. He may have been inspired by Marco Polo's accounts of Venetian and Arab sea voyages, but it was legitimate history, even if Marco's book doesn't mention anything of the sort."

"The Chinese had quite a nautical tradition of their own," said Everard. "Oh, it's all very natural. So how do we come in?"

He got his pipe lit and drew hard on it. Sandoval still hadn't spoken, so he asked, "How did you happen to find this expedition? It wasn't in Navajo country, was it?"

"Hell, I'm not confined to studying my own tribe," Sandoval answered. "Too few Amerinds in the Patrol as is, and it's a nuisance disguising other breeds. I've been working on Athabascan migrations generally." Like Keith Denison, he was an ethnic Specialist, tracing the history of peoples who never wrote their own so that the Patrol could know exactly what the events were that it safeguarded.

"I was working along the eastern slope of the Cascades, near Crater Lake," he went on. "That's Lutuami country, but I had reason to believe an Athabascan tribe I'd lost track of had passed that way. The natives spoke of mysterious strangers coming from the north. I went to have a look, and there the expedition was, Mongols with horses. I checked their back trail and found their camp at the mouth of the Chehalis River, where a few more Mongols were helping the Chinese sailors guard the ships. I hopped back upstairs like a bat out of Los Angeles and reported."

Everard sat down and stared at the other man. "How thorough an investigation did get made at the Chinese end?" he said. "Are you absolutely certain there was no extratemporal interference? It could be one of those unplanned blunders, you know, whose consequences aren't obvious for decades."

"I thought of that too, when I got my assignment," Sandoval nodded. "I even went directly to Yuan milieu HQ in Khan Baligh—Cambaluc, or Peking to you. They told me they'd checked it clear back to Genghis's lifetime, and spatially as far as Indonesia. And it was all perfectly okay, like the Norse and their Vinland. It simply didn't happen to have gotten the same publicity. As far as the Chinese court knew, an expedition had been sent out and had never returned, and Kublai decided it wasn't worthwhile to send another. The record of it lay in the Imperial archives, but was destroyed during the Ming revolt which expelled the Mongols. Historiography forgot the incident."

Still Everard brooded. Normally he liked his work, but there was something abnormal about this occasion.

"Obviously," he said, "the expedition met a disaster. We'd like to know what. But why do you need an Unattached agent to spy on them?"

Sandoval turned from the window. It crossed Everard's mind again, fleetingly, how little the Navajo belonged here. He was born in 1930, had fought in Korea and gone through college on the GI bill before the Patrol contacted him, but somehow he never quite fit the twentieth century.

Well, do any of us? Could any man with real roots stand knowing what will eventually happen to his own people?

"But I'm not supposed to spy!" Sandoval exclaimed. "When I'd reported, my orders came straight back from Danellian headquarters. No explanation, no excuses, the naked command: to arrange that disaster. To revise history myself!"

2

Anno Domini One Thousand Two Hundred Eighty:

The writ of Kublai Khan ran over degrees of latitude and longitude; he dreamed of world empire, and his court honored any guest who brought fresh knowledge or new philosophy. A young Venetian merchant named Marco Polo had become a particular favorite. But not all peoples desired a Mongol overlord. Revolutionary secret societies germinated throughout those several conquered realms lumped together as Cathay. Japan, with the Hojo family an able power behind the throne, had already repelled one invasion. Nor were the Mongols unified, save in theory. The Russian princes had become tax collectors for the Golden Horde; the Il-Khan Abaka sat in Baghdad.

Elsewhere, a shadowy Abbasid Caliphate had refuge in Cairo; Delhi was under the Slave Dynasty; Nicholas III was Pope; Guelphs and Ghibbelines were ripping up Italy; Rudolf of Habsburg was German Emperor, Philip the Bold was King of France, Edward Longshanks ruled England. Contemporaries included Dante Alighieri, Joannes Duns Scotus, Roger Bacon, and Thomas the Rhymer.

And in North America, Manse Everard and John Sandoval reined their horses to stare down a long hill.

"The date I first saw them is last week," said the Navajo. "They've come quite a ways since. At this rate, they'll be in Mexico in a couple of months, even allowing for some rugged country ahead."

"By Mongol standards," Everard told him, "they're proceeding leisurely."

He raised his binoculars. Around him, the land burned green with April. Even the highest and oldest beeches fluttered bright young leaves. Pines roared in the wind, which blew down off the mountains cold and swift and smelling of melted snow, through a sky where birds were homebound in such flocks that they could darken the sun. The peaks of the Cascade range seemed to float in the west, blue-white, distant, and holy. Eastward the foothills tumbled in clumps of forest and meadow to a valley, and so at last, beyond the horizon, to prairies thunderous under buffalo herds.

Everard focused on the expedition. It wound through the open areas, more or less following a small river. Some seventy men rode shaggy, dun-colored, short-legged, long-headed Asian horses. They led pack animals and remounts. He identified a few native guides, as much by their awkward seat in the saddle as by their physiognomy and clothing. But the newcomers held his attention most.

"A lot of pregnant mares toting packs," he remarked, half to himself. "I suppose they took as many horses in the ships as they could, letting them out to exercise and graze wherever they made a stop. Now they're breeding more as they go along. That kind of pony is tough enough to survive such treatment."

"The detachment at the ships is also raising horses," Sandoval informed him. "I saw that much."

"What else do you know about this bunch?"

"No more than I've told you, which is little more than you've now seen. And that record which lay for a while in Kublai's archives. But you recall, it barely notes that four ships under the command of the Noyon Toktai and the scholar Li Tai-Tsung were dispatched to explore the islands beyond Japan."

Everard nodded absently. No sense in sitting here and rehashing what they'd already gone over a hundred times. It was only a way of postponing action.

Sandoval cleared his throat. "I'm still dubious about both of us going down there," he said. "Why don't you stay in reserve, in case they get nasty?"

"Hero complex, huh?" said Everard. "No, we're better off together. I don't expect trouble anyhow. Not yet. Those boys are much too intelligent to antagonize anyone gratuitously. They've stayed on good terms with the Indians, haven't they? And we'll be a far more unknown quantity. . . . I wouldn't mind a drink beforehand, though."

"Yeh. And afterward, too!"

Each dipped in his saddlebag, took out a half-gallon canteen and hoisted it. The Scotch was pungent in Everard's throat, heartening in his veins. He clucked to his horse and both Patrolmen rode down the slope.

A whistling cut the air. They had been seen. He maintained a steady pace toward the head of the Mongol line. A pair of outriders closed in on either flank, arrows nocked to their short powerful bows, but did not interfere.

I suppose we look harmless, Everard thought. Like Sandoval, he wore twentieth-century outdoor clothes: hunting jacket to break the wind, hat to keep off the rain. His own outfit was a good deal less elegant than the Navajo's Abercrombie & Fitch special. They both bore daggers for show, Mauser machine pistols and thirtieth-century stun-beam projectors for business.

The troop reined in, so disciplined that it was almost like one man halting. Everard scanned them closely as he neared. He had gotten a pretty complete electronic education in an hour or so before departure—language, history, technology, manners, morals—of Mongols and Chinese and even the local Indians. But he had never before seen these people close up.

They weren't spectacular: stocky, bowlegged, with thin beards and flat, broad faces that shone greased in the sunlight. They were all well equipped, wearing boots and trousers, laminated leather cuirasses with lacquer ornamentation, conical steel helmets that might have a spike or plume on top. Their weapons were curved sword, knife, lance, compound bow. One man near the head of the line bore a standard of gold-braided yak tails. They watched the Patrolmen approach, their narrow dark eyes impassive.

The chief was readily identified. He rode in the van, and a tattered silken cloak blew from his shoulders. He was rather larger and even more hard-faced than his average trooper, with a reddish beard and almost Roman nose. The Indian guide beside him gaped and huddled back; but Toktai Noyon held his place, measuring Everard with a steady carnivore look.

"Greeting," he called, when the newcomers were in earshot. "What spirit brings you?" He spoke the Lutuami dialect, which was later to become the Klamath language, with an atrocious accent.

Everard replied in flawless, barking Mongolian: "Greeting to you, Toktai son of Batu. The Tengri willing, we come in peace."

It was an effective touch. Everard glimpsed Mongols reaching for lucky charms or making signs against the evil eye. But the man mounted at Toktai's

left was quick to recover a schooled self-possession. "Ah," he said, "so men
of the Western lands have also reached this country. We did not know that."

Everard looked at him. He was taller than any Mongol, his skin almost
white, his features and hands delicate. Though dressed much like the others,
he was unarmed. He seemed older than the Noyon, perhaps fifty. Everard
bowed in the saddle and switched to North Chinese: "Honored Li Tai-Tsung,
it grieves this insignificant person to contradict your eminence, but we belong
to the great realm farther south."

"We have heard rumors," said the scholar. He couldn't quite suppress
excitement. "Even this far north, tales have been borne of a rich and splendid
country. We are seeking it that we may bring your Khan the greeting of the
Kha Khan, Kublai son of Tuli, son of Genghis; the earth lies at his feet."

"We know of the Kha Khan," said Everard, "as we know of the Caliph, the
Pope, the Emperor, and all lesser monarchs." He had to pick his way with
care, not openly insulting Cathay's ruler but still subtly putting him in his
place. "Little is known in return of us, for our master does not seek the outside
world, nor encourage it to seek him. Permit me to introduce my unworthy self.
I am called Everard and am not, as my appearance would suggest, a Russian
or Westerner. I belong to the border guardians."

Let them figure out what that meant.

"You didn't come with much company," snapped Toktai.

"More was not required," said Everard in his smoothest voice.

"And you are far from home," put in Li.

"No farther than you would be, honorable sirs, in the Kirghiz marches."

Toktai clapped a hand to his sword hilt. His eyes were chill and wary.
"Come," he said. "Be welcome as ambassadors, then. Let's make camp and
hear the word of your king."

3

The sun, low above the western peaks, turned their snowcaps tarnished silver.
Shadows lengthened down in the valley, the forest darkened, but the open
meadow seemed to glow all the brighter. The underlying quiet made almost a
sounding board for such noises as existed: rapid swirl and cluck of the river,
ring of an ax, horses cropping in long grass. Woodsmoke tinged the air.

The Mongols were obviously taken aback at their visitors and this early halt.
They kept wooden faces, but their eyes would stray to Everard and Sandoval
and they would mutter formulas of their various religions—chiefly pagan, but
some Buddhist, Moslem, or Nestorian prayers. It did not impair the efficiency

with which they set up camp, posted guard, cared for the animals, prepared to cook supper. But Everard judged they were more quiet than usual. The patterns impressed on his brain by the educator called Mongols talkative and cheerful as a rule.

He sat cross-legged on a tent floor. Sandoval, Toktai, and Li completed the circle. Rugs lay under them, and a brazier kept a pot of tea hot. It was the only tent pitched, probably the only one available, taken along for use on ceremonial occasions like this. Toktai poured *kumiss* with his own hands and offered it to Everard, who slurped as loudly as etiquette demanded and passed it on. He had drunk worse things than fermented mare's milk, but was glad that everyone switched to tea after the ritual.

The Mongol chief spoke. He couldn't keep his tone smooth, as his Chinese amanuensis did. There was an instinctive bristling: what foreigner dares approach the Kha Khan's man, save on his belly? But the words remained courteous: "Now let our guests declare the business of their king. First, would you name him for us?"

"His name may not be spoken," said Everard. "Of his realm you have heard only the palest rumors. You may judge his power, Noyon, by the fact that he needed only us two to come this far, and that we needed only one mount apiece."

Toktai grunted. "Those are handsome animals you ride, though I wonder how well they'd do on the steppes. Did it take you long to get here?"

"No more than a day, Noyon. We have means."

Everard reached in his jacket and brought out a couple of small gift-wrapped parcels. "Our lord bade us present the Cathayan leaders with these tokens of regard."

While the paper was being removed, Sandoval leaned over and hissed in English: "Dig their expressions, Manse. We goofed a bit."

"How?"

"That flashy cellophane and stuff impresses a barbarian like Toktai. But notice Li. His civilization was doing calligraphy when the ancestors of Bonwit Teller were painting themselves blue. His opinion of our taste has just nosedived."

Everard shrugged imperceptibly. "Well, he's right, isn't he?"

Their colloquy had not escaped the others. Toktai gave them a hard stare, but returned to his present, a flashlight, which had to be demonstrated and exclaimed over. He was a little afraid of it at first, even mumbled a charm; then he remembered that a Mongol wasn't allowed to be afraid of anything except thunder, mastered himself, and was soon as delighted as a child. The best bet for a Confucian scholar like Li seemed to be a book, the *Family of Man* collection, whose diversity and alien pictorial technique might impress

him. He was effusive in his thanks, but Everard doubted if he was
overwhelmed. A Patrolman soon learned that sophistication exists at any level
of technology.

Gifts must be made in return: a fine Chinese sword and a bundle of sea otter
pelts from the coast. It was quite some time before the conversation could turn
back to business. Then Sandoval managed to get the other party's account
first.

"Since you know so much," Toktai began, "you must also know that our
invasion of Japan failed several years ago."

"The will of heaven was otherwise," said Li, with courtier blandness.

"Horse apples!" growled Toktai. "The stupidity of men was otherwise, you
mean. We were too few, too ignorant, and we'd come too far in seas too
rough. And what of it? We'll return there one day."

Everard knew rather sadly that they would, and that a storm would destroy
the fleet and drown who knows how many young men. But he let Toktai
continue:

"The Kha Khan realized we must learn more about the islands. Perhaps we
should try to establish a base somewhere north of Hokkaido. Then, too, we
have long heard rumors about lands farther west. Fishermen are blown off
course now and then, and have glimpses; traders from Siberia speak of a strait
and a country beyond. The Kha Khan got four ships with Chinese crews and
told me to take a hundred Mongol warriors and see what I could discover."

Everard nodded, unsurprised. The Chinese had been sailing junks for
hundreds of years, some holding up to a thousand passengers. True, these craft
weren't as seaworthy as they would become in later centuries under Portuguese
influence, and their owners had never been much attracted by any ocean, let
alone the cold northern waters. But still, there were some Chinese navigators
who would have picked up tricks of the trade from stray Koreans and
Formosans, if not from their own fathers. They must have a little familiarity
with the Kuriles, at least.

"We followed two chains of islands, one after another," said Toktai. "They
were bleak enough, but we could stop here and there, let the horses out, and
learn something from the natives. Though the Tengri know it's hard to do that
last, when you may have to interpret through six languages! We did find out
that there are two mainlands, Siberia and another, which come so close
together up north that a man might cross in a skin boat, or walk across the ice
in winter sometimes. Finally we came to the new mainland. A big country;
forests, much game and seals. Too rainy, though. Our ships seemed to want
to continue, so we followed the coast, more or less."

Everard visualized a map. If you go first along the Kuriles and then the
Aleutians, you are never far from land. Fortunate to avoid the shipwreck

which had been a distinct possibility, the shallow-draft junks had been able to find anchorage even at those rocky islands. Also, the current urged them along, and they were very nearly on a great-circle course. Toktai had discovered Alaska before he quite knew what had happened. Since the country grew ever more hospitable as he coasted south, he passed up Puget Sound and proceeded clear to the Chehalis River. Maybe the Indians had warned him the Columbia mouth, farther on, was dangerous—and, more recently, had helped his horsemen cross the great stream on rafts.

"We set up camp when the war was waning," said the Mongol. "The tribes thereabouts are backward, but friendly. They gave us all the food, women, and help we could ask for. In return, our sailors taught them some tricks of fishing and boatbuilding. We wintered there, learned some of the languages, and made trips inland. Everywhere were tales of huge forests and plains where herds of wild cattle blacken the earth. We saw enough to know the stories were true. I've never been in so rich a land." His eyes gleamed tigerishly. "And so few dwellers, who don't even know the use of iron."

"Noyon," murmured Li warningly. He nodded his head very slightly toward the Patrolmen. Toktai clamped his mouth shut.

Li turned to Everard and said, "There were also rumors of a golden realm far to the south. We felt it our duty to investigate this, as well as explore the country in between. We had not looked for the honor of being met by your eminent selves."

"The honor is all ours," Everard purred. Then, putting on his gravest face: "My lord of the Golden Empire, who may not be named, has sent us in a spirit of friendship. It would grieve him to see you meet disaster. We come to warn you."

"What?" Toktai sat up straight. One sinewy hand snatched for the sword which, politely, he wasn't wearing. "What in the hells is this?"

"In the hells indeed, Noyon. Pleasant though this country seems, it lies under a curse. Tell him, my brother."

Sandoval, who had a better speaking voice, took over. His yarn had been concocted with an eye to exploiting that superstition which still lingered in the half-civilized Mongols, without generating too much Chinese skepticism. There were really two great southern kingdoms, he explained. Their own lay far away; its rival was somewhat north and east of it, with a citadel on the plains. Both states possessed immense powers, call them sorcery or subtle engineering as you wished. The northerly empire, Badguys, considered all this territory as its own and would not tolerate a foreign expedition. Its scouts were certain to discover the Mongols before long, and would annihilate them with thunderbolts. The benevolent southern land of Goodguys could offer no protection, could only send emissaries warning the Mongols to turn home again.

"Why have the natives not spoken of these overlords?" asked Li shrewdly.

"Has every little tribesman in the jungles of Burma heard about the Kha Khan?" responded Sandoval.

"I am a stranger and ignorant," said Li. "Forgive me if I do not understand your talk of irresistible weapons."

Which is the politest way I've ever been called a liar, thought Everard. Aloud: "I can offer a small demonstration, if the Noyon has an animal that may be killed."

Toktai considered. His visage might have been scarred stone, but sweat filmed it. He clapped his hands and barked orders to the guard who looked in. Thereafter they made small talk against a silence that thickened.

A warrior appeared after some endless part of an hour. He said that a couple of horsemen had lassoed a deer. Would it serve the Noyon's purpose? It would. Toktai led the way out, shouldering through a thick and buzzing swarm of men. Everard followed, wishing this weren't needful. He slipped the rifle stock onto his Mauser. "Care to do the job?" he asked Sandoval.

"Christ, no."

The deer, a doe, had been forced back to camp. She trembled by the river, the horsehair ropes about her neck. The sun, just touching the western peaks, turned her to bronze. There was a blind sort of gentleness in her look at Everard. He waved back the men around her and took aim. The first slug killed her, but he kept the gun chattering till her carcass was gruesome.

When he lowered his weapon, the air felt somehow rigid. He looked across all the thick bandy-legged bodies, the flat, grimly controlled faces; he could smell them with unnatural sharpness, a clean odor of sweat and horses and smoke. He felt himself as nonhuman as they must see him.

"That is the least of the arms used here," he said. "A soul so torn from the body would not find its way home."

He turned on his heel. Sandoval followed him. Their horses had been staked out, the gear piled close by. They saddled, unspeaking, mounted and rode off into the forest.

4

The fire blazed up in a gust of wind. Sparingly laid by a woodsman, in that moment it barely brought the two out of shadow—a glimpse of brow, nose, and cheekbones, a gleam of eyes. It sank down again to red and blue sputtering above white coals, and darkness took the men.

Everard wasn't sorry. He fumbled his pipe in his hands, bit hard on it and drank smoke, but found little comfort. When he spoke, the vast soughing of trees, high up in the night, almost buried his voice, and he did not regret that either.

Nearby were their sleeping bags, their horses, the scooter—antigravity sled cum space-time hopper—which had brought them. Otherwise the land was empty; mile upon mile, human fires like their own were as small and lonely as stars in the universe. Somewhere a wolf howled.

"I suppose," Everard said, "every cop feels like a bastard occasionally. You've just been an observer so far, Jack. Active assignments, such as I get, are often hard to accept."

"Yeh." Sandoval had been even more quiet than his friend. He had scarcely stirred since supper.

"And now this. Whatever you have to do to cancel a temporal interference, you can at least think you're restoring the original line of development." Everard fumed on his pipe. "Don't remind me that 'original' is meaningless in this context. It's a consoling word."

"Uh-huh."

"But when our bosses, our dear Danellian supermen, tell *us* to interfere. . . . We know Toktai's people never came back to Cathay. Why should you or I have to take a hand? If they ran into hostile Indians or something and were wiped out, I wouldn't mind. At least, no more than I mind any similar incident in that goddamned slaughterhouse they call human history."

"We don't have to kill them, you know. Just make them turn back. Your demonstration this afternoon may be enough."

"Yeah. Turn back . . . and what? Probably perish at sea. They won't have an easy trip home—storm, fog, contrary currents, rocks—in those primitive ships meant mostly for rivers. And we'll have set them on that trip at precisely that time! If we didn't interfere, they'd start home later, the circumstances of the voyage would be different. . . . Why should we take the guilt?"

"They could even make it home," murmured Sandoval.

"What?" Everard started.

"The way Toktai was talking. I'm sure he plans to go back on a horse, not on those ships. As he's guessed, Bering Strait is easy to cross; the Aleuts do it all the time. Manse, I'm afraid it isn't enough simply to spare them."

"But they aren't going to get home! We know that!"

"Suppose they do make it." Sandoval began to talk a bit louder and much faster. The night wind roared around his words. "Let's play with ideas awhile.

Suppose Toktai pushes on southeastward. It's hard to see what could stop him. His men can live off the country, even the deserts, far more handily than Coronado or any of those boys. He hasn't terribly far to go before he reaches a high-grade neolithic people, the agricultural Pueblo tribes. That will encourage him all the more. He'll be in Mexico before August. Mexico's just as dazzling now as it was—will be—in Cortez's day. And even more tempting: the Aztecs and Toltecs are still settling who's to be master, with any number of other tribes hanging around ready to help a newcomer against both. The Spanish guns made, will make, no real difference, as you'll recall if you've read Diaz. The Mongols are as superior, man for man, as any Spaniard. . . . Not that I imagine Toktai would wade right in. He'd doubtless be very polite, spend the winter, learn everything he could. Next year he'd go back north, proceed home, and report to Kublai that some of the richest, most gold-stuffed territory on earth was wide open for conquest!"

"How about the other Indians?" put in Everard. "I'm vague on them."

"The Mayan New Empire is at its height. A tough nut to crack, but a correspondingly rewarding one. I should think, once the Mongols got established in Mexico, there'd be no stopping them. Peru has an even higher culture at this moment, and much less organization than Pizarro faced; the Quechua-Aymar, the so-called Inca race, are still only one power down there among several.

"And then, the land! Can you visualize what a Mongol tribe would make of the Great Plains?"

"I can't see them emigrating in hordes," said Everard. There was that about Sandoval's voice which made him uneasy and defensive. "Too much Siberia and Alaska in the way."

"Worse obstacles have been overcome. I don't mean they'd pour in all at once. It might take them a few centuries to start mass immigration, as it will take the Europeans. I can imagine a string of clans and tribes being established in the course of some years, all down western North America. Mexico and Yucatan get gobbled up—or, more likely, become khanates. The herding tribes move eastward as their own population grows and as new immigrants arrive. Remember, the Yuan dynasty is due to be overthrown in less than a century. That'll put additional pressure on the Mongols in Asia to go elsewhere. And Chinese will come here too, to farm and to share in the gold."

"I should think, if you don't mind my saying so," Everard broke in softly, "that you of all people wouldn't want to hasten the conquest of America."

"It'd be a different conquest," said Sandoval. "I don't care about the Aztecs; if you study them, you'll agree that Cortez did Mexico a favor. It'd be rough on other, more harmless tribes, too—for a while. And yet, the Mongols aren't such devils. Are they? A Western background prejudices us. We forget how much torture and massacre the Europeans were enjoying at the same time.

"The Mongols are quite a bit like the old Romans, really. Same practice of depopulating areas that resist, but respecting the rights of those who make submission. Same armed protection and competent government. Same unimaginative, uncreative national character; but the same vague awe and envy of true civilization. The *Pax Mongolica,* right now, unites a bigger area, and brings more different peoples into stimulating contact, than that piddling Roman Empire ever imagined.

"As for the Indians—remember, the Mongols are herdsmen. There won't be anything like the unsolvable conflict between hunter and farmer that made the white man destroy the Indian. The Mongol hasn't got race prejudices, either. And after a little fighting, the average Navajo, Cherokee, Seminole, Algonquin, Chippewa, Dakota, will be glad to submit and become allied. Why not? He'll get horses, sheep, cattle, textiles, metallurgy. He'll outnumber the invaders, and be on much more nearly equal terms with them than with white farmers and machine-age industry. And there'll be the Chinese, I repeat, leavening the whole mixture, teaching civilization and sharpening wits. . . .

"Good God, Manse! When Columbus gets here, he'll find his Grand Cham all right! The Sachem Khan of the strongest nation on earth!"

Sandoval stopped. Everard listened to the gallows creak of branches in the wind. He looked into the night for a long while before he said, "It could be. Of course, we'd have to stay in this century till the crucial point was past. Our own world wouldn't exist. Wouldn't ever have existed."

"It wasn't such a hell of a good world anyway," said Sandoval, as if in dream.

"You might think about your . . . oh . . . parents. They'd never have been born either."

"They lived in a tumbledown hogan. I saw my father crying once, because he couldn't buy shoes for us in winter. My mother died of TB."

Everard sat unstirring. It was Sandoval who shook himself and jumped to his feet with a rattling kind of laugh. "What have I been mumbling? It was just a yarn, Manse. Let's turn in. Shall I take first watch?"

Everard agreed, but lay long awake.

5

The scooter had jumped two days futureward and now hovered invisibly far above to the naked eye. Around it, the air was thin and sharply cold. Everard shivered as he adjusted the electronic telescope. Even at full magnification, the caravan was little more than specks toiling across green immensity. But no one else in the Western Hemisphere could have been riding horses.

He twisted in the saddle to face his companion. "So now what?"

Sandoval's broad countenance was unreadable. "Well, if our demonstration didn't work—"

"It sure as hell didn't! I swear they're moving south twice as fast as before. Why?"

"I'd have to know all of them a lot better than I do, as individuals, to give you a real answer, Manse. But essentially it must be that we challenged their courage. A warlike culture, nerve and hardihood its only absolute virtues . . . what choice have they got but to go on? If they retreated before a mere threat, they'd never be able to live with themselves."

"But Mongols aren't idiots! They didn't conquer everybody in sight by bull strength, but by jolly well understanding military principles better. Toktai should retreat, report to the Emperor what he saw, and organize a bigger expedition."

"The men at the ships can do that," Sandoval reminded. "Now that I think about it, I see how grossly we underestimated Toktai. He must have set a date, presumably next year, for the ships to try and go home if he doesn't return. When he finds something interesting along the way, like us, he can dispatch an Indian with a letter to the base camp."

Everard nodded. It occurred to him that he had been rushed into this job, all the way down the line, with never a pause to plan it as he should have done. Hence this botch. But how much blame must fall on the subconscious reluctance of John Sandoval? After a minute Everard said: "They may even have smelled something fishy about us. The Mongols were always good at psychological warfare."

"Could be. But what's our next move?"

Swoop down from above, fire a few blasts from the forty-first-century energy gun mounted in this timecycle, and that's the end. . . . No, by God, they can send me to the exile planet before I'll do any such thing. There are decent limits.

"We'll rig up a more impressive demonstration," said Everard.

"And if it flops too?"

"Shut up! Give it a chance!"

"I was just wondering." The wind harried under Sandoval's words. "Why not cancel the expedition instead? Go back in time a couple of years and persuade Kublai Khan it isn't worthwhile sending explorers eastward. Then all this would never have happened."

"You know Patrol regs forbid us to make historical changes."

"What do you call this we're doing?"

"Something specifically ordered by supreme HQ. Perhaps to correct some interference elsewhere, elsewhen. How should I know? I'm only a step on the evolutionary ladder. They have abilities a million years hence that I can't even guess at."

"Father knows best," murmured Sandoval.

Everard set his jaw. "The fact remains," he said, "the court of Kublai, the most powerful man on earth, is more important and crucial than anything here in America. No, you rang me in on this miserable job, and now I'll pull rank on you if I must. Our orders are to make these people give up their exploration. What happens afterward is none of our business. So they don't make it home. We won't be the proximate cause, any more than you're a murderer if you invite a man to dinner and he has a fatal accident on the way."

"Stop quacking and let's get to work," rapped Sandoval.

Everard sent the scooter gliding forward. "See that hill?" he pointed after a while. "It's on Toktai's line of march, but I think he'll camp a few miles short of it tonight, down in that little meadow by the stream. The hill will be in his plain view, though. Let's set up shop on it."

"And make fireworks? It'll have to be pretty fancy. Those Cathayans know about gunpowder. They even have military rockets."

"Small ones. I know. But when I assembled my gear for this trip, I packed away some fairly versatile gadgetry, in case my first attempt failed."

The hill bore a sparse crown of pine trees. Everard landed the scooter among them and began to unload boxes from its sizable baggage compartments. Sandoval helped, wordless. The horses, Patrol trained, stepped calmly off the framework stalls which had borne them and started grazing along the slope.

After a while the Indian broke his silence. "This isn't my line of work. What are you rigging?"

Everard patted the small machine he had half assembled. "It's adapted from a weather-control system used in the Cold Centuries era upstairs. A potential distributor. It can make some of the damnedest lightning you ever saw, with thunder to match."

"Mmm . . . the great Mongol weakness." Suddenly Sandoval grinned. "You win. We might as well relax and enjoy this."

"Fix us a supper, will you, while I put the gimmick together? No fire, naturally. We don't want any mundane smoke. . . . Oh, yes, I also have a mirage projector. If you'll change clothes and put on a hood or something at the appropriate moment, so you can't be recognized, I'll paint a mile-high picture of you, half as ugly as life."

"How about a PA system? Navajo chants can be fairly alarming, if you don't know it's just a *yeibichai* or whatever."

"Coming up!"

The day waned. It grew murky under the pines; the air was chill and pungent. At last Everard devoured a sandwich and watched through his binoculars as the Mongol vanguard checked that campsite he had predicted. Others came riding in with their day's catch of game and went to work cooking. The main body showed up at sundown, posted itself efficiently, and ate. Toktai was indeed pushing hard, using every daylight moment. As darkness closed down, Everard glimpsed outposts mounted and with strung bows. He could not keep up his own spirits, however hard he tried. He was bucking men who had shaken the earth.

Early stars glittered above snow peaks. It was time to begin work.

"Got our horses tethered, Jack? They might panic. I'm fairly sure the Mongol horses will! Okay, here goes." Everard flipped a main switch and squatted by the dimly lit control dials of his apparatus.

First there was the palest blue flicker between earth and sky. Then the lightnings began, tongue after forked tongue leaping, trees smashed at a blow, the mountainsides rocking under their noise. Everard threw out ball lightning, spheres of flame which whirled and curvetted, trailing sparks, shooting across to the camp and exploding above it till the sky seemed white hot.

Deafened and half blinded, he managed to project a sheet of fluorescing ionization. Like northern lights the great banners curled, bloody red and bone white, hissing under the repeated thunder cracks. Sandoval trod forth. He had stripped to his pants, daubed clay on his body in archaic patterns; his face was not veiled after all, but smeared with earth and twisted into something Everard would not have known. The machine scanned him and altered its output. That which stood forth against the aurora was taller than a mountain. It moved in a shuffling dance, from horizon to horizon and back to the sky, and it wailed and barked in a falsetto louder than thunder.

Everard crouched beneath the lurid light, his fingers stiff on the control board. He knew a primitive fear of his own; the dance woke things in him that he had forgotten.

Judas priest! If this doesn't make them quit. . . .

His mind returned to him. He even looked at his watch. Half an hour . . . give them another fifteen minutes, in which the display tapered off . . . They'd surely stay in camp till dawn rather than blunder wildly out in the dark; they had that much discipline. So keep everything under wraps for several hours more, then administer the last stroke to their nerves by a single electric bolt smiting a tree right next to them. . . . Everard waved Sandoval back. The Indian sat down, panting harder than his exertions seemed to warrant.

When the noise was gone, Everard said, "Nice show, Jack." His voice sounded tinny and strange in his ears.

"I hadn't done anything like that for years," muttered Sandoval. He struck a match, startling noise in the quietness. The brief flame showed his lips gone thin. Then he shook out the match and only his cigarette end glowed.

"Nobody I knew, on the reservation, took that stuff seriously," he went on after a moment. "A few of the older men wanted us boys to learn it to keep the custom alive, to remind us we were still a people. But mostly our idea was to pick up some change by dancing for tourists."

There was a longer pause. Everard doused the projector completely. In the murk that followed, Sandoval's cigarette waxed and waned, a tiny red Algol.

"Tourists!" he said at last.

After more minutes: "Tonight I was dancing for a purpose. It meant something. I never felt that way before."

Everard was silent.

Until one of the horses, which had plunged at its halter's end during the performance and was still nervous, whinnied.

Everard looked up. Night met his eyes. "Did you hear anything, Jack?"

The flashlight beam speared him.

For an instant he stared blinded at it. Then he sprang erect, cursing and snatching for his stun pistol. A shadow ran from behind one of the trees. It struck him in the ribs. He lurched back. The beam gun flew to his hand. He shot at random.

The flashlight swept about once more. Everard glimpsed Sandoval. The Navajo had not donned his weapons again. Unarmed, he dodged the sweep of a Mongol blade. The swordsman ran after him. Sandoval reverted to Patrol judo. He went to one knee. Clumsy afoot, the Mongol slashed, missed, and ran straight into a shoulder block to the belly. Sandoval rose with the blow. The heel of his hand jolted upward to the Mongol's chin. The helmeted head snapped back. Sandoval chopped a hand at the Adam's apple, yanked the sword from its owner's grasp, turned and parried a cut from behind.

A voice yammered above the Mongol yipping, giving orders. Everard backed away. He had knocked one attacker out with a bolt from his pistol. There were others between him and the scooter. He circled to face them. A lariat curled around his shoulders. It tightened with one expert heave. He went over. Four men piled on him. He saw half a dozen lance butts crack down on Sandoval's head; then there wasn't time for anything but fighting. Twice he got to his feet, but his gun was gone by now, the Mauser plucked from its holster—the little men were pretty good at *yawara*-style combat themselves. They dragged him down and hit him with fists, boots, dagger pommels. He never quite lost consciousness, but he finally stopped caring.

6

Toktai struck camp before dawn. The first sun saw his troop wind between scattered copses on a broad valley floor. The land was turning flat and arid, the mountains to the right farther away, fewer snow peaks visible and those ghostly in a pale sky.

The hardy small Mongol horses trotted ahead—plop of hoofs, squeak and jingle of harness. Looking back, Everard saw the line as a compact mass; lances rose and fell, pennants and plumes and cloaks fluttered beneath, and under that were the helmets, with a brown slit-eyed face and a grotesquely painted cuirass visible here and there. No one spoke, and he couldn't read any of those expressions.

His brain felt sandy. They had left his hands free, but lashed his ankles to the stirrups, and the cord chafed. They had also stripped him naked—sensible precaution, who knew what instruments might be sewn into his garments?—and the Mongol garb given him in exchange was ludicrously small. The seams had had to be slit before he could even get the tunic on.

The projector and the scooter lay back at the hill. Toktai would not take any risks with those things of power. He had had to roar down several of his own frightened warriors before they would even agree to bring the strange horses, with saddle and bedroll, riderless among the pack mares.

Hoofs thudded rapidly. One of the bowmen flanking Everard grunted and moved his pony a little aside. Li Tai-Tsung rode close.

The Patrolman gave him a dull stare. "Well?" he said.

"I fear your friend will not waken again," answered the Chinese. "I made him a little more comfortable."

But lying strapped on an improvised litter between two ponies, unconscious. . . . Yes, concussion, when they clubbed him last night. A Patrol hospital could put him to rights soon enough. But the nearest Patrol office is in Cambaluc, and I can't see Toktai letting me go back to the scooter and use its radio. John Sandoval is going to die here, six hundred and fifty years before he was born.

Everard looked into cool brown eyes, interested, not unsympathetic, but alien to him. It was no use, he knew; arguments which were logical in his culture were gibberish today; but one had to try. "Can you, at least, not make Toktai understand what ruin he is going to bring on himself, on his whole people, by this?"

Li stroked his fork beard. "It is plain to see, honored sir, your nation has arts

unknown to us," he said. "But what of it? The barbarians—" He gave
Everard's Mongol guards a quick glance, but evidently they didn't understand
the Sung Chinese he used. "—took many kingdoms superior to them in every
way but fighting skill. Now already we know that you, ah, amended the truth
when you spoke of a hostile empire near these lands. Why should your king
try to frighten us away with a falsehood, did he not have reason to fear us?"

Everard spoke with care: "Our glorious emperor dislikes bloodshed. But if
you force him to strike you down—"

"Please." Li looked pained. He waved one slender hand, as if brushing off
an insect. "Say what you will to Toktai, and I shall not interfere. It would not
sadden me to return home; I came only under Imperial orders. But let us two,
speaking confidentially, not insult each other's intelligence. Do you not see,
eminent lord, that there is no possible harm with which you can threaten these
men? Death they despise; even the most lingering torture must kill them in
time; even the most disgraceful mutilation can be made as naught by a man
willing to bite through his tongue and die. Toktai sees eternal shame if he turns
back at this stage of events, and a good chance of eternal glory and
uncountable wealth if he continues."

Everard sighed. His own humiliating capture had indeed been the turning
point. The Mongols had been very near bolting at the thunder show. Many had
groveled and wailed (and from now on would be all the more aggressive, to
erase that memory). Toktai charged the source as much in horror as defiance;
a few men and horses had been able to come along. Li himself was partly
responsible: scholar, skeptic, familiar with sleight-of-hand and pyrotechnic
displays, the Chinese had helped hearten Toktai to attack before one of those
thunderbolts did strike home.

*The truth of the matter is, son, we misjudged these people. We should have
taken along a Specialist, who'd have an intuitive feeling for the nuances of this
culture. But no, we assumed a brainful of facts would be enough. Now what?
A Patrol relief expedition may show up eventually, but Jack will be dead in
another day or two. . . .* Everard looked at the stony warrior face on his left.
*Quite probably I'll be also. They're still on edge. They'd sooner scrag me than
not.*

And even if he should (unlikely chance!) survive to be hauled out of this
mess by another Patrol band—it would be tough to face his comrades. An
Unattached agent, with all the special privileges of his rank, was expected to
handle situations without extra help. Without leading valuable men to their
deaths.

"So I advise you most sincerely not to attempt any more deceptions."

"What?" Everard turned back to Li.

"You do understand, do you not," said the Chinese, "that our native guides did flee? That you are now taking their place? But we expect to meet other tribes before long, establish communication. . . ."

Everard nodded a throbbing head. The sunlight pierced his eyes. He was not astonished at the ready Mongol progress through scores of separate language areas. If you aren't fussy about grammar, a few hours suffice to pick up the small number of basic words and gestures; thereafter you can take days or weeks actually learning to speak with your hired escort.

". . . again obtain guides from stage to stage, as we did before," continued Li. "Any misdirection you may have given will soon be apparent. Toktai will punish it in most uncivilized ways. On the other hand, faithful service will be rewarded. You may hope in time to rise high in the provincial court, after the conquest."

Everard sat unmoving. The casual boast was like an explosion in his mind.

He had been assuming the Patrol would send another force. Obviously *something* was going to prevent Toktai's return. But was it so obvious? Why had this interference been ordered at all, if there were not—in some paradoxical way his twentieth-century logic couldn't grasp—an uncertainty, a shakiness in the continuum right at this point?

Judas in hell! Perhaps the Mongol expedition was going to succeed! Perhaps all the future of an American Khanate which Sandoval had not quite dared dream of . . . was the real future.

There are quirks and discontinuities in space-time. The world lines can double back and bite themselves off, so that things and events appear causelessly, meaningless flutters soon lost and forgotten. Such as Manse Everard, marooned in the past with a dead John Sandoval, after coming from a future that never existed as the agent of a Time Patrol that never was.

7

At sundown their unmerciful pace had brought the expedition into sagebrush and greasewood country. The hills were steep and brown; dust smoked under hoofs; silvery-green bushes grew sparse, sweetening the air when bruised but offering little else.

Everard helped lay Sandoval on the ground. The Navajo's eyes were closed, his face sunken and hot. Sometimes he tossed and muttered a bit. Everard squeezed water from a wetted cloth past the cracked lips, but could do nothing more.

The Mongols established themselves more merrily than of late. They had overcome two great sorcerers and suffered no further attack, and the

implications were growing upon them. They went about their chores chattering
to each other, and after a frugal meal they broke out the leather bags of *kumiss*.

Everard remained with Sandoval, near the middle of camp. Two guards had
been posted on him. They sat with strung bows a few yards away but didn't
talk. Now and then one of them would get up to tend the small fire. Presently
silence fell on their comrades too. Even this leathery host was tired; men rolled
up and went to sleep, the outposts rode their rounds drowsy-eyed, other watch
fires burned to embers while stars kindled overhead, a coyote yelped across
miles. Everard covered Sandoval against the gathering cold; his own low
flames showed rime frost on sage leaves. He huddled into a cloak and wished
his captors would at least give him back his pipe.

A footfall crunched dry soil. Everard's guards snatched arrows for their
bows. Toktai moved into the light, his head bare above a mantle. The guards
bent low and moved back into shadow.

Toktai halted. Everard looked up and then down again. The Noyon stared
a while at Sandoval. Finally, almost gently, he said: "I do not think your friend
will live to next sunset."

Everard grunted.

"Have you any medicines which might help?" asked Toktai. "There are
some queer things in your saddlebags."

"I have a remedy against infection, and another against pain," said Everard
mechanically. "But for a cracked skull, he must be taken to skillful
physicians."

Toktai sat down and held his hands to the fire. "I'm sorry we have no
surgeons along."

"You could let us go," said Everard without hope. "My chariot, back at the
last camp, could get him to help in time."

"Now you know I can't do that!" Toktai chuckled. His pity for the dying
man flickered out. "After all, Eburar, you started the trouble."

Since it was true, the Patrolman made no retort.

"I don't hold it against you," went on Toktai. "In fact, I'm still anxious to
be friends. If I weren't, I'd stop for a few days and wring all you know out of
you."

Everard flared up. "You could try!"

"And succeed, I think, with a man who has to carry medicine against pain."
Toktai's grin was wolfish. "However, you may be useful as a hostage or
something. And I do like your nerve. I'll even tell you an idea I have. I think
maybe you don't belong to this rich southland at all. I think you're an
adventurer, one of a little band of shamans. You have the southern king in your
power, or hope to, and don't want strangers interfering." Toktai spat into the

fire. "There are old stories about that sort of thing, and finally a hero overthrew the wizard. Why not me?"

Everard sighed. "You will learn why not, Noyon." He wondered how correct that was.

"Oh, now." Toktai clapped him on the back. "Can't you tell me even a little? There's no blood feud between us. Let's be friends."

Everard jerked a thumb at Sandoval.

"It's a shame, that," said Toktai, "but he would keep on resisting an officer of the Kha Khan. Come, let's have a drink together, Eburar. I'll send a man for a bag."

The Patrolman made a face. "That's no way to pacify me!"

"Oh, your people don't like *kumiss?* I'm afraid it's all we have. We drank up our wine long ago."

"You could let me have my whisky." Everard looked at Sandoval again, and out into night, and felt the cold creep inward. "God, but I could use that!"

"Eh?"

"A drink of our own. We had some in our saddlebags."

"Well . . ." Toktai hesitated. "Very well. Come along and we'll fetch it."

The guards followed their chief and their prisoner, through the brush and the sleeping warriors, up to a pile of assorted gear also under guard. One of the latter sentries ignited a stick in his fire to give Everard some light. The Patrolman's back muscles tensed—arrows were aimed at him now, drawn to the barb—but he squatted and went through his own stuff, careful not to move fast. When he had both canteens of Scotch, he returned to his own place.

Toktai sat down across the fire. He watched Everard pour a shot into the canteen cap and toss it off. "Smells odd," he said.

"Try." The Patrolman handed over the canteen.

It was an impulse of sheer loneliness. Toktai wasn't such a bad sort. Not on his own terms. And when you sit by your dying partner, you'd bouse with the devil himself, just to keep from thinking. The Mongol sniffed dubiously, looked back at Everard, paused, and then raised the bottle to his lips with a bravura gesture.

"Whoo-oo-oo!"

Everard scrambled to catch the flask before too much was spilled. Toktai gasped and spat. One guardsman nocked an arrow, the other sprang to lay a hard hand on Everard's shoulder. A sword gleamed high. "It's not poison!" the Patrolman exclaimed. "It's only too strong for him. See, I'll drink some more myself."

Toktai waved the guards back and glared from watery eyes. "What do you make that of?" he choked. "Dragon's blood?"

"Barley." Everard didn't feel like explaining distillation. He poured himself another slug. "Go ahead, drink your mare's milk."

Toktai smacked his lips. "It does warm you up doesn't it? Like pepper." He reached out a grimy hand. "Give me some more."

Everard sat still for a few seconds. "Well?" growled Toktai.

The Patrolman shook his head. "I told you, it's too strong for Mongols."

"What? See here, you whey-faced son of a Turk—"

"On your head be it, then. I warn you fairly, with your men here as witnesses, you will be sick tomorrow."

Toktai guzzled heartily, belched, and passed the canteen back. "Nonsense. I simply wasn't prepared for it, the first time. Drink up!"

Everard took his time. Toktai grew impatient. "Hurry along there. No, give me the other flask."

"Very well. You are the chief. But I beg you, don't try to match me draught for draught. You can't do it."

"What do you mean, I can't do it? Why, I've drunk twenty men senseless in Karakorum. None of your gutless Chinks, either: they were all Mongols." Toktai poured down a couple of ounces more.

Everard sipped with care. But he hardly felt the effect anyway, save as a burning along his gullet. He was too tightly strung. Suddenly he was glimpsing what might be a way out.

"Here, it's a cold night," he said, and offered his canteen to the nearest guardsman. "You lads have one to keep you warm."

Toktai looked up, a trifle muzzily. "Good stuff, this," he objected. "Too good for. . . ." He remembered himself and snapped his words off short. Cruel and absolute the Mongol Empire might be, but officers shared equally with the humblest of their men.

The warrior grabbed the jug, giving his chief a resentful look, and slanted it to his mouth. "Easy, there," said Everard. "It's heady."

"Nothin's heady to me." Toktai poured a further dose into himself. "Sober as a bonze." He wagged his finger. "That's the trouble bein' a Mongol. You're so hardy you can't get drunk."

"Are you bragging or complaining?" said Everard. The first warrior fanned his tongue, resumed a stance of alertness, and passed the bottle to his companion. Toktai hoisted the other canteen again.

"Ahhh!" He stared, owlish. "That was fine. Well, better get to sleep now. Give him back his liquor, men."

Everard's throat tightened. But he managed to leer. "Yes, thanks, I'll want some more," he said. "I'm glad you realize you can't take it."

"Wha' d'you mean?" Toktai glared at him. "No such thing as too much.

Not for a Mongol!" He glugged afresh. The first guardsman received the other flask and took a hasty snort before it should be too late.

Everard sucked in a shaken breath. It might work out after all. It might.

Toktai was used to carousing. There was no doubt that he or his men could handle *kumiss*, wine, ale, mead, *kvass*, that thin beer miscalled rice wine—any beverage of this era. They'd know when they'd had enough, say good night, and walk a straight line to their bedrolls. The trouble was, no substance merely fermented can get over about twenty-four proof—the process is stopped by its waste product—and most of what they brewed in the thirteenth century ran well under five percent alcohol, with a high foodstuff content to boot.

Scotch whisky is in quite a different class. If you try to drink that like beer, or even like wine, you are in trouble. Your judgment will be gone before you've noticed its absence, and consciousness follows soon after.

Everard reached for the canteen held by one of the guards. "Give me that!" he said. "You'll drink it all up!"

The warrior grinned and took another long gulp, before passing it on to his fellow. Everard stood up and made an undignified scrabble for it. A guard poked him in the stomach. He went over on his backside. The Mongols bawled laughter, leaning on each other. So good a joke called for another drink.

When Toktai folded, Everard alone noticed. The Noyon slid from a cross-legged to a recumbent position. The fire sputtered up long enough to show a silly smile on his face. Everard squatted wire-tense.

The end of one sentry came a few minutes later. He reeled, went on all fours, and began to jettison his dinner. The other one turned, blinking, fumbling after a sword. "Wha's mattuh?" he groaned. "Wha' yuh done? Poison?"

Everard moved.

He had hopped over the fire and fallen on Toktai before the last guard realized it. The Mongol stumbled forward, crying out. Everard found Toktai's sword. It flashed from the scabbard as he bounded up. The warrior got his own blade aloft. Everard didn't like to kill a nearly helpless man. He stepped close, knocked the other weapon aside, and his fist clopped. The Mongol sank to his knees, retched, and slept.

Everard bounded away. Men stirred in the dark, calling. He heard hoofs drum, one of the mounted sentries racing to investigate. Somebody took a brand from an almost extinct fire and whirled it till it flared. Everard went flat on his belly.

A warrior pelted by, not seeing him in the brush. He glided toward deeper darknesses. A yell behind him, a machine-gun volley of curses, told that someone had found the Noyon.

Everard stood up and began to run.

The horses had been hobbled and turned out under guard as usual. They were a dark mass on the plain, which lay gray-white beneath a sky crowded with sharp stars. Everard saw one of the Mongol watchers gallop to meet him. A voice barked: "What's happening?"

He pitched his answer high. "Attack on camp!" It was only to gain time, lest the horseman recognize him and fire an arrow. He crouched, visible as a hunched and cloaked shape. The Mongol reined in with a spurt of dust. Everard sprang.

He got hold of the pony's bridle before he was recognized. Then the sentry yelled and drew sword. He hewed downward. But Everard was on the left side. The blow from above came awkwardly, easily parried. Everard chopped in return and felt his edge go into meat. The horse reared in alarm. Its rider fell from the saddle. He rolled over and staggered up again, bellowing. Everard already had one foot in a pan-shaped stirrup. The Mongol limped toward him, blood running black in that light from a wounded leg. Everard mounted and laid the flat of his own blade on the horse's crupper.

He got going toward the herd. Another rider pounded to intercept him. Everard ducked. An arrow buzzed where he had been. The stolen pony plunged, fighting its unfamiliar burden. Everard needed a minute to get it under control again. The archer might have taken him then, by coming up and going at it hand to hand. But habit sent the man past at a gallop, shooting. He missed in the dimness. Before he could turn, Everard was out of night view.

The Patrolman uncoiled a lariat at the saddlebow and broke into the skittish herd. He roped the nearest animal, which accepted it with blessed meekness. Leaning over, he slashed the hobbles with his sword and rode off, leading the remount. They came out the other side of the herd and started north.

A stern chase is a long chase, Everard told himself inappropriately. *But they're bound to overhaul me if I don't lose 'em. Let's see, if I remember my geography, the lava beds lie northwest of here.*

He cast a glance behind. No one pursued yet. They'd need a while to organize themselves. However. . . .

Thin lightnings winked from above. The cloven air boomed behind them. He felt a chill, deeper than the night cold. But he eased his pace. There was no more reason for hurry. That must be Manse Everard—

—who had returned to the Patrol vehicle and ridden it south in space and backward in time to this same instant.

That was cutting it fine, he thought. Patrol doctrine frowned on helping oneself thus. Too much danger of a close causal loop, or of tangling past and future.

But in this case, I'll get away with it. No reprimands, even. Because it's to rescue Jack Sandoval, not myself. I've already gotten free. I could shake pursuit in the mountains, which I know and the Mongols don't. The time-hopping is only to save my friend's life.

Besides (an upsurging bitterness), *what's this whole mission been, except the future doubling back to create its own past? Without us, the Mongols might well have taken over America, and then there'd never have been any us.*

The sky was enormous, crystalline black; you rarely saw that many stars. The Great Bear flashed above hoar earth; hoofbeats rang through silence. Everard had not felt so alone before now.

"And what am I doing back there?" he asked aloud.

The answer came to him, and he eased a little, fell into the rhythm of his horses and started eating miles. He wanted to get this over with. But what he must do turned out to be less bad than he had feared.

Toktai and Li Tai-Tsung never came home. But that was not because they perished at sea or in the forests. It was because a sorcerer rode down from heaven and killed all their horses with thunderbolts, and smashed and burned their ships in the river mouth. No Chinese sailor would venture onto those tricky seas in whatever clumsy vessel could be built here; no Mongol would think it possible to go home on foot. Indeed, it probably wasn't. The expedition would stay, marry into the Indians, live out their days. Chinook, Tlingit, Nootka, all the potlatch tribes, with their big seagoing canoes, lodges and copperworking, furs and cloths and haughtiness . . . well, a Mongol Noyon, even a Confucian scholar might live less happily and usefully than in creating such a life for such a race.

Everard nodded to himself. So much for that. What was harder to take than the thwarting of Toktai's bloodthirsty ambitions was the truth about his own corps, which was his own family and nation and reason for living. The distant supermen turned out to be not quite such idealists after all. They weren't merely safeguarding a perhaps divinely ordained history which led to them. Here and there they, too, meddled, to create their own past. . . . Don't ask if there ever was any "original" scheme of things. Keep your mind shut. Regard the rutted road mankind had to travel, and tell yourself that if it could be better in places, in other places it could be worse.

"It may be a crooked game," said Everard, "but it's the only one in town."

His voice came so loud, in that huge rime-white land, that he didn't speak any more. He clucked at his horse and rode a little faster northward.

Delenda Est

1

THE hunting is good in Europe twenty thousand years ago, and the winter sports are unexcelled anywhen. So the Time Patrol, always solicitous for its highly trained personnel, maintains a lodge in the Pleistocene Pyrenees.

Manse Everard stood on a glassed-in verandah and looked across ice-blue distances toward the northern slopes where the mountains fell off into woodland, marsh, and tundra. His big body was clad in loose green trousers and tunic of twenty-third century insulsynth, boots handmade by a nineteenth-century French-Canadian; he smoked a foul old briar of indeterminate origin. There was a vague restlessness about him, and he ignored the noise from within, where half a dozen agents were drinking and talking and playing the piano.

A Crô-Magnon guide went by across the snow-covered yard, a tall handsome fellow dressed rather like an Eskimo (why had romance never credited paleolithic man with enough sense to wear jacket, pants, and footgear in a glacial period?), his face painted, one of the steel knives he had earned at his belt. The Patrol could act quite freely, this far back in time; there was no danger of upsetting the past, for the metal would rust away and the strangers be forgotten in a few centuries. The main nuisance was that female agents from the more libertine periods upstairs were always having affairs with the native hunters.

Piet Van Sarawak (Dutch-Indonesian-Venusian, early twenty-fourth A.D.), a slim, dark young man whose looks and technique gave the guides some stiff competition, joined Everard. They stood for a moment in companionable silence. He was also Unattached, on call to help out in any milieu, and had worked with the American before. They had taken their first vacation together.

He spoke first, in Temporal. "I hear they've spotted a few mammoths near Toulouse." The city would not be built for a long while yet, but habit was powerful.

"I've bagged one," said Everard impatiently. "I've also been skiing and mountain-climbing and watched the native dances."

Van Sarawak nodded, took out a cigarette, and puffed it into lighting. The bones stood out in his lean brown face as he sucked the smoke inward. "A pleasant loafing spell, this," he agreed, "but after a bit the outdoor life begins to pall."

There were still two weeks left of their furlough. In theory, since he could return almost to the moment of departure, an agent could take indefinite vacations; but actually he was supposed to devote a certain percentage of his probable lifetime to the job. (They never told you when you were scheduled to die, and you had better sense than to try finding out for yourself. It wouldn't have been certain anyhow, time being mutable. One perquisite of an agent's office was the Danellian longevity treatment.)

"What I would enjoy," continued Van Sarawak, "is some bright lights, music, girls who've never heard of time travel—"

"Done!" said Everard.

"Augustan Rome?" asked the other eagerly. "I've never been there. I could get a hypno on language and customs here."

Everard shook his head. "It's overrated. Unless we want to go 'way upstairs, the most glorious decadence available is right in my own milieu. New York, say. . . . If you know the right phone numbers, and I do."

Van Sarawak chuckled. "I know a few places in my own sector," he replied, "but by and large, a pioneer society has little use for the finer arts of amusement. Very good, let's be off to New York, in—when?"

"Make it 1960. That was the last time I was there, in my public *persona*, before coming here-now."

They grinned at each other and went off to pack. Everard had foresightedly brought along some midtwentieth garments in his friend's size.

Throwing clothes and razor into a small suitcase, the American wondered if he could keep up with Van Sarawak. He had never been a high-powered roisterer, and wouldn't have known how to buckle a swash anywhere in space-time. A good book, a bull session, a case of beer—that was about his speed. But even the soberest men must kick over the traces occasionally.

Or a little more than that, if he was an Unattached agent of the Time Patrol; if his job with the Engineering Studies Company was only a blind for his wanderings and warrings through all history; if he had seen that history rewritten in minor things—not by God, which would have been endurable, but by mortal and fallible men—for even the Danellians were somewhat less than God; if he was forever haunted by the possibility of a major change, such that he and his entire world would never have existed at all. . . . Everard's battered, homely face screwed into a grimace. He ran a hand through his stiff brown hair, as if to brush the idea away. Useless to think about. Language and logic broke down in the face of the paradox. Better to relax at such moments as he could.

He picked up the suitcase and went to join Piet Van Sarawak.

Their little two-place antigravity scooter waited on its skids in the garage. You wouldn't believe, to look at it, that the controls could be set for any place on Earth and any moment of time. But an airplane is wonderful too, or a ship, or a fire.

> *Auprés de ma blonde*
> *Qu'il fait bon, fait bon, fait bon,*
> *Auprés de ma blonde*
> *Qu'il fait bon dormir!*

Van Sarawak sang it aloud, his breath steaming from him in the frosty air as he hopped onto the rear saddle. He'd picked up the song once when accompanying the army of Louis XIV. Everard laughed. "Down, boy!"

"Oh, come, now," warbled the younger man. "It is a beautiful continuum, a merry and gorgeous cosmos. Hurry up this machine."

Everard was not so sure; he had seen enough human misery in all the ages. You got case-hardened after a while, but down underneath, when a peasant stared at you with sick brutalized eyes, or a soldier screamed with a pike through him, or a city went up in radioactive flame, something wept. He could understand the fanatics who had tried to change events. It was only that their work was so unlikely to make anything better. . . .

He set the controls for the Engineering Studies warehouse, a good confidential place to emerge. Thereafter they'd go to his apartment, and then the fun could start.

"I trust you've said good-bye to all your lady friends here," Everard remarked.

"Oh, most gallantly, I assure you. Come along there. You're as slow as molasses on Pluto. For your information, this vehicle does not have to be rowed home."

Everard shrugged and threw the main switch. The garage blinked out of sight.

2

For a moment, shock held them unstirring.

The scene registered in bits and pieces. They had materialized a few inches above ground level—the scooter was designed never to come out inside a solid object—and since that was unexpected, they hit the pavement with a teeth-rattling bump. They were in some kind of square. Nearby a fountain jetted, its stone basin carved with intertwining vines. Around the plaza, streets led off between squarish buildings six to ten stories high, of brick or concrete, wildly painted and ornamented. There were automobiles, big clumsy-looking things of no recognizable type, and a crowd of people.

"Jumping gods!" Everard glared at the meters. The scooter had landed them in lower Manhattan, 23 October 1960, at 11:30 A.M. and the spatial coordinates of the warehouse. But there was a blustery wind throwing dust and soot in his face, the smell of chimneys, and. . . .

Van Sarawak's sonic stunner jumped into his fist. The crowd was milling away from them, shouting in some babble they couldn't understand. It was a mixed lot: tall, fair roundheads, with a great deal of red hair; a number of Amerinds; half-breeds in all combinations. The men wore loose colorful blouses, tartan kilts, a sort of Scotch bonnet, shoes and knee-length stockings. Their hair was long and many favored drooping mustaches. The women had full skirts reaching to the ankles and tresses coiled under hooded cloaks. Both sexes went in for massive bracelets and necklaces.

"What happened?" whispered the Venusian. "Where are we?"

Everard sat rigid. His mind clicked over, whirling through all the eras he had known or read about. Industrial culture—those looked like steam cars, but why the sharp prows and figurehead?—coal-burning—postnuclear Reconstruction? No, they hadn't worn kilts then, and they had spoken English. . . .

It didn't fit. There was no such milieu recorded.

"We're getting out of here!"

His hands were on the controls when the large man jumped him. They went over on the pavement in a rage of fists and feet. Van Sarawak fired and sent someone else down unconscious; then he was seized from behind. The mob piled on top of them both, and things became hazy.

Everard had a confused impression of men in shining coppery breastplates and helmets, who shoved a billy-swinging way through the riot. He was fished out and supported in his grogginess while handcuffs were snapped on his wrists. Then he and Van Sarawak were searched and hustled off to a big enclosed vehicle. The Black Maria is much the same in all times.

He didn't come back to full consciousness until they were in a damp and chilly cell with an iron-barred door.

"Name of a flame!" The Venusian slumped on a wooden cot and put his face in his hands.

Everard stood at the door, looking out. All he could see was a narrow concrete hall and the cell across it. The map of Ireland stared cheerfully through those bars and called something unintelligible.

"What's going on?" Van Sarawak's slim body shuddered.

"I don't know," said Everard very slowly. "I just don't know. That machine was supposed to be foolproof, but maybe we're bigger fools than they allowed for."

"There's no such place as this," said Van Sarawak desperately. "A dream?" He pinched himself and managed a rueful smile. His lip was cut and swelling, and he had the start of a gorgeous shiner. "Logically, my friend, a pinch is no test of reality, but it has a certain reassuring effect."

"I wish it didn't," said Everard.

He grabbed the bars so hard they rattled. "Could the controls have been askew, in spite of everything? Is there any city, anywhen on Earth—because I'm damned sure this is Earth, at least—any city, however obscure, which was ever like this?"

"Not to my knowledge."

Everard hung on to his sanity and rallied all the mental training the Patrol had ever given him. That included total recall; and he had studied history, even the history of ages he had never seen, with a thoroughness that should have earned him several Ph.D.'s.

"No," he said at last. "Kilted brachycephalic whites, mixed up with Indians and using steam-driven automobiles, haven't happened."

"Coordinator Stantel V," said Van Sarawak faintly. "In the thirty-eighth century. The Great Experimenter—colonies reproducing past societies—"

"Not any like this," said Everard.

The truth was growing in him, and he would have traded his soul for things to be otherwise. It took all the strength he had to keep from screaming and bashing his brains out against the wall.

"We'll have to see," he said in a flat tone

A policeman (Everard assumed they were in the hands of the law) brought them a meal and tried to talk to them. Van Sarawak said the language sounded

Celtic, but he couldn't make out more than a few words. The meal wasn't bad.

Toward evening, they were led off to a washroom and got cleaned up under official guns. Everard studied the weapons: eight-shot revolvers and long-barreled rifles. There were gas lights, whose brackets repeated the motif of wreathing vines and snakes. The facilities and firearms, as well as the smell, suggested a technology roughly equivalent to the earlier nineteenth century.

On the way back he spied a couple of signs on the walls. The script was obviously Semitic, but though Van Sarawak had some knowledge of Hebrew through dealing with the Israeli colonies on Venus, he couldn't read it.

Locked in again, they saw the other prisoners led off to do their own washing: a surprisingly merry crowd of bums, toughs, and drunks. "Seems we get special treatment," remarked Van Sarawak.

"Hardly astonishing," said Everard. "What would you do with total strangers who appeared out of nowhere and had unheard-of weapons?"

Van Sarawak's face turned to him with an unwonted grimness. "Are you thinking what I'm thinking?" he asked.

"Probably."

The Venusian's mouth twisted, and horror rode his voice: "Another time line. Somebody *has* managed to change history."

Everard nodded.

They spent an unhappy night. It would have been a boon to sleep, but the other cells were too noisy. Discipline seemed to be lax here. Also, there were bedbugs.

After a bleary breakfast, Everard and Van Sarawak were allowed to wash again and shave with safety razors not unlike the familiar type. Then a ten-man guard marched them into an office and planted itself around the walls.

They sat down before a desk and waited. The furniture was as disquietingly half-homelike, half-alien, as everything else. It was some time before the big wheels showed up. They were two: a white-haired, ruddy-cheeked man in cuirass and green tunic, presumably the chief of police, and a lean, hard-faced half-breed, gray-haired but black-mustached, wearing a blue tunic, a tam-o'-shanter, and on his left breast a golden bull's head which seemed an insigne of rank. He would have had a certain aquiline dignity had it not been for the thin hairy legs beneath his kilt. He was followed by two younger men, armed and uniformed much like himself, who took up their places behind him as he sat down.

Everard leaned over and whispered: "The military, I'll bet. We seem to be of interest."

Van Sarawak nodded sickly.

The police chief cleared his throat with conscious importance and said something to the—general? The latter answered impatiently, and addressed himself to the prisoners. He barked his words out with a clarity that helped Everard get the phonemes, but with a manner that was not exactly reassuring.

Somewhere along the line, communication would have to be established. Everard pointed to himself. "Manse Everard," he said. Van Sarawak followed the lead and introduced himself similarly.

The general started and went into a huddle with the chief. Turning back, he snapped, "*Yrn Cimberland?*"

Then: "*Gothland? Svea? Nairoin Teutonach?*"

"Those names—if they are names—they sound Germanic, don't they?" muttered Van Sarawak.

"So do our names, come to think of it," answered Everard tautly. "Maybe they think we're Germans." To the general: "*Sprechen sie Deutsch?*" Blankness rewarded him. "*Taler ni svensk? Niederlands? Dönsk tunga? Parlez-vous français?* Goddammit, *¿habla usted español?*"

The police chief cleared his throat again and pointed to himself. "Cadwallader Mac Barca," he said. The general hight Cynyth ap Cecrn. Or so, at least, Everard's Anglo-Saxon mind interpreted the noises picked up by his ears.

"Celtic, all right," he said. Sweat prickled under his arms. "But just to make sure. . . ." He pointed inquiringly at a few other men, being rewarded with monikers like Hamilcar ap Angus, Asshur yr Cathlan, and Finn O'Carthia. "No . . . there's a distinct Semitic element here too. That fits in with their alphabet."

Van Sarawak wet his lips. "Try classical languages," he urged harshly. "Maybe we can find out where this history went insane."

"*Loquerisne latine?*" That drew a blank. " '*Ελλευίζεις'?*"

General ap Ceorn jerked, blew out his mustache, and narrowed his eyes. "*Hellenach?*" he demanded. "*Yrn Parthia?*"

Everard shook his head. "They've at least heard of Greek," he said slowly. He tried a few more words, but no one knew the tongue.

Ap Ceorn growled something to one of his men, who bowed and went out. There was a long silence.

Everard found himself losing personal fear. He was in a bad spot, yes, and might not live very long; but whatever happened to him was ludicrously unimportant compared to what had been done to the entire world.

God in Heaven! To the universe!

He couldn't grasp it. Sharp in his mind rose the land he knew, broad plains and tall mountains and prideful cities. There was the grave image of his father, and yet he remembered being a small child and lifted up skyward while his father laughed beneath him. And his mother . . . they had a good life together, those two.

There had been a girl he knew in college, the sweetest little wench a man would ever have been privileged to walk in the rain with; and Bernie Aaronson, the nights of beer and smoke and talk; Phil Brackney, who had picked him out of the mud in France when machine guns were raking a ruined field; Charlie and Mary Whitcomb, high tea and a low cannel fire in Victoria's London; Keith and Cynthia Denison in their chrome-plated eyrie above New York; Jack Sandoval among tawny Arizona crags; a dog he had once had; the austere cantos of Dante and the ringing thunder of Shakespeare; the glory which was York Minster and the Golden Gate Bridge—Christ, a man's life, and the lives of who knew how many billions of human creatures, toiling and enduring and laughing and going down into dust to make room for their sons . . . It had never been.

He shook his head, dazed with grief, and sat devoid of real understanding.

The soldier came back with a map and spread it out on the desk. Ap Ceorn gestured curtly, and Everard and Van Sarawak bent over it.

Yes, Earth, a Mercator projection, though eidetic memory showed that the mapping was rather crude. The continents and islands were there in bright colors, but the nations were something else.

"Can you read those names, Van?"

"I can make a guess, on the basis of the Hebraic alphabet," said the Venusian. He began to read out the words. Ap Ceorn grunted and corrected him.

North America down to about Columbia was Ynys yr Afallon, seemingly one country divided into states. South America was a big realm, Huy Braseal, and some smaller countries whose names looked Indian. Australasia, Indonesia, Borneo, Burma, eastern India, and a good deal of the Pacific belonged to Hinduraj. Afghanistan and the rest of India were Punjab. Han included China, Korea, Japan, and eastern Siberia. Littorn owned the rest of Russia and reached well into Europe. The British Isles were Brittys, France and the Low Countries were Gallis, the Iberian peninsula was Celtan. Central Europe and the Balkans were divided into many small nations, some of which had Hunnish-looking names. Switzerland and Austria made up Helveti; Italy was Cimberland; the Scandinavian peninsula was split down the middle, Svea in the north and Gothland in the south. North Africa looked like a confederacy, reaching from Senegal to Suez and nearly to the equator under the name of Carthagalann; the southern part of the continent was partitioned among minor sovereignties, many of which had purely African titles. The Near East held Parthia and Arabia.

Van Sarawak looked up. He had tears in his eyes.

Ap Ceorn snarled a question and waved his finger about. He wanted to know where they were from.

Everard shrugged and pointed skyward. The one thing he could not admit was the truth. He and Van Sarawak had agreed to claim they were from another planet, since this world hardly had space travel.

Ap Ceorn spoke to the chief, who nodded and replied. The prisoners were returned to their cell.

3

"And now what?" Van Sarawak slumped on his cot and stared at the floor.

"We play along," said Everard grayly. "We do anything to get at our scooter and escape. Once we're free, we can take stock."

"But what happened?"

"I don't know, I tell you! Offhand, it looks as if something upset the Graeco-Romans and the Celts took over, but I couldn't say what it was." Everard prowled the room. A bitter determination was growing in him.

"Remember your basic theory," he said. "Events are the result of a complex. There are no single causes. That's why it's so hard to change history. If I went back to, say, the Middle Ages, and shot one of FDR's Dutch forebears, he's still be born in the late nineteenth century—because he and his genes resulted from the entire world of his ancestors, and there'd have been compensation. But every so often, a really key event does occur. Some one happening is a nexus of so many world lines that its outcome is decisive for the whole future.

"Somehow, for some reason, somebody has ripped up one of those events, back in the past."

"No more Hesperus City," mumbled Van Sarawak. "No more sitting by the canals in the blue twilight, no more Aphrodite vintages, no more—did you know I had a sister on Venus?"

"Shut up!" Everard almost shouted it. "I know. To hell with that. What counts is what we can do.

"Look," he went on after a moment, "the Patrol and the Danellians are wiped out. (Don't ask me why they weren't 'always' wiped out; why this is the first time we came back from the far past to find a changed future. I don't understand the mutable-time paradoxes. We just did, that's all.) But anyhow, such of the Patrol offices and resorts as antedate the switch point won't have been affected. There must be a few hundred agents we can rally."

"If we can get back to them."

"We can then find that key event and stop whatever interference there was with it. We've got to!"

"A pleasant thought. But. . . ."

Feet tramped outside. A key clicked in the lock. The prisoners backed away. Then, all at once, Van Sarawak was bowing and beaming and spilling gallantries. Even Everard had to gape.

The girl who entered in front of three soldiers was a knockout. She was tall, with a sweep of rusty-red hair past her shoulders to the slim waist; her eyes were green and alight, her face came from all the Irish colleens who had ever lived; the long white dress was snug around a figure meant to stand on the walls of Troy. Everard noticed vaguely that this time-line used cosmetics, but she had small need of them. He paid no attention to the gold and amber of her jewelry, or to the guns behind her.

She smiled, a little timidly, and spoke: "Can you understand me? It was thought you might know Greek."

Her language was Classical rather than modern. Everard, who had once had a job in Alexandrine times, could follow it through her accent if he paid close heed—which was inevitable anyway.

"Indeed I do," he replied, his words stumbling over each other in their haste to get out.

"What are you snakkering?" demanded Van Sarawak.

"Ancient Greek," said Everard.

"It would be," mourned the Venusian. His despair seemed to have vanished, and his eyes bugged.

Everard introduced himself and his companion. The girl said her name was Deirdre Mac Morn. "Oh, no," groaned Van Sarawak. "This is too much. Manse, teach me Greek. Fast."

"Shut up," said Everard. "This is serious business."

"Well, but can't I have some of the business?"

Everard ignored him and invited the girl to sit down. He joined her on a cot, while the other Patrolman hovered unhappily by. The guards kept their weapons ready.

"Is Greek still a living language?" asked Everard.

"Only in Parthia, and there it is most corrupt," said Deirdre. "I am a Classical scholar, among other things. *Saorann* ap Ceorn is my uncle, so he asked me to see if I could talk with you. Not many in Afallon know the Attic tongue."

"Well"—Everard suppressed a silly grin—"I am most grateful to your uncle."

Her eyes rested gravely on him. "Where are you from? And how does it happen that you speak only Greek, of all known languages?"

"I speak Latin, too."

"Latin?" She frowned in thought. "Oh, the Roman speech, was it not? I am afraid you will find no one who knows much about it."

"Greek will do," said Everard firmly.

"But you have not told me whence you came," she insisted.

Everard shrugged. "We've not been treated very politely," he hinted.

"I'm sorry." It seemed genuine. "But our people are so excitable. Especially now, with the international situation what it is. And when you two appeared out of thin air. . . ."

That had an unpleasantly familiar ring. "What do you mean?" he inquired.

"Surely you know. With Huy Braseal and Hinduraj about to go to war, and all of us wondering what will happen. . . . It is not easy to be a small power."

"A small power? But I saw a map. Afallon looked big enough to me."

"We wore ourselves out two hundred years ago, in the great war with Littorn. Now none of our confederated states can agree on a single policy." Deirdre looked directly into his eyes. "What is this ignorance of yours?"

Everard swallowed and said, "We're from another world."

"What?"

"Yes. A planet (no, that means 'wanderer') . . . an orb encircling Sirius. That's our name for a certain star."

"But—what do you mean? A world attendant on a star? I cannot understand you."

"Don't you know? A star is a sun like. . . ."

Deirdre shrank back and made a sign with her finger. "The Great Baal aid us," she whispered. "Either you are mad or. . . . The stars are mounted in a crystal sphere."

Oh, no!

"What of the wandering stars you can see?" asked Everard slowly. "Mars and Venus and—"

"I know not those names. If you mean Moloch, Ashtoreth, and the rest, of course they are worlds like ours, attendant on the sun like our own. One holds the spirits of the dead, one is the home of witches, one. . . ."

All this and steam cars too. Everard smiled shakily. "If you'll not believe me, then what do you think I am?"

Deirdre regarded him with large eyes. "I think you must be sorcerers," she said.

There was no answer to that. Everard asked a few weak questions, but learned little more than that this city was Catuvellaunan, a trading and manufacturing center. Deirdre estimated its population at two million, and that of all Afallon at fifty million, but wasn't sure. They didn't take censuses here.

The Patrolmen's fate was equally undetermined. Their scooter and other possessions had been sequestrated by the military, but no one dared monkey with the stuff, and treatment of the owners was being hotly debated. Everard got the impression that all government, including the leadership of the armed forces, was rather a sloppy process of individualistic wrangling. Afallon itself was the loosest of confederacies, built out of former nations—Brittic colonies and Indians who had adopted European culture—all jealous of their rights. The old Mayan Empire, destroyed in a war with Texas (Tehannach) and annexed, had not forgotten its time of glory, and sent the most rambunctious delegates of all to the Council of Suffetes.

The Mayans wanted to make an alliance with Huy Braseal, perhaps out of friendship for fellow Indians. The West Coast states, fearful of Hinduraj, were toadies of the Southeast Asian empire. The Middle West (of course) was isolationist; the Eastern States were torn every which way, but inclined to follow the lead of Brittys.

When he gathered that slavery existed here, though not on racial lines, Everard wondered briefly and wildly if the time changers might not have been Dixiecrats.

Enough! He had his own neck, and Van's, to think about. "We are from Sirius," he declared loftily. "Your ideas about the stars are mistaken. We came as peaceful explorers, and if we are molested, there will be others of our kind to take vengeance."

Deirdre looked so unhappy that he felt conscience-stricken. "Will they spare the children?" she begged. "The children had nothing to do with it." Everard could imagine the vision in her head, small crying captives led off to the slave markets of a world of witches.

"There need be no trouble at all if we are released and our property returned," he said.

"I shall speak to my uncle," she promised, "but even if I can sway him, he is only one man on the Council. The thought of what your weapons could mean if we had them has driven men mad."

She rose. Everard clasped both her hands—they lay warm and soft in his—and smiled crookedly at her. "Buck up, kid," he said in English. She shivered, pulled free of him, and made the hex sign again.

"Well," demanded Van Sarawak when they were alone, "what did you find out?" After being told, he stroked his chin and murmured. "That was one glorious little collection of sinusoids. There could be worse worlds than this."

"Or better," said Everard roughly. "They don't have atomic bombs, but neither do they have penicillin, I'll bet. Our job is not to play God."

"No. No, I suppose not." The Venusian sighed.

4

They spent a restless day. Night had fallen when lanterns glimmered in the corridor and a military guard unlocked the cell. The prisoners were led silently to a rear exit where two automobiles waited; they were put into one, and the whole troop drove off.

Catuvellaunan did not have outdoor lighting, and there wasn't much night traffic. Somehow that made the sprawling city unreal in the dark. Everard paid attention to the mechanics of his car. Steam-powered, as he had guessed, burning powdered coal; rubber-tired wheels; a sleek body with a sharp nose and serpent figurehead; the whole simple to operate and honestly built, but not too well designed. Apparently this world had gradually developed a rule-of-thumb engineering, but no systematic science worth talking about.

They crossed a clumsy iron bridge to Long Island, here also a residential section for the well-to-do. Despite the dimness of oil-lamp headlights, their speed was high. Twice they came near having an accident: no traffic signals, and seemingly no drivers who did not hold caution in contempt.

Government and traffic . . . hm. It all looked French, somehow, ignoring those rare interludes when France got a Henry of Navarre or a Charles de Gaulle. And even in Everard's own twentieth century, France was largely Celtic. He was no respecter of windy theories about inborn racial traits, but there was something to be said for traditions so ancient as to be unconscious and ineradicable. A Western world in which the Celts had become dominant, the Germanic peoples reduced to a few small outposts. . . . Yes, look at the Ireland of home; or recall how tribal politics had queered Vercingetorix's revolt. . . . But what about Littorn? Wait a minute! In *his* early Middle Ages, Lithuania had been a powerful state; it had held off Germans, Poles, and Russians alike for a long time, and hadn't ever taken Christianity till the fifteenth century. Without German competition, Lithuania might very well have advanced eastward. . . .

In spite of the Celtic political instability, this was a world of large states, fewer separate nations than Everard's. That argued an older society. If his own Western civilization had developed out of the decaying Roman Empire about, say, A.D. 600, the Celts in this world must have taken over earlier than that.

Everard was beginning to realize what had happened to Rome, but reserved his conclusions for the time being.

The cars drew up before an ornamental gate set in a long stone wall. The drivers talked with two armed guards wearing the livery of a private estate and the thin steel collars of slaves. The gate was opened and the cars went along a graveled driveway between lawns and trees. At the far end, almost on the beach, stood a house. Everard and Van Sarawak were gestured out and led toward it.

It was a rambling wooden structure. Gas lamps on the porch showed it painted in gaudy stripes; the gables and beam ends were carved into dragon heads. Close by he heard the sea, and there was enough light from a sinking crescent moon for Everard to make out a ship standing in close: presumably a freighter, with a tall smokestack and a figurehead.

The windows glowed yellow. A slave butler admitted the party. The interior was paneled in dark wood, also carved, the floors thickly carpeted. At the end of the hall was a living room with overstuffed furniture, several paintings in a stiff conventionalized style, and a merry blaze in an enormous stone fireplace.

Saorann ap Ceorn sat in one chair, Deirdre in another. She laid aside a book as they entered and rose, smiling. The officer puffed a cigar and glowered. Some words were swapped, and the guards disappeared. The butler fetched in wine on a tray, and Deirdre invited the Patrolmen to sit down.

Everard sipped from his glass—the wine was an excellent burgundy—and asked bluntly, "Why are we here?"

Deirdre dazzled him with a smile. "Surely you find it more pleasant than the jail."

"Of course. As well as more ornamental. But I still want to know. Are we being released?"

"You are. . . ." She hunted for a diplomatic answer, but there seemed to be too much frankness in her. "You are welcome here, but may not leave the estate. We hope you can be persuaded to help us. You would be richly rewarded."

"Help? How?"

"By showing our artisans and druids how to make more weapons and magical carts like your own."

Everard sighed. It was no use trying to explain. They didn't have the tools to make the tools to make what was needed, but how could he get that across to a folk who believed in witchcraft?

"Is this your uncle's home?" he asked.

"No, my own," said Deirdre. "I am the only child of my parents, who were wealthy nobles. They died last year."

Ap Ceorn clipped out several words. Deirdre translated with a worried frown: "The tale of your advent is known to all Catuvellaunan by now; and that includes the foreign spies. We hope you can remain hidden from them here."

Everard, remembering the pranks Axis and Allies had played in little neutral nations like Portugal, shivered. Men made desperate by approaching war would not likely be as courteous as the Afallonians.

"What is this conflict going to be about?" he inquired.

"The control of the Icenian Ocean, of course. In particular, certain rich islands we call Ynys yr Lyonnach." Deirdre got up in a single flowing movement and pointed out Hawaii on a globe. "You see," she went on earnestly, "as I told you, Littorn and the western alliance—including us— wore each other out fighting. The great powers today, expanding, quarreling, are Huy Braseal and Hinduraj. Their conflict sucks in the lesser nations, for the clash is not only between ambitions, but between systems: the monarchy of Hinduraj against the sun-worshipping theocracy of Huy Braseal."

"What is your religion, if I may ask?"

Deirdre blinked. The question seemed almost meaningless to her. "The more educated people think that there is a Great Baal who made all the lesser gods," she answered at last, slowly. "But naturally, we maintain the ancient cults, and pay respect to the more powerful foreign gods too, such as Littorn's Perkunas and Czernebog, Wotan Ammon of Cimberland, Brahma, the Sun. . . . Best not to chance their anger."

"I see."

Ap Ceorn offered cigars and matches. Van Sarawak inhaled and said querulously, "Damn it, this would have to be a time line where they don't speak any language I know." He brightened. "But I'm pretty quick to learn, even without hypno. I'll get Deirdre to teach me."

"You and me both," said Everard in haste. "But listen, Van." He reported what he had learned.

"Hm." The younger man rubbed his chin. "Not so good, eh? Of course, if they'd just let us aboard our scooter, we could make an easy getaway. Why not play along with them?"

"They're not such fools," answered Everard. "They may believe in magic, but not in undiluted altruism."

"Funny they should be so backward intellectually, and still have combustion engines."

"No. It's quite understandable. That's why I asked about their religion. It's always been purely pagan; even Judaism seems to have disappeared, and Buddhism hasn't been very influential. As Whitehead pointed out, the medieval idea of one almighty God was important to the growth of science, by inculcating the notion of lawfulness in nature. And Lewis Mumford added that the early monasteries were probably responsible for the mechanical clock—a very basic invention—because of having regular hours for prayer. Clocks seem to have come late in this world." Everard smiled wryly, a shield against the sadness within. "Odd to talk like this. Whitehead and Mumford never lived."

"Nevertheless—"

"Just a minute." Everard turned to Deirdre. "When was Afallon discovered?"

"By white men? In the year 4827."

"Um . . . when does your reckoning start from?"

Deirdre seemed immune to further startlement. "The creation of the world. At least, the date some philosophers have given. That is 5964 years ago."

Which agreed with Bishop Ussher's famous 4004 B.C., perhaps by sheer coincidence—but still, there was definitely a Semitic element in this culture. The creation story in Genesis was of Babylonian origin too.

"And when was steam *(pneuma)* first used to drive engines?" he asked.

"About a thousand years ago. The great druid Boroihme O'Fiona—"

"Never mind." Everard smoked his cigar and mulled his thoughts for a while before looking back at Van Sarawak.

"I'm beginning to get the picture," he said. "The Gauls were anything but the barbarians most people think. They'd learned a lot from Phoenician traders and Greek colonists, as well as from the Etruscans in cisalpine Gaul. A very energetic and enterprising race. The Romans, on the other hand, were a stolid lot, with few intellectual interests. There was little technological progress in our world till the Dark Ages, when the Empire had been swept out of the way.

"In *this* history, the Romans vanished early. So, I'm pretty sure, did the Jews. My guess is, without the balance-of-power effect of Rome, the Syrians did suppress the Maccabees; it was a near thing even in our history. Judaism disappeared and therefore Christianity never came into existence. But anyhow, with Rome removed, the Gauls got the supremacy. They started exploring, building better ships, discovering America in the ninth century. But they weren't so far ahead of the Indians that those couldn't catch up . . . could even be stimulated to build empires of their own, like Huy Braseal today. In the eleventh century, the Celts began tinkering with steam engines. They seem to have gotten gunpowder too, maybe from China, and to have made several other inventions. But it's all been cut-and-try, with no basis of real science."

Van Sarawak nodded. "I suppose you're right. But what did happen to Rome?"

"I don't know. Yet. But our key point is back there somewhere."

Everard returned his attention to Deirdre. "This may surprise you," he said smoothly. "Our people visited this world about twenty-five hundred years ago. That's why I speak Greek but don't know what has occurred since. I would like to find out from you; I take it you're quite a scholar."

She flushed and lowered long dark lashes such as few redheads possess. "I will be glad to help as much as I can." With a sudden appeal: "But will you help us in return?"

"I don't know," said Everard heavily. "I'd like to. But I don't know if we can."

Because after all, my job is to condemn you and your entire world to death.

5

When Everard was shown to his room, he discovered that local hospitality was more than generous. He was too tired and depressed to take advantage of it . . . but at least, he thought on the edge of sleep, Van's slave girl wouldn't be disappointed.

They got up early here. From his upstairs window, Everard saw guards pacing the beach, but they didn't detract from the morning's freshness. He came down with Van Sarawak to breakfast, where bacon and eggs, toast and coffee added the last touch of dream. Ap Ceorn had gone back to town to confer, said Deirdre; she herself had put wistfulness aside and chattered gaily of trivia. Everard learned that she belonged to an amateur dramatic group which sometimes gave Classical Greek plays in the original: hence her fluency. She liked to ride, hunt, sail, swim—"And shall we?" she asked.

"Huh?"

"Swim, of course." Deirdre sprang from her chair on the lawn, where they had been sitting under flame-colored leaves, and whirled innocently out of her clothes. Everard thought he heard a dull clunk as Van Sarawak's jaw hit the ground.

"Come!" she laughed. "Last one in is a Sassenach!"

She was already tumbling in the gray surf when Everard and Van Sarawak shuddered their way down to the beach. The Venusian groaned. "I come from a warm planet. My ancestors were Indonesians. Tropical birds."

"There were some Dutchmen too, weren't there?" Everard grinned.

"They had the sense to move to Indonesia."

"All right, stay ashore."

"Hell! If she can do it, I can!" Van Sarawak put a toe in the water and groaned again.

Everard summoned up all the control he had ever learned and ran in. Deirdre threw water at him. He plunged, got hold of a slender leg, and pulled her under. They frolicked about for several minutes before running back to the house for a hot shower. Van Sarawak followed in a blue haze.

"Speak about Tantalus," he mumbled. "The most beautiful girl in the whole continuum, and I can't talk to her and she's half polar bear."

Toweled dry and dressed in the local garb by slaves, Everard returned to stand before the living-room fire. "What pattern is this?" he asked, pointing to the tartan of his kilt.

Deirdre lifted her ruddy head. "My own clan's," she answered. "An honored guest is always taken as a clan member during his stay, even if a blood feud is going on." She smiled shyly. "And there is none between us, Manslach."

It cast him back into bleakness. He remembered what his purpose was.

"I'd like to ask you about history," he said. "It is a special interest of mine."

She nodded, adjusted a gold fillet on her hair, and got a book from a crowded shelf. "This is the best world history, I think. I can look up any details you might wish to know."

And tell me what I must do to destroy you.

Everard sat down with her on a couch. The butler wheeled in lunch. He ate moodily, untasting.

To follow up his hunch—"Did Rome and Carthage ever fight a war?"

"Yes. Two, in fact. They were allied at first, against Epirus, but fell out. Rome won the first war and tried to restrict Carthaginian enterprise." Her clean profile bent over the pages, like a studious child's. "The second war broke out twenty-three years later, and lasted . . . hmm . . . eleven years all told, though the last three were only a mopping up after Hannibal had taken and burned Rome."

Ah-hah! Somehow, Everard did not feel happy at his success.

The Second Punic War (they called it the Roman War here)—or, rather, some crucial incident thereof—was the turning point. But partly out of curiosity, partly because he feared to tip his hand, Everard did not at once try to identify the deviation. He'd first have to get straight in his mind what had actually happened, anyway. (No . . . what had not happened. The reality was here, warm and breathing beside him; he was the ghost.)

"So what came next?" he asked tonelessly.

"The Carthaginian empire came to include Hispania, southern Gaul, and the toe of Italy," she said. "The rest of Italy was impotent and chaotic, after the Roman confederacy had been broken up. But the Carthaginian government was too venal to remain strong. Hannibal himself was assassinated by men who thought his honesty stood in their way. Meanwhile, Syria and Parthia fought for the eastern Mediterranean, with Parthia winning and thus coming under still greater Hellenic influence than before.

"About a hundred years after the Roman Wars, some Germanic tribes overran Italy." (That would be the Cimbri, with their allies the Teutones and

Ambrones, whom Marius had stopped in Everard's world.) "Their destructive path through Gaul had set the Celts moving too, eventually into Hispania and North Africa as Carthage declined. And from Carthage the Gauls learned much.

"A long period of wars followed, during which Parthia waned and the Celtic states grew. The Huns broke the Germans in middle Europe, but were in turn defeated by Parthia; so the Gauls moved in and the only Germans left were in Italy and Hyperborea." (That must be the Scandinavian peninsula.) "As ships improved, trade grew up with the Far East, both form Arabia and directly around Africa." (In Everard's history, Julius Caesar had been astonished to find the Veneti building better vessels than any in the Mediterranean.) "The Celtanians discovered southern Afallon, which they thought was an island—hence the 'Ynys'—but they were thrown out by the Mayans. The Brittic colonies farther north did survive, though, and eventually won their independence.

"Meanwhile Littorn was growing apace. It swallowed up most of Europe for a while. The western end of the continent only regained its freedom as part of the peace settlement after the Hundred Years' War I've told you about. The Asian countries have shaken off their exhausted European masters and modernized themselves, while the Western nations have declined in their turn." Deirdre looked up from the book, which she had been skimming as she talked. "But this is only the barest outline, Manslach. Shall I go on?"

Everard shook his head. "No, thanks." After a moment: "You are very honest about the situation of your own country."

Deirdre said roughly, "Most of us won't admit it, but I think it best to look truth in the eyes."

With a surge of eagerness: "But tell me of your own world. This is a marvel past belief."

Everard sighed, switched off his conscience, and began lying.

The raid took place that afternoon.

Van Sarawak had recovered his poise and was busily learning the Afallonian language from Deirdre. They walked through the garden hand in hand, stopping to name objects and act out verbs. Everard followed, wondering vaguely if he was a third wheel or not, most of him bent to the problem of how to get at the scooter.

Bright sunlight spilled from a pale cloudless sky. A maple was a shout of scarlet, a drift of yellow leaves scudded across the grass. An elderly slave was raking the yard in a leisurely fashion, a young-looking guard of Indian race lounged with his rifle slung on one shoulder, a pair of wolfhounds dozed under a hedge. It was a peaceful scene; hard to believe that men prepared murder beyond these walls.

But man was man, in any history. This culture might not have the ruthless will and sophisticated cruelty of Western civilization; in fact, in some ways it looked strangely innocent. Still, that wasn't for lack of trying. And in this world, a genuine science might never emerge, man might endlessly repeat the cycle of war, empire, collapse, and war. In Everard's future, the race had finally broken out of it.

For what? He could not honestly say that this continuum was worse or better than his own. It was different, that was all. And didn't these people have as much right to their existence as—as his own, who were damned to nullity if he failed?

He knotted his fists. The issue was too big. No man should have to decide something like this.

At the showdown, he knew, no abstract sense of duty would compel him, but the little things and the little folk he remembered.

They rounded the house and Deirdre pointed to the sea. *"Awarkinn,"* she said. Her loose hair burned in the wind.

"Now does that mean 'ocean' or 'Atlantic' or 'water'?" laughed Van Sarawak. "Let's go see." He led her toward the beach.

Everard trailed. A kind of steam launch, long and fast, was skipping over the waves, a mile or two offshore. Gulls trailed it in a snowstorm of wings. He thought that if he'd been in charge, a Navy ship would have been on picket out there.

Did he even have to decide anything? There were other Patrolmen in the pre-Roman past. They'd return to their respective eras and. . . .

Everard stiffened. A chill ran down his back and congealed in his belly.

They'd return, and see what had happened, and try to correct the trouble. If any of them succeeded, this world would blink out of spacetime, and he would go with it.

Deirdre paused. Everard, standing in a sweat, hardly noticed what she was staring at, till she cried out and pointed. Then he joined her and squinted across the sea.

The launch was standing in close, its high stack fuming smoke and sparks, the gilt snake figurehead agleam. He could see the forms of men aboard, and something white, with wings. . . . It rose from the poop deck and trailed at the end of a rope, mounting. A glider! Celtic aeronautics had gotten that far, at least.

"Pretty," said Van Sarawak. "I suppose they have balloons, too."

The glider cast its tow and swooped inward. One of the guards on the beach shouted. The rest pelted from behind the house. Sunlight flashed off their guns. The launch headed straight for the shore. The glider landed, plowing a furrow in the beach.

An officer yelled and waved the Patrolmen back. Everard had a glimpse of Deirdre's face, white and uncomprehending. Then a turret on the glider swiveled—a detached part of his mind guessed it was manually operated—and a light cannon spoke.

Everard hit the dirt. Van Sarawak followed, dragging the girl with him. Grapeshot plowed hideously through the Afallonian soldiers.

There followed a spiteful crack of guns. Men sprang from the aircraft, dark-faced men in turbans and sarongs. *Hinduraj!* thought Everard. They traded shots with the surviving guards, who rallied about their captain.

The officer roared and led a charge. Everard looked up from the sand to see him almost upon the glider's crew. Van Sarawak leaped to his feet. Everard rolled over, caught him by the ankle, and pulled him down before he could join the fight.

"Let me *go!*" The Venusian writhed, sobbing. The dead and wounded left by the cannon sprawled nightmare red. The racket of battle seemed to fill the sky.

"No, you bloody fool! It's us they're after, and that wild Irishman's done the worst thing he could have—" A fresh outburst yanked Everard's attention elsewhere.

The launch, shallow-draft and screw-propelled, had run up into the shallows and was retching armed men. Too late the Afallonians realized that they had discharged their weapons and were now being attacked from the rear.

"Come on!" Everard hauled Deirdre and Van Sarawak to their feet. "We've got to get out of here—get to the neighbors. . . ."

A detachment from the boat saw him and veered. He felt rather than heard the flat smack of a bullet into soil, as he reached the lawn. Slaves screamed hysterically inside the house. The two wolfhounds attacked the invaders and were gunned down.

Crouched, zigzag, that was the way: over the wall and out onto the road! Everard might have made it, but Deirdre stumbled and fell. Van Sarawak halted to guard her. Everard stopped also, and then it was too late. They were covered.

The leader of the dark men snapped something at the girl. She sat up, giving him a defiant answer. He laughed shortly and jerked his thumb at the launch.

"What do they want?" asked Everard in Greek.

"You." She looked at him with horror. "You two—" The officer spoke again. "And me to translate. . . . No!"

She twisted in the hands that had closed on her arms, got partly free and clawed at a face. Everard's fist traveled in a short arc that ended in a squashing of nose. It was too good to last. A clubbed rifle descended on his head, and he was only dimly aware of being frog-marched off to the launch.

6

The crew left the glider behind, shoved their boat into deeper water, and revved it up. They left all the guardsmen slain or disabled, but took their own casualties along.

Everard sat on a bench on the plunging deck and stared with slowly clearing eyes as the shoreline dwindled. Deirdre wept on Van Sarawak's shoulder, and the Venusian tried to console her. A chill noisy wind flung spindrift in their faces.

When two white men emerged from the deckhouse, Everard's mind was jarred back into motion. Not Asians after all. Europeans! And now when he looked closely, he saw the rest of the crew also had Caucasian features. The brown complexions were merely greasepaint.

He stood up and regarded his new owners warily. One was a portly, middle-aged man of average height, in a red silk blouse and baggy white trousers and a sort of astrakhan hat; he was clean-shaven and his dark hair was twisted into a queue. The other was somewhat younger, a shaggy blond giant in a tunic sewn with copper links, legginged breeches, a leather cloak, and a purely ornamental horned helmet. Both wore revolvers at their belts and were treated deferentially by the sailors.

"What the devil?" Everard looked around once more. They were already out of sight of land, and bending north. The hull quivered with the haste of the engine, spray sheeted when the bows hit a wave.

The older man spoke first in Afallonian. Everard shrugged. Then the bearded Nordic tried, first in a completely unrecognizable dialect but afterward: *"Taelan thu Cimbric?"*

Everard, who knew several Germanic languages, took a chance, while Van Sarawak pricked up his Dutch ears. Deirdre huddled back, wide-eyed, too bewildered to move.

"Ja," said Everard, *"ein wenig."* When Goldilocks looked uncertain, he amended it: "A little."

"Ah, aen litt. Gode!" The big man rubbed his hands. *"Ik hait Boierik Wulfilasson ok main gefreond heer erran Boleslav Arkonsky."*

It was no language Everard had ever heard of—couldn't even be the original Cimbric, after all these centuries—but the Patrolman could follow it reasonably well. The trouble came in speaking; he couldn't predict how it had evolved.

"What the hell erran thu maching, anyway?" he blustered. "Ik bin aen man auf Sirius—the stern Sirius, mit planeten ok all. Set uns gebach or willen be der Teufel to pay!"

Boierik Wulfilasson looked pained and suggested that the discussion be continued inside, with the young lady for interpreter. He led the way back into the deckhouse, which turned out to include a small but comfortably furnished saloon. The door remained open, with an armed guard looking in and more on call.

Boleslav Arkonsky said something in Afallonian to Deirdre. She nodded, and he gave her a glass of wine. It seemed to steady her, but she spoke to Everard in a thin voice.

"We've been captured, Manslach. Their spies found out where you were kept. Another group is supposed to steal your traveling machine. They know where that is, too."

"So I imagined," replied Everard. "But who in Baal's name are they?"

Boierik guffawed at the question and expounded lengthily on his own cleverness. The idea was to make the Suffetes of Afallon think Hinduraj was responsible. Actually, the secret alliance of Littorn and Cimberland had built up quite an effective spy service. They were now bound for the Littornian embassy's summer retreat on Ynys Llangollen (Nantucket), where the wizards would be induced to explain their spells and a surprise prepared for the great powers.

"And if we don't do this?"

Deirdre translated Arkonsky's answer word for word: "I regret the consequences to you. We are civilized men, and will pay well in gold and honor for your free cooperation. If that is withheld, we will get your forced cooperation. The existence of our countries is at stake."

Everard looked closely at them. Boierik seemed embarrassed and unhappy, the boastful glee evaporated from him. Boleslav Arkonsky drummed on the tabletop, his lips compressed but a certain appeal in his eyes. *Don't make us do this. We have to live with ourselves.*

They were probably husbands and fathers, they must enjoy a mug of beer and a friendly game of dice as well as the next man, maybe Boierik bred horses in Italy and Arkonsky was a rose fancier on the Baltic shores. But none of this would do their captives a bit of good, when the almighty Nation locked horns with its kin.

Everard paused to admire the sheer artistry of this operation, and then began wondering what to do. The launch was fast, but would need something like twenty hours to reach Nantucket, as he remembered the trip. There was that much time, at least.

"We are weary," he said in English. "May we not rest awhile?"

"Ja deedly," said Boierik with a clumsy graciousness. *"Ok wir skallen gode gefreonds bin, ni?"*

—Sunset smoldered in the west. Deirdre and Van Sarawak stood at the rail, looking across a gray waste of waters. Three crewmen, their makeup and costumes removed, poised alert and weaponed on the poop; a man steered by compass; Boierik and Everard paced the quarterdeck. All wore heavy clothes against the wind.

Everard was getting some proficiency in the Cimbrian language; his tongue still limped, but he could make himself understood. Mostly, though, he let Boierik do the talking.

"So you are from the stars? These matters I do not understand. I am a simple man. Had I my way, I would manage my Tuscan estate in peace and let the world rave as it will. But we of the Folk have our obligations." The Teutonics seemed to have replaced the Latins altogether in Italy, as the English had done the Britons in Everard's world.

"I know how you feel," said the Patrolman. "Strange that so many should fight when so few want to."

"Oh, but this is necessary." A near whine. "Carthagalann stole Egypt, our rightful possession."

"Italia irredenta," murmured Everard.

"Hunh?"

"Never mind. So you Cimbri are allied with Littorn, and hope to grab off Europe and Africa while the big powers are fighting in the East."

"Not at all!" said Boierik indignantly. "We are merely asserting our rightful and historic territorial claims. Why, the king himself said. . . ." And so on and so on.

Everard braced himself against the roll of the deck. "Seems to me you treat us wizards rather hard," he remarked. "Beware lest we get really angered at you."

"All of us are protected against curses and shapings."

"Well—"

"I wish you would help us freely. I will be happy to demonstrate to you the justice of our cause, if you have a few hours to spare."

Everard shook his head, walked off and stopped by Deirdre. Her face was a blur in the thickening dusk, but he caught a forlorn fury in her voice: "I hope you told him what to do with his plans, Manslach."

"No," said Everard heavily. "We are going to help them."

She stood as if struck.

"What are you saying, Manse?" asked Van Sarawak. Everard told him.

"No!" said the Venusian.

"Yes," said Everard.

"By God, no! I'll—"

Everard grabbed his arm and said coldly: "Be quiet. I know what I'm doing. We can't take sides in this world; we're against everybody, and you'd better realize it. The only thing to do is play along with these fellows for a while. And don't tell that to Deirdre."

Van Sarawak bent his head and stood for a moment, thinking. "All right," he said dully.

7

The Littornian resort was on the southern shore of Nantucket, near a fishing village but walled off from it. The embassy had built in the style of its homeland: long, timber houses with roofs arched like a cat's back, a main hall and its outbuildings enclosing a flagged courtyard. Everard finished a night's sleep and a breakfast which Deirdre's eyes had made miserable by standing on deck as they came in to the private pier. Another, bigger launch was already there, and the grounds swarmed with hard-looking men. Arkonsky's excitement flared up as he said in Afallonian: "I see the magic engine has been brought. We can go right to work."

When Boierik interpreted, Everard felt his heart slam.

The guests, as the Cimbrian insisted on calling them, were led into an outsize room where Arkonsky bowed the knee to an idol with four faces, that Svantevit which the Danes had chopped up for firewood in the other history. A fire burned on the hearth against the autumn chill, and guards were posted around the walls. Everard had eyes only for the scooter, where it stood gleaming on the door.

"I hear the fight was hard in Catuvellaunan to gain this thing," remarked Boierik. "Many were killed; but our gang got away without being followed." He touched a handlebar gingerly. "And this wain can truly appear anywhere its rider wishes, out of thin air?"

"Yes," said Everard.

Deirdre gave him a look of scorn such as he had rarely known. She stood haughtily away from him and Van Sarawak.

Arkonsky spoke to her, something he wanted translated. She spat at his feet. Boierik sighed and gave the word to Everard:

"We wish the engine demonstrated. You and I will go for a ride on it. I warn you, I will have a revolver at your back. You will tell me in advance everything you mean to do, and if aught untoward happens, I will shoot. Your friends will remain here as hostages, also to be shot on the first suspicion. But I'm sure," he added, "that we will all be good friends."

Everard nodded. Tautness thrummed in him; his palms felt cold and wet. "First I must say a spell," he answered.

His eyes flickered. One glance memorized the spatial reading of the position meters and the time reading of the clock on the scooter. Another look showed Van Sarawak seated on a bench, under Arkonsky's drawn pistol and the rifles of the guards. Deirdre sat down too, stiffly, as far from him as she could get. Everard made a close estimate of the bench's position relative to the scooter's, lifted his arms, and chanted in Temporal:

"Van, I'm going to try to pull you out of here. Stay exactly where you are now, repeat, exactly. I'll pick you up on the fly. If all goes well, that'll happen about one minute after I blink off with our hairy comrade."

The Venusian sat wooden-faced, but a thin beading of sweat sprang out on his forehead.

"Very good," said Everard in his pidgin Cimbric. "Mount on the rear saddle, Boierik, and we'll put this magic horse through her paces."

The blond man nodded and obeyed. As Everard took the front seat, he felt a gun muzzle held shakily against his back. "Tell Arkonsky we'll be back in half an hour," he instructed. They had approximately the same time units here as in his world, both descended from the Babylonian. When that had been taken care of, Everard said, "The first thing we will do is appear in midair over the ocean and hover."

"F-f-fine," said Boierik. He didn't sound very convinced.

Everard set the space controls for ten miles east and a thousand feet up, and threw the main switch.

They sat like witches astride a broom, looking down on greenish-gray immensity and the distant blur which was land. The wind was high, it caught at them and Everard gripped tight with his knees. He heard Boierik's oath and smiled stiffly.

"Well," he asked, "how do you like this?"

"Why . . . it's wonderful." As he grew accustomed to the idea, the Cimbrian gathered enthusiasm. "Balloons are as nothing beside it. With machines like this, we can soar above enemy cities and rain fire down on them."

Somehow, that made Everard feel better about what he was going to do.

"Now we will fly ahead," he announced, and sent the scooter gliding through the air. Boierik whooped exultantly. "And now we will make the instantaneous jump to your homeland."

Everard threw the maneuver switch. The scooter looped the loop and dropped at a three-gee acceleration.

Forewarned, the Patrolman could still barely hang on. He never knew whether the curve or the dive had thrown Boierik. He only got a moment's glimpse of the man, plunging down through windy spaces to the sea, and wished he hadn't.

For a little while, then, Everard hung above the waves. His first reaction was a shudder. Suppose Boierik had had time to shoot? His second was a thick guilt. Both he dismissed, and concentrated on the problem of rescuing Van Sarawak.

He set the space verniers for one foot in front of the prisoners' bench, the time unit for one minute after he had departed. His right hand he kept by the controls—he'd have to work fast—and his left free.

Hang on to your hats, fellas. Here we go again.

The machine flashed into existence almost in front of Van Sarawak. Everard clutched the Venusian's tunic and hauled him close, inside the spatiotemporal drive field, even as his right hand spun the time dial back and snapped down the main switch.

A bullet caromed off metal. Everard had a moment's glimpse of Arkonsky shouting. And then it was all gone and they were on a grassy hill sloping down to the beach. It was two thousand years ago

He collapsed shivering over the handlebars.

A cry brought him back to awareness. He twisted around to look at Van Sarawak where the Venusian sprawled on the hillside. One arm was still around Deirdre's waist.

The wind lulled, and the sea rolled in to a broad white strand, and clouds walked high in heaven.

"Can't say I blame you, Van." Everard paced before the scooter and looked at the ground. "But it does complicate matters."

"What was I supposed to do?" the other man asked on a raw note. "Leave her there for those bastards to kill—or to be snuffed out with her entire universe?"

"Remember, we're conditioned. Without authorization, we couldn't tell her the truth even if we wanted to. And I, for one, don't want to."

Everard glanced at the girl. She stood breathing heavily, but with a dawn in her eyes. The wind ruffled her hair and the long thin dress.

She shook her head, as if to clear it of nightmare, ran over and clasped their hands. "Forgive me, Manslach," she breathed. "I should have known you'd not betray us."

She kissed them both. Van Sarawak responded as eagerly as expected, but Everard couldn't bring himself to. He would have remembered Judas.

"Where are we?" she continued. "It looks almost like Llangollen, but no dwellers. Have you taken us to the Happy Isles?" She spun on one foot and danced among summer flowers. "Can we rest here a while before returning home?"

Everard drew a long breath. "I've bad news for you, Deirdre," he said.

She grew silent. He saw her gather herself.

"We can't go back."

She waited mutely.

"The . . . the spells I had to use, to save our lives—I had no choice. But those spells debar us from returning home."

"There is no hope?" He could barely hear her.

His eyes stung. "No," he said.

She turned and walked away. Van Sarawak moved to follow her, but thought better of it and sat down beside Everard. "What'd you tell her?" he asked.

Everard repeated his words. "It seems the best compromise," he finished. "I can't send her back to what's waiting for this world."

"No." Van Sarawak sat quiet for a while, staring across the sea. Then: "What year is this? About the time of Christ? Then we're still upstairs of the turning point."

"Yeh. And we still have to find out what it was."

"Let's go back to some Patrol office in the farther past. We can recruit help there."

"Maybe." Everard lay down in the grass and regarded the sky. Reaction overwhelmed him. "I think I can locate the key event right here, though, with Deirdre's help. Wake me when she comes back."

She returned dry-eyed, though one could see she had wept. When Everard asked if she would assist in his own mission, she nodded, "Of course. My life is yours who saved it."

After getting you into the mess in the first place. Everard said carefully: "All I want from you is some information. Do you know about . . . about putting people to sleep, a sleep in which they may believe anything they're told?"

She nodded doubtfully. "I've seen medical druids do that."

"It won't harm you. I only wish to make you sleep so you can remember everything you know, things you believe forgotten. It won't take long."

Her trustfulness was hard for him to endure. Using Patrol techniques, he put her in a hypnotic state of total recall and dredged out all she had ever heard or read about the Second Punic War. That added up to enough for his purposes.

Roman interferences with Carthaginian enterprise south of the Ebro, in direct violation of treaty, had been the final goading. In 219 B.C. Hannibal Barca, governor of Carthaginian Spain, laid siege to Saguntum. After eight months he took it, and thus provoked his long-planned war with Rome. At the beginning of May, 218, he crossed the Pyrenees with 90,000 infantry, 12,000 cavalry, and 37 elephants, marched through Gaul, and went over the Alps. His losses en route were gruesome: only 20,000 foot and 6,000 horse reached Italy late in the year. Nevertheless, near the Ticinus River he met and broke a superior Roman force. In the course of the following year, he fought several bloodily victorious battles and advanced into Apulia and Campania.

The Apulians, Lucanians, Bruttians, and Samnites went over to his side. Quintus Fabius Maximus fought a grim guerrilla war, which laid Italy waste and decided nothing. But meanwhile Hasdrubal Barca was organizing Spain, and in 211 he arrived with reinforcements. In 210 Hannibal took and burned Rome, and by 207 the last cities of the confederacy had surrendered to him.

"That's it," said Everard. He stroked the coppery mane of the girl lying beside him. "Go to sleep now. Sleep well and wake up glad of heart."

"What'd she tell you?" asked Van Sarawak.

"A lot of detail," said Everard. The whole story had required more than an hour. "The important thing is this: her knowledge of those times is good, but she never mentioned the Scipios."

"The whos?"

"Publius Cornelius Scipio commanded the Roman army at Ticinus. He was beaten there all right, in our world. But later he had the intelligence to turn westward and gnaw away the Carthaginian base in Spain. It ended with Hannibal being effectively cut off in Italy, and what little Iberian help could be sent him was annihilated. Scipio's son of the same name also held a high command, and was the man who finally whipped Hannibal at Zama; that's Scipio Africanus the Elder.

"Father and son were by far the best leaders Rome had. But Deirdre never heard of them."

"So . . ." Van Sarawak stared eastward across the sea, where Gauls and Cimbri and Parthians were ramping through the shattered Classical world. "What happened to them in this time line?"

"My own total recall tells me that both the Scipios were at Ticinus, and very nearly killed. The son saved his father's life during the retreat, which I imagine was more like a stampede. One gets you ten that in *this* history the Scipios died there."

"Somebody must have knocked them off," said Van Sarawak. His voice tightened. "Some time traveler. It could only have been that."

"Well, it seems probable, anyhow. We'll see." Everard looked away from Deirdre's slumbrous face. "We'll see."

8

At the Pleistocene resort—half an hour after having left it for New York—the Patrolmen put the girl in charge of a sympathetic Greek-speaking matron and summoned their colleagues. Then the message capsules began jumping through spacetime.

All offices prior to 218 B.C.—the closest was Alexandria, 250–230—were "still" there, with two hundred or so agents altogether. Written contact with the future was confirmed to be impossible, and a few short jaunts upstairs clinched the proof. A worried conference met at the Academy, back in the Oligocene Period. Unattached agents ranked those with steady assignments, but not each other; on the basis of his own experience, Everard found himself the chairman of a committee of top-bracket officers.

That was a frustrating job. These men and women had leaped centuries and wielded the weapons of gods. But they were still human, with all the ingrained orneriness of their race.

Everyone agreed that the damage would have to be repaired. But there was fear for those agents who had gone ahead into time before being warned, as Everard himself had done. If they weren't back when history was realtered, they would never be seen again. Everard deputized parties to attempt rescue, but doubted there'd be much success. He warned them sternly to return within a day, local time, or face the consequences.

A man from the Scientific Renaissance had another point to make. Granted, the survivors' plain duty was to restore the "original" time track. But they had a duty to knowledge as well. Here was a unique chance to study a whole new phase of humankind. Several years' anthropological work should be done before—Everard slapped him down with difficulty. There weren't so many Patrolmen left that they could take the risk.

Study groups had to determine the exact moment and circumstances of the change. The wrangling over methods went on interminably. Everard glared out the window, into the prehuman night, and wondered if the sabertooths weren't doing a better job after all than their simian successors.

When he had finally gotten his various gangs dispatched, he broke out a bottle and got drunk with Van Sarawak.

Reconvening next day, the steering committee heard from its deputies, who had run up a total of years in the future. A dozen Patrolmen had been rescued from more or less ignominious situations; another score would simply have to be written off. The spy group's report was more interesting. It seemed that two Helvetian mercenaries had joined Hannibal in the Alps and won his confidence. After the war, they had risen to high positions in Carthage. Under the names of Phrontes and Himilco, they had practically run the government, engineered Hannibal's murder, and set new records for luxurious living. One of the Patrolmen had seen their homes and the men themselves. "A lot of improvements that hadn't been thought of in Classical times. The fellows looked to me like Neldorians, two-hundred-fifth millennium."

Everard nodded. That was an age of bandits who had "already" given the Patrol a lot of work. "I think we've settled the matter," he said. "It makes no difference whether they were with Hannibal before Ticinus or not. We'd have hell's own time arresting them in the Alps without such a fuss that we'd change the future ourselves. What counts is that they seem to have rubbed out the Scipios, and that's the point we'll have to strike at."

A nineteenth-century Britisher, competent but with elements of Colonel Blimp, unrolled a map and discoursed on his aerial observations of the battle. He'd used an infrared telescope to look through low clouds. "And here the Romans stood—"

"I know," said Everard. "A thin red line. The moment when they took flight is the critical one, but the confusion then also gives us our chance. Okay, we'll want to surround the battlefield unobtrusively, but I don't think we can get away with more than two agents actually on the scene. The baddies are going to be alert, you know, looking for possible counterinterference. The Alexandria office can supply Van and me with costumes."

"I say," exclaimed the Englishman, "I thought I'd have the privilege."

"No. Sorry." Everard smiled with one corner of his mouth. "No privilege, anyway. Just risking your neck, in order to negate a world full of people like yourself."

"But dash it all—"

Everard rose. "I've got to go," he said flatly. "I don't know why, but I've got to."

Van Sarawak nodded.

They left their scooter in a clump of trees and started across the field.

Around the horizon and up in the sky waited a hundred armed Patrolmen, but that was small consolation here among spears and arrows. Lowering clouds hurried before a cold whistling wind, there was a spatter of rain; sunny Italy was enjoying its late fall.

The cuirass was heavy on Everard's shoulders as he trotted across blood-slippery mud. He had helmet, greaves, a Roman shield on his left arm and a sword at his waist; but his right hand gripped a stunner. Van Sarawak loped behind, similarly equipped, eyes shifting under the wind-ruffled officer's plume.

Trumpets howled and drums stuttered. It was all but lost among the yells of men and tramp of feet, screaming riderless horses and whining arrows. Only a few captains and scouts were still mounted; as often before stirrups were invented, what started to be a cavalry battle had become entirely a fight on foot after the lancers fell off their mounts. The Carthaginians were pressing in, hammering edged metal against the buckling Roman lines. Here and there the struggle was already breaking up into small knots, where men cursed and cut at strangers.

The combat had passed over this area already. Death lay around Everard. He hurried behind the Roman force, toward the distant gleam of the eagles. Across helmets and corpses, he made out a banner that fluttered triumphant red and purple. And there, looming monstrous against the gray sky, lifting their trunks and bawling, came a squad of elephants.

War was always the same: not a neat affair of lines across maps, nor a hallooing gallantry, but men who gasped and sweated and bled in bewilderment.

A slight, dark-faced youth squirmed nearby, trying feebly to pull out the javelin which had pierced his stomach. He was a slinger from Carthage, but the burly Italian peasant who sat next to him, staring without belief at the stump of an arm, paid no attention.

A flight of crows hovered overhead, riding the wind and waiting.

"This way," muttered Everard. "Hurry up, for God's sake! That line's going to break any minute."

The breath was raw in his throat as he jogged toward the standards of the Republic. It came to him that he'd always rather wished Hannibal had won. There was something repellent about the frigid, unimaginative greed of Rome. And here he was, trying to save the city. Well-a-day, life was often an odd business.

It was some consolation that Scipio Africanus was one of the few decent men left after the war.

Screaming and clangor lifted, and the Italians reeled back. Everard saw something like a wave smashed against a rock. But it was the rock which advanced, crying out and stabbing, stabbing.

He began to run. A legionary went past, howling his panic. A grizzled Roman veteran spat on the ground, braced his feet, and stood where he was till they cut him down. Hannibal's elephants squealed and blundered about. The ranks of Carthage held firm, advancing to an inhuman pulse of drums.

Up ahead, now! Everard saw men on horseback, Roman officers. They held the eagles aloft and shouted, but nobody could hear them above the din.

A small group of legionaries trotted past. Their leader hailed the Patrolmen: "Over here! We'll give 'em a fight, by the belly of Venus!"

Everard shook his head and continued. The Roman snarled and sprang at him. "Come here, you cowardly. . . ." A stun beam cut off his words. He crashed into the muck. His men shuddered, someone wailed, and the party broke into flight.

The Carthaginians were very near, shield to shield and swords running red. Everard could see a scar livid on the cheek of one man, the great hook nose of another. A hurled spear clanged off his helmet. He lowered his head and ran.

A combat loomed before him. He tried to go around, and tripped on a gashed corpse. A Roman stumbled over him in turn. Van Sarawak cursed and dragged him clear. A sword furrowed the Venusian's arm.

Beyond, Scipio's men were surrounded and battling without hope. Everard halted, sucked air into starved lungs, and looked into the thin rain. Armor gleamed wetly as a troop of Roman horsemen galloped closer, with mud up to their mounts' noses. That must be the son, Scipio Africanus to be, hastening to rescue his father. The hoofbeats made thunder in the earth.

"Over there!"

Van Sarawak cried out and pointed. Everard crouched where he was, rain dripping off his helmet and down his face. From another direction, a Carthaginian party was riding toward the battle around the eagles. And at their head were two men with the height and craggy features of Neldor. They wore G.I. armor, but each of them held a slim-barreled gun.

"This way!" Everard spun on his heel and dashed toward them. The leather in his cuirass creaked as he ran.

The Patrolmen were close to the Carthaginians before they were seen. Then a horseman called the warning. Two crazy Romans! Everard saw how he grinned in his beard. One of the Neldorians raised his blast rifle.

Everard flopped on his stomach. The vicious blue-white beam sizzled where he had been. He snapped a shot, and one of the African horses went over in a roar of metal. Van Sarawak stood his ground and fired steadily. Two, three, four—and there went a Neldorian, down in the mud!

Men hewed at each other around the Scipios. The Neldorians' escort yelled with terror. They must have had the blaster demonstrated beforehand, but these invisible blows were something else. They bolted. The second of the bandits got his horse under control and turned to follow.

"Take care of the one you potted, Van," gasped Everard. "Drag him off the battlefield—we'll want to question—" He himself scrambled to his feet and made for a riderless horse. He was in the saddle and after the Neldorian before he was fully aware of it.

Behind him, Publius Cornelius Scipio and his son fought clear and joined their retreating army.

Everard fled through chaos. He urged speed from his mount, but was content to pursue. Once they had gotten out of sight, a scooter could swoop down and make short work of his quarry.

The same thought must have occurred to the time rover. He reined in and took aim. Everard saw the blinding flash and felt his cheek sting with a near miss. He set his pistol to wide beam and rode in shooting.

Another firebolt took his horse full in the breast. The animal toppled and Everard went out of the saddle. Trained reflexes softened the fall. He bounced to his feet and lurched toward his enemy. The stunner was gone, fallen into the mud, no time to look for it. Never mind, it could be salvaged later, if he lived. The widened beam had found its mark; it wasn't strong enough at such dilution to knock a man out, but the Neldorian had dropped his blaster and the horse stood swaying with closed eyes.

Rain beat in Everard's face. He slogged up to the mount. The Neldorian jumped to earth and drew a sword. Everard's own blade rasped forth.

"As you will," he said in Latin. "One of us will not leave this field."

9

The moon rose over mountains and turned the snow to a sudden wan glitter. Far in the north, a glacier threw back the light, and a wolf howled. The Crô-Magnons chanted in their cave, the noise drifted faintly through to the verandah.

Deirdre stood in darkness, looking out. Moonlight dappled her face and caught a gleam of tears. She started as Everard and Van Sarawak came up behind her.

"Are you back so soon?" she asked. "You only came here and left me this morning."

"It didn't take long," said Van Sarawak. He had gotten a hypno in Attic Greek.

"I hope—" she tried to smile—"I hope you have finished your task and can rest from your labors."

"Yes," said Everard, "we finished it."

They stood side by side for a while, looking out on a world of winter.

"Is it true what you said, that I can never go home?" Deirdre spoke gently.

"I'm afraid so. The spells. . . ." Everard swapped a glance with Van Sarawak.

They had official permission to tell the girl as much as they wished and take her wherever they thought she could live best. Van Sarawak maintained that would be Venus in his century, and Everard was too tired to argue.

Deirdre drew a long breath. "So be it," she said. "I'll not waste of life lamenting. But the Baal grant that they have it well, my people at home."

"I'm sure they will," said Everard.

Suddenly he could do no more. He only wanted to sleep. Let Van Sarawak say what had to be said, and reap whatever rewards there might be.

He nodded at his companion. "I'm turning in," he declared. "Carry on, Van."

The Venusian took the girl's arm. Everard went slowly back to his room.

IVORY, AND APES, AND PEACOCKS

WHILE Solomon was in all his glory and the Temple was a-building, Manse Everard came to Tyre of the purple. Almost at once, he was in peril of his life.

That mattered little in itself. An agent of the Time Patrol was expendable, the more so if he or she enjoyed the godlike status of Unattached. Those whom Everard sought could destroy an entire reality. He had come to help rescue it.

One afternoon, 950 E.C., the ship that bore him approached his destination. The weather was warm, nearly windless. Sail furled, the vessel moved under manpower, creak and splash of sweeps, drumbeat of a coxswain posted near the sailors who had the twin steering oars. Around the broad seventy-foot hull, wavelets glittered blue, chuckled, swirled. Farther out, dazzlement off the water blurred sight of other craft upon it. They were numerous, ranging from lean warships to tublike rowboats. Most were Phoenician, though many hailed from different city-states of that society. Some were quite foreign, Philistine, Assyrian, Achaean, or stranger yet; trade through the known world flowed in and out of Tyre.

"Well, Eborix," said Captain Mago genially, "there you have her, queen of the sea like I told you she is, eh? What d'you think cf my town?"

He stood in the bows with his passenger, just behind a fishtail ornament that curled upward and aft toward its mate at the stern. Lashed to that figurehead and to the latticework rails which ran down either side was a clay jar as big as himself. The oil was still within it; there had been no need to calm any billows, as easily as the voyage from Sicily had gone.

Everard glanced down at the skipper. Mago was a typical Phoenician, slender, swarthy, hook-nosed, eyes large and a bit slant, cheekbones high; neatly bearded, he wore a red-and-yellow kaftan, conical hat, sandals. The Patrolman towered over him. Since he would be conspicuous whatever guise he assumed, Everard took the part of a Celt from central Europe, complete with breeches, tunic, bronze sword, and sweeping mustache.

"A grand sight, indeed, indeed," he replied in a diplomatic, heavily accented voice. The electrocram he had taken, uptime in his native America, could have given him flawless Punic, but that wouldn't have fit his character; he settled for fluency. "Daunting, almost, to a simple backwoodsman."

His gaze went forward again. Truly, in its way Tyre was as impressive as New York—perhaps more, when you recalled how much King Hiram had accomplished in how short a span, with only the resources of an Iron Age that was not yet very old.

Starboard the mainland rose toward the Lebanon Mountains. It was summer-tawny, save where orchards and woodlots spotted it with green or villages nestled. The appearance was richer, more inviting than when Everard had seen it on his future travels, before he joined the Patrol.

Usu, the original city, lay along the shore. Except for its size, it was representative of the milieu, adobe buildings blocky and flat-roofed, streets narrow and twisty, a few vivid façades indicating temple or palace. Battle-mented walls and towers ringed three sides of it. Along the docks, gates between warehouses let those double as defenses. An aqueduct ran in from heights beyond Everard's view.

The new city, Tyre itself—Sor to its dwellers, meaning "Rocks"—was on an island half a mile offshore. Rather, it covered what had been two skerries until men filled in between and around them. Later they dug a canal straight through, from north to south, and flung out jetties and breakwaters to make this whole region an incomparable haven. With a burgeoning population and a bustling commerce thus crowded together, houses climbed upward, story upon story until they loomed over the guardian walls like small skyscrapers. They seemed to be less often of brick than of stone and cedarwood. Where earth and plaster had been used, frescos or inlaid shells ornamented them. On the eastward side, Everard glimpsed a huge and noble structure which the king had had built not for himself but for civic uses.

Mago's ship was bound for the outer or southern port, the Egyptian Harbor as he called it. Its piers bustled, men loading, unloading, fetching, bearing off, repairing, outfitting, dickering, arguing, chaffering, a tumble and chaos that somehow got its jobs done. Dock wallopers, donkey drivers, and other laborers, like the seamen on this cargo-cluttered deck, wore merely loincloths, or kaftans faded and patched. But plenty of brighter garments were in sight, some flaunting the costly colors that were produced here. Occasional women passed among the men, and Everard's preliminary education told him that they weren't all hookers. Sound rolled out to meet him, talk, laughter, shouts, braying, neighing, footfalls, hoofbeats, hammerbeats, groan of wheels and cranes, twanging music. The vitality was well-nigh overwhelming.

Not that this was any prettified scene in an Arabian Nights movie. Already he made out beggars crippled, blind, starveling; he saw a lash touch up a slave who toiled too slowly; beasts of burden fared worse. The smells of the ancient East roiled forth, smoke, dung, offal, sweat, as well as tar, spices, and savory roastings. Added to them was a stench of dyeworks and murex-shell middens on the mainland; but sailing along the coast and camping ashore every night, he had gotten used to that by now.

He didn't take the drawbacks to heart. His farings through history had cured him of fastidiousness and case-hardened him to the cruelties of man and nature—somewhat. For their era, these Canaanites were an enlightened and happy people. In fact, they were more so than most of humanity almost everywhere and everywhen.

His task was to keep them that way.

Mago hauled his attention back. "Aye, there are those who'd shamelessly swindle an innocent newcomer. I don't want that to happen to you, Eborix, my friend. I've grown to like you as we traveled, and I want you to think well of my town. Let me show you to an inn that a brother-in-law of mine has— brother of my junior wife, he is. He'll give you a clean doss and safe storage for your valuables at a fair exchange."

"It's thankful to you I am," Everard replied, "but my thought was I'd seek out that landsman I've bespoken. Remember, 'twas his presence emboldened me to fare hither." He smiled. "Sure, and if he's died or moved away or whatever, glad I'll be to take your offer." That was mere politeness. The impression he had gathered along the way was that Mago was as cheerfully rapacious as any other merchant adventurer, and hoped to get him plucked.

The captain regarded him for a moment. Everard counted as big in his own era, which made him gigantic here. A dented nose in the heavy features added to the impression of toughness, while blue eyes and dark-brown hair bespoke the wild North. One had better not push Eborix too hard.

At the same time, the Celtic persona was no great wonder in this cosmopolitan place. Not only did amber come from the Baltic littoral, tin from Iberia, condiments from Arabia, hardwoods from Africa, occasional wares from farther still: men did.

Engaging passage, Eborix had told of leaving his mountainous homeland because of losing out in a feud, to seek his fortune in the South. Wandering, he had hunted or worked for his keep, when he didn't receive hospitality in return for his tales. He fetched up among the Umbrians of Italy, who were akin to him. (The Celts would not begin overrunning Europe, clear to the Atlantic, for another three centuries or so, when they had become familiar with iron; but already some had won territory far from the Danube Valley that was the cradle of their race.) One of them, who had served as a mercenary, described opportunities in Canaan and taught Eborix the Punic tongue. This induced the latter to seek a bay in Sicily where Phoenician traders regularly called and buy passage with goods he had acquired. A man from his area of birth was said to be living in Tyre, after an adventurous career of his own, and probably willing to steer a compatriot in a profitable direction.

This line of bull, carefully devised by Patrol specialists, did more than slake local curiosity. It made Everard's trip safe. Had they supposed the foreigner to be a waif with no connections, Mago and the crew might have been tempted to set upon him while he slept, bind him, and sell him for a slave. As was, the journey had been interesting, yes, rather fun. Everard had come to like these rascals.

That doubled his wish to save them from ruin.

The Tyrian sighed. "As you wish," he said. "If you do need me, my home is on the Street of Anat's Temple, near the Sidonian Harbor." He brightened. "In any case, do come look me up, you and your host. He's in the amber trade, you mentioned? Maybe we can work out a little deal of some kind. . . . Now, stand aside. I've got to bring us in." He shouted profane commands.

Deftly, the sailors laid their vessel along a quay, got it secured, put out a gangplank. Folk swarmed close, yelling for news, crying for stevedore work, chanting the praises of their wares or of their masters' business establishments. None boarded, however. That prerogative belonged initially to the customs officer. A guard, helmeted, scale-mailed, armed with spear and shortsword, went before him, pushing a way through the crowd, leaving a wake of fairly good-natured curses. At the officer's back trotted a secretary, who bore a stylus and waxed tablet.

Everard went below decks and fetched his baggage, which he had stowed among the blocks of Italian marble that were the ship's principal cargo. The officer required him to open the two leather sacks. Nothing surprising was in them. The whole purpose of traveling all the way from Sicily, instead of time-hopping directly here, was to pass the Patrolman off as what he claimed to be. It was well-nigh certain that the enemy was keeping watch on events, as they neared the moment of catastrophe.

"You can provide for yourself a while, at least." The Phoenician official nodded his grizzled head when Everard displayed some small ingots of bronze. Coinage would not be invented for several centuries, but the metal could be swapped for whatever he wanted. "You must understand that we cannot let in one who might feel he has to turn robber. In fact—" He looked dubiously at the barbarian sword. "What is your purpose in coming?"

"To find honest work, sir, as it might be a caravan guard. I'll be seeking out Conor the amber factor." The existence of that resident Celt had been a major reason for Everard's adoption of his specific disguise. The chief of the local Patrol base had suggested it.

The Tyrian reached a decision. "Very well, you may go ashore, your weapon too. Remember that we crucify thieves, bandits, and murderers. If you fail to get other work, seek out Ithobaal's hiring house, near the Hall of the Suffetes. He can always find something in the way of day labor for a husky fellow like you. Good luck."

He returned to dealing with Mago. Everard lingered, awaiting a chance to bid the captain farewell. Discussion went quickly, almost informally, and the tax to be paid in kind would be modest. This race of businessmen had no use for the ponderous bureaucracy of Egypt or Mesopotamia.

Having said what he wanted to, Everard picked up his bags by the cords around them and went ashore. The crowd surged about him, staring, chattering. At first he was amazed; after a couple of tentative approaches, nobody begged alms or beset him to buy trinkets. Could this be the Near East?

He recalled the absence of money. A newcomer wouldn't likely have anything corresponding to small change. Usually you made a bargain with an innkeeper, food and lodging for so-and-so much of the metal, or whatever else of value, you carried. For lesser purchases, you sawed a piece off an ingot, unless some different trade was arranged. (Everard's fund included amber and nacre beads.) Sometimes you called in a broker, who made your transaction part of a complicated one involving several other individuals. If you felt charitable, you'd carry around a little grain or dried fruit and drop it in the bowls of the indigent.

Everard soon left most of the people behind. They were mainly interested in the crew. A few idle curiosity-seekers, and many stares, trailed him. He strode over the quay toward an open gate.

A hand plucked his sleeve. Startled enough to miss a step, he looked down.

A brown-skinned boy grinned back. He was sixteen or so, to judge from the fuzz on his cheeks, though small and scrawny even by local standards. Nonetheless, he moved lithely, barefoot, clad only in a ragged and begrimed kilt at which hung a pouch. Curly black hair fell in a queue behind a sharp-nosed, sharp-chinned face. His smile and his eyes—big, long-lashed Levantine eyes—were brilliant.

"Hail, sir, hail to you!" he greeted. "Life, health, and strength be yours! Welcome to Tyre! Where would you go, sir, and what can I do for you?"

He didn't burble, but spoke very clearly, in hopes the stranger would understand. When he got a response in his own language, he jumped for joy. "What do you want, lad?"

"Why, sir, to be your guide, your advisor, your helper, and, yes, your guardian. Alas, our otherwise fair city is afflicted with scoundrels who like nothing better than to prey on innocent newcomers. If they do not outright steal everything you have, the first time you blink, they'll at least wish the most worthless trash on you, at a cost which'll leave you paupered almost as fast—"

The boy broke off. He had spied a seedy-looking young man approaching. At once he sped to intercept, windmilling his fists, yelling too quickly and shrilly for Everard to catch more than a few words. "—louse-bitten jackal! . . . I saw him first. . . . Begone to the latrine that spawned you—"

The young man stiffened. He reached for a knife hung at his shoulder. Hardly had he moved before the stripling snatched a sling from his pouch and a rock to load it. He crouched, leered, swung the leather strap to and fro. The man spat, said something nasty, turned on his heel, and stalked off. Laughter barked from such passersby as had paid attention.

The boy laughed too, gleefully, loping back to Everard. "Now that, sir, was a prime example of what I meant," he crowed. "I know yon villain well. He's a runner for his father—maybe his father—who keeps the inn at the Sign of the Blue Squid. There you'd be lucky to get a rotten piece of goat's tail for your dinner, the single wench is a shambling farm of diseases, the pallets hang together only because the bedbugs hold hands, and as for the wine, why, I think the wench must have infected somebody's horse. You'd soon be too sick to notice that grandsire of a thousand hyenas when he plundered your baggage, and if you sought to complain, he'd swear by every god in the universe that you gambled it away. Little does he fear hell after this world is rid of him; he knows they'd never demean themselves there by letting him in. That is what I've saved you from, great lord."

Everard felt a grin tug at his lips. "Well, son, you might be stretching things just a trifle," he said.

The boy smote his thin breast. "No more than needful to give your magnificence the proper impression. Surely you are a man of the widest experience, a judge of the best as well as a generous rewarder of faithful service. Come, let me bring you to lodgings, or whatever else you may desire, and then see for yourself whether or not Pummairam has led you aright."

Everard nodded. The map of Tyre was engraved in his memory; he had no need of a guide. However, it would be natural for a yokel to engage one. Also, this kid would keep others from pestering him, and might give him a few useful tips.

"Very well, lead me whither I would go. Your name is Pummairam?"

"Yes, sir." Since the youth didn't mention his father, as was customary, he probably didn't know who that had been. "May I ask how my noble master should be addressed by his humble servant?"

"No title. I am Eborix, son of Mannoch, from a country beyond the Achaeans." With none of Mago's folk listening, the Patrolman could add: "He whom I seek is Zakarbaal of Sidon, who deals for his kin in this city." That meant Zakarbaal represented his family firm among the Tyrians, and handled its affairs here in between visits by its ships. "I've heard tell his house is on, uh, the Street of the Chandlers. Can you be showing me the way?"

"Indeed, indeed." Pummairam took Everard's bags. "Only deign to accompany me."

Actually, it wasn't hard to get around. As a planned city, rather than one which had grown organically through centuries, Tyre was laid out more or less on a gridiron pattern. The thoroughfares were paved, guttered, and reasonably wide, considering how short of acreage the island was. They lacked sidewalks, but that didn't matter, because except for a few trunk routes, beasts of burden were not allowed on them outside the wharf areas; nor did people dump stuff on them. They also lacked signs, of course, but that didn't matter either, since almost anybody would have been glad to give directions for the sake of some words with an outlander and perhaps a deal to propose.

Walls rose sheer to right and left, mostly windowless, enclosing the inward-looking houses that would prevail in Mediterranean countries for millennia to come. They shut off breezes and radiated back the heat of the sun. Noise echoed off them, odors rolled thick between. Yet Everard found himself enjoying the place. Still more than at the waterfront, crowds moved, jostled, gestured, laughed, talked at machine-gun speed, chanted, clamored. Porters beneath their yokes, litter-bearers conveying the occasional wealthy burgher, forced a way among sailors, artisans, vendors, laborers, housewives, entertainers, mainland farmers and shepherds, foreigners from end to end of the Midworld Sea, every variety and condition of life. If most clothes were of dull hue, many were gaudy, and none seemed to cover a body that was not overflowing with energy.

Booths lined the walls. Everard couldn't resist lingering now and then, to look at what they offered. That did not include the famous purple dye; it was too expensive, sought after by garmentmakers everywhere, destined to become the traditional color of royalty. But there was no dearth of bright fabrics, draperies, rugs. Glassware abounded, anything from beads to beakers; it was another specialty of the Phoenicians, their own invention. Jewelry and figurines, often carved in ivory or cast in precious metals, were excellent; this culture originated little or nothing artistic, but copied freely and skillfully. Amulets, charms, gewgaws, food, drink, utensils, weapons, instruments, games, toys, endlessness—

Everard remembered how the Bible gloated (would gloat) over the wealth of Solomon, and whence he got it. *"For the king had at sea a navy of Tharshish with the navy of Hiram: once in three years came the navy of Tharshish, bringing gold, and silver, ivory, and apes, and peacocks.—"*

Pummairam was quick to switch off conversations with shopkeepers and start Everard onward. "Let me show my master where the really good stuff is." Doubtless that meant a commission for Pummairam, but what the hell, the youngster had to live somehow, and didn't seem ever to have lived terribly well.

For a while they followed the canal. To a bawdy chant, sailors towed a laden ship along. Its officers stood on deck, wrapped in the dignity that behooved businessmen. The Phoenician bourgeoisie tended to be a sober lot . . . except in their religion, some of whose rites were orgiastic enough to compensate.

The Street of the Chandlers led off from this waterway. It was fairly long, being hemmed in by massive buildings that were warehouses as well as offices and homes. It was quiet, too, despite its far end giving on a thronged avenue; no shops crouched against the high, hot walls, and few people were in sight. Captains and shipowners came here for supplies, merchants came to negotiate, and, yes, two monoliths flanked the entrance of a small temple dedicated to Tanith, Our Lady of the Waves. Several little children who must belong to resident families—boys and girls together, naked or nearly so—darted about at play while a gaunt, excited mongrel dog barked.

A beggar sat, knees drawn up, by the shady entrance to an alley. His bowl rested at his bare feet. A kaftan muffled his body and a cowl obscured his face. Everard did see the rag tied over the eyes. Poor, blind devil; ophthalmia was among the countless damnations that made the ancient world not so glamorous after all. . . . Pummairam darted past the fellow, to overtake a man in a priestly robe who was leaving the temple. "Hoy, sir, your reverence, if you please," he called, "which is the door of Zakarbaal the Sidonian? My master condescends to visit him—" Everard, who already knew the answer, lengthened his stride to follow.

The beggar rose. His left hand plucked away his bandage, to reveal a lean, thick-bearded visage and a pair of eyes that had surely been watching through the cloth. From that flowing sleeve, his right hand drew something that gleamed.

A pistol!

Reflex flung Everard aside. Pain whipped through his own left shoulder. Sonic gun, he realized, from futureward of his home era, soundless, recoilless. If that invisible beam got him in the head or heart, he'd be dead, and never a mark upon him.

No place to go but forward. "Haaa!" he roared, and plunged zigzag to the attack. His sword hissed forth.

The other grinned, drifted back, took careful aim.

A *smack!* resounded. The assassin lurched, yelled, dropped his weapon, grabbed at his ribs. Pummairam's spent slingstone clattered over the cobbles.

Children scattered, screaming. The priest returned prudently through his temple door. The stranger whirled and ran. He vanished down the lane. Everard was too slow. His injury wasn't serious, but for the moment it hurt abominably. Half dazed, he stopped at the alley mouth, stared down the emptiness before him, panted, and rasped in English, "He's escaped. Oh, God damn it, anyway."

Pummairam darted to him. Anxious hands played over the Patrolman's form. "Are you wounded, my master? Can your servant help? Ah, woe, woe, I'd no time for a proper windup, nor to aim right, else I'd have spattered the evildoer's brains for yon dog to lick up."

"You . . . did mighty well . . . just the same." Everard drew shuddering breaths. Strength and steadiness began to return, agony to recede. He was still alive. That was miracle enough for one day.

He had work to do, though, and urgent it was. Having obtained the gun, he laid a hand on Pummairam's shoulder and made their gazes meet. "What did you see, lad? What d'you think happened this while?"

"Why, I—I—" Ferret-fast, the youth collected his wits. "It seemed to me that the beggar, though such he scarcely was, threatened my lord's life with some talisman whose magic did inflict harm. May the gods pour abominations on the head of him who would have extinguished the light of the universe! Yet, naturally, his wickedness could not prevail against the valor of my master—" The voice dropped to a confidential whisper: "—whose secrets are assuredly locked away safe in the bosom of his worshipful servant."

"Good," Everard grunted. "Sure, and these be matters about which common folk should never dare talk, lest they be stricken with palsy, deafness, and emerods. You've done well, Pum." *Saved my life, probably,* he thought, and stooped to untie the cord on a fallen bag. "Here, small reward it is, but this ingot ought to buy you something you'd like. And now, before the brannigan started, you did learn which is the house I want, did you not?"

Underneath the business of the minute, fading pain and shock from the assault, exhilaration of survival, grimness rose. After all his elaborate precautions, within an hour of arrival, his cover was blown. The enemy had not only had Patrol headquarters staked out, somehow their agent had instantly seen that it was no ordinary wanderer come into this street, and had not hesitated a second before trying to kill him.

This was a hairy mission for sure. And more was at stake than Everard liked to think about—first the existence of Tyre, later the destiny of the world.

Zakarbaal closed the door to his inner chambers and latched it. Turning around, he held out his hand in the manner of Western civilization. "Welcome," he said in Temporal, the Patrol language. "My name, you may remember, is Chaim Zorach. May I present my wife Yael?"

They were both of Levantine appearance and in Canaanite garb, but here, shut away from office staff and household servants, their entire bearing changed, posture, gait, facial expressions, tone of voice. Everard would have recognized them as being of the twentieth century even if he had not been told. The atmosphere was as refreshing to him as a wind off the sea.

He introduced himself. "I am the Unattached agent you sent for," he added.

Yael Zorach's eyes widened. "Oh! An honor. You . . . you are the first such I have met. The others who've been investigating, they are just technicians."

Everard grimaced. "Don't be too awestruck. I'm afraid I haven't made much of a showing so far."

He described his journey and the contretemps at its end. She offered him some painkiller, but he said he was pretty well over hurting, and her husband thereupon produced what was better anyway, a bottle of Scotch. Presently they were seated at their ease.

The chairs were comfortable, not unlike those of home—a luxury in this milieu, but then, Zakarbaal was supposed to be a wealthy man, with access to every kind of imported goods. Otherwise the apartment was austere by future standards, though frescos, draperies, lamps, furnishings were tasteful. It was cool and dim; a window opening on a small cloister garden had been curtained against the heat of the day.

"Why don't we relax a while and get acquainted before we buckle down to duty?" Everard suggested.

Zorach scowled. "You can do that right after you almost got killed?"

His wife smiled. "I think he might need to all the more, dear," she murmured. "We too. The menace can wait a little longer. It's been waiting, hasn't it?"

From the pouch at his belt, Everard drew anachronisms he had permitted himself, hitherto used only in solitude: pipe, tobacco, lighter. Zorach's tension eased a trifle; he chuckled and fetched cigarettes out of a locked coffer which held various such comforts. His language changed to Brooklyn-accented English: "You're American, aren't you, Agent Everard?"

"Yes. Recruited in 1954." How many years of his lifespan had passed "since" he answered an ad, took certain tests, and learned of an organization that guarded a traffic through the epochs? He hadn't added them up lately. It didn't matter much, when he and his fellows were the beneficiaries of a treatment that kept them unaging. "Uh, I thought you two were Israelis."

"We are," Zorach explained. "In fact, Yael's a *sabra*. Me, though, I didn't immigrate till I'd been doing archaeology there for a spell and had met her. That was in 1971. We got recruited into the Patrol four years later."

"How'd that happen, if I may ask?"

"We were approached, sounded out, finally told the truth. Naturally, we jumped at the chance. The work's often hard and lonesome—twice as lonesome, in a way, when we're home on furlough and can't tell our old friends and colleagues what we've been up to—but it's totally fascinating." Zorach winced. His words became a near mumble. "Also, well, *this* post is special for us. We don't just maintain a base and its cover business, we manage to help local people now and then. Or we try to, as much as we can without causing anybody to suspect there's anything peculiar about us. That makes up, somehow, a little bit, for . . . for what our countrymen will do hereabouts, far uptime."

Everard nodded. The pattern was familiar to him. Most field agents were specialists like these, passing their careers in a single milieu. They had to be, if they were to learn it thoroughly enough to serve the Patrol's purposes. What a help it would be to have native-born personnel! But such were very rare before the eighteenth century A.D., or still later in most parts of the world. How could a person who hadn't grown up in a scientific-industrial society even grasp the idea of automatic machinery, let alone vehicles that jumped in a blink from place to place and year to year? An occasional genius, of course; however, most identifiable geniuses carved niches for themselves in history, and you didn't dare tell them the facts for fear of making changes. . . .

"Yeah," Everard said. "In a way, a free operative like me has it easier. Husband-and-wife teams, or women generally— Not to pry, but what do you do about children?"

"Oh, we have two at home in Tel Aviv," Yael Zorach answered. "We time our returns so we've never been gone from them for more than a few days of their lives." She sighed. "It is strange, of course, when to us months have passed." Brightening: "Well, when they're of age, they're going to join the outfit too. Our regional recruiter has examined them already and decided they'll be fine material."

If not, Everard thought, *could you stand it, watching them grow old, suffer the horrors that will come, finally die, while you are still young of body?* Such a prospect had made him shy away from marriage, more than once.

"I think Agent Everard means children here in Tyre," Chaim Zorach said. "Before traveling from Sidon—we took ship, like you, because we were going to become moderately conspicuous—we quietly bought a couple of infants from a slave dealer, took them along, and have been passing them off as ours. They'll have lives as good as we can arrange." Unspoken was the likelihood that servants had the actual raising of those two; their foster parents would not dare invest much love in them. "That keeps us from appearing somehow unnatural. If my wife's womb has since closed, why, it's a common misfortune. I do get twitted about not taking a second wife or at least a concubine, but on the whole, Phoenicians mind their own business pretty well."

"You like them, then?" Everard inquired.

"Oh, yes, by and large, we do. We have excellent friends among them. We'd better—as important a nexus as this is."

Everard frowned and puffed hard on his pipe. The bowl had grown consolingly warm in his clasp, aglow like a tiny hearthfire. "You think that's correct?"

The Zorachs were surprised. "Of course!" Yael said. "We *know* it is. Didn't they explain to you?"

Everard chose his words with care. "Yes and no. After I'd been asked to look into this matter, and agreed, I got myself crammed full of information about the milieu. In a way, too full; it became hard to see the forest for the trees. However, my experience has been that I do best to avoid grand generalizations in advance of a mission. It could get hard to see the trees for the forest, so to speak. My idea was, once I'd been dropped off in Sicily and taken ship for Tyre, I'd have leisure to digest the information and form my own ideas. But that didn't quite work out, because the captain and crew were infernally curious about me; my mental energy went into answering their questions, which were often sharp, without letting any cat out of the bag." He paused. "To be sure, the role of Phoenicia in general, and Tyre in particular, in Jewish history—that's obvious."

On the kingdom that David had cobbled together out of Israel, Judah, and Jerusalem, this city soon became the main civilizing influence, its principal trading partner and window on the outside world. Now Solomon continued his father's friendship with Hiram. The Tyrians were supplying most of the materials and nearly all the skilled hands for the building of the Temple, as well as structures less famous. They would embark on joint exploratory and commercial ventures with the Hebrews. They would advance an immensity of goods to Solomon, a debt which he could only pay off by ceding them a score of his villages . . . with whatever subtle long-range consequences that had.

The subtleties went deeper, though. Phoenician customs, thoughts, beliefs permeated the neighboring realm, for good or ill; Solomon himself made sacrifices to gods of theirs. Yahweh would not really be the sole Lord of the Jews until the Babylonian Captivity forced them to it, as a means of preserving an identity that ten of their tribes had already lost. Before then, King Ahab of Israel would have taken the Tyrian princess Jezebel as his queen. Their evil memory was undeserved; the policy of foreign alliance and domestic religious tolerance which they strove to carry out might well have saved the country from its eventual destruction. Unfortunately, they collided with fanatical Elijah—"the mad mullah from the mountains of Gilead," Trevor-Roper would call him. And yet, had not Phoenician paganism spurred them to fury, would the prophets have wrought that faith which was to endure for thousands of years and remake the world?

"Oh, yes," Chaim said. "The Holy Land's aswarm with visitors. Jerusalem Base is chronically swamped, trying to regulate the traffic. We get a lot fewer here, mostly scientists from different eras, traders in artwork and the like, the occasional rich tourist. Nevertheless, sir, I maintain that this place, Tyre, is the real nexus of the era." Harshly: "And our opponents seem to have reached the same conclusion, right?"

The starkness took hold of Everard. Precisely because the fame of Jerusalem, in future eyes, overshadowed that of Tyre, this station was still worse undermanned than most; therefore it was terribly vulnerable; and if indeed it was a root of the morrow, and that root was cut away—

The facts passed before him as vividly as if he had never known them before.

When humans built their first time machine, long after Everard's home century, the Danellian supermen had arrived from farther yet, to organize the police force of the temporal lanes. It would gather knowledge, furnish guidance, aid the distressed, curb the wrongdoer; but these benevolences were incidental to its real function, which was to preserve the Danellians. A man has not lost free will merely because he has gone into the past. He can affect the course of events as much as ever. True, they have their momentum, and it is enormous. Minor fluctuations soon even out. For instance, whether a certain ordinary individual has lived long or died young, flourished or not, will make no noticeable difference several generations later. Unless that individual was, say, Shalmaneser or Genghis Khan or Oliver Cromwell or V. I. Lenin; Gautama Buddha or Kung Fu-Tze or Paul of Tarsus or Muhammad ibn Abdallah; Aristotle or Galileo or Newton or Einstein— Change anything like that, traveler from tomorrow, and you will still be where you are, but the people who brought you forth do not exist, they never did, it is an entirely other Earth up ahead, and you and your memories bespeak the uncausality, the ultimate chaos, which lairs beneath the cosmos.

Before now, along his own world line, Everard had had to stop the reckless and the ignorant before they worked that kind of havoc. They weren't too common; after all, the societies which possessed time travel screened their emissaries pretty carefully as a rule. However, in the course of a million years or more, mistakes were bound to happen.

So were crimes.

Everard spoke slowly: "Before going into detail about that gang and its operation—"

"What pitiful few details we have," Chaim Zorach muttered.

"—I'd like some idea of what their reasoning was. Why did they pick Tyre for the victim? Aside from its relationship to the Jews, that is."

"Well," Zorach began, "for openers, consider political events futureward of today. Hiram's become the most powerful king in Canaan, and that strength will outlive him. Tyre will stand off the Assyrians when they come, with everything that that implies. It'll push seaborne trade as far as Britain. It'll found colonies, the main one being Carthage." (Everard's mouth tightened. He had cause to know, far too well, how much Carthage mattered in history.) "It'll submit to the Persians, but fairly willingly, and among other things provide most of their fleet when they attack Greece. That effort will fail, of course, but imagine how the world might have gone if the Greeks had not faced that particular challenge. Eventually Tyre will fall to Alexander the Great, but only after a siege of months—a delay in his progress that also has incalculable consequences.

"Meanwhile, more basically, as the leading Phoenician state, it will be in the forefront of spreading Phoenician ideas abroad. Yes, to the Greeks themselves. There are religious concepts—Aphrodite, Adonis, Herakles, and other figures originate as Phoenician divinities. There's the alphabet, a Phoenician invention. There's the knowledge of Europe, Africa, Asia that Phoenician navigators will bring back. There's the progress in shipbuilding and seamanship."

Enthusiasm kindled in his tone: "Above everything else, I'd say, there's the origin of democracy, of the worth and rights of the individual. Not that the Phoenicians have any such theories; philosophy, like art, never will be a strong point of theirs. Just the same, the merchant adventurer—explorer or entrepreneur—he's their ideal, a man out on his own, deciding for himself. Here at home, Hiram's no traditional Egyptian or Oriental god-king. He inherited his job, true, but essentially he presides over the suffetes—the magnates, who must approve every important thing he does. Tyre is actually quite a bit like the medieval Venetian republic in its heyday.

"We don't have the scientific personnel to trace the process out step by step, no. But I'm convinced that the Greeks developed their democratic institutions under strong Phoenician influence, mainly Tyrian—and where will your country or mine get those ideas from, if not the Greeks?"

Zorach's fist smote the arm of his chair. His other hand brought the whisky to his lips for a long and fiery gulp. "That's what those devils have learned!" he exclaimed. "They're holding Tyre up for ransom because that's how to put the future of the whole human race at gunpoint!"

Having broken out a holocube, he showed Everard what would happen, a year hence.

He had taken pictures with a sort of minicamera, actually a molecular recorder from the twenty-second century, disguised as a gem on a ring. ("Had" was the ludicrous single way to express in English how he doubled back and forth in time. The Temporal grammar included appropriate tenses.) Granted, he was not a priest or acolyte, but as a layman who made generous donations so that the goddess would favor his ventures, he had access.

The explosion took place (would take place) along this very street, in the little temple of Tanith. Occurring at night, it didn't hurt anybody, but it wrecked the inner sanctum. Rotating the view, Everard studied cracked and blackened walls, shattered altar and idol, strewn relics and treasures, twisted scraps of metal. Horror-numbed hierophants sought to placate the divine wrath with prayers and offerings, on the site and everywhere else in town that was sacred.

The Patrolman selected a volume of space within the scene and magnified. The bomb had fragmented its carrier, but there was no mistaking the pieces. A standard two-seat hopper, such as plied the time lanes in untold thousands, had materialized, and instantly erupted.

"I collected some dust and char when nobody was looking, and sent it uptime for analysis," Zorach said. "The lab reported the explosive had been chemical—fulgurite-B, the name is."

Everard nodded. "I know that stuff. In common use for a rather long period, starting a while after the origin span of us three. Therefore easy to obtain in quantity, untraceably—a hell of a lot easier than nuke isotopes. Wouldn't need a large amount to do this much damage, either. . . . I suppose you've had no luck intercepting the machine?"

Zorach shook his head. "No. Or rather, the Patrol officers haven't. They went downtime of the event, planted instruments of every kind that could be concealed, but—everything happens too fast."

Everard rubbed his chin. The stubble felt almost silky; a bronze razor and a lack of soap didn't make for a close shave. He thought vaguely that he would have welcomed some scratchiness, or anything else familiar.

What had happened was plain enough. The vehicle had been unmanned, autopiloted, sent from some unknown point of space-time. Start-off had activated the detonator, so that the bomb arrived exploding. Though Patrol agents could pinpoint the instant, they could do nothing to head off the occurrence.

Could a technology advanced beyond theirs do so—Danellian, even? Everard imagined a device planted in advance of the moment, generating a force field which contained the violence when it smote. Well, this had not happened, therefore it might be a physical impossibility. Likelier, though, the Danellians stayed their hand because the harm *had* been done—the saboteurs could try again—all by itself, such a cat-and-mouse game might warp the continuum beyond healing. He shivered and asked roughly: "What explanation will the Tyrians themselves come up with?"

"Nothing dogmatic," Yael Zorach replied. "They don't have our kind of *Weltanschauung*, remember. To them, the world isn't entirely governed by laws of nature; it's capricious, changeable, magical."

And they're fundamentally right, aren't they? The chill struck deeper into Everard.

"When nothing else of the kind occurs, excitement will die down," she went on. "The chronicles that record the incident will be lost; besides, Phoenicians aren't especially given to writing chronicles. They'll think that somebody did something wrong that provoked a thunderbolt from heaven. Not necessarily any human; it could have been a quarrel among the gods. Therefore nobody will become a scapegoat. After a generation or two, the incident will be forgotten, except perhaps as a bit of folklore."

Chaim Zorach fairly snarled: "That's if the extortionists don't do more and worse."

"Yeah, let's see their ransom note," Everard requested.

"I have a copy only. The original went uptime for study."

"Oh, sure, I know. I've read the lab report. Sepia ink on a papyrus scroll, no clue there. Found at your door, probably dropped from another unmanned hopper that just flitted through."

"Certainly dropped in that way," Zorach reminded him. "The agents who came in set up instruments for that night, and detected the machine. It was present for about a millisecond. They might have tried to capture it, but what would have been the use? It was bound to be devoid of clues. And in any case, the effort would have entailed making a racket that could have brought the neighbors out to see what was going on."

He fetched the document for Everard to examine. The Patrolman had pored over a transcript as part of his briefing, but hoped that sight of the actual hand would suggest something, anything to him.

The words had been formed with a contemporary reed pen, rather skillfully used. (This implied that the writer was well versed in the milieu, but that was obvious already.) They were printed, not cursive, though certain flamboyant flourishes appeared. The language was Temporal.

"To the Time Patrol from the Committee for Aggrandizement, greeting." At least there was none of the cant about being a people's army of national liberation, such as nauseated Everard in the later part of his home century. These fellows were frank bandits. Unless, of course, they pretended to be, in order to cover their tracks the more thoroughly. . . .

"Having witnessed the consequences when one small bomb was delivered to a carefully chosen location in Tyre, you are invited to contemplate the results of a barrage throughout the city."

Once more, heavily, Everard nodded. His opponents were shrewd. A threat to kill or kidnap individuals—say, King Hiram himself—would have been nugatory, if not empty. The Patrol would mount guard on any such person. If somehow an attack succeeded, the Patrol would go back in time and arrange for the victim to be elsewhere at the moment of the assault; it would make the event "unhappen." Granted, that involved risks which the outfit hated to take, and at best would require a lot of work to make sure that the future did not get altered by the rescue operation itself. Nevertheless, the Patrol could and would act.

But how did you move a whole islandful of buildings to safety? You could, perhaps, evacuate the population. The town would remain. It wasn't physically large, after all, no matter how large it loomed in history—about twenty-five thousand people crowded into about 140 acres. A few tons of high explosive would leave it in ruins. The devastation needn't even be total. After such a terrifying manifestation of supernatural fury, no one would come back here. Tyre would crumble away, a ghost town, while all the centuries and millennia, all the human beings and their lives and civilizations, which it had helped bring into existence . . . those would be less than ghosts.

Everard shivered anew. *Don't tell me there is no such thing as absolute evil,* he thought. *These creatures—* He forced himself to read on:

"—The price of our forbearance is quite reasonable, merely a little information. We desire the data necessary for the construction of a Trazon matter transmuter—"

When that device was being developed, during the third Technological Renaissance, the Patrol had covertly manifested itself to the creators, though they lived downtime of its own founding. Forever afterward, its use—the very knowledge of its existence, let alone the manner of its making—had been severely restricted. True, the ability to convert any material object, be it just a heap of dirt, into any other, be it a jewel or a machine or a living body, could have spelled unlimited wealth for the entire species. The trouble was, you could as easily produce unlimited amounts of weapons, or poisons, or radioactive atoms. . . .

"—You will broadcast the data in digital form from Palo Alto, California, United States of America, throughout the 24 hours of Friday, 13 June, 1980. The waveband to employ . . . the digital code. . . . Your receipt will be the continued reality of your time line.—"

That was smart, too. The message wasn't one that would be picked up accidentally by some native, yet electronic activity in the Silicon Valley area was so great as to rule out any possibility of tracking down a receiver.

"—We will not use the device upon the planet Earth. Therefore the Time Patrol need not fear that it is compromising its Prime Directive by this helpfulness to us. On the contrary, you have no other way to preserve yourselves, do you?

"Our compliments, and our expectations."

No signature.

"The broadcast won't be made, will it?" Yael asked low. In the shadows of the room, her eyes glimmered enormous. *She has children uptime,* Everard remembered. *They would vanish with their world.*

"No," he said.

"And yet our reality remains!" burst from Chaim. "You came here, out of it, starting uptime of 1980. So we must have caught the criminals."

Everard's sigh seemed to leave a track of pain through his breast. "You know better than that," he said tonelessly. "The quantum nature of the continuum—If Tyre explodes, why, here we'll be, but our ancestors, your kids, everything we knew, they won't. It'll be a whole different history. Whether whatever is left of the Patrol can restore it—somehow head off the disaster—that's problematical. I'd call it unlikely."

"But what would the criminals have gained, then?" The question was raw, almost a screech.

Everard shrugged. "A certain wild satisfaction, I guess. The temptation to play God slinks around in the best of us, doesn't it? And the temptation to play Satan isn't unrelated. Besides, they'd be careful to lurk downtime of the destruction; they'd stay existent. They'd have a good chance of making themselves overlords of a future where nothing but bits and pieces of the Patrol were left to oppose them. Or at a minimum, they'd have a lot of fun trying."

Sometimes I myself have chafed at the restrictions on me. "Ah, Love! could thou and I with Fate conspire To grasp this sorry Scheme of Things entire—"

"Besides," he added, "conceivably the Danellians will countermand the decision and order us to release the secret. I could return home to find that feature of my world wasn't the same any longer. A trivial variation as far as the twentieth century is concerned, affecting nothing noticeable."

"But later centuries?" the woman gasped.

"Yeah. We've only the gang's word that it'll confine its attentions to planets in the far future and beyond the Solar System. I'll bet whatever you like that that word is worthless. Given the capabilities of the transmuter, why shouldn't they play fast and loose with Earth? It'll always be *the* human globe, and I don't see how the Patrol can stop them."

"Who are they?" Chaim whispered. "Have you any idea?"

Everard drank whisky and smoke, as if warmth could seep through his tongue into his spirit. "Too early to say, on my personal world line . . . or yours, hm? Plain to see, they're from far uptime, though short of the Era of Oneness that precedes the Danellians. In the course of many millennia, information about the transmuter was bound to leak out—enough to give somebody a clear notion of the thing and of what he might do with it. Certainly he and his buddies are rootless desperados; they don't give a damn that their action threatens to eliminate the society that begot them, and everybody living in it whom they ever knew. But I don't think they are, say, Neldorians. This operation is too sophisticated. The enemy's got to have spent a lot of lifespan, a lot of effort, getting to know the Phoenician milieu well and establishing that it is in fact a nexus.

"The organizing brain must be of genius level. But with a touch of childishness—did you notice that Friday-the-thirteenth date? Likewise, performing the sabotage practically next door to you. The MO—and my being recognized as a Patrolman—those do suggest—Merau Varagan?"

"Who?"

Everard didn't reply. He went on mumbling, mostly to himself: "Could be, could be. Not that that's much help. The gang did its homework, downtime of today, surely—yes, they'd want an informational baseline covering quite a few years. And this post is undermanned. The whole goddamn Patrol is." *Regardless of agents' longevity. Sooner or later, something or other will get each and every one of us. And we don't go back to cancel the deaths of our comrades, nor to see them again while they lived, because that could start an eddy in time, which might grow into a maelstrom; or if not, it would at least rack us too cruelly.* "We can detect time vehicles arriving and departing, if we know where and when to aim our instruments. That may be how the gang discovered this is Patrol HQ, if they didn't learn it routinely in the guise of honest visitors. Or they could have entered this era elsewhere and come by ordinary transportation, looking like any of countless legitimate contemporary people, the same way I tried to.

"We can't ransack every bit of local space-time. We haven't the manpower, nor dare we risk the disruption that so much activity of ours could cause. No, Chaim, Yael, we've got to find ourselves some clues, to narrow down our search. But how? Where do I start?"

His disguise being penetrated, Everard accepted the Zorachs' offer of a guest room. He'd be more comfortable here than in an inn, and handier to whatever gadgets he might need. However, he'd also be cut off from the real life of the city.

"I'll arrange an interview with the king for you," his host promised. "No difficulty; he's a brilliant man, bound to be interested in an exotic like you." He chuckled. "Therefore it will be very natural for Zakarbaal the Sidonian, who needs to cultivate the friendship of the Tyrians, to inform him of a chance meeting with you."

"That's fine," Everard replied, "and I'll enjoy paying the call. Maybe he can even be some help to us. Meanwhile, uh, we've got several hours of daylight left. I think I'll stroll around town, start getting the feel of it, pick up a scent if I'm lucky."

Zorach scowled. "You might be what's picked up. The killer is skulking yet, I'm sure."

Everard shrugged. "A chance I take; and could be him that comes to grief. Lend me a gun, please. Sonic."

He set the weapon to stun, not slay. A live prisoner was at the top of his birthday list. Since the enemy would be aware of that, he didn't really expect another attempt on him—today, at any rate.

"Take a blaster, too," Zorach urged. "I wouldn't put it past them to come after you from the air. Bring a hopper to an instant where you are, hover on antigravity, and pot-shoot, hm? They don't have our motivation to stay inconspicuous."

Everard holstered the energy gun opposite the other. Any Phoenician who noticed would take them for charms or something of the kind, and besides, he'd let a cloak fall over them. "I scarcely think I'd be worth that much effort and risk," he said.

"You were worth trying for earlier, weren't you? How did that guy know you for an agent, anyway?"

"He may have had a description. Merau Varagan would realize that just a few Unattached operatives, me among them, were likely choices for this assignment. Which inclines me more and more to think he is behind the plot. If I'm right, we've got a mean and slippery opponent."

"Stay in public view," Yael Zorach pleaded. "Be sure to get back before dark. Violent crime is rare here, but there are no lights, the streets grow nearly deserted, you'd become easy prey."

Everard imagined himself hunting his hunter through the night, but decided not to attempt provoking such a situation unless he became desperate. "Okay, I'll return for dinner. I'm interested in what Tyrian food is like—ashore, not ship rations."

She mustered a smile. "Not awfully good, I'm afraid. The natives aren't sensualists. However, I've taught our cook several uptime recipes. Do you like gefilte fish for an appetizer?"

Shadows had lengthened and air cooled somewhat when Everard stepped forth. Traffic bustled along the street crossing Chandlers, though no more than earlier. Situated on the water, Tyre and Usu were generally free of the extreme midday heat that dictated a siesta in many countries, and no true Phoenician would waste hours asleep in which he might turn a profit.

"Master!" warbled a joyful voice.

Why, it's my little wharf rat. "Hail, uh, Pummairam," Everard said. The boy bounced up from his squat. "What are you waiting for?"

The slight brown form bowed low, albeit eyes and lips held as much merriment as reverence. "What but the fervently prayed-for hope that I might again be of service to his luminosity?"

Everard stopped and scratched his head. The kid had been almighty quick, had possibly saved his bacon, but—"Well, I'm sorry, but I've no further need of help."

"Oh, sir, you jest. See how I laugh, delighted by your wit! A guide, an introducer, a warder off of rogues and . . . certain worse persons—surely a lord of your magnanimity will not deny a poor sprig the glory of his presence, the benefit of his wisdom, the never-to-be-forgotten memory in after years of having trotted at his august heels."

While the words were sycophantic, that was conventional in this society, the tone was anything but. Pummairam was having fun, Everard saw. Doubtless he was curious, too, as well as eager to earn more. He fairly quivered where he stood looking straight up at the huge man.

Everard made his decision. "You win, you rogue," he said, and grinned when Pummairam whooped and danced. It wasn't a bad idea to have such an attendant, anyway. Wasn't his purpose to get to know the city, rather than merely its sights? "Now tell me what it is you are thinking you can do for me."

The boy poised, cocked his head, laid finger to chin. "That depends upon what my master's desire may be. If business, what kind and with whom? If pleasure, likewise. My lord has but to speak."

"Hm-m. . . ." *Well, why not level with him, to the extent that is allowable? If he proves unsatisfactory, I can always fire him, though I expect he'd cling like a tick.* "Then hear me, Pum. I do have weighty matters to handle in Tyre. Yes, they may well concern the suffetes and the king's self. You saw how a magician tried to stop me. Aye, you aided me against him. That may happen anew, and I not so lucky next time. It's barred I am from saying more about that. Yet I think you'll understand my need to learn a great deal, to meet people of many kinds. What would you suggest? A tavern, maybe, and I buying drinks for the house?"

Pum's quicksilver mood froze to seriousness. He frowned and stared into space for a few heartbeats, before he snapped his fingers and cackled. "Ah, indeed! Well, excellent master, I can recommend no better beginning than a visit to the High Temple of Asherat."

"Hey?" Startled, Everard flipped through the information planted in his brain. Asherat, whom the Bible would call Astarte, was the consort of Melqart, the patron god of Tyre—Baal-Melek-Qart-Sor. . . . She was a mighty figure in her own right, goddess of fruitfulness in man, beast, and land, a female warrior who had once dared hell itself to recall her lover from the dead, a sea queen of whom Tanith might be simply an avatar . . . yes, she was Ishtar in Babylon, and she would enter the Grecian world as Aphrodite. . . .

"Why, the vast learning of my lord surely includes the fact that it would be foolish for a visitor, most especially a visitor as important as he, *not* to pay homage to her, that she may smile upon his enterprise. Truly, if the priests heard of such an omission, they would set themselves against you. That has, indeed, caused difficulties with some of the emissaries from Jerusalem. Also, is it not a good deed to release a lady from bondage and yearning?" Pum leered, winked, and nudged Everard. "Besides being a pleasurable romp."

The Patrolman remembered. For a moment, he was taken aback. Like most other Semites of this era, the Phoenicians required that every freeborn woman sacrifice her virginity in the fane of the goddess, as a sacred prostitute. Not until a man had paid for her favor might she marry. The custom was not lewd in origin; it traced back to Stone Age fertility rites and fears. To be sure, it also attracted profitable pilgrims and foreign visitors.

"I trust my lord's folk do not forbid such an act?" the boy inquired anxiously.

"Well. . . . They do not."

"Good!" Pum took Everard by the elbow and steered him off. "If my lord will allow his servant to accompany him, quite likely I shall recognize someone whom he would find it useful thus to get acquainted with. In all abasement, let me say that I do get around and I do keep eyes and ears open. They are utterly at the service of my master."

Everard grinned, on one side of his mouth, and strode along. Why shouldn't he? To be honest with himself, after his sea voyage he felt damnably horny; and it was true, patronizing the holy whorehouse was, in this milieu, not an exploitation but a kindness; and he might even get some lead in his mission. . . .

First I'd better try to find out how reliable my guide is. "Tell me something about yourself, Pum. We may be together for, well, several days if not more."

They came out on the avenue and threaded their way through jostling, shouting, odorous throngs. "There is little to tell, great lord. The annals of the poor are short and simple." That coincidence startled Everard too. Then, as Pum talked, he realized that the phrase was false in this case.

Father unknown, presumably one of the sailors and laborers who frequented a certain low-life hostel while Tyre was under construction and had the wherewithal to enjoy its serving wench, Pum was a pup in a litter, raised catch-as-catch-can, a scavenger from the time he could walk and, Everard suspected, a thief, and whatever else might get him the local equivalent of a buck. Nonetheless, early on he had become an acolyte at a dockside temple of the comparatively unimportant god Baal Hammon. (Everard harked back to tumbledown churches in the slums of twentieth-century America.) Its priest had been a learned man once, now gentle and drunken; Pum had garnered considerable vocabulary and other knowledge from him, like a squirrel garnering acorns in a wood, until he died. His more respectable successor kicked the raffish postulant out. Despite that, Pum went on to make a wide circle of acquaintances, which reached into the palace itself. Royal servants came down to the waterfront in search of cheap fun. . . . Still too young to assume any kind of leadership, he was wangling a living however he could. His survival to date was no mean accomplishment.

Yes, Everard thought, *I may have lucked out, just a little.*

The temples of Melqart and Asherat confronted each other across a busy square near the middle of town. The former was the larger, but the latter was amply impressive. A porch of many columns, with elaborate capitals and gaudy paint, gave on a flagged courtyard wherein stood a great brass basin of water for ritual cleansing. The house rose along the farther side of the enclosure, its squareness relieved by stone facing, marble, granite, jasper. Two pillars flanked the doorway, overtopping the roof and shining. (In Solomon's Temple, which copied Tyrian design, these would be named Jachin and Boaz.) Within, Everard knew, was a main chamber for worshippers, and beyond it the sanctuary.

Some of the forum crowd had spilled into the court and stood about in little groups. The men among them, he guessed, simply wanted a quiet place to discuss business or whatever. Women outnumbered them—housewives for the most part, often balancing loads on their scarved heads, taking a break from marketing to make a brief devotion and indulge in a bit of gossip. While the attendants of the goddess were male, here females were always welcome.

Stares followed Everard as Pum urged him toward the temple. He began to feel self-conscious, even abashed. A priest sat at a table, in the shade behind the open door. Except for a rainbow-colored robe and a phallic silver pendant, he looked no different from a layman, his hair and beard well trimmed, his features aquiline and lively.

Pum halted before him and said importantly, "Greeting, holy one. My master and I wish to honor Our Lady of Nuptials."

The priest signed a blessing. "Praises be. A foreigner confers double fortune." Interest gleamed in his eyes. "Whence come you, worthy stranger?"

"From north across the waters," Everard replied.

"Yes, yes, that's clear, but it's a vast and unknown territory. Might you be from a land of the Sea Peoples themselves?" The priest waved at a stool like that which he occupied. "Pray be seated, noble sir, take your ease for a while, let me pour you a cup of wine."

Pum jittered about for several minutes in an agony of frustration, before he hunkered down under a column and sulked. Everard and the priest conversed for almost an hour. Others drifted up to listen and join in.

It could easily have lasted all day. Everard was finding out a lot. Probably none of it was germane to his mission, but you never knew, and anyway, he enjoyed the gab session. What brought him back to earth was mention of the sun. It had dropped below the porch roof. He remembered Yael Zorach's warning, and cleared his throat.

"Och, how I regret it, friends, but time passes and I must soon begone. If we are first to pay our respects—"

Pum brightened. The priest laughed. "Aye," he said, "after so long a faring, the fire of Asherat must burn hotly. Well, now, the free-will donation is half a shekel of silver or its value in goods. Of course, men of wealth and rank are wont to give more."

Everard paid over a generous chunk of metal. The priest repeated his blessing and gave him and Pum each a small ivory disc, rather explicitly engraved. "Go in, my sons, seek whom you will do good, cast these in their laps. Ah . . . you understand, do you not, great Eborix, that you are to take your chosen one off the sacred premises? Tomorrow she will return the token and receive the benison. If you have no place of your own nigh to here, then my kinsman Hanno rents clean rooms at a modest rate, in his inn just down the Street of the Date Sellers. . . ."

Pum fairly zoomed inside. Everard followed with what he hoped was more dignity. His talk mates called raunchy good wishes. That was part of the ceremony, the magic.

The chamber was large, its gloom not much relieved by oil lamps. They picked out intricate murals, gold leaf, inset semiprecious stones. At the far end shimmered a gilt image of the goddess, arms held out in a compassion which somehow came through the rather primitive sculpturing. Everard sensed fragrances, myrrh and sandalwood, and an irregular undertone of rustles and whispers.

As his pupils widened, he discerned the women. Perhaps a hundred altogether, they sat on stools, crowded along the walls to right and left. Their garb ranged from fine linen to ragged wool. Some slumped, some stared blankly, some made gestures of invitation as bold as the rules permitted, most looked timidly and wistfully at the men who strolled by them. Those visitors were few, at this hour of an ordinary day. Everard thought he identified three or four mariners on shore leave, a fat merchant, a couple of young bucks. Their deportment was reasonably polite; it *was* a church here.

His pulses pounded. *Damnation,* he thought, irritated, *why am I making such a production in my head? I've been with enough women before.*

Sadness touched him. *Only two virgins, though.*

He walked along, watching, wondering, avoiding glances. Pum sought him and tugged his sleeve. "Radiant master," the youth hissed, "your servant may have found that which you require."

"Huh?" Everard let his attendant drag him out to the center of the room, where they could murmur unheard.

"My lord understands that this child of poverty could never hitherto enter these precincts," spilled from Pum. "Yet, as I said earlier, I do have acquaintanceship reaching into the royal palace itself. I know of a lady who has come each time her duties and the moon allow, to wait and wait, these past three years. She is Sarai, daughter of shepherd folk in the hills. Through an uncle in the guard, she got a post in the king's household, at first only as a scullery maid, but now working closely with the chief steward. And she is here today. Since my master wishes to make contacts of that sort—"

Bemused, Everard followed his guide. When they halted, he gulped. The woman who, low-voiced, responded to Pum's greeting, was squat, big-nosed—he decided to think of her as homely—and verging on spinsterhood. But the gaze she lifted to the Patrolman was bright and unafraid. "Would you like to release me?" she asked quietly. "I would pray for you for the rest of my life."

Before he could change his mind, he pitched his token onto her skirt.

Pum had found himself a beauty, arrived this same day and engaged to the scion of a prominent family. She was dismayed when such a ragamuffin picked her. Well, that was her problem. And perhaps his too, though Everard doubted it.

The rooms in Hanno's inn were tiny, equipped with straw mattresses and little else. Slit windows, giving on the inner court, admitted a trickle of evening light, also smoke, street and kitchen smells, chatter, plaintiveness of a bone flute. Everard drew the reed curtain that served as a door and turned to his companion.

She knelt before him as if huddling into her garments. "I do not know your name or your country, sir," she said, low and not quite steadily. "Do you care to tell your handmaiden?"

"Why, sure." He gave her his alias. "And you are Sarai from Rasil Ayin?"

"Did the beggar boy send my lord to me?" She bowed her head. "No, forgive me, I meant no insolence, I was thoughtless."

He ventured to push back her scarf and stroke her hair. Though coarse, it was abundant, her best physical feature. "No offense taken. See here, shall we get to know each other a bit? What would you say to a cup or two of wine before—Well, what would you say?"

She gasped, astounded. He went out, found the landlord, made the provision.

Presently, as they sat side by side on the floor with his arm around her shoulders, she was talking freely. Phoenicians had scant concept of personal privacy. Also, while their women got more respect and independence than those of most societies, still, a little consideration on a man's part went a long ways.

"—no, no betrothal yet for me, Eborix. I came to the city because my father is poor, with many other children to provide for, and it did not seem anybody in our tribe would ever ask my hand for his son. You wouldn't possibly know of someone?" He himself, who would take her maidenhead, was debarred. In fact, her question bent the law that forbade prearrangement, as for example with a friend. "I have won standing in the palace, in truth if not in name. I wield some small power among servants, purveyors, entertainers. I have scraped together a dowry for myself, not large, but . . . but it may be the goddess will smile on me at last, after I have made this oblation—"

"I'm sorry," he answered in compassion. "I'm a stranger here."

He understood, or supposed he did. She wanted desperately to get married: less to have a husband and put an end to the barely veiled scorn and suspicion in which the unwedded were held, than to have children. Among these people, few fates were more terrible than to die childless, to go doubly into the grave. . . . Her defenses broke apart and she wept against his breast.

The light was failing. Everard decided to forget Yael's fears (and—a chuckle—Pum's exasperation) and take his time, treat Sarai like a human being simply because that was what she in fact was, wait for darkness and then use his imagination. Afterward he'd see her back to her quarters.

The Zorachs were mainly upset because of the anxiety their guest caused them, not returning until well past sunset. He didn't tell them what he had been doing, nor did they press him about it. After all. they were agents in place, able persons who coped with a difficult job often full of surprises, but they were not detectives.

Everard did feel obliged to apologize for spoiling their supper. That was to have been an unusual treat. Normally the main meal of the day occurred about midafternoon, and folk had little more than a snack in the evening. A reason for this was the dimness of lamplight, which made it troublesome to prepare anything elaborate.

Nonetheless, the technical accomplishments of the Phoenicians deserved admiration. Over breakfast, which was also a sparse meal, lentils cooked with leeks and accompanied by hardtack, Chaim mentioned the waterworks. Rain-catching cisterns were helpful but insufficient. Hiram didn't want Tyre dependent on boats from Usu, nor linked to the mainland by an extended aqueduct that could serve an enemy as a bridge. Like the Sidonians before him, he had a project in train that would draw fresh water from springs beneath the sea.

And then, of course, there was the skill, the accumulated knowledge and ingenuity, behind dyeworks and glassworks, not to mention ships less frail than they looked, since in the future they would ply as far as Britain. . . .

"The Purple Empire, somebody in our century called Phoenicia," Everard mused. "Almost makes me wonder if Merau Varagan has a thing for that color. Didn't W. H. Hudson call Uruguay the Purple Land?" His laugh clanked. "No, I'm being foolish. The murex dyes generally have more red than blue in them. Besides, Varagan was doing his dirty work a lot farther north than Uruguay when we collided 'earlier.' And so far I've no proof he's involved in this case; only a hunch."

"What happened?" asked Yael. Her glance sought him across the table, through sunlight that slanted in a doorway open to the garden court.

"No matter now."

"Are you certain?" Chaim persisted. "Conceivably your experience will call something to our minds that will be a clue. Anyhow, we do get starved for outside news in a post like this."

"Especially adventures as wonderful as yours," Yael added.

Everard smiled wryly. "To quote still another writer, adventure is somebody else having a hell of a tough time a thousand miles away," he said. "And when the stakes are high, like here, that really makes a situation feel bad." He paused. "Well, no reason not to spin you the yarn, though in very sketchy form, because the background's complicated. Uh, if a servant isn't going to come in soon, I'd like to light my pipe. And is any of that lovely clandestine coffee left in the pot?"

—He settled himself, rolled smoke across his tongue, let the rising warmth of the day bake his bones after the night's nippiness. "My mission was to South America, the Colombia region, late in the year 1826. Under Simón Bolívar's leadership, the patriots had cast off Spanish rule, but they still had plenty troubles of their own. That included worries about the Liberator himself. He'd put through a constitution for Bolivia that gave him extraordinary powers as lifetime president; was he going to turn into a Napoleon and bring all the new republics under his heel? The military commander in Venezuela, which was then a part of Colombia, or New Granada as it called itself—he revolted. Not that this José Páez was such an altruist; a harsh bastard, in fact.

"Oh, never mind details. I don't remember them well myself anymore. Essentially, Bolívar, who was a Venezuelan by birth, made a march from Lima to Bogotá. Only took him a couple of months, which was *fast* in those days over that terrain. Arriving, he assumed martial-law presidential powers, and moved on into Venezuela against Páez. Bloodshed was becoming heavy there.

"Meanwhile Patrol agents, monitoring the history, turned up indications that all was not kosher. (Um-m, pardon me.) Bolívar wasn't behaving quite like the selfless humanitarian that his biographers, by and large, described. He'd acquired a friend from . . . somewhere . . . whom he trusted. This man's advice had, on occasion, been brilliant. Yet it seemed as if he might be turning into Bolívar's evil genius. And the biographies never mentioned him. . . .

"I was among the Unattached operatives dispatched to investigate. This was because I, before ever hearing of the Patrol, had kicked around some in those boonies. That gave me a slight special sense for what to do. I could never pass myself off as a Latin American, but I could be a Yankee soldier of fortune, in part starry-eyed over the liberation, in part hoping somehow to cash in on it—and, mainly, though *macho* enough, free of the kind of arrogance that would have put those proud people off.

"It's a long and generally tedious story. Believe me, my friends, ninety-nine percent of an operation in the field amounts to patient collection of dull and usually irrelevant facts, in between interminable periods of hurry-up-and-wait. Let's say that, aided by a good deal of luck, I managed to infiltrate, make my connections, pass out my bribes, gather my informers and my evidence. At last there was no reasonable doubt. This obscurely originating Blasco López had to be from the future.

"I called in our troops and we raided the house where he was staying in Bogotá. Most of those we collared were harmless local people, hired as servants, though what they had to tell proved useful. López's mistress, accompanying him, turned out to be his associate. She told us a lot more, in exchange for comfortable accommodations when she'd go to the exile planet. But the ringleader himself had broken free and escaped.

"One man on horseback, headed for the Cordillera Oriental that rises beyond the town—one man like ten thousand genuine Creoles—we couldn't go after him on time hoppers. The search could too damn easily get too damn noticeable. Who knew what effect that might have? The conspirators had already made the time stream unstable. . . .

"I grabbed a horse, a couple of remounts, some jerky and vitamin pills for myself, and set off in pursuit."

Wind boomed hollowly down the mountainside. Grass and low, scattered shrubs trembled beneath its chill. Up ahead, they gave way to naked rock. Right, left, behind, peaks reared into a blue bleakness. A condor wheeled huge, on watch for any death. Snowfields on the heights above glowed beneath a declining sun.

A musket cracked. At its distance, the noise it made was tiny, though echoes flew. Everard heard the bullet buzz. Close! He hunched down in the saddle and spurred his steed onward.

Varagan can't really expect to drop me at this range, passed through him. *What, then? Does he hope I'll slow down? If so, if he gains a little on me, what use is that to him? What goal has he got?*

His enemy still led him by half a mile, but Everard could see how yonder animal lurched along, exhausted. To get on Varagan's trail had taken some while, going from this peon to that sheepherder and asking if a man of the given description had ridden by. However, Varagan had only the single horse, which he must spare if it was not to collapse under him. After Everard found

the traces, a wilderness-trained eye had readily been able to follow them, and
the pace of the hunt picked up.

It was also known that Varagan had fled bearing no more than a
muzzle-loader. He'd been spending powder and balls pretty freely ever since
the Patrolman hove in view. Since he was a fast recharger and an excellent
shot, it did have its delaying effect. But what refuge was in these wastes?
Varagan appeared to be making for a particular crag. It was conspicuous, not
only high but its shape suggestive of a castle tower. It was no fortress, though.
If Varagan took shelter behind it, Everard could use the blaster he carried to
bring the rock molten down upon his head.

Maybe Varagan wasn't aware the agent had such a weapon. Impossible.
Varagan was a monster, yes, but not a fool.

Everard pulled down his hat brim and drew his poncho tight against the
wind. He didn't reach for the blaster, no point in that yet, but as if by instinct,
his left hand dropped to the flintlock pistol and saber at his hip. They were
mainly part of his costume, intended to make him an authority figure to the
inhabitants, but there was an odd comfort in their massiveness.

Having reined in to shoot, Varagan continued straight on uphill, this time
without lingering to reload. Everard brought his own horse from trot to canter
and closed the gap further. He kept alert—not tensed, but alert against
contingencies, ready to swing aside or even jump down behind the beast.
Nothing happened, just that lonesome trek on through the cold. Could Varagan
have fired his last ammunition? *Have a care, Manse, old son.* The sparse
alpine grass ended, save for tufts between boulders, and rock rang beneath
hoofs.

Varagan halted near the crag and sat waiting. The musket was sheathed and
his hands rested empty on the saddlebow. His horse quivered and swayed,
neck a-droop, utterly blown, lather swept freezingly off its hide and out of its
mane.

Everard took forth his energy gun and clattered nigh. Behind him, a
remount whickered. Still Varagan waited.

Everard stopped three yards off. "Merau Varagan, you are under arrest by
the Time Patrol," he called in Temporal.

The other smiled. "You have the advantage of me," he replied in a soft tone
that, somehow, carried. "May I request the honor of learning your name and
provenance?"

"Uh . . . Manson Everard, Unattached, born in the United States of
America about a hundred years uptime. No matter. You're coming back with
me. Hold on while I call a hopper. I warn you, at the least suspicion you're
about to try something, I'll shoot. You're too dangerous for me to be
squeamish."

Varagan made a gentle gesture. "Really? How much do you know about me, Agent Everard, or think you know, to justify this violent an attitude?"

"Well, when a man takes potshots at me, I reckon he's not a very nice person."

"Might I perhaps have believed you were a bandit, of the sort who haunt these uplands? What crime am I alleged to have committed?"

Everard's free hand paused on its way to get out the little communicator in his pocket. For a moment, eerily fascinated, he stared through the wind at his prisoner.

Merau Varagan seemed taller than he actually was, as straight as he held his athletic frame. Black hair tossed around a skin whose whiteness the sun and the weather had not tinged at all. There was no sign of beard. The face might have been a young Caesar's, were it not too finely chiseled. The eyes were large and green, the smiling lips cherry-red. His clothes, down to the boots, were silver-trimmed black, like the cape that flapped about his shoulders. Seen against the turreted crag, he made Everard remember Dracula.

Yet his voice remained mild: "Evidently your colleagues have extracted information from mine. I daresay you have been in touch with them as you fared. Thus you know our names and somewhat of our origin—"

Thirty-first millennium. Outlaws after the failure of the Exaltationists to cast off the weight of a civilization grown older than the Old Stone Age was to me. During their moment of power, they possessed themselves of time machines. Their genetic heritage—

Nietzsche might have understood them. I never will.

"—But what do you truly know of our purpose here?"

"You were going to change events," Everard retorted. "We barely forestalled you. At that, our corps has a lot of tricky restoration work ahead. Why did you do it? How could you be so . . . so selfish?"

"I think 'egoistic' might be a better word," Varagan gibed. "The ascendancy of the ego, the unconfined will— But think. Would it have been altogether bad if Simón Bolívar had founded a true empire in Hispanic America, rather than a gaggle of quarrelsome successor states? It would have been enlightened, progressive. Imagine how much suffering and death would have been averted."

"Come off that!" Everard felt anger rise and rise within himself. "You must know better. It's impossible. Bolívar hasn't the cadre, the communications, the support. If he's a hero to many, he's at least got many others furious with him: like the Peruvians, after he detached Bolivia. He'll cry on his deathbed that he 'plowed the sea' in all his efforts to build a stable society.

"If you meant it about unifying even part of the continent, you'd have tried earlier and elsewhere."

"Indeed?"

"Yes. The only chance. I've studied the situation. In 1821 San Martín was negotiating with the Spanish in Perú, and playing with the idea of setting up a monarchy under somebody like Don Carlos, King Ferdinand's brother. It could have included the territories of Bolivia and Ecuador, maybe later Chile and Argentina, because it would have had the advantages Bolívar's inner sphere lacks. But why am I telling you this, you bastard, except to prove I know you're lying? You must have done your own homework."

"What then do you suppose my real objective was?"

"Obvious. To make Bolívar overreach himself. He's an idealist, a dreamer, as well as a warrior. If he pushes too hard, everything hereabouts will break up in a chaos that could well spread to the rest of South America. And there would be your chance for seizing power!"

Varagan shrugged, as a were-cat might have shrugged. "Concede me this much," he said, "that such an empire would have had a certain dark magnificence."

The hopper flashed into being and hovered twenty feet aloft. Its rider grinned and aimed the firearm he carried. From the saddle of his horse, Merau Varagan waved at his time-traveling self.

Everard never quite knew what happened next. Somehow he made it out of the stirrups and onto the ground. His horse screamed as an energy bolt struck. Smoke and a stench of seared flesh spurted forth. Even while the slain animal crumpled, Everard shot back from behind it.

The enemy hopper must veer. Everard skipped clear of the falling mass and maintained fire, upward and sideways. Varagan leaped from his own horse, behind the rock. Lightnings blazed and crackled. Everard's free hand yanked forth his communicator and thumbed the Mayday spot.

The vehicle dropped, rearward of the crag. Displaced air made a popping noise. Wind blew away the stinging ozone.

A Patrol machine appeared. It was too late. Merau Varagan had already borne his earlier self away to an unknowable point of space-time.

Everard nodded heavily. "Yeah," he finished, "that was his scheme, and it worked, God damn it. Reach an obvious landmark and note the time on his watch. That meant he'd know, later along his world line, where-when to go, in mounting his rescue operation."

The Zorachs were appalled. "But, but a causal loop of that sort," Chaim stammered, "didn't he have any idea of the dangers?"

"Doubtless he did, including the possibility that he would make himself never have existed," Everard replied. "But then, he'd been quite prepared to wipe out an entire future, in favor of a history where he could have ridden high. He's totally fearless, the ultimate desperado. That was built into the genes of the Exaltationist princes."

He sighed. "They lack loyalty, also. Varagan, and whatever associates he had left, made no attempt to save those we'd captured. They just vanished. We've been wary of their reappearance ever 'since then,' and this new caper does bear similarities to that one. But of course—time loop hazard again—I can't go read whatever report I'll have filed at the conclusion of the present affair. If it has a conclusion, and if I don't."

Yael patted his hand. "I'm sure you'll prevail, Manse," she said. "What happened next in South America?"

"Oh, once the bad counsel, which he hadn't recognized was bad—once they stopped, Bolívar went back to his natural ways," Everard told them. "He made a peaceful settlement with Páez and issued a general amnesty. More troubles broke out later, but he handled them capably and humanely, too, while fostering both the interests and the culture of his people. When he died, most of the great wealth he'd inherited was gone, because he'd never taken a centavo of public money for himself. A good ruler, one of the few that humankind will ever know.

"So's Hiram, I gather—and now his rule is threatened likewise, by whatever devil is loose in the world."

When Everard emerged, sure enough, there was Pum waiting. The boy skipped to meet him.

"Where would my glorious master go today?" he caroled. "Let his servant conduct him whithersoever he wills. Perhaps to visit Conor the amber factor?"

"Huh?" In slight shock, the Patrolman goggled at the native. "What makes you think I've aught to do with . . . any such person?"

Pum returned a look whose deference failed to mask its shrewdness. "Did not my lord declare this was his intention, while aboard Mago's ship?"

"How do you know that?" Everard barked.

"Why, I sought out men of the crew, engaged them in talk, lured forth their memories. Not that your humble servant would pry into that which he should not hear. If I have transgressed, I abase myself and beg forgiveness. My aim was merely to learn more of my master's plans in order that I might think how best to assist them." Pum beamed in undiminished cockiness.

"Oh. I see." Everard tugged his mustache and peered around. Nobody else was in earshot. "Well, then, know that that was a pretense. My true business is different." *As you must have guessed already, from the fact of my going straight to Zakarbaal and lodging with him,* he added silently. This was far from the first time that experience reminded him that people in any given era could be intrinsically as sharp as anybody futureward of them.

"Ah, indeed! Business of the greatest moment, assuredly. The lips of my master's servant are sealed."

"Understand that my aims are in no way hostile. Sidon is friendly to Tyre. Let's say I'm involved in an effort to organize a large joint venture."

"To increase trade with my master's people? Ah, but then you do want to visit your countryman Conor, no?"

"I do not!" Everard realized he had shouted. He curbed his temper. "Conor is not my countryman, not in the way that Mago is yours. My folk have no single country. Aye, most likely Conor and I would not be understanding each other's languages."

That was more than likely. Everard had too much intellectual baggage to carry as was, information about Phoenicia, to pile on a heap about the Celts. The electronic calculator had simply taught him enough to pass for one among outsiders who didn't know them intimately—he hoped.

"What I've in mind," he said, "is just to stroll about the city today, whilst Zakarbaal seeks to get me an audience with the king." He smiled. "Sure, and for this I could well put myself in your hands, lad."

Pum's laughter pealed. He clapped his palms together. "Ah, my lord is wise! Come evening, let him deem whether or not he was led to pleasure and, yes, knowledge such as he seeks, and perhaps he . . . will in his magnanimity see fit to bestow largesse on his guide."

Everard grinned. "Give me the grand tour, then."

Pum assumed shyness. "May we first seek the Street of the Tailors? Yesterday I took it upon myself to order new garb that should be ready now. The cost will bear hard on a poor youth, despite the munificence his master has already shown, for I must pay for speed as well as fine material. Yet it is not fitting that a great lord's attendant should go in rags like these."

Everard groaned, though he didn't really mind. "I catch your drift. Och, how I do! 'Tis unsuited to my dignity that you buy your own garments. Well, let's go, and 'tis I will be standing you your coat of many colors."

Hiram did not quite resemble his average subject. He was taller, lighter-complexioned, hair and beard reddish, eyes gray, nose straight. His appearance recalled the Sea Peoples—that buccaneer horde of displaced Cretans and European barbarians, some of them from the far North, who raided Egypt a couple of centuries before, and eventually became the principal ancestors of the Philistines. A lesser number, ending up in Lebanon and Syria, interbred with certain Bedouin types who were themselves getting interested in nautical things. From that cross arose the Phoenicians. The invader blood still showed in their aristocrats.

Soloman's palace, of which the Bible was to boast, would when finished be a cut-rate imitation of the house in which Hiram already dwelt. The king himself, though, usually went simply clad, in a white linen kaftan with purple trim, slippers of fine leather, a gold headband and a massive ruby ring to signify royalty. His manner, likewise, was direct and unaffected. Middle-aged, he looked younger, and his vigor remained unabated.

He and Everard sat in a room broad, gracious, and airy, that opened on a cloister garden and fish pond. The carpet was of straw, but dyed in fine patterns. Frescoes on the plaster walls had been done by an artist imported from Babylonia, depicting arbors, flowers, and winged chimeras. A low table between the men was of ebony inlaid with mother-of-pearl. It held unwatered wine in glass cups, and dishes of fruit, bread, cheese, sweets. A pretty girl in a diaphanous gown knelt nearby and strummed a lyre. Two manservants awaited orders in the background.

"You are being right mysterious, Eborix," murmured Hiram.

"Sure, and 'tis not my wish to withhold aught from your highness," Everard replied carefully. A word of command could bring in guardsmen to kill him. No, that was unlikely; a guest was sacred. But if he offended the king, his whole mission was compromised. "Aye, vague I am about certain things, but only because my knowledge of them is slight. Nor would I risk laying baseless charges against anyone, should my information prove in error."

Hiram bridged his fingers and frowned. "Still, you claim to bear word of danger—word which contradicts what you have said elsewhere. You are scarcely the bluff warrior you pass yourself off as."

Everard constructed a smile. "My lord in his wisdom knows well that an unlettered tribesman is not necessarily a fool. To him I admit having, ah, earlier shaded the truth a wee bit. 'Twas because I had to, even as any Tyrian tradesman does in the normal course of business. Is that not so?"

Hiram laughed and relaxed. "Say on. If you are a rogue, you are at least an interesting one."

Patrol psychologists had invested considerable thought in Everard's yarn. There was no way for it to be immediately convincing, nor was that desirable; the king should not be stampeded into actions that might change known history. Yet the tale must be sufficiently plausible that he would cooperate in the investigation which was Everard's real purpose.

"Know, then, O lord, that my father was a chieftain in a mountain land far over the waves"—the Hallstatt region of Austria.

Eborix went on to relate how various Celts who had been among the Sea Peoples fled back there after the shattering defeat which Rameses III inflicted on those quasi-vikings in 1149 B.C. Their descendants had maintained tenuous connection, mostly along the amber route, with the descendants of kinsmen who settled in Canaan by leave of victorious Pharaoh. Old ambitions were unforgotten; Celts have always had a long racial memory. Talk went on about reviving the great Mediterranean push. That dream strengthened as wave after wave of barbarians came down into Greece, over the wreckage of Mycenaean civilization, and chaos spread through the Adriatic and far into Anatolia.

Eborix knew of spies who had also served as emissaries to the kings of the Philistine city-states. Tyre's amicability toward the Jews did not exactly endear it to the Philistines; and of course the riches of Phoenicia provided ever more temptation. Schemes developed fitfully, slowly, over a period of generations. Eborix himself was not sure how far along arrangements might be, to bring south an army of Celtic adventurers.

To Hiram he admitted frankly that he would have considered joining such a troop, his handfast men at his back. However, a feud between clans had ended in the overthrow and slaying of his father. Eborix had barely escaped alive. Wanting revenge as much as he wanted to mend his fortunes, he made the trek hither. A Tyre grateful for his warning might, if nothing else, give him the means to hire soldiers of his own and bring them home to reinstate him.

"You offer me no proof," said the king slowly, "naught but your naked word."

Everard nodded. "My lord sees clearly as Ra, the Falcon of Egypt. Did I not agree beforehand that I could be mistaken, that there may in truth be no real menace, just the scutterings and chatterings of vainglorious apes? Nonetheless I do urge that my lord have the matter looked into as closely as may be, for safety's sake. In that effort, 'tis I his servant that could be of help. Not only do I know my folk and their ways, but in wandering across their continent I met many different tribes, aye, and civilized nations too. I might therefore be a better hound than most, upon this particular scent."

Hiram tugged his beard. "Perhaps. Such a conspiracy must needs involve more than a few wild mountaineers and Philistine magnates. Men of several origins—but foreigners come and go like vagrant breezes. Who shall track the wind?"

Everard's heart slugged. Here was the moment toward which he had striven. "Your highness, I've thought much upon this, and the gods have sent me some ideas. I'm thinking we should first search not for common merchants, skippers, and seamen, but for strangers from lands which Tyrians have seldom or never visited, strangers who ask questions that often do not pertain to trade, or even to ordinary inquisitiveness. They would be inserting themselves into high places as well as low, seeking to learn everything. Does my lord recall any such?"

Hiram shook his head. "No, none unaccountable like that. And I would have heard about them and wanted to see them. My followers are aware of how I always hunger for new knowledge, fresh news." He chuckled. "As witness the fact I was willing to receive you."

Everard swallowed his disappointment. It tasted sour. *But I shouldn't have imagined the enemy would be openly active now, this close to the time when he's going to strike. He'd know the Patrol would be busy. No, he'd do his preliminary research, acquire his detailed information about Phoenicia and its vulnerabilities, earlier. Maybe quite a bit earlier.*

"My lord," he said, "if there is indeed a menace, it must have been a long while in the egg. Dare I ask your highness to think back? The king in his omniscience might recollect something from years agone."

Hiram lowered his gaze and concentrated. Sweat prickled Everard's skin. He forced himself to sit still. Finally, softly, he heard:

"Well, late in the reign of my illustrious father King Abibaal . . . yes . . . he had certain guests for a spell, about whom rumors flew. They were not of any land familiar to us. . . . Seekers of wisdom from the Far East, they said. . . . What was the name of their country? Shee-an? No, belike not." Hiram sighed. "Memory fades. Especially memory of mere words."

"My lord did not meet them himself, then?"

"No, I was gone, spending some years in travel through our hinterlands and abroad, so as to prepare myself for the throne. And now Abibaal sleeps with his fathers. As, I fear, do well-nigh all who may have encountered those men."

Everard suppressed a sigh of his own and struggled to ease off. The lead was fog-tenuous, if it was a lead. But what could he expect? The enemy wouldn't have left engraved announcements.

Nobody here kept journals or saved letters, nor did anybody number years in the manner of later civilizations. Everard would not be able to learn precisely when Abibaal entertained his curious visitors. The Patrolman would be lucky to find one or two individuals who remembered them well. Hiram had reigned for two decades now, and life expectancy was not great.

I've got to try, though. It's the single lonely clue I've turned up. Or else it's a false scent, of course. Those could have been legitimate contemporaries— explorers from Chou Dynasty China, maybe.

He cleared his throat. "Does my lord grant permission for his servant to ask questions, in the royal household as well as in the city? I'm thinking that humble folk might speak a little more free and open before a plain fellow like me, than they would in the awe of his highness's presence."

Hiram smiled. "For a plain fellow, Eborix, you've a smooth tongue. But—yes, you may try. Abide for a while as my guest, with your young footman whom I noticed outside. We'll talk further. If nothing else, you are a fanciful talker."

A page conducted Everard and Pum through corridors to their quarters, as evening closed. "The noble visitor will dine with the guards officers and men of like rank, unless he is bidden to the royal board," he explained obsequiously. "His attendant is welcome at the freeborn servants' mess. If aught be desired, let him only inform a butler or steward; his highness's generosity knows no bounds."

Everard resolved not to try that generosity too far. The household seemed more status-conscious than Tyrians generally were—no doubt the presence of many out-and-out slaves reinforced that—but Hiram was probably not above thrift.

Yet when the Patrolman reached his room, he found that the king was a thoughtful host. Hiram must have issued orders after their discussion, while the newcomers were shown the rights of the palace and given a light supper.

The chamber was large, well-furnished, lit by several lamps. A window, which could be shuttered, overlooked a court where flowers and pomegranates grew. Doors were solid wood on bronze hinges. The interior one stood open on an adjacent cubicle, sufficient for a straw tick and a pot, where Pum would sleep.

Everard halted. Lamplight fell soft over carpet, draperies, chairs, a table, a cedar chest, a double bed. Shadows stirred as a young woman arose and genuflected.

"Does my lord wish more?" asked the page. "If not, let this lowly person bid him a good night." He bowed and departed.

Breath hissed between Pum's teeth. "Master, she's beautiful!"

Everard's cheeks smoldered. "Uh-huh. Good night to you, too, lad."

"Noble sir—"

"Good night, I said."

Plum rolled eyes toward the ceiling, shrugged elaborately, and trudged to his kennel. The door slammed behind him.

"Stand straight, my dear," Everard mumbled. "Don't be afraid. I'd never hurt you."

The woman obeyed, arms crossed over bosom and head meekly lowered. She was tall for this milieu, slender, stacked. The wispy gown decked a fair skin. The hair knotted loosely at her nape was ruddy-brown. Feeling almost diffident, he laid a finger beneath her chin. She lifted a face that was blue-eyed, pert-nosed, full-lipped, piquantly freckled.

"Who are you?" he wondered. His throat felt tight.

"Your handmaiden sent to attend you, lord." Her words bore a lilting foreign accent. "What is your pleasure?"

"I . . . I asked who you are. Your name, your people."

"They call me Pleshti, master."

"Because they can't pronounce your real name, I'll be bound, or won't bother to. What is it?"

She swallowed. Tears glimmered. "I was Bronwen once," she whispered.

Everard nodded to himself. Glancing around, he saw a jug of wine as well as water on the table, plus a beaker and a bowl of fruit. He took her hand. It lay small and tender in his. "Come," he said, "let's sit down, take refreshment, get acquainted. We'll share yon glass."

She shuddered and half shrank away. Sadness touched him afresh, though he achieved a smile. "Don't be afraid, Bronwen. I'm not leading up to anything that could hurt you. I simply wish us to be friends. You see, macushla, I think you're of my folk."

She fought off the weeping, squared her shoulders, and gulped, "My lord is, is g-godlike in his kindness. How shall I ever thank him?"

Everard led her to the table, got her seated, and poured. Before long her story came forth.

It was all too ordinary. Though her concepts of geography were vague, he deduced that she belonged to a Celtic tribe which had migrated south from the Danubian *Urheimat*. Hers was a village at the head of the Adriatic Sea, and she had been the daughter of a well-to-do yeoman, as Bronze Age primitives reckoned prosperity.

She hadn't counted birthdays before nor years after, but he figured she was about thirteen when the Tyrians came, about a decade ago. They were in a single ship, boldly questing north in search of new trade possibilities. They camped on the shore and dickered in sign language. Evidently they decided there was nothing worth coming back for, because when they left, they kidnapped several children who had wandered near to look at the marvelous foreigners. Bronwen was among them.

The Tyrians hadn't raped their female captives, nor mistreated any of either sex more than they found necessary. A virgin in sound condition was worth too much on the slave market. Everard admitted that he couldn't even call the sailors evil. They had just done what came naturally in the ancient world, and most subsequent history for that matter.

Bronwen lucked out, everything considered. She was acquired for the palace: not the royal harem, though the king had had her unofficially a few times, but for him to lend to such houseguests as he would favor. Men were seldom deliberately cruel to her. The pain that never ended lay in being captive among aliens.

That, and her children. She had borne four over the years, of whom two died in infancy—a good record, especially when they hadn't cost her much in the way of teeth or health. The surviving pair were still small. The girl would probably become a concubine too when she reached puberty, unless she was passed on to a brothel. (Slave women did not get deflowered as a religious rite. Who cared about their fortunes in later life?) The boy would probably be castrated at that age, since his upbringing at court would have made him a potential harem attendant.

As for Bronwen, when she lost her looks she'd be assigned to labor. Not having been trained in skills such as weaving, she'd likeliest end in the scullery or at a quern.

Everard had to coax all this out of her, piece by harsh little piece. She didn't lament nor beg. Her fate was what it was. He remembered a line Thucydides would pen centuries hence, about the disastrous Athenian military expedition whose last members ended their days in the mines of Sicily. "Having done what men could, they suffered what men must."

And women. Especially women. He wondered if, way down inside, he had Bronwen's courage. He doubted it.

About himself he was short-spoken. After avoiding one Celt and then getting another thrust upon him, so to speak, he felt he'd better play very close to his vest.

Nonetheless, at last she looked at him, flushed, aglow, and said in a slightly wine-slurred voice, "Oh, Eborix—" He couldn't follow the rest.

"I fear my tongue is too unlike yours, my dear," he said.

She returned to Punic: "Eborix, how generous of Asherat that she brought me to you for, for whatever time she grants. How wonderful. Now come, sweet lord, let your handmaiden give you back some of the joy—" She rose, came around the table, cast her warmth and suppleness into his lap.

He had already consulted his conscience. If he didn't do what everybody expected, word was bound to reach the king. Hiram might well take umbrage, or wonder what was wrong with his guest. Bronwen herself would be hurt, bewildered; she might get in trouble. Besides, she was lovely, and he'd been much deprived. Poor Sarai scarcely counted.

He gathered Bronwen to him.

Intelligent, observant, sensitive, she had well learned how to please a man. He hadn't figured on more than once, but she changed his mind about that, more than once. Her own ardor didn't seem faked, either, Well, he was probably the first man who had ever tried to please *her*. After the second round, she whispered brokenly into his ear: "I've . . . borne no further . . . these past three years. How I am praying the goddess will open my womb for you, Eborix, Eborix—"

He didn't remind her that any such child would be a slave also.

Yet before they slept she murmured something else, which he thought she might well not have let slip if she were fully awake: "We have been one flesh tonight, my lord, and may we be so often again. But know that I know we are not of one people."

"What?" An iciness stabbed him. He sat bolt upright.

She snuggled close. "Lie down, my heart. Never, never will I betray you. But . . . I remember enough things from home, small things, and I do not believe Geyils in the mountains can be that different from Geyils by the sea . . . Hush, hush, your secret is safe. Why should Bronwen Brannoch's daughter betray the only person here who ever cared about her? Sleep, my nameless darling, sleep well in my arms."

At dawn a servant roused Everard—apologizing, flattering all the while— and took him away to a hot bath. Soap was for the future, but a sponge and a pumice stone scrubbed his skin, and afterward the servant gave him a rubdown with fragrant oil and a deft shave. He met the guards officers, then, for a meager breakfast and lively conversation.

"I'm going off duty today," proposed a man among them. "What say we ferry over to Usu, friend Eborix? I'll show you around. Later, if daylight remains, we can go for a ride outside the walls." Everard wasn't sure whether that would be on a donkeyback or, more swiftly if less comfortably, in a war chariot. To date, horses were almost always draft animals, too valuable for any purposes but combat and pomp.

"Many thanks," the Patrolman answered. "First, though, I've need to see a woman called Sarai. She works in the steward's department."

Brows lifted. "What," scoffed a soldier, "do you Northerners prefer grubby housekeepers to the king's choice?"

What a gossipy village the palace is, Everard thought. *I'd better restore my reputation fast*. He sat straight, cast a cold look across the table, and growled, "I am present at the king's behest, to conduct inquiries that are no concern of anybody else's. Is that clear, gossoon?"

"Oh, yes, oh, yes! I did but jest, noble sir. Wait, I'll go find somebody who'll know where she is." The man scrambled from his bench.

Guided to an offside room, Everard had a few minutes alone. He spent them reflecting upon his sense of urgency. Theoretically, he had as much time as he wanted; if need be, he could always double back, provided he took care to keep people from seeing him next to himself. In practice, that entailed risks acceptable only in the worst emergencies. Besides the chance of starting a causal loop that might expand out of control, there was the possibility of something going wrong in the mundane course of events. The likelihood of that would increase as the operation grew more long-drawn and complex. Then too, he had a natural impatience to get on with his job, complete it, nail down the existence of the world that begot him.

A dumpy figure parted the door curtain. Sarai knelt before him. "Your adorer awaits her lord's bidding," she said in a slightly uneven voice.

"Rise," Everard told her. "Be at ease. I want no more than to ask a question or two of you."

Her eyelids fluttered. She blushed to the end of her large nose. "Whatever my lord commands, she who owes him so much shall strive to fulfill."

He understood she was being neither slavish nor coquettish. She neither invited nor expected forwardness on his part. Once she had made her sacrifice to the goddess, a pious Phoenician woman stayed chaste. Sarai was simply, humbly grateful to him. He felt touched.

"Be at ease," he repeated. "Let your mind roam free. On behalf of the king, I seek knowledge of certain men who once visited his father, late in the life of glorious Abibaal."

Her gaze widened. "Master, I can scarcely have been born."

"I know. But what of older attendants? You must know everybody on the staff. A few might remain who served in those days. Would you inquire among them?"

She touched brow, lips, bosom, the sign of obedience. "Since my lord wills it."

He passed on what scant information he had. It disturbed her. "I fear—I fear naught will come of this," she said. "My lord must have seen how much we make of foreigners. If any were as peculiar as that, the servants would talk about them for the rest of their days." She smiled wryly. "After all, we've no great store of newness, we menials within the palace walls. We chew our gossip over and over again. I think I would have heard about those men, were anybody left who remembered them."

Everard cursed to himself in several languages. *Looks like I'll have to go back to Usu in person, twenty-odd years ago, and scratch around—regardless of the danger of my machine getting detected by the enemy and alerting him, or me getting killed.* "Well," he said, strained, "ask anyway, will you? If you learn nothing, that won't be your fault."

"No," she breathed, "but it will be my sorrow, kind lord." She knelt again before she departed.

Everard went to join his acquaintance. He had no real hope of discovering a clue on the mainland today, but the jaunt should work some tension out of him.

The sun was low when they came back to the island. A thin mist lay over the sea, diffusing light, making the high walls of Tyre golden, not altogether real, like an elven castle that might at any moment glimmer away into nothingness. Landing, Everard found that most dwellers had gone home. The soldier, who had a family, bade farewell, and the Patrolman made his way to the palace through streets that, after their daytime bustle, seemed ghostly.

A dark shape stood beside the royal porch, ignored by the sentries. Those climbed to their feet and hefted their spears as Everard approached, prepared to check his identity. Standing at attention had never been thought of. The woman scuttled to intercept him. As she bent the knee, he recognized Sarai.

His heart sprang. "What do you want?" ripped from him.

"Lord, I have been awaiting your return much of this day, for it seemed you were anxious to get whatever word I might bear."

She must have delegated her regular duties. The street had been hot, hour after hour. "You . . . have found something?"

"Perhaps, master; perhaps a scrap. Would it were more."

"Speak, for—for Melqart's sake!"

"For yours, lord, yours, since you did ask this of your servant." Sarai drew breath. Her gaze met his, and stayed. Her tone became strong, matter-of-fact:

"As I feared, of those few retainers who are old enough, none had the knowledge you seek. They had not yet entered service, or if they had, they worked elsewhere for King Abibaal than at the palace—on a farm or a summer estate or some such place. At best, a man or two said he might have heard a little talk once; but what he remembered about that was no more than what my lord had already conveyed to me. I despaired, until I thought to seek a shrine of Asherat. I prayed that she be gracious unto you who had served her through me, when for so long no other man would. And lo, she answered. Praises be unto her. I recalled that an under-groom named Jantin-hamu has a father alive who was formerly on the steward's staff. I sought Jantin-hamu out, and he brought me to Bomilcar, and, aye, Bomilcar can tell about those strangers."

"Why, that, that is splendid," he blurted. "I don't believe I myself could ever have done what you did. I wouldn't have known."

"Now I pray that this may prove to be in truth helpful to my lord," she said mutedly, "he who was good to an ugly hill-woman. Come, I will guide you."

—In filial piety, Jantin-hamu gave his father a place in the one-room apartment he shared with his wife and a couple of children still dependent on them. A single lamp picked out, through monstrous shadows, the straw pallets, stools, clay jugs, brazier that were about all the furniture. The woman cooked in a kitchen shared with other tenants, then brought the food here to eat; the air was close and greasy. Everybody else squatted, staring, while Everard interrogated Bomilcar.

The old man was bald except for white remnants of beard, toothless, half deaf, gnarled and crippled by arthritis, eyes turned milky by cataracts. (His chronological age must be about sixty. So much for the back-to-nature crowd in twentieth-century America.) He hunched on a stool, hands weakly clasped around a stick. His mind worked, though—reached forth out of the ruin where it was trapped like a plant reaching for sunlight.

"Aye, aye, they come and stand before me as I speak, as if 'twere yesterday. Could I but remember that well what happened in the real yesterday. Well, nothing did, nothing ever does anymore. . . .

"Seven, they were, who said they had come on a ship from the Hittite coast. Now young Matinbaal got curious, he did, and went down and asked around, and never found a skipper who'd carried any such passengers. Well, maybe 'twas a ship that went right onward, toward Philistia or Egypt. . . . Sinim they called themselves, and told of faring thousands upon thousands of leagues from the Sunrise Lands, that they might bring home an account of the world to their king. They spoke fair Punic, albeit with an accent like none else I ever heard. . . . Taller than most, well built; they walked like wildcats, and were as mannerly and, I guessed, as dangerous if aroused. No beards; 'twasn't that they shaved, their faces were hairless, like women's. Not eunuchs, however, no, the wenches lent 'em were soon sitting down careful, heh, heh. Their eyes were light, their skins whiter even than a yellow-haired Achaean's, but *their* straight locks were raven-black. . . . Ever there was an air of wizardry about them, and I heard tales of eldritch things they'd shown the king. Be that as it may, they did no harm, they were only curious, oh, how curious about every least thing in Usu, and about the plans that were then being drawn up for Tyre. They won the king's heart; he commanded they see and hear whatever they liked, though it be the deepest secrets of a sanctuary or a merchant house. . . . I did often wonder, afterward, if this was what provoked the gods against them."

Judas priest! slashed through Everard. *That's almost got to be my enemies. Yes, them, Exaltationists, Varagan's gang. "Sinim"—Chinese? A red herring, in case the Patrol stumbled onto their trail? No, I suspect not, I think probably they just used that alias so as to have a ready-made story to hand Abibaal and his court. For they didn't bother to disguise their appearance. As in South America, Varagan must have felt sure his cleverness would be too much for the plodding Patrol. Which it might well have been, except for Sarai.*

Not that I'm very far along on the trail yet.

"What became of them?" he demanded.

"Ah, that was a pity, unless it was punishment for something wrong they did, like maybe poking into a Holy of Holies." Bomilcar clicked his tongue and wagged his head. "After several weeks, they asked leave to go. 'Twas late in the season, most ships were already put away for the winter, but against advice they offered a rich payment for passage to Cyprus, and got a daring skipper to agree. I went down to the wharf myself to watch them depart, I did. A cold, blustery day, 'twas. I watched that ship dwindle away under the racing clouds till she vanished in the brume, and something made me stop by the temple of Tanith on my way back and put oil in a lamp—not for them, understand, but for all poor mariners, on whom rests the well-being of Tyre."

Everard restrained himself from shaking that withered frame. "And then? Anything?"

"Aye, my feeling was right. My feelings have always been right, haven't they, Jantin-hamu? Always. I should've been a priest, but too many boys were trying for what few acolytes' berths there were. . . . Ah, yes. That day a gale sprang up. The ship foundered. Everybody lost. I heard about that, I did, because we naturally wanted to know what'd happened to those strangers. Her figurehead and some other bits and pieces drifted onto the rocks where this city now is."

"But—wait, gaffer—are you sure everybody drowned?"

"No, I suppose I couldn't swear to that, no. I suppose a man or two could've clung to a plank and been borne ashore likewise. They'd've made landfall elsewhere and trudged home unremarked. Who in the palace cares about a common sailor? Certain is, the ship was lost, and the Sinim—for if *they'd* returned, we'd know, wouldn't we, now?"

Everard's mind whirred. *Time travelers might well have arrived here by machine, directly. The Patrol base, with instruments to detect it, wasn't yet established. (We can't man every instant of the millennia. At best, at need, we send agents back and forth within a milieu, out of those stations we do keep.) If they weren't to cause a sensation that would endure, though, they would have to depart in contemporary wise, by land or sea. But surely, before embarking, they'd have checked out what the weather was going to be like. Ships in this age practically never sail during the winter; they're too fragile.*

Could this be a false scent regardless? Bomilcar's memory may not be as clear as he claims. And the visitors could have been from one of those odd, short-lived little civilizations that history and archaeology afterward lost sight of, and time-traveling scientists discover mainly by accident. For instance, a city-state off in the Anatolian mountains somewhere, which'd learned things from the Hittites, and whose aristocracy is so inbred that its members have a unique physiognomy—

On the other hand, of course, this could be the real means of breaking the trail, this shipwreck. That would explain why enemy agents didn't trouble to make themselves look Chinese.

How to find out, before Tyre explodes?

"When did this happen, Bomilcar?" he asked as gently as he was able.

"Why, I told you," the old man said. "Back in the days of King Abibaal, when I worked for his steward in the palace in Usu."

Everard felt acutely, annoyingly conscious of the family around and their eyes. He heard them breathe. The lamp guttered, shadows thickened, the air was cooling fast. "Could you tell me more closely?" he pursued. "Do you recall which year of Abibaal's reign it was?"

"No. No. Nor anything else special. Let me think. . . . Was it two years, or three, after Captain Rib-adi brought back such a treasure trove from— from—where was it? Somewhere beyond Tharshish. . . . No, wasn't that later? . . . My first wife died in childbed a while afterward, that I remember, but 'twas several years before I could arrange a second marriage, and meanwhile I had to make do with harlots, heh, heh. . . ." With the abruptness of the aged, Bomilcar's mood changed. Tears trickled forth. "And my second wife, my Batbaal, she died too, of a fever. . . . Crazed, she was, didn't know me any longer. . . . Don't plague me, my lord, don't plague me, leave me in peace and darkness and the gods will bless you."

I'll get nothing further here. What did I get? Maybe nothing.

Before he went, Everard made Jantin-hamu a present of metal which should allow the family to live in more comfort. The ancient world had some few advantages over his; it was free of gift and income taxes.

A couple of hours past sunset, Everard returned to the palace. That was late in local eyes. The sentries raised rushlights, squinted at him, and summoned their officer. When Eborix had been identified, they let him in with apologies. His indulgent laugh was better than a large tip would have been.

He didn't really feel like laughing. Lips gone tight, he followed a lamp bearer to his room.

Bronwen lay asleep. A single flame still burned. He undressed and stood for a minute or three looking down at her through the flickery dimness. Unbound, her hair glowed across the pillow. One arm, out of the blanket, didn't quite cover a bare young breast. It was her face he regarded, though. How innocent she looked, childlike, woundable even now, even after everything she had endured.

If only. No. We may be a little bit in love already. But no possible way could it last, could we ever really live together, unless as a mere pair of bodies. Too much time sunders us.

What shall become of her?

He started to get into bed, intending simply slumber. She roused. Slaves learn to sleep alertly. He saw joy blossom in her. "My lord! Welcome, a thousand welcomes!"

They held each other close. Just the same, he found he wanted to talk with her. "How did your day go?" he asked into the warmth where her jaw met her ear.

"What? I—O master—" She was surprised that he would ask. "Why, it was pleasant, surely because your dear magic lingered. Your servant Pummairam and I chatted a long while." She giggled. "He's an engaging scoundrel, isn't he? Some of his questions struck too near the bone, but have no fear, my lord; those I refused to answer, and he backed off at once. Later I sallied forth, leaving word where I could be found should my lord return, and spent the afternoon in the nursery where my children are. They are such darlings." She didn't venture to inquire if he would care to meet them.

"Hm." A thought nudged Everard. "What did Pum do meanwhile?" *I can't see him sitting idle all day, that squirrel.*

"I know not. Well, I glimpsed him twice, on his errands down the corridors, but took it for given that my lord must have commanded—My lord?"

Alarmed, she sat straight as Everard left the bed. He flung open the door to the cubicle. It stood empty. What in hell was Pum up to?

Perhaps nothing much. Yet a servant who got into mischief might cause trouble for his master.

Standing there in a brown study, the floor cold beneath his feet, Everard grew aware of arms around his waist, and a cheek stroking across his shoulder blades, and a voice that crooned: "Is my lord overly weary? If so, let his handmaiden sing him a lullaby from her homeland. But if not—"

To hell with my worries. They'll keep. Everard turned his attention elsewhere, and himself.

The boy was still missing when the man awoke. Discreet questions revealed that he had spent hours the day before talking with various members of the staff. They agreed he was inquisitive and amusing. Finally he had gone out, and no one had seen him since.

Probably he got restless and flitted off to spend what I've given him in the wineshops and cathouses. Too bad. In spite of his scapegrace style, I thought he was basically reliable, and meant to do something or other that'd give him a chance at a better life.

Never mind. I've Patrol business on hand.

Everard excused himself from further activities and went alone into the city. As a hireling admitted him to the house of Zakarbaal, Yael Zorach appeared. Phoenician dress and hairdo became her charmingly well, but he was too preoccupied to appreciate it. The same strain showed on her features. "This way," she said, unwontedly curt, and led him to the inner chambers.

Her husband sat in conference with a craggy-faced bushy-bearded man whose costume varied in numerous ways from local male dress. "Oh, Manse," Chaim exclaimed. "What a relief. I wondered if we'd have to send for you, or what." He switched to Temporal: "Agent Manson Everard, Unattached, let me present Epsilon Korten, director of Jerusalem Base."

The other man rose in a future-military fashion and snapped a salute. "An honor, sir," he said. Nonetheless, his rank was not much below Everard's. He was responsible for temporal activities throughout the Hebrew lands, between the birth of David and the fall of Judah. Tyre might be more important in secular history, but it would never draw a tenth of the visitors from uptime that Jerusalem and its environs did. The position he held told Everard immediately that he was both a man of action and a scholar of profundity.

"I'll have Hanai bring in refreshments, and then tell the household to stay out of here and not let anybody in," Yael proposed.

Everard and Korten spent those minutes getting an acquaintance started. The latter was born in twenty-ninth-century New Edom on Mars. While he didn't brag, Everard gathered that his computer analyses of early Semitic texts had joined his exploits as a spaceman in the Second Asteroid War to attract Patrol recruiters. They sounded him out, got him to take tests which proved him trustworthy, revealed the existence of the organization, accepted his enlistment, trained him—the usual procedure. What was less usual was his level of competence. In many ways, his job was more demanding than Everard's.

"You'll understand that this situation is especially alarming to my office," he said when the foursome had settled down by themselves. "If Tyre is destroyed, Europe may take decades to show any major effects, the rest of the world centuries—millennia, in the Americas or Australasia. But it will be an immediate catastrophe for Solomon's kingdom. Lacking Hiram's support and the prestige it confers, he probably can't hold his tribes together long; and without Tyre at their backs, the Philistines won't be slow to seek revenge. Judaism, Yahwistic monotheism, is new and frail, still half pagan. My extrapolation is that it won't survive either. Yahweh will sink to being one more character in a crude and mutable pantheon."

"And there goes a good deal of Classical civilization," Everard added. "Judaism influenced philosophy as well as events among both the Alexandrine

Greeks and the Romans. Obviously, no Christianity, therefore no Western civilization, or Byzantine, or any of their successors. No telling what will arise instead." He thought of another altered world, which he had helped abort, and a wound twinged that he would bear throughout his life.

"Yes, of course," said Korten impatiently. "The point is, granted that the resources of the Patrol are finite—and, yes, spread terribly thin over a continuum that has many nexuses as critical as this one—I don't believe it should concentrate all available effort on rescuing Tyre. If that happens, and we fail, everything is lost; the chances of our being able to restore the original world become vanishingly small. No, let us establish a strong standby— personnel, organization, plans—in Jerusalem, ready to minimize the effects there. The less that Solomon's kingdom suffers, the less powerful the change vortex will be. That should give us more likelihood of damping it out altogether."

"Do you mean to, to write Tyre off?" Yael asked, dismayed.

"No, certainly not. But I do want us to have some insurance against its loss."

"That in itself is playing fast and loose with history." Chaim's tone trembled.

"I know. But extreme situations call for extreme measures. I came here first to discuss it with you, but please be advised that I intend to press for this policy in the highest echelons." Korten turned to Everard. "Sir, I regret the need to reduce further the slender resources you have at your command, but my judgment is that we must."

"They aren't slender," the American grumbled, "they're downright emaci-ated." *Following the preliminary legwork, what has the Patrol got here other than me?*

Does that mean the Danellians know I'll succeed? Or does it mean they'll agree with Korten—even, that Tyre is "already" doomed? If I fail—if I die—

He straightened, reached into his pouch for pipe and tobacco, and said: "My lady and gentlemen, this could too easily turn into a shouting match. Let's talk it over like reasonable people. The beginning of that is to assemble what hard facts we have, and look at them. Not that I've collected many so far."

The debate went on for hours.

It was afternoon before Yael suggested they break for food. "Thanks," Everard said, "but I think I'd better get back to the palace. Otherwise Hiram might suspect I'm loafing, at his expense. I'll check in again tomorrow, okay?"

The truth was that he had no appetite for the usual heavy meal of the day, roast lamb or whatever else it would be. He'd rather get a slab of bread and a hunk of goat cheese at some food stall, while he tried to sort out this new problem. (Thank technology again. Without the gene-tailored protective microbes the Patrol medics had implanted in him, he'd never have dared touch local stuff that wasn't cooked dead. And vaccinations against every sort of disease that came and went through the ages would long since have overloaded his immune system.)

Twentieth-century style, he shook hands all around. Korten might be wrong, or he might not be, but he was pleasant, able, and well-intentioned. Everard went forth into a street that brooded and simmered beneath the sun.

Pum waited. He rose less exuberantly than before. An odd gravity was on the thin young face. "Master," he breathed, "can we talk unheard?"

They found themselves a tavern where they were the only customers. In actuality, it was a lean-to roof shading a small area on which cushions lay; you sat cross-legged, and the landlord fetched clay goblets of wine from inside his home. Everard paid him in beads, after desultory haggling. Foot traffic swarmed and babbled up and down the street on which the shop intruded, but at this hour men were generally busied. They'd relax here, those who could afford to, when cooling shadows had fallen between the walls.

Everard sipped the thin, sour drink and grimaced. In his opinion, nobody understood wine before about the seventeenth century A.D. Beer was worse. No matter. "Speak, son," he said. "And you needn't waste breath or time calling me the radiance of the universe and offering to lie down for me to wipe my feet on. What have you been doing?"

Pum gulped, shivered, leaned forward. "O lord of mine," he began, and his voice broke in an adolescent squeak, "your underling has dared take much upon his head. Upbraid me, beat me, have me whipped, whatever your will may be, if I have transgressed. But never, I beg, never think I have sought anything but your welfare. My sole wish is to serve you as far as my poor abilities allow."

A brief grin flashed. "You see, you pay so well!"

Soberness returned: "You are a strong man, a man of great powers, in whose service I may hope to flourish. Now for that, I must prove myself worthy. Any lout can carry your baggage or lead you to a pleasure house. What can Pummairam do, over and above this, that my lord will wish to keep him as a retainer? Well, what does my lord require? What does he need?"

"Master, it pleases you to pose as a rude tribesman, but from the very first I had a feeling there was far more to you. Of course you would not confide in a chance-met guttersnipe. So, without knowledge of you, how could I tell what use I might be?"

Yeah, Everard thought, *in his kind of hand-to-mouth existence, he had to develop a pretty keen intuition, or else go under.* He kept his tone mild: "I am not angry. But tell me what you did."

Pum's big, russet-hued eyes met his and stayed, almost as equal to equal. "I made bold to query others about my master. Always carefully, never letting out what my purpose was or, in sooth, letting the person suspect what he or she revealed. As proof of this, has anyone seemed to doubt my lord?"

"M-m . . . no . . . not any more than I could expect. Who did you talk with?"

"Well, the lovely Pleshti—Bo-ron-u-wen, for a start." Pum lifted a palm. "Master! She said never a word you would not have approved. I read her face, her movements, while I asked certain questions. No more. She refused me answers, now and then, herself, and those refusals told me something too. And her body does not know how to keep secrets. Is that her fault?"

"No." *Also, I wouldn't be surprised but what you reopened your door a crack that night and eavesdropped. Never mind. I don't want to know.*

"Thus I learned you are not of the . . . the Geyil folk, is that their name? It was no surprise. I had already guessed as much. You see, although I am sure my master is terrible in battle, he is as forbearing with women as a mother with her child. Would a half-savage wanderer be?"

Everard laughed ruefully. *Touché!* On previous missions, he'd sometimes heard remarks about his lack of normal callousness, but nobody else had drawn conclusions from it.

Encouraged, Pum hurried on: "I shan't weary my lord with details. Menials are always watching the mighty, and love to gossip about them. I may have deceived Sarai the housekeeper a tiny bit. Since I was your footman, she saw no reason to bid me begone. Not that I asked her very much directly. That would have been both foolish and unnecessary. I was content to get myself steered toward the dwelling of Jantin-hamu, where they were agog over their visitor yesterday eventide. Thus did I get a hint of what it is my lord seeks."

He puffed himself up. "That, resplendent master, was what his servant required. I hied myself down to the docks and started gadding about. Lo!"

A billow passed through Everard. "What did you find?" he nearly yelled.

"What," Pum declaimed, "but a man who lived through the shipwreck and onslaught of demons?"

Gisgo appeared to be in his mid-forties, short but wiry, his weathered nutcracker face full of life. Over the years, he had risen from deckhand to coxswain, a skilled and well-rewarded post. Over the years, too, his cronies had tired of hearing about his remarkable experience. They took it for just another tall tale, anyway.

Everard appreciated what a fantastic piece of detective work Pum had done, tracing the man down by getting sailors in wineshops to talk about who told what kind of yarns. He himself could never have managed it; they'd have been too leery of such an outsider, who moreover was a royal guest. Like sensible people throughout history, the average Phoenician wanted as little to do with his government as possible.

It had been a lucky break that Gisgo was home in voyaging season. However, he had attained enough seniority and saved enough wealth that he need no more join long expeditions, hazardous and uncomfortable. His ship was on the Egypt run, and took layovers between passages.

In his neat fifth-floor apartment, his two wives brought refreshments while he lolled back and spouted at his guests. A window gave on a court between tenements. The view was of clay walls and laundry strung on lines between. Yet sunlight came in alongside an eddy of breeze, to touch souvenirs of many a trip—a miniature Babylonian cherub, a syrinx from Greece, a faience hippopotamus from the Nile, an Iberian juju, a leaf-shaped bronze dagger from the North. . . . Everard had made a substantial golden gift, and the mariner waxed expansive.

"Aye," Gisgo said, "that was an eldritch journey, 'twas. Bad time of year, equinox drawing nigh, and those there Sinim from who knows where, carrying misfortune in their bones for aught we knew. But we were young, the whole crew of us, from the captain on down; we reckoned on wintering in Cyprus, where the wines are strong and the girls are sweet; those Sinim, they'd pay well, they would. For that kind of metal, we were ready to give the fig to death and hell. I've since grown wiser, but won't claim I'm gladder, no, no. I'm still spry, but I feel the teeth gnawing, and believe me, my friends, it was better to be young."

He signed himself. "The poor lads who went down, may their shades rest peaceful." With a glance at Pum: "One of them looked like you, younker. Gave me a start, you did, when first we met. Adiyaton, was that his name? Aye, I think so. Maybe he was your grandsire?"

The boy gestured ignorance. He had no way of knowing.

"I've made my offerings for the lot of them, I have," Gisgo went on, "as well as in thanks for my own deliverance. Always stand by your friends and pay your debts, then the gods will help you in your need. They surely helped me.

"The Cyprus run is tricky at best. Can't make camp; it's overnight on the open sea, sometimes for days on end if the wind's foul. This time—ah, this time! Scarce were we beyond sight of land when the gale struck, and little did it avail us to spread oil on those waters. Out oars and keep her head to the waves, it was, till breath failed and sinews cracked but we must row regardless. Black as a pig's bowels, it was, and howling and lashing and rolling and pitching while the salt crusted my eyes and stung the cracks in my lips—and how to keep stroke when we couldn't hear the cox's drum through the wind?

"But on the midships catwalk I saw the chief of the Sinim, cloak flapping about him, faced straight into the blast, and laughing, laughing!

"I don't know whether he was bold, or landlubber-ignorant of the danger, or wiser than I then was in the ways of the sea. Afterward I've harked back, in the light of much hard-won knowledge, and decided that with any luck we could have ridden out the storm. That was a well-found ship, and her officers knew their trade. However, the gods, or the demons, would have it otherwise.

"For suddenly, crack and blaze! The brightness blinded me. I lost hold of my oar, like most of us did. Somehow I fumbled out and got a grip on it again before it slid away between the tholes. That may have saved my sight, because I wasn't looking up when the second bolt smote.

"Aye, we'd been hit by lightning. Twice. I'd heard no thunder, but maybe the roar of the waves and shriek of the wind covered that. When the dazzle began to clear from my eyes, I saw the mast aflame like a torch. The hull was slashed and weakened. I felt the sea shiver my skull, and my arse, too, as it broke the ship apart under me.

"That scarce seemed to matter right away. For by that fitful, ragged light I glimpsed things in heaven, like yonder winged bull but huge as real oxen and ashine as if cast in iron. Men were astride them. They swooped downward—

"Then everything went to pieces. I found myself in the water, clutching my oar. A couple other men in my sight had got hold of flotsam also. But the fury wasn't done with us. A lightning bolt struck down, straight into poor Hurum-abi, my drinking friend since I was a kid. He must've been killed right off. Me, I ducked below and held my breath as long's I could.

"When I must needs bring my nose up for air, I seemed to be alone in the sea. But overhead was a swarm of those dragons or chariots or whatever they were, a-dart through the wind. Flame raged between them. I went under again.

"I think they were soon gone to wherever in the Beyond they'd come from, but I was too busy staying alive to pay any more heed. Finally I made it to land. What had happened seemed unreal, like a mad dream. Maybe it was. I don't know. What I do know is that I'm the single man on that ship who ever came back. Praise Tanith, eh, girls?" Undaunted by memory, Gisgo pinched the bottom of his nearest wife.

More reminiscence followed, which took a couple of hours to disentangle. Finally Everard could ask, his tongue dry despite the wine: "Do you remember just when this was? How many years ago?"

"Why, sure I do, sure I do," Gisgo answered. "An even one score and six years, come fifteen days before the fall equinox, or pretty near to that."

He waved a hand. "How do I know, you wonder? Well, it's like the Egyptian priests, that keep such a close calendar because their river floods and falls every year. A seaman who doesn't take care, he's not likely to get old. Did you know that beyond the Pillars of Melqart the sea rises and falls like the Nile, but twice a day? You'd better watch those times sharp, if you'd fare in those parts.

"But the Sinim, they were what really drove the idea home in this head. There I was, attendant on my captain while they bargained with him for passage, and they kept talking about exactly which day we'd depart—talking him into it, you understand. I listened, and I thought what gains might lie in that kind of remembering, and told myself I'd make a point of it. Back then, I couldn't read or write, but what I could do was mark whatever special things happened each year, and keep those happenings in order and count back over them when I needed to. So this was the year in between a venture to the Red Cliff Shores and the year when I caught the Babylonian disease—"

Everard and Pum emerged and began walking from the Sidonian Harbor quarter, down a Street of the Ropemakers now filling with dusk and quietness, toward the palace.

"My lord gathers his forces, I see," murmured the boy after a while.

The Patrolman nodded absently. His mind was in a storm of its own.

Varagan's procedure seemed clear to him. (Everard felt well-nigh certain it was Merau Varagan, perpetrating a fresh enormity.) From wherever in space-time his hideout was, he and half a dozen of his confederates had sought the Usu area, twenty-six years ago. Others must have carried them on hoppers, which let them off and immediately returned. The Patrol couldn't hope to catch the vehicles in that brief an interlude, when the exact place and moment were unknown. Varagan's band had gone afoot into town and ingratiated themselves with King Abibaal.

They must have done this *after* bombing the temple, leaving the ransom note, and probably making the attempt on Everard—after, that is, in terms of their world lines, their continuity of experience. It would not have been hard to pick such a target, or even plant such an assassin. Scientists studying Tyre had written books which were readily available. The preliminary mischief would give Varagan an idea as to the feasibility of his entire scheme. Having decided that it would be worth a substantial investment of lifespan and effort, he thereupon sought the detailed knowledge, the kind that seldom gets into books, which he would need in order to do a really thorough job of wrecking this society.

When they had learned as much at the court of Abibaal as they felt was called for, Varagan and his followers left town in conventional wise, so as not to engender stories among the people that would spread and persist and eventually give the Patrol a lead. For the same reason, the dying out of public interest in them, they wanted it thought that they had perished.

Hence their departure date, on which they had insisted; a scouting flight had revealed that a storm would suddenly rise within hours. Those of the gang who were to pick them up had fired energy beams to destroy the ship and kill the witnesses. Had they not chanced to miss Gisgo, they would have covered their tracks almost completely. In fact, without Sarai's assistance, Everard would most likely never have heard of those Sinim who were unfortunately lost at sea.

From his base, Varagan had "already" dispatched agents to keep an eye on Patrol HQ in Tyre, as the time of his demonstration attack drew near. If such a gunman succeeded in recognizing and killing one or more of the scarce, valued Unattached officers, excellent! It would increase the probability of the Exaltationists getting what they wanted—whether that be the matter transmuter or the destruction of the Danellian future. Everard didn't think Varagan cared which. Either would gratify his power hunger and *Schadenfreude*.

Well, but Everard had found the spoor. He could loose the hounds of the Patrol—

Can I?

He gnawed his Celtic mustache and thought irrelevantly how glad he'd be to mow the damned fungus off, once this operation was finished.

Will it be?

Outnumbered, outgunned, Varagan was not necessarily outsmarted. His scheme had a built-in fail-safe that might be impossible to break.

The trouble was, the Phoenicians possessed neither clocks nor accurate navigation instruments. Gisgo didn't know, any closer than a week or two, when his ship suffered disaster; nor did he know, any closer than fifty miles or so, where it had been at the time. Therefore Everard didn't.

Of course, the Patrol could easily ascertain the date, and the course for Cyprus was known. But anything more precise required keeping watch from the air nearby, didn't it? And the enemy must have detectors which would warn him of that. The pilots who were to scuttle the ship and take away Varagan's group could arrive prepared for a dogfight. They wouldn't need but a few minutes to carry out their mission, then they'd be untraceably gone.

Worse, they might cancel the mission altogether. They could wait for a more favorable instant to recover their associates—or, worse yet, do it at an earlier time, before the ship ever sailed. In either case, Gisgo would not have (had) the experience which Everard had just heard him relate. The trail that the Patrolman had so painfully uncovered would never have existed. *Probably* the long-range consequences to history would be trivial, but there was no guarantee of that, once you started monkeying around with events.

For the same reasons, certain nullification of clues and possible upheaval in the continuum, the Patrol could not anticipate Varagan's plan. It dared not, for instance, swoop down on the ship and arrest the passengers before the gale and the Exaltationists struck.

Looks like the only way we can proceed is to appear exactly where they are, within that time-slot of five minutes or less when the riders carry out their dirty work. But how are we to pinpoint it without alerting them?

"I think," said Pum, "my lord intends to do battle, in a strange realm where wizards are his foes."

Am I that transparent to him? "Yes, it may be," Everard replied. "I'll first recompense you well, for you've been a right-hand man to me."

The youth plucked his sleeve. "Lord," he implored, "let your servant follow you."

Astounded, Everard stopped in midstride. "Huh?"

"I would not be parted from my master!" cried Pum. Tears gleamed in his eyes and down his cheekbones. "Better death at his side—aye, better the demons cast me down to hell—then return to that cockroach life you raised me from. Teach me what I should do. You know I learn fast. I shall not be afraid. You have made me into a man!"

By God, I do believe that for once his passion is perfectly genuine.

It's out of the question, of course.

IS it? Everard stood thunderstruck.

Pum danced before him, laughing and weeping. "My lord will do it, my lord will take me!"

And maybe, maybe, after this is all over, if he's survived—maybe we'll have gained something very precious.

"The danger will be great," Everard said slowly. "Moreover, I await things and happenings from which hardy warriors would flee, screaming. And earlier, you'll have to acquire knowledge which most of the wise men in this world could not even understand, were it told them."

"Try me, my lord," answered Pum. A sudden calm had come upon him.

"I will! Let's go!" Everard strode so fast that the youth must trot to keep up.

Basic indoctrination would take days, assuming Pum could handle it. That was okay, though. It would take a while anyway to collect the necessary intelligence and organize a task force. Besides, meanwhile there would be Bronwen. Everard couldn't tell if he himself would live through the conflict. Let him first receive whatever joy came his way, and try to give it back.

Captain Baalram was reluctant. "Why should I enroll your son?" he demanded. "I've a full crew already, including two apprentices. This one is a landlubber born, small, and scrawny."

"He's stronger than he seems," replied the man who called himself Adiyaton's father. (A quarter century hence, he would call himself Zakarbaal.) "You'll find him clever and willing. As for experience, everybody begins with none, true? See here, sir. I'm anxious for him to get into a trading career. For the sake of that, I'll be happy to . . . make it worth your while personally."

"Well, now." Baalram smiled and stroked his beard. "That's different. What amount of tuition had you in mind?"

Adiyaton (who, a quarter century hence, would have no precautionary need not to call himself Pummairam) looked gleeful. Inwardly, he shivered, for he gazed upon a man who must soon die.

From where the Patrol squadron waited, high in heaven, the storm was a blue-black mountain range crouched on the northern horizon. Elsewhere the sea reached argent and sapphire across the curve of the planet, save where islands broke the sheen and, eastward, the Syrian coast made a darkling line. Low in the west, the sun shone as cold as the blue around it. Wind whittered in Everard's ears.

On the front saddle of his time hopper, he huddled into a parka. The rear seat was empty, like those of about half the twoscore vehicles that shared the sky with him. Their pilots hoped to transport prisoners. The rest were guncraft, eggs of armor wherein fire waited to hatch. Light clanged off metal.

Damn! Everard thought. *I'm freezing. How much longer? Has something gone wrong? Did Pum betray himself to the enemy, or has his equipment failed, or what?*

A receiver dial secured to the steering bar beeped and winked red. Breath exploded out of him, white vapor that the wind strewed and swallowed. Despite his years as a hunter of men, he must gulp before he could snap into his throat mike: "Signal received by commander. Triangulation stations, report."

Down ahead, in wrack and spindrift, the enemy band had appeared. They had commenced their evil labors. But Pum had reached inside his garb and pressed the button on a miniature radio transmitter.

Radio. The Exaltationists wouldn't anticipate something that primitive. Everard hoped.

Now, Pum, boy, are you able to find shelter, protect yourself, the way you were told to? Fear laid fingers around the Patrolman's gullet. He'd doubtless begotten sons, here and there through the ages, but this was the closest he had ever come to having one.

Words crackled in his earphones. Numbers followed. Instruments a hundred miles apart had precisely found the beleaguered ship. Clocks had already recorded the first split second of reception.

"Okay," Everard said. "Compute spatial coordinates for each vehicle according to our strategy. Troopers, stand by for instructions."

That required several minutes. He felt a chilly peace welling up within him. His unit was committed. At this exact moment, it was in battle yonder. Let that happen which the Norns willed.

The data came crisply. "Everybody set?" he called. "Advance!"

He himself verniered controls and flipped the main drive toggle. His machine sprang forward through space, backward through time, to the moment when Pum had hailed it.

Wind raved. The hopper rocked and yawed in its antigrav field. Fifty yards below, black in this gloom, waves roared. The spume blown off them was sleet-colored. Everard saw by the light of a great torch some ways off. A resinous mast, fanned by the storm, burned fiercely. Tarry, flaming pieces of the ship were quenched in steam as it broke apart.

Everard tugged down his optical amplifiers. Vision became stark. It showed him that his command had arrived correctly, so as to englobe the half-dozen enemy vehicles everywhere above the billows.

It had not come soon enough to prevent them from starting their butchery. They had done that on the instant of their own appearance. Not knowing where any one of them would be, but knowing that each was lethally well armed, Everard had perforce caused his group to show up at a distance where it could assess the situation before the killers noticed it.

They would, in a heartbeat or two. "Attack!" Everard roared needlessly. His steed hurtled forward.

A blue-white hell-beam speared through murk. Zigzagging as he flew, he felt it miss him by inches: heat, sting of ozone, crack of air. He didn't see it, for his goggles had automatically stopped down a glare that would have blinded.

Nor did he shoot back, though he drew his blaster. That wasn't his business.

Heaven was already lurid with such lightnings. The waters reflected them as if also afire.

There was no good way to seize any enemy pilots. Everard's gunner had orders to kill, at once, before the reavers realized how outnumbered they were and skipped off into space-time. The job of the single-riding Patrolmen was to capture those spies who had been aboard the ship.

He didn't expect he'd find them clinging to the sections of hull that swung to and fro in the swells and disintegrated. Men would check those, of course, just in case. But likeliest the travelers were afloat by themselves. They'd surely taken the precaution of wearing cartridge-inflatable life jackets under their contemporary kaftans.

Pum could not risk doing so. As a crewboy, he'd have looked wrong in much more than a loincloth. It served to conceal his transmitter, but nothing else. Everard had made certain he learned to swim.

Few Punic sailors could. Everard glimpsed one who gripped a plank. Almost, he went to the rescue. But no, he mustn't. Baalram and his mariners had gone under—except for Gisgo, whose survival revealed itself to be no accident. The Patrol had pounced in time to save him from being hunted down as he drifted; and he had the strength to keep hold of his heavy sweep till it washed ashore. The rest, his shipmates, his friends—they died and their kin mourned them, as would be the fate of seafarers for the next several thousand years . . . and afterward spacefarers, timefarers . . . . At least these men perished so that their people, and untold billions of people in the future, might live.

It was a bleak consolation.

Everard's reheightened vision brought him sight of another head, unmistakable, yes, a man who bobbed about free as a cork—an enemy to take. He swung low. The man looked up out of froth and turmoil. Malignancy wrenched at his mouth. A hand rose from the water. It carried an energy pistol.

Everard was quicker to shoot. A thin beam stabbed. The man's scream was lost in the gale. Likewise was his weapon. He gaped at seared flesh and naked bone on that wrist.

Here Everard felt no pity. But he had not wanted to slay, in this encounter. Live captives, under painless, harmless, absolute psychointerrogation, could direct the Patrol to the lairs of all sorts of interesting villainies.

Everard lowered his vehicle. Its motor throbbed, holding it in place against the waves that crashed over it, the wind that tore and hooted and chilled. His legs clenched tight on the frame. He leaned from his saddle, got a hold on the semiconscious man, lifted him and laid him across the bow. *Okay, let's get some altitude!*

It was sheer chance, but not the less satisfying, that he, Manse Everard, turned out to be the Patrol agent who clapped hands on Merau Varagan.

The squadron sought a quiet place, to make assessment before it went uptime. Its choice was an uninhabited Aegean islet. White cliffs rose out of cerulean waters, whose calm was stirred only by glitter of sunlight and foam. Gulls flew equally lucent, and mewed through the lulling of the breeze. Shrubs thrust forth among boulders. Warmth baked pungencies out of their leaves. Far and far away, a sail passed by. It could have been driving the ship of Odysseus.

The constables held conference. They had suffered no harm apart from a few wounds. For those, analgesics and antishock medications were directly available, and later hospital treatment would restore whatever had been lost. They had shot down four Exaltationist vehicles; three got away, but would be hunted, would be hunted. They had taken a full complement of captives.

One of the Patrolmen, homing on the transmitter, had plucked Pummairam from the sea.

"Good show!" Everard bawled, and hugged the boy to him.

They sat on a bench at the Egyptian Harbor. It was as private a spot as any, since everyone roundabout was too busy to eavesdrop; and soon the pulse of Tyre would beat no more for either of them. They did draw stares. In honor of the occasion, which had included various recreations around town, Everard had bought them both kaftans of the finest linen and most beautiful dye, fit for the kings they felt themselves to be. He didn't care about the clothing, except that it would make duly impressive his farewell at Hiram's court, but Pum was ecstatic.

The quay resounded—slap of feet, thud of hoofs, creak of wheels, rumble of rolled barrels. A cargo was in from Ophir, by way of Sinai, and stevedores were unloading its costly bales. Sweat beneath the sun made their muscled bodies shine. Sailors lounged in a nearby lean-to tavern, where a girl danced to music of flute and tabor; they drank, gambled, laughed, boasted, swapped yarns of countries beyond and beyond. A vendor sang the praises of the sweetmeats on his tray. A donkey cart passed laden. A priest of Melqart, in gorgeous robes, talked with an austere foreigner who served Osiris. A couple of red-haired Achaeans swaggered piratically by. A long-bearded warrior from Jerusalem and a bodyguard for a visiting Philistine dignitary exchanged glares, but the peace of Hiram stayed their swords. A black man in leopard skin and ostrich plumes drew a swarm of Phoenician urchins. An Assyrian walked weightily, holding his staff like a spear. An Anatolian and a blond man from the North of Europe reeled arm in arm, beerful and cheerful. . . . The air smelled of dyeworks, dung, smoke, tar, but also of sandalwood, myrrh, spice, and salt spray.

It would die at last, all of this, centuries hence, as everything must die; but first, how mightily would it have lived! How rich would be its heritage!

"Yes," Everard said, "I don't want you to get above yourself—" He chuckled. ". . . though are you ever below yourself? Still, Pum, you're a remarkable find. We didn't simply rescue Tyre, we won you."

A trifle more hesitant then usual, the youngster stared before him. "You explained that, lord, when teaching me. That hardly anybody in this age of the world is able to imagine travel through time and the marvels of tomorrow. It is no use to tell them, they merely get bewildered and frightened." He cradled his downy chin. "Maybe I am different because I was always on my own, never cast into a mold and let harden." Happily: "Then I praise the gods, or whatever they were, that kicked me into such a life. It prepared me for a new life with my master."

"Well, no, not really that," Everard replied. "We won't see each other often again, you and I."

"What?" exclaimed Pum, stricken. "Why? Has your servant offended you, O my lord?"

"Not in any way." Everard patted the thin shoulder beside him. "On the contrary. But mine is a roving commission. What we want you for is an agent in place, here in your home country, which you know in and out as a foreigner like me—or Chaim and Yael Zorach—never can. Don't worry. It will be a colorful task, and require as much of you as you can give."

Pum gusted a sigh. His smile flashed white. "Well, that will do, master! In truth, I was a little daunted at the thought of faring always among aliens." His tone dropped. "Will you ever come visit me?"

"Sure, once in a while. Or if you like, you can join me in assorted interesting future locales when you take your furloughs. We Patrollers work hard, and sometimes dangerously, but we have our fun."

Everard paused, then went on: "Of course, first you need training, education, every kind of knowledge and skill you lack. You'll go to the Academy, elsewhere in space and time. There you'll spend years, and they won't be easy years—though I believe on the whole you'll revel in them. At last you'll return to this same year in Tyre, aye, this same month, and take up your duties."

"I will be full-grown?"

"Right. In fact, they'll put quite a bit of height and weight on you, as well as information into you. You'll need a new identity, but that won't be hard to arrange. The same name will serve; it's common enough. You'll be Pummairam the sailor, who shipped out years before as a youthful deckhand, won a fortune in trade goods, and is ready to buy a ship and organize his own ventures. You won't be especially conspicuous, that would defeat our purpose, but you'll be a prosperous and well-regarded subject of King Hiram."

The boy clasped hands together. "Lord, your benevolence overwhelms his servant."

"It isn't done with doing that," Everard answered. "I have discretionary authority in a case like this, you know, and I am going to make certain arrangements on your behalf. You can't pass for a respectable man when you settle down unless you get married. Very well, you'll marry Sarai."

Pum squeaked. His gaze upon the Patrolman was dismayed.

Everard laughed. "Oh, come!" he said. "She may not be any beauty, but she's not hideous either; we owe her much; and she's loyal, intelligent, versed in the ways of the palace, lots of useful stuff. True, she'll never know who you really are. She'll just be the wife of Captain Pummairam and mother of his children. If any questions arise in her mind, I think she'll be too wise to ask them." Sternly: "You will be good to her. Do you hear?"

"Well—ah, well—" Pum's attention strayed to the dancing girl. Phoenician males lived by the double standard, and Tyre held more than its share of joyhouses. "Yes, sir."

Everard slapped the other's knee. "I read your mind, son. However, you may find you're not so interested in roaming. For a second wife, what would you say to Bronwen?"

It was a pleasure to watch Pum being flabbergasted.

Everard grew serious. "Before leaving," he explained, "I mean to give Hiram a gift, not the sort of present that's customary but something spectacular, like a gold ingot. The Patrol has unlimited wealth and a relaxed attitude toward requisitions. For the sake of his honor, Hiram can refuse me nothing in his turn. I'll ask for his slave Bronwen and her children. When they are mine, I'll formally manumit them and furnish her a dowry.

"I've sounded her out. If she can have freedom in Tyre, she doesn't really want to go back to her homeland and share a wattle-and-daub hut with ten or fifteen fellow tribesfolk. But to stay here, she must have a husband for herself, a stepfather for her kids. How about you?"

"I—would I—might she—" The blood came and went through Pum's face.

Everard nodded. "I promised I'd find her a decent man."

She was wistful. Still, practicality takes precedence over romance in this era, as it does in most.

It may be hard on him later, seeing his family grow old while he only fakes it. But what with his missions through time, he'll have them for many decades of his life; and he's not brought up to the American kind of sensitivity, after all.

It should go reasonably well. No doubt the women will become friends, and league to quietly rule Captain Pummairam's roost for him.

"Then . . . oh, my lord!" The youth leaped to his feet and pranced.

"Easy, easy." Everard grinned. "On your calendar, remember, you've years to go before you're established. Why delay? Seek the house of Zakarbaal and report to the Zorachs. They'll get you started."

For my part . . . well, it'll take me a few days yet to wind up my stay at the palace in graceful and plausible fashion. Meanwhile, Bronwen and I—Everard sighed, with a wistfulness of his own.

Pum was gone. Feet flying, kaftan flapping, the purple wharf rat sped to the destiny he would make for himself.

THE SORROW OF
ODIN THE GOTH

"Then I heard a voice in the world: 'O woe
for the broken troth,
And the heavy Need of the Niblungs, and
the Sorrow of Odin the Goth!'"
— William Morris, *Sigurd the Volsung*

372

WIND gusted out of twilight as the door opened. Fires burning down the length of the hall flared in their trenches; flames wavered and streamed from stone lamps; smoke roiled bitter back from the roof-holes that should have let it out. The sudden brightness gleamed off spearheads, axheads, swordguards, shield bosses, where weapons rested near the entry. Men, crowding the great room, grew still and watchful, as did the women who had been bringing them horns of ale. It was the gods carved on the pillars that seemed to move amidst unrestful shadows, one-handed Father Tiwaz, Donar of the Ax, the Twin Horsemen—they, and the beasts and heroes and entwining branches graven into the wainscot. *Whoo-oo* said the wind, a noise as cold as itself.

Hathawulf and Solbern trod through. Their mother Ulrica strode between them, and the look upon her face was no less terrible than the look on theirs. The three of them halted for a heartbeat or two, a long time for those who awaited their word. Then Solbern shut the door while Hathawulf stepped forward and raised his right arm. Silence clamped down on the hall, save for the crackling of fires and seething of breath.

Yet it was Alawin who spoke first. Rising from his bench, his slim frame aquiver, he cried, "So we'll take revenge!" His voice cracked; he had but fifteen winters.

The warrior beside him hauled at his sleeve and growled, "Sit. It is for the lord to tell us." Alawin gulped, glared, obeyed.

A smile of sorts brought forth teeth in Hathawulf's yellow beard. He had been in the world nine years longer than yon half-brother, four years more than his full brother Solbern, but he seemed older, and not only because of height, wide shoulders, wildcat gait; leadership had been his for the last five of those years, after his father Tharasmund's death, and hastened the growth of his soul. There were those who whispered that Ulrica kept too strong a grip on him, but any who questioned his manhood would have had to meet him in a fight and been unlikely to walk away from it.

"Yes," he said, without loudness, nevertheless heard from end to end of the building. "Bring forth the wine, wenches; drink well, all my men, make love to your wives, break out your war gear; friends who have come hither offering help, take my deepest thanks: for tomorrow dawn we ride to slay my sister's murderer."

"Ermanaric," uttered Solbern. He was shorter and darker than Hathawulf, more given to tending his farm and to shaping things with his hands than to war or the chase; but he spat forth the name as if it had been a foulness in his mouth.

A sigh, rather than a gasp, ran around the throng, though some of the women shrank back, or moved closer to husbands, brothers, fathers, youths whom they might have married someday. A few thanes growled, almost gladly, deep in their throats. Grimness came upon others.

Among the latter was Liuderis, who had quelled Alawin. He stood up on his bench, so as to be seen above heads. A stout, grizzled, scarred fellow, formerly Tharasmund's trustiest man, he asked heavily: "You would fare against the king, to whom you gave your oath?"

"That oath became worthless when he had Swanhild trodden beneath the hoofs of horses," answered Hathawulf.

"Yet he says Randwar plotted his death."

"He says!" Ulrica shouted. She stalked forth until what light there was flickered more fully across her: a big woman, her coiled braids half gray and half still ruddy around a face whose lines had frozen into the sternness of Weard herself. Costly furs trimmed Ulrica's cloak; the gown beneath was of Eastland silk; amber from the Northlands glowed around her neck: for she was the daughter of a king, who had married into the god-descended house of Tharasmund.

She halted, fists clenched, and flung at Liuderis and the rest: "Well might Randwar the Red have sought to overthrow Ermanaric. Too long have the Goths suffered from that hound. Yes, I call him hound. Ermanaric, unfit to live. Tell me not how he made us mighty and his sway reaches from the Baltic Sea to the Black. It is *his* sway, not ours, and it will not outlast him. Tell yourselves, rather, of scot well-nigh ruinous to pay, of wives and maidens dishonored, of lands unrightfully seized and folk driven from their homes, of men hewn down or burned in their surrounded dwellings merely because they dared speak against his deeds. Remember how he slew his nephews and their families when he did not get their treasure. Think how he had Randwar hanged, on nothing more than the word of Sibicho Mannfrithsson—Sibicho, that viper forever hissing in the king's ear. And ask yourselves this. Even if Randwar had indeed become Ermanaric's foe, betrayed before he could strike to avenge outrage upon his kin—even if this be so, why should Swanhild die too? She was only his wife." Ulrica drew breath. "She was also the daughter of Tharasmund and myself, the sister of your chief Hathawulf and of Solbern his brother. They, who sprang from Wodan, shall send Ermanaric below to be her slave."

"You talked to your sons alone for half a day, my lady," said Liuderis. "How much of this is your will, not theirs?"

Hathawulf brought hand to sword. "You overspeak yourself," he snapped.

"I meant no ill—" the warrior began.

"The earth is tearful with the blood of Swanhild the fair," said Ulrica. "Will it bear for us ever again, if we do not wash it with the blood of her murderer?"

Solbern stayed more calm: "You Teurings know well how trouble has been waxing for years between the king and our tribe. Why else did you rally to us when you heard what happened? Do you not all think that belike this deed of his was done to test our mettle? If we sit quietly at our hearths—if Heorot takes whatever weregild he might deign to offer—he will know he is free to crush us altogether."

Liuderis nodded, folded arms across breast, and answered steadily, "Well, you shall not fare to battle without my sons and me, while this old head remains above ground. I did but wonder if you and Hathawulf are being rash. Ermanaric is strong indeed. Would it not be better if we bide our time, make quite ready, gather men of neighbor tribes, before we strike?"

Hathawulf smiled afresh, a little more warmly than erstwhile. "We thought about that," he said in a level tone. "If we give ourselves time, we give the king time, too. Nor do I believe we can raise very many spears against him. Not while the Huns prowl the marches, vassal folk are sullen about paying tribute, and the Romans might see, in a war of Goth upon Goth, a chance to enter and lay all beneath them. Besides, Ermanaric will not sit idle long before he moves to humble the Teurings. No, we must attack now, before he awaits us—catch him unawares, overwhelm his guardsmen—they do not much outnumber you who are here—slay Ermanaric in one quick, clean blow, and afterward call a folkmoot to pick a new king who shall be righteous."

Liuderis nodded again. "I have spoken my mind, you have spoken yours. Now let us have an end of speaking. Tomorrow we ride." He sat down.

"It is a risk," Ulrica said. "These are my last living sons, and maybe they fare to their deaths. That is as Weard wills, who sets the doom of gods and men alike. But rather would I have my sons die boldly than kneel to their sister's murderer. No luck would come of that."

Young Alawin leaped anew to his feet on the bench. His knife flashed forth. "We don't die!" he shouted. "Ermanaric will, and Hathawulf will be king of the Ostrogoths!"

A slow roar, like an incoming tide, lifted from the men.

Solbern the sober walked down the hall. The crowd made way for him. Strewn rushes rustled and the clay floor thudded beneath his boots. "Did I hear you say 'we'?" he asked through the rumbling. "No, you're a boy. You stay home."

The downy cheeks reddened. "I am man enough to fight for my house!" Alawin shrilled.

Ulrica stiffened where she stood. Cruelty lashed from her: "'Your' house, by-blow?"

The growing din died away. Men traded uneasy stares. It did not bode well, such an unleashing of olden hatred at such an hour as this. Alawin's mother Erelieva had not merely been a leman of Tharasmund's, she had become the one woman for whom he really cared, and Ulrica had gloated almost openly when every child that Erelieva bore him, save for this firstborn, died small. After the chieftain himself went down hell-road, friends of hers had gotten her hastily married off to a yeoman who lived far from the hall. Alawin stayed, the seemly thing for a lord's son to do, but Ulrica was always stinging him.

Eyes clashed through smoke and shadow-haunted firelight. "Yes, my house," Alawin called, "and Swanhild m-m-my sister too." His stammer made him bite his lip for shame.

"Easy, easy." Hathawulf raised his arm again. "You have the right, lad, and do well to claim it. Yes, ride with us, come dawn." His glance defied Ulrica.

She twisted her mouth but said naught. Everybody guessed she was hoping the stripling would be killed.

Hathawulf strode toward the high seat at the middle of the hall. His words rang: "No more bickering! We'll be merry this eventide. But first, Anslaug"— this to his wife—"come sit beside me, and together we'll drink the beaker of Wodan."

Feet stamped, fists pounded wood, knives lifted like torches. The women themselves began to yell with the men: "Hail, hail, hail!"

The door flew open.

Dusk had deepened fast, when autumn was on hand, so that the newcomer stood in the middle of blackness. Wind flapped the edges of his blue cloak, flung a few dead leaves in past him, whistled and chilled along the room. Folk turned to see who had come, drew a sharp breath, and those who had been seated now scrambled to stand. It was the Wanderer.

Tallest he stood among them, holding his spear more like a staff than a weapon, as if he had no need of iron. A broad-brimmed hat shaded his face, but not the wolf-gray hair and beard, nor the gleam of his gaze. Few of them here had ever seen him before, most had never happened to be nigh when he made his seldom showings; but none failed to know the forefather of the Teuring headmen.

Ulrica was first to muster hardihood. "Greeting, Wanderer, and welcome," she said. "You honor our roof. Come, take the high seat, and I will bring you a horn of wine."

"No, a goblet, a Roman goblet, the best we have," said Solbern.

Hathawulf came back to the door, squared his shoulders, and stood before the Elder. "You know what is afoot," he said. "What word have you for us?"

"This," answered the Wanderer. His voice was deep, and did not sound like the southern Goths', or like any's whom they had met. Men supposed his mother tongue was the tongue of the gods. Tonight it fell heavily, as if grief weighted it. "You are bound upon vengeance, Hathawulf and Solbern, and that stands not to be altered; it is the will of Weard. But Alawin shall not go with you."

The youth shrank back, whitening. A near sob broke harsh from his throat.

The Wanderer's look ranged down the hall to lay hold upon him. "This is needful," he went on, word by slow word. 'I lay no slur on you when I say that you are only half-grown, and would die bravely but uselessly. All who are men have first been boys. No, I tell you instead that yours shall be another task, more hard and strange than vengeance for the welfare of that kindred which sprang from your father's father's mother Jorith—" did his tone waver the least bit?—"and myself. Abide, Alawin. Your time will come soon enough."

"It . . . shall be done . . . as you will, lord," said Hathawulf out of a stiffened gullet. "But what does this mean . . . for those of us who ride forth?"

The Wanderer regarded him for a while that grew very still before answering: "You do not wish to know. Be the word good or ill, you do not wish to know."

Alawin sank to his bench, laid head in hands, and shuddered.

"Farewell," said the Wanderer. His cloak swirled, his spear swung about, the door shut, he was gone.

1935

I didn't change clothes till my vehicle had brought me across space-time. Then, in a Patrol base which masqueraded as a warehouse, I shed the garb of the Dnieper basin, late fourth century, and donned that of the United States, middle twentieth century.

The basic patterns, shirts and trousers for men, gowns for women, were the same. Differences of detail were countless. Despite its coarse fabrics, the Gothic outfit was more comfortable than a tie and jacket. I stowed it in the baggage box of my hopper, along with such special items as the little gadget I'd used to listen in, from outside, on the proceedings in the hall of Teuring sachem. Since my spear wouldn't fit, I left it strapped to the side of the machine. I wouldn't be going anyplace on that except back to the milieu where such weapons belonged.

The officer on duty today was in his early twenties—young by current standards; in most eras he'd long since have been an established family man—and somewhat in awe of me. True, my status as a member of the Time Patrol was almost as much a technicality as his. I had no part in policing the spatiotemporal lanes, rescuing travelers in distress, or anything glamorous like that. I was merely a scientist of sorts; "scholar" was probably more accurate. However, I did make trips on my own, which he was not qualified to do.

He peered at me as I emerged from the hangar to the nondescript office, allegedly of a construction company, which was our front in this town during these years. "Welcome home, Mr. Farness," he said. "Uh, you had a pretty rough go-around, didn't you?"

"What makes you think so?" I replied automatically.

"Your expression, sir. The way you walk."

"I was in no danger," I rapped. Not caring to talk about it, except to Laurie and maybe not her either for a while, I brushed past him and stepped out onto the street.

Here also it was fall, the kind of crisp and brilliant day New York often enjoyed until it became uninhabitable; this year chanced to be the one before I was born. Masonry and glass gleamed higher than high, up into a blueness where a few bits of cloud scudded along on the breeze that gave me its cool kiss. Cars were not so many that they put more than a tang into it, less than the aroma of the roast-chestnut carts that were beginning to come out of estivation. I went over to Fifth Avenue and walked uptown past glamorous shops, among some of the most beautiful women in the world, as well as people from all the rich diversity of our planet.

My hope was that by going afoot to my place, I'd work out part of the tension and misery in me. The city could not only stimulate, it could heal, right? This was where Laurie and I had chosen to dwell, we who could have settled practically anywhere in the past or the future.

No, of course that isn't quite correct. Like most couples, we wanted a nest in reasonably familiar surroundings, where we didn't have to learn everything from scratch and stay always on guard. The thirties were a marvelous milieu if you were a white American, in good health and with money. What amenities were lacking, such as air conditioning, could be unobstrusively installed, not to be used when you had visitors who would never know that time travelers exist. Granted, the Roosevelt gang was in charge, but the conversion of the Republic to the Corporate State was not very far along as yet and didn't affect Laurie's and my private lives; the outright disintegration of this society wouldn't become a fast and obvious process till (my opinion) after the 1964 election.

In the Middle West, where my mother was now carrying me, we'd have had to be annoyingly circumspect. But most New Yorkers were tolerant, or at least incurious. A beard down to my chest, and shoulder-length hair which I'd pulled into a queue while at the base, didn't draw many stares, nor more than a few cries of "Beaver!" from little boys. To our landlord, our neighbors, and other contemporaries, we were a retired professor of Germanic philology and his wife, our oddities to be expected. It was no lie, either, as far as it went.

Therefore my walk should have eased me somewhat, restored that perspective which Patrol agents must have, lest certain of the things they witness drive them mad. We must understand that what Pascal said is true of every human being in the whole of space-time, ourselves included—"The last act is tragic, however pleasant all the comedy of the other acts. A little earth on our heads, and all is done with forever."—understand it in our bones, so that we can live with it calmly if not serenely. Why, those Goths of mine were getting off lightly compared to, say, millions of European Jews and Gypsies, less than ten years futureward, or millions of Russians at this very moment.

It was no good. They *were* my Goths. Their ghosts crowded around me till street, buildings, flesh and blood became the unreal, the half-remembered dream.

Blindly, I hastened my steps, toward whatever sanctuary Laurie could give.

We occupied a huge flat overlooking Central Park, where we liked to stroll on mild nights. The doorman at the apartment need not double as an armed guard. I hurt him today by the curtness with which I returned his greeting, and realized it when in the elevator, but then my regret was too late. To jump back through time and change the incident would have violated the Prime Directive of the Patrol. Not that something that trivial would have threatened the continuum; it's flexible within limits, and the effects of alterations usually damp out fast. Indeed, there's an interesting metaphysical question about the extent to which time travelers discover the past, versus the extent to which they create it. Schrödinger's cat lurks in history as well as in its box. Yet the Patrol exists in order to assure that temporal traffic does not abort that scheme of events which will at last bring forth the Danellian superhumans who founded the Patrol when, in their own remote past, ordinary men learned how to travel temporally.

My thoughts had fled into this familiar territory while I stood caged in the elevator. It made the ghosts more distant, less clamorous. Nevertheless, when I let myself into our home, they followed.

A smell of turpentine drifted amidst the books which lined the living room. Laurie was winning somewhat of a name as a painter, here in the 1930s when she was no longer the preoccupied faculty wife she had been later in our century. Offered a job in the Patrol, she had declined; she lacked the physical strength that a field agent—male or, especially, female—was bound to need upon occasion, while routine clerical or reference work didn't interest her. To be sure, we'd shared vacations in mighty exotic milieus.

She heard me enter and ran from her studio to meet me. The sight lifted my spirits a tiny bit. In spattered smock, red hair tucked under a kerchief, she was still slender, supple, and handsome. The lines around her green eyes were too fine to notice until she got near enough to embrace me.

Our local acquaintances tended to envy me a wife who, besides being delightful, was far younger than myself. In fact, the difference in birth dates is a mere six years. I was in my mid-forties, and prematurely gray, when the Patrol recruited me, whereas she had kept most of her youthful looks. The antithanatic treatment that our organization provides will arrest the aging process but not reverse its effects.

Besides, she spent most of her life in ordinary time, sixty seconds to the minute. As a field agent, I'd go through days, weeks, or months between saying good-bye to her in the morning and returning for dinner—an interlude during which she could pursue her career without me underfoot. My cumulative age was approaching a hundred years.

Sometimes it felt like a thousand. That showed.

"Hi, there, Carl, darling!" Her lips pulsed against mine. I drew her close. If a dab of paint got onto my suit, what the hell? Then she stepped back, took both my hands, and sent her gaze across me and into me.

Her voice dropped low: "It's hurt you, this trip."

"I knew it would," I answered out of my weariness.

"But you didn't know how much. . . . Were you gone long?"

"No. Tell you about it in a while, the details. I was lucky, though. Hit a key point, did what I needed to do, and got out again. A few hours of observation from concealment, a few minutes of action, and *fini*."

"I suppose you might call it luck. Must you return soon?"

"In that era, yes, quite soon. But I want a while here to—to rest, get over what I saw was about to happen. . . . Can you stand me around, brooding at you, for a week or two?"

"Sweetheart." She came back to me.

"I have to work up my notes, anyway," I said into her ear, "but evenings we can go out to dinner, the theater, have fun together."

"Oh, I hope you'll be able to have fun. Don't pretend for my sake."

"Later, things will be easier," I assured us. "I'll simply be carrying out my original mission, recording the stories and songs they'll make about this. It's just . . . I've got to get through the reality first."

"Must you?"

"Yes. Not for scholarly purposes, no, I guess not. But those are my people. They are."

She hugged me tighter. She knew.

What she did not know, I thought in an uprush of pain—what I hoped to God she did not know—was why I cared so greatly about yonder descendants of mine. Laurie wasn't jealous. She'd never begrudged the while that Jorith and I had had. Laughing, she'd said it deprived her of nothing, while it gave me a position in the community I was studying which might well be unique in the annals of my profession. Afterward she'd done her best to console me.

What I could not bring myself to tell her was that Jorith was not simply a close friend who happened to be a woman. I could not say to her that I had loved one who lay dust these sixteen hundred years as much as I loved her, and still did, and maybe always would.

300

The home of Winnithar the Wisentslayer stood on a bluff above the River Vistula. It was a thorp, half a dozen houses clustered around a hall, with barns, sheds, cookhouse, smithy, brewery, and other workplaces nearby: for his family had long dwelt here, and waxed great among the Teurings. Westward reached meadows and croplands. Eastward, across the water, wilderness remained, though settlement was encroaching heavily upon it as the tribe grew in numbers.

They might have logged off the woods altogether, save that more and more of them were moving away. This was a time of unrest. Not only were plundering war bands on the trail; whole folk were pulling up stakes, and clashing when they met. Word drifted from afar that the Romans were often at each other's throats too, while the mightiness which their forefathers had built crumbled. As yet, few Northerners had done anything bolder than to raid along the Imperial borders. But the southlands just outside those borders, warm, rich, scantily defended by their dwellers, beckoned many a Goth to come carve out a new home for himself.

Winnithar stayed where he was. However, that forced him to pass almost as much of each year in fighting—especially against Vandals, though sometimes against Gothic tribes, Greutungs or Taifals—as he passed in farming. As his sons neared manhood, they began to yearn elsewhere.

Thus matters stood when Carl arrived.

He came in winter, when hardly anybody traveled. On that account, men made strangers doubly welcome, who broke the sameness of their lives. At first, spying him at a mile's reach, they took him for a mere gangrel, since he fared alone and afoot. Nonetheless they knew their chief would want to see him.

He drew nigh, striding easily over the frozen ruts of the road, making a staff of his spear. His blue cloak was the only color in that landscape of snow-decked fields, stark trees, dull sky. Hounds bayed and growled at him; he showed no fear, and afterward the men came to understand that he could have stricken those dead that attacked him. Today they called the beasts to heel and met the newcomer with sudden respect—for it became plain that his garments were of the finest, and not the least way-stained, while he himself was awesome. Taller than the tallest here he loomed, lean but sinewy, a graybeard as lithe as a youth. What had those pale eyes of his beheld?

A warrior went ahead to greet him. "I hight Carl," he said when asked:

nothing further. "Fain would I guest you a while." The Gothic words came readily from him, but their sound, and sometimes their order or endings, were not of any dialect known to the Teurings.

Winnithar had stayed in his hall. It would have been unseemly for him to gape like an underling. When Carl entered, Winnithar said from his high seat, "Be welcome if you come in peace and honesty. May Father Tiwaz ward you and Mother Frija bless you."—as was the ancient custom of his house.

"My thanks," Carl answered. "That was kindly spoken to a fellow you may well think is a beggar. I am not, and hope this gift will be found worthy." He reached in the pouch at his belt and drew forth an arm-ring which he handed over to Winnithar. Gasps arose from those who had jostled close to watch, for the ring was heavy, of pure gold, cunningly wrought and set with gems.

The host kept his calmness, barely. "That is a gift a king might have given. Share my seat, Carl." It was the place of honor. "Abide for as long as you wish." He clapped his hands. "Ho," he shouted, "bring mead for our guest, and for me that I may drink his health!" To the swains, wenches, and children milling about: "Back to your work, you. We can all hear whatever he chooses to tell us after the evening meal. Now he's doubtless weary."

Grumblingly, they heeded. "Why say you that?" Carl asked him.

"The nearest dwelling where you might have spent last night is a goodly walk from this," Winnithar replied.

"I was at none," Carl said.

"What?"

"You would be bound to find that out. I would not have you believe I lied to you."

"But—" Winnithar peered at him, tugged his mustache, and said slowly: "You are not of these parts; aye, you must have fared far. Yet your garb is clean, though you carry no change of clothes, nor food or aught else that a traveler should. Who are you, whence have you come, and . . . how?"

Carl's tone was mild, but those who listened heard what steel underlay it. "There are things I may not talk about. I do give you my oath—may Donar's lightning smite me if it is false—that I am no outlaw, nor foe to your kindred, nor a sort whom it would shame you to have beneath your roof."

"If honor demands that you keep certain secrets, none shall pry," said Winnithar. "But you understand that we cannot help wondering—" Clear to see was the relief with which he broke off and exclaimed: "Ah, here comes the mead. That's my wife Salvalindis who bears your horn to you, as befits a guest of rank."

Carl hailed her courteously, though his gaze kept straying to the maiden at her side, who brought Winnithar his draught. She was sweetly formed and moved like a deer; unbound hair streamed golden past a face with fine bones, shyly smiling lips, eyes big and the hue of summer heaven.

Salvalindis noticed. "You meet our oldest child," she told Carl, "our daughter Jorith."

1980

After basic training at the Patrol Academy, I returned to Laurie on the same day as I'd left her. I'd need a spell to rest and readapt; it was rather a shock transferring from the Oligocene period to a Pennsylvania college town. We must also set our mundane affairs in order. For my part, I should finish out the academic year before resigning "to take a better-paying job abroad." Laurie saw to the sale of our house and the disposal of goods we didn't want to keep—wherever and whenever else we were going to establish residence.

It wrenched us, bidding goodbye to the friends of years. We promised to make occasional visits, but knew that those would be few and far between, until they ceased entirely. The required lies were too great a strain. As was, we left an impression that my vaguely described new position was a cover for a post in the CIA.

Well, I had been warned at the beginning that a Time Patrol agent's life becomes a series of farewells. I had yet to learn what that really meant.

We were still in the course of uprooting ourselves when I got a phone call. "Professor Farness? This is Manse Everard, Unattached operative. I wonder if we could meet for a talk, like maybe this weekend."

My heart bounded. Unattached is about as high as you can get in the organization; throughout the million or more years that it guards, such personnel are rare. Normally a member, even if a police officer, works within a single milieu, so that he or she can get to know it inside out, and as part of a closely coordinated team. The Unattached may go anyplace they choose and do virtually anything they see fit, responsible only to their consciences, their peers, and the Danellians.

"Uh, sure, certainly, sir," I blurted. "Saturday would be fine. Do you want to come here? I guarantee you a good dinner."

"Thanks, but I'd prefer it was my digs—the first time, anyway. Got my files and computer terminal and things like that handy. Just the two of us, please. Don't worry about airline schedules. Find a spot, as it might be your basement, where nobody will see. You've been issued a locator, haven't you? . . . Okay, read off the coordinates and call me back. I'll pick you up on my hopper."

I found out later that that was characteristic of him. Large, tough-looking, wielding more power than Caesar or Genghis ever dreamed of, he was as comfortable as an old shoe.

Me on the saddle behind his, we skipped through space, rather than time, to the current Patrol base in New York City. From there we walked to the apartment he maintained. He didn't like dirt, disorder, and danger any better than I did. However, he felt he needed a *pied-à-terre* in the twentieth century, and had grown used to these lodgings before decay had advanced overly far.

"I was born in your state in 1924," he explained. "Entered the Patrol at age thirty. That's why I decided I should be the guy who interviewed you. We have pretty much the same background; we ought to understand each other."

I took a steadying gulp of the whisky and soda he'd poured for us and said cautiously, "I'm not too sure, sir. Heard something about you at the school. Seems you led quite an adventurous life even before you joined. And afterward— Me, I've been a quiet, stick-in-the-mud type."

"Not really." Everard glanced at a sheet of notes he held. His left hand curled around a battered briar pipe. Once in a while he'd take a puff or a sip. "Let's refresh my memory, shall we? You didn't see combat during your Army hitch, but that was because you served your two years in what we laughingly call peacetime. You did, though, make top scores on the target range. You've always been an outdoorsman, mountaineering, skiing, sailing, swimming. In college, you played football and won your letter in spite of that lanky build. In grad school your hobbies included fencing and archery. You've traveled a fair amount, not always to the safe and standard places. Yes, I'd call you adventurous enough for our purposes. Possibly a tad too adventurous. That's one thing I'm trying to sound you out about."

Feeling awkward, I glanced again around the room. On a high floor, it was an oasis of quiet and cleanliness. Bookshelves lined the walls, save for three excellent pictures and a pair of Bronze Age spears. Else the only obvious souvenir was a polar bear rug that he had remarked was from tenth-century Greenland.

"You've been married twenty-three years, to the same lady," Everard remarked. "These days, that indicates a stable character."

There was no sign of femininity here. To be sure, he might well keep a wife, or wives, elsewhen.

"No children," Everard went on. "Hm, none of my business, but you do know, don't you, that if you want, our medics can repair every cause of infertility this side of menopause? They can compensate for a late start on pregnancies, too."

"Thanks," I said. "Fallopian tubes— Yes, Laurie and I have discussed it. We may well take advantage someday. But we don't think we'd be wise to begin parenthood and my new career simultaneously." I formed a chuckle. "If simultaneity means anything to a Patroller."

"A responsible attitude. I like that." Everard nodded.

"Why this review, sir?" I ventured. "I wasn't invited to enlist merely on the strength of Herbert Ganz's recommendation. Your people put me through a whole battery of far-future psych tests before they told me what it meant."

They'd called it a set of scientific experiments. I'd cooperated because Ganz had asked me to, as a favor to a friend of his. It wasn't his field; he was in Germanic languages and literature, the same as me. We'd met at a professional gathering, become drinking buddies, and corresponded quite a bit. He'd admired my papers on *Deor* and *Widsith*, I'd admired his on the Gothic Bible.

Naturally, I did not know then that it was his. It was published in Berlin in 1853. Later he was recruited into the Patrol, and eventually he came uptime under an alias, in search of talent for his undertaking.

Everard leaned back. Across the pipe, his gaze probed at me. "Well," he said, "the machines told us you and your wife are trustworthy, and would both be delighted by the truth. What they could not measure was how competent you'd be in the job for which you were proposed. Excuse me, no insult intended. Nobody is good at everything, and these missions will be tough, lonesome, delicate." He paused. "Yes, delicate. The Goths may be barbarians, but that doesn't mean they are stupid, or that they can't be hurt as badly as you or me."

"I understand," I said. "But look, all you need do is read the reports I'll have filed in my own personal future. If the early accounts show me bungling, why, just tell me to stay home and become a book researcher. The outfit needs those too, doesn't it?"

Everard sighed. "I have inquired, and been told you performed—will perform—will have performed—satisfactorily. That isn't enough. You don't realize, because you haven't experienced it, how overburdened the Patrol is, how ghastly thin we're spread across history. We can't examine every detail of what a field agent does. That's especially true when he or she isn't a cop like me, but a scientist like you, exploring a milieu poorly chronicled or not chronicled at all." He treated himself to a swallow of his drink. "That's why the Patrol does have a scientific branch. So it can get a slightly better idea of what the hell the events *are* that it is supposed to keep careless time travelers from changing."

"Would it make a significant difference, in a situation as obscure as that?"

"It might. In due course, the Goths play an important role, don't they? Who knows what a happening early on—a victory or a defeat, a rescue or a death, a certain individual getting born or not getting born—who knows what effect that could have, as its results propagate through the generations?"

"But I'm not even concerned with real events, except indirectly," I argued. "My objective is to help recover various lost stories and poems, and unravel how they evolved and how they influenced later works."

Everard grinned ruefully. "Yeah, I know. Ganz's big deal. The Patrol has bought it because it is an opening wedge, the single such wedge we've found, to getting the history of that milieu recorded."

He knocked back his drink and rose. "How about another?" he proposed. "And then we'll have lunch. Meanwhile, I wish you'd tell me exactly what your project is."

"Why, you must have talked to Herbert—to Professor Ganz," I said, astonished. "Uh, thanks, I would like a refill."

"Sure," Everard said, pouring. "Retrieve Germanic literature of the Dark Ages. If 'literature' is the right word for stuff that was originally word of mouth, in illiterate societies. Mere chunks of it have survived on paper, and scholars don't agree on how badly garbled those copies are. Ganz's working on the, um-m, the Nibelung epic. What I'm vague about is where you fit in. That's a story from the Rhineland. You want to go gallivanting solo away off in eastern Europe, in the fourth century."

His manner did more than his whisky to put me at ease. "I hope to track down the Ermanaric part," I told him. "It isn't properly integral, but a connection did develop, and besides, it's interesting in its own right."

"Ermanaric? Who dat?" Everard gave me my glass and settled himself to listen.

"Maybe I better backtrack a little," I said. "How familiar are you with the Nibelung-Volsung cycle?"

"Well, I've seen Wagner's *Ring* operas. And when I had a mission once in Scandinavia, toward the close of the viking period, I heard a yarn about Sigurd, who killed the dragon and woke the Valkyrie and afterward mucked everything up."

"That's a fraction of the whole story, sir."

"'Manse' will do, Carl."

"Oh, uh, thanks. I feel honored." Not to grow fulsome, I hurried on in my best classroom style:

"The Icelandic *Volsungasaga* was written down later than the German *Nibelungenlied*, but contains an older, more primitive, and lengthier version of the story. The *Elder* and the *Younger Edda* have some of it too. Those are the sources that Wagner mainly borrowed from.

"You may recall that Sigurd the Volsung got tricked into marrying Gudrun the Gjuking instead of Brynhild the Valkyrie, and this led to jealousy between the women and at last to his getting killed. In German, those persons are called Siegfried, Kriemhild of Burgundy, Brunhild of Isenstein; and the pagan gods don't appear; but no matter now. According to both stories, Gudrun, or Kriemhild, later married a king called Atli, or Etzel, who is none other than Attila the Hun.

"Then the versions really diverge. In the *Nibelungenlied*, Kriemhild lures her brothers to Etzel's court and has them set on and destroyed, as her revenge for their murder of Siegfried. Theodoric the Great, the Ostrogoth who took over Italy, gets into that episode under the name of Dietrich of Bern, though in historical fact he flourished a generation later than Attila. A follower of his, Hildebrand, is so horrified at Kriemhild's treachery and cruelty that he slays her. Hildebrand, by the way, has a legend of his own, in a ballad whose entirety Herb Ganz wants to find, as well as in derivative works. You see what a cat's cradle of anachronisms this is."

"Attila the Hun, eh?" Everard murmured. "Not a very nice man. But he operated in the middle fifth century, when those bully boys were already riding high in Europe. You're going to the fourth."

"Correct. Let me give you the Icelandic tale. Atli enticed Gudrun's brothers to him because he wanted the Rhinegold. She tried to warn them, but they came anyway under pledge of safe conduct. When they wouldn't surrender the hoard or tell Atli where it was, he had them put to death. Gudrun got even for that. She butchered the sons she'd borne him and served them to him as ordinary food. Later she stabbed him as he slept, set his hall afire, and left Hunland. With her she took Svanhild, her daughter by Sigurd."

Everard frowned, concentrating. It couldn't be easy to keep track of these characters.

"Gudrun came to the country of the Goths," I said. "There she married again and had two sons, Hamther and Sorli. The king of the Goths is called Jormunrek in the saga and in the Eddic poems, but there is no doubt that he was Ermanaric, who is a real if shadowy figure around the middle and late fourth century. Accounts differ whether he married Svanhild and she was falsely accused of infidelity, or she married somebody else whom the king caught plotting against him and hanged. In either case, he had poor Svanhild trampled to death by horses.

"By this time, Gudrun's boys, Hamther and Sorli, were young men. She egged them on to kill Jormunrek in vengeance for Svanhild. Along the way they met their half-brother Erp, who offered to accompany them. They cut him down. The manuscripts are vague as to the reason why. My guess is he was their father's child by a concubine and there was bad blood between them and him.

"They proceeded to Jormunrek's headquarters and the attack. They were two alone, but invulnerable to steel, so they slew men right and left, reached the king, and wounded him severely. Before they could finish the job, though,

Hamther let slip that stones could hurt them. Or, according to the saga, Odin suddenly appeared, in the guise of an old man with one eye, and betrayed this information. Jormunrek called to his remaining warriors to stone the brothers, and that is how they died. There the tale ends.¨

"Grim, hey?" said Everard. He pondered for a minute. "But it seems to me that whole last episode—Gudrun in Gothland—must've been tacked on at a much later date. The anachronisms have gotten completely out of hand."

"Of course," I agreed. "That very commonly happens in folklore. An important story will attract lesser ones to it. Even in trifling ways. For instance, it wasn't W. C. Fields who said that a man who hates children and dogs can't be all bad. It was somebody else, I forget who, introducing Fields at a banquet."

Everard laughed. "Don't tell me the Patrol should monitor Hollywood history!" He grew serious again. "If that sanguinary little yarn doesn't really belong in the Nibelung canon, why do you want to trace it? Why does Ganz want you to?"

"Well, it did reach Scandinavia, where it did inspire a couple of pretty good poems—if those weren't just redactions of something earlier—and did hook up to the Volsung saga. The connections, the whole evolution, interest us. Also, Ermanaric gets mention elsewhere—in certain Old English lays, for instance. So he must have figured in a lot of legend and bardic work that was since forgotten. He *was* powerful in his day, though apparently not a very nice man himself. The lost Ermanaric cycle might well be as important and brilliant as anything that has come down to us from the West and the North. It may have influenced Germanic literature in scores of unsuspected ways."

"Do you intend to go straight to his court? I wouldn't recommend that, Carl. Too many field agents get killed because they got careless."

"Oh, no. Something horrible happened, from which stories sprang and traveled far, even reaching into historical chronicles. I think I can bracket when it happened, too, within about ten years. But I mean to familiarize myself thoroughly with the whole milieu before I venture into that episode."

"Good. What is your plan?"

"I'll take an electronic cram in the Gothic language. I can read it already, but want to speak it fluently, though doubtless my accent will be odd. I'll also want a cram on what little is known about customs, beliefs, *et cetera*. That'll be very little. The Ostrogoths, if not the Visigoths, were still on the bare fringes of Roman awareness. Surely they changed considerably before they moved west.

"So I'll begin well downtime of my target dates; somewhat arbitrarily, I'm thinking of A.D. 300. I'll get acquainted with people. Next I'll reappear at intervals and learn what's been going on in my absence. In short, I'll keep track of events as they march toward *the* event. When it finally comes, I shouldn't be caught by surprise. Afterward I'll drop in here and there, from time to time, and listen to the poets and storytellers, and get their words on a concealed recorder."

Everard scowled. "Um-m, that kind of procedure—Well, we can discuss the possible complications. You'll move around a fair amount geographically too, won't you?"

"Yes. According to what traditions of theirs got written down in the Roman Empire, the Goths originated in what's now central Sweden. I don't believe that numerous a breed could have come from that limited an area, even allowing for natural increase, but it may have furnished leaders and organization, the way the Scandinavians did for the nascent Russian state in the ninth century.

"I'd say the bulk of the Goths started as dwellers along the southern Baltic littoral. They were the easternmost of the Germanic peoples. Not that they were ever a single nation. By the time they reached western Europe, they were separated into the Ostrogoths, who took over Italy, and the Visigoths, who took over Iberia. Gave those regions fairly good government, by the way, the best government they'd had for a long while. Eventually the invaders were overrun in their turn, and vanished into the general populations."

"But earlier?"

"Historians make unclear mention of tribes. By A.D. 300 Goths were firmly established along the Vistula, in the middle of what's currently Poland. Before the end of that century, the Ostrogoths were in the Ukraine and the Visigoths just north of the Danube, the Roman frontier. A great folk migration, apparently, over the course of generations, because they seem at last to have abandoned the North entirely; there, Slavic tribes moved in. Ermanaric was an Ostrogoth, so that's the branch I mean to follow."

"Ambitious," Everard said doubtfully. "And you a new chum."

"I'll gain experience as I go along, uh, Manse. You admitted yourself, the Patrol is shorthanded. Moreover, I'll be acquiring a lot of that history which you want."

He smiled. "You should, at that." Rising: "Come on, finish your drink and let's go eat. We'll need a change of clothes, but it'll be worth the trouble. I know a local saloon, back in the eighteen-nineties, that sets out a magnificent free lunch."

300-302

Winter descended and then slowly, in surges of wind, snow, icy rain, drew back. For those who dwelt in the thorp by the river, and soon for their neighbors, the dreariness of the season was lightened that year. Carl abode among them.

At first the mystery surrounding him roused fear in many; but they came to see that he bore neither ill will nor bad luck. The awe of him did not dwindle. Rather, it grew. From the beginning, Winnithar said that for such a guest to sleep on a bench, like a common thane, was unfitting, and turned a shut-bed over to him. He offered Carl the pick of the thrall women to warm it, but the stranger made refusal, in mannerly wise. He did accept food and drink, and he did bathe and seek the outhouse. However, the whisper went about that maybe these things were not needful for him, save as a show of being mortal.

Carl was soft-spoken and friendly, in a somewhat lofty way. He could laugh, crack a joke, tell a funny tale. He went forth afoot or ahorse, in company, to hunt or call on the nearer yeomen or join in offerings to the Anses and in the feasting that followed. He took part in contests such as shooting or wrestling, until it had become clear that no man could best him. When he played at knucklebones or board games, he did not always win, though the idea arose that this was because he chose not to make folk afraid of witchcraft. He would talk to anybody, from Winnithar to the lowliest thrall or littlest toddler, and listen with care; indeed, he drew them out, and was kindly toward underlings and animals.

But as for his own inward self, that remained hidden.

This did not mean that he sat sullen. No, he made words and music come forth asparkle as none had ever done before. Eager to hear songs, lays, stories, saws, everything that went about, he gave overflowing measure in return. For he seemed to know all the world, as if he had wandered it himself for longer than a lifetime.

He told of Rome, the mighty and troubled, of its lord Diocletian, his wars and his stern laws. He answered questions about the new god, him of the Cross, of whom the Goths had heard a bit from traders or from slaves sold this far north. He told of the Romans' great foes, the Persians, and what wonders they had wrought. Onward his words ranged, evening after evening—on southward to lands where it was always hot, and people had black skins, and beasts prowled that were akin to lynxes but the size of bears. Other beasts did he show them, drawing pictures in charcoal on slabs of wood, and they cried aloud in their astonishment; set beside an elephant, an aurochs or even a troll-steed was nothing! Near the ends of the East, he said, lay a realm larger, older, more marvelous than Rome or Persia. Its dwellers were of a hue like wan amber, and had eyes that appeared to be aslant. Plagued by wild tribes north of them, they had built a wall as long as a mountain range, and had since then been striking back out of that redoubt. This was why the Huns had come west. They, who had broken the Alans and were vexing the Goths, were only a rabble in the slanting gaze of Khitai. And all this vastness was not all there was. If you traveled westward till you had crossed the Roman holding called Gaul, you would come to the World Sea of which you had heard fables, and if there you took ship—but craft such as plied the rivers were not big enough—and sailed on and on, you would find the home of the wise and wealthy Mayas. . . .

Tales Carl also had of men, women, and their deeds—Samson the strong, Deirdre the fair and unhappy, Crockett the hunter. . . .

Jorith, daughter of Winnithar, forgot she was of age to be wedded. She would sit among the children on the floor, at Carl's feet, and hearken while her eyes caught firelight and became suns.

He was not steadily on hand. Often he would say he must be by himself, and stride off out of sight. Once a lad, brash but skilled at stalking, followed him unseen, unless it was that Carl deigned not to heed him. The boy came back white and ashudder, to stammer forth that the graybeard had gone into Tiwaz's Shaw. None went under those darkling pines save on Midwinter Eve, when three blood offerings—horse, hound, and slave—were made so that the Binder of the Wolf would bid darkness and cold begone. The boy's father flogged him, and thereafter nobody spoke openly of it. If the gods allowed it to happen, best not ask into their reasons.

Carl would return in a few days, freshly clothed and bearing gifts. Those were small things, but beyond price, be it a knife whose steel held an edge uncommonly long, a scarf of lustrous foreign fabric, a mirror outdoing buffed brass or a still pond—the treasures arrived and arrived, until everybody of any standing, man or woman, had gotten at least one. About this he said merely, "I know the makers."

Spring stole northward, snow melted, buds burst into leaf and flower, the river brawled in spate. Homebound birds filled heaven with wings and clamor. Lambs, calves, foals tottered across paddocks. Folk came forth, blinking in sudden brightness; they aired out their houses, garments, and souls. The Spring Queen drove Frija's image from farm to farm to bless the plowing and sowing, while garlanded youths and maidens danced around her oxcart. Longings quickened.

Carl went away still, but now he would be back on the same evening. More and more were he and Jorith together. They would even stroll into woods, down blossoming lanes, over meadows, out of everybody else's ken. She walked as though lost in dreams. Salvalindis her mother scolded her about unseemliness—did she care naught for her good name?—until Winnithar quelled his wife. The chieftain was a shrewd reckoner. As for Jorith's brothers, they glowed.

At length Salvalindis took her daughter aside. They sought an outbuilding where the household's women met to weave and sew when there was no other work for them. There was now, so that these two were alone in its dimness. Salvalindis put Jorith between herself and the broad, stone-weighted loom, as if to trap her, and asked bluntly, "Have you been less idle with that man Carl than you've become at home? Has he had you?"

The maiden flushed, twisted fingers together, stared downward. "No," she breathed. "He can, whenever he wants. How I wish he would. But we've only held hands, kissed a little, and—and—"

"And what?"

"Talked. Sung songs. Laughed. Been grave. Oh, Mother, he's not aloof. With me, he's kinder and, and sweeter than . . . than I knew a man could be. He talks to me as he would to somebody who can think, not just be a wife—"

Salvalindis's lips pinched. "*I* never stopped thinking when I married. Your father may see a powerful ally in Carl. But I see in him a man without land or kin, belike a warlock but rootless, rootless. What gain can our house have of linking with him? Goods, aye; knowledge; but what use are those when foemen threaten? What would he leave to his sons? What would bind him to you after the freshness is gone? Girl, you're being a fool."

Jorith clenched her fists, stamped her foot, and yelled through tears that were more of rage than woe: "Hold your tongue, old crone!" At once she shrank back, as aghast as Salvalindis.

"You speak thus to your mother?" the latter said. "Aye, a warlock he is, who's cast a spell on you. Throw that brooch he gave you into the river, do you hear?" She turned and left the room. Her skirts made an angry rustling.

Jorith wept, but did not obey.

And soon everything changed.

On a day when rain blew like spears, while Donar's wagon boomed aloft and the flash of his ax blinded heaven, a man galloped into the thorp. He sagged in the saddle, and his horse was near falling from weariness. Nevertheless he shook an arrow on high and shrilled to those who had come out through the mud to meet him: "War! The Vandals draw nigh!"

Brought into the hall, he said before Winnithar: "My word is from my father, Aefli of Staghorn Dale. He had it from a man of Dagalaif Nevittasson,

who fled the slaughter at Elkford so as to carry warning. But already we at
Aefli's had marked a ruddiness on the skyline, where surely farmsteads were
afire."

"Two bands of them, then," Winnithar muttered. "At least. Belike more.
They're out early this year, and in strength."

"How could they leave their grounds untended in seeding time?" asked a
son of his.

Winnithar gusted a sigh. "They've bred more hands than they need for
work. Besides, I hear of a King Hildaric, who's brought their clans beneath
him. Thus they can field greater hosts than erstwhile, which move faster and
under a better plan than we're able. Aye, could be Hildaric means to rid these
lands of us, for the good of his own overflowing realm."

"What shall we do?" an iron-steady old warrior wanted to know.

"Gather the neighborhood men and go to meet as many others as time
allows, like Aefli's, if he hasn't already been overrun. At the Rock of the Twin
Horsemen as aforetime, eh? It may be that, together, we'll not hit a Vandal
troop too big for us."

Carl stirred where he sat. "But what of your homes?" he asked. "Raiders
could outflank you, unbeknownst, and fall on steadings like yours." He left
the rest unspoken: plunder, burning, women in their best years borne off,
everybody else cut down.

"We must risk that. Else we'll be whipped piecemeal." Winnithar grew
silent. The longfires leaped and flickered. Outside, wind hooted and rain
dashed against walls. His gaze sought Carl's. "We have no helmet or mail that
would fit you. Maybe you can fetch gear for yourself from wherever you get
things."

The outsider sat stiff. Lines deepened in his face.

Winnithar's shoulders slumped. "Well, this is no fight of yours, is it?" he
sighed. "You're no Teuring."

"Carl, oh, Carl!" Jorith came out from among the women.

For a while that reached onward, she and the gray man looked at each other.
Then he shook himself, turned to Winnithar, and said: "Fear not. I'll abide by
my friends. But it must be in my own way, and you must follow my redes,
whether or not you understand them. Are you willing to that?"

Nobody cheered. A sound like the wind passed down the shadowy length of
the hall.

Winnithar mustered heart. "Yes," he said. "Now let riders of ours take war
arrows around. But the rest of us shall feast."

—What happened in the next few weeks was never really known. Men
fared, pitched camp, fought, came home afterward or did not. Those who did,
which was most of them, often had wild tales to tell. They spoke of a

blue-cloaked spearman who rode through the sky on a mount that was not a horse. They spoke of dreadful monsters charging at Vandal ranks, and eerie lights in the dark, and blind fear coming upon the foe, until he cast his weapons from him and fled screaming. They spoke of somehow always finding a Vandal gang before it had quite reached a Gothic thorp, and putting it to flight, making sheer lack of loot cause clan after clan to give up and trek off. They spoke of victory.

Their chiefs could say slightly more. It was the Wanderer who had told them where to go, what to await, how best to form array for battle. It was he who outsped the gale as he brought warning and summons, he who got Greutung and Taifal and Amaling help, he who overawed the haughty till they worked side by side as he ordered.

These stories faded away in the course of the following lifetime or two. They were so strange. Rather, they sank back among the older stories of their kind. Anses, Wanes, trolls, wizards, ghosts, had not such beings again and again joined the quarrels of men? What mattered was that for a half-score years, the Goths along the upper Vistula knew peace. Let us get on with the harvest, said they: or whatever else they wanted to do with their lives.

But Carl came back to Jorith as the rescuer.

—He could not really wed her. He *had* no acknowledged kin. Yet men who could afford it had always taken lemans; the Goths held that to be no shame, if the man provided well for woman and children. Besides, Carl was no mere swain, thane, or king. Salvalindis herself brought Jorith to him, where he waited in a flower-decked loftroom, after a feast at which splendid gifts passed to and fro.

Winnithar had timber cut and ferried across the river, and a goodly house raised for the two. Carl wanted some odd things in the building, such as a bedroom by itself. There was also another room, kept locked save when he went in alone. He was never there long, and no more did he go off to Tiwaz's Shaw.

Men said between themselves that he made far too much of Jorith. They were apt to swap looks, or walk away from others, like some fuzz-cheeked boy and a thrall girl. However . . . she ran her home well enough, and anyway, who dared mock at him?

He himself left most of a husband's tasks to a steward. He did bring in the goods that the household needed, or the wherewithal to trade for them. And he became a great trader. These years of peace were not years of listlessness. No, they brought more chapmen than ever before, carrying amber, furs, honey, tallow from the North, wine, glass, metalwork, cloth, fine pottery from the South and West. Ever eager to meet somebody new, Carl guested passersby lavishly, and went to the fairs as well as the folkmoots.

In those moots he, who was not a tribesman, only watched; but after the day's talk, things would get lively around his booth.

Nonetheless, men wondered, and women too. Word trickled back that a man, gray but hale, whom nobody formerly knew, was often seen among other Gothic tribes. . . .

It may be that those absences of his were the reason why Jorith was not at once with child; or it may be that she was rather young, just sixteen winters, when she came to his bed. A year had gone by before the signs were unmistakable.

Although her sicknesses grew harsh, joy shone from her. Again his behavior was strange, for he seemed to care less about his get that she bore than about her own well being. He even oversaw what she ate, providing her with things like out land fruits regardless of season though forbidding her as much salt as she was wont to. She obeyed gladly, saying this showed he loved her.

Meanwhile life went on in the neighborhood, and death. At the burials and grave-ales, nobody made bold to speak freely with Carl; he was too close to the unknown. On the other hand, the heads of household who had chosen him were taken aback when he refused the honor of being the man hereabouts who would swive the next Spring Queen.

Remembering what else he had done and was doing on their behalf, they got over that.

Warmth; harvest; bleakness; rebirth; summer again; and Jorith was brought to her childbed.

Long was her toil. She suffered the pains bravely, but the women who attended her became very glum. The elves would not have liked it had a man seen her during that time. Bad enough how Carl had demanded unheard-of cleanliness. They could only hope that he knew what he was about.

He waited it out in the main room of his house. When callers came, he had mead and drink set forth as was right, but stayed curt in his speech. When they left at nightfall, he did not sleep but sat alone in the dark until sunrise. Now and then the midwife or a helper would shuffle out to tell him how the birth was going. By the light of the lamp she bore, she saw how his glance sought the door he kept locked.

Late in the second day, the midwife found him among his friends. Silence fell upon them. Then that which she bore in her arms let out a wail—and Winnithar a shout. Carl rose, his nostrils white.

The woman knelt before him, unfolded the blanket, and on the earthen floor, at the father's feet, laid a man-child, still bloody but lustily sprattling and crying. If Carl did not take the babe up onto his knee, she would carry it into the woods and leave it for the wolves. He never stopped to see if aught might be wrong with it. He snatched the wee form to him while he croaked, "Jorith, how fares Jorith?"

"Weak," said the midwife. "Go to her now if you will."

Carl gave her back his son and hastened to the bedroom. The women who were there stood aside. He bent over Jorith. She lay white, sweat-clammy, hollowed out. But when she saw her man, she reached feebly upward and smiled the ghost of a smile. "Dagobert," she whispered. That was the name, old in her family, that she had wished for, were this a boy.

"Dagobert, yes," Carl said low. Unseemly though it was in sight of the rest, he bent to kiss her.

She lowered her lids and sank back onto the straw. "Thank you," came from her throat, barely to be heard. "The son of a god."

"No—"

Suddenly Jorith shuddered. For a moment she clutched at her brow. Her eyes opened again. The pupils were fixed and wide. She grew bonelessly limp. Breath rattled in and out.

Carl straightened, whirled, and sped from the room. At the locked door, he took forth his key and went inside. It banged behind him.

Salvalindis moved to her daughter's side. "She is dying," she said flatly. "Can his witchcraft save her? Should it?"

The forbidden door swung back. Carl came out, and another. He forgot to close it. Men glimpsed a thing of metal. Some remembered what he had ridden who flew above the battlefields. They huddled close, gripped amulets or drew signs in the air.

Carl's companion was a woman, though clad in rainbow-shimmery breeks and tunic. Her countenance was of a kind never seen before—broad and high in the cheekbones like a Hun's, but short of nose, coppery-golden of hue, beneath straight blue-black hair. She held a box by its handle.

The two dashed to the bedroom. "Out, out!" Carl roared, and chased the Gothic women before him like leaves before a storm.

He followed them, and now remembered to shut the door on his steed. Turning around, he saw how everybody stared at him, while they shrank away. "Be not afraid," he said thickly. "No harm is here. I have but fetched a wise-woman to help Jorith."

For a while they all stood in stillness and gathering murk.

The stranger trod forth and beckoned to Carl. There was that about her which drew a groan from him. He stumbled to her, and she led him by the elbow into the bedroom. Silence welled out of it.

After another while folk heard voices, his full of fury and anguish, hers calm and ruthless. Nobody understood that tongue.

They returned. Carl's face looked aged. "She is sped," he told the others.

"I have closed her eyes. Make ready her burial and feast, Winnithar. I will be back for that."

He and the wise-woman entered the secret room. From the midwife's arms, Dagobert howled.

2319

I'd flitted uptime to nineteen-thirties New York, because I knew that base and its personnel. The young fellow on duty tried to make a fuss about regulations, but him I could browbeat. He put through an emergency call for a top-flight medic. It happened to be Kwei-fei Mendoza who had the opportunity to respond, though we'd never met. She asked no more questions than were needful before she joined me on my hopper and we were off to Gothland. Later, however, she wanted us both at her hospital, on the moon in the twenty-fourth century. I was in no shape to protest.

She had me take a kettle-hot bath and sent me to bed. An electronic skullcap gave me many hours of sleep.

Eventually I received clean clothes, something to eat (I didn't notice what), and guidance to her office. Seated behind an enormous desk, she waved me to take a chair. Neither of us spoke for a minute or three.

Evading hers, my gaze shifted around. The artificial gravity that kept my weight as usual did nothing to make the place homelike for me. Not that it wasn't quite beautiful, in its fashion. The air bore a tinge of roses and new-mown hay. The carpet was a deep violet in which star-points twinkled. Subtle colors swirled over the walls. A big window, if window it was, showed the grandeur of mountains, a craterscape in the distance, heaven black but reigned over by an Earth nearly full. I lost myself in the sight of that glorious white-swirled blueness. Jorith had lost herself there, two thousand years ago.

"Well, Agent Farness," Mendoza said at length in Temporal, the Patrol language, "how do you feel?"

"Dazed but clear-headed," I muttered. "No. Like a murderer."

"You should certainly have left that child alone."

I forced my attention toward her and replied, "She wasn't a child. Not in her society, or in most throughout history. The relationship helped me a lot in getting the trust of the community, therefore in furthering my mission. Not that I was cold-blooded about it, please believe me. We were in love."

"What has your wife to say on that subject? Or did you never tell her?"

My defense had left me too exhausted to resent what might else have seemed nosiness. "Yes, I did. I . . . asked her if she'd mind. She thought it over and decided not. We'd spent our younger days in the nineteen-sixties and seventies, remember . . . No, you'd scarcely have heard, but that was a period of revolution in sexual mores."

Mendoza smiled rather grimly. "Fashions come and go."

"We'd stayed monogamous, my wife and I, but more out of preference than principle. And look, I always kept visiting her. I love her, I really do."

"And she doubtless reckoned it best to let you have your middle-aged fling," Mendoza snapped.

That stung. "It wasn't! I tell you, I loved Jorith, the Gothic girl, I loved her too." Grief took me by the throat. "Was there absolutely nothing you could do?"

Mendoza shook her head. Her hands rested quietly on the desk. Her tone softened. "I told you already. I'll tell you in detail if you wish. The instruments—no matter how they work, but they showed an aneurysm of the anterior cerebral artery. It hadn't been bad enough to produce symptoms, but the stress of a long and difficult primiparous labor caused it to rupture. No kindness to revive her, after such extensive brain damage."

"You couldn't repair it?"

"Well, we could have brought the body uptime, restarted the heart and lungs, and used neuron cloning techniques to produce a person that resembled her, but who would have had to learn almost everything over from the beginning. My corps does not do that sort of operation, Agent Farness. It isn't that we lack compassion, it's simply that we have too many calls on us already, to help Patrol personnel and their . . . proper families. If ever we started making exceptions, we'd be swamped. Nor would you have gotten your sweetheart back, you realize. She would not have gotten herself back."

I rallied what force of will was left me. "Suppose we went downtime of her pregnancy," I said. "We could bring her here, fix that artery, blank her memories of the whole trip, and return her to—live out a healthy life."

"That's your wishfullness speaking. The Patrol does not change what has been. It preserves it."

I sank deeper into my chair. Variable contours sought in vain to comfort me.

Mendoza relented. "But don't feel too much guilt, you," she said. "You couldn't have known. If the girl had married somebody else, as she surely would have, the end would have been the same. I get the impression you made her happier than most females of her era."

Her tone gathered strength: "You, though, you've given yourself a wound that will take long to scar over. It never will, unless you resist the supreme temptation—to keep going back to her lifetime, seeing her, being with her. That is forbidden, under severe penalties, and not only because of the risks it might pose to the time stream. You'd wreck your spirit, even your mind. And we need you. Your wife needs you."

"Yes," I achieved saying.

"Hard enough will be watching your descendants and hers endure what they must. I wonder if you should not transfer entirely from your project."

"No. Please."

"Why not?" she flung at me.

"Because I—I can't just abandon them—as if Jorith had lived and died for nothing."

"That will be for your superiors to decide. You'll get a stiff reprimand at the very least, as close to the black hole as you've orbited. Never again may you interfere to the degree you did." Mendoza paused, glanced from me, stroked her chin, and murmured, "Unless certain actions prove necessary to restore equilibrium . . . But that is not my province."

Her look returned to my misery. Abruptly she leaned forward over the desk, made a reaching gesture, and said:

"Listen, Carl Farness. I'm going to be asked for my opinion of your case. That's why I brought you here, and why I want to keep you a week or two—to get a better idea. But already—you're not unique, my friend, in a million years of Patrol operations!—already I've begun to see you as a decent sort, who may have blundered but largely through inexperience.

"It happens, has happened, will happen, over and over. Isolation, in spite of furloughs at home and liaisons with prosaic fellow members like me. Bewilderment, in spite of advance preparation; culture shock; human shock. You witnessed what to you were wretchedness, poverty, squalor, ignorance, needless tragedy—worse, callousness, brutality, injustice, wanton man-slaughter—You couldn't encounter that without it hurting you. You had to assure yourself that your Goths were no worse than you are, merely different; and you had to seek past that difference to the underlying identity; and then you had to try to help, and if along the way you suddenly found a door open on something dear and wonderful—

"Yes, inevitably, time travelers, including Patrollers—many of them form ties. They perform actions, and sometimes those are intimate. It doesn't normally pose a threat. What matters the precise, the obscure and remote, ancestry of even a key figure? The continuum yields but rebounds. If its stress limits aren't exceeded, why, the question becomes unanswerable, meaning-less, whether such minor doings change the past, or have 'always' been a part of it.

"Do not feel too guilty, Farness," she ended, most quietly. "I would also like to start you recovering from that, and from your grief. You are a field agent of the Time Patrol; this is not the last mourning you will ever have reason to do."

302-330

Carl kept his word. Stone-silent, he leaned on his spear and watched while her kinfolk laid Jorith in the earth and heaped a barrow above her. Afterward he and her father honored her by an arval to which they bade the whole neighborhood come, and which lasted three days. There he spoke only when spoken to, though at those times polite enough in his lordly way. While he did not seek to dampen anybody's merriment, that feast was quieter than most.

When guests had departed, and Carl sat alone by his hearth save for Winnithar, he told the chieftain: "Tomorrow I go too. You will not see me often again."

"Have you then done whatever you came for?"

"No, not yet."

Winnithar did not ask what it was. Carl sighed and added: "As far as Weard allows, I mean to watch over your house. But that may not be so far."

At dawn he bade farewell and strode off. Mists lay heavy and chill, soon hiding him from the sight of men.

In years that followed, tales grew. Some thought they had glimpsed his tall form by twilight, entering the grave-mound as if by a door. Others said no; he had led her away by the hand. Their memories of him slowly lost humanness.

Dagobert's grandparents took the babe in, found a wet nurse, and raised him like their own. Despite his uncanny begetting, he was not shunned nor let run wild. Instead, folk reckoned his friendship well worth having, for he must be destined to mighty deeds—on which account, he should learn honor and seemly ways, as well as the skills of a warrior, hunter, and husbandman. Children of gods were not unheard of. They became heroes, or women passing wise and fair, but were nonetheless mortal.

After three years, Carl came briefly calling. As he watched his son, he murmured, "How he does look like his mother."

"Aye, in the face," Winnithar agreed, "but he'll not lack manliness; that's already plain to see, Carl."

None else made bold anymore to bespeak the Wanderer by that name—nor by the name they supposed was right. At drinking time they did as he wished, saying forth what tales and verses they had lately heard. He asked whence those sprang, and they could tell him of a bard or two, whom he said he would visit. He did, later, and the makers reckoned themselves lucky to have *his* notice. For his part, he told spellbinding things as of yore. However, now he was shortly gone again, not to return for years.

Meanwhile Dagobert grew apace, a lad brisk, merry, handsome, and well liked. He was but twelve when he accompanied his half-brothers, Winnithar's two oldest sons, on a trip south with a crew of traders. They wintered there, and came back in spring brimful of wonders. Yes, yonder were lands for the taking, rich, wide, watered by a Dnieper River that made this Vistula seem a brook. The northern valleys there were thickly wooded but farther south the countryside lay open, pastureland for herds and flocks, bride-like awaiting the farmer's plow. Whoever held it would also sit astride a flow of goods through the Black Sea ports.

As yet, not many Goths had moved thither. It was the westerly tribes that had made the really great trek, into the Danube. There they were at the Roman frontier, which meant a spate of barter. On the bad side, should it come to war, the Romans remained formidable—especially if they could put an end to their civil strife.

The Dnieper flowed safely from the Empire. True, Heruls had come from the North and settled along the Azov shore: wild men, who would doubtless give trouble. Yet because they were such wolfish beings, who scorned to wear mail or fight in ranks, they were less fearsome than the Vandals. Likewise true, north and east of them laired the Huns, horsemen, stockbreeders, akin to trolls in their ugliness, filth, and bloodlust. They were said to be the direst warriors in the world. But the more glory in beating them if they attacked; and a Gothic league could beat them, for they were split into clans and tribes, likelier to fight each other than to raid farms and towns.

Dagobert was ablaze to be off, and his brothers eager. Winnithar urged caution. Let them learn more ere making a move that could not be unmade. Besides, come the time, they should go not as a few families, prey to reavers, but in force. It looked as though that would soon be possible.

For these were the days when Geberic of the Greutung tribe was drawing the eastern Goths together. Some he fought and broke to his will, others he won over by talk, whether threat or promise. Among the latter were the Teurings, who in Dagobert's fifteenth year hailed Geberic their king.

This meant that they paid scot to him, which was not heavy; sent men to fight for him when he wanted, unless it was the season of sowing or harvest; and heeded such laws as the Great Moot made for the whole realm. In return, they need no longer beware of fellow Goths who had joined him, but rather had the help of these against common foes; trade bloomed; and they themselves had men at each year's Great Moot, to speak and to vote.

Dagobert did well in the king's wars. In between, he would fare south, as a captain of guards for the chapmen's bands. There he went around and learned much.

Somehow, the rare visits of his father always took place when he was at home. The Wanderer gave him fine gifts and sage counsel, but talk between them was awkward, for what can a young fellow say to one like that?

Dagobert did lead in making sacrifice at a shrine which Winnithar had built where the house formerly stood in which the boy was born. That house Winnithar had burned, for her to have whose howe stood behind it. Strangely, at this halidom the Wanderer forbade bloodshed. Only first fruits of the earth might be offered. The story arose that apples cast in the fire before the stone became the Apples of Life.

When Dagobert was full grown, Winnithar sought a good wife for him. This became Waluburg, a maiden strong and comely, daughter of Optaris at Staghorn Dale, who was the second most powerful man among the Teurings. The Wanderer blessed the wedding by his presence.

He was also there when Waluburg bore her first child, a boy whom they named Tharasmund. In the same year was born the first son of King Geberic that lived to manhood, Ermanaric.

Waluburg throve, giving her man healthy children. Dagobert stayed unrestful, though; folk said that was the blood of his father in him, and that he heard the wind at the edge of the world forever calling. When he came back from his trip south, he brought news that a Roman lord hight Constantine had finally put down his rivals and become master of the whole Empire.

It may be that this fired Geberic, however forcefully the king had already gone forth. He spent a few more years rallying the East Goths; then he summoned them to follow him and make an end of the Vandal pest.

Dagobert had by now decided he would indeed move south. The Wanderer had told him that that would not be unwise; it was the fate of the Goths, and he might as well be early and get a better pick of holdings. He went about talking this over with yeomen great and small, for he knew his grandfather was right about going in strength. Yet when the war arrow came, in honor he could not but heed. He rode off at the head of better than a hundred men.

That was a grim struggle, ending in a battle which fattened wolves and ravens. There fell the Vandal King Visimar. There too died the older sons of Winnithar, who had hoped to be off with Dagobert. He himself lived, not even badly wounded, and won ringing fame by his doughtiness. Some said that the Wanderer had warded him on the field, spearing foemen, but this he denied. "My father was there, yes, to be with me on the night before the last clash—naught else. We spoke of many and strange things. I asked him not to demean me by doing my fighting for me, and he said that was not the will of Weard."

The upshot was that the Vandals were routed, overrun, and forced to depart their lands. After scouring to and fro for several years beyond the River Danube, dangerous but wretched, they besought the Emperor Constantine for leave to settle in his realm. Not loth to have fresh warriors guarding his marches, he let them cross into Pannonia.

Meanwhile Dagobert found himself the leader of the Teurings, through his marriage, his inheritance, and the name he had won. He spent a time making them ready, and thereupon took them south.

Few stayed behind, so glittering was the hope. Among those who did were old Winnithar and Salvalindis. When the wagons had creaked away, the Wanderer sought those two out, one last time, and was kind to them, for the sake of what had been and of her who slept by the River Vistula.

1980

Manse Everard was not the officer who raked me over the coals for my recklessness, and barely agreed to let me continue in the mission—largely, he grumbled, at Herbert Ganz's urging, because there was nobody to replace me. Everard had his reasons for holding back. Those eventually became evident, as did the fact he'd been studying my reports.

Between the fourth century and the twentieth, I'd passed about two years of personal lifespan since losing Jorith. My grief had dwindled to wistfulness—if only she could have had more of the life she loved and made lovely!—except once in a while when it rose in full force and struck again. In her quiet way, Laurie had helped me toward acceptance. Never before had I understood in full what a wonderful person she was.

I was at home on furlough, New York, 1932, when Everard called and asked for another conference. "Just a few questions, a couple hours' bull-shooting," he said, "and afterward you can go out on the town. Your wife too, of course. Ever see Lola Montez in her heyday? I've got tickets, Paris, 1843."

Winter had fallen uptime. Snow tumbled past the windows of his apartment, making a cave of white stillness for us. He gave me a toddy and inquired what I particularly liked in the way of music. We agreed on a koto performance, by a player in medieval Japan whose name the chronicles have forgotten but who was the finest that ever lived. Time travel has its rewards as well as its pains.

Everard made a production of stuffing and lighting his pipe. "You never filed an account of your relationship to Jorith," he said in a tone almost casual. "It only came out in the course of the inquiry, after you'd sent for Mendoza. Why?"

"It was . . . personal," I answered. "Didn't see that it was anybody else's business. Oh, they cautioned us about that sort of thing at the Academy, but regs don't actually forbid it."

Looking at his dark, bowed head, I had the eerie knowledge that he must have read everything I would write. He knew my personal future as I did not—as I would not until I had been through it. The rule is very seldom waived that keeps an agent from learning his or her destiny; a causal loop is the least undesirable thing that could all too easily result.

"Well, I don't aim to repeat a scolding you've already had," Everard said. "In fact, between the two of us, I feel that Coordinator Abdullah got needlessly stuffy. Operatives must have discretion, or they'd never get their jobs done, and plenty of them have sailed closer to the wind than you did."

He spent a minute kindling his tobacco before he went on, through the blue haze: "However, I would like to ask you about a couple of details. More to get your reaction than on any deep philosophical grounds—though I admit to being curious, too. You see, on that basis, maybe I can give you a few useful procedural suggestions. I'm not a scientist myself, but I have kicked around history, prehistory, and even posthistory, quite a lot."

"You have that," I agreed with enormous respect.

"Well, okay, for openers, the most obvious. Early on, you intervened in a war between Goths and Vandals. How do you justify that?"

"I answered that question at the inquiry, sir . . . Manse. I knew better than to kill anybody, since my own life was never in jeopardy. I helped organize, I collected intelligence, I inspired fear in the enemy—flying around on antigrav, throwing illusions, projecting subsonic beams. If anything, by making them panic, I saved lives on both sides. But my essential reason was that I'd spent a lot of effort—Patrol effort—establishing a base in the society I was supposed to study, and the Vandals threatened to destroy that base."

"You weren't afraid of touching off a change in uptime events?"

"No. Oh, perhaps I should have thought it over more carefully, and gotten expert opinions, before acting. But it did look like almost a textbook case. That was merely a large-scale raid the Vandals were mounting. Nowhere did history record it. The outcome either way was insignificant . . . except to individuals, certain of whom were important to my mission as well as to me. And as for the lives of those individuals—and the line of descent that I started myself, back yonder—why, those are minor statistical fluctuations in the gene pool. They soon average out."

Everard scowled. "You're giving me the standard arguments, Carl, same as you did the board of inquiry. They got you off the hook there. But don't bother today. What I'm trying to make you know, not in your forebrain but in your marrow, is that reality never conforms very well to the textbooks, and sometimes it doesn't conform at all."

"I believe I am beginning to see that." My humility was genuine. "In the lives I've been following downtime. We have no *right* to take people over, do we?"

Everard smiled, and I felt free to savor a long draught from my glass. "Good. Let's drop generalities and get into the details of what you're actually after. For instance, you gave your Goths things they'd never have had without you. The physical presents are not to worry about; those'll rust or rot or be lost quickly enough. But accounts of the world and stories from foreign cultures."

"I had to make myself interesting, didn't I? Why else should they recite old, familiar stuff for me?"

"M-m, yeah, sure. But look, wouldn't whatever you told them get into their folklore, alter the very matter you went to study?"

I allowed myself a chuckle. "No. There I did have a psychosocial calculation run in advance, and used it for a guide. Turns out that societies of this kind have highly selective collective memories. Remember, they're illiterate, and they live in a mental world where marvels are commonplace. What I said about, say, the Romans merely added detail to information they already had from travelers; and those details would shortly be garbled down to the general noise level of their concepts of Rome. As for more exotic material, well, what was somebody like Cuchulainn but one more foredoomed hero, such as they'd heard scores of yarns about? What was the Han Empire but one more fabulous country beyond the horizon? My immediate listeners were impressed; but afterward they passed it on to others, who merged everything into their existing sagas."

Everard nodded. "M-m-m-hm." He smoked for a bit. Abruptly: "What about yourself? You're not a clutch of words; you're a concrete and enigmatic person who keeps appearing among them. You propose to do it for generations. Are you setting up in business as a god?"

That was the hard question, for which I'd spent considerable time preparing. I let another swallow of my drink glow down my throat and warm my stomach before I replied, slowly: "Yes, I'm afraid so. Not that I intended it or want it, but it does seem to have happened."

Everard scarcely stirred. Lazily as a lion, he drawled, "And you maintain that doesn't make a historical difference?"

"I do. Please listen. I've never claimed to be a god, or demanded divine prerogatives, or anything like that. Nor do I propose to. It's just come about. In the nature of the case, I arrived alone, dressed like a wayfarer but not like a bum. I carried a spear because that's the normal weapon for a man on foot. Being of the twentieth century, I'm taller than the average for the fourth, even among Nordic types. My hair and beard are gray. I told stories, described distant places, and, yes, I did fly through the air and strike terror into enemies—it couldn't be helped. But I did not, repeat not, establish a new god. I merely fit an image they'd long worshiped, and in the course of time, a generation or so, they came to assume I must be him."

"What's his name?"

"Wodan, among the Goths. Cognate to western German Wotan, English Woden, Frisian Wons, *et cetera*. The late Scandinavian version is best known: Odin."

I was surprised to see Everard surprised. Well, of course the reports I filed with the guardian branch of the Patrol were much less detailed than the notes I was compiling for Ganz. "Hm? Odin? But he was one-eyed, and the boss god, which I gather you are not . . . Or are you?"

"No." How soothing it was to get back into lecture gear. "You're thinking of the Eddic, the viking Odin. But he belongs to a different era, centuries later and hundreds of miles northwestward.

"For my Goths, the boss god, as you put it, is Tiwaz. He goes straight back to the old Indo-European pantheon, along with the other Anses, as opposed to aboriginal chthonic deities like the Wanes. The Romans identified Tiwaz with Mars, because he was the war god, but he was much else as well.

"The Romans thought Donar, whom the Scandinavians called Thor, must be the same as Jupiter, because he ruled over weather; but to the Goths, he was a son of Tiwaz. Likewise for Wodan, whom the Romans identified with Mercury."

"So mythology evolved as time passed, eh?" Everard prompted.

"Right," I said. "Tiwaz dwindled to the Tyr of Asgard. Little memory of him was left, except that it was he who'd lost a hand in binding the Wolf that shall destroy the world. However, 'tyr' as a common noun is a synonym in Old Norse for 'god.'

"Meanwhile Wodan, or Odin, gained importance, till he became the father of the rest. I think—though this is something we have to investigate someday—I think that was because the Scandinavians grew extremely warlike. A psychopomp, who'd also acquired shamanistic traits through Finnish influence, was a natural for a cult among aristocratic warriors; he brought them to Valhalla. At that, Odin was most popular in Denmark and maybe Sweden. In Norway and its Icelandic colony, Thor loomed larger."

"Fascinating." Everard gusted a sigh. "So much more to know than any of us will ever live to learn. . . . Well, but tell me about your Wodan figure in fourth-century eastern Europe."

"He still has two eyes," I explained, "but he already has the hat, the cloak, and the spear, which is really a staff. You see, he's the Wanderer. That's why the Romans thought he must be Mercury under a different name, same as they thought the Greek god Hermes must be. It all goes back to the earliest Indo-European traditions. You can find hints of it in India, Persia, the Celtic and Slavic myths—but those last are even more poorly chronicled. Eventually, my service will—

"Anyhow. Wodan-Mercury-Hermes is the Wanderer because he's the god of the wind. This leads to his becoming the patron of travelers and traders. Faring as widely as he does, he must have learned a great deal, so he likewise becomes associated with wisdom, poetry . . . and magic. Those attributes join with the idea of the dead riding on the night wind—they join to make him the psychopomp, the conductor of the dead down to the Afterworld."

Everard blew a smoke ring. His gaze followed it, as if some symbol were in its twistings. "You've gotten latched onto a pretty strong figure, seems," he said low.

"Yes," I agreed. "Repeat, it was none of my intention. If anything, it complicates my mission without end. And I'll certainly be careful. But . . . it is a myth which already existed. There were countless stories about Wodan's appearances among men. That most were fable, while a few reflected events that really happened—what difference does it make?"

Everard drew hard on his pipe. "I dunno. In spite of my study of this episode, as far as it's gone, I don't know. Maybe nothing, no difference. And yet I've learned to be wary of archetypes. They have more power than any science in history has measured. That's why I've been quizzing you like this, about stuff that should be obvious to me. It isn't, down underneath."

He did not so much shrug as shake his shoulders. "Well," he growled, "never mind the metaphysics. Let's settle a couple of practical matters, and then get hold of your wife and my date and go have fun."

337

Throughout that day, battle had raged. Again and again had the Huns dashed themselves over the Gothic ranks, like storm waves that break on a cliff. Their arrows darkened the sky ere lances lowered, banners streamed, earth shook to the thunder of hoofs, and the horsemen charged. Fighters on foot, the Goths stood fast in their arrays. Pikes slanted forward, swords and axes and bills gleamed at the ready, bows twanged and slingstones flew, horns brayed. When the shock came, deep-throated shouts made answer to the yelping Hunnish war cries.

Thereafter it was hew, stab, pant, sweat, kill, die. When men fell, feet as well as hoofs crushed rib cages and trampled flesh to red ruin. Iron dinned on helmets, rattled on ring mail, banged the wood of shields and the hardened leather of breastplates. Horses wallowed and shrieked, throats pierced or hocks hamstrung. Wounded men snarled and sought to thrust or grapple. Seldom was anybody sure whom he had struck or who had smitten him. Madness filled him, took him unto itself, whirled black through his world.

Once had the Huns broken an enemy line. They yelled their glee as they reined mounts around to butcher from behind. But as if out of nowhere, a fresh Gothic troop rolled upon them, and now it was they who were trapped. Few escaped. Otherwise, Hunnish captains who saw a charge fail would sound the retreat. Those riders were well drilled; they pulled out of bowshot, and for a while the hosts breathed hard, slaked thirst, cared for their hurt, glared across the ground between.

The sun sank westward, blood-red in a greenish heaven. Its light glimmered on the river and on the wings of carrion fowl awheel overhead. Shadows ran long down slopes of silvery grass, welled upward in dales, turned clumps of trees black and shapeless. A breeze flitted cold across gore-muddied earth, ruffled the hair of the corpses that lay in windrows, whistled as if to call them hence.

Drums thuttered. The Huns drew into squadrons. A last trumpet shrilled, and they made their last onslaught.

Bone-weary though they were, the Goths cast it back, and reaped men by the hundreds. Well and truly had Dagobert sprung his trap. When first he heard of an invader army—slaying, raping, looting, burning—he called for his folk to gather beneath a single standard. Not only the Teurings, but kindred settlers heeded. He lured the Huns into this hollow that led down to the Dnieper, where cavalry was cramped, before his main body poured over the ridges on either side and barred retreat.

His small round shield lay gnawed to splinters. His helmet was battered, his mail ragged, sword blunt, body a single bruise. Yet he stood in the forefront of the Gothic center, and his banner flew above him. When the attack came, he moved like a wildcat.

A horse reared huge. He glimpsed the man in the saddle: short but broad, clad in stenchful skins beneath what armor he had, head shaven save for a pigtail, thin beard braided in twain, big-nosed face made hideous by patterned scars. The Hun wielded a single-hand ax. Dagobert stepped aside while the hoofs crashed down. He struck, and met the other weapon on its way. Steel rang. Sparks showered athwart dusk. Dagobert slewed his blade around and raked it over the rider's thigh. That would have been a deadly slash had the edge still been sharp. As was, blood runneled forth. The Hun yammered and smote anew. He hit the Gothic helmet full on. Dagobert staggered. He regained his feet—and his enemy was gone, swept off in the whirlwind of struggle.

From another horse, suddenly there, a lance struck forward. Dagobert, half dazed, took it between neck and shoulder. The Hun saw him sink, and pressed ahead at the hole opened in the Gothic line. From the ground, Dagobert threw his sword. It hit the Hun's arm and shook loose the spear. Dagobert's nearest fellow hacked with a bill. The Hun toppled. His body dragged from a stirrup.

All at once, there was no fight. Broken, snatched by terror, those of the foe that lived fled. Not as a host, but each for himself, they stampeded.

"After them," Dagobert gasped where he lay. "Let none go free—avenge our dead, make safety for our land—" Weakly, he slapped the ankle of his standard bearer. The man bore the banner forward, and the Goths followed, slaying and slaying. Few indeed were the Huns that returned home.

Dagobert pawed at his neck. The point had gone in on the right. Blood pumped forth. The racket of war moved off. Nearer were the cries of the crippled, man and horse, and of the ravens that circled low. Those also grew dim in his hearing. His eyes sought the last glimpse of sun.

Air shimmered and stirred. The Wanderer had arrived.

He dismounted from his eldritch steed, knelt in the muck, sent hands across the wound in his son. "Father," Dagobert whispered, a gurgle through the blood that filled his mouth.

Anguish went over the face that he remembered as stern and aloof. "I cannot save—I may not—they would not—" the Wanderer mumbled.

"Have . . . we . . . won?"

"Yes. We'll be rid of the Huns for many a year. Your doing."

The Goth smiled. "Good. Now take me away, Father—"

Carl held Dagobert in his arms till death had come, and for a long while afterward.

1933

"Oh, Laurie!"

"Hush, darling. It was to be."

"My son, my son!"

"Come close. Don't be afraid to cry."

"But he was so young, Laurie."

"A man grown, just the same. You won't forsake *his* children, your grandchildren. Will you?"

"No, never. Though what can I do? Tell me what I can do for them. They're doomed, Jorith's d-d-descendants will die, I may not change that, how can I help them?"

"We'll think about it later, dear. First, please rest, be quiet, sleep."

337-344

Tharasmund was in his thirteenth winter when his father Dagobert fell. Nonetheless, after they had buried their leader in a hill-high barrow, the Teurings hailed the lad their chieftain. A stripling he was, but full of promise, and they would have no other house than his over them.

Besides, after the battle on the Dnieper, they awaited no danger in the morrow. That had been an alliance of several Hunnish tribes which they smashed. The rest would not be hasty to move on Goths, nor would the Heruls. Whatever warfare got waged would likeliest be afar, and not in defense but on behalf of King Geberic. Tharasmund should have time in which to grow and learn. Moreover, would he not have the favor and counsel of Wodan?

Waluburg his mother married again, a man named Ansgar. He was of lesser station than she, but well-to-do, not greedy for power. He and she ruled well over their holdings and gave good leadership to their folk until Tharasmund came of age. If they stayed on thus somewhat beyond that year, before withdrawing to live quietly, it was at his wish. The restlessness of his line was in him too, and he wanted freedom to travel.

This was well, for in those days many changes passed through the world. A chieftain must know them before he could hope to deal with them.

Rome lay once more at peace with itself, though before he died Constantine had divided rule of the Empire between East and West. For the Eastern seat of lordship he had chosen the city Byzantium, renaming it after himself. It waxed swiftly in size and wealth. After clashes in which they took a drubbing, the Visigoths made treaty with Rome, and traffic became brisk across the River Danube.

Constantine had declared Christ the single god of the state. Spokesmen for that faith went far and wide. More and more of the West Goths hearkened. Those who stayed by Tiwaz and Frija misliked that greatly. Not only might the old gods grow angry and bring woe to a thankless people; to take the new one opened a way for Constantinople to win mastery, slowly but without ever a sword being drawn. The Christians said this counted for less than salvation; besides, from a worldly standpoint, it was better to be in the Empire than out. Year by year, embitterment crept between the factions.

At their distance, the Ostrogoths were slow to become much aware of these matters. Christians among them were mostly slaves brought from western parts. There was a church at Olbia, but it was for the use of Roman traders—wooden, small and shabby when set against the ancient marble temples, emptily though those now echoed. However, as the trade grew, dwellers inland also began to meet Christians, some of them priests. Here and there, free women took baptism, and a few men.

The Teurings would have none of this. Their gods were doing well by them, as by all the East Goths. Broad acres yielded riches; likewise did barter north and south, and their share of tribute paid by folk whom the king had overcome.

Waluburg and Ansgar built a new hall that would be worthy of Dagobert's son. On the right bank of the Dnieper it rose, upon a height overlooking the river's gleam, ripple of wind through grass and croplands, stands of timber where birds nested in flocks to becloud heaven. Carven dragons reared over its gables; horns of elk and aurochs above the doors were gilded; pillars within bore the images of gods—save for Wodan, who had a richly bedecked halidom nearby. Outbuildings sprang up around it, and lesser homes, until the thorp could almost be called a village. Life boomed about, men, women, children, horses, hounds, wagons, weapons, sounds of talk, laughter, song, footfalls on cobblestones, hammer, saw, wheels, fire, oaths, or now and then somebody weeping. A shed down by the water held a ship, when it was not faring abroad, and the wharf often welcomed vessels that plied the stream with their wonderful cargoes.

Heorot, they named the hall, because the Wanderer, wryly smiling, had said that was the name of a famous dwelling in the North. He came by every few years, for a few days at a time, to hear what there was to hear.

Tharasmund grew up darker than his father, brown-haired, heavier of bone and features and soul. That was not bad, thought the Teurings. Let him burn off his lust for adventure early, and gain knowledge as he did; then he ought to settle down and steer them soberly. They felt they were going to need a steadfast man at their head. Stories had reached them of a king who was hauling the Huns together as Geberic had done the Ostrogoths. Word from the northern mother country was that Geberic's son and likely heir, Ermanaric, was a cruel and overbearing sort. Moreover, the odds were that erelong the royal house would move south, out of the swamps and damps, down to these sunny lands where the bulk of the nation was now found. The Teurings wanted a leader who could stand up for their rights.

The last journey that Tharasmund made began when he was of seventeen winters, and lasted for three years. It took him through the Black Sea to Constantinople itself. Thence his ship returned; that was the only news his kin had of him. Yet they did not fear—because the Wanderer had offered to accompany his grandson throughout.

Afterward Tharasmund and his men had stories to brighten evenings for as long as they lived. Following their stay in New Rome—marvel upon marvel, happening upon happening—they went overland, across the province of Moesia and thus to the Danube. On its far side they settled down among the Visigoths for a year. The Wanderer had insisted on that, saying that Tharasmund must form friendships with them.

And indeed it came to pass that the youth met Ulrica, a daughter of King Athanaric. That mighty man still offered to the old gods; and the Wanderer had sometimes appeared in his realm too. He was glad to make an alliance with a chieftainly house in the East. As for the young ones, they got along. Already Ulrica was haughty and hard, but she bade fare to run her household well, bear sound children, and uphold her man in his doings. Agreement was reached: Tharasmund would proceed home, gifts and pledges would go back and forth, in a year or so his bride would come to him.

The Wanderer stayed but a single night at Heorot before he said farewell. Of him, Tharasmund and the rest related little other than that he had led them wisely, albeit he often disappeared for a while. He was too strange for them to chatter about.

Once, though, years later, when Erelieva lay at his side, Tharasmund told her: "I opened my heart to him. He wanted that, and heard me out, and somehow it was as if love and pain dwelt together behind his eyes."

1858

Unlike most Patrol agents above the rank of routineer, Herbert Ganz had not abandoned his former surroundings. Middle-aged when recruited, and a confirmed bachelor, he liked being Herr Professor at the Friedrich Wilhelm University in Berlin. As a rule, he would come back from his time trips within five minutes of departure to resume an orderly, slightly pompous academic existence. For that matter, his jaunts were seldom to anywhere but a superbly equipped office centuries uptime, and scarcely ever to the early Germanic milieus which were his field of research.

"They are unsuitable for a peaceful old scholar," he had said when I asked why. "And *vice versa*. I would make a fool of myself, earn contempt, arouse suspicion, perhaps get killed. No, my usefulness is in study, organization, analysis, hypothesis. Let me enjoy my life in these decades that suit me. Too soon will they end. Yes, of course, before Western civilization begins self-destruction in earnest, I must needs have aged my appearance, until I stimulate my death. . . . What next? Who knows? I will inquire. Perhaps I should simply start over elsewhere: *exempli gratia*, post-Napoleonic Bonn or Heidelberg."

He felt it incumbent on him to give hospitality to field operatives when they reported in person. For the fifth time in my lifespan thus far, he and I followed a gargantuan midday meal by a nap and a stroll along Unter den Linden. We came back to his house through a summer twilight. Trees breathed fragrance, horse-drawn vehicles clop-clopped past, gentlemen raised their tall hats to ladies of their acquaintance whom they met, a nightingale sang in a rose garden. Occasionally a uniformed Prussian officer strode by, but his shoulders did not obviously carry the future.

The house was spacious, though books and bric-a-brac tended to disguise that fact. Ganz led me to the library and rang for a maid, who entered arustle in black dress, white cap and apron. "We shall have coffee and cakes," he directed. "And, yes, put on the tray a bottle of cognac, with glasses. Thereafter we are not to be disturbed."

When she had left on her errand, he lowered his portly form onto a sofa. "Emma is a good girl," he remarked while he polished his pince-nez. Patrol medics could easily have corrected his eyeballs, but he'd have had trouble explaining why he no longer required lenses, and declared it made no particular difference. "Of a poor peasant family—*ach*, they breed fast, but the nature of life is that it overflows, not true? I take an interest in her. Avuncular only, I assure you. She is to leave my service in three years because she marries a fine young man. I will provide a modest dowry in the guise of a wedding present, and stand godfather to their firstborn." Trouble crossed the ruddy, jowly visage. "She dies of tuberculosis at the age of forty-one." He ran a hand over his bare scalp. "I am allowed to do nothing about that except provide some medicines that make her comfortable. We dare not mourn, we of the Patrol: certainly not beforehand. I should save pity, sense of guilt, for my poor unwitting friends and colleagues, the brothers Grimm. Emma's life is better than most of mankind will ever have known."

I made no reply. Our privacy being assured, I got more intent than necessary on setting up the apparatus I'd brought in my luggage. (Here I passed for a visiting British scholar. I'd practiced my accent. An American would have been pestered with too many questions about Red Indians and slavery.) While Tharasmund and I were among the Visigoths, we'd met Ulfilas. I'd recorded that event, as I did all of special interest. Surely Ganz would want a look at Constantinople's chief missionary, the Apostle to the Goths, whose translation of the Bible was virtually the sole source of information about their language which survived until time travel came along.

The hologram sprang into being. Suddenly the room—chandelier, book-shelves, up-to-date furniture which I knew was Empire, busts, framed etchings and oils, crockery, Chinese-motif wallpaper, maroon drapes—became the mystery, darkness around a campfire. Yet I was not there, in my own skull: for it was myself on whom I looked, and he was the Wanderer.

(The recorders are tiny, operating on the molecular level, self-directing as they collect full sensory input. Mine, one of several I took along, was hidden in the spear that I had leaned against a tree. Wanting to encounter Ulfilas informally, I'd laid out the route of my party to intercept that of his as we both traveled through what the Romans had known as Dacia before they withdrew from it, and I in my day knew as Rumania. After mutual avowals of peaceful intentions, my Ostrogoths and his Byzantines pitched tents and shared a meal.)

Trees walled the forest meadow in gloom. Flame-lit smoke rose to hide stars. An owl hooted, over and over. The night was still mild, but dew had begun chilling the grass. Men sat cross-legged near the coals, save for Ulfilas and me. He had stood up in his zeal, and I could not let myself be dominated before the others. They stared, listened, furtively drew signs of Ax or Cross.

Despite his name—Wulfila, originally—he was short, thickset, fleshy-nosed; for he took after Cappadocian grandparents, carried off in the Gothic raid of 264. In accordance with the treaty of 332, he had gone to Constanti-nople as both hostage and envoy. Eventually he returned to the Visigoths as missionary. The creed he preached was not that of the Nicean Council, but the austere doctrine of Arius, which it had rejected as heresy. Nonetheless he moved in the vanguard of Christendom, the morrow.

"—No, we should not merely trade stories of our farings," he said. "How can those be sundered from our faiths?" His tone was soft and reasonable, but keen was the gaze he leveled at me. "You are no ordinary man, Carl. That I see plain upon you, and in the eyes of your followers. Let none take offense if I wonder whether you are entirely human."

"I am no evil demon," I said.

Was it truly me looming over him, lean, gray, cloaked, doomed and resigned to foreknowledge—yon figure out of darkness and the wind? On this night, one and a half thousand years after that night, I felt as if it were somebody else, Wodan indeed, the forever homeless.

Ulfilas's fervor burned at him: "Then you will not fear to debate."

"What use, priest? You know well that the Goths are not a people of the Book. They would offer to Christ in his lands, they often do. But you never offer to Tiwaz in his."

"No, for God has forbidden that we bow down to any save him. It is only God the Father who may be worshiped. To the Son, let men give due reverence, yes: but the nature of Christ—" And Ulfilas was off on a sermon.

It was not a rant. He knew better. He spoke calmly, sensibly, even good-humoredly. He did not hesitate to employ pagan imagery, nor did he try to lay more than a groundwork of ideas before he let conversation go elsewhere. I saw men of mine nodding thoughtfully. Arianism better fitted their traditions and temperament than did a Catholicism of which they had no knowledge anyway. It would be the form of Christianity that all Goths finally took; and from this would spring centuries of trouble.

I had not made a particularly good showing. But then, how could I in honesty have argued for a heathenism in which I had no belief and which I knew was going under? For that matter, how could I in honesty have argued for Christ?

My eyes, 1858, sought Tharasmund. Much lingered in his young countenance of Jorith's dear features. . . .

—"And how goes the literary research?" Ganz asked when my scene was done.

"Quite well." I escaped into facts. "New poems; lines in them that definitely look ancestral to lines in *Widsith* and *Walthere*. To be specific, since the battle at Dnieper side—" That hurt, but I brought forth my notes and recordings, and plowed ahead.

344-347

In the same year that Tharasmund returned to Heorot and took up chieftainship over the Teurings, Geberic died in the hall of his fathers, on a peak of the High Tatra. His son Ermanaric became king of the Ostrogoths.

Late in the next year Ulrica, daughter of Visigothic Athanaric, came to her betrothed Tharasmund, at the head of a great and rich retinue. Their marriage was a feast long remembered, a week where food, drink, gifts, games, merriment, and brags went unstinted for hundreds of guests. Because his grandson had asked him to, the Wanderer himself hallowed the pair, and by torchlight led the bride to the loft where the groom awaited her.

There were those, not of the Teuring tribe, who muttered that Tharasmund seemed overweening, as though he would fain be more than his king's handfast man.

Shortly after the wedding he must hasten off. The Heruls were out and the marches aflame. To beat them back and lay waste some of their own country became a winter's work. No sooner was it done but Ermanaric sent word that he wanted all heads of tribes to meet with him in the motherland.

This proved worthwhile. Plans got hammered out for conquests and other

things that needed doing. Ermanaric shifted his court south to where the bulk
of his people were. Besides many of his Greutungs, the tribal chiefs and their
warriors went along. It was a splendid trek, on which bards lavished words
that the Wanderer soon heard chanted.

Therefore Ulrica was late in becoming fruitful. However, after Tharasmund
met her again, he soon filled her belly for her, and mightily well. She said to
her women that of course it would be a man-child, and live to become as
renowned as his forebears.

She gave him birth one winter night—some said easily, some said scornful
of any pains. Heorot rejoiced. The father sent word around that he would hold
a naming feast.

This was a welcome break in the season's murk, added to the Yuletide
gatherings. People flocked thither. Among them were men who thought it
might be a chance to draw Tharasmund aside for a word or two. They bore
grudges against King Ermanaric.

The hall was bedight with evergreen boughs, weavings, burnished metal,
Roman glass. Though day reigned yet over snowfields outside, lamps
brightened the long room. Clad in their best, the leading yeomen and wives
among the Teurings ringed the high seat, where rested crib and babe. Lesser
folk, children, hounds crowded along the walls. Sweetness of pine and mead
filled air and heads.

Tharasmund stepped forth. In his hand was a holy ax, to hold above his son
while he called down Donar's blessing. From her side Ulrica bore water out of
Frija's well. None there had witnessed anything like this erenow, save for the
firstborn of a royal house.

"We are met—" Tharasmund broke off. All eyes swung doorward, and
breath went like a wave. "Oh, I hoped! Be welcome!"

Spear slowly thumping floor, the Wanderer neared. He bent his grayness
over the child.

"Will you, lord, bestow his name?" Tharasmund asked.

"What shall it be?"

"From his mother's kin, to bind us closer to the West Goths, Hathawulf."

The Wanderer stood altogether still for a while that went on and on. At last
he lifted his head. The hat brim shadowed his face. "Hathawulf," he said low,
as if to himself. "Oh, yes. I understand now." A little louder: "Weard will
have it so. Well, then, so be it. I will give him his name."

1934

I came out of the New York base into the cold and early darkness of December, and went uptown afoot. Lights and window displays threw Christmas at me, but shoppers were not many. On street corners in the wind, Salvation Army musicians blatted or Santa Clauses rang bells at their kettles for charity, while sad vendors offered this or that. They didn't have a Depression among the Goths, I thought. But the Goths had less to lose. Materially, anyway. Spiritually—who could tell? Not I, no matter how much history I had seen or would ever see.

Laurie heard my tread on the landing and flung our apartment door wide. We had set the date beforehand for my latest return, after she'd be back from Chicago, where she had a show. She embraced me hard.

As we went on inside, her joy dimmed. We stopped in the middle of the living room. She took both my hands in hers, regarded me for a mute spell, and asked low, "What stabbed you . . . this trip?"

"Nothing I shouldn't have foreseen," I answered, hearing my voice as dull as my soul. "Uh, how'd the exhibition go?"

"Fine," she replied efficiently. "In fact, two pictures have already sold for a nice sum." Concern welled forth: "With that out of the way, sit down. Let me bring you a drink. God, you look blackjacked."

"I'm all right. No need to wait on me."

"Maybe I feel a need to. Ever think of that?" Laurie hustled me into my usual armchair. I slumped down in it and stared out the window. Lights afar made a hectic glimmer along the sill, at the feet of night. The radio was tuned to a program of carols. "*O little town of Bethlehem—*"

"Kick off your shoes," Laurie advised from the kitchen. I did, and it was as if that were the real act of homecoming, like a Goth unbuckling his sword belt.

She brought in a pair of stiff Scotch-and-lemons, and brushed lips across my brow before settling herself in the chair opposite. "Welcome," she said. "Welcome always." We raised glasses and drank.

She waited quietly for me to be ready.

I got it out in a rush: "Hamther has been born."

"Who?"

"Hamther. He and his brother Sorli died trying to avenge their sister."

"I know," she whispered. "Oh, Carl, darling."

"First child of Tharasmund and Ulrica. The name is actually Hathawulf, but it's easy to see how that got elided to Hamther as the story flowed north over centuries. And they want to call their next son Solbern. The timing is right, too. Those will be young men—will have been—when—" I couldn't go on.

She leaned forward just long enough that a touch of her hand reached my awareness.

Afterward, her tone stark, she said: "You don't have to go through with this. Do you, Carl?"

"What?" Astonishment made me stop hurting for an instant. "Of course I do. My job, my duty."

"Your job is to trace out whatever people put into verses and stories. Not what they actually did. Skip forward, dear. Let . . . Hathawulf be safely dead when next you return there."

"No!"

I realized I'd shouted, took a deep and warming draught, made myself confront her and state levelly: "I've thought about that. Believe me, I have. And I can't. Can't abandon them."

"Can't help them, either. It's predestined, everything."

"We don't know just what will . . . did happen. Or how I might be able to—No, Laurie, please don't say any more about that."

She sighed. "Well, I can understand. You've been with generations of them, as they grew and lived and suffered and died; but to you it hasn't been so long." To you, she did not say, Jorith is a very near memory. "Yes, do what you must, Carl, while you must."

I had no words, because I could feel her own pain.

She smiled shakily. "You've got a furlough now, though," she said. "Put your work aside. I went out today and brought back a small Christmas tree. How'd you like if we trimmed it this evening, after I've fixed a gourmet dinner?"

> " 'Peace on the earth, good will to men,
> From Heav'n's all-gracious King—' "

348-366

Athanaric, king of the West Goths, hated Christ. Besides holding fast to the gods of his fathers, he feared the Church as a sly agent of the Empire. Let it gnaw away long enough, he said, and folk would find themselves bending the knee to Roman overlords. Therefore he egged men on against it, thwarted the kin of murdered Christians when they sought weregild, at last rammed laws through his Great Moot that left them open to wholesale slaughter as soon as some happening made tempers flare. Or so he thought. For their part, the baptized Goths, who by now were not few, drew together and spoke of letting the Lord God of Hosts decide the outcome.

Bishop Ulfilas called them unwise. Martyrs became saints, he agreed, but it was the body of the faithful that kept the Word alive on earth. He sought and obtained permission from Emperor Constantius for his flock to move into Moesia. Leading them across the Danube, he saw them settled under the Haemus Mountains. There they became a peaceable lot of herdsmen and farmers.

When this news reached Heorot, Ulrica laughed aloud. "Then my father is rid of them!"

She cried that too soon. For the next thirty years and more, Ulfilas worked on in his vineyard. Not every Christian Visigoth had followed him south. Some remained, among them chieftains strong enough to protect themselves and their underlings. These received missionaries, whose labors bore fruit. Athanaric's persecutions caused the Christians to seek a leader of their own. They found one in Frithigern, also of the royal house. While it never came to open war between the factions, there were clashes aplenty. Younger, soon wealthier than his rival because of being favored by traders from the Empire, Frithigern brought many West Goths to join the Church as the years wore on, merely because that seemed a promising thing to do.

It touched the Ostrogoths little. The number of Christians among them did swell, but slowly and without rousing undue trouble. King Ermanaric cared naught about gods of any sort or about the next world. He was too busy seizing as much as he could of this one.

Up and down eastern Europe his wars raged. In several seasons' fierce campaigning he broke the Heruls. Those who did not submit moved off to join westerly tribes bearing the same name. Aestii and Vendi were easier prey for Ermanaric. Unsated, he took his armies north, beyond the lands that his father had made tributary. In the end, a sweep of earth from the Elbe River to the Dnieper mouth acknowledged him overlord.

In these farings Tharasmund gained renown and booty. Yet he liked not the king's harshness. Often in the moots he stood up not only for his own tribe but for others, on behalf of their ancient rights. Then Ermanaric must needs back down, however sullenly. The Teurings were as yet too powerful, or he not powerful enough, for him to make foemen of. This was the more true since many Goths would have feared to draw blade against a house whose strange forebear still guested it from time to time.

The Wanderer was there when they gave name to the third child of Tharasmund and Ulrica, Solbern. The second had died in its crib, but Solbern, like his brother, grew up strong and handsome. The fourth child was a girl, whom they called Swanhild. For her, too, the Wanderer appeared, but fleetingly, and thereafter he was not seen for years. Swanhild became very fair to look upon, and of a sweet and merry nature.

Ulrica bore three more children. They were far apart and none lived long. Tharasmund was mostly away from home, fighting, trading, taking counsel with men of worth, leading his Teurings in their common business. Upon his returns he was apt to sleep with Erelieva, the leman he had taken soon after Swanhild's birth.

She was neither slave nor base-born, but the daughter of a well-to-do yeoman. Indeed, on the distaff side she too descended from Winnithar and Salvalindis. Tharasmund met her while he rode about among the tribesfolk, as was his yearly wont when he was abroad, to hear whatever they had on their minds. He lengthened his stay at that home, and they two were much in each other's company. Later he sent messengers to ask if she would come to him. They brought rich gifts for her parents, as well as promises of honor for her and bonds between the families. This was no offer to refuse lightly, and the lass was eager, so erelong she went off with Tharasmund's men.

He kept his word and cherished her. When she bore him a son, Alawin, he gave as lavish a feast as he had done for Hathawulf and Solbern. She had few future children, and sickness took them away early on, but he did not care for her the less.

Ulrica grew bitter. It was not that Tharasmund kept another woman. Most men who could afford it did that, and he had gone through more than his share. What galled Ulrica was the standing he gave Erelieva—second only to her own in the household, and above it in his heart. She was too proud to start a fight she would be bound to lose, but her feelings were plain. Toward Tharasmund she became cold, even when he sought her bed. This made him do so seldom, and merely in hopes of more offspring.

During his lengthy absences, Ulrica went out of her way to scorn Erelieva and say barbed words about her. The younger woman flushed but bore it quietly. She had won her friends. It was Ulrica the overbearing who grew lonely. Therefore she gave much heed to her sons; they grew closely bound to her.

Withal, they were mettlesome lads, quick to learn everything that beseemed a man, well-liked wherever they fared. They were unlike, Hathawulf the hotter, Solbern the more thoughtful, but fondness linked them. As for their sister Swanhild, all the Teurings—Erelieva and Alawin among them—loved her.

Throughout that time, years passed between visits by the Wanderer, and then they were short. This brought folk still more into awe of him. When his craggy form came striding over the hills, men blew a call on horns, and from

Heorot riders galloped forth to greet and escort him. He was even quieter than
of yore. It was as if some secret grief weighed upon him, though none dared
ask what. This showed most sharply whenever Swanhild passed by in her
budding loveliness, or came prideful and atremble if her mother had allowed
her to bring the guest his wine, or sat among the other youngsters at his feet
while he told tales and uttered wise sayings. Once he sighed to her father, "She
is like her great-grandmother."

The hardy warrior shivered a little in his coat. How long had that woman
lain dead?

At an earlier guesting the Wanderer showed surprise. Since his last
appearance, Erelieva had come to Heorot and had borne her son. Shyly, she
brought the babe to show the Elder. He sat unspeaking for many heartbeats
before he asked, "What is his name?"

"Alawin, lord," she answered.

"Alawin!" The Wanderer laid hand over brow. "Alawin?" After another
while, almost in a whisper: "But you are Erelieva. Erelieva—Erp—yes,
maybe that's how you'll be remembered, my dear." Nobody understood what
he meant.

—The years blew by. Throughout, the might of King Ermanaric waxed.
Likewise did his greed and cruelty.

When he and Tharasmund were in their fortieth winter, the Wanderer called
again. Those who met him were grim of face and curt of speech. Heorot was
aswarm with armed men. Tharasmund greeted the guest in a bleak gladness.
"Forefather and lord, have you come to our help—you who once drove the
Vandals from olden Gothland?"

The Wanderer stood as if graven in stone. "Best you tell me from the
beginning what this is about," he said at last.

"So that we may make it clear in our own heads? But it is. Well . . . your
will be done." Tharasmund pondered. "Let me send for two more."

Those proved an odd pair. Liuderis, stout and grizzled, was the chieftain's
trustiest man. He served as steward of Tharasmund's lands and as captain of
fighters when Tharasmund was not there himself. The second was a red-haired
youth of fifteen, beardless but strong, with a wrath beyond his years in the
green eyes. Tharasmund named him as Randwar, son of Guthric, not a Teuring
but a Greutung.

The four withdrew to a loft-room where they could talk unheard. A short
winter day was drawing to its close. Lamps gave light to see by and a brazier
some warmth, though men sat wrapped in furs and their breath smoked white
through gloominess. It was a room richly furnished, with Roman chairs and a
table where mother-of-pearl was inlaid. Tapestries hung on walls and carvings
were on the shutters across the windows. Servants had brought a flagon of

wine and glass goblets from which to drink it. Sounds of the life everywhere
around boomed up through an oak floor. Well had the son and the grandson of
the Wanderer done for themselves.

Yet Tharasmund scowled, shifted about in his seat. ran fingers through
unkempt brown locks and over close-cropped beard, before he could turn to
his visitor and rasp: "We ride to the king, five hundred strong. His latest
outrage is more than anyone may bear. We will have justice for the slain, or
else the red cock shall crow on his roof."

He meant fire—uprising, war of Goth upon Goth, overthrow and death.

None could tell whether the Wanderer's face stirred. Shadows did, across
the furrows therein, as lamps flickered and murk prowled. "Tell me what he
has done," he said.

Tharasmund nodded stiffly at Randwar. "You tell, lad, as you told us."

The youth gulped. Fury rose through the bashfulness he had felt in this
presence. Fist smote knee, over and over, while he related roughly:

"Know, lord—though I think you already know—that King Ermanaric had
two nephews, Embrica and Fritla. They were sons of a brother of his, Aiulf,
who fell in war upon the Angles in the North. Ever did Embrica and Fritla fight
well themselves. Here in the South, two years ago, they led a troop eastward
against the Alanic allies of the Huns. They bore home a mighty booty, for they
had sacked a place where the Huns kept tribute wrung from many a region.
Ermanaric heard of it and declared it was his, as king. His nephews said no,
for they had carried out that raid on their own. He asked them to come talk the
matter over. They did, but first they hid the treasure away. Although he had
plighted their safety, Ermanaric had them seized. When they would not tell
him where the hoard was, he first had them tortured. then put to death.
Thereafter he sent men to scour their lands for it. Those failed; but they
ravaged widely about, burned the homes of Aiulf's sons, cut down their
families—to teach obedience, he said. My lord," Randwar screamed, "was
that rightful?"

"It is apt to be the way of kings." The Wanderer's tone was like iron given
a voice. "What is your part in the business?"

"My . . . my father was also a son of Aiulf, who died young. My uncle
Embrica and his wife raised me. I'd been on a long hunting trip. When I came
back, the steading was an ash heap. Folk told me how Ermanaric's men had
had their way with my foster mother before they slit her throat. She . . . was
kin to this house. I sought hither."

He sank back in his chair, struggled not to sob, tossed off his beaker of
wine.

"Aye," Tharasmund said heavily, "she, Mathaswentha, was my cousin.
You know that high families often marry across tribal lines. Randwar here is

more distant kin to me; nonetheless, we share some of that blood which has been spilt. Also, he knows where the treasure is, sunken beneath the Dnieper. It is well that Weard sent him off just then and so spared him from capture. That gold would buy the king too much might."

Liuderis shook his head. "I don't understand," he muttered. "After everything I've heard, I still don't. Why does Ermanaric behave thus? Has a fiend possessed him? Or is he only mad?"

"I think he is neither," Tharasmund said. "I think in some measure his counselor Sibicho—not even a Goth, but a Vandal in his service—Sibicho has hissed evil into his ear. But Ermanaric was always ready to listen, oh, yes." To the Wanderer: "For years has he been raising the scot we must pay, and calling freeborn women to his bed whether they will or no, and otherwise riding roughshod over the folk. I think he means to break the will of those chieftains who have withstood him. If we yield to this latest thing, we will be the readier to yield to the next."

The Wanderer nodded. "Yes, you're doubtless right. I would say, besides, that Ermanaric envies the power of the Roman Emperor, and wants the same for himself over the Ostrogoths. Moreover, he hears of Frithigern rising to oppose Athanaric among the Visigoths, and means to scotch any such rival in his kingdom."

"We ride to demand justice," Tharasmund said. "He must pay double weregild, and at the Great Moot vow upon the Stone of Tiwaz to abide henceforward by olden law and right. Else I will raise the whole country against him."

"He has many on his side," the Wanderer warned: "some for troth given him, some for greed or fear, some who feel you must have a strong king to keep your borders, now when the Huns are gathering themselves together like a snake coiling to strike."

"Yes, but that king need not be Ermanaric!" blazed from Randwar.

Hope kindled in Tharasmund. "Lord," he said to the Wanderer, "you who smote the Vandals, will you stand by your kindred again?"

Trouble freighted the answer. "I . . . cannot fight in your battles. Weard will not have it so."

Tharasmund was mute for a space. At last he asked, "Will you at least come with us? Surely the king will heed *you*."

The Wanderer was wordless longer, until there dragged from him: "Yes, I will see what I can do. But I make no promises. Do you hear me? I make no promises."

And thus he fared off beside the others, at the head of the band.

Ermanaric kept dwellings throughout the realm. He and his guards, wisemen, servants traveled between them. News was that soon after the killings he had boldly moved to within three days' ride of Heorot.

Those were three days of scant cheer. Snow lay in a crust over the lands. It creaked beneath hoofs. The sky was low and flat gray, the air still and raw. Houses huddled under thatch. Trees stood bare, save where firs made a gloom. Nobody said much or sang at all, not even around the campfire before crawling into bedrolls.

But when they saw their goal, Tharasmund winded his horn and they arrived at a full gallop.

Cobblestones rang, horses neighed as the Teurings drew rein in the royal courtyard. Guards to about the same number stood ranked before the hall, spearheads agleam though pennons adroop. "We will have speech with your master!" Tharasmund roared.

That was the chosen insult, a word used as if yonder men were not free but kept to heel like hounds or Romans. The captain flushed before he snapped, "A few of you may get leave to enter, but the rest must first pull back."

"Yes, do," Tharasmund murmured to Liuderis. The elder warrior growled aloud, "Oh, we will, since we make you troopers uneasy—but not far, nor idle for long before we get knowledge that our leaders are safe from treachery."

"We have come to talk," said the Wanderer in haste.

He, Tharasmund, and Randwar dismounted. Doorkeepers stood aside for them and they passed through. More guardsmen filled the benches within. Against common usage, they were armed. At the middle of the east wall, flanked by his courtiers, Ermanaric sat waiting.

He was a big man who bore himself unbendingly. Black locks and spade beard ringed a stern, lined face. In splendor was he attired, golden bands heavy over brow and wrists; flamelight shimmered across the metal. His clothes were of foreign dyed stuffs, trimmed with marten and ermine. In his hand was a wine goblet, not glass but cut crystal; and rubies sparkled on his fingers.

Silent he abided until the three wayworn, mud-splashed newcomers reached his high seat. A time longer did he glower at them before he said, "Well, Tharasmund, you go in unusual company."

"You know who these are," answered the Teuring chief, "and what our errand must be."

A scrawny, ash-pale man on the king's right, Sibicho the Vandal, whispered in his ear. Ermanaric nodded. "Sit down, then," he said. "We will drink and eat."

"No," Tharasmund told him. "We will take no salt or stoup of you before you have made peace with us."

"You talk over-boldly, you."

The Wanderer lifted his spear on high. A hush fell, which made the

longfires seem to crackle the louder. "If you are wise, king, you will hear this
man out," he said. "Your land lies bleeding. Wash that wound and bind on
herbs ere it swells and sickens."

Ermanaric met his gaze and replied, "I do not brook mockery, old one. I
will listen if he keeps watch on his tongue. Tell me in few words what you
want, Tharasmund."

That was like a slap on the cheek. The Teuring must swallow thrice before
he could bark out his demands.

"I thought you would want some such," Ermanaric said. "Know that
Embrica and Fritla fell on their own deeds. They withheld from their king what
was rightly his. Thieves and forsworn men are outlaw. However, I am forgiving.
I am willing to pay weregild for their families and holdings . . . after that hoard
has been turned over to me."

"What?" yelled Randwar. "You dare speak thus, you murderer?"

The guardsmen rumbled. Tharasmund laid a warning hand on the boy's
arm. To Ermanaric he said: "We call for double weregild as an acknowledg-
ment of the wrong you did. No less can we take and still keep our honor. But
as for the ownership of the treasure, let the Great Moot decide; and whatever
it decides, let all of us handsel peace."

"I do not haggle," Ermanaric answered in a frosty voice. "Take my offer
and begone—or refuse it and begone, lest I make you sorry for your
insolence."

The Wanderer trod forth. Again he raised his spear to bring silence. The hat
shadowed his face, making him twice uncanny to behold; the blue cloak fell
from his shoulders like wings. "Hear me," he said. "The gods are righteous.
Whoso flouts the law and grinds down the helpless, him will they bring to
doom. Ermanaric, hearken before it is too late. Hearken before your kingdom
is rent asunder."

A mumble and rustle went along the hall. Men stirred, made signs, gripped
hafts as though for comfort. Eyeballs rolled white amidst smoke and dimness.
This was the Wanderer who spoke.

Sibicho tugged the king's sleeve and muttered something. Ermanaric
nodded. He leaned forward, his forefinger stabbed like a knife, and he said so
that it rang back from the rafters:

"You have guested houses of mine erenow, old one. Ill does it become you
to threaten me. And unwise you are, whatever children and crones and
doddering gaffers may babble of you—unwise you are, if you think I fear you.
Yes, they tell that you're Wodan himself. What care I? I trust in no wispy
gods, but in the strength that is mine."

He sprang to his feet. His sword whirred forth and gleamed aloft. "Do you
care to meet me in fight, old gangrel?" he cried. "We can go stake out a

ground this very hour. Meet me there, man to man, and I'll cleave that spear of yours in twain and drive you howling hence!"

The Wanderer did not stir; his weapon shuddered a bit. "Weard will not have that," he well-nigh whispered. "But I warn you most gravely, for the sake of every Goth, make peace with these men you have aggrieved."

"I will make peace if they will," Ermanaric said, grinning. "You have heard my offer, Tharasmund. Do you take it?"

The Teuring braced himself, while Randwar snarled like a wolf at bay, the Wanderer stood as if he were only an idol, and Sibicho leered from the bench. "No," he croaked. "I cannot."

"Then go, the lot of you, before I have you whipped back to your kennels."

At that, Randwar drew blade. Tharasmund and Liuderis snatched for theirs; iron flashed everywhere. The Wanderer said aloud: "We will go, but only for the sake of the Goths. Bethink you again, king, while yet you are a king."

He urged his companions away. Ermanaric began to laugh. His laughter hounded them down the length of the hall.

1935

Laurie and I went walking in Central Park. March gusted boisterous around us. A few patches of snow lingered, otherwise grass had started to green. Shrubs and trees were in bud. Beyond those boughs, the city towers gleamed newly washed by weather, on into a blueness where some clouds held a regatta. The chill was just enough to make blood tingle.

Lost in my private winter, I scarcely noticed.

She gripped my hand. "You shouldn't have, Carl." I felt how she shared the pain, as far as she was able.

"What else could I do?" I replied out of the dark. "Tharasmund asked me to come along, I told you. How could I refuse and ever sleep easy again?"

"Do you now?" She dropped that question fast. "Okay, maybe it was all right, allowable, to lend whatever consolation there might be in your presence, but you spoke up. You tried to head off the conflict."

"Blessed are the peacemakers, they taught me in Sunday school."

"That clash is inescapable. Isn't it? In the self-same tales and poems you went back to study."

I shrugged. "Tales. Poems. How much fact is in them? Oh, yes, history knows what became of Ermanaric at the end. But *did* Swanhild, Hathawulf, Solbern die as the saga says? If anything of the kind ever happened—if it isn't just a romantic imagining, centuries later, that a chronicler chanced to take seriously—did it necessarily happen to *them*?" I cleared my stiffened throat. "My job in the Patrol is to help discover what the events really were that it exists to preserve."

"Dearest, dearest," she sighed, "you're hurting so much. It's twisting your judgment. Think. I've thought—oh, but I've thought—and of course I haven't been there myself, but maybe that's given me a perspective you . . . you've chosen not to have. Everything you've reported, throughout this whole affair, everything shows events driving toward a single goal. If you, as a god, could have bluffed the king into reconciliation, you would have, surely. But no, that isn't the shape of the continuum."

"It flexes, though! What difference can a few barbarians' lives make?"

"You're raving, Carl, and you know it. I . . . lie awake a lot myself, afraid of what you might blunder into. You're too close again to what is forbidden. Maybe you've already crossed the threshold."

"The time lines would adjust. They always do."

"If that were true, we wouldn't need a Patrol. You must understand the risk you've been running."

I did. I made myself confront it. Nexus points do occur, where it matters how the dice fell. They aren't oftenest the obvious ones, either.

An example bobbed into my memory, like a drowned corpse rising to the surface. An instructor at the Academy had given it as being suitable for cadets out of my milieu.

Enormous consequences flowed from the Second World War. Foremost was that it left the Soviets in control of half Europe. (Nuclear weapons were indirect; they would have come into being at approximately that time regardless, since the principles were known.) Ultimately, that military-political situation led to happenings which affected the destiny of humankind for hundreds of years afterward—therefore forever, because those centuries had their own nexuses.

And yet Winston Churchill was right when he called the struggle of 1939–1945 "the Unnecessary War." The weakness of the democracies was important in bringing it on, true. Nonetheless, there would not have been a threat to make them quail, had Nazism not taken control of Germany. And that movement, originally small and scoffed at, later chastised (though far too mildly) by the Weimar authorities—that movement would not, could not have come to power in the country of Bach and Goethe, except through the unique genius of Adolf Hitler. And Hitler's father had been born as Alois Schickl-gruber, illegitimate, result of a chance affair between an Austrian bourgeois and a housemaid of his. . . .

But if you headed off that liaison, which you could easily have done without harming anybody, then you aborted all history that followed. By 1935, say, the world would already be different. Maybe it would become better than the original (in some respects; for a while) or maybe it would become worse. I could imagine, for example, that humans never got into space. Surely they would not have done it anywhere near as soon; it might well have occurred too late to rescue a gutted Earth. I could *not* imagine that any peaceful utopia would have resulted.

No matter. If things back in Roman times changed significantly because of me, I'd still be there; but when I returned to this year, my whole civilization would never have existed. Laurie would never have.

"I . . . don't agree I was taking risks," I argued. "My superiors read my reports, honest reports they are. They'll let me know if I'm going off the track."

Honest? I wondered. Well, yes, they related what I observed and did, without any lies or concealment, though in spare style. But the Patrol didn't want emotional breast-beating, did it? And I wasn't expected to render every last trivial detail, was I? Impossible to do, anyway.

I drew breath. "Look," I said, "I know my place. I'm simply a literary and linguistic scholar. But wherever I can help—wherever I safely can—I've got to. Don't I?"

"You're you, Carl."

We walked on. Presently she exclaimed, "Hey, man, you're on furlough, vacation, remember? We're supposed to relax and enjoy life. I've been making plans for us. Just listen."

I saw tears in her eyes, and did my best to return the cheerfulness she laid over them.

366-372

Tharasmund led his men back to Heorot. There they disbanded and sought their own homes. The Wanderer bade farewell. "Do not rush into action," was his counsel. "Bide your time. Who knows what may happen?"

"I think you do," said Tharasmund.

"I am no god."

"You have told me that more than once, but naught else. What are you, then?"

"I may not unhood it. But if this house owes me anything for what I have done over the years, I claim the debt now, and lay upon you that you gang slowly and warily."

Tharasmund nodded. "I would in any case. It will take time and skill to bring enough men into a brotherhood that Ermanaric cannot stand against. After all, most would rather sit on their farms and hope trouble passes them by, whoever else it may strike. Meanwhile, the king will likeliest not risk an open breach before he feels he is ready. I must keep ahead of him, but I know full well that a man can walk farther than he can run."

The Wanderer took his hand, made as if to speak, but blinked hard, wheeled, strode off. The last sight Tharasmund had of him was his hat, cloak, and spear, away down the winter road.

Randwar settled into Heorot, a living remembrance of wrongs. Yet he was too young and full of life to brood very long. Soon he, Hathawulf, and Solbern were fast friends, together in hunt, sport, games, every kind of merriment. He likewise saw much of their sister Swanhild.

Equinox brought melting ice, bud, blossom, and leaf. During the cold season Tharasmund had gone widely around among the Teurings and beyond, to speak in private with leading men. In spring he stayed home and busied himself with work upon his lands; and every night he and Erelieva had joy of each other.

The day came when he cried cheerily: "We've plowed and sown, cleaned and rebuilt, midwifed our kine and sent them to pasture. Let's be free for a while! Tomorrow we hunt."

On that dawn he kissed Erelieva in front of all the men who were going with him, before he sprang to the saddle and led them off. Hounds bayed, horses whinnied, hoofs thudded, horns lowed. At the edge of sight, where the road swung around a shaw, he turned about to wave at her.

She saw him again that eventide, but then he was a reddened lich.

The men who bore him indoors, on a litter made of a cloak lashed to two spearshafts, told in dulled voices what had happened. Entering the forest that began several miles hence, they found the trace of a wild boar and set off after it. Long was the chase before they caught up to the beast. It was a mighty one, silvery-bristled, tusks like curved dagger blades. Tharasmund roared his glee. But the heart in this swine was as great as its body. It did not stand while some hunters got down and others goaded it to charge. At once it attacked. Tharasmund's horse screamed, knocked off its feet, belly gashed open. The chief fell heavily. The boar saw, and was upon him. Tusks ripped, amidst monstrous grunts. Blood spurted.

Though the men did soon kill the brute, they muttered that it might well have been a demon, or bewitched—a sending of Ermanaric's, or of his cunning counselor Sibicho? However that was, Tharasmund's wounds were too deep to staunch. He had barely time to reach up and take the hands of his sons.

Women keened in the hall and the lesser houses—save for Ulrica, who kept stony, and Erelieva, who went off to weep alone.

While the first of them washed and laid out the corpse, as was her wifely right, friends of the second hustled her elsewhere. Not much later they got her married off to a yeoman, a widower whose children needed a stepmother and who dwelt well away from Heorot. Although only ten years of age, her son Alawin did the manly thing and stayed. Hathawulf, Solbern, and Swanhild fended the worst of their mother's spite off him, thereby winning his utter love.

Meanwhile the news of their father's death had flown widely about. Folk had flocked to the hall, where Ulrica did her man and herself honor. The body was brought forth from an icehouse where it had rested, richly attired. Liuderis led those warriors who laid it down in a grave-chamber of logs, together with sword, spear, shield, helm, ring-byrnie, treasures of gold, silver, amber, glass, and Roman coins. Hathawulf, son of the house, killed the horse and the hound that would follow Tharasmund down hell-road. A fire roared at the shrine of Wodan as men heaped earth over the tomb until the howe stood high. Thereafter they rode around and around it, clanging blade on shield and howling the wolf-howl.

An arval followed that went for three days. On the last of these, the Wanderer appeared.

Hathawulf yielded the high seat to him. Ulrica brought him wine. In a hush that had fallen through the whole glimmering dimness, he drank to the ghost, to Mother Frija, and to the wellbeing of the house. Else he said little. Presently he beckoned Ulrica to him and whispered. They two left the hall and sought the women's bower.

Dusk was closing in, blue-gray in the open windows, murky in the room. Coolness bore smells of leaf and soil, trill of nightingale, but those seemed distant, not quite real, to Ulrica. She stared a while at the half-finished cloth in the loom. "What next does Weard weave?" she asked low.

"A shroud," said the Wanderer, "unless you send the shuttle on a new path."

She turned to face him and replied, almost as if in mockery, "I? But I am only a woman. It is my son Hathawulf who steers the Teurings."

"*Your* son. He is young, and has seen less of the world than his father had at that age. You, Ulrica, Athanaric's daughter, Tharasmund's wife, have both knowledge and strength, as well as the patience that women must learn. You can give Hathawulf wise redes if you choose. And . . . he is used to listening to you."

"What if I marry again? His pride will raise a wall between us."

"Somehow I do not think you will."

Ulrica gazed out at the gloaming. "It is not my wish, no. I've had my fill of that." She turned back to the shadowy countenance. "You bid me stay here and keep whatever sway I have over him and his brother. Well, what shall I tell them, Wanderer?"

"Speak wisdom. Hard will it be for you to swallow your own pride and not pursue vengeance on Ermanaric. Harder still will it be for Hathawulf. Yet surely you understand, Ulrica, that without Tharasmund to lead, the feud can have only one end. Make your sons see that unless they come to terms with the king, this family is doomed."

Ulrica was long mute. At last she said, "You are right, and I will try." Anew her eyes sought his through the deepening dark. "But it will be out of need, not wish. If ever the chance should come for us to work Ermanaric harm, I will be the first to urge that we take it. And never will we bow down to that troll, nor meekly suffer fresh ills at his hands." Her words struck like a stooping hawk: "You know that. Your blood is in my sons."

"I have said what I must," the Wandered sighed. "Now do what you can."

They returned to the feast. In the morning he departed.

Ulrica took his counsel to heart, however bitterly. She had no light task, making Hathawulf and Solbern agree. They yelled about honor and their good names. She told them that boldness was not the same as foolishness. Young, untried, without skill in leadership, they simply had no hope of talking enough Goths into rebellion. Liuderis, whom she called in, unwillingly bore her out. Ulrica told her sons that they had no right to bring down destruction upon the house of their father.

Instead let them bargain, she urged. Let them bring the case before the Great Moot, and abide by its decision if the king did too. Those who had been wronged were no very close kin; the heirs could better use the weregild that had been offered than they could use somebody else's revenge; many a chief and yeoman would be glad that Tharasmund's sons had held back from splitting the realm, and in years to come would heed them with respect.

"But you recall what Father feared," Hathawulf said. "If we give way to him, Ermanaric will but press us the harder."

Ulrica's lips tightened. "I did not say you should allow that," she answered. "No, if he tries, then by the Wolf that Tiwaz bound, he'll know he was in a fight! But my hope is that he's too shrewd. He'll hold off."

"Until he has the might to overwhelm us."

"Oh, that will take time, and meanwhile, of course, we shall be quietly building our own strength. Remember, you are young. If naught else happens, you will outlive him. But it may well be you need not wait that long. As he grows older—"

Thus day by day, week by week, Ulrica wore her sons down, until they yielded to her wishes.

Randwar raged at them for treacherous cravens. It well-nigh came to blows. Swanhild cast herself between her brothers and him. "You are *friends*!" she cried. They could not but grumble their way toward a kind of calm.

Later Swanhild soothed Randwar the more. She and he walked together down a lane where blackberries grew, trees soughed and caught sunlight, birds sang. Her hair flowed golden, her eyes were big and heaven-blue in the fine-boned face, she moved like a deer. "Need you always mourn?" she asked. "This day is too lovely for it."

"But they who, who fostered me," he stammered, "they lie unavenged."

"Surely they know you'll see about that as soon as you can, and are patient. They have till the end of the world, don't they? You're going to win a name that will make theirs remembered too; just you wait and see—Look, look! Those butterflies! A sunset come alive!"

Though Randwar never again told Hathawulf and Solbern everything that was in his heart, he grew easy enough with them. After all, they were Swanhild's brothers.

Men who knew how to speak softly went between Heorot and the king. Ermanaric surprised them by granting more than hitherto. It was as if he felt, once his opponent Tharasmund was gone, he could afford a little mildness. He would not pay double weregild, because that would be to admit wrongdoing. However, he said, if those who knew where the treasure lay hidden would bring it to the next Great Moot, he would let the assembly settle its ownership.

Thus was agreement made. But while the chaffering went on, Hathawulf, guided by Ulrica, had other men going around; and he himself spoke to many householders. This kept on until the gathering after autumnal equinox.

There the king set forth his claim to the hoard. It was usage from of old, he said, that whatever of high value a handfast man might gain while fighting in the service of his lord should go to that lord, who would deal the booty out as gifts to those who deserved it or whose goodwill he needed. Else warfare would become each trooper for himself; the strength of the host would be blunted, since greed counted for more than glory; quarrels over loot would rive the ranks. Embrica and Fritla knew this well, but chose not to heed the law.

Thereupon spokesmen whom Ulrica had picked took the word, to the king's astonishment. He had not expected such a number of them. In their different ways, they brought the same thought forward. Yes, the Huns and their Alanic vassals were foemen to the Goths. But Ermanaric had not been fighting them that year. The raid was a deed that Embrica and Fritla carried out by and for themselves, as they would have a trading venture. They had fairly won the treasure and it was theirs.

Long and heated went the wrangling, both in council and around the booths set up at the field. Here was more than a question of law; it was a matter of whose will should prevail. Ulrica's words, in the mouths of her sons and their messengers, had convinced enough men that even though Tharasmund was gone—yes, *because* Tharasmund was gone—best for them would be if the king was chastened.

Not everybody agreed, or dared admit he agreed. Hence the Goths finally voted to split the hoard in three equal shares, one for Ermanaric, one each for the sons of Embrica and Fritla. The king's men having slain those, the two-thirds fell to Randwar the fosterling. Overnight he became wealthy.

Ermanaric rode livid and mum from the meeting. It was long before anyone got the courage to speak to him. Sibicho was the first. He drew him aside and they talked for hours. What they said, nobody else heard; but thereafter Ermanaric was in a better mood.

When word of this reached Heorot, Randwar muttered that if yonder weasel was happy, it boded ill for all birds. Yet the rest of the year passed quietly.

A strange thing happened in the following summer, which had also been peaceful. The Wanderer appeared on the road from the west, as ever he did. Liuderis led men forth to welcome and escort him. "How fare Tharasmund and his kin?" the newcomer hailed.

"What?" replied Liuderis, astounded. "Tharasmund is dead, lord. Have you forgotten? You yourself were at the grave-ale."

The Gray One stood leaning on his spear like a man stunned. Suddenly, to the others, the day felt less warm and sunny than before. "Indeed," he said at last, well-nigh too low to be heard. "I misspoke me." He shook his shoulders, looked up at the horsemen, and went on louder, faster: "There has been much on my mind. Forgive me, but I find I cannot guest you this time after all. Give them my greetings. I will see you later." He swung around and strode back the way he had come.

Men stared, wondered, drew signs against evil. A while afterward, a cowherd came home and told that the Wanderer had met him in a meadow and asked him at length about Tharasmund's death. Nobody knew what any of this portended, though a Christian serving-woman at the hall said it showed how the old gods were failing and fading.

Nonetheless, the sons of Tharasmund received the Wanderer with deference when he returned in the autumn. They did not venture to ask what had been the trouble earlier. For his part, he was more outgoing than erstwhile, and instead of a day or two, he stayed a pair of weeks. Folk marked how much heed he paid to the younger siblings, Swanhild and Alawin.

Of course, it was with Hathawulf and Solbern that he talked in earnest. He urged that either or both fare west next year, as their father had done in his youth. "It will pay you well to get to know the Roman countries, and to cultivate friendship with your kin among the Visigoths," he said. "I myself can be along to guide, counsel, and interpret."

"I fear we cannot," Hathawulf answered heavily. "Not as yet. The Huns wax ever stronger and bolder. They've begun reaving our marches again. Little though we like him, we must agree that King Ermanaric is right when he calls for war, come summer; and Solbern and I would not be laggards therein."

"No," said his brother, "and not only for honor's sake. Thus far the king has stayed his hand, but it's no secret that he loves us not. If we get the name of cowards or sluggards, and then a threat arises, who will dare or care to stand beside us?"

The Wanderer seemed more grieved by this than might have been awaited. Finally he said, "Well, Alawin will be twelve—too young to go with you, but old enough to go with me. Let him."

They allowed that, and Alawin went wild for joy. Watching him cartwheel over the ground, the Wanderer shook his head and murmured, "How like Jorith he still looks. But then, his descent on both sides is close to her." Sharply, to Hathawulf: "How well do you and Solbern and he get along?"

"Why, very well indeed," said the chieftain, taken aback. "He's a good lad."

"There's never a quarrel between you and him?"

"Oh, no more than his brashness brings on every once in a while." Hathawulf stroked his youthfully silky beard. "Yes, our mother has ill will toward him. She was ever one for nursing grudges. But regardless of what some fools babble, she keeps no bridle on her sons. If her rede seems wise to us, we follow it. If not, then not."

"Cleave fast to the kindness you have for each other." The Wanderer seemed to plead, rather than advise or command. "Such is all too rare in this world."

—True to his word, he came back in spring. Hathawulf had furnished Alawin a proper outfit, horses, followers, gold as well as furs to trade. The Wanderer showed forth the precious gifts he carried, which should help win good understanding abroad. Taking his leave, he hugged both brothers and their sister to him.

They stood long watching the caravan trek off. Alawin seemed so small, and his fluttering hair so bright, against the gray and blue that rode at his side. They did not utter the thought that was in them: how yonder sight recalled that Wodan was the god who led away the souls of the dead.

—Yet after a whole year everyone returned safely. Alawin's limbs were lengthened, his voice deepened, he himself ablaze with what he had seen and heard and done.

Hathawulf and Solbern bore news less heartening. The war against the Huns had not gone well last summer. Always made terrible mounted fighters by their skill and stirrups, the plainsmen had now learned to move under the taut control of canny leadership. They had not overrun the Goths in any of the pitched battles that took place, but they had inflicted heavy losses, and one could not say they had suffered defeat. Gnawed down by sneak attacks, hungry, bootyless, Ermanaric's host must at length trudge home over the endless grasslands. He would not try afresh this year; he could not.

It was thus a relief to listen to Alawin, evening after evening when folk were gathered over drink. The fabled realms of Rome awakened dreams. Nonetheless, some of what he told brought a frown to the brows of Hathawulf and Solbern, puzzlement to Randwar and Swanhild, an angry sneer to Ulrica. Why had the Wanderer fared as he did?

He had not taken his band first by sea to Constantinople, as with Tharasmund. Instead, he brought them overland to the Visigoths, where they abode for months. They paid their respects to heathen Athanaric, but were more at the court of Christian Frithigern. True, the latter was not only younger but by now had greater numbers at his beck than did the former, even though Athanaric still harried Christians in the parts over which he ruled.

When at last the Wanderer got leave to enter the Empire and crossed the Danube into Moesia, again he lingered among Christian Goths, Ulfilas's settlement, and encouraged Alawin to make friends here too. Later the group did visit Constantinople, but not for very long. The Wanderer spent much of that time explaining Roman ways to the youth. They went north again late in the autumn, and wintered at Frithigern's court. The Visigoth wanted them to take baptism, and Alawin might have done so, after the churches and other majesties he had seen along the Golden Horn. In the end he refused, but politely, explaining that he must not set himself at odds with his brothers. Frithigern took that well, saying merely, "Let the day be soon when things are otherwise for you."

Come spring, mire having dried in the roads, the Wanderer brought the youngster and their men home. He did not remain there.

That summer Hathawulf married Anslaug, daughter of the Taifal chief. Ermanaric had tried to forestall this linking.

Shortly after, Randwar sought Hathawulf out and asked if they two could talk alone. They saddled horses and went for a ride through the pastures. It was a windy day, abloom and aripple across miles of tawny grass. Clouds scudded dazzling white through the deeps above; their shadows raced over the world. Cattle grazed ruddy, in far-scattered herds. Game birds burst from underfoot, and high overhead a hawk was at hover. The coolness of the wind was veined with a smell of sun-baked earth and of growth.

"I can guess what you want," Hathawulf said shrewdly.

Randwar passed a hand through his red mane. "Yes. Swanhild for my wife."

"Hm. She does seem glad of your nearness."

"We will have each other!" Randwar cried. He checked himself. "It would be well for you. I am rich; and broad acres lie fallow, awaiting me, in the Greutung land."

Hathawulf scowled. "That's rather far hence. Here we can stand together."

"Plenty of yeoman there will welcome me. You'll not lose a comrade, you'll gain an ally."

Still Hathawulf hung back, until Randwar blurted: "It'll happen regardless. Our hearts will have it so. Best you go along with Weard."

"You've ever been rash," said the chieftain, not unkindly though trouble weighed his tones. "Your belief that mere feelings between man and woman are enough to make a sound marriage—it speaks ill of your judgment. Left to yourself, what might you undertake of unwisdom?"

Randwar gasped. Before he had time to grow angry, Hathawulf laid a hand on his shoulder and went on, smiling a bit sadly: "I meant no insult there. I only want to make you think twice. That's not your wont, I know, but I ask that you try. For Swanhild."

Randwar showed he could hold his tongue.

When they came back, Swanhild sped into the courtyard. She caught her brother's knee. Her eagerness tumbled upward: "Oh, Hathawulf, it's all right, isn't it? You said yes, I know you did. Never have you made me happier."

The upshot was that a huge wedding feast swirled and shouted through Heorot that autumn. For Swanhild there was but one shadow upon it, that the Wanderer was elsewhere. She had taken it for given that he would hallow her and her man. Was he not the Watcher over this family?

In the meantime Randwar had sent men east to his holdings. They raised a new home where Embrica's had been and staffed it well. The young couple journeyed thither in a splendid company. Swanhild carried over the threshold those evergreen boughs that called on Frija's blessing, Randwar gave a feast for the neighborhood, and there they were.

Soon, however, much though he loved his bride, he was often away for days on end. He rode around the Greutung countryside, getting to know the dwellers. When a man seemed of the right mind, Randwar would take him aside and they would take about other matters than kine, trade, or even the Huns.

On a dark day before solstice, when a few snowflakes drifted down onto frozen earth, hounds barked outside the hall. Randwar took a spear at the doorway and stepped forth to see what this was. Two burly farmhands came after, likewise armed. But when he spied the tall form that strode into his courtyard, Randwar grounded his weapon and cried, "Hail! Welcome!"

Hearing that no danger threatened, Swanhild hurried out too. Her eyes and hair, beneath a wife's kerchief, and the white gown that hugged her litheness were the only things bright, anywhere around. Joy lilted from her: "Oh, Wanderer, dear Wanderer, yes, welcome!"

He trod nigh until she could see beneath the shadowing hat. She raised hand to parted lips. "But you are full of woe," she breathed. "Are you not? What's wrong?"

"I am sorry," he answered in words that fell like stones. "Some things must stay secret. I kept away from your wedding because I would not cast gloom over it. Now—Well, Randwar, I have traveled a troublous road. Let me rest before we speak of this. Let us drink something hot and remember earlier times."

A little of his olden interest kindled that eventide, when a man chanted a lay about the last campaign into Hunland. In return he told new stories, though in less lively wise than of yore, as if he must flog himself to do it. Swanhild sighed happily. "I cannot wait till my children sit and hear you," she said, albeit she did not yet have any on the way. She was the least bit frightened to see him flinch.

Next day he led Randwar off. They spent hours by themselves. Later the Greutung told his woman:

"He warned me over and over of what hatred Ermanaric bears us. Here we are in the king's own tribal country, he said, our strength not firm while our wealth is a glittering lure. He wanted us to pull up stakes and move away—far away, clear to West Gothland—soon. Of course I would have none of that. Whatever the Wanderer is, right and honor are mightier. Then he said he knew I'd already been sounding men out about getting together against the king, to withstand his overbearingness and, if need be, fight. The Wanderer said I could not hope to keep this hidden, and it was madness."

"What did you answer to that?" she asked half fearfully.

"Why, I said free Goths have the right to open their minds to each other. And I said my foster parents never have been avenged. If the gods will not do justice, men must."

"You should hearken to him. He knows more than we ever will."

"Well, I'm not about to try anything reckless. I'll watch for my chance. More may not be needful. Men often die untimely; if good men like Tharasmund, why not evil ones like Ermanaric? No, my darling, never will we skulk off from these our lands, that belong to our unborn sons. Therefore we must make ready to defend them; true?" Randwar drew Swanhild to him. "Come," he laughed, "let's begin by doing something about those children."

The Wanderer could not move him, and after a few more days said farewell. "When will we see you again?" Swanhild asked as they stood in the doorway.

"I think—" he faltered. "I can't—Oh, girl who is like Jorith!" He embraced her, kissed her, let her go, and hurried off. Shocked, folk heard him weeping.

Yet back among the Teurings he was steely. Much was he there in the months that followed, both at Heorot and widely among yeomen, chapmen, or common field hands, workers, sailors.

Even coming from him, that which he urged upon them was naught they were quick to agree to. He wanted them to make closer ties with the West. They did not merely stand to gain from heightened trade. If woe came upon them here—carried, say, by the Huns—then they would have a place to go. Next summer, let them send men and goods to Frithigern, who would safeguard those; and let them keep ships, wagons, gear, food standing by; and let many of them learn about the lands in between and how to get through unharmed.

The Ostrogoths wondered and muttered. They were doubtful about a fast growth of trade across such distances, therefore unwilling to gamble work or wealth. As for leaving their homes, that was unthinkable. Did the Wanderer speak sooth? What was he, anyhow? He was often called a god, and did seem to have been around for a very long time; but he made no claims for himself. He might be a troll, a black wizard, or—said the Christians—a devil sent to lure men astray. Or he might simply be getting foolish at his high age.

The Wanderer kept on. Some who listened found his words worth further thought; and some, young, he kindled. Foremost among the latter was Alawin at Heorot—though Hathawulf grew wistful, while Solbern hung back.

To and fro the Wanderer went on earth, talking, scheming, ordering. By autumnal equinox he had gotten a skeleton of what he wanted. Gold, goods, men to attend these were now at Frithigern's seat in the West; Alawin would go there the following year to push for more trade, regardless of how young he was; at Heorot and numerous other households, dwellers could depart on short notice, should the need arise.

"You have worn yourself out for us," Hathawulf said to him at the end of his last stay in the hall. "If you are of the Anses, then they are not tireless."

"No," sighed the Wanderer. "They too shall perish in the wreck of the world."

"But that is far off in time, surely."

"World after world has gone down in ruin erenow, my son, and will in the years and thousands of years to come. I have done for you what I was able."

Hathawulf's wife Anslaug entered, to say her own farewell. At her breast she suckled their firstborn. The Wanderer gazed long upon the babe. "There lies tomorrow," he whispered. Nobody understood what he meant. Soon he was walking off, he and his spear-staff, down a road where lately fallen leaves flew on a chill blast.

And soon after that, the terrible news came to Heorot.

Ermanaric the king had given out that he intended a foray into Hunland. This would not be an outright war, such as had failed before. Hence he did not call up a levy, but only his full troop of guards, several hundred warriors well-known and faithful to him. The Huns had been wasting the borders again. He would punish them. A swift, hard strike should at least kill off many of their cattle. With luck, it might surprise a camp or three of theirs. Goths nodded when that word reached their steadings. Fatten ravens in the East, and the filthy landloupers of the steppe might slouch back to wherever their forebears had spawned them.

But when his troop had gathered, Ermanaric did not lead it so far. Suddenly, there it was at Randwar's hall, while the homes of Randwar's friends stood afire from horizon to horizon.

Scant was the fighting, as great a strength as the king had brought against an unwarned young man. Shoved along, hands tied behind his back, Randwar stumbled forth into his courtyard. Blood trickled and clotted over his scalp. He had killed three of those who set on him, but their orders were to take him alive, and they wielded clubs and spearbutts until he sank.

This was a bleak evening, where wind shrilled. Tatters of smoke mingled with scudding wrack. Sunset smoldered. A few slain defenders sprawled on the cobbles. Swanhild stood dumb in the grip of two warriors, near Ermanaric on his horse. It was as if she did not understand what had happened, as if nothing was real save the child that bulged her belly.

The king's men brought Randwar before him. He peered downward at the prisoner. "Well," he greeted, "what have to say for yourself?"

Randwar spoke thickly, though he held his battered head aloft: "That I did not fall by stealth on one who had done me no wrong."

"Well, now." Ermanaric's fingers combed a beard turning white. "Well, now. Is is right to plot against your lord? Is it right to slink about heel-biting?"

"I . . . did none of that. . . . I would but ward the honor and freedom . . . of the Goths—" Randwar's dried throat could get no more out.

"Traitor!" screamed Ermanaric, and launched into a long tirade. Randwar stood hunched, belike not hearing much of it.

When he saw that, Ermanaric stopped. "Enough," he said. "Hang him by the neck and leave him for the crows, like any thief."

Swanhild shrieked and struggled. Randwar threw her a blurred look before he turned it on the king and answered, "If you hang me, I go to Wodan my forefather. He . . . will avenge—"

Ermanaric shot forth a foot and kicked Randwar in the mouth. "Up with him!"

A haylift beam jutted from a barn. Men had already thrown a rope over it. They put the noose about Randwar's neck, hauled him aloft, and made the rope fast. He struggled long before he swung free in the wind.

"Yes, the Wanderer will have you, Ermanaric!" Swanhild yelled. "I lay the widow's curse on you, murderer, and I call Wodan against you! Wanderer, lead him down to the coldest cave in hell!"

Greutungs shuddered, drew signs or clutched at talismans. Ermanaric himself showed unease. Sibicho, perched on horseback beside him, yelped: "She calls on her witchy ancestor? Suffer her not to live! Let earth purify itself of that blood she bears!"

"Aye," Ermanaric said in an uprush of will. He rapped forth his command.

Fear more than aught else gave haste to the men. Those who had held Swanhild cuffed her till she staggered, and booted her out into the middle of the yard. She lay stunned on the stones. Riders crowded around, forcing their horses, which neighed and reared. When they withdrew, nothing was left but red mush and white splinters.

Night fell. Ermanaric led his troop into Randwar's hall for a victory feast. In the morning they found the treasure and took it back with them. The rope creaked where Randwar swung above that which had been Swanhild.

Such was the news that men bore to Heorot. They had hastily buried the dead. Most dared do no more than that, but a few Greutungs felt vengeful, as did all Teurings.

Rage and grief overwhelmed the brothers of Swanhild. Ulrica was colder, locked into herself. Yet when they wondered what they could do, even though tribesmen of theirs had swarmed to them from widely about . . . she drew her sons aside, and they talked until the restless darkness fell.

Those three entered the hall. They said they had decided. Best to strike back at once. True, the king would be wary of that, and keep his guard on hand for a while. However, by the accounts of witnesses who had seen it ride past, it was hardly larger than the band which crowded this building tonight. A surprise onslaught by brave men could vanquish it. To wait would give Ermanaric time he needed and was doubtless counting on—time to crush every last East Goth who would be free.

Men bellowed their willingness. Young Alawin joined them. But suddenly the door opened, and there was the Wanderer. Sternly, he bade Tharasmund's last-born son abide here, before he went back into the night and the wind.

Undaunted, Hathawulf, Solbern, and their men rode forth at dawn.

1935

I had fled home to Laurie. But next day, when I let myself into our place after a long walk, she was not waiting. Instead, Manse Everard rose from my armchair. His pipe had made the air hazed and acrid.

"Huh?" I could only exclaim.

He stalked close. I felt his footfalls. As tall as I and heavier-boned, he seemed to loom. His face was expressionless. The window at his back framed him in sky.

"Laurie's okay," he said like a machine. "I asked her to absent herself. This'll be plenty rough on you without watching her get shocked and hurt."

He took my elbow. "Sit down, Carl. You've been through the wringer, plain to see. Figured you'd take a vacation, did you?"

I slumped into my seat and stared down at the rug. "Got to," I mumbled. "Oh, I'll make sure of any loose ends, but first—God, it's been ghastly—"

"No."

"What?" I lifted my gaze. He stood above me, feet apart, fists on hips, overshadowing. "I tell you, I can't."

"Can and will," he growled. "You'll come back with me to base. Right away. You've had a night's sleep. Well, that's all you'll get till this is over. No tranquilizers, either. You'll have to feel everything to the hilt as it happens. You'll need full alertness. Besides, there's nothing like pain for driving a lesson in permanently. Most important, maybe—if you don't let that pain go through you, the way nature intended, you'll never really be rid of it. You'll be a haunted man. The Patrol deserves better. So does Laurie. And even you yourself."

"What are you talking about?" I asked while the horror rose in a tide around me.

"You've got to finish the business you started. The sooner the better, for you above all. What kind of vacation could you have if you knew that duty lay ahead? It'd destroy you. No, do the job at once, get it behind you on your world line; *then* you can rest and start recovering."

I shook my head, not in negation but in bewilderment. "Did I go wrong? How? I filed my reports regularly. If I was straying off the reservation again, why didn't some officer call me in and explain?"

"That's what I'm doing, Carl." A ghost of gentleness passed into Everard's voice. He sat down opposite me and busied his hands with his pipe.

"Causal loops are often very subtle things," he said. Despite the soft tone, that phrase shocked me to full awareness. He nodded. "Yeah. We've got one here. The time traveler becomes a cause of the selfsame events he set out to study or otherwise deal with."

"But—no, Manse, how?" I protested. "I've not forgotten the principles, I never did forget them, in the field or anywhere, anywhen else. Sure, I became part of the past, but a part that fit into what was already there. We went through this at the inquiry—and I corrected what mistakes I had been making."

Everard's lighter cast a startling *snap* through the room. "I said they can be very subtle," he repeated. "I looked deeper into your case mainly because of a hunch, an uneasy feeling that something wasn't right. It involved a lot more than reading your reports—which, by the way, are satisfactory. They're simply insufficient. No blame to you for that. Even with a long experience under your belt, you'd probably have missed the implications, as closely involved in the events as you've been. Me, I had to steep myself in knowledge of that milieu, and rove it from end to end, over and over, before the situation was clear to me."

He drew hard on his pipe. "Never mind technical details," he went on. "Basically, your Wanderer became stronger than you realized. It turns out that poems, stories, traditions which flowed on for centuries, transmuting, crossbreeding, influential on people—a number of those had their sources in him. Not the mythical Wodan, but the physically present person, you yourself."

I had seen this coming and mustered my defense. "A calculated risk from the outset," I said. "Not uncommon. If feedback like that occurs, it's no disaster. What my team is tracing are simply the words, oral and literary. Their original inspirations are beside the point. Nor does it make any difference to subsequent history . . . whether or not, for a while, a man was there whom certain individuals took for one of their gods . . . as long as the man didn't abuse his position." I hesitated. "True?"

He dashed my wan hope. "Not necessarily. Not in this instance, for sure. An incipient causal loop is always dangerous, you know. It can set up a resonance, and the changes of history that that produces can multiply catastrophically. The single way to make it safe is to close it. When the Worm Ouroboros is biting his own tail, he can't devour anything else."

"But . . . Manse, I left Hathawulf and Solbern bound off to their deaths . . . Okay, I confess attempting to prevent it, not supposing it was of any importance to mankind as a whole. I failed. Even in something that minor, the continuum was too rigid."

"How do you know you failed? Your presence through the generations, the veritable Wodan, did more than put genes of yours into the family. It heartened the members, inspired them to become great. Now at the end—the battle against Ermanaric looks like touch and go. Given the conviction that Wodan is on their side, the rebels may very well carry the day."

"What? Do you mean—oh, Manse!"

"They mustn't," he said.

Agony surged higher still. "Why not? Who'll care after a few decades, let alone a millennium and a half?"

"Why, you will, you and your colleagues," the pitying, implacable voice declared. "You set out to investigate the roots of a specific story about Hamther and Sorli, remember? Not to mention the Eddic poets and saga writers before you, and God knows how many tellers before them, affected in small ways that could add up to a big final sum. Mainly, though, Ermanaric is a historical figure, prominent in his era. The date and manner of his death are a matter of record. What came immediately afterward shook the world.

"No, this is no slight ripple in the time stream. This is a maelstrom abuilding. We've got to damp it out, and the only way to do that is to complete the causal loop, close the ring."

My lips formed the useless, needless "How?" which throat and tongue could not.

Everard pronounced sentence on me: "I'm sorrier than you imagine, Carl. But the *Volsungasaga* relates that Hamther and Sorli were almost victorious, when for unknown reasons Odin appeared and betrayed them. And he was you. He could be nobody else but you."

372

Night had lately fallen. The moon, while little past the full, was not yet up. Stars threw a dimness over hills and shaws, where shadows laired. Dew had begun to gleam on stones. The air was cold, quiet save for a drumroll of many galloping hoofs. Helmets and spearheads shimmered, rose and sank like waves under a storm.

In the greatest of his halls, King Ermanaric set at drink with his sons and most of his warriors. The fires flared, hissed, crackled in their trenches. Lamplight glowed through smoke. Antlers, furs, tapestries, carvings seemed to move along walls and pillars, as the darkness did. Gold gleamed on arms and around necks, beakers clashed together, voices dinned hoarsely. Thralls scuttled about, attending. Overhead, murk crouched on the rafters and filled the roof peak.

Ermanaric would fain be merry. Sibicho pestered him: "—Lord, we should not dawdle. I grant you, a straightforward raid on the Teurings' chieftain would be dangerous, but we can start work at once to undermine his standing among them."

"Tomorrow, tomorrow," said the king impatiently. "Do you never weary of plots and tricks, you? Tonight is for that toothsome slave maiden I bought—"

Horns clamored outside. A man staggered in through the entry room that this building had. Blood smeared his face. "Foemen—attack—" An uproar drowned his cry.

"At this hour?" Sibicho wailed. "And by surprise? They must have killed horses traveling hither—yes, and cut down everybody along the way who might have outsped them—"

Men boiled off the benches and went for their mail and weapons. Those being stacked in the entry room, there was a sudden jam of bodies. Oaths lifted, fists flailed. The guards who had stayed equipped sprang to make a bulwark in front of the king and his nearest. He always kept a score of them full-armed.

In the courtyard, royal warriors spent their lives on time for their comrades within to make ready. The newcomers bore against them in overwhelming numbers. Axes thundered, swords clanged, knives and spears bit deep. In that press, slain men did not always fall down at once; wounded who dropped never got up again.

At the head of the onslaught, a big young man shouted, "Wodan with us! Wodan, Wodan! Haa!" His blade flew murderous.

Hastily outfitted defenders took stance at the front door. The big young man was first to shock upon them. Right and left, his followers broke through, smote, stabbed, kicked, shoved, burst the line and stamped in over the pieces of it.

As their van pierced through to the main room, the unarmored troopers beyond stumbled back. The attackers halted, panting, when their leader called, "Wait for the rest of us!" The racket of battle died away inside, though outside it still raged.

Ermanaric sprang onto his high seat and looked across the helmets of his bodyguards. Even in the dancing gloom, he saw who stood at the door. "Hathawulf Tharasmundsson, what new misdeed would you wreak?" he flung through the lodge.

The Teuring lifted his dripping sword on high. "We have come to cleanse the earth of you," rang from him.

"Beware. The gods hate traitors."

"Yes," answered Solbern at his brother's shoulder, "this night Wodan fetches you, oathbreaker, and ill is that house to which he will take you."

More invaders poured through; Liuderis pushed them into ragged ranks. "Onward!" Hathawulf bawled.

Ermanaric had been giving his own orders. His men might mostly lack helmet, byrnie, shield, long weapon. But each bore a knife, at least. Nor did the Teurings have much iron to wear. They were mainly yeomen, who could afford little more than a metal cap and a coat of stiffened leather, and who went to battle only when the king raised a levy. Those whom Ermanaric had gathered were warriors by trade; any of them might have a farm or a ship or the like, but he was first and foremost a warrior. He was well drilled in standing side by side with his fellows.

The king's troopers snatched at trestles and the boards that had lain on top. These they used to ward themselves. Those that had axes, having retreated before the inroad, chopped cudgels for their fellows out of wainscots and pillars. Besides a knife, a stag's tine off the wall, the narrow end of a drinking horn, a broken Roman goblet, a brand from the fire trenches made a deadly weapon. As tightly wedged as the struggle became—flesh against flesh, friend in the way of friend, pushing, stumbling, slipping in blood and sweat—sword or ax was of scant more help. Spears and bills were useless, save that from their stance on the benches by the high seat, the armored guards could strike downward.

Thus the fight became formless, blind, a fury as of the Wolf unbound.

Yet Hathawulf, Solbern, and their best men beat a path onward, pushed, rammed, hewed, slashed, stabbed, amidst bellow and shriek, thud and clash, onward, living storm winds—until at last they came to their mark.

There they sat shield against shield, loosed steel upon steel, they and the king's household troopers. Ermanaric was not in that front line, but he boldly stood above on the seat, before the gaze of all, and wielded a spear. Often did he trade a look with Hathawulf or Solbern, and then each grinned his hatred.

It was old Liuderis who broke through the line. His lifeblood spurted from thigh and forearm, but his ax beat right and left; he won as far as the bench and clove the skull of Sibicho. Dying, he rasped, "One snake the less."

Hathawulf and Solbern passed over his body. A son of Ermanaric threw himself before his father. Solbern cut the boy down. Hathawulf struck beyond. Ermanaric's spear shaft cracked across. Hathawulf struck again. The king reeled back against the wall. His right arm dangled half severed. Solbern slashed low, at the left leg, and hamstrung him. He crumpled, still snarling. The brothers moved in for the kill. Their followers strove to keep the last of the royal guard off their backs.

Someone appeared.

A stop to the fighting spread through the hall like the wave when a rock falls in a pool. Men stood agape and agasp. Through the unrestful gloom, made the thicker by their crowding, they barely saw what hovered above the high seat.

On a skeletal horse, whose bones were of metal, sat a tall gray-bearded man. Hat and cloak hid any real sight of him. In his right hand he bore a spear. Its head, above every other weapon and limned against the night under the roof, caught fire-glow—a comet, a harbinger of woe?

Hathawulf and Solbern let their blades sink. "Forefather," the elder breathed into the sudden hush. "Have you come to our help?"

The answer rolled forth unhumanly deep, loud, and ruthless: "Brothers, your doom is upon you. Meet it well and your names will live.

"Ermanaric, this is not yet your time. Send your men out the rear and take the Teurings from behind.

"Go, all of you here, to wherever Weard will have you go."

He was not there.

Hathawulf and Solbern stood stunned.

Crippled, bleeding, Ermanaric could nonetheless shout: "Heed! Stand fast where you're up against the foe—the rest of you take the hinder door, swing around—heed the word of Wodan!"

His bodyguards were the first to understand. They yelled their glee and fell on their enemies. These lurched back, aghast, into the reborn turmoil. Solbern stayed behind, sprawled under the high seat in a pool of blood.

King's men streamed through the small postern. They hastened past the building to the front. Most of the Teurings had gotten inside. Greutungs overran those in the yard. Had they no better weapons, they ripped cobblestones out of the earth and cast them. A risen moon gave light enough.

Howling, the warriors next cleared the entryroom. They outfitted themselves and fell on the invaders both fore and aft.

Grim was that battle. Knowing they would die whatever happened, the Teurings fought till they dropped. Hathawulf alone heaped a wall of slain before him. When he fell, few were left to be glad of it.

The king himself would not have been among them, had not folk of his been quick to stanch his wounds. As was, they bore him, barely aware, out of a hall where none but the dead then dwelt.

1935

Laurie, Laurie!

372

Morning brought rain. Driven on a hooting wind, hail-cold, hail-hard, it hid everything but the thorp that huddled beneath it, as if the rest of the world had gone down in wreck. The roar on the roof resounded through hollow Heorot.

Darkness within seemed deepened by emptiness. Fires burned, lamps shone well-nigh for naught amidst the shadows. The air was raw.

Three stood near the middle. That of which they spoke would not let them sit. Breath puffed ghost-white out of their lips.

"Slain?" mumbled Alawin numbly. "Every last one of them?"

The Wanderer nodded. "Yes," he told them again, "though there will be as much sorrow among Greutungs as Teurings. Ermanaric lives, but maimed and lamed, and poorer by two sons."

Ulrica gave him a whetted look. "If this happened last night," she said, "you have ridden no earthly horse to bring us the tale."

"You know who I am," he answered.

"Do I?" She lifted fingers toward him that were crooked like talons. Her voice grew shrill. "If you are indeed Wodan, he is a wretched god, who could not or would not help my sons in their need."

"Hold, hold," Alawin begged her, while he cast an abashed glance at the Wanderer.

The latter said softly: "I mourn with you. But the will of Weard stands not to be altered. As the story of what happened drifts west, belike you will hear that I was there, and even that it was Ermanaric whom I saved. Know that against time the gods themselves are powerless. I did what I was doomed to do. Remember that in meeting the end that was set for them, Hathawulf and Solbern redeemed the honor of their house, and won a name for themselves that shall abide as long as their race does."

"But Ermanaric remains above ground," Ulrica snapped. "Alawin, the duty of vengeance has passed to you."

"No!" said the Wanderer. "His task is more than that. It is to save the blood of the family, the life of the clan. This is why I have come."

He turned to the youth, who stared wide-eyed. "Alawin," he went on, "foreknowledge is mine, and a heavy load that is. Yet I may sometimes use it to fend off harm. Listen well, for this is the last time you will ever hear me."

"Wanderer, no!" Alawin cried. Breath hissed between Ulrica's teeth.

The Gray One lifted the hand that did not hold his spear. "Winter will soon be upon you," he said, "but spring and summer follow. The tree of your kindred stands bereft of leaves, but its roots slumber in strength, and it shall be green anew—if an ax does not hew it down.

"Hasten. Hurt though he is, Ermanaric will seek to make an end, once for all, of your troublesome breed. You cannot raise as much force as he can. If you stay here, you will die.

"Think. You have readiness to fare west, and a welcome awaiting you among the Visigoths. It will be the warmer for the rout Athanaric suffered this year from the Huns at the River Dnestr; they all need fresh and hopeful souls. Within a few days, you can be leading the trek. Ermanaric's men, when they come, will find nothing but the ashes of this hall, which you set afire to keep from him and be a balefire in honor of your brothers.

"You will not be fleeing. No, you will be off to forge a mighty morrow. Alawin, you now keep the blood of your fathers. Ward it well."

Wrath twisted Ulrica's face. "Yes, you've always dealt in smooth words," shuddered out of her. "Heed not his slyness, Alawin. Hold fast. Avenge my sons—the sons of Tharasmund."

The youth swallowed hard. "Would you really . . . have me go . . . while the murderer of Swanhild, Randwar, Hathawulf, Solbern—while he lives?" he stammered.

"You must not stay," said the Wanderer gravely. "If you do, you will give up the last life that was in your father—give it up to the king, along with Hathawulf's son and wife, and your own mother. There is no dishonor in withdrawal when outnumbered."

"Y-yes. . . . I could hire a Visigothic host—"

"You will have no call to. Hearken. Within three years, you will hear word about Ermanaric that will gladden you. The justice of the gods shall fall upon him. On this I give you my oath."

"What is that worth?" fleered Ulrica.

Alawin filled his lungs, straightened his shoulders, stood for a while and then said quietly, "Stepmother, be still. I am the man of the house. We will follow the Wanderer's rede."

The boy in him burst through for a moment: "Oh, but lord, forebear—will we indeed never see you again? Do not forsake us!"

"I must," answered the Gray One. "It is needful for you." Suddenly: "Yes, best I go at once. Farewell. Fare ever well."

He strode through the shadows, out the door, into the rain and the wind.

43

Here and there amidst the ages, the Time Patrol keeps places where its members may rest. Among them is Hawaii before the Polynesians arrived. Although that resort exists through thousands of years, Laurie and I counted ourselves lucky to get a cottage for a month. In fact, we suspected Manse Everard had pulled a string or two on our behalf.

He made no mention of that when he visited us late in our stay. He was simply affable, went picnicking and surfing in our company, afterward tucked into Laurie's dinner with the gusto it deserved. Not till later did he speak of what lay behind us and before us on our world lines.

We sat on a deck which abutted the building. Dusk gathered cool and blue in the garden, across the flowering forest beyond. Eastward, land dropped steeply to where the sea glimmered quicksilver; westward, the evening star trembled above Mauna Kea. A brook chimed. Here was the peace that heals.

"So you feel ready to return?" Everard inquired.

"Yes," I said. "And it'll be a lot easier, too. The groundwork has been laid, the basic information collected and assimilated. I just have to record the songs and stories as they are composed and evolve."

"Just!" exclaimed Laurie. Her mockery was tender, and became solace as she laid a hand over mine. "Well, at least you are free of your grief."

Everard's voice dropped low: "Are you sure of that, Carl?"

I could be calm as I replied, "Yes. Oh, there will always be memories that hurt, but isn't that the common fate of man? There are more that are good, and I'm able to draw on them once again."

"You realize, of course, you mustn't get obsessed the way you were. That's a hazard which claims many of us—" Did his tone stumble, ever so slightly? It grew brisk. "When it does, the victim has to overcome it and recover."

"I know," I said, and chuckled a bit. "Don't you know I know?"

Everard puffed on his pipe. "Not exactly. Since the rest of your career seems free of any more disarray than is normal for a field agent, I couldn't justify spending lifespan and Patrol resources on further investigation. This isn't official business. I'm here as a friend, who'd simply like to find out how you're doing. Don't tell me anything you don't care to."

"You're a sweet old bear, you are," Laurie said to him.

I could not stay entirely comfortable, but a sip of my rum collins soothed. "Well, sure, you're welcome to the information," I began. "I did assure myself that Alawin would be all right."

Everard stirred. "How?" he demanded.

"Not to worry, Manse. I proceeded cautiously, for the most part indirectly. Different identities on different occasions. The few times he glimpsed me, he recognized nothing." My fingers passed over a smooth-shaven chin—Roman style, like my close-cropped hair; and when the need arises, a Patrolman has advanced disguise technology at his service. "Oh, yes, I've laid the Wanderer to rest."

"Good!" Everard relaxed back into his chair. "What did become of that lad?"

"Alawin, you mean? Well, he led a fair-sized group, including his mother Erelieva and her household, he led them west to join Frithigern." (He *would* lead them, three centuries hence. But we were talking our native English. The Temporal language has appropriate tenses.) "He enjoyed favor there, especially after he was baptized. That by itself was reason for letting the Wanderer fade away, you understand. How could a Christian stay close to a heathen god?"

"Hm. I wonder what he thought about those experiences, later."

"I get the impression he kept his mouth shut. Naturally, if his descendants—he married well—if his descendants preserved any tradition about it, they'd suppose that some kind of spook had been running around in the old country."

"The old country? Oh, yes. Alawin never got back to the Ukraine, did he?"

"No, hardly. Would you like me to sketch the history for you?"

"Please. I did study it somewhat, in connection with your case, but not much of the aftermath. Besides, that was quite a spell ago, on my world line."

And plenty must have happened to you since, I thought. Aloud: "Well, in 374 Frithigern's people crossed the Danube, by permission, and settled in Thrace. Athanaric's soon followed, although into Transylvania. Hunnish pressure had gotten too severe.

"The Roman officials abused and exploited the Goths—in other words, were a government—for several years. Finally the Goths decided they'd had a bellyful, and revolted. The Huns had given them the idea and technique of developing cavalry, which they made heavy; at the battle of Adrianople in 378 it rode the Romans down. Alawin distinguished himself there, by the way, which started him toward the prominence he achieved. A new Emperor, Theodosius, made peace with the Goths in 381, and most of their warriors entered the Roman service as *foederati*: allies, we'd say.

"Afterward came renewed conflicts, battles, migrations—the *Völkerwanderung* was under way. I'll sum it up for my Alawin by saying that after a turbulent but basically happy life, he died, at a ripe old age, in the kingdom which by then the Visigoths had carved out for themselves in southern Gaul. Descendants of his took a leading part in founding the Spanish nation.

"So you can see how I can let that family go from me, and get on with my work."

Laurie's hand closed hard around mine.

Twilight was becoming night. Stars blinked forth. A coal in Everard's pipe made its own red twinkle. He himself was a darkling bulk, like the mountain that lifted above the western horizon.

"Yes," he mused, "it comes back to me, sort of. But you've been speaking about the Visigoths. The Ostrogoths, Alawin's original countrymen—didn't they take over in Italy?"

"Eventually," I said. "First they had dreadful things to undergo." I paused. What I was about to utter would touch wounds that were not fully scarred over. "The Wanderer spoke truth. There was vengeance for Swanhild."

374

Ermanaric sat alone beneath the stars. Wind whimpered. From afar he heard wolves howl.

After the messengers had brought their news, he could soon endure no more of the terror and the gabble that followed. At his command, two warriors had helped him up the stairs to the flat roof of this blockhouse. They set him down on a bench by the parapet and wrapped a fur cloak about his hunched shoulders. "Go!" he barked, and they went, fear upon them.

He had watched sunset smolder away in the west, while thunderheads gathered blue-black in the east. Those clouds now loomed across a fourth of heaven. Lightnings played through their caverns. Before dawn, the storm would be here. As yet, though, only its forerunner wind had arrived, winter-cold in the middle of summer. Elsewhere the stars still shone in their hordes.

They were small and strange and without pity. Ermanaric's gaze tried to flee the sight of Wodan's Wain, where it wheeled around the Eye of Tiwaz that forever watches from the north. But always the sign of the Wanderer drew him back. "I did not heed you, gods," he mumbled once. "I trusted in my own strength. You are more tricky and cruel than I knew."

Here he sat, he the mighty, lame of hand and foot, able to do naught but hear how the foe had crossed the river and smashed underhoof the army that sought to stay them. He should be thinking what next to try, giving his orders, rallying his folk. They were not undone, if they got the right leadership. But the king's head felt hollow.

Hollow, not empty. Dead men filled that hall of bone, the men who fell with Hathawulf and Solbern, the flower of the East Goths. Had they been alive during these past days, together they would have hurled back the Huns, Ermanaric at their forefront. But Ermanaric had died too, in the same slaughter. Nothing was left but a cripple, whose endless pains gnawed holes in his mind.

Naught could he do for his kingdom but let go of it, in hopes that his oldest living son might be worthier, might be victorious. Ermanaric bared teeth at the stars. Too well did he know how that hope lied. Before the Ostrogoths lay defeat, rapine, butchery, subjection. If ever they became free again, it would be long after he had moldered back into the earth.

He—how blessed that would be—or merely his flesh? What waited for him beyond the dark?

He drew his knife. Starlight and lightninglight shimmered on the steel. For a while it trembled in his hand. The wind whittered.

"Have done!" he screamed. He ruffled his beard aside and brought the point under the right corner of his jaw. Eyes lifted anew, as if of themselves, to the Wain. Something white flickered yonder—a scrap of cloud, or Swanhild riding behind the Wanderer? Ermanaric called forth all the courage that remained to him. He thrust the knife inward and hauled it across.

Blood spurted from the slashed throat. He sagged and fell to the deck. The last thing he heard was thunder. It sounded like the hoofs of horses bearing westward the Hunnish midnight.

STAR OF THE SEA

I

BY day Niaerdh roamed among the seals and whales and fish she had made. From her fingertips she cast gulls and spindrift onto the wind. At the rim of the world her daughters danced to her song, which called rain from heaven or sent light ashiver across the waters. When darkness flowed out of the east, she sought her bed that it blanketed yonder. But often she rose early, long before the sun, to watch over her sea. Upon her brow shone the morning star.

Then once Frae rode to the strand. "Niaerdh, I call you!" he shouted. Only the surf gave answer. He put the horn Gatherer to his lips and blew. Cormorants flew shrieking from the skerries. Last he drew sword and with the flat of it smote the flanks of the bull Earthshaker whereon he sat. At the bellow that sounded forth, wells spouted and dead kings woke in their barrows.

Thereat Niaerdh sought him. Angered, she sailed on an iceberg, herself clad in the fog and bearing in one hand the net in which she takes ships. "Why have you dared trouble me?" she flung at him, words like hailstones.

"I would wed you," he told her. "From afar, the light shining off your breasts blinded me. I have sent my sister away. Earth sickens and all growth withers in the heat of my longing."

Niaerdh laughed. "What can you give me that my brother does not?"

"A high-roofed house," he said, "rich offerings, warm flesh in your trencher and hot blood in your cup, sway over sowing and reaping, over begetting and birth and old age."

"Those things are great," she yielded him, "but what if I still turn from them?"

"Then life will die from the land and, dying, curse you," he warned. "My arrows will fly to the horses of the Sun Car and slay them. When it falls aflame, the sea will boil; afterward it will freeze beneath a night that has no dawn."

"No," she said, "for first I will bring the waves in over your kingdom and drown it."

They were silent a while.

"We are both strong," she said at last. "Best that we not wreck the world between us. I will come to you in springtime with my dowry of rain, and together we will fare about the land to bless it. Your gift to me shall be the bull that you are riding."

"That is too much," said Frae. "In him is the might to fill earth's womb. He scatters the foe, gores and tramples them, lays waste their fields. Rock shudders beneath his hoofs."

"You may keep him ashore and use him as aforetime," answered Niaerdh, "save when I have need for him. But mine he shall be, and in the end I will call him to me forever." After another while she went on: "Each autumn I will leave you and go back to my sea. But in spring I will come again. This shall be the year and every year henceforward."

"I had hoped for more," said Frae, "and I think that if we sunder our doings, the gods of war will rove more free than erstwhile. Yet it is foredoomed that you will have it thus. I will await you when the sun turns north."

"I will come to you on the rainbow," Niaerdh plighted.

So it was. So it is.

1

Seen from the ramparts of Old Camp, nature was terrifying enough. Eastward, in this drought year, the Rhine gleamed shrunken. The Germans crossed it with ease, while supply vessels bound for the outposts along its left bank ran often aground and, before they could escape, might well fall into enemy hands. It was as if the very rivers, the ancient defenses of the Empire, were deserting Rome. Where forest on the farther side, woodlots on this, rose out of the plain, parched leaves were already browning and dropping. Farm plots had been sere until war made them not mud, but dust beneath a brazen sky, to gray the ash and charcoal of houses.

Now that soil bore a new crop, dragon's teeth sprouted, a barbarian horde. Big blond men surged around emblems brought from sacred groves and bloody rites, poles or litters that held skulls or rude carvings of bear, boar, wisent, aurochs, elk, stag, wildcat, wolf. Sunset light flashed on spearheads, shield bosses, the occasional helmet, rarely a coat of ring mail or a cuirass taken off a slain legionary. Most went unarmored, in tunic and close-fitting trousers or stripped to the waist, perhaps with the skin of a beast shaggy above. They growled, barked, shouted, roared, stamped, a sound akin to ongoing distant thunder.

Distant indeed. Peering past the shadows stretched toward them, Munius Lupercus made out long hair knotted at the temple or atop the head. That was the style of the Suebian tribes in the heart of Germany. It wasn't common, those must be small bands who had followed adventurer captains here, but it showed how far the word of Civilis had gone.

The majority braided their manes; some dyed them red or soaped them into spikes, in the manner of Gauls. They were Batavi, Canninefates, Tungri, Frisii, Bructeri, others native to these parts—and more to be feared, less because of their numbers than because they had knowledge of Roman ways. Hoo, there went a squadron of Tencteri, galloping on their ponies as flowingly as centaurs, lances and pennons aloft, axes at saddle bows, cavalry for the rebels!

"We'll have a busy night," Lupercus said.

"How can you tell, sir?" The orderly's voice was not quite steady. He was just a boy, hastily picked for the job after experienced Rutilius fell. When five thousand soldiers had been driven off the field and into the nearest fort, with two or three times as many camp followers, you grabbed what you could.

Lupercus shrugged. "One gets a feeling for their moods."

Not all the signs were subtle. Beyond the river and behind the male tumult on this side, smoke curled past kettles and spits. Women and children of the region had come along to egg their men on to battle. Now again the keening had begun among them. It spread and strengthened while he listened, saw-edged, with an underlying beat, *ha*-ba-da *ha*-ba, *ha*-ba-da-da. More and more ears turned toward it, more and more of the chaos eddied its way.

"I shouldn't think Civilis would want action," said Aletus. Lupercus had detached the veteran centurion from the fragments of his command that survived, to be staff officer and counselor. Aletus gestured down the palisade topping the earthworks. "The last couple of attacks cost him plenty."

Corpses sprawled, bloated, discolored, amidst entrails and clotted blood, broken weapons, ruins of crude testudines under which the barbarians had tried to storm the gates. In places they filled the ditch. Mouths gaped around tongues that ants and beetles were eating. Crows had plucked out many of the eyes. Several birds still pecked away, tucking in a supper before nightfall. Noses had gotten used to the stench, except when a breeze bore it straight at them, and the eventide cooling had damped it.

"He has plenty to spare," Lupercus said.

"Still, sir, he's no fool, nor ignorant, is he?" the centurion persisted. "He marched with us twenty years or more, I've heard, clear down into Italy, and got as much rank as an auxiliary can get. He must know we're short of food and everything. Starving us out makes better sense than charging at regulars and their machines."

"True," Lupercus agreed. "I daresay that's been his intent since he failed to break in. But he hasn't got Roman control over those wild men, you know." Wryly: "Not that our legions haven't been known to kick over the traces of late, eh?"

His gaze sought a center of steadiness around which the enemy weltered. Metal gleamed in arrays where men rested beneath the standards of their units; horses, tethered, fed quietly on oats brought them; newly built, its wood raw but solidly carpentered, a two-story siege tower waited on its wheels. Yonder lay Claudius Civilis, who formerly served Rome, and the tribesmen who had campaigned and learned beside him.

"Something's set the Germans afire again," the legate went on. "Some news or inspiration or whim or . . . whatever. I'd like to know what. But I repeat, we've a busy time ahead of us. Let's make ready."

He led the way back down from the watchtower. It was almost a descent into peace. In the decades since its establishment, Old Camp had enlarged, become a kind of settlement, not everywhere in military gridiron fashion. At the moment it was choked with fugitives as well as the remnants of his expeditionary force. But he had gotten order imposed, soldiers properly quartered and posted, civilians assigned to useful work or at least out from underfoot.

Quietness dwelt in the shadows; for a moment he could close his ears to the savage chant. His mind flew free, across miles and years, over the Alps and south along blue, blue sea to the bay and majestic mountain, nestling town, house and its courtyard of roses, Julia, the children . . . Why, Publius must be shooting up toward manhood, Lupercilla quite the young lady, and had Marcus overcome those problems of his with reading? . . . Letters arrived so infrequently, so irregularly. How were they doing, how was it for them at this exact hour in Pompeii?

Dismiss them. I have my own business to handle. He went about it, inspecting, planning, issuing instructions.

Night fell. Fires leaped huge around the fort, where warriors sat at feast and drink. They had plundered countless amphorae of wine. Presently they started their hoarse war songs. In the background, their women shrilled like hawks.

One by one, gang by gang, they lumbered to their feet, took arms, and dashed themselves against the walls. In the dark, their spears, arrows, and throwing-axes clove only air. The Romans saw them plainly by the light of their fires. Javelin, sling, catapult picked them off, the gaudiest and bravest first. "An Egyptian bird hunt, by Hercules!" Aletus exulted.

"Civilis sees it too," Lupercus replied.

In fact, after a couple of hours sparks whirled high and blinked into nothing, rakes spread wood and coals apart, boots and blankets obliterated flames. The precaution seemed to madden the Germans further. The night was moonless and a haze had blurred stars. Fighting turned well-nigh blind, hand to hand, strike where you heard a noise and spied a deeper darkness coming at you. Still the legionaries kept their discipline. From the walls they tossed stones and iron-shod stakes as well as they could aim. Where the racket told them of a ladder brought up, they pushed it back with shields, and javelins followed. In those men who reached the top, they sheathed their swords.

Sometime after midnight, combat faded away. For a space there was near silence, not even the sounds that the dying make. The Germans had found and borne off their wounded, regardless of any danger, and the Romans' lay by lamplight under care of the surgeons. Lupercus remounted his observation post to listen. Soon he heard a voice haranguing, then shouts, then again the death chant. He shook his head. "They'll be back." He sighed.

First light showed him the siege tower rocking toward the praetorian gate. It went slowly, sweated along by a score or two of warriors while the rest milled impatient behind and Civilis's elite waited aside. Lupercus had ample time to study the situation, make his decisions, get his men positioned and his military engines deployed. He had kept both soldiers and refugee artisans at the task of building those.

The tower approached the gate. Fighters climbed into it, brandishing weapons, hurling missiles, poising to spring down from above. The legate spoke. Romans on the wall brought poles and beams to the entry point. Under cover of shields and their slingers, they shoved, battered, hacked. They beat the tower to a standstill and began smashing it apart. Meanwhile their companions sallied from both sides and attacked the surrounding enemy.

Civilis led his veterans in aid. Roman engineers extended a crane arm over the top of the wall. Iron jaws at the end of a chain swung through an arc, closed on a man, plucked him off his feet. Gleeful, the engineers shifted counterweights. The arm swiveled around, the jaws opened, the captive fell to earth inside the camp. A squad awaited him.

"Prisoners!" Lupercus shouted. "I want prisoners!"

The crane reached forth again, and yet again. That was a device slow and clumsy, but also new and weird, demoralizing. Lupercus never knew how much it did toward throwing dismay into the foe. Most likely nobody could say. The destruction of the tower and the assault by trained, coordinated infantry were amply bad.

Good troops would have stood their ground, enveloped the outnumbered men of the sortie, and cut them to pieces. In the packs of the barbarians, nobody had clear command save over his immediate followers, nor any way of knowing what went on anywhere else. Those who encountered deadliness got no reinforcement. They were weary after their long night, many had lost blood, neither comrades nor gods came to their help. The heart went from them and they ran. Avalanche-like, the rest of the horde tumbled after.

"Shouldn't we pursue, sir?" wondered the orderly.

"That would be fatal." A part of Lupercus wondered why he explained, why he didn't simply tell the boy to shut up. "They aren't in real panic. Look, they're coming to a halt by the river. Their chiefs will rally them and Civilis will bring them more or less to their senses. However, I don't expect he'll allow any further such attempts. He'll settle down to blockade us."

And try to seduce his countrymen among us, the legate's mind added. *But at least now I can get some sleep.* How tired he was. His skull felt full of sand, his tongue like a strip of leather.

First he had duties. He went downstairs and along the pomoerium lane to the spot where the crane had dumped its prey. A pair lay killed, whether because they resisted too hard or the squad grew overexcited. One moaned and writhed feebly on the dust. His legs never stirred, he must have a broken back, best cut his throat. Three slumped bound under the eyes of their guards. The seventh, also with wrists tied and ankles hobbled, stood straight. The outfit of a Batavian auxiliary covered his broad frame.

Lupercus stopped before him. "Well, soldier, what have you to say for yourself?" he asked quietly.

Beard was growing around the lips and the Latin they uttered bore a guttural accent, but it came firmly. "You've got us. That's all you've got, though."

A legionary half lifted his sword. Lupercus waved it aside. "Mind your manners," he advised. "I'll have some questions for you fellows. Cooperate, and you won't suffer the worst that can happen to traitors."

"I'll not betray my lord, whatever you do," said the Batavian. His own exhaustion made the defiance toneless. "Woen, Donar, Tiw be witness."

Mercury, Hercules, Mars. Their main gods, or so we Romans identify them. No matter. I think he means it, and torture won't break him. We have to try, of course. Maybe his comrades will be less resolute. Not that I really believe any of them knows anything useful. What a waste all around.

Hm, one thing, A faint eagerness prickled the legate's skin. *He might well be willing to say this.* "Tell me, anyhow, what possessed you? It was crazy, rushing us. Civilis must have torn his hair out."

"He wanted to stop it," the prisoner admitted. "But the warriors got out of hand, and he—we—could only try to make them effective." A canine grin. "Maybe now they've learned their lesson and will go about the business right."

"But what set the attack off?"

Suddenly the voice throbbed, the eyes kindled. "They were wrong about the tactics, yah, but the word was true. It is true. It came through the Bructeri who joined us. Veleda has spoken."

"Uh, Veleda?"

"The sibyl. She's called on every tribe to rise. Rome is doomed, the goddess tells her, and ours shall be the victory." The Batavian squared his shoulders. "Do what you like to me, Roman. You're a dead man. you with your whole stinking Empire."

2

In the closing decades of the twentieth century, a minor export-import business fronted for the Amsterdam office of the Time Patrol. Its warehouse, with attached office, was in the Indische Buurt, where exotic-looking people drew scant attention.

Manse Everard's timecycle appeared in the secret part of the building early one May morning. He had to wait a minute or so at the exit when the door indicated that somebody was passing by on the other side who shouldn't see that it wasn't merely a wainscot—doubtless an ordinary employee of the company. Then it opened to his key. The arrangement seemed a bit clumsy to him, but he supposed it suited local conditions.

He found his way to the manager, who was also chief of Patrol operations throughout this corner of Europe. Those were usually routine, or as routine as is possible when you deal with traffic up and down the lanes of history. This wasn't milieu headquarters, after all. It hadn't even appeared to be overseeing an especially important sector, till now.

"We weren't expecting you yet, sir," said Willem Ten Brink, surprised. "Shall I call Agent Floris?"

"No, thanks," Everard replied. "I'll meet her later as arranged. Just thought

I'd first look around the city a little. Haven't been here since, uh, 1952, when I spent a few days on a vacation trip. I liked it."

"Well, I hope you enjoy yourself. Things have changed, you know. Do you wish a guide, a car, any kind of assistance? No? What about facilities for your conference?"

"No need, I think. Her message said she could best explain matters, at least to start with, at her place." Despite the other man's obvious disappointment, Everard let forth no hint of what the matters were. They were plenty delicate without leaking information to anybody who didn't require it and didn't work outside his birth era. Besides, Everard wasn't quite sure what did threaten.

Equipped with a map, a walletful of *gulden,* and a few practical cues, he strolled off. At a tobacconist's he bought refills for his pipe and a *strippenkart* for the public transit system. He hadn't had Dutch instilled, but everybody he encountered possessed excellent English. Footloose, he drifted.

Thirty-four years was a long absence. (Longer than that on his personal world line, of course. He had meanwhile joined the Patrol and become an Unattached agent and snaked around through the ages, across most of the planet. Now the London of Elizabeth the First or the Pasargadae of Cyrus the Great stood him nearer than did the streets he would walk today. Had that summer really been so golden, or had he simply been young, unburdened with too much knowledge?) He half dreaded what he might find.

The following hours relieved him. Amsterdam had not become the sewer that some people nowadays called it. From the Dam to the Central Station, it pullulated with scruffy youth, but he saw no one making trouble. In alleys directly off the Damrak you could idle a delightful while in a sidewalk café or a small bar with a huge beer selection. The sleaze shops were at fairly wide intervals, tucked in among ordinary businesses and extraordinary bookstores. When he took a canal tour and the guide insouciantly pointed out the red-light district, what Everard saw was more of the centuried houses that dignified the entire old part of town. He'd been warned about pickpockets but had no need to take precautions against muggers. He'd breathed worse smog in New York and dodged more dog droppings around Gramercy Park than in any residential section here. For lunch he found a friendly little place where they cooked a mean dish of eel. The Stedelijke Musem was a letdown—as regarded modern art, he admitted being an unreconstructed philistine—but he lost himself in the Rijks, forgetting all else, till closing time.

By then he was soon due at Floris's. The hour had been his suggestion, in their preliminary phone conversation. She hadn't demurred. A field agent, Specialist second class, ranked fairly high, but still didn't normally argue with an Unattached. It wasn't too eccentric a time of day anyhow, when you could hop straight to it from whenever you were. Probably she'd skipped uptime shortly after breakfast.

For his part, this relaxed interlude hadn't dulled alertness. On the contrary. Also, by giving him some slight acqaintance with her hometown, the background whence she sprang, it started him on a knowledge of her. He needed that. They might be working very closely together.

His route afoot from the Museumplein took him along the Singelgracht and down through part of Vondelpark. Water gleamed, leaves and grass glowed with sunlight. A boy paddled a hired canoe, his girl in the bow before his eyes; a gray-haired couple walked hand in hand under trees with more years than themselves; a band of bicyclists swept by him in a storm of shouts and laughter. He harked back to the Oude Kerk, the Rembrandts, yes, the Van Goghs he hadn't yet seen, all the life that pulsed in the city today and in past and future, everything that begot and nourished it. And he knew their whole reality for a spectral flickering, diffraction rings across abstract, unstable space-time, a manifold brightness that at any instant could not only cease to be but cease ever having been.

> The cloud-capp'd towers, the gorgeous palaces,
> The solemn empires, the great globe itself,
> Yea, all which it inherit, shall dissolve
> And like this insubstantial pageant faded
> Leave not a wrack behind—

No! He must never let himself brood so. It would merely shake him in his duty, which was to get on with whatever pragmatic, prosaic operations were necessary to safeguard this existence. He lengthened his stride.

The apartment building he sought was one of a row on a quiet street, handsome relics from around 1910. A directory in the entry told him that Janne Floris lived on the fourth floor. It gave her profession vaguely as *bestuurder*, administrator; for purposes of maintaining a local persona, she was on the payroll of Ten Brink's company.

Otherwise Everard knew only that she did field research in the Roman Iron Age, that period when the archaeology of northern Europe began fitfully merging with recorded history. He'd been tempted to call up her service record, which he had authority to do within limits. That was surely no easy milieu for a woman of any kind, let alone a scientist from its future. He'd decided against it, at any rate till they'd talked. Better that his first impression be direct. Also, the business might turn out not to be a real crisis. Maybe investigation would show nothing worse than some kind of mistake or misunderstanding, with no corrective action required.

He found her door and pushed the bell. She opened it. For a moment they stood mute.

Was she taken aback too? Had she expected the Unattached agent to be something more impressive than a big, homely guy with a battle-dented nose and still, after all he'd been through, "Midwesterner" written upon him? He'd certainly not awaited as goodly a sight as this tall blonde in her elegantly understated gown.

"How do you do," he managed in English. "I am—"

She smiled, broad mouth baring large teeth. Snub-nosed, heavy-browed, her features weren't conventionally pretty, apart from eyes of changeable turquoise, but he admired them, and her figure could have belonged to an athletic Juno. "Agent Everard," she finished for him. "An honor, sir." The tone was warm without being subservient and she shook hands as if with an equal. "Welcome."

Passing close as he entered, he saw that she wasn't really young. That clear complexion had known much weather; fine lines crinkled around eyes and lips. Well, she couldn't have accomplished what she must have to earn her rank in any few years of lifespan, and longevity treatment didn't expunge every trace.

In the living room he glanced around. It was furnished plainly and comfortably, like his, though her things weren't battered or faded and she displayed no souvenirs. Maybe she didn't care to explain them away to mundane visitors—and lovers? On the walls he recognized a copy of a Cuyp landscape and an astronomical photograph of the Veil Nebula. Among books in a floor-to-ceiling case he spied stuff by Dickens, Mark Twain, Thomas Mann, Tolkien. A shame that Dutch titles conveyed nothing to him.

"Please sit down," Floris urged. "Smoke if you wish. I have made coffee, or tea can be ready in a few minutes."

"Thanks, coffee will be fine." Everard took an armchair. She brought pot, cups, cream, sugar from the kitchen, put them on a low table, and settled on the couch opposite him.

"Do you prefer we use English or Temporal?" she asked.

He liked her approach, straightforward yet not brusque. "English for now," he decided. The Patrol speech had a grammar capable of handling chronokinesis, variable time, and the associated paradoxes, but when it came to human things was as weak as artificial languages generally are. (An Esperantist who hits his thumb with a hammer will not likely yell, *"Excremento!"*) "I'm after a sketchy, preliminary understanding of what this is about."

"Why, I thought you would arrive prepared. What I have here that is not at the office is—oh, pictures, small objects, the kind of things one brings back from missions, things that have no particular value to science or anyone else but hold memories. Doesn't one?" Everard nodded. "Well, I thought if I took them from their drawer they might help give you a better feel for the milieu, or remind me of observations I made that you may find useful."

He sipped. The coffee was the way he preferred it, hot and strong. "Good thinking. We'll look them over later. But whenever it's practicable, I'd rather start by hearing about a case in direct, first-hand terms. The precise details, the scholarly analysis, the broad picture, those mean more to me afterward." *In other words, I'm not an intellectual, I'm a farm boy who became first an engineer and then a cop.*

"But I have not been on the scene either," she said.

"I know. None of the corps have yet, have they? However, you've been informed of the problem in some circumstantiality, and I'm sure you've given it much thought in the light of your experience, your particular expertise. That makes you the closest thing to an observer we've got."

Everard leaned forward. "Okay," he went on, "what I can tell you is this. The Middle Command asked me if I'd investigate. They'd received a report of inconsistencies in a chronicle of Tacitus's, and it has them worried. The events concerned evidently center on the Low Countries in the first century A.D. That happens to be your field, and you and I are more or less contemporaries"—*a generation between our births, is it?*—"so we should be able to cooperate more or less efficiently. That's why I'm the Unattached agent they contacted." Everard gestured at *David Copperfield.* He'd show her the two of them had something more in common. "Barkis is willin'. I called Ten Brink and then you almost immediately, and followed close behind. Maybe I should first have studied my Tacitus. I'd read him, of course, but quite a while ago on my world line and it's gotten vague. I did glance over the material again, but just a glance, and he gets sort of convoluted, doesn't he? Go ahead and fill me in from the ground up. If you repeat something I already know, what harm?"

Floris smiled. "You have a most disarming manner, sir," she murmured. "Is it on purpose?" Momentarily he wondered if she was being flirtatious; but she tautened and proceeded, businesslike, well-nigh academic:

"You are certainly aware that both the *Annals* and the *Histories* came down to later centuries incomplete. Of the *Histories,* the oldest copy that survived contained only four books of the original twelve, and part of the fifth. That part broke off in the middle of describing what we have become troubled about. Naturally, when time travel is developed, an expedition will in due course go to his era and recover the lost sections. They are much desired. Tacitus is not the most reliable chronicler who ever wrote, but he is a notable stylist, a moralist—and for some occurrences, the single written source of any importance."

Everard nodded. "Yeah. Explorers read the historians for clues to what they should look for and look out for, before they set off to chart what really happened." He coughed. "Why am I telling you your business? Pardon me. Mind if I light a pipe?"

"Not at all," Floris said absently before she continued. "Yes, the complete *Histories*, as well as the *Germania*, have been among my principal guides. I found countless details are different from what he wrote, but that is to be expected. In broad outline, and usually in particulars, his account of the great rebellion and its aftermath is trustworthy."

She paused, then, stubbornly honest: "I have not done my research alone, you realize. Far from it. Others are busy in hundreds of years before and after my special period, in areas from Russia to Ireland. And there are those, the truly indispensable ones, who sit at home to assemble, correlate, and analyze our reports. But it chances that I operate in and around what are now the Netherlands and the nearby parts of Belgium and Germany, during the time when the Celtic influence was dying away—after the Roman conquest of Gaul—and the Germanic peoples were beginning to develop truly distinctive cultures. It is not much we have learned, either, set beside everything we do not know. We are too few."

Too few indeed, Everard thought. *With half a million years or more to guard, the Patrol's forever undermanned, stretched thin, compromising, improvising. We get some help from civilian scientists, but most of them work out of civilizations millennia uptime; their interests are often too alien. And yet we've got to uncover the hidden truths of history, to have an inkling of what the moments are when it could too easily be changed. . . . From a god's-eye viewpoint, Janne Floris, you're probably worth more to the cause of preserving the reality that brought us into being than I am.*

Her rueful laugh pulled him back from his recollections. He felt grateful; they kept recurring to plague him. "How professorish, no?" she exclaimed. "And how shopworn obvious. Please believe I generally talk better to the point. Today I am nervous." Humor faded. Did she shiver? "I am not used to this. Confronting death, yes, but oblivion, the nothingness of everything I ever knew—" Her mouth firmed. She sat straight. "Forgive me."

Having stoked his pipe, Everard struck a match and sent the first pungency across his tongue. "You'll find you're plenty tough," he assured her. "You've proved it. I want to hear about your field experiences."

"Later." For an instant she looked away. He thought he saw hauntedness. Her gaze returned to him, her words became crisp. "Three days ago a special agent had me in for a long consultation. A research team had obtained their own text of the *Histories*. You heard?"

"Uh-huh." Brief though his briefing was, Everard had been told. Sheer happenstance; or was it? (Causality can double back on itself in strange ways.)

Sociologists studying Rome, early second century A.D., found on short notice that they needed to know what the upper classes thought of the Emperor Domitian, who died a couple of decades earlier. Did they really remember him as a Stalin, or concede that he'd done a few worthwhile things? The later sections of Tacitus eloquently expressed the negative view. It seemed easier to borrow his work from a private library and surreptitiously duplicate it than to send uptime for a data file. "They noticed differences from the standard version as they remembered it—if it is the standard version—and comparison showed the differences are radical."

"Far beyond copyist's errors, author's revisions, or anything else reasonable," Floris emphasized. "Detective work proved it was not a forgery, but an authentic copy of a manuscript by Tacitus himself. And, while the phrasing varies between them, as one would expect if they led toward two separate endings—the chronicle as such, the narrative line, does not split until the fifth book, very soon after the scene where the copy that survived breaks off. Is this coincidence?"

"I dunno," Everard replied, "and better we pass that question by. Kind of spooky, huh?" He forced himself to lean back, cross shank over thigh, drain his cup, trail out a slow streamer of smoke. "Suppose you give me a synopsis of the story—the two stories. Don't be afraid of repeating what's elementary to you. I confess what I remember is simply that the Dutch and some of the Gauls rose against Roman rule and gave the Empire a stiff fight before they were put down. Afterward they, their descendants, were placid Roman subjects, eventually citizens."

Starkness responded. "Tacitus goes into detail, and I have—we have—confirmed that on the whole he reports it fairly well. It began with the Batavi, a tribe living in what is now South Holland, between the Rhine and the Waal. They, with a number of others in this area, had not formally been brought under the Empire, but they had been made tributaries. All furnished soldiers to Rome, auxiliary troops, who served their terms with the legions and retired on nice pensions, whether they settled down where they were at discharge or returned to the homeland.

"But under Nero the Roman government became more and more extortionate. For instance, the Frisii were supposed to furnish a certain amount of leather every year for making shields. Instead of the hides of the dwarfish domestic cattle, the governor now demanded the much bigger and thicker hides of wild bulls, which were growing scarce, or the equivalent. It was ruinous."

Everard grinned on the left side of his face. "Tax collection. Sounds familiar. Go on."

Floris's tone intensified. She stared before her, fists clenched on her lap.

"You remember, at the overthrow of Nero, civil war broke out. The year of the three emperors—Galba, Otho, Vitellius—then, in the Near East, Vespasian—devastating the Empire as they contended. Each raised what forces he could, any kind, anywhere, by any means, including conscription. The Batavi, especially, saw their sons haled off, and not only to fight in a war that was meaningless to them. Some Roman officials had an appetite for comely youths."

"Yeah. Give government an inch, and that's what it'll do to the people every time. Which is why the founding fathers of the United States tried to limit federal powers. Too bad their success was temporary. Sorry, didn't mean to interrupt."

"Well, there was a Batavian family of noble birth—property, influence, descent claimed from the gods—which had supplied Rome with a number of soldiers. Prominent among them was a man who had taken the Latin name Claudius Civilis. At home, we have learned, he was Burhmund. He distinguished himself in many actions through a long career. Now he called the tribes to arms, the Batavi and their neighbors. He was no naive rustic, you understand."

"I do. Half civilized, and doubtless a smart, observant sort."

"Ostensibly, he declared for Vespasian as against Vitellius, and told his followers that Vespasian would give them justice. That made it easy for Germanic troops elsewhere to set their orders aside and come join him. He scored several major victories. Northeastern Gaul took fire. Under Julius Classicus and Julius Tutor, the Gallic auxiliaries went over to Civilis, while they proclaimed their province an empire in its own right. In the Germanic tribe of the Bructeri, a prophetess called Veleda predicted the fall of Rome. It inspired the natives further, to heroic efforts, and their aim also became an independent confederation."

That too sounds familiar to an American. We started in 1775 fighting for our rights as Englishmen. Then one thing led to another. Everard refrained from speaking.

Floris sighed. "Well, Vespasian's cause prevailed. He himself remained in the Near East several months, having much on his hands there, but he wrote to Civilis requiring an end of hostilities. He was refused, of course. After that he dispatched an able general, Petillius Cerialis, to take charge in the North. Meanwhile the Gauls and the Germanic tribes quarreled, could not coordinate, bungled what opportunities came to them. You see, unified command was something outside their mental horizon. The Romans reduced them in detail. Finally Civilis agreed to meet with Cerialis and discuss terms. It is a dramatic scene in Tacitus—a bridge across the Ijssel, from which workers first removed the middle—the two men stood each at an end of the broken span and talked—"

"I remember that," Everard said. "It's where the manuscript ended, till the rest was recovered. As I recall, the rebels got a pretty fair offer, which they accepted."

Floris nodded. "Yes. An end to outrages, guarantees for the future, and amnesty. Civilis retired to private life. Veleda—Tacitus does not say, except that she apparently helped arrange the armistice. I would like to find out what became of her."

"Any ideas?"

"A sort of guess. If you go to the museums in Leiden and in Middelburg on Walcheren you will see stones from the second or third centuries, altars, votive blocks, carved and inscribed in Latin—" Floris shrugged. "No matter, probably. The fact is that those ancestors of us Dutch became provincial Romans, reasonably well content." Her eyes widened. She clutched at the border of her cushion. "The fact *was*."

Stillness dropped over them. How fragile the late afternoon sunlight and rustle of traffic seemed, beyond the windowpanes.

"That's Tacitus One, right?" Everard said low after a while. "The version we've always used, and that I skimmed yesterday. I'm not quite clear on Tacitus Two. What does it tell?"

Floris answered no louder. "That Civilis did not yield, in large part because Veleda preached against peace. The war went on for another year, till the tribes were wholly subjugated. Civilis killed himself rather than go in chains to Rome for a triumph. Veleda escaped into free Germany. Many followed her. Tacitus—Two—remarks near the end of the *Histories* that the religion of the wild Germans has changed since he wrote his book about them. A female deity is becoming prominent, the Nerthus he described in his *Germania*. Now he compares her to Persephone, Minerva, and Bellona."

Everard tugged his chin. "The goddesses of death, wisdom, and war, eh? Strange. The Anses or Aesir or whatever you call them—the male sky-gods— should've long since reduced the old chthonic figures to second place. . . . What does he have to say about happenings in Rome itself and elsewhere?"

"Essentially the same things as in the first text. The phrases often vary. Likewise do conversations and a number of incidents; but ancient and medieval chroniclers freely invented those, you know, or drew on traditions that might have drifted considerably from the facts. These variations do not prove that actual events changed."

"Aside from in Germany. Well, it was the boondocks. Whatever happened there, for the first several decades, wouldn't particularly touch the high civilizations. The long-range consequences, though—"

"They were not significant, were they?" Floris's words trembled. "We are still here, we still exist, don't we?"

Everard pulled hard on his pipe. "So far. And 'so far' is meaningless in English or Dutch or whatever. But let's not go to Temporal yet. What we've got is an anomaly that needs investigation. I daresay it escaped notice earlier—yes, 'earlier' is meaningless too—because of its dates. Nearly all attention is elsewhere."

Annis Domini 69 and 70. Those weren't just the years of the Northern revolt. Nor were they just when Kwang Wu-Ti was nailing down the rule of the Later Han dynasty, or the Satavahanas were overrunning India, or Vologaeses the First was struggling against rebels and invaders of his own in Persia. (I checked the records before leaving for here. Nothing ever quite happens in isolation.) It wasn't even when Rome was ripping itself apart, after the legions had discovered that emperors could be made elsewhere than in Rome. No, it was the time of the Jewish War. That was what detained Vespasian and his son Titus after their victory over Vitellius. The rising of the Jews, the bloody suppression of it, the destruction of the Third Temple—with everything that that was to mean for the future, Judaism, Christianity, the Empire, Europe, the world.

"A nexus, then, is it not?" Floris whispered.

Everard nodded heavily. Somehow he preserved outward calm. "Patrol units are concentrated on guarding Palestine. You can well imagine what emotions are engaged, through how many centuries. Fanatics or freebooters who want to change what took place in Jerusalem, researchers crowding in and multiplying the chances of a fatal blunder, and the situation itself, the near-infinity of causes radiating into that episode and effects radiating out from it. . . . I don't pretend to understand the physics, but I can sure believe what I've been taught, that the continuum is especially vulnerable around such moments. As far away as barbarian Germany, reality is unstable."

"But what could have shifted it?"

"That's what we've got to find out. Could be somebody taking advantage of the Patrol's preoccupation. Or could be accident, could be—I don't know. Maybe a Danellian could spell out the possibilities. Our job—" Everard drew breath. "Since they don't have some improbable but safe explanation, like a forgery, these two variant texts are . . . a warning. An early sign, a ripple of change, something that *may have had* consequences which caused history to flow into a different channel till at last you and I and everything around us never existed—unless we heed the warning and take steps to see that this *did not happen*— Oh, Lord, we had better talk Temporal."

Floris stared into her cup. "Can that wait?" she asked, barely audibly. "I need to think about this, to, to assimilate it. It was never more than theory to me. I did my fieldwork like, oh, a nineteenth-century explorer in darkest Africa. There were precautions to take, yes, but I was told that the pattern of events is not easily disturbed and that whatever I did, within reason, would 'always' have been a part of the past. Today it is as if earth dissolved beneath my feet."

"I know." *How nightmarishly well I know. The Second Punic War*— "Sure, take your time." *Time!* "Collect your wits." His smile surprised him by its genuineness. "Mine are still kind of scattered too. Look, suppose we relax and gab freely, whether about the subject on hand or anything else. In a while, let's go out for a drink and dinner, enjoy ourselves, start getting acquainted. Tomorrow we can buckle down in earnest."

"Thank you." She passed a hand over the thick yellow braids coiled around her head. He recalled that ancient Germanic tribeswomen wore their hair long. As if she felt that magic which folk around the world laid to the human mane, strength rang anew: "Yes, tomorrow we shall cope."

3

Winter brought rain, snow, rain again, flogged by harsh winds, weather that raged on into the springtime. Rivers ran gorged, meadows flooded, swamps overflowed. Men doled out what grain they still had stored, killed more of their huddled and shivering livestock than they wished, went hunting oftener and with less gain than they had been wont. They wondered whether the gods had wearied of last year's drought but not of harrowing earth.

Maybe it was a hopeful sign that the night when the Bructeri met at their halidom was clear, though cold. Rags of cloud flew on the wind, ghost-white next to the full moon that sped among them. A few stars flickered wan. Trees of the grove were huge darknesses, formless save where boughs nearly bare tossed against heaven. Their creakings went like an unknown tongue, answers to the skirl and snarl of the wind.

The balefire roared. Flames leaped red and yellow from its white heart. Sparks whirled aloft to mock the stars and die. Light barely touched the great boles around the glade and made them seem to stir, uneasy as the shadows. It gleamed off the spears and eyeballs of the gathered men, brought grim faces forth out of gloom, but lost itself in their beards and shaggy coats.

Behind the fire loomed the images, rough-hewn from whole logs. Woen, Tiw, and Donar were cracked and gray, begrown with moss and toadstools. Nerha was newer, freshly painted to shine beneath the moon, and the skill of a slave from the Southlands had gone into the carving of her. In the restless glow, she might have been alive, the goddess herself. The wild boar roasting over the coals had been killed more to her than to the others.

They were not many, the men, nor were any but a few young. All who could had followed their chiefs across the Rhine last summer, to fight with Burhmund the Batavian against the Romans. They were there yet, and sorely missed at home. Wael-Edh had sent word around that the heads of households among the Bructeri should meet this night, make offering, and hear her.

The breath soughed between their teeth as she trod into sight. Her garb was moon-white, trimmed with dark fur, a necklace of raw amber aglow over her bosom. The wind made waves in her skirts and her cloak fluttered like great wings. Who knew what thoughts laired within its hood? She raised her arms, the gold rings coiled upon them shimmered snakish, and every spear dipped to her.

Heidhin, who had led in readying the boar, stood nearest the fire, apart from the others. He drew his knife, lifted blade to lips, sheathed it again. "Welcome, lady of ours," he greeted. "Behold, they are come as you bade, they who speak for the folk, that through you the gods may speak to them. If you will, say forth."

Edh lowered her hands. While not loud, her voice struck to its mark past the noises of the night. More than Heidhin's, it kept an outland tone, a rise and fall like surf beating on some far shore. Maybe from this came a little of the awesomeness that forever enwrapped her.

"Hear me, sons of Brucht, for great are my tidings. The sword is aloft, the wolves and ravens eat well, the witches of Nerha fly free. Hail to the heroes!

"Let me first give you the older truth. When I called you hither, my wish was only to hearten you. The time has been long, homes guest hunger, and still the foe has stood fast. Many among you begin to wonder why we are allied with our kin beyond the river. We have shames to avenge but no yoke to cast off. We have a kingdom to build together with them but cannot if they fail.

"Yes, tribes among the Gauls have risen too, but they are a flighty lot. Yes, Burhmund has ravaged among the Ubii, those dogs of Rome, but the Romans have wasted the country of our friends the Gugernes. Yes, we have laid Moguntiacum and Castra Vetera under siege, but from the first we had to withdraw and the second has held out month after month. Yes, we have had our victories on the field, but we have had our defeats too, and always our losses were heavy. Therefore would I renew my promise to you, that Rome shall fall, the bones of the legions lie strewn and the red cock crow on every Roman roof—the vengeance of Nerha. We have but to fight on.

"Then, only today, surely by the will of the goddess, a rider reached me from Burhmund himself. Castra Vetera, the Old Camp of the enemy, has yielded. Vocula the legate, victor of Moguntiacum, is dead, and Novesium, where he died, has likewise surrendered. Colonia Agrippinensis, proud city among the Ubii, asks for terms.

"Nerha keeps faith, sons of Brucht. This is the beginning of the pledge she will wholly redeem. Rome shall fall!"

Their yells tore at the sky.

She harangued them longer, though not much longer, and ended quietly: "When at last your warriors come home, Nerha will bless their loins and they will father men to bestride the world. Now feast before her, and tomorrow bring hope to your women." She lifted a hand. Once more they lowered their spears. She took a brand from the fire to light her way and departed into the darkness.

Heidhin led them as they pulled the offering off the grill, carved it, and devoured the smellsome flesh. However, he said little while they talked into each other's mouths of the wonder told them. Often such a silent spell came upon him. Folk had grown used to it. Enough that he was Wael-Edh's trusty man and, in his own right, a shrewd, swift leader. He was lean, with narrow features, white streaks in the blackness of hair and close-trimmed beard.

When the bones were cast aside onto the midden and the fire was guttering low, on behalf of everyone he bade the gods good night. Men sought the lodge nearby, where they would rest before starting back in the morning. Heidhin went a different way. His torch helped him along a dim trail until he came out from under the trees to a broad clearing, where he dropped it to die. Here the moon ran above western woodland, amidst the wind and the witchy clouds.

Before him hunched a house. Frost glistened on thatch. Within it, he knew, kine slept along one wall, folk along the other, mingled with their stores and tools, as they might anywhere else; but these served Wael-Edh. Her tower hulked beyond, heavy-timbered, iron-bound, raised for her to dwell in alone with her dreams. Heidhin walked onward.

A man stepped into his path, slanted spear, and cried, "Halt!"—then, peering through the moonlight: "Oh, you, my lord. Do you want a doss?"

"No," Heidhin said. "Dawn's nigh, and I've a horse at the lodge to bear me home. First I would call on the lady."

The guard stood unsure. "You'd not wake her, would you?"

"I do not think she has slept," Heidhin said. Helpless, the man let him go by.

He knocked on the door of the tower. A thrall girl woke and drew the bolt. Seeing him, she held a pine splinter to her clay lamp and used it to light a second, which he took. He climbed the ladder to the loft-room.

As he awaited—they had known one another so long—Edh sat on her high stool, staring into the shadows cast by her own lamp. They wavered big and ill-formed among the beams, the chests, the pelts and hides, the things of

witchcraft and the things brought along from her wanderings. In the chill she
kept her cloak wrapped around her, the hood up; when she looked his way he
saw her face nighted. "Hail," she said low. A wraith out of her lips glimmered
in the dull light.

Heidhin sat down on the floor, leaning back against the panel of the
shut-bed. "You should rest," he said.

"You knew I could not, this soon."

He nodded. "Nevertheless, you should. You grind yourself thin."

He thought he glimpsed a half smile. "I have been doing that for many
years, and am still above ground."

Heidhin shrugged. "Well, then, sleep when you can." It would be fitfully.
"What have you been thinking of?"

"Everything, of course," she said wearily. "What these victories mean.
What we should do next."

He sighed. "I thought so. But why? It is clear."

The hood crinkled and uncrinkled, shadowful, as she took her head. "It is
not. I understand you, Heidhin. A Roman host has fallen into our hands, and
you believe we should do what warriors of old did, give everything to the
gods. Cut throats, break weapons, smash wagons, cast all into a bog, that Tiw
be slaked."

"A mighty offering. It would quicken the blood in our men."

"And enrage the Romans."

Heidhin grinned. "I know the Romans better than you, my Edh." Did she
wince? He hastened on: "I mean, I have dealt with them and theirs, I, a war
chieftain. The goddess says little to you about such everyday things, does she?
I say the Romans are not like our kind. They are coldly forethoughtful—"

"Therefore you understand them well."

"Men do call me cunning," he said, unabashed. "Then let us make use of
my wits. I tell you a slaughter will rouse the tribes and bring new warriors to
us, more than it will set the foe on vengeance." He donned gravity. "Also, the
gods themselves will be glad. They will remember."

"I have thought on this," she told him. "The word from Burhmund is that
he means to spare their men—"

Heidhin stiffened. "Ha," he said. "Thus. He, half Roman."

"Only in knowing them still better than you. He deems a butchery unwise.
It could well enrage them into bringing their full strength against us, whatever
that costs them elsewhere in their realm." Edh raised a palm. "But wait. He
also knows what the gods may want—what we here at home may think the
gods want. He is sending a headman of theirs to me."

Heidhin sat straight. "Well, that's something!"

"Burhmund's word is that we may kill the man in the halidom if we must, but his rede is that we stay our hands. A hostage, to swap for something worth more—" She was still for a bit. "I have spent this while mutely calling on Niaerdh. Does she want yon blood or no? She has given me no sign. I believe that means no."

"The Anses—"

Seated above him, Edh said with sudden stiffness: "Let Woen and the rest grumble at Niaerdh, Nerha, if they like. I serve *her*. The captive shall live."

He scowled at the floor and gnawed his lip.

"You know I am foe to Rome, and why," she went on. "But this talk of bringing it down in wreck—more and more, as the war wears on, I come to see that as mere rant. It is not truly what the goddess bade me say, it is what I have told myself she wants me to say. I must needs utter it again tonight, or the gathering would have been bewildered and shaken. Yet can we really win anything but Roman withdrawal from these lands?"

"Can we gain even that much if we forsake the gods?" he blurted.

"Or is it your hopes of power and fame that we may have to forgo?" she snapped.

He glared. "From none but you would I brook that."

She left the stool. Her voice went soft. "Heidhin, old friend, I am sorry. I meant no hurt. We should never lie at odds, we twain."

He rose too. "I did swear once . . . I would follow you."

She took both his hands in hers. "And well you have. How very well." When she threw her head back to look at him, the hood fell off and he saw her face lamplit. Shadows filled the furrows in it and underlined the cheekbones but masked the gray in the brown tresses. "We've fared far together."

"I did not swear I would blindly obey," he muttered. Nor had he done so. Sometimes he went dead against her wishes. Afterward he showed her he had been right.

"Far and far," she whispered as though she had not heard. Hazel eyes sought the murk behind him. "Did we end here, east of the great river, because the years and miles had worn us out? We should have wandered on, maybe to the Batavi. Their land opens onto the sea."

"The Bructeri made us wholly welcome. They did everything for you that you asked."

"Oh, yes. I was thankful. I am. But someday—a single kingdom of all the tribes—and I shall again watch the star of Niaerdh shine above the sea."

"No such kingdom can be unless first we bleed Rome dry."

"Do not talk of that. Later we shall have to. Now let us remember gentle things."

Sunrise reddened heaven when he bade her farewell. Dew sheened on the mud outside. Black above it, he passed the holy grove, bound for the lodge and his horse. Peace had been on her brow, she was ready for sleep, but his fingers drew taut around the hilt of his knife.

4

Castra Vetera, Old Camp, stood near the Rhine, about where Xanten in Germany did when Everard and Floris were born. But the whole of this land in this age was Germany—Germania, reaching across upper Europe from the North Sea to the Baltic, from the River Scheldt to the Vistula, and south to the Danube. Sweden, Denmark, Norway, Austria, Switzerland, the Netherlands, the German state would arise out of it in the course of almost two thousand years. Today it was wilderness broken here and there by cultivation, grazing, villages, steadings, held by tribes that came and went in war, migration, eternal turbulence.

Westward, in what would be France, Belgium, Luxembourg, much of the Rhineland, the dwellers were Gauls, of Celtic language and Celtic ways. With a high culture and military capability, they had dominated the Germans with whom they were in contact—though the distinction was never absolute, and blurred in the border country—until Caesar conquered them. That was not so long ago, assimilation was not yet so far along, that memory of the old free days had died out of everyone.

It had seemed the same would befall their rivals to the east; but when Augustus lost three legions in the Teutoburg Forest, he decided to draw the frontier of the Empire at the Rhine rather than the Elbe, and only a few German tribes stayed under Roman rule. For the outermost of these, such as the Batavi and Frisii, it was not actual occupation. Like native states in India of the British Raj, they were required to pay tribute and, in general, behave as the nearest proconsul directed. They furnished a good many auxiliary troops, originally volunteers, lately conscripts. It was they that first rose in revolt; then they got allies from among their kindred to the east, while southwest of them Gauls took fire.

"Fire—I hear of a sibyl who prophesies that Rome itself shall burn," said Julius Classicus. "Tell me about her."

Burhmund's bulk shifted uneasily in the saddle. "With words like that, she brought the Bructeri, Tencteri, and Chamavi to our cause," he acknowledged, with somewhat less enthusiasm than might have been expected. "Her fame has overleaped the rivers to lay hold on us." He glanced at Everard. "You must have heard of her too as you fared. Your trail would have crossed hers, and yon tribes have not forgotten. Warriors of theirs have been coming to us because they learned she was here, calling for war."

"Certainly I heard," lied the Patrolman, "but I did not know what to make of those stories. Do tell more."

The three sat mounted under a gray sky, in a bleak breeze, near the road from Old Camp. It was a military road, paved and arrow-straight, running south along the Rhine to Colonia Agrippinensis. The Roman legions had been here that many years. Now those remnants of them that had held this fortress through fall and winter moved under guard toward Novesium, which had yielded much more quickly.

They were a sorry lot to behold, ragged, dirty, skeletally thin. Most shambled empty-eyed, making no attempt to form ranks. They were mainly Gauls, both regulars and auxiliaries, and it was to the Empire of Gaul that they had surrendered and pledged allegiance, according to the demands and cajolements of Classicus's spokesmen. Not that they could have stood off a determined attack, as they had done again and again early in the siege. The blockade had brought them down to eating grass and whatever cockroaches a man might catch.

Their escort was nominal, a handful of fellow Gauls, well fed and smartly outfitted, soldiers themselves before they became followers of Classicus and his colleagues. More men kept watch over the ox-drawn wagons that lumbered behind, laden with spoils. Those were Germans, a few legionary veterans officering backwoodsmen armed with spears, axes, and long swords. It was plain to see that Claudius Civilis—Burhmund the Batavian—had limited faith in his Celtic associates.

He frowned. He was a big man, blunt-featured, his left eye blind and milky from an infection in the past, the right coldly blue. Since disavowing Rome he had let his beard grow, brown shot with white, and had his hair, also unclipped, dyed red in barbarian wise. But ring mail rustled about his body, a Roman helmet shone on his head, and at his hip hung a legionary blade meant for stabbing, not hewing.

"It would take the whole day to speak of Wael-Edh—Veleda," he said. "Nor am I sure it would be lucky. That's a strange goddess she serves."

"Wael-Edh!" whispered in Everard's hearing. "Her proper name, then. Latin speakers would naturally change it a little—" The three men were using the language of the Romans, the one they had in common.

Startled in his tension, Everard involuntarily glanced up. He saw only cloud cover. Above it, Janne Floris hovered on a timecycle. A woman could not very well have ridden into the rebel camp. Though he could have explained her presence away, the risk of trouble was idiotic to assume, on a mission dicey enough. Besides, she was most useful where she was. Her instruments pierced the deck, ranged widely, magnified or amplified when she desired. Through the electronics in his ornamental-looking headband, she saw and heard what he did, while bone conduction brought her words to him. Should he get into serious difficulties, she might be able to rescue him. That depended on whether she could do it without creating a sensation. No telling how these people would react—even the most sophisticated Roman believed in omens, if nothing else—and the object of the game was to preserve history. If necessary, you let your partner die.

"Anyhow," Burhmund went on, obviously anxious to dismiss the subject, "her fierceness is lessening. Perhaps the goddess herself wants an end to the war. What gain in it, after we've won what we began it for?" His sigh gusted in to the wind. "I too, I've had my fill of strife."

Classicus bit his lip. He was a short man, which may have fueled the ambition that blazed in him, though an aquiline countenance betokened the royal descent he claimed. In Roman service he had commanded the Treverian cavalry, and it was in the city of that Gallic tribe, Trier to be, that he and others first conspired to take advantage of the German uprising. "We have dominion to win," he snapped, "greatness, wealth, glory."

"Well, I'm a man of peace myself," Everard said on impulse. If he could not stop what was to happen this day, he must at least, in so small and futile a way, protest it.

He sensed skepticism in the looks upon him. He'd better fend it off. He, a pacifist? His persona was that of a Goth, come from lands that would one day be Poland, where his tribe still dwelt. Everard Amalaric's son was among its king's—its war chief's—numerous progeny, thus of a social standing that entitled him to speak freely to Burhmund. Born too late for any inheritance worth mentioning, he went into the amber trade, personally conducting the costly ware down to the Adriatic, which was where he acquired his accented Latin. Eventually he quit and struck off westward because he felt adventurous and had heard rumors of fortunes to be made in these parts. Also, he hinted, some trouble at home needed a few years to cool down.

It was an unusual but not unbelievable story. A large and formidable man, who carried little worth robbing, might well travel by himself without ever being assaulted. Indeed, he would be welcome most places, a break in monotony, a bearer of news and tales and songs. Claudius Civilis had been glad to receive Everard when the wanderer arrived. Whether or not Everard had anything helpful to tell, he offered a bit of distraction from the long campaigning.

But it was *not* believable that he had never fought, or that he lost any sleep after having cut a human being apart. Before he should be suspected as a spy, the Patrolman said fast, "Oh, I've had my share of battles, and single combats too. Whoever calls me coward will feed the ravens before nightfall." He paused. *I've a notion I can appeal to something in Burhmund, make him open up to me a little. We need an idea of how he, the key man in all this, thinks, if we're to discover how it is that the time stream forks—and which is the right course, which the wrong one, for us and our world.* "But I'm sensible. When you can do it, trade is better than war."

"You will find rich commerce among us in future," Classicus declared. "The Empire of Gaul—" Pensively: "Why not? Bring the amber straight west, overland as well as by sea. . . . I will think about that when I have time."

"Hold," Burhmund interrupted. "I've a task " He put heels to horse and trotted off.

Classicus's regard followed him warily. The Batavian rode to the line of surrendered troops. The tail of the sad procession was just passing by. He drew alongside a man, almost the only one, who walked erect and proudly. Ignoring practicality, the man had wrapped a toga, clean and pipe-clayed, around his starveling frame. Burhmund leaned over and spoke to him.

"What's gotten into his head?" Classicus muttered. Immediately he turned his own and glowered at Everard. He must have remembered the newcomer would overhear. Friction between allies should not be displayed to outsiders.

I've got to divert him, or he may well order me begone, the Patrolman considered. Aloud: "The Empire of Gaul, did you say? Do you mean that part of the Roman Empire?"

He foreknew the answer. "It is the independent nation of all the Gallic peoples. I have proclaimed it. I am its emperor "

Everard acted duly impressed. "I beg your pardon, sir! I hadn't heard, being so lately arrived."

Classicus smiled sardonically. There was more to him than vainglory. "The empire itself is very lately founded. It will be a while before I reign from a throne instead of a saddle."

Everard drew him out. That was easy. Uncouth and uninfluential, this Goth was nevertheless somebody to talk to and, after all, an impressive figure of a man, who had seen a lot, whose interest therefore held a subtly unique flattery.

Classicus's dream was fascinating in detail, and by no means insane. He would detach Gaul from Rome. That would cut off Britain. Thinly garrisoned, its natives restive and resentful, the island should presently fall to him. Everard knew Classicus grossly underestimated Roman strength and determination. It was a natural mistake. He could not tell that the civil wars were over and Vespasian would henceforward rule competently, unchallenged.

"But we require allies," he admitted. "Civilis shows signs of wavering—" He clipped his mouth shut, again realizing he had said too much. "What are your intentions, Everard?" he demanded.

"I am only rambling around, sir," the Patrolman assured him. *Get the tone right, neither humble nor arrogant.* "You honor me by sharing your plans. The trade prospects—"

Classicus made a dismissive gesture and looked away. Hardness settled on his face. *He's thinking, he's reaching a decision that he may have been brooding on. I can guess what.* Chill went along Everard's backbone.

Burhmund had completed his brief discussion with the Roman. He issued an order to a guard, who accompanied the prisoner from the train toward the crude wattle-and-daub shelters the Germans had made for themselves during the siege. Meanwhile Burhmund rode over to a score of bully boys who sat mounted ten or fifteen yards off, his household troops. He addressed the smallest and slenderest of them. The lad nodded obedience and hurried toward the abandoned encampment himself, overtaking the Roman and escort. Some Germans were there yet, to keep an eye on the civilians left in the fortress. They had extra horses, supplies, and equipment he could claim.

Burhmund returned to his companions. "What was that about?" Classicus asked sharply.

"A legate of theirs, as I thought he must be," Burhmund said. "I had resolved I would send one such to Veleda. Guthlaf goes ahead, my fastest rider, to let her know."

"Why?"

"I have heard grumbles among my men. I know folk at home feel the same. We have had our victories, but we have suffered our defeats as well, and the war drags on. At Ascibergium—I will be honest—we lost the flower of our army, and I suffered injuries that kept me days disabled. Fresh soldiers have been reaching the enemy. Men say it's high time we gave the gods a blood-feast, and here is this herd of foes dropped into our hands. We should slay them, wreck their gear, offer everything to the gods. Then we shall overcome."

Everard heard a gasp from high above.

"If it will satisfy your followers, you can." Classicus sounded more eager than cool, though the Romans had weaned the Gauls away from human sacrifice.

Burhmund cast him a steely one-eyed stare. "What? Those defenders surrendered to *you*, they gave you their oath." It was clear he had disliked that idea and had gone along with it only because he must.

Classicus shrugged. "They'll be worthless till we've fed them up, and afterward unreliable. Kill them if you wish."

Burhmund stiffened. "I do not wish. And it would provoke the Romans further. Unwise." He hesitated. "However, best we make a gesture. I am sending Veleda that dignitary. She can choose what to do with him, and persuade the people it's the right thing."

"As you will. Now, for my part, I have business of my own. Farewell." Classicus clucked to his horse and cantered southward. Rapidly he passed the wagons and prisoners, dwindled in sight, disappeared where the road entered a thick stand of forest.

Yonder, Everard knew, most of the Germans were camped. Some had recently come in Burhmund's train, some had lain outside Castra Vetera for months and were sick of huts grown filthy. Though still thinly leaved, the woods provided windbreak; they were clean and alive, like the woods of home; the wind in their treetops spoke with the voices of the darkling gods. Everard suppressed a shudder.

Burhmund squinted after his retreating confederate. "I wonder what," he said in his native tongue. "Hm." It could not have been a conscious idea, just a vague hunch, that made him wheel about, ride after the man in the toga and his keeper, gesture at his bodyguards. They hurried to meet him. Everard ventured to join them.

Guthlaf the courier emerged from among the huts, riding a fresh pony and leading three remounts. He trotted to the river and boarded a waiting ferry. It shoved off.

Approaching the legate, Everard got a good look at him. From his appearance, swarthily handsome despite the haggardness, he was of Italian birth. He had stopped upon command and waited with antique impassivity for whatever might befall him.

"I want to take care of this at once, lest something go awry," Burhmund said. To the Gaul, in Latin: "Go back to your duty." To a pair of his warriors: "You, Saeferth, Hraef, I want you to bring this fellow to Wael-Edh among the Bructeri. Guthlaf's barely gone, carrying word of it, but that's as well. You'll have to fare much easier lest you kill the Roman, the shape he's in." Half kindly, he told the captive in Latin: "You are going to a holy woman. I think you will be well treated if you behave yourself."

Awe upon them the designated warriors hustled their charge toward the former encampment to prepare for the journey. Floris's voice trembled in Everard's head. "*Ach, nie, de arme*— That must be Munius Lupercus. You know what will happen to him."

The Patrolman subvocalized his answer. "I know what will happen all around."

"Is there nothing we can do?"

"Not a God damned thing. This is written. Hang tough, Janne."

"You look grim, Everard," said Burhmund in his Germanic tongue.

"I am . . . weary," Everard replied. Knowledge of the language had been instilled in him before he left the twentieth century (as well as Gothic, just in case). It was akin to what he had used in Britain some four centuries furtureward, when the descendants of tribesmen on these North Sea shores were invading it.

"I too," Burhmund murmured. For an instant he seemed oddly, endearingly vulnerable. "We've both been long on the trail, eh? Let us rest while we may."

"Your path has been harder than mine, I think," Everard said.

"Well, a man fares easiest alone. And earth clings to the boots when blood has made it muddy."

A thrill drove his forebodings from Everard. This was what he'd hoped for, had been working toward since he arrived here two days ago. In many ways the Germans were childlike, unreserved, devoid of any concept of privacy. More than Julius Classicus, who simply displayed his ambitions, Claudius Civilis—Burhmund—yearned to speak into a sympathetic ear, unburden himself to somebody who laid no claims on him.

"Listen close, Janne," Everard transmitted to Floris. "Tell me whatever questions occur to you." In their short but intense time of readymaking, he had found she was quick to understand people. Between them they might gain insight, a feel for what was going on and what it could lead to.

"I will," she agreed jaggedly, "but I had better also keep watch on Classicus."

"You fought for Rome since you were a youth, did you not?" Everard prompted in Germanic.

Burhmund barked a laugh. "Aye, and marched, drilled, built roads, barracked, squabbled, diced, whored, got drunk, got sick, yawned through endless dullness— the soldier's life."

"Yet I've heard you have a wife, children, landholdings."

Burhmund nodded. "It wasn't all pack and hike. For me and my close kinsmen, less than for the ruck of the men. We were of the kingly house, you see. Rome wanted us as much for keeping our folk quiet as for soldiering. So we made officer fast, and often got long furloughs when our units were stationed in Lower Germany. Which they were, mostly, till the troubles began. We'd go home on leave, take part in the folkmoots, speak well of Rome, besides seeing our families." He spat. "What thanks our services gained us!"

Recollection flowed from him. The exactions of Nero's ministers had kindled increasing anger among the tributaries, riots broke out, tax collectors and other plague dogs got killed. Civilis and a brother of his were arrested on charges of conspiracy. To Everard Burhmund said that they had merely protested, albeit in strong words. The brother was beheaded. Civilis went in chains to Rome for further interrogation, no doubt under torture, probably to be followed by crucifixion. The overthrow of Nero stalled proceedings. Galba pardoned Civilis, among various goodwill gestures, and sent him back to his duties.

Very soon Otho in turn cast Galba down, while the armies in Germany hailed Vitellius emperor and the armies in Egypt elevated Vespasian. Civilis's debt to Galba almost got him condemned again, but that was forgotten when the Fourteenth Legion was withdrawn from Lingonian territory, taking along the auxiliaries he commanded.

Seeking to secure Gaul, Vitellius entered Treverian lands. His soldiers looted and murdered in Divodurum, Metz to be. (That helped account for the instant popular support Classicus obtained when he rebelled.) A brawl between the Batavi and the regulars could have become catastrophic but was quelled in time. Civilis took the lead in bringing matters under control. With Fabius Valens for their general, the troops marched south to aid Vitellius against Otho. Along the way Valens took large bribes from communities to keep his army from sacking them.

When he ordered the Batavi to Narbonensis, southern Gaul, to relieve beleaguered forces there, his legionaries mutinied. They cried that this would deprive them of their bravest men. The disagreement was composed and the Batavi went on as before. After he crossed the Alps and word came of another defeat for their side, at Placentia, the soldiers mutinied again, this time at his inaction. They *wanted* to go help.

Burhmund chuckled, deep in his throat. "He obliged us."

The two warriors rode from the huts. The Roman was between them, clad for travel. Remounts loaded with food and gear came behind. They went down to the Rhine. The ferry was back. They boarded.

"The Othonianists tried to stop us at the Po," Burhmund said. "That was when Valens found the legionaries had been right to keep us Germans. We swam across and cut a foothold, which we kept till the rest could follow. Once we'd forced the river, the enemy broke and fled. Great was the slaughter at Bedriacum. Shortly afterward, Otho killed himself." He grimaced. "But Vitellius had no stronger rein on his troops. They ran wild through Italy. I saw some of that. It was ugly. This wasn't an enemy land they'd taken, it was the land they were supposed to defend. Wasn't it?"

That might have been part of the reason why the Fourteenth grew restless and snarly. A riot between the regulars and the auxiliaries nearly became a pitched battle. Civilis was among the officers who got things quieted. The new Emperor Vitellius ordered the legionaries to Britain and attached the Batavi to his palace troops. "But that wasn't good either. He had no grasp of how to handle men. Mine got slack, drank on duty, fought in barracks. At last he returned us to Germany. He could do naught else, unless he wanted blood spilled, which could have included his precious own. We were sick of him."

The ferry, a broad-beamed scow with oars, had crossed the stream. The travelers debarked and vanished into the forest.

"Vespasian held Africa and Asia," Burhmund went on. "His general Primus now landed in Italy and wrote to me. Aye, by then I had that much of a name."

Burhmund sent word around to his widespread connections. A feckless Roman legate agreed. Men went to hold the passes of the Alps; no Vitellianist Gauls or Germans would cross northward, while the Italians and Iberians had plenty to engage their attention where they were. Burhmund called an assembly of his tribe. Vitellius's conscription had been the last outrage they would take. They clashed blade on shield and shouted.

Already the neighboring Canninefates and Frisii knew what was afoot. Their folkmoots yelled for men to rally to the cause. A Tungrian cohort left its base and joined. German auxiliaries, bound south for Vitellius, heard the news and defected.

Two legions moved against Burhmund. He smashed them and drove the remnants into Castra Vetera. Crossing the Rhine, he won a clash near Bonna. His couriers urged the defenders of Old Camp to come forth on behalf of Vespasian. They refused. That was when he proclaimed secession, open war for the sake of freedom.

The Bructeri, Tencteri, and Chamavi entered his league. He dispatched couriers far and wide through Germany. Adventurers flocked from the wilds to his banners. Wael-Edh foretold the doom of Rome.

"And then the Gauls," Burhmund said, "those of them Classicus and his friends could raise. Just three tribes thus far— What's the matter?"

Everard had started at a scream that he alone heard. "Nothing," he said. "I thought I spied a movement, but it was nothing. Weariness does that, you know."

"They are killing them in the forest," Floris's voice choked. "It is ghastly. Oh, why did we have to come to this day?"

"You remember why," he told her. "Don't watch it."

They could not take years to feel out the whole truth. The Patrol could ill spare that much lifespan of theirs. Moreover, this segment of space-time was unstable; the less they from the future moved about in it, the better. Everard had decided to start with a visit to Civilis several months downtime from the split in events. Preliminary scouting suggested the Batavian would be most easily accessible when he accepted the surrender of Castra Vetera; and the occasion would add a chance to meet Classicus. Everard and Floris had hoped to get sufficient information and depart before that happened which Tacitus related.

"Did Classicus instigate it?" he asked.

"I can't be sure," Floris said around a sob. He didn't blame her. He would have hated witnessing the massacre himself, and he was case-hardened. "He is among the Germans, yes, but the trees interfere with seeing and the wind with sound pickup. Does he speak their language?"

"Little if any, as far as I know, but some among them know Latin—"

"Your soul is elsewhere, Everard," Burhmund said.

"I do feel a . . . foreboding," the Patrolman replied. *Might as well give him a hint I've got a bit of foresight, a touch of elflore. It could come in handy later.*

Burhmund's visage was stark. "I too, though for reasons more earthly. Best I gather my trusty men. Hold aside, Everard. Your sword is keen, yes, but you've not marched with the legions, and I think I'll have need of tight discipline." The last word was Latin.

The truth reached them, borne by a horseman a-gallop out of the woods. In a suddenly rising, roaring mob, the Germans had fallen on the prisoners. The few Gallic guards scrambled out of the way. The Germans were butchering every unarmed man and smashing the treasures. They would give the gods their hecatomb.

Everard suspected Classicus had egged them on to it. That would have been simple. Classicus wanted them committed beyond the possibility of making a separate peace. No doubt Burhmund shared the suspicion, as furious as the Batavian was. But what could he do about it?

He could not even stop his barbarians when they swarmed kill-crazy from the woods into Old Camp. Fire leaped up behind the walls. Shrieks mingled with the stench of burning human flesh.

Burhmund wasn't actually horrified. This kind of thing was common in his world. What maddened him was the disobedience and the underhandedness that had brought it on.

"I will hale them to a weaponmoot," he growled. "I will flay them with shame. That they may know I mean it, in their sight I will cut this hair of mine, Roman-short again, and wash the dye from it. As for plighting faith to Classicus and his empire—if he mislikes what I'll have to say about that, let him dare take arms against me."

"I think best I go," Everard said. "I would only be underfoot here. Maybe we will meet anew."

When, in the unhappy days ahead of you?

5

Wind rushed bitter, driving low clouds like smoke before it. Spatters of rain flew slantwise past unrestful boughs. Hoofs splashed puddles in the trail where horses plodded, heads drooping. Saeferth rode first; Hnaef came after, leading the laden relief animals. Between them, hunched in a sodden cloak, was the Roman. With hand-signs and the like when they stopped to eat or rest, the Batavi had learned his name was Lupercus.

From around a bend appeared a group of five, surely Bructeri, for the wayfarers had reached that land. They were, however, still in the belt where nobody lived, which German tribes liked to keep around themselves. He at the forefront was gaunt as a ferret, black as a crow save where the years had strewn whiteness over hair and beard. His right hand gripped a spear. "Hold!" he cried.

Saeferth reined in. "We come peacefully, sent by our lord Burhmund to the wise-woman Wael-Edh," he said.

The dark man nodded. "We have had word of this."

"That can be but a short while ago, for we left well-nigh on the heels of his messenger, though we must needs fare slower."

"Aye. Now the time has come to act swiftly. I am Heidhin, Viduhada's son, Wael-Edh's foremost man."

"I recall you," Hnaef said, "from when my lord visited her last year. What would you of us?"

"The man you bring," Heidhin told them. "He is the one Burhmund gives to Wael-Edh, is he not?"

"Yes."

Aware that they talked about him, Lupercus tightened. His glance went from face to face while the guttural words rolled around his head.

"She in her turn gives him to the gods," Heidhin said. "I have watched for you that I may do the deed."

"What, not in your halidom, with a feast to follow?" wondered Saeferth.

"I told you there is need of haste. Several great men among us would liefer keep him in hopes of ransom, did they know. We cannot afford to aggrieve them. Yet the gods are wrathful. Look about you." Heidhin swept his spear athwart the drenched and moaning forest.

Saeferth and Hnaef could not well gainsay him. The Bructeri outnumbered them. Besides, everybody knew how he had been with the wise-woman since leaving their faraway birthland. "Witness, all, that we fully meant to seek her, and are taking your word that this is her will instead," Saeferth spoke.

Hnaef scowled. "Let's get it finished," he said.

They dismounted, as did the others, and beckoned Lupercus to do likewise. He required help, though that was because he remained weak and shaky from starvation. When they bound his wrists behind him and Heidhin uncoiled a rope with a noose, his eyes widened and he drew one sharp breath. Thereafter he steadied himself on his feet and murmured what might be something to his own gods.

Heidhin looked heavenward. "Father Woen, warrior Tiw, Donar of the thunder, hear me," he said slowly and weightily. "Know this offering for what it is, the gift of Nerha to you. Know she was never your foe nor any thief of your honor. If men have lately given you less than erstwhile, what she received was ever on behalf of all the gods. Stand again at her side, mighty ones, and bestow on us victory!"

Saefeth and Hnaef grasped Lupercus's arms. Heidhin trod forward to him. With the spearpoint he marked on the Roman's brow the sign of the hammer; on his breast, slashing the tunic, he cut a fylfot. Blood welled shoutingly red into the gray air. Lupercus kept silent. They led him to the ash tree Heidhin chose, tossed the rope over a branch, laid the noose about his neck. "Oh, Julia," he called softly. Two of Heidhin's men hauled him aloft while the rest beat sword on shield and howled. He kicked the wind until Heidhin drove the spear into him, up the belly to the heart.

When the rest had been done that should be, Heidhin said to Saeferth and Hanaef, "Come along. I will guest you at my hall ere you go back to lord Burhmund."

"What shall we tell him about this?" asked Hnaef.

"The truth," answered Heidhin. "Tell the whole host. At last the gods have gotten their rightful share as of old. Now they ought wholeheartedly to fight for us."

The Germans rode off. A raven flapped around the dead man, perched on his shoulder, pecked and swallowed. Another came, and another, and another. Their cries rang hoarse through the wind that rocked him to and fro.

6

Everard allowed Floris two days at home for rest and recovery. She was no weak sister, but she was a civilized person with a conscience, who had been witness to horror. Luckily, she hadn't known any of the victims; there should be no survivor's guilt to overcome. "Ask for psychotech help if the nightmares won't go away," he suggested. "Of course, we also have to think things over, in the light of what we've now directly observed, and figure out a program for ourselves."

Toughened though he was, he too welcomed a respite in which to come to terms with the sights and sounds and smells of Old Camp. He walked the Amsterdam streets for hours on end, bathing in the decency of the twentieth-

326

326

century Netherlands. Otherwise he was at the Patrol office retrieving data files—history, anthropology, political and physical geography, everything available—and having the most essential-looking items imprinted.

His advance preparation had been on the cursory side. Not that he now acquired an encyclopedic knowledge. It wasn't available. Germanic prehistory drew few investigators; they scattered across a vast stretch of miles and centuries. So much else appeared to be so much more interesting and important. Hard information was sparse. Nobody besides him and Floris had personally researched Civilis. The rebellion hadn't seemed worth the considerable hazards of fieldwork, when nothing came of it but a change for the better in Roman treatment of a few obscure people.

And maybe that is all, Everard thought. *Maybe those variations in text have a safe origin that the Patrol detectives missed, and we're chasing shadows. Certainly we have no evidence of anybody trying to monkey with events. Well, whatever the answer, we've got to find it.*

On the third day he phoned Floris from his hotel and proposed dinner, as they had had on their first meeting. "We'll relax, talk small talk, touch on our mission lightly if at all. Tomorrow we'll lay our plans. Okay?" At his request, she named the restaurant and met him there.

The Ambrosia dealt in Surinam-Caribbean food. On Stadthouderskade, in a quiet neighborhood near the Museumplein, it was intimate, right on a canal. Besides the pretty waitress, the black cook came forth to discuss their meal with them beforehand in fluent English. The wine was just right, too. Maybe the sense of evanescence, this warmth and light and savor no more than a moment in an unbounded darkness, something that could come to never having been, gave depth to pleasure.

"I will walk back," said Floris at the end. "The evening is so beautiful." Her place was a mile or two distant.

"I'll see you to your door, if I may," Everard replied gladly.

She smiled. Her hair shone against the dusk in the windows like remembered sunlight. "Thank you. I hoped."

They went out into mild air. It smelled of spring, for rain had cleansed it earlier and traffic was rather thin, mostly a background pulsing. A canal boat chugged by, wake a-glisten. "Thank you," she repeated. "That was delightful. Exactly what would cheer me up."

"Well, good." He took tobacco pouch from pocket and started filling his pipe. "Though I'm sure you'd have rebounded quite fast in any case."

They turned from the water and passed between old façades. "Yes, I have met terrible things before," she assented. The mood at dinner, which they had both carefully maintained carefree, was slipping off, though her tone stayed level and her expression calm. "Not violence on that scale, no, but men dead or wounded after fights, and mortal sickness, and—many cruel fates."

Everard nodded. "Yeah, this era of ours has seen all hell let out for noon, but scarcely more than others. The main difference is, nowadays they imagine it *could* be better."

Floris sighed. "At first it was romantic, the living past, but then—"

"Well, you did pick a mighty rough milieu. At that, though, the real guignol was in Rome."

She gave him a close look. "I cannot believe you harbor any illusions about the barbarians being nature's noblemen. I soon lost mine. They were every bit as ruthless. They were simply less efficient."

Everard struck match to bowl. "Why did you choose them for your specialty, if I may ask? Sure, somebody had to do the job, but with your capabilities you could have taken your pick of a lot of societies."

She smiled. "They tried to persuade me of that, after I graduated from the Academy. One agent spent hours telling me how I would like his Duchy of Brabant. He was sweet. But I was stubborn."

"How come?"

"The more I think back, the less clear to me my motives are. It seemed at the time that— Yes, if you don't mind, I would like to tell you."

He held his arm toward her. She took it. Her stride easily matched his and was more supple. His free hand cradled the little hearth of his pipe. "Please do," he said. "I haven't pried into your records beyond the indispensable minimum, but I can't help feeling curious. They wouldn't contain the true explanation anyway."

"I suppose it goes back to my parents." She was gazing beyond them both, the tiniest line between her brows. Her voice flowed almost dreamily. "I am their only child, born in 1950." *And by now a good deal older, along your world line, than the calendar shows,* he knew. "My father grew up in what was the Dutch East Indies. Do you recollect, we Dutch founded Jakarta, and our name for it was Batavia? He was young when first the Nazi Germans invaded the Netherlands, then later the Japanese overran Southeast Asia. He fought them as a sailor in what navy we had left. My mother, at home, a schoolgirl, was involved with the resistance, the underground press."

"Proud people," Everard murmured.

"My parents met and married after the war, settled in Amsterdam. They are still alive, retired, he from his business, she from teaching history, Dutch history." *Yes,* he thought, *you return from each expedition to the day you left, because you don't want to miss time you can see them in before they die, never knowing what you truly do. Bad enough that they're disappointed of grandchildren.* "They did not boast about their parts in the war. But I was . . . was bound? . . . yes, bound to live always with the knowledge of it, and with the whole past of my country. Patriotism? Call it what you like. These are my folk. What made them what they are? What seed, what roots? The origins fascinated me, and at the university I studied to be an archaeologist."

Everard knew that already, as well as the fact that she had been an athlete at close to championship standards and had traveled off the tourist routes into a couple of difficult, somewhat dangerous places. It caught the attention of a Patrol recruiter, who got her to take the tests and, when she passed, revealed their meaning. His induction had gone similarly.

"Just the same," he said, "you elected a culture where a woman is badly hampered."

She responded a little sharply. "You must at least have seen a resumé showing that I managed. You must know about Patrol disguises."

"Sorry. No offense. They're fine for short visits." It wasn't far uptime from this year that things like whiskers and vocal registers could be faked to near perfection. Coarse, baggy fabrics, suitably padded, hid curves. Hands might be a giveaway, but hers were big for a woman and if she claimed youthfulness, their shape and lack of hair need not excite comment. "But—" Occasions could too readily arise when clothes should come off among companions, as when bathing. Or something like a fight could, perhaps brought on by a countenance that remained inescapably muliebral—effeminate, barbarians would think. No matter how well trained, a woman, in a situation where high-tech weapons were forbidden, lacked the upper-body musculature and surge strength of a man.

"Limited uses," she admitted. "It was often frustrating. I actually considered—" She broke off.

"Changing your sex?" he inquired gently after half a minute.

Her nod was stiff.

"It needn't have been permanent, you know." Future operations didn't involve surgery or hormone shots; they took place at the molecular level, rebuilding the organism from the DNA up. "Of course, it's a pretty big deal. You'd only do it for a mission years long, at a minimum."

Her glance challenged him. "Would you?"

"Hell, no!" he exclaimed. Thereupon he thought, *Was that too strong a reaction? Intolerant?* "But remember, I was born in Middle America, 1924."

Floris laughed and squeezed his arm. "I doubted my mind, my basic personality, could change. Male, I would be a complete homosexual. In that society, a worse handicap than being a woman. Which, furthermore, I like."

He grinned. "That's been obvious right along."

Down, boy. No personal involvement on the job. It could prove lethal. Intellectually, I wish she were a man.

Her feeling must have corresponded, for she shied off as well and they went on a while without speaking. It was a companionable silence, though. They were crossing the park, greenness fragrant around them, lamplight falling through leafage to dapple the path, when he broke it:

"In spite of this, I gather, you've carried out a major project. I didn't pull the file on it, expecting you'd rather tell me yourself, which would be better." He had hinted a time or two, but she had avoided, or evaded, the topic. That wasn't hard, when they had such a heap of material to cover.

He heard and saw her drew breath. "Yes, I must," she agreed. "You need to know what experience I have. A long story, but I could make a start here." She hesitated. "I have come to feel more easy with you. At first I was terrified. I, to work with an Unattached agent?"

"You hid it well," he drawled around a puff on his pipe.

"One learns in the field to hide emotions, no? But tonight I can talk freely. You are a, a comfortable kind of man."

He didn't know what to say to that.

"I lived fifteen years with the Frisii," she told him.

He caught the pipe before it hit the pavement. "Huh?"

"From A.D. 22 to 37," she continued earnestly. "The Patrol wanted knowledge, more than a sketch, of life at the far western end of the Germanic range, in the period when Roman influence was replacing Celtic. Specifically, they were concerned about the upheavals among the tribes that followed the murder of Arminius. The consequences were potentially large."

"But nothing alarming turned up, eh? Whereas Civilis, whom the Patrol figured it could safely ignore— Well, it's staffed by fallible humans. And, of course, a detailed report on a typical society is valuable in a lot of different contexts. Go on, please."

"Colleagues helped me establish myself. My persona was a young woman of the Chasuarii, widowed when the Cherusci attacked. She fled to Frisian territory with some possessions and a pair of men who had served her husband and stayed faithful to her. The headman of the village we found received us generously. I did bring in gold as well as news; and to them, hospitality was sacred."

Didn't hurt that you were, are, almighty attractive.

"Before long, I married a younger son of his," Floris said, resolutely matter-of-fact. "My 'servants' excused themselves to go on a 'venture' and were never heard of again. Everybody supposed they had come to grief. How many ways there were to perish!"

"And?" Everard watched her profile. Vermeer might have summoned it from the surrounding twilight, under its cap of gold.

"Those were hard years. I was often homesick, sometimes in despair. But then I would think how I was learning, discovering, exploring a whole universe of ways and beliefs, knowledge, skills, people. I became very fond of the people. They were good-hearted in their rough way—within the tribe, that is—and my Garulf and I . . . we grew close. I bore him two children, and secretly made sure they would live. He hoped for more, naturally, but that was another thing I saw to, and it was common for a woman to go barren." Her mouth bent ruefully upward. "He had his others by a farmhand girl. She and I got along, she deferred to me and— Never mind. It was a normal, accepted thing, no slur on me, and . . . I knew that someday I would be gone."

"How did that happen?" Everard asked low.

Her voice flattened. "Garulf died. He was hunting aurochs, and a bull gored him. I grieved, but it did simplify matters for me. I should have left well before, disappeared like my attendants, but he and our children—boys in their early teens, which meant they were nearly men. Garulf's brothers would see to their welfare."

Everard nodded. His studies had taught him that the ancient Germans hallowed the relationship between uncle and nephew. Among the tragedies Burhmund, Civilis, endured was a break with a sister's son, who fought and died in the Roman army.

"Nevertheless it hurt to leave them," Floris ended. "I said I was going away for a while to mourn alone, and let them wonder ever afterward what became of me."

And you wonder what became of them, and no doubt always shall, Everard thought. *Unless, scanning from afar, you've followed their lives till their deaths. But I expect you're wiser than that. So much for the adventure and glamour of service in the Time Patrol.*

Floris gulped. Swallowing a few tears? Forlorn gaiety followed. "You can imagine what a cosmetic rejuvenation I needed when I returned! And hot baths, electric lights, books, shows, airplanes, everything!"

"Not least, being equal again," Everard added.

"Yes, yes. Women had a high standing, they were more free than they would be later until the nineteenth century, but still—oh, yes."

"It seems Veleda was out-and-out dominant."

"That was different. She spoke for the gods, I think."

We need to make sure.

"The mission was terminated several years ago on my personal world line," Floris said. "My subsequent efforts have been less ambitious. Until now."

Everard bit hard on his pipestem. "M-m, we do have that problem of sex.

I don't want to fool around with disguises, except maybe briefly. Too many limitations."

She halted. Perforce he did. They were close to a lamp. It gave her eyes a cat-gleam. She raised her voice. "I will not merely sit in the sky and watch you, Agent Everard. I will not."

A bicyclist sibilated past, threw them a look, continued on his way.

"It'd be useful, having you with me on the ground," Everard granted. "Not constantly. You must agree it's often best if one partner stays in reserve. But when we get down to the real Sherlock Holmes work, then you, with your experience— The question is, how can we?"

Turning from angry to eager, she pressed her advantage. "I will be your wife. Or your concubine or handmaiden or whatever suits the circumstances. It is not unheard of among the Germani, that a woman accompanies a man when he travels."

Damnation! Do my ears actually feel hot? "We dare not complicate matters for ourselves."

Her gaze caught his and held fast. "I am not worried about that, sir. You are a professional and a gentleman."

"Well, thanks," he said, relieved. "I guess I can mind my manners."

If you mind yours!

7

Suddenly springtime billowed over the land. Warmth and lengthening days lured forth leaves. Grass glowed. The sky filled with wings and clamor. Lambs, calves, foals rollicked through meadows. Folk came from the gloom of houses, the smoke and stink of winter; they blinked in the brightness, breathed the sweetness, and set to work readying for summer.

Yet they were hungry after last year's niggard yields. Many a man was at war beyond the Rhine, and already few of them would ever come back. Edh and Heidhin still bore frost in their hearts.

They walked about her grounds, heedless of light or breeze. Workers in her fields saw how she went and dared not hail or come question her. Though the woods westward shone beneath the sun, the holy grove in the offing eastward seemed dark, as if her tower had cast its shadows that far.

"I am wrathful with you," she said. "Oh, I should send you from me forever."

"Edh—" His voice had gone harsh. Knuckles whitened above his spearshaft. "I did what I must needs do. It was clear you would have spared that Roman. The Anses had enough of a grudge against us."

"So fools have babbled."

"Then most of the tribe are fools. Edh, I go among them as you cannot, for I am a man, and only a man, not the chosen of a goddess. Folk tell me what they would quail to say straight to you." Heidhin paced on while he gathered his words together. "Nerha has been taking too much of what formerly went to the sky gods. I mind well what you and I owe her, but it is otherwise for the Bructeri, and even we twain owe much to the Anses also. If we do not make our peace with them, they will withdraw victory from us. I have read this in the stars, the weather, the flight of ravens, the bones I cast. And what if I am mistaken? The fear itself is real in men's hearts. They will begin to hang back in battle, and the foe will break them.

"Now I, in your name, have given the Anses a man, no mere thrall but a chieftain. Let this news go abroad, and see how hope comes to fresh birth among the warriors!"

Edh's look struck at him like a sword. "Ha, do you think your one little slaying will reck aught to them? Know, while you were gone, another messenger from Burhmund found me. His men killed everyone and destroyed everything at Castra Vetera. They glutted their gods."

The spear jerked in Heidhin's grip before he locked his face shut. A time went by. At last he said slowly, "How could I foresee that? It is well."

"It is *not*. Burhmund was enraged. He knows it is bound to stiffen Roman will. And now you, you have robbed me of a captive who might have been a go-between for us."

Heidhin clenched his jaws. "I could not have known," he muttered. "And what use would one man be, anyhow?"

"You have robbed me of yourself, too, it seems," Edh went on bleakly. "I had thought you would go to Colonia for me."

Surprised, he twisted his neck around to stare at her. The high cheekbones, long straight nose, full mouth stayed forward-aimed, away from him. "Colonia?"

"That was in Burhmund's message too. From Castra Vetera he is going on to Colonia Agrippinensis. He thinks they may yield. But once they hear of the slaughter—and they will ere he reaches them—why should they? Why not fight on, in hopes of relief, when they have nothing to lose? Burhmund wants me to lay my curse, the withering wrath of Nerha, on whoever breaks the terms of surrender."

His wonted shrewdness returned to Heidhin and calmed him. "Hm, so." His free hand stroked his beard. "Yes, that may well sway them in Colonia. They must know of you. The Ubii are Germans, for all they call themselves Roman.

If your avouching was spoken aloud to Burhmund's host, near the wall where the defenders could see and hear—"

"Who shall utter it, now?"

"Yourself?"

"Hardly."

He nodded. "No, that's right. Best you hold aloof. Few outside the Bructeri have seen you. There is more awesomeness in a tale than in flesh and blood."

Her laugh was wolfish. "Flesh and blood which must eat, drink, sleep, rid itself of wastes, maybe catch cold, surely grow weary." The tone dropped. She lowered her head. "Indeed I am weary," she whispered. "Liefest would I be alone."

"That may well be wise," Heidhin said. "Yes. Withdraw for a while into your tower. Make known that you are thinking, brewing witchcraft, calling the goddess to you. I will bear your word into the world."

She straightened. "So I thought," she snapped. "But after what you did, how can I trust you?"

"You can. I'll swear to it"—Heidhin's voice stumbled a bit—"if our years together are not enough." At once he donned pride. "You understand you have no better spokesman. I am more than the first among your followers, I am a leader in my own right. Men heed me."

She was long silent. They walked by a paddock where a bull stood, Tiw's beast, his horns mighty beneath the sun. At last she asked: "You will give forth my words unwarped, and work in good faith to have their meaning carried out?"

He shaped his answer with skill. "It hurts that you should mistrust me, Edh."

Then she looked at him. Her eyes thawed. "All these years—dear old friend—"

They stopped where they were, on a muddy track through the swelling grass. "I would have been more than friend to you, had you let me," he said.

"You knew I never could. And you honored it. How can I do other than forgive you? Yes, go to Colonia for me."

Sternness came upon him. "I will, and wherever else you may send me, serving you as best I can, if only you do not tell me to break the vow I made on the shore of the Eyn."

"That—" Color flowed and ebbed in her face "It was long ago."

"To me it is as if I swore it yesterday. No peace with the Romans. War while I live, and after I am dead I will harry them on their way down hell-road."

"Niaerdh could release you from it."

"I could never release myself." Like a heavily striking hammer, Heidhin bade her: "Either send me from you this day, for always, or swear that you will never ask me to make peace with Rome."

She shook her head. "I cannot do that. If they offer us, our kinfolk, all of us, our freedom—"

He turned that over in his mind before he said unwillingly, "Well, if they do, take it of them. I daresay you would have to."

"Niaerdh herself would want it. She is no bloodthirsty Ans."

"Hm, aforetime you said otherwise." Heidhin grinned. "I do not await the Romans will gladly let the western tribes and their scot to them go. But should they, then I will take me off, with whatever men will follow me, and raid them in their lands till I fall under their blades."

"May that never be!" she cried.

He laid his hands on her shoulders. "Swear to me—bring Niaerdh to witness—that you will call for war without end until the Romans leave these lands or . . . or, at the least, I am dead. If you do this, then I can work for anything else you wish, yes, even for the sparing of what Romans we catch alive."

"If you will have it thus." Edh sighed. She stepped back from him. Command rang: "Come, then, let us seek the halidom, mingle our blood on the earth and our words in the air, to fasten this bond. I want you riding to Burhmund tomorrow. Time is on our heels."

8

Once the city had been Oppidum Ubiorum, or so the Romans called it. Otherwise Germans did not build towns; but the Ubii, on the left bank of the Rhine, were under heavy Gallic influence. After Caesar's conquest, they soon came into the Empire and, unlike most of their kinsmen, were content with this, the trade, the learning, the openings to the world outside. In the reign of Claudius the town was made a Roman colony and named for his wife. Eagerly Latinizing themselves, the Ubii changed their own name to the Agrippinenses. The city waxed. It would be Köln—Cologne, to French and English speakers—but that was far in the future.

On this day the ground below its massive Roman-built walls seethed. Smoke rose from a hundred campfires, barbarian standards reared above leather tents, pelts and blankets lay spread about where those slept who had brought no shelter along. Horses neighed and stamped. Cattle lowed, sheep bleated in the wattled pens that held them until they were butchered for the army. Men milled to and fro, wild warriors from beyond the river, Gallic rabble from this side. Quieter were the armed yeomen of Batavia and its near neighbors; disciplined were Civilis's and Classicus's veterans. Apart huddled the dispirited legionaries who had been marched here from Novesium. Along the way they had endured such taunts that at last a cavalry troop of theirs said to hell with it, repudiated the pledge of allegiance given the Empire of Gaul, and struck south to rejoin Rome.

A small set of tents stood by itself near the stream. No rebel ventured within yards of it unless he had cause, and then he approached most quietly. Bructerian men-at-arms kept watch at the corners, but only as an honor guard. What warded it was a sheaf of grain to which was tied several apples, atop an erected pole—from last year, dried and faded, yet emblems of Nerha.

"Whence came you?" asked Everard.

Heidhin peered at him. The answer hissed. "If you trekked hither out of the east as you say, you know. The Angrivarri remember Wael-Edh; the Langobardi do, the Lemovii, and more. Did none among them ever say aught of her to you?"

"She passed through years ago—"

"I know they remember, for we hear from them through traders, land-loupers, and the fighters lately come to Burhmund." A cloud shadow swept over the men where they sat, on a rude bench before Heidhin's pavilion. Darkening his visage, it seemed to whet the piercing stare. Wind bore a puff of smoke, a clang of iron. "Who are you truly, Everard, and what would you here in our midst?"

This is one smart cookie, and a fanatic to boot, the Patrolman realized. Quickly: "I was about to say, it struck me how her name lives on among tribes far away, long after she passed by."

"Hm." Heidhin relaxed a trifle. His right hand, which had strayed close to his sword hilt, drew the black cloak more snugly against the wind. "I wonder why you trailed Burhmund, when you have no wish to go beneath his banner."

"It is as I told you, my lord." Heidhin didn't rate the honorific from Everard, who had not sworn him fealty, but it didn't hurt. And in truth Heidhin had become an important man among the Bructeri, a chieftain with lands and holdings, married into a noble family, above all the confidant and frequent spokesman of Veleda. "I called on him at Castra Vetera because I had heard of his fame and am seeking to learn how things are in these countries. On my way elsewhere I heard that the wise-woman was bound hither. I hoped to meet her, or at least see and hear her."

Burhmund, who made Everard welcome, had explained that the sibyl sent her representative instead. The Batavian's hospitality was perfunctory, though, as busy as he was. When he saw a chance, Everard sought Heidhin out on his own hook. A Goth was unusual enough to be received, but the conversation went awkwardly, Heidhin's thoughts on other matters until abruptly suspicion awoke.

"She has withdrawn into her tower to be alone with the goddess," he said. Belief burned in him.

Everard nodded. "So Burhmund told me. And I listened to your speech yesterday, at the gate of the city. My lord, let's not plow the same soil over again. What I asked was merely—whence came you and holy Wael-Edh? Where did you begin your wanderings, and when and why?"

"We come of the Alvarings," Heidhin said. "Belike most men in this host were unborn when we left. Why did we? The goddess called her forth." Intensity gave way to brusqueness: "I have better work on hand than enlightening a stranger. If you will abide among us, Everard, you will hear more, and maybe you and I can talk further. Today I must bid you farewell."

They stood up. "Thank you for your time, my lord," the Patrolman said. "Someday I will go back to my folk. Should you or kin of yours ever seek to the Goths, that man shall have good guesting."

Heidhin did not let the routine courtesy go by. "It may be," he replied. "Nerha's messengers—but first is this war to win. Fare you well."

Everard walked through the surrounding turbulence to a pen near Civilis's headquarters, where he claimed his horses. They were shaggy German ponies; his feet dangled just inches above ground when he mounted. But then, he was big even among these men, and they would have wondered too much about him had he lacked animals to bear him and his possessions. He rode north. Colonia Agrippinensis fell from sight behind him.

Evening light sheened golden on the river. Hills were nearly as he recalled them from his home era, but the countryside lay marred by weed-grown fields and ruined buildings where Civilis had ravaged it months before. Here and there he glimpsed bones, some human.

Desolation served his purpose. Nevertheless he waited till dark to tell Floris, "Okay, send down the truck." He mustn't be seen departing the road, and a vehicle capable of accommodating horses was more noticeable than a timecycle. She dispatched it by remote control, he led the beasts aboard, and in an instant overleaping of space he reached their camp. She joined him a minute later.

They could have sprung back to Amsterdam's comforts, but it would have wasted lifespan, not in the shuttling but in the commuting to and from quarters there, the shucking and redonning of barbarian garb, perhaps most the changes back and forth of mind-set. Let them rather dwell in this archaic land, become intimate not only with its people but with its natural world. Nature—the wilderness, the mysteries of day and night, summer and winter, storm, stars, growth, death—pervaded it and the souls of the folk. You could not really understand them, feel with them, until you had yourself entered into the forest and let it enter into you.

Floris had chosen the site, a remote hilltop overlooking woodlands that reached to every horizon. None but a rare hunter ever saw it, and quite likely none had ever climbed to the bare ridge. Northern Europe was so thinly populated; a tribe numbering fifty thousand was large, and spread over a wide territory. Another planet would have been less alien to this country than was the twentieth century.

Two one-person shelters rested side by side in soft radiance, and savory odors drifted from a cook unit, technology futureward of his and her birthtime. Just the same, after he had gotten his horses settled by hers, Everard kindled firewood he had prepared earlier. They ate in musing silence, then turned off the lamp. The cook unit became another shadow, unobtrusively cleaning up. They sat down on the grass by the flames. Neither had said anything about it; they simply knew, in some blind way, that this was right for them.

A breeze wandered chilly. Now and then an owl hooted, low, as if asking a question of an oracle. Treetops glimmered like a sea beneath the stars. The Milky Way stretched hoar above them in the north. Higher gleamed the Great Bear, which men here knew as the Wain of the Sky Father. *But what do they call it in Edh's home country?* wondered Everard. *Wherever that is. If Janne didn't recognize the name "Alvaring," then it's so obscure that nobody in the Patrol has heard of it.*

He lit his pipe. The fire crackled, gave him its own smoke, brought Floris's face out of the dark in flickery highlights across the braids she had uncoiled and the strong bones. "I think we've got to search pastward," he said.

She nodded. "These last few days, they have confirmed Tacitus, have they not?"

Throughout them, he had necessarily still been the operative on the ground, she observing from on high. But her role had been as active as his. He was confined to his immediate vicinity. She scanned widely, and then dispatched her minute robotic spies by night to lurk unseen and relay what went on beneath selected roofs.

They witnessed— The senate of Colonia knew its position was desperate. Could they get terms of surrender less than disastrous, and would those be honored? The tribe of the Tencteri, living across the Rhine from them, sent envoys proposing unity independent of Rome. Among their demands was that the city walls be razed. Colonia demurred; it would accept only a loose league, and unhindered passage over the river only by daylight, until usage had bred more trust. It also proposed that the mediators of any such treaty be Civilis and Veleda. The Tencteri agreed. About then, Civilis-Burhmund and Classicus arrived.

Classicus would as soon, or sooner, have Colonia given to sack. Burhmund was reluctant. Among other reasons for that, the city held a son of his, taken for a hostage in the ambiguous period last year when he was still ostensibly fighting to make Vespasian emperor. Despite everything that had happened since, the boy was well treated, and Burhmund stood to get him back. Veleda's influence could make a negotiated peace possible.

It did.

"Yeah," Everard said. "I guess the rest will go according to the book too." Colonia would yield, suffer no harm, and join the rebel alliance. It would, however, get new hostages, Burhmund's wife and sister and a daughter of Classicus. That those men would lay so much on the line spoke of more than realpolitik, the value of the agreement; it spoke of Veleda's power.

("How many divisions does the Pope have?" Stalin would gibe. His successors would find it had never mattered. In the long run, humans live mainly by their dreams, and die by them.)

"Well, we are not at the divergence point yet," Floris said needlessly. "We are exploring the background of it."

"And we're stiffening our notion that Veleda is a key to it all. Do you think we—meaning you, I suppose—could approach her directly and get acquainted?"

Floris shook her head. "No. Especially not now, when she has isolated herself. Probably she is in a state of emotional, perhaps religious crisis. An interruption could bring on . . . anything."

"Uh-huh." Everard puffed on his pipe for a minute. "Religion—Did you hear Heidhin's speech to the army yesterday, Janne?"

"In part. I knew you were there, taking note."

"You're not an American. Nor are you any of your Calvinist ancestors. I suspect you don't appreciate what he was doing."

She held her hands toward the fire and waited.

"If ever I heard a stem-winding, hellfire-and-damnation revival sermon, throwing the fear of the Lord into the meeting, Heidhin delivered it," Everard said. "Almighty effective, too. There won't be any more Castra Vetera atrocities."

Floris shivered. "I should hope not."

"But . . . the whole approach. . . . I realize it wasn't unknown to the Classical world. Especially after Jews were living everywhere around the Mediterranean. The prophets of the Old Testament came to have their influence even on paganism. But up here, among the Nordics—wouldn't a speaker have appealed to their machismo? At most, to their obligation to abide by a promise?"

"Yes, of course. Their gods are cruel, but, well, tolerant. Which will make them, the people, vulnerable to the Christian missionaries."

"Veleda seems to have hit the same unshielded spot," Everard said thoughtfully, "six or seven hundred years before any Christian missionaries reach these parts."

"Veleda," Floris murmured. "Wael-Edh. Edh the Foreign, Edh the Strange. She has borne her message, whatever it is, across Germany. Tactitus Two says she will carry it back there after Civilis falls—and the faith of the Germans will begin to change— Yes, I believe we must follow her spoor through the past, to wherever she began."

9

The months toiled on, slowly grinding down Burhmund's victory.

Tacitus would record how it happened, the confusions and mistakes, dissensions and treacheries, while the weight of Roman reinforcement inexorably mounted. Already then, memory would have blurred or lost much and any single man staring at the wound from which his life drained would be quite forgotten. Such details as did survive are of interest, but for the most part unnecessary to understanding the end result. A sketch suffices.

At first Burhmund continued to enjoy success. He occupied the country of the Sunici and recruited intensively among them. At the Moselle River he defeated a band of Imperialist Germans, took some into his host, and chased the rest and their leader south.

That was a bad error. While he struggled through the Belgic woods, Classicus sat idle and Tutor was fatally slow to occupy the defenses of the Rhine and the Alps. The Twenty-first Legion took advantage, crossing into Gaul. There it linked with its auxiliaries, including a cavalry troop commanded by Julius Briganticus, nephew and implacable enemy of Civilis. Tutor was beaten, his Treveri routed. Before then, a rebel attempt on the Sequani had met disaster, and Roman units had begun moving in from Italy, Spain, and Britain.

Petillius Cerialis was now in overall charge of the Imperial effort. Though worsted nine years before by Boadicea in Britain, this relative of Vespasian had since redeemed himself by taking a major part in the capture of Rome from the Vitellianists. At Moguntiacum, Mainz to be, he sent the Gallic conscripts home, declaring that his legions would be ample. The gesture practically completed the pacification of Gaul.

Thereupon he entered Augusta Treverorum, Trier to be, city of Classicus and Tutor, birthplace of the Gallic rebellion. He gave a general amnesty and took those units that had defected back into his army. Addressing an assembly of Treveri and Lingones in bleakly reasonable style, he convinced them that they had nothing to gain and everything to lose by further insurgency.

Burhmund and Classicus had regrouped their scattered forces, minus a substantial contingent that Cerialis had trapped. They sent a herald to him, offering him the imperium of Gaul if he would join them. He merely passed the letter on to Rome.

Busy with the political side of the war, he was not well prepared for the onslaught that followed. In a hard-fought battle, the rebels captured the bridge over the Moselle. Cerialis personally led the assault that took it back. Rallying his cohorts when the barbarians were in his very camp, he caught them in disarray, plundering, and put them to flight.

Northward down the Rhine, the Agrippinenses—Ubii that were—had made their treaty with Burhmund reluctantly. Now they surprised and massacred the German garrisons among them, and appealed to Cerialis for help. He advanced by forced marches to relieve their city.

Despite some minor reverses, he got the capitulation of the Nervii and Tungri. When fresh legions had doubled his strength, he set forth for a showdown with Burhmund. In a two-day battle near Old Camp, aided by a Batavian deserter, who guided his men in a flanking movement, he broke the Germans. The war might have ended there, had the Romans had ships on hand to block their escape across the Rhine.

Upon learning of this, the remaining Treverian rebel leaders also withdrew over the river. Burhmund retreated into the Batavian island, where the men left to him waged for a while a guerrilla campaign. Among those they killed was Briganticus. Yet they could keep no ground. The fiercest fight saw Burhmund and Cerialis pitted directly against one another. The German, trying to rally his troops as they reeled back, was recognized; missiles hailed about him; he barely got away by jumping off his horse and swimming across the stream. His boats took off Classicus and Tutor, who were thenceforward no more than disconsolate hangers-on.

Cerialis had one contretemps. After going to inspect the winter quarters being constructed for the legions at Novesium and Bonna, he was on his way back down the Rhine with his fleet. From their coverts, German scouts saw a sloppiness born of overconfidence. They gathered a pair of strong bands and, on a clouded night, attacked. Those who invaded the Roman camp cut the tent ropes and slaughtered the men within. Their companions threw grapnels on several vessels and dragged them off. The great prize was the praetorian trireme, where Cerialis should have been sleeping. As it chanced, he was elsewhere—with an Ubian woman, rumor said—and emerged groggy, nearly naked, to take charge.

It was only a hit-run action. No doubt its main result was that the Romans smartened in a hurry. The Germans towed the captured trireme up the River Lippe and gave it to Veleda.

Small though it was, that setback to the Imperial cause might later have been taken for an omen. Cerialis advanced deeper into the tribal homelands. None could withstand him. But neither could he come to final grips with his foes. Rome could spare him no more troops. Supplies grew scant and irregular. All the while, marching down upon him was the Northern winter.

10

A.D. 60.

Over the highlands east of the Rhine valley trekked a caravan of thousands. For the most part the hills were thickly wooded, the ways through them little better than game trails. Horses, oxen, men strained to move wagons along; wheels groaned, brush crackled, breath rasped. Mainly folk trudged afoot, dumb with weariness and hunger.

From a height two or three miles off, Everard and Floris watched the exodus as it crossed a grassy open stretch. Hand-held opticals brought it into arm's-length view. They could have used auditory pickups as well, but the sight was hard enough to take.

Straight-shouldered yet, a white-headed man rode at the front. Mail and spearheads gleamed where his household guards walked behind. That was the only brightness, and no merriment stirred beneath the helmets. After them, some boys herded what few scrawny cattle, sheep, and pigs were left. Here and there in the line, a cart bore a wicker cage of chickens or geese. Hardtack bread and the rare piece of cured meat went more closely watched than the bundled-up clothes, tools, and other chattels—even the crude wooden idol on its wain where gold glinted meaningless. What use had any gods been to the Ampsivarii?

Everard pointed. "That old guy in the lead," he said. "Their chief, Boiocalus, do you think?"

"As Tacitus wrote the name," Floris replied. "Yes, surely he. Not many in this milieu reach an age like his." Sadly: "I imagine he regrets that he did."

"And that he spent most of his life in Roman service. Yeah."

A young woman, a girl really, shuffled by, cradling a baby in her arms. It wailed at a breast bared for it, from which no more milk would flow. A middle-aged man, perhaps her father, using a spear for a staff, kept his free arm ready to help her when she staggered. Her husband no doubt lay slain, tens or hundreds of miles behind them.

Everard shifted in the saddle. "Let's go," he said roughly. "It's a ways to the meeting place, isn't it? Why'd you route us by here?"

"I thought we should have a close look at this," Floris explained. "Yes, it will haunt me too. But the Tencteri have experienced it directly. We need to know well what it is, if we hope to understand their reaction to it, and Veleda's, and theirs to her."

"I s'pose." Everard clucked to his horse, pulled on the tether of his spare, which at present carried his modest baggage, and picked a way downhill. "Though compassion is mighty scarce in this century. The nearest society that ever encouraged it much is in Palestine, and that one will get scattered to the winds."

Thereby sowing Judaism throughout the Empire, of which the harvest will be Christianity. No wonder that strife and death in the North would become the barest footnote to history.

"Kin loyalty is overwhelmingly strong," Floris reminded, "and in the face of Rome, a feeling is in embryo among the western Germans, of a basic kinship reaching past tribal borders."

Uh-huh, Everard remembered, *and you suspect Veleda has a lot to do with it. That's why we're tracking her back through time—to try and discover what she signifies*.

They reentered forest. Summer-green arches reached high before them, above a path walled with underbrush. Sunlight struck between leaves to spatter on moss and shadow. Squirrels ran fiery along boughs. Birdsong and fragrance wove through a mighty stillness. Already nature had swallowed up the agony of the Ampsivarii.

Like a spiderweb he saw snaring brightness in a hazel, pity reached between them and Everard. He must fare a goodly ways before it stretched so far that it broke. No use telling himself that they all died obscurely eighteen hundred years before he was born. They were here, now, as real as the refugees he had seen no great distance east of this ground, fleeing west, 1945. But these would find no succor.

Tacitus apparently got the general outline of the story right. The Ampsivarii were driven from their homes by the Chauci. A land grab; people were becoming too many for their available technology to support them on ancestral acres; overpopulation is relative, as old as the famine and war it raises, and as immortally reborn. The defeated sought the lower Rhine. They knew a considerable territory lay vacant there, cleared of its former inhabitants by the Romans, who meant to reserve it for purposes of military supply and settlement of discharged soldiers. Already two Frisian tribes had tried to take it over. They were ordered out and, when they stalled, expelled by an attack that killed many and sent many more to the slave markets. But the Ampsivarii were loyal federates. Boiocalus had suffered imprisonment when he would not go along with Arminius's revolt forty years ago. Afterward he served under Tiberius and Germanicus, until he retired from the army to become the leader of his folk. Surely Rome would grant him and his exiles a place to lay their heads.

Rome would not. Privately, hoping to avoid trouble, the legate offered Boiocalus property for himself and his family. The chieftain refused the bribe: "We may lack a land to live in; we cannot lack one to die in." He brought his tribe upstream to the Tencteri. Before a massed gathering he called on them, the Bructeri, and any others who found the nearness of the Empire oppressive to join him in war.

While they argued about it in their disorganized quasi-democratic fashion, the legate took his legions across the Rhine into the same country. He threatened extermination unless the newcomers were evicted. Northward out of Upper Germany marched a second army, to stand at the backs of the Bructeri. In the jaws of the vise, the Tencteri bade their guests begone.

I better not feel too self-righteous. The United States will commit a worse betrayal in Vietnam, with less excuse.

The trail debouched on something vaguely like a road, narrow, rutted, maintained solely by the feet, hoofs, and wheels that used it. Everard and Floris wound over its ups and downs for hours. Spying from invisibly high above and with the help of her robot bugs, cut-and-try work, patiently fitting together scraps of possibly useful observation, she had planned their course. It was a little dangerous for a man and woman to travel thus unescorted, though the Tencteri didn't go in much for banditry. However, they had to be seen arriving in ordinary wise. They could use stun pistols in self-defense if they were assailed *and* if there weren't a bunch of witnesses whose tale might significantly affect the society.

In the event, they had no trouble. More and more travelers came onto the road, bound the same way. All were men; almost all seemed preoccupied or anxious and talked little. An exception was a large fellow with a beer belly, who introduced himself as Gundicar. He rode beside the unusual couple and chatted away, incurably cheerful. In the nineteenth or twentieth century, Everard thought, he'd have been a well-to-do grocer or baker and daily patron of the local *Brauhaus*. "And how came you hither unscathed, you twain?"

The Patrolman gave him a prepared story. "Hardly that, my friend. I am of the Reudigni, north of the River Elbe; you have heard of us? . . . Trading southward. . . . The war between the Hermunduri and Chatti. . . . We were swept off, I believe I alone of my band escaped alive, my goods gone save for this bit of gear. . . . A woman left widowed, bereft of kin, happy to join me. . . . Wending homeward along the Rhine and the seaboard, hoping for fewer woes. . . . Having heard of the wise-woman from the east, and that she would speak to you Tencteri. . . ."

"Ach, in truth these are fearsome times." Gundicar sighed. "Huge fires grieving the Ubii across the river, too." He brightened. "I think that's the wrath of the gods for their licking Roman boots. Maybe soon an ill doom will fall on yon whole bunch."

"Then you'd fain have fought when the legions thrust into your land?"

"Well, now, that would have been unwise, we were unready, and hay harvest well-nigh upon us, you know. But I am not ashamed to say I howled in mourning for those poor homeless. May the Mother be kind to them! I'm hoping the spaewife Edh gives us word of a morrow when we may indeed right such wrongs. Good plunder in that Colonia burh, eh?"

Floris took over most of the conversation. Woman in a frontier society normally enjoys respect, if not complete equality. She runs everything when her man is gone from the lonely steading; should the feud-foe, the Vikings, the Indians then appear, it is she who commands the defense. Still more than the Greeks or the Hebrews did the Germanic peoples believe in the sibyl, the prophetess, the female—almost shamanistic among them—to whom a god gave powers and told of the future. Edh's reputation had run long ahead of her, and Gundicar gossiped with everybody.

"No, it's unknown whence she came at the first. She fared hither from among the Cherusci, and I've heard that ere then she abode for a time with the Langobardi. . . . I think this Nerha goddess of hers is of the Wanes, not the Anses . . . unless it's another name for Mother Fricka. And yet . . . they say Nerha is as terrible in her rage as Tiw himself. . . . There's something about a star and the sea, but I know nothing of that, we're inlanders here. . . . She reached us soon after the Romans withdrew. The king guests her. He bade men come and hearken. That must have been at her wish. He would hardly gainsay it. . . ."

Floris led him on. What he told would much help her plan the next step in the search. Edh herself, the Patrol agents had better avoid meeting. Until they had more knowledge of her and whatever the forces were that she was unleashing, they would be crazy to interfere.

Late in the afternoon they arrived at a cleared vale, fields and pastures, the king's main estate. He was basically a landholder, not above joining his tenants, hirelings, and slaves in the farm work. He presided over councils and the great seasonal sacrifices, he took command in war, but law and tradition bound him as fast as anyone else; his often riotous folk would overrule or overthrow him if that was their mood, and any scion of the royal house had a claim to the post that was as good as the fighting men he could muster to support it. *No wonder these Germans can't overcome Rome,* Everard reflected. *They never will, either. When their descendants—Goths, Vandals, Burgundians, Lombards, Saxons, and the rest—take over, it'll be by default, because the Empire has crumbled from within. And besides, it'll have taken them over before then—spiritually, by converting them to Christianity, so that the new Western civilization comes to birth where the old Classical one did, on the Mediterranean shore, not along the Rhine or the gray North Sea.*

It was a flitting thought at the back of his mind, repeating what he well knew, gone again as his attention focused ahead.

The king and his household dwelt in a long, thatch-roofed timber hall. Sheds, barns, a pair of hovels where the lowly slept, and other outbuildings formed, with it, a square. A way behind it loomed a grove of ancient trees, the halidom, where the gods received their offerings and gave their omens. Most arrivals pitched camp in front, filling a meadow. Nearby, calves and swine roasted over big fires, while servants dished up horns or wooden cups of beer for all. Lavish hospitality was essential to maintaining a lord's reputation, on which his life might well depend.

Everard and Floris established themselves inconspicuously offside and mingled with the crowd. Passing a gap between the buildings, they got a look into the courtyard. Rudely cobbled, at present it was occupied by the horses of the important visitors, who would stay in the royal house. Amidst them stood four white oxen and the wagon they had surely drawn. It was an extraordinary vehicle, beautifully carpentered, elaborately carved. Behind a driver's seat, windowless sides rose to a shake roof. "A van," Everard murmured. "Got to be Veleda's—Edh's. I wonder, does she sleep in it on the road?"

"Doubtless," Floris said. "To preserve dignity and mystery. I suspect an image of the goddess is in there too."

"M-m, Gundicar mentioned several men who travel with her. She may not need an armed guard, if the tribes respect her as much as I gather, but it's impressive, and besides, somebody has to do the chores. Though I suppose being her attendants makes them heap big medicine, and they're putting up in the sachem's lodge along with his braves and the local chiefs. She too, do you think?"

"Certainly not. She, to lie on a bench among a lot of snoring men? Either she will use her car or the king has arranged some kind of private room for her."

"How does she do it, anyway? What gives her that power?"

"We are trying to learn what."

The sun slipped below western treetops. Dusk began to rise in the vale. A wind slithered chilly. Now that the guests were fed, it smelled only of woodsmoke and forest deeps. Thralls stoked the fires; flames flickered aloft, growled, spat. Overhead winged nest-bound crows and darting swallows, runes changeably scrawled on a sky gone purple in the east, cold green in the west. The evening star trembled into sight.

Horns sounded. Warriors trod from the hall, through the courtyard, onto the trampled ground outside. Their spearheads caught the dying daylight. Before them went a man in a richly patterned tunic, gold helices entwining his arms, the king. Breath hissed in the shadowed gathering until, silent, men waited. The heart knocked in Everard's breast.

The king spoke loudly but gravely. Everard thought that, underneath, he was shaken. To them from afar, he said, had come Edh, of whose wonder-working all had heard. She wanted to prophesy for the Tencteri. In honor to her and the goddess who fared with her, he had therefore bidden the nearest dwellers tell the next, and thus across the land. In these unhappy times, whatever signs the gods sent must be carefully weighed. He warned that the words of Edh would hurt. Bear them manfully, as one bears the setting of a broken bone. Think what it meant, and what folk could or should do hereafter.

The king stood aside. Two women—wives of his?—bore out a high, three-legged stool. Edh came forth and seated herself on it.

Everard strained through the gloaming. How he wished he could use his optical to help this uneasy firelight! What he saw surprised him. He had half expected a ragged hag. She was well clad, in a short-sleeved long-skirted gown of plain white wool, a fur-trimmed blue cloak held with a gilt bronze brooch, thin leather shoes. Her head was bare, like a maiden's, but the long brown hair hung in braids, rather than loosely, beneath a snakeskin fillet. Tall, full-boned but thin, she moved just a little awkwardly, as if she and her body were not quite one. Big eyes glowed in a long, handsomely sculptured face. When she opened her mouth, what appeared to be a full set of teeth flashed white. *Why, she's young,* he thought; and: *No. Mid-thirties, I'd guess. That's middle-aged here. She could be a grandmother, though actually they say she's never married.*

His gaze left her for an instant and, with a start, he recognized the man who had accompanied her and stood at her side, dark, saturnine, somberly garbed. *Heidhin. Of course. Ten years younger than when I first saw him. He doesn't look it, or, rather, he already looks as old as then.*

Edh spoke. She made no gestures, kept hands on lap, and her voice, a husky contralto, stayed soft. It carried, though; and steel was in it, and winter winds.

"Hear me and heed ye," she uttered, eyes turned beyond them toward the evenstar, "highborn or lowborn, still in your strength or stumbling graveward, doomed to death and dreeing the weird boldly or badly. I bid ye hearken.

When life is lost, alone is left, for yourself and your sons, what is said of you. Doughty deeds shall never die, but in minds of men remain forever—night and nothingness for the names of cravens! No good the gods will give to traitors, nor aught but anger unto the slothful. Who fears to fight will lose his freedom, will cringe and crawl to get moldy crusts, his children chafing in chains and shame. Hauled into whoredom, helplessly, his women weep. These woes are his. Better a brand should burn his home while he, the hero, harvests foemen till he falls defiant and fares on skyward.

"Hoofs in heaven heavily ring. Lightning leaps, blazing lances. All the earth resounds with anger. Seas in surges smite the shores. Now will Nerha naught more suffer. Wrathful she rides to bring down Rome, the war gods with her, the wolves and ravens."

She recalled humiliations endured, wealth paid over, dead lying unavenged. Icily she lashed the Tencteri for yielding to invaders and forsaking the kindred who called on them. Yes, it had seemed they had no choice; but what they in truth chose was infamy. Let them slaughter as much as they would in the halidoms, it could not buy them back their honor. The weregild they would pay was sorrow unbounded. Rome would gather it in.

But a day would yet dawn. Abide it, and be ready when that red sun rose.

Afterward, pondering the audiovisual they had recorded, Everard and Floris felt again a little of the spell. They had well-nigh been swept away too, humbled, exalted, with the throng that lifted weapons and shouted as Edh walked back to the hall. "Total conviction," Floris said.

"More to it than that," Everard answered. "A gift, a power—real leadership has a touch of mystery, something transhuman. . . . But I wonder if also the time stream isn't bearing her along."

"North to the Bructeri, where she will settle, and then—"

As for the Ampsivarii, they wandered year after year, sometimes briefly finding refuge, sometimes harried onward, until, Tacitus wrote, "all their young were killed in a foreign country, and those who could not fight were shared out as booty."

‖

Out of the east, the morning behind them, rode the Anses into the world. Sparks flew across heaven from the wheels of their wains, which rumbled so that mountains shook. The tracks of their horses smoldered black. Their arrows darkened the air. The sound of their battle horns woke a killing rage in men.

Against these newcomers went the Wanes. Froh was at the forefront, astride his bull, the Living Sword in his hand. Wind scourged the sea until its waves foamed near the feet of the moon, who fled. Over them in her ship came Naerdha. Her right hand steered with the Ax of the Tree for oar. Her left hand cast eagles to shriek, strike, and tear. Upon her brow a star burned white as the fire's heart.

Thus did the gods war on each other, while the eotans of the high North and the low South watched and talked of how it would clear the way for them. But the birds of Wotan saw and warned him. The head of Mim heard and warned Froh. Thereat the gods called truce, gave hostages, and held council.

In the peace they made, they apportioned the world between them. They held weddings, Anse to Wane—father to mother, wizard to wife—and Wane to Anse—huntress to craftsman, witch to warrior. By him whom they hanged, by her whom they drowned, and by their own blood that they mingled, they swore faith, which should abide until the day of doom.

Then they raised walls for their defense, a wooden stockade in the North, high-piled stones in the South; and they set themselves to their sway over those things that are under the Law.

But one among the Anses, Leokaz the Thief, half eotan, grew restless. He longed for the old wild years and felt himself now reckoned of little worth. At last he slipped unbeknownst away. South he fared to the wall of stone. At the gate he threw a sleep spell on its watchman, took the key from its hiding place, and passed into the Iron Land. There he bargained with its lords. When they gave him the spear Summer's Bane, he gave them the key.

In this wise did the Iron Lords gain a way into the Earthworld. Their hosts came through bringing slavery and slaughter. It was the West that first knew them, and often the sun goes down into a lake of blood.

But the giant Hoadh strode northward, thinking to reach the Frost Land and make alliance with the eotans there. Wherever he went, he took what he wanted. Kine he plucked from the meadows. Houses he clubbed asunder to reave his bread. Fire he sowed and men he slew for his sport. The road he made was of wreckage.

He reached the seashore. Afar he spied Naerdha. Unawares she sat on a skerry, combing her hair. The locks shone like gold and her breasts like snow where shadows lie blue. Lust swelled. Night-softly for all his hugeness, Hoadh crept nigh, until he waded out and seized her. When she struggled, he knocked her head against the rock and stunned her. There in the surf, he ravished her.

The waters have risen over that reef, to hide the shame even at low tide. Because of this, many a ship has struck, and the breakers have taken their crews. It does not slake the wrath and grief of Naerdha.

She roused with a wildcat scream to find herself alone again. On wings of storm she rushed to her hall beyond the sunrise. "Whither has he gone?" she cried.

"We know not," wailed her daughters, "save that he went from the sea."

"Vengeance will follow him," said Naerdha. She returned landward and sought the dwelling she shared with Froh, to bid him help her. But the season was spring and he had gone to quicken life, the round on which she ought to have come likewise. Hence she could not claim the bull Earthshaker either, as was her right.

Instead she called their eldest son to her and changed him into a tall black stallion. Mounting, she rode to Ansaheim. Wotan lent her his spear that never misses, Tiwaz his Helm of Dread. Off she hastened on Hoadh's track. That was a gaunt year, when she had forsaken Froh and her sea.

Hoadh heard her coming after him. He climbed a mountain and lifted his club for battle. Night fell. The moon rose. By its light he saw, across many furlongs, the spear, the helm, and the grim stallion. His heart failed him and he bolted west. So fast did he run that she could barely keep him in sight.

Hoadh reached his fellow Iron Lords and begged their help. Shield to shield they stood before him. Naerdha cast the spear above their heads and pierced her foe. His blood flooded the lowlands.

She wended home full of anger yet at Froh for his broken promise. "I will take the bull when I choose," she said, "and sorely will you miss him on the day of doom." He was angry too, for what she had made of their son. They dwelt apart.

On Midwinter Eve she bore Hoadh's get, nine sons. She turned them into hounds as black as her horse.

Thonar of the Thunders drove to her hall. "Froh left his sister and you left your brother that you twain might be together," he said. "If you no longer are, life will die from land and sea alike. What then shall feed the gods?" Therefore in spring Naerdha returned to her husband, but not gladly. She left him once more in autumn. So has it been ever since.

"Leokaz broke the oath we swore," said Wotan to her. "Henceforward the world will never know peace. We have dire need of my spear."

"I will recover it for you," answered Naerdha, "if you will lend it again and Tiwaz the helm when I go hunting."

The flood had borne it out to sea. Long did Naerdha range in search. Many are the tales of a strange woman who came to this land or that. She repaid those who guested her by healing their hurts, righting their wrongs, and foretelling their morrows. Still she sends women wandering across the world who do as she did, in her name and at her behest. In the end she found the spear floating below the evening star.

Vengefulness cannot die within her. At the turnings of the year, and whenever else her heart freezes at the memory, she goes forth. With horse and hounds, helm and spear, she rides in the night wind, to raid the Iron Lords, harry the ghosts of evildoers, and bring ill on the foes of those folk who worship her. Fearful it is to hear that rush and clamor in the sky, horn, hoofs, howls, the Wild Hunt. Yet men who bear weapons against them she hates shall have her stern blessing.

11

A.D. 49.

Westward from the Elbe, south of where Hamburg would someday arise, stretched the realm of the Langobardi. Centuries futureward their posterity ended a migration lifetimes long by conquering northern Italy and founding what became known as the Lombard kingdom. At present they were only another German tribe, albeit a powerful one that had dealt many of the hardest blows Rome took in Teutoburger Wald. Lately their axes had hewn out the decision of who should be king among their neighbors the Cherusci. Wealthy, haughty, they drew trade and news from the Rhine to the Vistula, from the Cimbri in Jutland to the Quadi along the Danube. Floris decided she and Everard couldn't simply ride in, claiming to be distressed travelers from somewhere else. That was feasible in 70 and 60, among peoples on the western fringe who were engaged with Rome—hostilely, servilely, or peacefully—more than with easterlings. Here the risk of making a slip would be too great.

But here and now Edh was, in a sojourn of two years. Here was where the next clue to her origin must be, as well as an opportunity to observe in more depth her effect on the folk through whom her pilgrimage went.

Luckily, though logically, an ethnographer was in residence, like Floris among her Frisii. The Patrol also wanted a sampling of central Europe during the first century, and this was a better locale than most.

Jens Ulstrup had settled down a dozen years ago. He related that he was Domar, from what was to become the Bergen area of Norway, virtual terra incognita to the landlocked Langobardi. A family feud drove him into exile. He took passage to Jutland; the southern Scandinavians had already developed rather large vessels. Thence he wandered on shank's mare, welcomed for his songs and poetry. As was customary, the king rewarded some flattering verses with gold and an invitation to stay. Domar invested in trade goods, parlayed his fortune remarkably fast, and in due course acquired a homestead of his own. Both his mercantile interests and his curiosity about the world, natural in a scop, accounted for his frequent lengthy absences. Many of his trips really were within contemporary lands, though he might expedite them by his timecycle.

Having walked to a spot where he knew he was unobserved, he summoned the machine from its hiding place. Moments later but days earlier, he was at the camp of Everard and Floris. They had established themselves farther north, in the uninhabited stretch—the American called it the DMZ—between Langobardian and Chaucian territory.

From a bluff screened by trees they looked down over the river. It flowed broad between deeply green banks; reeds rustled, frogs croaked, fish splashed silvery, waterfowl flew in their tumultuous thousands; occasionally men paddled a boat along the opposite, Suarinian shore. "We will be a little in the life of the country," Floris had said, "not quite like disembodied spirits flitting through."

They sprang to their feet when Ulstrup appeared. He was a slender, sandy-haired man, as barbaric-looking as them. That did not mean bearskin kilts. His shirt, coat, and pants were of cloth well woven, tastefully patterned, and skillfully tailored. The goldsmith who made the brooch at his throat did not go by Hellenic canons, but was nonetheless an artist. His hair was combed and tied in a knot on the right side. His mustache was trimmed, and if his chin was stubbly, it was because razors were not of Gillette sharpness.

"What have you found?" Floris exclaimed.

Ulstrup's smile showed how tired he was. "That will take a stretch to tell," he answered.

"Give the guy a break," Everard said. "Here, sit down." He gestured at a mossy log. "Want some coffee? You can smell it's fresh."

"Coffee," Ulstrup crooned. "I often drink it in my dreams."

Odd, Everard thought momentarily, *that we should be using twentieth-century English, we three in this scene. But no. He happens to be from then too, doesn't he? For a while, English will sort of play the role that Latin does today. Not for as long a while.*

They made very little small talk before Ulstrup turned earnest. His stare fixed upon the others as an animal might stare from a trap. He spoke with care. "Yes, I do believe you are right. This is something unique. I confess the potentials frighten me; and I have no experience with variable reality or expertise in it.

"As I told you before, I had heard tales of an itinerant sibyl or witch or whatever she was, but paid no special attention. That kind is . . . oh, not common in this culture, but not extraordinary either. I was concerned about the ongoing civil strife among the Cherusci and, frankly, resented your demand that I investigate her, an outsider. My apologies, Agent Floris, Unattached

Agent Everard. Now I have encountered her. I have listened to her. I have spoken at length with a number of men about her. My Langobardian wife has told me what women are saying to each other.

"You related what a tremendous impact Edh will have on the western tribes. I suspect you did not anticipate how strong it is here, already, or how swiftly it increases. She arrived in a primitive wagon. I heard the Lemovii gave it to her, after she had come to them afoot. She will leave in a magnificent van the king is having made, drawn by his finest oxen. She arrived with four men in her train. She will leave with a dozen. She could have had far more than that—and women, too—but chose them and set the limit with intelligent practicality. I think that was on the advice of the Heidhin you described. . . . No matter. I have seen proud young warriors begging to abandon everything and follow her as servants. I have seen their lips tremble and their eyes blink hard when she refused them."

"How does she do it?" Everard whispered.

"She bears a myth," Floris said. "Isn't that correct?"

Surprised, Ulstrup nodded. "How did you guess?"

"I heard her uptime, and I know well what could influence the Frisii. They cannot be greatly unlike these easterners."

"No. Perhaps a difference comparable to that between Dutch and Germans in our period. Of course, Edh is not proclaiming the gospel of a whole new religion. That is outside the pagan mentality. In fact, I rather imagine her ideas are evolving as she goes along. She is not even adding a new deity. Her goddess is known through most of the Germanic range. The local name is Naerdha. She must be more or less identical with the Nerthus whose cult Tacitus describes. Do you remember?"

Everard nodded. The *Germania* told of a covered oxcart that each year drew an image in procession around the land. That was a time when war was set aside, a time of rejoicing and fertility rites. After the goddess returned to her grove, the idol was taken to a secluded lake and washed by slaves, who immediately afterward were drowned. Nobody asked "what that sight is that may only be seen by the eyes of the dying."

"A pretty grim sort," Everard said. The neopagans of his home milieu did not include her in their fairy tales of a prehistoric matriarchy when everybody was nice.

"It is a pretty grim life they lead," Floris observed.

The scholar in Ulstrup took over. "This is clearly a figure in an aboriginal chthonic pantheon, the Wanes or Vanir," he said. "It originated before the Indo-Europeans reached these parts. They brought their characteristic warlike, masculine sky-gods, the Anses or Aesir. Dim memories of the conflict between cultures survived in myths of a war between the two divine races, which was finally settled by negotiations and intermarriage. Nerthus—

Naerdha—is still female. In centuries ahead she will become male, the Eddic god Njordh, father of Freyja and Frey—who today is still her husband. Njordh will be a sea god, as Nerthus is associated with the sea, though she is also an agricultural deity."

Floris touched Everard's arm. "Suddenly you look bleak," she murmured.

He shook himself. "Sorry. My mind strayed. I was remembering an episode that hasn't happened yet, among the Goths. It involved their gods. But that was quite a minor eddy in the time stream, easily damped except for what it cost the persons involved. This is different. I don't know how it is, but I feel it in my marrow."

Floris turned to Ulstrup. "What is Edh preaching, then?" she asked him.

He shivered. "'Preaching.' What a spooky word. Pagans don't preach—at least, heathen Germans don't—and at this moment Christianity is hardly more than a persecuted Jewish heresy. No, Edh does not deny Wotan and the rest. She simply tells new stories about Naerdha and Naerdha's powers. But there is nothing simple about what they imply. And . . . by sheer intensity and eloquence, yes, it is fair to say that she delivers sermons. These tribes have never known anything of the kind before. They are . . . not immunized. It is why so many will so readily turn Christian, once those missionaries get here." As if defensively, his tone dried. "To be sure, there will also be political and economic reasons to convert, which no doubt decide the issue in most cases. Edh offers nothing like that, unless you count her hatred of Rome and her prophecies of its downfall."

Everard rubbed his chin. "Then she's invented preaching, religious fervor, independently," he said. "How? Why?"

"We must find out," Floris responded.

"What are these new myths?" Everard inquired.

Ulstrup frowned into the distance. "It will take me long to tell you everything I have learned. And it is inchoate, not a neat theological system, you realize. And I doubt I have heard all of it, listening to her or at second hand. Certainly I have not heard what will develop as time goes on.

"But—well, she does not say it outright, perhaps she herself is not conscious of it, but she is making her goddess into a being at least as powerful, as . . . cosmic . . . as any. Naerdha is not exactly usurping Wotan's authority over the dead, but she too receives them in her hall, she too leads them in a hunt through heaven. She is becoming as much a deity of war as Tiwaz, and the destined destroyer of Rome. Like Thonar, she commands elemental forces, weather, storm, together with the sea, rivers, lakes, all water. Hers is the moon—"

"Hecate," Everard muttered.

"But she keeps her ancient precedence over begetting and birth," Ulstrup finished. "Women who die in childbed go directly to her, like fallen warriors to the Eddic Odin."

"That must appeal to women," Floris said.

"It does, it does," Ulstrup agreed. "Not that they have a separate faith—mystery cults, and sects for that matter, are unknown among the Germans—but here is a, a special devotion for them."

Everard paced to and fro in the glen. His fist beat his palm. "Yeah," he said. "That was important to the success of Christianity, in both the South and the North. It had more for women than any paganism did, even the Magna Mater. They might not convert their husbands, but they'd sure influence their children."

"Men can behold visions too." Ulstrup regarded Floris. "Do you see the same possibility that I do?"

"Yes," she answered, not quite steadily. "It could happen. Tacitus Two . . . Veleda went back into free Germany after Civilis was crushed, bearing her message, and a new religion spread among the barbarians. . . . It could grow and develop onward after her death. It would have no real competition. Oh, it would not become monotheistic or anything like that. But this goddess would be the supreme figure, around whom everything gathered. She would give folk as much, spiritually, or almost as much, as Christ could. Few would ever join the Church."

"The more so if they lacked political reason to," Everard added. "I watched the process in viking Scandinavia. Baptism was the admission ticket to civilization, with all its commercial and cultural advantages. But a collapsed West Roman Empire won't be anywhere near that attractive, and Byzantium is a long ways off."

"True," Ulstrup said. "Quite conceivably the Nerthus faith can become the seed and core of a Germanic civilization—not barbarism but a civilization, however turbulent—which has the inner richness to resist Christendom, as Zoroastrian Persia will. Already they are not mere woods-runners here, you know. They are aware of an outside world, they interact with it. When the Langobardi intervened in the dynastic quarrels of the Cherusci, it was to restore a king who had been overthrown because he was Roman-reared and sent by request from Rome. Not that the Langobardi are cat's-paws; it was a Machiavellian move. Trade with the South increases year by year. Roman or Gallo-Roman ships sometimes ply as far as Scandinavia. The archaeologists of our time will speak of a Roman Iron Age, followed by a Germanic Iron Age. Yes, they are learning, these barbarians. They are assimilating what they find useful. It does not follow that they must inevitably be assimilated themselves."

His voice dropped. "Of course, if they are not it will be a different future. *Our* twentieth century will never exist."

"That's what we're trying to head off," Everard said harshly.

A silence fell. Wind lulled, leaves rustled, sunlight skipped on the ruffled stream. The peacefulness made the landscape feel unreal.

"But we've got to learn how this deviation started, before we can do anything about it," Everard went on. "Did you find where Veleda hails from?"

"I am afraid not," Ulstrup confessed. "Poor communications, vast reaches of wilderness—and Edh does not talk about her past, nor does her associate Heidhin. He may feel a little more at ease with himself twenty-one years hence, when he mentions the Alvarings to you, whoever they are. Even then, I think, it would be dangerous to ask him for details. At present he and she are totally reticent.

"However, I did hear that she appeared first among the Rugii on the Baltic littoral, five or six years ago as nearly as I can determine from the vague accounts. They say she came in a ship, as befits the prophetess of a sea deity. That and her accent suggest to me a Scandinavian origin. I'm sorry I cannot do better for you."

"It'll serve," Everard replied. "You did okay, buddy. With patience and instruments, maybe occasional inquiries on the ground, we'll track down the place and moment of her landing."

"And then—" Floris's words trailed away. She gazed past the river and the forest beyond, northeasterly toward an unseen shore.

12

A.D. 43.

Right and left the strand reached, sand rising into dunes where stiff grass grew, until haze blurred sight. Kelp, shells, bones of fish and birds lay sparsely strewn on the darker stretch below the high-water line. A few gulls rode the wind. It whistled raw-cold. A taste of salt was on it, and smells from the deeps. Waves washed low onto the shore, hissed back down, came again a little higher up. Farther out they ran strong, hollowly booming, white-capped above steely gray, to a horizon that likewise lost itself in the sky. It pressed in on the world, did that sky, hueless as the sea. Tatters of cloud scudded murky beneath it. Rain walked in the west.

Inland, sedge swayed around pools whose algal green was the only lightness. Forest gloomed in the distance. A brook seeped through the marsh to the beach. Doubtless the dwellers used it to move whatever boats they owned. Their hamlet lay a mile from the coast, some wattle-and-daub cabins hunched below turf roofs. Smoke blew out of louvers, otherwise nothing stirred.

The ship brought abrupt vividness. She was a beauty, long and lean, clinker-built, stem- and sternposts curving high, mastless but swiftly driven by thirty oars. Though her red paint had weathered, the oak remained stout. To the chant of the helmsman, her crew brought her aground, leaped over the sides, and hauled her partway out.

Everard approached. They waited for him in restrained wariness. Nearing, they had seen that he stood alone. He drew close and put the butt of his spearshaft on the sand. "Hail," he greeted.

A grizzled, scarred fellow who must be the captain asked, "Are you from yon houses?" His dialect would have been hard to understand had Everard and Floris not received an imprint. (It was of a Danish tongue four centuries uptime, the closest available. Fortunately, early Nordic languages didn't change fast. However, the agents could not hope to pass for natives, either of the ship's home or of this region.)

"No, I am a wayfarer. I was bound for there, wanting shelter tonight, but spied you and thought I would hear your tale first. It should be better than aught that any homefast hinds can tell. I hight Maring."

Ordinarily the Patrolman would just have said, "Everard," which sounded like a name in some other patois. But he'd be using it uptime when he met Heidhin, whom he hoped to buttonhole this day. He couldn't afford recognition then—another shift in reality, with unguessable consequences. Floris had suggested this monicker, authentically southern German. She had also assisted him with a flowing blond wig and false beard, plus a Jimmy Durante nose that would keep attention off the rest of him. Given the fading of memory with years, that should serve.

A grin creased and crinkled the mariner's face. "And I am Vagnio Thuthevar's son, from Hariu thorp in the land of the Alvarings. Whence come you?"

"From afar." The Patrolman jerked a thumb at the settlement. "They're staying within their walls, hey? Afraid of you?"

Vagnio shrugged. "We could be reavers, for aught they know. This is nobody's port of call. It's merely the landfall we made—"

Everard already realized that. On timecycles aloft, he and Floris had observed the ship, once scanning revealed that she, among all they had checked, carried a woman. A jump into the future showed where she would halt; a jump back into the past deposited him close by. Floris stayed above the clouds. Explaining her presence away would have been too much trouble.

"—where we'll camp the night," Vagnio went on, "and fill our water casks in the morning. But then we coast west to the Anglii, with goods for a great market they hold this time of year. If yon folk like, they can call on us, else we'll leave them be. Their kind has naught worth robbing."

"Not even themselves, to sell for thralls?" The question was foul in Everard's mouth, but natural in this age.

"No, they'd run off as soon as they saw us bound for them, and scatter what livestock they have. That's why they built where they did." Vagnio squinted. "You must be a landlubber not to ken that."

"Yes, of the Marcomanni." The tribe was safely remote, about where western Czechoslovakia would lie. "You are, uh, from Scania?"

"No. The Alvarings hold half of an island off the Geatish coast. Stay the night with us, Maring, and we'll swap yarns— What're you peering at?"

Sailors had crowded around, eager to hear. They were mostly tall blonds, who blocked the Patrolman's view of their vessel. A couple of them had shifted, restless, and he got a clear look. A slender youth had just sprung out of the prow to the beach. He lifted his arms and helped the woman follow. *Veleda.*

No mistaking her. *I'd know that face, those eyes, at the bottom of her goddess's ocean.* But how young she was today, a girl in her teens, withy-thin. The wind tossed loose brown tresses and flapped skirt around ankles. Across the ten or fifteen yards between, Everard thought he saw—what? A look that sought something beyond this place, lips that would suddenly quiver and maybe whisper, a grief, a lostness, a dream, he couldn't say.

Certainly she showed none of the interest in him he had counted on. He wondered if she had so much as cast him a glance. The pale countenance turned away. She spoke briefly with her dark-haired companion. They walked off together, down the strand from the ship.

"Ah, her," Vagnio deduced. Unease touched him. "An uncanny twain, those."

"Who are they?" Everard asked. That too was a natural question, when women crossing the sea other than as captives were well-nigh unheard of. Eventually invaders from the Frisian and Jutish shores would bring their families along to Britain, but that wouldn't happen for centuries.

Unless Scandinavian women occasionally took ship at this early date? His information didn't say. Those lands in those years were little studied. It hadn't seemed they would make much difference to the rest of the world until the *Völkerwanderung.* Surprise, surprise.

"Edh Hlavagast's daughter and Heidhin Viduhada's son," Vagnio said. Everard noticed that he named her first. "They bought aboard, but not to trade alongside us. Indeed, she'd not seek the market at all, but wants we let her—them—off somewhere else, she has not yet said where."

"Best we make ready for night, skipper," growled a man. A mutter of agreement went among others. Darkness was hours off, and it wasn't likely the rain would come this way. *They'd rather not have talk about her,* Everard realized. *They've nothing against her, I'm sure, but she is, yes, uncanny.* Vagnio was quick to assent.

Everard offered to lend a hand with setting up. Bluffly polite, for a guest was sacred, the captain expressed doubt that a landlubber could expedite matters. Everard strolled off, the way Edh and Heidhin had gone.

He saw them stop, well ahead of him. They appeared to argue. She made a gesture strangely imperious for such a slip of a lass. Heidhin wheeled about and started back with long stiff strides. Edh went onward.

"This may be my chance," Everard subvocalized. "I'll see if I can get the boy into conversation."

"Have a care," Floris replied. "I think he is upset."

"Yeah. I've got to try, though, don't I?"

It was the reason for making this rendezvous, instead of simply tracing the ship across the water, backward through time. They dared not charge blind into what might well be the source of the instability, the obscure and easily annulled event from which an entire future could spring. Here, they hoped, was an opportunity to learn something beforehand at minimal risk.

Heidhin jarred to a halt, glowering, before the foreigner. He also was in his teens, perhaps a year or two older than Edh. In this milieu that made him an adult, but he was still gangly, not quite filled out, the sharp countenance darkened by no more than fuzz. He wore wadmal, odorous in the damp air, and salt-stained boots. A sword hung at his flank.

"Hail," said Everard amiably. That was on the surface. Cold prickles went over his scalp.

"Hail," grunted Heidhin. The surliness would have been considered appropriate to his years in twentieth-century America. Here it meant real trouble. "What would you?" He paused before adding roughly, "Follow not the woman. She wants to be alone."

"Is that safe for her?" Everard asked: another natural question.

"She'll not go too far, and will return ere nightfall. Besides—" Again Heidhin fell mute. He seemed to be wrestling with himself. Everard guessed that a youthful desire to be important and mysterious won out over discretion. Yet he heard an almost frightening sincerity: "Whoso offends her shall suffer worse than death. She is the chosen of a goddess."

Did the wind really blow keener all at once? "You know her well, then?"

"I . . . fare at her side."

"Whither?"

"Why would you know?" flared Heidhin. "Let me be!"

"Easy, friend, easy," Everard said. It helped being large and mature. "I do but ask, I, an outlander. Gladly would I hear more about—Edh, did the shipmaster call her? And you Heidhin, I think."

Curiosity awoke. The boy relaxed a bit. "What of you? We wondered as we drew nigh."

"I am a wayfarer, Maring of the Marcomanni, a folk you may never have heard of. You'll get my tale this evening."

"Where are you bound?"

"Wherever my luck may lead me."

Heidhin stood still a moment. The small surf mumbled. A gull mewed. "Could you be sent?" he breathed.

Everard's pulse raced. He forced his tone to stay casual. "Who might have sent me, and why?"

"See you," Heidhin blurted, "Edh is going whither Niaerdh bids her, by dreams or signs. She's now had a thought that this is where we should leave the ship and wend overland. I tried to tell her it's a niggard country, dwellings wide-scattered, maybe outlaws running free. But she—" He gulped. The goddess was supposed to protect her. Faith struggled with common sense and found a compromise. "If a second warrior fared along—"

"Oh, wonderful!" crowed Floris's voice.

"I don't know how well I can act like somebody that destiny has tapped," Everard warned her.

"At least you can draw him out in conversation."

"I'll try."

To Heidhin: "This is news to me, you understand. But we can talk about it. I've naught else to do at once, have you? Come, let's walk to and fro while you tell me about yourself and Edh."

The boy looked downward. He bit his lip, reddened, whitened, reddened again. "That's less easy than you think," he grated.

"Yet I must know—eh?—ere I can plight faith." Everard clapped the stooped shoulder before him. "Take your time, but tell me the whole of it."

"Edh— She should— She will decide—"

"What is it about her that makes you, a man, wait on her word?" *Show plenty of respect.* "Is she a spaewife, she, a girl to behold? That would be a mighty thing."

Heidhin looked up. He trembled. "Yes, that and more than that. The goddess came to her and, and now she is Niaerdh's, she shall bear Niaerdh's wrath across the world."

"What? At whom is the goddess angry?"

"The folk of Romaburh!"

"Why, what harm have they done?" *In these distant parts.*

"They—they— No, this is too holy to speak of. Wait till you meet her. She will make you as wise as she deems needful."

"This is asking much of me," Everard protested reasonably, as a practical-minded hobo would. "You say naught of what has happened aforetime, naught of whither you would fare or why, though you'd have me ward with my life a maiden who'll rouse lust in any rover, greed in any slaver—"

Heidhin screamed. His sword flashed from the sheath. "You dare!" The blade whirred down.

Drilled-in reflex saved Everard. He brought his spear aslant fast enough to block. Iron slammed deep. The seasoned ash did not quite break. Heidhin whipped the blade high again. Everard swept his weapon quarterstaff style. *Mustn't kill him, he's alive in the future, and anyway he's just a kid—* Impact thudded. The blow to the head would have knocked Heidhin woozy, had the shaft not snapped. As was, he lurched.

"Hold off, you murderous lout!" Everard roared. Alarm and rage buzzed in his skull. *What the hell is going on?* "D'you want men for your girl or not?"

Yowling, Heidhin sprang at him. This sword slash was weak, easily sidestepped. Everard dropped the spear, got in close, grasped the tunic, took the moving body on his hip, and sent Heidhin asprawl six feet away.

The youth crawled to his feet. He fumbled for the knife at his belt. *Got to end this.* Everard delivered a karate kick to the solar plexus. He kept it mild. Heidhin doubled over, collapsed, lay heaving for breath. Everard hunkered down to make sure there was no serious damage or choking on vomit or any such thing.

"*Wat drommel*— What is this?" Floris cried in dismay.

Everard straightened. "I dunno," he answered dully, "except that somehow, in my ignorance, I touched the wrong, inflamed nerve. He must've been overwrought, maybe after days or weeks of brooding. He's very young, remember. Something I said or did triggered a hysterical break. In this culture, you know, among males, that's apt to take the form of a killing frenzy."

"I don't suppose . . . you can . . . mend the situation."

"Nope. Especially as precarious as the whole business is." Everard looked down the beach. Edh was a dwindled bit of fluttering darkness, half lost in the sea mist, into which she drifted onward. Wrapped in her dreams, or nightmares, or whatever they were, she had not noticed the fight. "I'd better clear out. The sailors will accept that I'm bewildered—true enough, huh?— but unwilling to cut Heidhin's throat while he's helpless, or chance him cutting mine later, or bother negotiating a reconciliation. He's nothing to me, I'll say, and walk off."

He picked up his spearhead, as Maring would, and started in the direction of the ship. *They'll be disappointed*, he thought wryly. *Gossip from afar is a rare treasure. Well, I'm spared rehashing that elaborate story we concocted.*

"Then we may as well go straight to Öland," said Floris, equally toneless.

"Hm?"

"Edh's home. The captain identified it unmistakably. It is a long, narrow island off the Baltic coast of Sweden. The city of Kalmar will be built opposite it. I was there once on holiday." The voice became wistful. "It was, will be, quite charming. Old windmills everywhere, ancient barrows, snuggled villages, and at either tip a lighthouse overlooking a sea where sailboats bob along— But that is then."

"Sounds like a place I'd visit to visit myself," Everard said. "Then." *Maybe. Depends on what memories I bring back from it now, nineteen hundred years earlier.* He trudged on up the beach.

13

Hlavagast Unvod's son was king of the Alvarings. His wife was Godhahild. They dwelt in Laikian, the biggest thorp their tribe had, more than a score of houses within a wall of dry-laid stone. Around it reached heath, where only sheep could thrive. Neither, though, could foemen fall on it without being seen from afar. The walk was short to the eastern strand, nor much longer to the western, and there timber grew. Southward, also, one soon found good grazing and cropland, which went for some ways before it came to its own shore.

Once the Alvarings held all the Eyn, until Geats crossed over from the mainland and, in the course of lifetimes, overran the richer northern half. At last the Alvarings fought them to a standstill. Many among the Geats said the south was not worth taking; many among the Alvarings said the fear of Niaerdh had gripped them. The Alvarings still paid her as much worship as they did the Anses, or more, whereas the Geats gave the goddess only a cow in springtime. Be that as it may, since then the two tribes had done more trading than warring.

Both had men who rowed cargoes over the sea to swap, as far as the Rugii southward or the Anglii westward. The Geats of the Eyn also held a yearly market at Kaupavik haven, which drew traffickers from widely about. To this, Alvarings brought their woolen goods, salt fish, sealskins, blubber oil, feathers and down, amber when a storm had left a hoard of it on their coast. Now and then a young man of theirs joined the crew of an outland ship; if he lived, he would come home with tales of strange countries.

Hlavagast and Godhahild lost three children early on. Then he vowed that if Niaerdh saved those who came after, when the first of them had shed all its milk teeth he would give her a man—not the two thralls, usually old and sick, that she got when she had blessed the fields, but a hale youth. A girl was born. He named her Edh, Oath, to keep the goddess reminded. The sons for whom he hoped followed her.

When the time was ripe, he took a ship and warriors across the channel. Not to stir up the mainland Geats, he fared north well beyond them and fell on a Skridhfennian camp. Of the captives he brought back, he slaughtered the choicest one in Niaerdh's grove. The rest he sold in Kaupavik. Otherwise Hlavagast did not go warlike abroad, for he was a mild and thoughtful man.

Maybe because of her beginnings, maybe because she had only brothers, Edh grew up a quiet, withdrawn child. She had friends among the others in the thorp, but none close, and when they played together she was always at the rim of it. She was quick to learn her tasks and carried them out faithfully, but was best at those, such as weaving, that she could do by herself. She seldom chattered or giggled.

Yet when she spoke freely, girls listened. After a while boys did, and sometimes the full-grown: for she could make stories. These became more wonderful as the years passed, and she began to put verses into them, almost like a skald. They were of wide-faring men, lovely maidens, wizards, witches, talking animals, merfolk, lands beyond the sea where anything could happen. Ofttimes Niaerdh came into them, a counselor or rescuer. At first Hlavagast feared the goddess might wax wroth; but no ill smote, so he did not forbid it. After all, his daughter had a certain tie to her.

In the thorp Edh was never alone. Nobody ever was. Houses crowded against the wall. In each, stalls for cows or the horses that a few men owned ran along one side, bedsteads along the other. A stone-weighted loom stood near the door for light to weave and sew by, a bench and table at the far end, a clay hearth in the middle. Food and housewares hung from the roof beams or lay across them. The buildings opened on a yard where pigs, sheep, fowl, and gaunt dogs wandered loose around a well. Life crammed together, talking, laughing, singing, weeping, lowing, neighing, grunting, bleating, cackling, barking. Hoofs thumped, wagon wheels creaked, hammer clashed on anvil. Lying in the dark between straw and sheepskin, among the warm smells of animals, dung, hay, embers, you could hear a baby cry till Mother gave it suck, or she and Father thrash about for a while gasping and groaning, or from outside a howl at the moon, a rush of rain, the wind sough or whine or roar—and that other noise, somewhere, what was it, a night-raven, a troll, a dead man out of his howe?

There was much for a little girl to watch whenever she was free, comings and goings, breeding and bearing, hard work and hard frolic, skilled hands shaping wood, bone, leather, metal, stone, the holy days when folk offered to the gods and feasted. . . . When you grew bigger they took you with them and you saw the car of Niaerdh go by, covered that none might behold her; you wore an evergreen garland and strewed last year's flowers in her path and sang to her in your thin voice, it was joy and renewal but also awe and an unspoken underlying fear. . . .

Edh grew onward. Bit by bit she got new tasks that took her farther and farther off. She gathered dry twigs for kindling, woad and madder for dyes, berries and blossoms in season. Later she went in a band to the woods for nuts and to the strand beyond for shells. Later yet, first with a gleaning basket, a year or two after with a sickle, she helped harvest the fields to the south. Boys herded the livestock, but often girls brought them food and might well linger most of a long, long summer's day. Outside the brief busy times of year, folk seldom had anything to hurry for. Neither did they fear anything but sickness, baneful witchcraft, night-beings, and the anger of the gods. No bears or wolves prowled the Eyn, and no foes had sought this poor part of it within living memory.

Thus, more and more as she changed from child to maiden, Edh could stray off by herself, over the heath till her moodiness blew from her. Commonly she ended by the sea, and there she might well sit, lost in the sight, until shadows and a breeze plucked at her sleeve to say she had better go home. From the limestone heights on the western shore she looked across to the mainland, dim with distance; from the sandy east she saw only water. It was enough. In every weather it was enough. Waves danced bluer than heaven, snow streaks of foam on their shoulders, snowstorms of gulls above. They ran heavy, green and gray, their manes flew in the wind, their galloping beat through the ground into her bones. They surged, battered, bellowed, embittered the air with spindrift. They laid a molten road toward her from a low sun, they dimpled beneath oncoming rain and gave it back its rushing noise, they cloaked themselves in fog and whispered unseen of things unknown. Niaerdh was in them with dread and blessing. Hers were the kelp and upcast amber, hers the fish, fowl, seals, great whales, and ships. Hers was the quickening in the land when she came ashore to her Frae, for her sea embraced it, warded it, mourned for its winter death and called it back to life in spring. Very small amidst these things, hers was the child she had kept in this world.

So Edh grew toward womanhood, a tall, shy, slightly awkward girl with a gift for words when she chose to speak of things other than the everyday. She wondered much about them, and spent much time in a waking dream, and when alone might suddenly break into tears, not knowing quite why. Nobody shunned her, but nobody sought her out either, for she had stopped sharing the tales she made and there was otherwise something a little odd about

Hlavagast's daughter. This was the more true after her mother died and he took a new wife. They two did not get along well. Folk muttered that Edh sat too often by Godhahild's grave.

Then one day a youth of the thorp saw her walk by. Wind blew hard over the heath and her loose brown hair tossed full of sunlight. He, who had never hung back, found that his throat froze tight and the heart fluttered in his breast. A long time passed before he could utter a word to her. She lowered her eyes and he barely heard how she answered. After a while, though, they learned to feel easier.

This was Heidhin Viduhada's son. He was a lean, dark lad, short on merriment but sharp of wits, tough and lithe, good at weapon-play, a leader among his fellows albeit some of them hated him for his toploftiness. None cared to tease him about Edh.

When they saw how it was going, Hlavagast and Viduhada went aside for a talk. They agreed that such a linking of their families would be welcome, but a betrothal should wait. Edh's courses had begun just last year; the youngsters might fall out, and an unhappy marriage meant trouble for everybody; abide and see, and meanwhile drink a stoup of ale to the hope of a glad outcome.

Winter passed, rain, snow, cavernous darknesses, the night of fear before the sun turned back and the day of feast that followed, lightening skies, thaw, newborn lambs, budding boughs. Spring brought leaves and northbound wings; Niaerdh rode about the land; men and women coupled in the fields where they would plow and sow. The Sun Car rolled ever higher and slower, green swelled, thunderstorms flashed and banged above the heath, rainbows glimmered far out at sea.

Time came for the market at Kaupavik. Alvaring men gathered their wares and busked themselves. Word thrilled from homestead to homestead: this year a ship had arrived from beyond the Anglii and Cimbri, from realms of the very Romans.

No one knew much about Romaburh. It lay somewhere remote in the South. But its warriors were like locusts, they had eaten land after land; and finely made things trickled out of those realms, glass and silver vessels, metal discs bearing faces, unbelievably lifelike little figures. The stream must be strengthening, for more such goods reached the Eyn every year. Now, at last, Roman chapmen had themselves made it to the country of the Geats! Those who stayed behind in Laikian watched with envy those who left.

Having scant work to do just then, they took comfort in idleness. No sign of evil marked that day a sennight later when Edh and Heidhin strolled west to the shore.

Huge reached the heath, man-empty once they left the thorp out of sight, treeless and flat, so that most of the world was sky. Dizzyingly tall the clouds loomed, dazzlingly white, in a blue without bounds. Light and heat fell from the sun like rain. Poppies flared red, gorse yellow, amidst the murky ling. When they sat down for a while they caught a scorched smell of spurrey; bees hummed in a silence through which larksong drifted earthward; then wings racketed, a grouse hastened low overhead, they looked into one another's eyes and laughed aloud at their own astonishment. Walking, they held hands, no more, for theirs was a chaste folk and he felt himself the warder of a fragile sacredness.

Their path skirted the bluffs that stretched north from the farms and brought them through woods to a strand. Starred with wildflowers, grass grew nearly to the water's edge. Wavelets chuckled on stones they had long since worn smooth. Farther out they gleamed and glinted. Across the channel, the mainland shadowed the horizon. Closer, cormorants on a rock dried their wings in the breeze. A stork flew by, white bearer of luck and growth.

Heidhin caught his breath. His finger leaped to point. "Look!" he cried.

Edh squinted north against the brightness. Her voice wavered. "What *is* it?"

"A ship," he said, "bound this way. A big, big ship."

"No, it can't be. That thing above it—"

"I've heard about such. Men who've been abroad have sometimes seen them. They catch the wind and push the hull along. Yon's the Roman ship, Edh, it has to be, headed home from Kaupavik, and we came right in time to behold!"

Rapt, they stared, forgetting all else. The vessel glided nigh. Indeed she was a wonder. Black with gold trim, she was no longer than a large Northern craft, but much wider, round-bellied to hold an untellable freight of treasures. She was decked over, men standing high above the hold. They seemed a swarm, plenty to fight off any rovers. The stempost curved grandly up and aft, while the carving of a giant swan's neck lifted at the stern. Between them rested a wooden house. No oars drove this ship. From a great pole with a crosspiece swelled a cloth as broad as the beam. She moved along noiseless, a wave at her bow and wake aswirl behind the double steering blades.

"Surely they are beloved of Niaerdh," Edh breathed.

"Now I can see how they clutch half the world," Heidhin said shakenly. "What can withstand them?"

The ship changed course, nearer to the island. Youth and maiden saw crewmen peer their way. A hail rang faintly in their ears. "Why, I, I do think it's us they look at," Edh stammered. "What could they want?"

"Maybe . . . they would like me to join them," Heidhin said. "I've heard from travelers to western parts that the Romans will take tribesmen into their war-hosts. If those are shorthanded because of sickness or something—"

Edh cast him a stricken glance. "Would you go with them?"

"No, never!" Her fingers closed tight around his. He squeezed back. "But let's hear them out anyway, if they do land. They may want something else, and pay us well for our help." A pulse throbbed in his throat.

The yard rattled down. What must be an anchor, though it was not a stone but a hook, went out at the end of a line. A boat trailed on another line. Sailors hauled it alongside and lowered a rope ladder. Men climbed down and seated themselves on the thwarts. Their mates handed them oars. One stood up and flapped a fine cloak he carried. "He smiles and beckons," said Heidhin. "Yes, they have a wish they hope we can grant."

"How beautiful, that garment," Edh murmured. "I think Niaerdh wears the like when she visits the other gods."

"Maybe ere sundown it will be yours."

"Oh, I dare not ask."

"Ho, there!" bawled a man in the boat. He was the biggest, fair-haired, doubtless a German-born interpreter. The rest were a mixed lot, some also light of hue, some darker than Heidhin. But of course the Romans had many different folk to draw on. All wore knee-length tunics over bare legs. Edh flushed and kept her gaze from the ship, where most went naked.

"Be not afraid," the German called. "We'd fain deal with you."

Heidhin reddened too. "An Alvaring knows no fear," he shouted. As his voice cracked he grew redder yet.

The Romans rowed in. The two ashore waited, blood loud in their heads. The boat grounded. A man jumped forth and made fast. The one with the cloak led them up the strand. He smiled and smiled.

Heidhin clasped hard his spear. "Edh," he said, "I like not the look of them. I think we'd be wisest if we kept out of reach—"

He was too late. The leader yelled an order. His followers dashed forward. Before Heidhin could raise his weapon, new hands grabbed it. A man stepped behind him and caught his arms in a wrestler's lock. He struggled, screeching. A short stick, to which he had paid no heed—the gang was unarmed save for knives—struck his nape. That was a skillful blow, to stun without real harm. He sagged, and they bound him.

Edh had whirled to run. A sailor caught her hair. Two more closed in. They flung her down on the grass. She screamed and kicked. Another pair grabbed her ankles. The leader knelt between her spraddled legs. He grinned. Spit ran from a corner of his mouth. He hiked up her skirt.

"You trolls, you dog turds, I'll kill you," Heidhin raged weakly, out of the pain that stabbed through his skull. "I swear by every god of war, no peace shall your breed ever have with me. Your Romaburh shall burn—" Nobody listened. Where Edh lay pinned, the thing went on and on.

14

A.D. 43.

Tracing Vagnio's voyage back to his departure from Öland was easy. With skill and persistence, it was possible to find that a boy and a girl had walked to his home from a village about twenty miles south. But what happened earlier? Some cautious inquiries on the ground were in order. First, though, Everard and Floris planned an aerial survey over the previous several months. The more clues they collected in advance, the better. Vagnio would not necessarily hear of an event such as a murder; perhaps the family could hush it up. Or he and his men might keep silent about it before a stranger. Or Everard might simply get no chance to ask before circumstances forced him from the camp on the beach.

Leaving behind their van and horses, the agents flitted off together on separate hoppers. Their search pattern was a set of leaps from point to point of a precalculated space-time grid. If they spied anything unusual, they would take as close a look through as long a duration as needful. The procedure wasn't guaranteed to pay off, but it was better than nothing and they didn't have infinite lifespan to spend here.

A mile above the village, they flashed from midsummer balefires to a couple of weeks later and hung in an enormous blue. Wind whittered thin and cold. The view wheeled over a sunlit Baltic Sea, Sweden's hills and forests to the west, Öland a straitness mottled with heather, grass, woods, rock, sand—names no dweller would speak for unchronicled centuries to come.

Everard swept his scanner around. Abruptly he stiffened. "Yonder!" he exclaimed into the transmitter at his neck. "About seven o'clock—see?"

Floris whistled. "Yes. A Roman ship, is it not, anchored offshore?" Thoughtfully: "Gallo-Roman, most likely, out of some such port as Bordeaux or Boulogne, rather than the Mediterranean. They never had a regular trade directly with Scandinavia, you know, but records mention a few official visits, and occasional entrepreneurs sail to Denmark and beyond, bypassing the long chain of middlemen. Amber, especially."

"This might be significant for us. Let's check." Everard increased magnification.

Floris had already done it. She screamed.

"Oh, my God," Everard choked.

Floris swooped downward. Cloven air boomed behind her.

"Stop, you fool!" Everard yelled. "Come back!"

Floris ignored him, her popping ears, everything but that which was ahead of her dive. Still her shriek trailed after. So might a plunging hawk scream, or a wrathful Valkyrie. Everard struck fist on control console, cursed, and grimly, all but helplessly, trailed at a slower pace. He halted a few hundred feet aloft, keeping the sun at his back.

The men, clustered to watch the show or wait their turns, heard. They looked up and saw the death-horse bound for them. They wailed and scrambled in every direction. The one on the girl pulled from her, got to his knees, yanked out his knife. Maybe he meant to kill her, maybe it was only defensive reflex. No matter. A sapphire-blue energy bolt smote him through the mouth. He crumpled at her feet. From a hole in the back of his skull curled the smoke off his brain.

Floris whipped her cycle about. A man's height above ground, she fired at the next nearest. Gut-shot, he yammered and threshed on the grass, to Everard like an overturned beetle. Floris chased a third and dropped him cleanly. She ceased then, motionless in the saddle for a minute. Sweat mingled with tears on her face, as cold as her hands.

Breath shuddered into her. She holstered her pistol and leaf-gentle descended by Edh.

Done is done, tolled through Everard. Swiftly he considered his options. In blind panic, surviving sailors spurted along the shore or toward the woods. Two had kept some wits, had waded out and were swimming for the ship, where horror boiled. The Patrolman bit his lip till blood ran. "Okay," he said aloud, tonelessly. With jumps around space and precise aim, he killed each of those who had landed. Finally he put the wounded man out of his misery. *I don't suppose Janne left him on purpose. She just forgot.* Everard rode back to a fifty-foot altitude and poised. By scanner and amplifier he observed what went on below him.

Edh sat up. Her stare was blank, but she plucked at her skirt and got it down over the red-streaked thighs. Hog-tied, Heidhin writhed toward her. "Edh, Edh," he groaned. He stopped when the timecycle settled between. "Oh, goddess, avenger—"

Floris dismounted and knelt beside Edh. She laid her arms about the girl. "It is over, dear," she sobbed. "It will be well with you. Nothing like this, ever again. You are free now."

"Niaerdh," she heard. "All-Mother, you came."

"No use denying your divinity," Everard snarled in Floris's receiver. "Get the hell out before you make matters worse."

"No," the woman answered. "You don't understand. I have to give her what little comfort I am able."

Everard sat mute. The crewmen in the channel heaved frantic on halyard and anchor rode. "Loose me," Heidhin pleaded "Let me to her."

"Maybe I do understand," Everard said. "Be as quick as possible, can you?"

The daze was lifting from Edh, but unearthliness brimmed the hazel eyes. "What do you want of me, Niaerdh?" she whispered. "I am yours. As I always was?"

"Slay the Romans, all the Romans!" Heidhin bawled. "I'll pay you for it with my life if you will."

Poor muchacho, Everard thought, *your life is already ours to take, anytime we might choose. But I could hardly expect you to act sensible right off the bat, could I?*

Or ever, by my lights. You are not a scientifically educated post-Christian Western European. To you, the gods are real and your highest duty is avenging a wrong.

Floris stroked the matted hair. Her free arm drew the reeking, shivering, slight body close. "I want only your well-being, only your gladness," she said. "I love you."

"You saved me," Edh stammered, "because . . . because I must— what?"

"Listen to me, Floris, for everything's sake," Everard called between his teeth. "The time is out of joint and you can't set it right today. You *can't.* Meddle any more, and I swear there'll never be a Tacitus One book, maybe never a Tacitus Two. We don't belong in these events, and that's why the future is in danger. Leave them be!"

His partner fell altogether still.

"Are you troubled, Niaerdh?" Edh asked as a child might. "What can trouble you, the goddess? That the Romans befoul your world?"

Floris closed her eyes, opened them, and let go of the girl. "It . . . is . . . your woe, my dear," she said. Rising: "Fare you well. Fare you bravely, free from fear and sorrow. We shall meet again." To Everard: "Shall I release Heidhin?"

"No, Edh can take a knife and cut the rope. He can help her back to the village."

"True. And that should do both of them good, shouldn't it? A pitiful tiny bit of good."

Floris mounted her timecycle. "I suppose we'd best ascend, instead of winking out of sight," Everard said. "Come on."

He threw a last glance down. It was as if he felt the two there looking and looking. Out on the water, sail filled, the ship bore west. Lacking several hands and, no doubt, at least a couple of officers, she might or might not make it home. If she did, the crew might or might not relate what they had seen. It would scarcely win credence. They'd be smarter to invent something more plausible. Of course, any tale could well be taken for a fabrication, an attempt to cover up a mutiny. In that case, they had an unpleasant death in store. Maybe they'd try their luck among the Germans instead, slim though the prospects be. Knowing their fate would not affect history, Everard didn't give a damn what it was.

15

A.D. 70.

The sun was newly down, clouds lay red and gold in the west, eastward the sky deepened while night rose in a tide over the wilderness. Light lingered on a treeless hilltop in central Germany, but already the grass there was full of shadows and warmth draining from the quiet air.

Having seen to the horses, Janne Floris squatted at the blackened spot in front of the twin shelters and began assembling wood for a fire. Some remained, split and stacked, from the last time the Patrol agents had used the site, a few days ago if you counted by the turning of the planet. A gust and thump brought her to her feet. Everard swung off his vehicle.

"Why are you—I expected you back sooner," she said half timidly.

He shrugged his heavy shoulders. "I figured you might as well do the camp chores while I did mine," he replied. "And nightfall is a logical return point. I don't want more than a bite to eat, but then a clock dial's worth of sleep. I'm wrung out. Aren't you?"

She looked away. "Not yet. Too tense." With a gulp, she made herself confront him. "Where did you go? You just told me to wait, immediately after we got here, and left."

"I guess I did. Sorry. Wasn't thinking. It seemed obvious."

"I thought I was being punished."

He shook his head more vigorously than his words would have suggested. "Good Lord, no. In fact, I'd a vague notion of sparing you a discussion. What I did was skip back to Öland, after dark on . . . that day. The kids were gone and nobody else was around, as I'd hoped. I lifted the corpses one after another, took them well out to sea, and dumped them. Not a fun job. No reason for you to be in on it."

She stared. "Why?"

"Isn't that obvious either?" he snapped. "Think. Same reason I shot the swine that you didn't get around to. Minimize impact on local people, because we've got too flinking many variables as is. I daresay they'll believe Edh and Heidhin, more or less, but they live in a world of gods and trolls and magic anyway. Material evidence or independent witnesses would hit them a lot harder than a doubtless incoherent story."

"I see." She twisted her hands together. "I am being quite stupid and unprofessional, am I not? I wasn't trained for this kind of mission, but that is no excuse. I am very sorry."

"Well, you caught me by surprise," he growled. "When you skited off into action, I was dumbfounded for a second. And then what could I do? Not mess around with causality anymore, for certain, nor risk Heidhin seeing my face, to recognize it in Colonia this year. Duck back uptime, get a different disguise from the one I used on the beach, and return to the same minute? No, it wouldn't do for mortals to see the gods quarreling; that'd confuse things worse yet. I could only play along with you."

"I *am* sorry," she said desperately. "I couldn't help myself. There was Edh, Veleda whom I saw among the Langobardi—no woman ever impressed me more—I *knew* her—but this was a young girl, and those animals—"

"Yeah. Berserk rage, followed by overwhelming sympathy."

Floris straightened. Fists doubled, she gazed squarely at Everard and said, "I am explaining, not making excuses. I will take whatever penalty the Patrol gives me, without complaint."

He stood a few heartbeats unspeaking before he made a crooked smile and answered, "There won't be any if you carry on honestly and competently. Which I'm sure you will. As an Unattached agent on this case, I can make summary judgments. You are hereby pardoned."

She blinked hard, rubbed wrist over eyes, and said unevenly, "Sir, you are too kind. Because we have worked together—"

"Hey, give me credit," he protested. "Yes, you've been a grand companion, but I wouldn't let that influence me . . . much. What counts is that you've proved yourself a crack operative, which the outfit is always short of. More important still, this hasn't actually been your fault."

Bemusement: "What? I allowed my emotions to take me over—"

"Under the circumstances, that isn't exactly to your discredit. I'm not at all sure what I'd've done myself, though maybe sneakier, and I'm not a woman. It didn't bother me killing those vermin. I didn't enjoy it, mind you, especially since they hadn't a chance against me, but as long as it had to be done, I'll sleep okay." Everard paused. "You know, in my salad days, before I joined the Patrol, I favored the death penalty for forcible rape, till a lady pointed out to me that then the bastard would have an incentive to murder his victim and no motive not to. My feelings stayed the same. If I remember right, you twentieth-century Dutch, in your civilized, clinical fashion, treat the problem with castration."

"Nevertheless, I—"

"Get off that guilt trip. What are you, some kind of a liberal or something? Let's put sentiment on the shelf and think about the matter from a Patrol point of view. Listen. It seems fairly clear—do you agree?—those were merchant seamen who'd finished whatever business they'd done on Öland, if any, and were bound elsewhere, probably home. They happened to see Edh and Heidhin on that lonely shore and seized an opportunity. That sort of thing is common throughout the ancient world. Maybe they didn't intend to come back, or maybe it'd be to a different tribe—from the air, I got an impression the island's divided—or maybe they figured nobody would know. Whichever, they trapped the kids. If we hadn't interfered, they'd have taken Heidhin off to sell for a slave. Edh too, unless they injured her so badly it was only worthwhile slitting her throat for one last bit of sport. That's what would have happened. An incident like thousands of others, important to nobody but those who suffer, and they soon dead, forgotten, lost forever."

Floris crossed fists over breasts. The waning light glimmered in her eyes. "Instead—"

Everard nodded. "Yeah. Instead, we appeared. We'll want to seek out her home town, a few years after she left it, settle down for a while as visitors, ask discreet questions, get to know her people. Then maybe we'll have some idea of how poor little Edh became terrible Veleda."

Floris grimaced. "I think I do. In a, a general way. I can imagine myself into her. I think she was more intelligent and sensitive than most, yes, devout, if we can say that of a heathen. This dreadful thing came upon her, fear, shame, despair, not simply her body but her spirit crushed under those heaving, thrusting weights; and suddenly the veritable goddess arrived, to slay them and embrace her. From the bottom of hell, up to glory. . . . But afterward, afterward! The defilement, the sense of having been made worthless, it will not ever quite leave a woman, Manse. Worse for her, because in Iron Age Germany the blood, the womb, is sacred to the clan and a wife's adultery is punished by the most brutal death. They would not blame her for what she could not help, I suppose, but she would be contaminated and—and the element of the supernatural would rouse fear, I think, more than reverence. Pagan gods are tricky, often cruel. I wonder if Edh and Heidhin dared say much. Perhaps they said nothing; and that would itself make a tearing conflict in them."

Everard wished for his pipe but didn't believe he should go to his hopper's carrier box for it. Floris had become too vulnerable. *She never called me by my first name before, as careful as we've been to avoid entanglements. I doubt she's aware she did.* "You're probably right," he agreed. "At the same time, there the supernatural occurrence was. It had left them alive and free. If her body was degraded, her soul couldn't really be. Somehow, she was worthy of the goddess. It must be because she had a destiny. she was chosen for something enormous. Only what? Well, with Heidhin talking to her, over and over, full of male revengefulness— In terms of her culture, it would make sense. She was appointed to bring about the destruction of Rome."

"She could accomplish nothing on her backwater island," Floris finished. "Nor could she any longer fit into its life. She would wander west, confident of the goddess's protection. Heidhin went with her. Between them they scraped together enough goods to buy passage across the sea. What they saw and heard of Roman doings as they traveled fueled their hatred, their sense of her mission. But I think, in spite of everything, and rare though it is in their society, I think he loved her."

"I suspect he does yet. Remarkable, when it's pretty plain she never let him into her bed."

"Understandable." Floris sighed. "For her, after that experience—and he, if nothing else, he would not force himself on a vessel of the goddess. I heard he has a wife and children among the Bructeri."

"Uh-huh. Well, what we've found is the irony that our investigation of a disturbance to the plenum is what brought it about. To be quite frank, that sort of nexus is by no means unprecedented. Another reason for not condemning you, Janne. Often a causal loop has a powerful and subtle force to it. What we've got to do is prevent it from developing into a causal vortex. We have to forestall the events that would lead to Tacitus Two, while not unduly perturbing those that are described in Tacitus One."

"How?" she asked despairingly. "Dare we meddle more? Should we not appeal for help from . . . the Danellians?"

Everard smiled the least bit. "M-m, the situation doesn't look that bad to me. We're expected to handle everything we can, you know, economizing on lifetime of other agents. First, as I remarked, it seems wise to spend a while on Öland, researching background. Then we'll return to this year, the Batavi, the Romans, and—well, I have some preliminary thoughts, but I want to discuss them with you in depth, and you'll be vital to whatever we do."

"I will try."

They stood silent. The air grew colder. Night rose up the hillside. Sunset colors smoldered to gray. Above them kindled the evening star.

Everard heard a ragged breath. Through the dusk, he saw Floris shudder and hug herself. "Janne, what's the matter?" he asked, already guessing.

She looked out over the darkness. "All this death and pain, loss and grief."

"The norm of history."

"I know, I know, but— And I thought living among the Frisii had hardened me, but today, in this today of mine, I killed men, and, and *I* will not sleep soundly—"

He stepped close, laid hands on shoulders, murmured. She spun about to throw her arms around him. What could he do but the same? When she raised her face to his, what could he do but kiss her?

She responded wildly. Her lips tasted salt. "Oh, Manse, yes, yes, please, don't you yourself need to forget for this night?"

16

Sleet hissed, blown out of unseen heaven across a land that rain had already half drowned. Vision soon lost itself; flat acres, withered grass, leafless trees tossing in the wind, the burnt-out remnant of a house, dissolved in a noontide murk. As dank as the chill was, clothing gave little defense. The north wind smelled of the swamps over which it had roared, of the sea beyond, and of winter striding down from the Pole.

Everard hunched in the saddle, cloak drawn tight. Water dripped from the hood past his face. The horse's hoofs went *plop-squelp*, *plop-squelp* in pastern-deep mud. Yet this was the entryway through an estate to a manor house.

The building hove in view before him. In modified Mediterranean style, tile-roofed, stuccoed, it had been raised by Burhmund when he was Civilis, ally and officer of Rome. His wife was its matron, his children filled it with laughter. Now it served as headquarters for Petillius Cerialis.

Two sentries stood in the portico. Like those at the gate, they challenged the Patrolman when he drew rein at the foot of the stairs. "I am Everardus the Goth," he told them. "The general is expecting me."

One soldier gave his companion an inquiring glance. The latter nodded. "I've been instructed," he said. "In fact, I escorted the preliminary courier." Was he snatching at any scrap of pride, of importance? He snuffled and sneezed. Probably the first man was a last-minute replacement for a ranker who lay fevered, teeth chattering, in sick bay. Although they appeared to be of Gallic breed, both these were pretty wretched themselves. Their metal was tarnished, their kilts hung sodden, gooseflesh studded their arms, sunken cheeks spoke of short rations.

"Pass," the second legionary said. "We'll call a groom to stable your mount."

Everard entered a gloomy atrium, where a slave took his cloak and knife.

Several men sitting slumped, staff with nothing to do, gave him stares in which, perhaps, a sudden feeble hope flickered. An aide came to conduct the visitor to a room in the south wing. He knocked on the door, heard a gruff "Open," obeyed, and announced: "Sir, the German delegate is here."

"Send him in," rumbled the voice. "Leave us alone but stand outside, just in case."

Everard entered. The door shut behind him. Scant light seeped through a leaded window. Candles stood around in holders. Tallow, not wax, they smoked and stank. Shadows bulked in corners and slid across a table strewn with papyrus dispatches. Otherwise there were a couple of stools and a chest that might hold changes of clothing. An infantry sword and its sheath hung side by side on a wall. A charcoal brazier had warmed the air but made it stuffy.

Cerialis sat behind the table. He wore merely a tunic and sandals: a burly man with a hard square face whose clean-shavenness revealed deep furrows. His eyes raked the newcomer. "You are Everardus the Goth, eh?" he greeted. "The go-between said you speak Latin. You'd better."

"I do." *This'll be tricky,* the Patrolman thought. *It wouldn't be in character for me to grovel, but he might decide I'm arrogant and he's not going to take any lip from any Jupiter-damned native. His nerves must be worn thin, like everybody else's.* "The general is both kind and wise to receive me."

"Well, frankly, by now I'd listen to a Christian, if he claimed he'd something to offer. If it turned out he didn't, I could at least have the pleasure of crucifying him."

Everard feigned puzzlement. "A Jew sect," Cerialis grunted. "Heard about the Jews? Another pack of mutinous ingrates. But you, your tribe's way to the east. Why in Tartarus are you running errands hereabouts?"

"I thought that was explained to the general. I am no enemy of yours, nor of Civilis either. I've spent time in the Empire as well as in different parts of Germany. I got to know Civilis a bit, and lesser chieftains a bit more. They trust me to speak straightforwardly for them, because of my being an outsider whom you have nothing against. And because of knowing Roman ways somewhat, I can bring them your words clear, not scrambled. As for myself, I'm a trader who'd like to do business with this region. I stand to benefit from peace and their thankfulness."

Persuading them had been more complicated than that, but not very much more. The rebels were in fact weary and discouraged. The Goth might be granted personal access to the Imperial commander, where he might do some good and could scarcely do worse harm than already went on. After heralds had carried the request, the ease with which arrangements were made surprised the Germans. Everard had awaited it. He knew better than they, from Tacitus and from aerial observation, how badly off the Romans were too.

"I do know!" Cerialis snapped. "Except that they didn't mention what was in it for you. Very well, we'll talk. I warn you, get that long-winded again and I'll boot you out myself. Sit down. No, pour us wine first. It makes this frog-marsh country a hair less horrible."

Everard filled two silver goblets from a graceful glass decanter. The seat he took was likewise handsome, and the drink tasted well, if a tad too sweet for his preferences. This must all have belonged to Civilis. To civilization.

I'll never be fond of the Romans, but they do bring other things with them than slave traders, tax farmers, and sadistic games. Peace, prosperity, a widened world—those don't last, but when the tide ebbs it leaves behind, scattered through the wreckage, books, technologies, faiths, ideas, memories of what once was, stuff for later generations to salvage and treasure and build with again. And among the memories is that there was, for a while, a life not given over entirely to naked survival.

"So the Germans are ready to surrender, are they?" Cerialis prompted.

"I beg the general's pardon if we gave the wrong impression. We are not masters of the Latin language."

Cerialis thumped the table. "I told you, stop pussyfooting or get out! You're royal at home, descended from Mercury. Got to be, the way you bear yourself. And I'm the emperor's kinsman, but he and I are plain soldiers who've pulled heavy duty. We two can be blunt with each other, here while we're alone."

Everard ventured a grin. "As you wish, sir. I daresay you did not really misunderstand us. Then why don't *you* come to the point? The chieftains who sent me do not propose to go under the yoke or chained in a triumph. But they'd like an end to this war."

"What gall have they got, to demand terms? What have they left to fight with? We hardly even see a hostile any more. Civilis's last attempt worth mentioning was a naval demonstration in fall. I wasn't worried, I was astonished that he bothered. Nothing came of it and he withdrew across the Rhine. Since then we've ravaged his homeland."

"I've seen, including the fact that you spared his properties."

Cerialis fired off a laugh. "Of course. Drive a wedge between him and the rest. Make 'em wonder why they should bleed and die for his benefit. I know they're pretty well fed up. You came on behalf of a clutch of tribal chiefs, not him."

That's true, and you're shrewd, mister. "Communication is slow. Besides, we Germans are used to acting independently. It does not mean that they sent me to betray him."

Cerialis swallowed from his cup, slammed it down, and said, "All right, let's hear. What am I offered?"

"Peace, I told you," Everard declared. "Can you afford to refuse? You're in as much trouble as they are. You claim you don't see enemy fighters any more. That's because you aren't advancing any farther. You're bogged down in a land picked bare, every road a quagmire, your troops cold, wet, hungry, sickening, miserable. Your supply problems are hideous, and it won't get better till the state has recovered from the civil war, which will take longer than you can wait." *I wish I could quote that great line of Steinbeck's, about the flies having conquered the flypaper.* "Meanwhile Burhmund, Civilis, is recruiting in Germany. You could lose, Cerialis, the way Varus lost in the Teutoburg Forest, with the same long-range consequences. Better come to terms while you've got the chance. There, was that plain-spoken enough?"

The Roman had flushed and knotted his hands. "It was insolent. We'll not reward rebellion. We cannot."

Everard softened his tone. "It seems to . . . those whose mouth I'm being . . . that you've punished it adequately. If the Batavi and their allies return to their allegiance and to quietness beyond the river, haven't you reached your objective? What they ask in exchange is no more than they owe to their people to get. No decimation, no enslavements, no captives for the triumph or the arena. Instead, amnesty for all, including Civilis. Restoration of tribal lands, where these are occupied. Correction of the abuses that brought the revolt on in the first place. This means, mostly, reasonable tribute, local autonomy, access to trade, and an end to conscription. Given that, you'll once again get as many volunteers enlisting as Rome can use."

"That's no small set of demands," Cerialis said. "It goes beyond my authority."

Ah, he's willing to consider it. A thrill coursed through Everard. He leaned forward. "General, you're of Vespasian's house, Vespasian for whom Civilis fought too. The emperor will listen to you. Everybody says he's a hardheaded man who's interested in making things work, not in hollow glory. The Senate will . . . listen to the emperor. You can bring this treaty about, general, if you want to, if you'll make the effort. You can be remembered not as a Varus but as a Germanicus."

Cerialis peered slit-eyed across the table. "You talk almighty knowing for a barbarian," he said.

"I've been around, sir," Everard answered.

Oh, I have, I have, around the whole globe, up and down the centuries. Most recently at the wellspring of your sorest woes, Cerialis.

How long ago it already felt, that idyll on Ölanc, no, on the Eyn. Twenty-five years past by the calendar. Hlavagast and Viduhada and most of those who had been so hospitable were likeliest dead by now, bones in the earth and names on tongues wearing down toward oblivion. Gone with them were the pain and puzzlement left behind by children whom strangeness had called away. But for Everard it was scarcely a month since he and Floris bade farewell to Laikian. Man and wife, wanderers from the far South who had gotten passage over the sea for themselves and their horses, and would like to pitch their tent for a while close to this friendly thorp. . . . It was extraordinary, therefore enchanting; it caused people to talk more freely than ever before in their lives; but there were also the hours alone, in the tent or out on the summery heath. . . . Afterward the Patrol agents got floggingly busy.

"And I have my connections," Everard said.

The histories, the data files, the great coordinating computers, the experts of the Time Patrol. The knowledge that this *is the proper configuration of a plenum that has powerful negative feedback. We've identified the random factor that could bring on an avalanching change; what we must do is damp it.*

"Hm," Cerialis said. "I'll want a fuller account." He cleared his throat. "Later. Today we'll stick to business. I do want my men out of the mud."

I find that I kind of like this guy. In many ways he reminds me of George Patton. Yes, we can dicker.

Cerialis weighed his words. "Tell your lordlings this, and have them pass it on to Civilis. I see one big stumbling block. You speak of the Germans beyond the Rhine. I can't concede what he wants and pull the legions out while they are faunching for somebody to whistle them up all over again."

"He would not, I assure you," Everard said. "Under the conditions proposed, he'd have won what he was fighting for, or at least a decent compromise. Who else might start a new war?"

Cerialis's mouth tightened. "Veleda."

"The sibyl among the Bructeri?"

"The witch. D'you know, I've thought about a strike into that country just to seize her. But she'd vanish into the woods."

"And if you did somehow succeed, it'd be like snatching a hornets' nest."

Cerialis nodded. "Every crazy tribesman from the Rhine to the Suebian Sea up in arms." He meant the Baltic, and he was right. "But it might well be worse, for my grandchildren if not me, to let her go on spewing her venom amongst them." He sighed. "Except for that, the furor could die down. But as is—"

"I think," said Everard weightily, "if Civilis and his allies are promised honorable terms, I think we can get her to call for peace."

Cerialis goggled. "You mean that?"

"Try it," Everard said. "Negotiate with her as well as with the male leaders. I can carry word between you."

Cerialis shook his head. "We couldn't leave her running loose. Too dangerous. We'd have to keep an eye on her."

"But not a hand."

Cerialis blinked, then chuckled. "Ha! I see what you mean. You've got a gift of gab, Everardus. True, if ever we arrested her or anything like that, we'd likely get a whole new rebellion. But what if she provoked it? How can we know she'll behave herself?"

"She will, once she's reconciled with Rome."

"What's that worth? I know barbarians. Flighty as geese." Evidently it didn't occur to the general that he might offend the emissary, unless he didn't care. "From what I've gathered, that's a war goddess she serves. What if Veleda takes it into her head that this Bellona's hollering for blood once more? We could have another Boadicea on our hands."

A sore point with you, huh? Everard sipped of his wine. The sweetness glowed down his throat, invoking summers and southlands against the weather that ramped outside. "Give it a try," he said. "What can you lose by exchanging messages with her? I think a settlement that everybody can live with is possible."

Whether in superstition or in metaphor, Cerialis replied, surprisingly quietly, "That will depend on the goddess, won't it?"

17

The early sunset smoldered above the forest. Boughs were like black bones athwart it. Puddles in field and paddock glowed dull red with it beneath a greenish sky as cold as the wind that eddied whimpering across them. A flight of crows passed. Their hoarse cries sounded for a while after the dusk had swallowed them up.

A hind carrying hay between stack and house shivered, not only because of the weather, when he saw Wael-Edh go by. She was not unkindly, in her stark way, but she was in league with the Powers, and now she walked from the halidom. What there had she heard and said? For months no man had fared hither to speak with her, as often erstwhile. By day she paced her grounds or sat under a tree and brooded, alone. It was surely at her own behest—but why? This was a grim time, even for the Bructeri. Too many of their men had come home from Batavian or Frisian lands with tales of mishap or woe, or had not come home at all. Could the gods be turning from their spaewife? The hind muttered a luck-spell and hastened his steps.

Her tower loomed dark ahead of the woman. The warrior on watch dipped his spear to her. She nodded and opened the door. In the room beyond, a pair of thralls sat cross-legged at a low hearthfire, palms held close. Smoke drifted around bitter until it found its outlet. Their breath mingled with it, wan in the light of two lamps. They scrambled to their feet. "Does my lady want food or drink?" the man asked.

Wael-Edh shook her head. "I will sleep," she answered.

"We will guard your dreaming well," the girl said. It was needless, nobody save Heidhin would dare climb the ladder unbidden, but she was new here. She gave her mistress one of the lamps and Wael-Edh went up.

A ghost of daylight lingered in a window covered with thin-scraped gut, and the flame burned yellow. Nonetheless the loft-room was already heavy with gloom, wherein her things crouched like trolls underground. Not yet wishing for her shut-bed, she put the lamp on a shelf and sat down on her high three-legged witch-seat, cloak drawn tight. Her gaze sought the shifty shadows.

Air whuffed in her face. The floor groaned beneath a sudden heavy weight. Edh leaped back. The stool clattered to the boards. She gasped.

Soft radiance flowed out of a ball atop the horns of the thing that stood before her. Two saddles were on its back, it was the bull of Frae, cast in iron, and on it rode the goddess who had claimed it from him.

"Niaerdh, oh, Niaerdh—"

Janne Floris got off the timecycle and stood as stately as might be. Last time, caught unawares, she had been garbed like any Germanic woman of the Iron Age. It hadn't mattered then, but no doubt memory made her more impressive, and for this visit she had outfitted herself with care. Her gown draped lustrous white, jewels glinted in the belt, a silver pectoral had the pattern of a fishnet, and her hair hung in twin amber-hued braids below a diadem.

"Fear not," she said. The tongue she used was the dialect of Edh's girlhood. "Speak low. I have returned to you as I promised."

Edh straightened, pressed hands to breasts, swallowed once or twice. Her eyes stood huge in the thin, strong-boned countenance. The hood had fallen back and light picked out the gray that was stealing across her head. For a few seconds she only breathed. Then, amazingly fast, a sort of calm flowed into her, an acceptance more stoic than exalted but altogether willing.

"Ever I knew you would," she said. "I am ready to go." A whisper: "How very ready."

"Go?" asked Floris.

"Down hell-road. You will bring me to darkness and peace." Anxiety fluttered. "Will you not?"

Floris tautened. "Ach, what I want of you is harder than death."

Edh was silent a little before she replied, "As you will. I am no stranger to pain."

"I would not hurt you!" Floris blurted. She regained due gravity. "You have served me for long years."

Edh nodded. "Since you gave me back my life."

Floris could not stifle a sigh. "A life lamed and twisted, I fear."

Emotion quickened. "You did not save me for nothing, I know. It was for all the others, wasn't it? All the women ravished, men slain, children bereft, free folk laid in bonds. I was to call their avenging down upon Rome. *Was I not?*"

"You are no longer sure?"

Tears glinted on lashes. "If I was wrong, Niaerdh, why did you let me go on?"

"You were not wrong. But child, hearken." Floris held out her hands. Like a small girl in truth, Edh took them. Hers were cold and faintly atremble. Floris drew breath. The majestic words rolled forth.

"To every thing there is a season, and a time to every purpose under heaven: A time to be born, and a time to die; a time to plant, and a time to pluck up that which is planted; a time to kill, and a time to heal; a time to break down, and a time to build up; a time to weep, and a time to laugh; a time to mourn, and a time to dance; a time to cast away stones, and a time to gather stones together; a time to embrace, and a time to refrain from embracing; a time to get, and a time to lose; a time to keep, and a time to cast away; a time to rend, and a time to sew; a time to keep silence, and a time to speak; a time to love, and a time to hate; a time of war, and a time of peace."

Awe looked at her. "I hear you, goddess."

"It is olden wisdom, Edh. Hear onward. You have wrought well, you have sown for me as I would have you. But your work is not yet done. Now gather in the harvest."

"How?"

"Thanks to the will that you aroused in them, the westfolk have fought for their rights, until at last the Romans would fain yield them back what was robbed. But they, the Romans, still fear Veleda. As long as you might cry again for their downfall, they dare not withdraw their hosts. It is time that you, in my name, call for peace."

Rapture blazed. "They will go away then? We shall be rid of them?"

"No. They will take their tribute and have their warders among the tribes as erstwhile." In haste: "But they will be righteous; and dwellers on this side of the Rhine will also gain by the trade and the lawfulness."

Edh blinked, shook her head violently, crooked fingers into claws at her sides. "No real freedom? No revenge? Goddess, I cannot—"

"This is my will," Floris commanded. "Obey." Once more she gentled her voice. "And for you, child, there shall be reward, a new home, a place of calm and comfort, where you shall tend my shrine, that will henceforward be the halidom of peace."

"No," Edh stammered. "You, you must be aware—I have sworn—"

"Tell me!" Floris exclaimed. After an instant: "I . . . wish you to make yourself clear to yourself."

The shaking, straining figure before her gained back its balance. Edh had long coped with menaces and horrors. She could overcome bewilderment. Briefly, she sounded almost wistful. "I wonder if I ever have been. . . ." She stiffened herself. "Heidhin and I, he got me to swear I would never make peace while he lives and Romans remain in German lands. We mingled our blood in the grove before the gods. Were you elsewhere?"

Floris scowled. "He had no right."

"He—invoked the Anses—"

Floris donned haughtiness. "I will deal with the Anses. You are free of that oath."

"Heidhin would never— He has been faithful through all these years," Edh faltered. "Would you have me cast him out like a dog? For *he* will never end war against the Romans, whatever other men or you gods yourselves may do."

"Tell him I gave you my bidding."

"I know not, I know not!" ripped from Edh's throat. She sank to the floor and buried her face on the knees she hugged. Her shoulders quivered.

Floris glanced aloft. Roof beams and rafters were lost in blackness. Light had left the window and cold crept inward. The wind hooted.

"We have a crisis, I fear," she subvocalized. "Loyalty is the highest morality these people know. I'm not certain Edh can bring herself to break that pledge. Or if she does, she may be shattered."

"Which'd leave her incapable," sounded Everard's English in her head, "and we've got to have her authority to make this deal work. Besides, poor tortured woman—"

"We must make Heidhin release her from the vow. I hope he will heed me. Where is he?"

"I was just checking on that. He's at home." They had bugged it some time ago. "M-m, it happens Burhmund is with him, riding circuit among the trans-Rhine chiefs, you know. I'll find another day for you to approach him."

"No, wait. This may be a stroke of luck." *Or the world lines tightening as they seek to regain their proper configuration?* "Since Burhmund is trying to rouse the tribes to a new effort—"

"We'd better not pull any epiphanies on him. No telling how he'd react."

"Of course not. I mean, I won't appear directly to him. But if he sees Heidhin the implacable suddenly converted—"

"Well . . . okay. It's dicey whatever we do, so I'll trust your judgment, Janne."

"Hsh!"

Edh looked up. Tears streaked her cheekbones, but she had fought the weeping off. "What can I do?" she asked colorlessly.

Floris moved to stand above her, bent, again offered her hands. She helped the other rise, clasped arms about her, stood thus for a minute giving what warmth her body was able. Stepping back, she said: "Yours is a clean soul, Edh. You need not betray your friend. We will go together and speak with him. Then he ought to understand."

Wonder and dread became one. "We twain?"

"Is that wise?" Everard questioned. "M-m, yeah, I suppose having her along will reinforce you."

"Love may be as strong as religion, Manse," Floris said.

To Edh: "Come, mount my steed behind me. Hold fast to my waist."

"The holy bull," Edh breathed. "Or the hell horse?"

"No," Floris said. "I told you, yours is a harder road than the way under."

18

Fire sprang and crackled in a trench down the middle of Heidhin's house. Smoke did not rise well toward the louvers, but hazed and made stinging an air that the flames hardly warmed. Their red light wrestled with darknesses among the pillars and beams. It wavered across the men on the benches and the women who brought them drink. Most sat wordless. Although Heidhin's home was as grand as many a royal hall, it had commonly known less mirth than a crofter's hut. This eventide there was none. Outside, wind shrilled through a deepening dusk.

"Naught can come of it save treachery," Heidhin snarled.

Seated beside him, Burhmund slowly shook his grizzled head. The fire threw a bloodshot shimmer over the milkiness of his blind eye. "I know not," he answered. "Yon Everard is an odd one. He may be able to bring something about."

"The best he, or anybody, could bear back to us is a refusal. Any offer would be meant for our ruin. You should never have let him go."

"How could I have stopped him? It was the lords of the tribes whom he spoke with, and they who sent him off. I told you how I did not hear till lately, when I was already on this quest."

Heidhin's lips writhed. "They dared!"

"They had the right." Burhmund's tone fell dull to the ground. "They do not forswear themselves merely by talk with the foe. I think, now, I would not have tried to forbid them, had I been on hand. They are sick of this war. Maybe Everard can find them a hope. I too am death-weary."

"I thought better of you," fleered Heidhin.

Burhmund showed no anger; but then, Wael-Edh's oath-brother stood well-nigh as high as he did. "Easy for you," said the Batavian patiently. "Your house has not been riven. My sister's son fell in battle against me. My wife and another sister lie hostage in Colonia; I know not whether they yet live. My homeland is laid waste." He stared down into his drinking horn. "Are the gods done with me?"

Heidhin sat spear-straight. "Only if you yield," he said. "I never will."

A knock sounded on the door. The man seated nearest took an ax and went to open it. Wind gusted in; the flames jumped and streamed sparks. Murk rimmed the shaped that trod through.

Heidhin leaped up. "Edh!" he cried, and started toward her.

"Lady," Burhmund whispered. A mumble went around the hall. Men got to their feet.

Unhooded, she moved a ways alongside the fire trench. They saw she was stiff and pale, and that her gaze went beyond them. "How, how came you here?" Heidhin stumbled. The sight of him, the relentless, thus shaken, daunted every heart. "Why?"

She halted. "I must speak with you alone," she said. Fate rang in her low voice. "Follow me. None else."

"But—you—what—"

"Follow me, Heidhin. Mighty tidings are come. You others, abide them." Wael-Edh turned and strode back out.

Like a sleepwalker, Heidhin went after her. At the entry, his hand of itself plucked a spear from the weapons left leaning against the wall. The two of them passed into the dark. Shuddering, a man crept to close the door.

"No, bar it not," Burhmund told him. "We will wait here as she bade till she returns or morning does."

The first stars winked faint overhead. Buildings crouched shapeless. Edh led the way from the yard to the open ground beyond. Sere grass and wind-ruffled puddles faded off into blindness. Near the edge of sight stood a great oak at which Heidhin offered to the Anses. From behind it spilled a steady white light. Heidhin jarred to a stop. He made a noise in his gullet.

"You must be brave tonight," Edh said. "Yonder is the goddess."

"Niaerdh . . . she . . . has come back?"

"Yes, to my tower, whence she fetched me hither. Come." Edh went steadily on. Her cloak flapped in the wind, which threw the loosened hair about the head she bore so high. Heidhin gripped his spearshaft hard and trailed her.

Gnarled boughs reached widely, half seen by the glow. The wind clicked their twigs together. Dead leaves squelched wet underfoot. The two came around the bole and saw her who stood next to a bull or a horse cast in steel.

"Goddess," Heidhin moaned. He dropped to a knee and bent his neck. But when he rose again, he held firm. If his spear shook, it was with the same wild gladness that burst from his lips. "Will you now lead us to the last fight?"

Floris's look searched over him. He stood lean and dark, somberly clad, face etched and locks streaked by the hunter years, the iron of his weapon asheen above them. Her lamp cast his shadow across Edh. "No," said Floris. "The time for war is past."

Breath rattled between his jaws. "The Romans are dead? You slew them all for us?"

Edh flinched.

"They live," Floris said, "as your folk shall live. Too many have died in every tribe, theirs also. They will make peace."

Heidhin's left hand joined his right, clutching the spearshaft. "I never will," he rasped. "The goddess heard my vow I made at the shore. When they go, I will dog their heels, I will harry them by day and raid them by night— Shall I give you my kills, Niaerdh?"

"The Romans are not going. They will remain. But they will restore to the folk their rights. Let that suffice."

Heidhin shook his head as if smitten. He gaped from woman to woman for a whole minute before he whispered, "Goddess, Edh, do you both betray them? I will not believe it."

He seemed unaware that Edh reached toward him. The wind ran between them. Her tone pleaded. "The Batavi and the rest, they are no tribe of ours. We have done enough for them."

"I tell you, the terms will be honorable," Floris said. "Your work is ended. You have won what will content Burhmund himself. But Veleda must make known that this is what the gods want and men should lay down their arms."

"I—you—We swore, Edh." Heidhin sounded puzzled. "Never would you make peace while the Romans held on and I lived. We swore to it. We mingled our blood in the earth."

"You will set her free of that vow," Floris commanded, "as I already have done."

"I cannot. I *will* not." Raw with pain, the words suddenly lashed at Edh. "Have you forgotten how they made you their slut? Do you no longer care for your honor?"

She fell to her knees. Her hands fended. Her mouth stretched wide. "No," she keened, "don't, no, no."

Floris moved toward the man. In the night above, Everard aimed a stun pistol. "Have done," she said. "Are you a wolf, to rip her whom you love?"

Heidhin flung an arm wide, baring his breast to her. "Love, hate—I am a man. I swore to the Anses."

"Do as you like," Floris said, "but spare my Edh. Remember you owe me your life."

Heidhin slumped. Leaning on his spear, Edh huddled at his feet, he shadowed her while the wind blew around them and the tree creaked like a gallows rope.

All at once he laughed, squared his shoulders, and looked straight into Floris' eyes. "You speak truth, goddess," he said. "Yes, I will let go."

He lowered the spear, gripped it with hands below the head, and stabbed the point into his throat. In a single swording motion he slashed the edge from side to side.

Edh's shriek overrode Floris's. Heidhin went down in a heap. Blood spouted, blackly aglisten. He kicked and clawed at the grass, blind reflex.

"Stop!" Everard rapped. "Don't try to save him. This damned warrior culture—it's his only way out."

Floris didn't trouble to subvocalize. A goddess might well use an unknown tongue to sing the soul on its way. "But the horror of it—"

"Yeah. Think, though, think about everybody who will not die, if we work this right."

"Can we, now? What will Burhmund think?"

"Let him wonder. Tell Edh not to answer any questions about it. An apparition of her, when she'd been miles away—the man who wanted no end to violence, dead by it—Veleda speaking for peace— The mystery will lend force, though I suppose people will draw the obvious conclusions, which'll be a big help."

Heidhin lay still. He looked shrunken. Blood pooled around him and soaked into the ground.

"It is Edh we must help first," Floris said.

She went to the other woman, who had risen and stood numbed. Blood had splashed onto Edh's cloak and gown. Heedless of it, Floris laid arms around her.

"You are free," Floris murmured. "He bought your freedom with his life. Cherish it."

"Yes," Edh said. She stared into the dark.

"Now you may cry peace over the land. You shall."

"Yes."

Floris warmed her for a while and a while.

"Tell me how," Edh said. "Tell me what to say. The world has gone empty."

"Oh, my child," Floris breathed into the graying tresses. "Be of good heart. I have promised you a new home, a new hope. Would you like to hear about it? It is an island, low and green, open to the sea."

Life stirred a little in the answer. "Thank you. You are kind. I will do my best . . . in your name."

"Now come," Floris said. "I will bear you back to your tower. Sleep. When you have slept your fill, send forth that you would fain speak to the kings and chiefs. When they are gathered before you, give them the word of peace."

19

New-fallen snow covered ash heaps that had been homesteads. Where junipers had caught some of it in their deep green, it lay like whiteness's self. Low to the south, the sun cast their shadows across it, blue as heaven. Thin ice on the river had thawed with morning but still crusted dried reeds along the banks, while bits of it drifted in midstream, slowly northward. A gloom on the eastern horizon marked the edge of wilderness.

Burhmund and his men rode west. Hoofs struck muffled on hard ground beneath, baring the ruts of a road. Breath steamed from nostrils and made rime in beards. Metal gleamed frosty. The riders spoke seldom. Shaggy in wadmal and fur, they rode from the forest to the river.

Ahead of them lifted the stump of a wooden bridge. Piers jutted naked out of the water beyond. On the opposite shore stood the other fragment. Workers who demolished the middle had rejoined the legionaries ranked on that side. They were few, like the Germans. Their armor gave back the light but kilts, cloaks, legwear, all cloth hung worn and dirty. The plumes of officers' helmets were faded.

Burhmund drew rein, got down, and stepped onto the bridge. His boots thudded hollow over the planks. He saw that Cerialis already stood in place. That was a friendly gesture, when it was Burhmund who requested a parley—though it did not mean much, because the understanding had been clear that they would hold one.

At the end of his section, Burhmund stopped. The two thick-set men regarded one another across a dozen feet of winter air. The river clucked below them on its way to the sea.

The Roman unfolded his arms and lifted his right hand. "Hail, Civilis," he greeted. Accustomed to addressing troops, he easily cast his voice the needful distance.

"Hail, Cerialis," Burhmund responded in like manner.

"You would discuss terms," said Cerialis. "That is difficult to do with a traitor."

His tone was matter-of-fact, his words an opening. Burhmund took it. "But I am no traitor," he replied gravely, in Latin. He pointed out that this was no legate of Vitellius with whom he met; Cerialis was Vespasian's. Burhmund the Batavian, Claudius Civilis, went on to number the services he had rendered over the years to Rome and its new emperor.

III

Gutherius was the name of a hunter who often went hunting in the wildwood, for he was poor and his acres meager. One blustery day in autumn he set forth, armed with bow and spear. He did not really expect to take any big game, which had grown scarce and wary. He would set snares for squirrel and hare, then leave them overnight while he pushed on in hopes of knocking down a capercaillie or the like. However, should he come on anything better, he would be ready.

His path took him around a bay. Surf dashed wildly over the reefs outside and whitecaps chopped on the half-sheltered water, although the tide was in ebb. An old woman walked the sand, stooped low, searching for whatever she might find, mussels laid bare or a fish dead but not too rotten. Toothless, fingers knotty and weak, she moved as if every step hurt. Her rags fluttered in the bitter wind.

"Good day, granny," said Gutherius. "How goes it?"

"Not at all," said the crone. "If nothing turns up for me to eat, I fear I cannot creep home."

"Well, now, that would be a pity," said Gutherius. From his pouch he took the bread and cheese he bore along. "I will give you half of this."

"You have a warm heart," she quavered.

"I remember my mother," he said, "and it honors Nehalennia."

"Could you spare me the whole of that?" she asked. "You are young and strong."

"No, I must keep that strength if I am to feed my wife and children," said Gutherius. "Take what I give and be grateful."

"I am that," said the old woman. "You shall have reward. But because you withheld some of it, first you shall have woe."

"Be still!" cried Gutherius. He hurried onward to get away from the ill-omened words.

Reaching the forest, he set off on trails he knew. Suddenly from the brush bounded a stag. It was a mighty beast, well-nigh big as an elk, and snowy white. Its antlers spread like an ancient oak. "Halloo!" shouted Gutherius. He flung his spear but missed. The stag did not leap in flight. It poised there ahead of him, a dimness against the shadows. He strung bow, nocked arrow, and shot. At the thrum of the string, the animal fled. Yet it went no faster than a man could run, and Gutherius did not see his arrow anywhere. He thought maybe it had struck and he could chase the wounded quarry down. Recovering his spear, he dashed in pursuit.

On and on that hunt went, ever deeper into the wilderness. Always the white stag glimmered just in sight. Somehow Gutherius never tired, the breath never failed him, he ran without cease. He was drunk with running, beyond himself, everything forgotten save the chase.

The sun sank. Twilight welled up. As light failed, the stag put on a burst of speed and vanished. Wind piped among the trees. Gutherius came to a halt, overwhelmed by weariness, hunger, and thirst. He saw that he was lost. "Did yon hag truly curse me?" he wondered. Fear blew through him, colder than the oncoming night. He rolled in the blanket he carried and lay wakeful the whole of the dark hours.

All the next day he blundered about, finding nothing he recognized. Indeed this was an eldritch part of the forest. No beast scuttered in its undergrowth, no bird called from its depths, there was only the wind soughing in the crowns and tearing dead leaves loose. No nuts or berries grew, nor even mushrooms, only moss on fallen logs and misshapen stones. Cloud veiled the sun, by which he might have taken bearings. Wildly he ranged.

Then at dusk he found a spring. He cast himself on his belly to quench his withering thirst. This gave him back his wits, and he looked around him. He had entered a glade, whence he got a sight of the sky, which was clearing. In violet-blue shone the evening star.

"Nehalennia," he prayed, "have mercy. To you I offer what I should have given freely." Thirsty as he was, he had been unable to chew his food. He scattered it under the trees for whatever creatures it might help. By the spring he lay down to sleep.

During the night a great storm roared up. Trees groaned and tossed. Branches torn loose hurtled on the wind. Rain flew like spears. Gutherius groped blind in search of shelter. He bumped into a trunk which he felt was hollow. There he huddled through the night.

Morning broke calm and sunny. Raindrops glittered many-hued on twigs and moss. Wings passed overhead. As Gutherius stretched his stiffened body, a dog stepped out of a brake and approached him. It was no mongrel but a tall gray hunting hound. Joy wakened in the man. "Whose are you?" he asked. "Lead me to your master."

The dog turned and trotted off. Gutherius followed. Presently they came on a game trail and took it. Yet he spied never a sign of humanity. The knowledge grew in him. "You are the hound of Nehalennia," he dared say. "She has bidden you lead me home, or at least to a berry bush or a hazel where I can still my hunger. I thank the goddess."

The dog answered naught, merely padded on. Nothing such as the man hoped for came in sight. Instead, after a while the woods opened. He heard the sea and smelled the salt wind off it. The dog sprang to one side and vanished among the shadows. Gutherius must needs trudge on ahead. Worn though he was, happiness burned in him, for he knew that if he followed the shoreline south, he would reach a fisher village where he had kinfolk.

At the strand he stopped, amazed. A ship lay in the shadows, driven aground by the storm, dismasted and unseaworthy though not wholly wrecked. The crew had survived. They sat about in despair, being foreigners who kenned nothing of this coast.

Gutherius went to them and discovered their plight. By signs he told them he could be their guide. They fed him and left some men on guard while others took rations and accompanied him.

In this wise did Gutherius gain the reward he had been promised: for the ship bore a rich cargo and the procurator ruled that he who saved the crew was entitled to a fair share. Gutherius thought the old woman must have been Nehalennia herself.

Because she is goddess of ships and trade, he invested his gains in a vessel that plied the Britain run. Ever did she enjoy fair weather and a following wind, while the wares she bore commanded high prices. Gutherius became a wealthy man.

Mindful of thanks he owed, he raised an altar to Nehalennia, where after each voyage he made generous offering; and whenever he saw the evening star or the morning star shine forth, he bowed low, for they too are Nehalennia's.

Hers are the trees, the vine, and the fruits thereof. Hers are the sea and the ships that plow it. Hers are the well-being of mortals and peace among them.

20

"I just got your letter," Floris had said on the phone. "Oh, yes, Manse, do come as soon as you can." Everard hadn't wasted time aboard a jet. He stuck his passport in a pocket and hopped directly from the Patrol's New York office to the one in Amsterdam. There he drew some Dutch money and got a cab to her place.

When he entered the apartment and they embraced, her kiss was tender rather than passionate and soon ended. He was unsure whether that surprised him or not, disappointed or relieved. "Welcome, welcome," she breathed in his ear. "It has been too long." Yet the litheness pressed lightly against him and moved quickly back. His pulse began to slow.

"You're looking great as always," he said. True. A brief black gown hugged the tall figure and set off the amber braids. Her sole jewelry was a silver thunderbird pin above her left breast. In his honor?

A small smile curved her mouth. "Thank you, but look closer. I am very tired, very ready for my holiday."

In and around the turquoise eyes he did see hauntedness. *What more has she witnessed since last we said good-bye?* he thought. *What have I been spared?* "I understand. Yeah, better than I like to. You had ten people's work loaded on you. I should have stayed and helped."

She shook her head. "No. I realized it then, and I still do. Once the crisis was resolved, the outfit had much better uses for you, the Unattached agent. You had authority to assign yourself to the remainder of the mission, but a higher claim on your lifespan." Again she smiled. "Old dutiful Manse."

Whereas you, the Specialist who really knows the milieu, must see the job through. With whatever assistance you got from your fellow researchers and from auxiliaries newly trained for the purpose—not much, huh?—you must watch over events; make certain they continued on the Tacitus One course; no doubt intervene, most carefully, now and then, here and there: till at last they were out of the unstable space-time zone and could safely be left to themselves.

Oh, you have earned your holiday, all right.

"How long were you in the field?" he asked.

"From 70 to 95 A.D. Of course, I skipped about, so on my world line it totalled . . . somewhat over a year. You, Manse? What have you been busy with?"

"Frankly, nothing except recuperation," he admitted. "I knew you'd return to this week because of your parents, as well as your public persona, so I went directly to it, allowed us a few days' rest, then wrote you."

Was that fair? I've bounced back. For one thing, I'm less sensitive than you; what happens in history racks me less savagely. For another, you've endured those added months yonder.

It was as if her gaze sought behind his face. "You're sweet." Hastily laughing, she seized his hands. "But why do we stand here? Come, let us be comfortable."

They proceeded to the room of pictures and books. She had set the low table with coffee, canapés, miscellaneous accessories, the Scotch she knew he liked—yes, the very Glenlivet, which he couldn't even recall ever mentioning specifically to her. Side by side they took the sofa. She leaned back and beamed. "Comfort?" she purred. "No, luxury. Once again I am learning to appreciate my birth era."

Is she really relaxing, or is that a pretense? I sure can't. Everard sat on the edge of his cushion. He poured coffee for them both and a neat whisky for himself. When he cast her a glance, she gestured no and took her cup. "This is early for me," she said.

"Hey, I wasn't proposing to tie one on," he assured her. "We'll take it easy, and talk, and go out to dinner, I hope. How about that delightful little Caribbean place? Or I can wreak havoc on a *rijstaffel,* if you prefer."

"And afterward?" she asked quietly.

"Well, uh—" He felt the blood in his cheeks.

"You see why I need to keep my head clear."

"Janne! Do you think I—"

"No, certainly not. You are an honorable man. More honorable than is quite good for you, I believe." She laid a hand on his knee. "We will, as you suggest, talk."

The hand lifted before he could throw an arm around her. Through an open window drifted the mildness of spring. Traffic sounded like distant surf.

"It is no use playing merry," she said after a while.

"I guess not. We may as well go straight to the serious." Oddly, that eased him a trifle. He sat back, glass in hand. You inhaled this delicate smokiness as much as you sipped it.

"What will you do next, Manse?"

"Who knows? We never have a dearth of problems." He turned to look at her. "I want to hear about your doings. You succeeded, obviously. I'd have been informed if there were any anomalies."

"Such as more copies of Tacitus Two?"

"None. That single manuscript exists, and whatever transcriptions the Patrol made of it, but now it's just a curiosity."

He felt her slight shiver. "An object uncaused, formed out of nothing for no reason. What a terrifying universe. It was easier being ignorant about variable reality. Sometimes I regret I was recruited."

"And also when you are present at certain episodes. I know." He wanted to kiss the unhappiness off her lips. *Should I try? Could I?*

"Yes." The bright head lifted, the voice throbbed. "But then I think of the exploring, the discovering, the helping, and I am glad again."

"Good lass. Well, tell me about your adventures." *A slow lead-up to the real question.* "I haven't retrieved your report yet, because I wanted to hear it from you personally."

Her spirit flagged. "You had better get the report if you are interested," she said, looking across the room to the picture of the Veil Nebula.

"What? . . . Oh. Tough for you to talk about."

"Yes."

"But you did succeed. You did get history secured, and in the right pattern, with peace and justice."

"A measure of peace and justice. For a time."

"That's the best human beings can ever expect, Janne."

"I know."

"We'll skip the details." *Were they really that gory? My impression was that reconstruction went pretty smoothly, and the Low Countries did rather well in the Empire till it started coming apart.* "But can't you tell me a few things? What about the people we met? Burhmund?"

Floris's tone lightened a bit. "He received amnesty, like everyone else. His wife and sister were restored to him unharmed. He retired to his lands in Batavia, where he ended his days modestly prosperous, a kind of elder statesman. The Romans, too, respected and often consulted him.

"Cerialis became governor of Britain, where he conquered the Brigantes. Tacitus's father-in-law Agricola served under him, and you may recall that the historian rates him well.

"Classicus—"

"Never mind for now," Everard interrupted. "Veleda—Edh?"

"Ah, yes. After bringing about that meeting at the river, she disappears from the chronicle." *The complete chronicle, retrieved by time travelers.*

"I remember. How come? Did she die?"

"Not for another twenty years. A ripe old age in that era." Floris frowned. *Did dread touch her anew?* "I wondered. You would think her fate would interest Tacitus enough for him to mention it."

"Not if she went into obscurity."

"She didn't, quite. Could it be that I was making my own change in the past? When I reported my doubts, I was ordered to proceed and told that in fact this was a proper part of history."

"Okay, then it was. Don't worry. It *could* be a trivial glitch in causality. If so, it doesn't matter. That kind happens a lot, and has no consequences of any importance. Or it could straightforwardly be due to Tacitus not knowing or caring what became of Veleda after she ceased to be a political force. She did, didn't she?"

"In a way. Although— The program I thought of and suggested, and that the Patrol approved, it occurred to me because of what I knew, what I had seen, before I had any idea the Patrol exists. I heartened Edh, foretold what she would and must do, saw to the necessary arrangements, watched over her, appeared to her whenever she seemed to need her goddess—" Again Everard saw Floris troubled. "The future was creating the past. I hope I will escape any more such experiences. Not that this was horrible. No, it was worthwhile, I felt that it justified my life. But—" Her voice faded away.

"Eerie," Everard supplied. "I know."

"Yes," she said softly, "you have your own secrets, don't you?"

"Not from the Patrol."

"From those you care about. Things that would hurt you too much to speak of, or would hurt them too much to hear."

This is cutting near the bone. "Okay, what about Edh? I trust you made her as happy as possible." Everard paused. "I'm sure you did."

"Were you ever on the island of Walcheren?" Floris asked.

"M-m, no. Down close to the Belgian border, isn't it? Wait. I've a vague recollection you once made a remark about archaeological finds there."

"Yes. They are mostly stones with Latin inscriptions, from about the second and third centuries. Thank offerings, usually for a safe voyage to Britain and back. The goddess to whom they are dedicated had a temple at one of the North Sea ports of embarkation. She is represented on some of the stones, with a ship or a dog, often bearing a horn of plenty or surrounded by fruit and grain. Her name was Nehalennia."

"Fairly important, then, at least in that area."

"She did what gods are supposed to do, gave courage and solace, made men a little more decent than they might otherwise have been, and sometimes opened their eyes to beauty."

"Wait!" Everard sat straight. A prickling went up his spine and over his scalp. "That deva of Veleda's—"

"The ancient Nordic goddess of fertility and the sea, Nerthus, Niaerdh, Naerdha, Nerha, many different versions of the name. Veleda made her the avenging deity of war."

Everard regarded Floris for an intense moment before he said, "And you got

Veleda to proclaim her once more peaceful and bring her south. That's as . . . as marvelous an operation as I've ever heard of."

Her glance dropped from his. "No, not really. The potential was there, above all in Edh herself. What a woman she was. What might she have done in a luckier age? . . . On Walcheren the goddess was called Neha. She had become minor, even as an agricultural and maritime divinity. A primitive association with hunting still clung to her. Veleda arrived, revitalized the cult, gave it fresh elements suited to the civilization that was transforming her people. They came to speak of the goddess with a Latin tag, Neha Lenis, Neha the Gentle. In time that turned into Nehalennia."

"She must have mattered a lot, if they worshiped her centuries later."

"Evidently. Sometime I would like to trace out the history, if the Patrol can spare that much lifespan of mine." Floris sighed. "In the end, of course, the Empire collapsed, the Franks and Saxons ravaged around, and when a new order of things arose it was Christian. But I like to imagine that something of Nehalennia lingered on."

Everard nodded. "Me too, from what you say. It could well have. A lot of medieval saints were pagan gods in disguise, and those that were historical often took on attributes of the gods, in folklore or in the Church itself. Midsummer fires were still lighted, though it was now the Eve of Saint John. Saint Olaf fought trolls and monsters like Thor before him. Even the Virgin Mary has aspects of Isis, and I daresay quite a few legends about her were originally local myths. . . ." He shook himself. "You're familiar with this. And it is straying kind of far. How was Edh's life?"

Floris looked beyond him and this year. Her words flowed slow. "She grew old in honor. She never married, but she was like a mother to the people. The island was low, a birthplace of ships, like her girlhood home, and the temple of Nehalennia stood on the edge of her beloved sea. I think—I can't be sure, for how much can a goddess know of a mortal's heart?—I think she became . . . serene. Is that what I am trying to say? Certainly as she lay dying—" The voice caught. "—as she lay on her deathbed—" Floris fought the tears and lost.

Everard drew her to him, put her head on his shoulder and stroked her hair. Her fingers clutched at his shirt. "Easy, lass, easy," he whispered. "Some memories will always hurt. You came to her that one last time, didn't you?"

"Yes," she mumbled against him. "What else could I do?"

"Sure. How could you not have? You eased her passing. What's wrong with that?"

"She—she asked—and I promised—"

Floris wept.

"A life beyond the grave," Everard realized. "A life with you, forever in the sea-home of Niaerdh. And she went happily into the dark."

Floris tore from him. "It was a lie!" she yelled. She sprang to her feet, stumbled around the coffee table, paced back and forth on the floor. Sometimes her hands strained against one another, sometimes fist beat palm, over and over. "All those years were a lie, a trick, I was *using* her! And she believed in me!"

Everard decided he had better stay seated. He poured himself a new drink. "Calm down, Janne," he urged. "You did what you had to, for the whole world's sake. And you did it lovingly. As for Edh, you gave her everything she could have wished for."

"*Bedriegerij*—false, empty, like so much else I have done."

Everard ran the silky fire over his tongue. "Listen, I've gotten to know you rather well. You're as honest a person as I've ever met. Too damn honest, in fact. You're also a very kind person by nature, which matters more. Sincerity is the most overrated virtue in the catalogue. Janne, you're wrong when you imagine there's anything here to forgive. But go ahead anyway, put your common sense in gear and forgive yourself."

She stopped, confronted him, gulped, wiped the tears, and spoke with a gradually strengthening steadiness: "Yes, I . . . understand. I, I thought about this . . . for days . . . before I made my proposal to the Patrol. Afterward I s-s-stuck by it. You are right, it was necessary, and I know that many stories people live by are myths, and many myths were manufactured. Pardon this scene. It was quite a short while ago, on my world line, that Veleda died in the arms of Nehalennia."

"And the memory overwhelmed you. Sure. I'm sorry."

"It was not your fault. How could you have known?" Floris drew a long breath. The hands clenched at her sides. "But I do not want to lie more than I must. I never want to lie to you, Manse."

"What do you mean?" he asked, half in fear, half in foreknowledge.

"I have been thinking about us," she said. "Thinking hard. I suppose what we did, coming together, was wrong—"

"Well, ordinarily it would've been, but in this case it didn't foul us up in our job. If anything, I felt inspired. It was damn wonderful."

"It was for me." Still she grew inexorably more and more calm. "You came here today in hopes of renewing it, did you not?"

He attempted a grin. "I plead guilty. You're hell on wheels in bed, darling."

"You are no *prutsener*." The faint smile died. "What further had you in mind?"

"More of the same. Often."

"Always?"

Everard sat mute.

"It would be difficult," Floris said. "You Unattached, I a Specialist field agent. We would spend most of our lives apart."

"Unless you transferred to data coordination or something else where you could work at home." Everard leaned forward. "You know, that's an excellent idea in itself. You've got the brains for it. Be done with all that risk and hardship and, yes, witness of suffering which you're forbidden to prevent."

She shook her head. "I do not wish to. In spite of everything, I feel I am worth most in the field, my field, and will be until I am too old and feeble."

If you survive so long. "Yeah. Challenge, adventure, fulfillment, and the occasional chance to help. You're that sort."

"I could come to hate the man who made me give them up. I do not wish this either."

"Well, uh—" Everard rose. "All right," he said. It felt like bailing out of a plane. You gave yourself to your parachute. "Not much domestic bliss, but in between missions, something extra special and entirely our own. Are you game?"

"Are *you?*" she answered.

In midstride toward her, he halted.

"You are aware of what my work can require," she said. Her face had gone pale. *It's not a blushing matter,* he thought at the back of his mind. "On this past mission, too. I was not all the time a goddess, Manse. Now and then I found it useful to be a Germanic woman far from home. Or I simply wanted a night's forgetfulness."

The blood thudded in his temples. "I'm no prude, Janne."

"But you are a Middle American farm boy. You have told me so, and I have learned it is true. I can be your friend, your partner, your mistress, but never, down inside you, anything more. Be honest."

"I'm trying," he said harshly.

"It would be worse for me," Floris finished. "I would have to keep too much from you. I would feel I was betraying you. That makes no sense, no, but it is what I would feel. Manse, we had better not fall more in love. We had better say good-bye."

They spent the next few hours together, talking. Then she laid her head on his breast, he hugged her for a minute, and he departed.

IV

Mary, mother of God, mother of sorrows, mother of salvation, be with us now and at the hour of our death.

Westward we sail, but night overtakes us. Watch over us through the dark and bring us on into day. Grant that this our ship bear the most precious of cargoes, your blessing.

Pure as yourself, your evenstar shines above the sunset. Guide us by your light. Lay your gentleness on the seas, breathe us forward in our faring and home again to our loves, carry us at last by your prayers into Heaven.

Ave Stella Maris!

THE YEAR OF THE RANSOM

10 September 1987

"EXCELLENT loneliness." Yes, Kipling could say it. I remember how those lines of his rolled up and down my spine when first I heard them, Uncle Steve reading aloud to me. Though that must have been a dozen years ago, they still do. The poem's about the sea and the mountains, of course; but so are the Galápagos, the Enchanted Islands.

Today I need just a little of their loneliness. The tourists were mostly bright, decent people. Still, a season of herding them along the trails, answering the same questions over and over, does begin to wear on a person. Now they've become fewer, my summer job has ended, soon I'll be home Stateside, commencing grad school. Here is my last chance.

"Wanda, dear!" The word Roberto used is *querida,* which could mean quite a lot. Not necessarily. I wonder about it for a flicker or two while he: "Please, at least let me come along."

Headshake. "I'm sorry, my friend." No, not exactly; *amigo* doesn't translate one-on-one into English, either. "I'm not sulking or anything. Far from it. All I want is a few hours by myself. Haven't you ever?"

I'm being honest. My fellow guides are fine. I wish the friendships I've made among them will keep. Surely they will if we can get back together. But that's uncertain. I may or may not be able to return next year. Eventually I may or may not make my dream of joining the research staff at Darwin Station. It can't take many scientists; or another dream could come along meanwhile and take me. This trip, where half a dozen of us are knocking around the archipelago with a boat and a camping permit, may well be the end of what we've called *el compañerismo*, the Fellowship. Oh, I suppose a Christmas card or two.

"You need protection." Roberto has put on his dramatic style. "That strange man we heard of, asking around Puerto Ayora about the blonde young North American woman."

Let Roberto escort me? Temptation. He's handsome, lively, and a gentleman. We haven't exactly carried on a romance, these past months, but we've gotten pretty close. While he's never told me in words, I know how much he's hoped we'd get closer yet. It hasn't been easy resisting.

Must be done, for his sake more than mine. Not because of his nationality. I think Ecuador is the Latin American country most yanquis feel most at home in. By our standards, things work right there. Quito is charming, and even Guayaquil—ugly, smog-choked, exploding with energy—reminds me of Los Angeles. However, Ecuador is not the USA, and from its standpoint I've got a lot wrong with me, starting with the fact that I'm not sure when I'll be ready to settle down, if ever.

Therefore, laughing, "Oh, yes, Señor Fuentes in the post office told me. Poor dear, how worried he was. The stranger's funny clothes and accent and everything. Hasn't he learned what can crawl off the cruise ships? And how many blondes do the Islands see, these days? Five hundred a year?"

"How would Wanda's secret admirer follow her, anyway?" Jennifer adds. "Swim?" We happen to know that none of the ships has touched at Bartolomé since we left Santa Cruz; no yachts are nearby; and everybody would have recognized a local fisherman.

Roberto goes red under the tan we share. With pity, I pat his hand while telling the group, "Go ahead, folks, snorkel or whatever else you feel like. I'll be back in time for my share of supper chores."

Quickly, then, striding from the bight. I really do need some solitude in this weird, harsh, beautiful nature.

I could merge myself in it skin-diving. The water's glass-clear, silky around me; now and then I see a penguin, not so much swimming as flying through it; fish dance like fireworks, seaweeds do a stately hula; I can get friendly with the sea lions. But other swimmers, never mind how dear they are, *will* talk. What I want is to commune with the land. In company I couldn't admit that. It'd sound too pompous, as though I were from Greenpeace or the People's Republic of Berkeley.

Now I've laid white-shell sand and mangroves behind me, I seem to have utter desolation underfoot. Bartolomé is volcanic, like its sisters, but bears hardly any soil. It's already hot beneath the morning sun, and never a cloud to soften the glare. Here and there sprawl gaunt shrubs or tussocks of grass, but they become few as I walk toward Pinnacle Rock. My Adidases whisper on dark lava, in simmering silence.

However . . . among boulders and tide pools, Sally Lightfoot crabs scuttle, brilliant orange-and-blue. Bound inland, I spy a lizard of a kind unique to this place. I'm within a yard of a blue-footed booby; she could flap off, but simply watches me, the naive creature. A finch flitting across my vision; it was the Galápagos finches that helped Darwin understand how life works through time. An albatross wheeling white. Higher cruises a frigate bird. Unship the binoculars hung at my neck and catch the arrogance of his wings in the spilling sunlight, the split tail like a buccaneer's twin swords.

Here are none of the paths I've generally required my tourists to stay on. Ecuadorian government strict about that. Given its all too limited resources, it's doing a great job, trying to protect and restore the environment. Care where I put my feet, as becomes a biologist.

I'll circle around to the eastern end of the islet and there take the trail and stairs leading to the central peak. The view from it, across to Santiago Island and widely over the ocean, is stunning; and today I'll have it to myself. Probably that's where I'll eat the lunch I've packed along. May later go down to the cove, peel off shirt and jeans, enjoy a private dip before turning westward.

Careful about that, kid! You're a bare twenty klicks below the Equator. This sun wants respect. Tilt my hat brim against it and stop for a drink from my canteen.

Catch a breath, take a look around. I've gained some altitude, which I must give back before reaching the trail head. Beach and camp are out of sight. Instead, I see a sweep and tumble of stone down to Sullivan Bay, fiery-blue water, Point Martínez lifting grayish on the big island. Is that a hawk there? Reach for the binoculars.

A flash in the sky. Light off metal. An airplane? No, can't be. It's gone.

Puzzled, I lower the glasses. I've heard enough about flying saucers, or UFOs to give them the more respectable name. Never taken them seriously. Dad gave his children a healthy inoculation of skepticism. Well, he's an electronics engineer. Uncle Steve, the archaeologist, has knocked around a lot more in the world, and claims it's full of things we don't understand. I suppose I'll simply never know what it was I glimpsed. Let's push on.

Out of nowhere, a moment's gust. The air thuds softly. A shadow falls over me. I turn my face upward.

Can't be!

An outsize motorcycle, except every last detail is different, and it has no wheels, and it hangs there, ten feet up, unsupported, silent. A man in the front saddle grips what might be handlebars. I see him with knife sharpness. Each second takes forever. Terror has me, like nothing since I was seventeen, driving along the cliff tops near Big Sur in a rainstorm, and the car went into a skid.

I pulled out of that one. This doesn't stop.

He's about five feet nine, rawboned but broad-shouldered, brown-skinned, pockmarked, hook-nosed, black hair falling past his ears, black beard and mustache trimmed to points though getting shaggy. His outfit is what's absolutely wrong, on top of such a machine. Floppy boots, saggy brown hose poking out of short puffed breeches, long-sleeved loose shirt that might be saffron below its grime—steel breastplate, helmet, red cloak, sword scabbarded at left hip—

As if across a hundred miles: "Are you the lady Wanda Tamberly?"

Somehow that snaps me back from the edge of screaming. Whatever is going on, I can meet it. Hysteria never has been compulsory. Nightmare, fever dream? I don't believe so. The sun is too warm on my back and off the rocks, the sea too steadily bright, and I could count every spine on yonder cactus. Prank, stunt, psychological experiment? Less possible than the thing itself. . . . His Spanish is the Castilian sort, but I never met that accent till now.

"Who are you?" I force out of my throat. "What are you after?"

His lips draw tight. Bad teeth. His tone is half fierce, half desperate. "Quickly! I must find Wanda Tamberly. Her uncle Esteban is in terrible danger."

"I am she," blurts my mouth.

He barks a laugh. His vehicle swoops down at me. Run!

He draws alongside, leans over, throws his right arm around my waist. Those muscles are titanium steel. Hauls me off my feet. That course I took in self-defense. My spread fingers jab for his eyes. He's too fast. Knocks my hand aside. Does something to a control board. Suddenly we're elsewhere.

3 June 1533 (Julian calendar)

This day the Peruvians brought to Caxamalca another load of the treasure that was to buy their king free. Luis Ildefonso Castelar y Moreno saw them from afar. He had been out exercising the horsemen under his command. They were now bound back, for the sun was low above western heights. Against shadows grown long throughout the valley, the river gleamed and vapors turned golden as they rose from the hot springs of the royal baths. Llamas and human porters plodded in a line down the road from the south, wearied by burdens and many leagues. Natives stopped their labor in the fields to stare, then got hastily on with it. Obedience was ingrained, no matter who their overlord might be.

"Take charge," Castelar ordered his lieutenant, and put spurs to stallion. He drew rein just outside the small city and waited for the caravan.

A movement on the left caught his glance. Another man emerged afoot from between two white-plastered, thatch-roofed clay buildings. The man was tall; were both standing, he would top the rider by three inches or more. The hair around his tonsure was the same dusty brown as his Franciscan robe, but age had scarcely marked a sharp, light-complexioned visage—nor had the pox— and not a tooth was missing. Even after weeks and adventures, Castelar knew Fray Estebán Tanaquil. The recognition was mutual.

"Greetings, reverend sir," he said.

"God be with you," answered the friar. He stopped by the stirrup. The treasure train reached them and went on. Shouts of jubilation sounded from within the city.

"Ah," Castelar rejoiced, "a splendid sight, no?"

When he got no reply, he looked down. Pain touched the other face. "Is something wrong?" Castelar asked.

Tanaquil sighed. "I cannot help myself. I see how worn and footsore those men are. I think what a heritage of ages they carry, and how it has been wrung from them."

Castelar stiffened. "Would you speak against our captain?"

This was an odd fellow at best, he thought: beginning with his order, when the religious with the expedition were nearly all Dominicans. It was something of a puzzle how Tanaquil had come along in the first place, and eventually won the confidence of Francisco Pizarro. Well, that last must be due his learning and gentle manners, both rare in this company.

"No, no, of course not," the friar said. "And yet—" His voice trailed off.

Castelar squirmed a bit. He believed he knew what went on beneath the shaven pate. He himself had wondered about the righteousness of what they did last year. The Inca Atahuallpa received the Spaniards peacefully; he let them quarter themselves in Caxamalca; he entered the city by invitation, to continue negotiations; and his litter carried him into an ambush, where his attendants were gunned down and cut down by the hundreds while he was made prisoner. Now, at his bidding, his subjects stripped the country of wealth to fill a room with gold and another room twice with silver, the price of his liberty.

"God's will," Castelar snapped. "We bring the Faith to these heathen. The king's well treated, isn't he? He even has his wives and servants to attend him.

As for the ransom, Christ"—he cleared his throat—"Sant'Iago, like every good leader, rewards his troops well."

The friar cast a wry smile upward. It seemed to retort that preaching was not the proper business of a soldier. Outwardly, he shrugged and said, "Tonight I will see how well."

"Ah, yes." Castelar felt relief at sheering away from a dispute. No matter that he too once studied for holy orders, was expelled because of trouble with a girl, enlisted in the war against the French, at last followed Pizarro to the New World in hopes of whatever fortune the younger son of an impoverished Estremaduran hidalgo might find: he remained respectful of the cloth. "I hear you look every load over before it goes into the hoard."

"Someone should, someone who has an eye for the art rather than the mere metal. I persuaded our captain and his chaplain. Scholars at the Emperor's court and in the Church will be pleased that a fragment of knowledge was saved."

"Hm." Castelar tugged his beard. "But why do you do it at night?"

"You have heard that too?"

"I've been back for days. My ears are full of gossip."

"I daresay you give much more than you get. I'd like to talk with you at length myself. That was a herculean journey your party made."

Through Castelar passed a jumbled pageant of the months gone by, when Hernando Pizarro, the captain's brother, led a band west over the cordillera, stupendous mountains, dizzyingly deep ravines, brawling rivers, to Pachaca-mac and its dark oracular temple on the coast. "We had little gain," he said. "Our best booty was the Indio general Challcuchima. Get the lot of them together, under control. . . . But you were going to tell me why you study the treasure only after sunset."

"To avoid exciting cupidity and discord worse than already afflict us. Men grow ever more impatient for division of the spoils. Besides, at night the forces of Satan are at their strongest. I pray over things that were consecrated to false gods."

The last porter trudged past and disappeared among walls.

"I'd like to see," Castelar said. Impulse flared. "Why not? I'll join you."

Tanaquil was startled. "What?"

"I won't disturb you. I'll simply watch."

Reluctance was unmistakable. "You must obtain permission first."

"Why? I have the rank. None would deny me. What have you against it? I should think you would welcome some company."

"You'll find it tedious. Others did. That is the reason they leave me alone at my task."

"I'm used to standing guard." Castelar laughed.

Tanaquil surrendered. "Very well, Don Luis, if you insist. Meet me at the Serpent House, as they're calling it, after compline."

—Stars glittered keen and countless over the uplands. Half or more of them were unknown to European skies. Castelar shivered and wrapped his cloak tighter around himself. His breath smoked, his boots rang on hard-packed streets. Caxamalca enclosed him, ghostly in the gloom. He felt glad of corselet, helmet, sword, needless though they might seem here. Tavantinsuyu, the Indios called this land, the Four Quarters of the World; and somehow that felt more right than Perú, a name whose meaning nobody was sure of, for a realm whose reach dwarfed the Holy Roman Empire. Was it subdued yet, or could it ever entirely be, its peoples and their gods?

The thought was unworthy of a Christian. He hastened on.

The watchmen at the treasury were a reassuring sight. Lantern glow sheened off armor, pikes, muskets. These were of the iron ruffians who had sailed from Panamá, marched through jungle and swamp and desert, shattered every foe, raised their strongholds, come in a handful over a range that stormed heaven, to seize the very king of the pagans and lay his country under tribute. No man or demon would get past them without leave, nor stop them when again they fared onward.

They knew Castelar and saluted him. Fray Tanaquil was waiting, a lantern in his own hand. He led the cavalryman beneath a lintel sculptured in the form of a snake, though not such a snake as had ever haunted white men's nightmares, into the building.

It was large, multiply chambered, of stone blocks cut and fitted together with exquisite care. The roof was timber, for this had been a palace. The Spaniards had supplied exterior entrances with stout doors, where the Indios had used curtains of reeds or cloth. Tanaquil shut the one through which he came.

Shadows filled corners and bobbed misshapen over wall paintings which priests had piously defaced. Today's consignment lay in an anteroom. Castelar saw gleams beyond. He wondered half dizzily how many hundredweight of precious metal were heaped there.

He must content himself for the present with gloating over what he had seen arrive. Pizarro's officers had hastily unwrapped the bundles, to assure themselves about the contents, and left everything where they tossed it. Tomorrow they would weigh the mass and put it with the rest. Cords and wrappings rustled under Castelar's boots, Tanaquil's sandals.

The friar set his lantern on the clay floor and hunkered down. He picked up a golden cup, brought it near the dim light, shook his head and muttered. The thing was dented, the figures cast in it crumpled. "The receivers dropped this, or kicked it aside." Did anger tremble in his tone? "They've no more care for workmanship than animals."

Castelar took the object from him and hefted it. Easily a quarter pound, he reckoned. "Why should they?" he asked. "It'll soon go to the smelter."

Bitterness: "True." After a moment: "They will send a few pieces intact to the Emperor, for the sake of whatever interest he may have. I've been picking out the best, hoping Pizarro will listen to me and choose them. But mostly he won't."

"What's the difference? Everything is just as unsightly."

Gray eyes turned aloft to reproach the warrior. "I thought you might be a little wiser, a little able to understand that men have many ways of . . . praising God through the beauty they create. You have an education, no?"

"Latin. Reading, writing, ciphering. A bit of history and astronomy. It's largely dropped out of me, I fear."

"And you've traveled."

"I fought in France and Italy. Gained a smattering of those languages."

"I have the impression you've acquired Quechua too."

"A minim. Can't let the natives play stupid, you know, or conspire in earshot." Castelar felt himself under inquisition, mild but probing, and changed the subject. "You told me you record what you see. Where are your quill and paper?"

"I have an excellent memory. As you observed, there is not much point in itemizing things that are to become ingots. But to make sure no curse, no witchcraft lingers—"

Tanaquil had been sorting and arranging articles as he talked, ornaments, plates, vessels, figurines, grotesque in Castelar's sight. When they were marshaled before him, he reached inside a pouch hung at his waist and drew forth a curiosum of his own. Castelar stooped and squinted for a better look. "What's that?" he asked.

"A reliquary. It holds a finger bone of Saint Ippolito."

Castelar signed himself. Nonetheless he peered closer. "I've never seen its like." It was a hand's breadth in size, smoothly rounded, black save for a cross of nacreous material inset on top and, in front, two crystals more suggestive of lenses than of windows.

"A rare piece," the friar explained. "Left behind when the Moors departed Granada, later sanctified by these contents and the blessing of the Church. The bishop who entrusted it to me declared it has special efficacy against infidel magic. Captain Pizarro and Fray Valverde agreed it could be wise, and would certainly be harmless, if I subject each piece of Inca treasure to its influence."

He assumed a more comfortable position on the floor, selected a small gold image of a beast, revolved it in his left hand before the crystals of the reliquary, which he held in his right. His lips moved silently. When he had finished, he put the object down and went on to another.

Castelar shifted from foot to foot.

After a while Tanaquil chuckled and said, "I warned you this would prove tedious. I'll be at it for hours. You may as well go to bed, Don Luis."

Castelar yawned. "I think you are right. Thank you for your courtesies."

A whoosh and thud brought him whirling around. For an instant he poised locked in unbelief.

Over by the wall, a thing had appeared. A thing—massive, dully slick, perhaps of steel, with a pair of handles and two stirrupless saddles— He saw it clear, for light radiated from a baton the rearmost rider held. Both men wore form-fitting black. It made their hands and faces stand forth bone-white, unweathered, unnatural.

The Friar sprang up. He yelled. The words were not Spanish.

In that eyeblink of time, Castelar saw amazement on the aliens. Be they wizards or devils straight from hell, they were not all-powerful, not before God and His saints. Castelar's sword whipped into his grasp. He plunged forward. "Sant'Iago and at them!" he roared, the ancient battle cry of his people as they drove the Moors from Spain back to Africa. Make such a racket that the guards outside would hear and—

The rider in front lifted a tube. It blinked. Castelar spun down into nothingness.

15 April 1610

Machu Picchu! was the immediate recognition as Stephen Tamberly awoke. And then: *No. Not quite. Not as I've known it. When am I?*

He climbed to his feet. Clarity of mind and senses told him he had been knocked out by an electronic stunner, probably a twenty-fourth-century model or later. No surprise. The deadly shock had been the apparition of those men on a machine such as was not to be made for thousands of years after he was born.

Around him lifted the peaks he knew, misty, tropically green even at their altitudes save for snow on the most remote. A condor hovered aloft. A blue-and-gold morning flooded the Urubamba gorge with light. But he saw no railway down there, no station, and the only road in sight was up here, built by engineers of the Incas.

He stood on a platform that had been attached, with a descending ramp, to a high point on a wall above a ditch. Below him the city spread over acre upon acre; it clung, it soared, in buildings of dry-laid stone, staircases, terraces, plazas, as powerful as the mountains themselves. If those heights might almost have been from a Chinese painting, the human works might almost have been from medieval southern France; and yet not really, for they were too foreign, too imbued with their own spirit.

A breeze blew cool. Its whittering was the single sound amidst the bloodbeat in his temples. Nothing stirred throughout the fastness. With the mind-speed of desperation, he saw that it had not long lain deserted. Weeds and shrubs were everywhere, but they and the weather had hardly begun the work of demolition. That didn't reveal much, for it still had far to go when Hiram Bingham discovered the place in 1911. However, he spied structures almost intact which he remembered as ruins or not at all. Traces remained of wood and thatch roofs. And—

And Tamberly was not alone. Luis Castelar crouched beside him, stupefaction fading out before a snarl. Men and women stood around, themselves tense. The timecycle rested near the platform edge.

First Tamberly was aware of weapons aimed at him. Then he stared at the people. They were like none he had met in his wanderings. Their very alienness made them look somehow alike. Faces were finely chiseled, high in the cheekbones, thin in the noses, large in the eyes. Despite raven darkness of hair, skin was alabaster and irises were light, while men seemed never to have had any growth of beard. Bodies poised tall, slender, supple. Basic clothing for both sexes was a close-fitted one-piece garment with no visible seams or fastenings, and soft half-boots of the same lustrous black. Silver patterns, an Oriental-like tracery, ornamented most, and several persons added cloaks of flamboyant red, orange, or yellow. Wide belts held pockets and holsters. Hair fell to the shoulders, held in place by a simple headband, arabesqued fillet, or diamond-glittery coronet.

They numbered about thirty. All seemed young—or ageless? Tamberly thought he perceived many years of lifespan behind them. It showed in both the pride and the alertness, above a feline self-composure.

Castelar glared from side to side. He had been deprived of knife and sword. The latter flashed in the hand of a stranger. He tautened as if to attack. Tamberly caught him by the arm. "Peace, Don Luis," he urged. "This is hopeless. Call on the saints if you wish, but stay quiet."

The Spaniard growled before he subsided. Tamberly felt him shiver beneath sleeve and skin. Somebody in the group said something in a language that purred and trilled. Another gestured, as if for silence, and stepped forward. The grace of the motion was such that one could say he flowed. Clearly, he dominated the rest. His features were aquiline, green-eyed. Full lips curved in a smile.

"Greeting," he said. "You are unexpected guests."

He used fluent Temporal, the common speech of the Time Patrol and many civilian travelers; and the machine was scarcely different from a Patrol runabout; but he must surely be an outlaw, an enemy.

Breath shuddered into Tamberly. "What . . year is this?" he mumbled. Peripherally, he noticed Castelar's reactions when Fray Tanaquil replied in the unknown tongue—astonishment, dismay, grimness.

"By the Gregorian calendar, which I suppose you are accustomed to, it is the fifteenth of April, 1610," said the stranger. "I daresay you recognize the site, although your companion obviously does not."

Of course he doesn't, passed through Tamberly. *What the natives of a later day called Machu Picchu was built by the Inca Pachacutec as a holy city, a center for the Virgins of Sun. It lost its purpose when the headquarters of resistance to the Spaniards became Vilcabamba, till they captured and killed Tupac Amaru, the last who bore the name of Inca before the Andean Resurgence of the twenty-second century. So nothing led the Conquistadores to find it, and it lay empty, forgotten by everyone but a few poor countryfolk, till 1911.* . . . He barely heard: "I suppose, likewise, you are an agent of the Time Patrol."

"Who are *you?*" Tamberly choked.

"Let us discuss matters in a more convenient location," said the man. "This is merely the place to which our scouts have returned."

Why? A timecycle could appear within seconds and centimeters of any point, any moment within its range—from here to Earth orbit, from now to the age of the dinosaurs, or, futureward, the age of the Danellians, though that was forbidden— Tamberly guessed these conspirators built this landing stage, exposed to outside eyes, in order to keep the local Indians frightened and therefore distant. Stories about magical comings and goings would die out in the course of generations, but Machu Picchu would remain shunned.

Most of those who had been watching dispersed to whatever their business was. Four guards with drawn stunners walked behind the leader and prisoners. One also carried the sword, perhaps as a souvenir. By ramp, paths, and staircases they made their way down among the compounds of the city. Silence lay thick about them until the chieftain said, "Apparently your companion is just a soldier who happened to be with you." At the American's nod: "Well, then, we'll put him aside while you and I talk. Yaron, Sarnir, you know his language. Interrogate him. Psychological means only, for the time being."

They had reached that structure which Tamberly, if he remembered aright, knew as the King's Group. An outer wall marked off a small courtyard where another timecycle was parked. Curtains of nacreous iridescence shimmered in doorways and across the roofless tops of the buildings that bounded the rest of the open space. Those were force fields, Tamberly recognized, impervious to anything short of a nuclear blast.

"In God's name," Castelar cried when a boot nudged him, "what is this? Tell me before I go mad!"

"Easy, Don Luis, easy," Tamberly answered fast. "We're captives. You've seen what their weapons can do. Go as they command. Heaven may have mercy on us, but by ourselves we're helpless."

The Spaniard clenched his jaws and went with the two assigned him, into a lesser unit. The leader's group sought the largest. Barriers blinked out of existence to admit both parties. They stayed off, giving a look at stones and sky and freedom. Tamberly supposed that was to let fresh air in; the room he entered did not appear to have been used lately.

Sunshine joined radiance from the canopy overhead to illuminate its windowlessness. The floor had been given a deep-blue covering that responded slightly to footfalls, like living muscles. A couple of chairs and a table bore halfway familiar shapes, though their darkly glowing material was new to him. He could not identify the things shelved in what might have been a cabinet.

The guards took stance on either side of the entrance. One was male, one a woman no less steely. The leader settled into a chair and invited Tamberly to take the other. It fitted itself to his contours, to his every motion. The leader pointed at a carafe and glasses on the table. Those were enameled—made in Venice about now, Tamberly judged. Bought? Stolen? Looted? The man glided forward to fill two vessels. His master and Tamberly took them.

Smiling, the leader lifted his goblet and murmured, "Your health." The implication was: *You'd better do whatever is necessary to keep it.* The wine was a tart chablis type, so refreshing that Tamberly thought it might contain a stimulant. They had broad and subtle knowledge of human chemistry in his future.

"Well, then," the leader said. His tone continued mild. "You are obviously of the Patrol. That was a holographic recorder in your hand. And the Patrol would never permit any visitor out of time to prowl about a moment so critical, except its own."

Tamberly's throat contracted. His tongue stiffened. It was the block laid in his mind during his training, a reflex to keep him from revealing to any unauthorized person, ever, that traffic went up and down the tiers of history. "Uh, uh—I—" Sweat sprang forth cold upon his skin.

"My sympathies." Did laughter run through the words? "I am quite aware of your conditioning. I also realize that it operates within the bounds of common sense. We being time travelers, you are free to discuss that subject, if not those details the Patrol prefers to keep secret. Will it help if I introduce myself? Merau Varagan. If you have heard of my race, it is probably under the name of the Exaltationists."

Tamberly recalled enough to make this an hour of nightmare. *The thirty-first millennium was—is—will be—only Temporal grammar has the verbs and tenses to deal with these concepts—it is far earlier than the development of the first time machines, but chosen members of its civilization know about the travel, take part in it; some join the Patrol, like individuals in most milieus. Only . . . this era had its supermen, their genes created for adventurousness on the space frontier; and they came to chafe beneath the weight of that civilization of theirs, which to them was older than the Stone Age is to me; and they rebelled, and lost, and must flee; but they had learned the great fact, that timefaring exists, and had, incredibly, managed to seize some vehicles; and "since then" the Patrol has been on their track, lest they do worse mischief, but I know of no report that the Patrol "will" catch them. . . .*

"I can't tell you more than you've deduced," he protested. "If you torture me to death, I can't."

"When a man plays a dangerous game," replied Merau Varagan, "he should prepare for contingencies. I admit we failed to anticipate your presence. We thought the treasure vault would be deserted at night, except for sentries outside. However, the possibility of an encounter with the Patrol has been very much on our minds. Raor, the kyradex."

Before Tamberly could wonder what that word meant, the woman was at his side. Horror surged through him as he divined her purpose. He started to rise, scramble free, get himself killed, anything.

Her pistol blinked. It was set to less than knockout force. His sinews gave way, he flopped back onto his chair. Only its embrace kept him from sliding to the carpet.

She sought the cabinet, returned with an object. It was a box and a sort of luminous helmet, joined by a cable. The hemisphere went over his head. Raor's fingers danced across glow-spots that must be controls. Symbols appeared in the air. Meter readings? A humming took hold of Tamberly. It grew and grew until it was all there was, he was lost in it, he spun down into the darkness at its heart.

Slowly he ascended. He regained use of his muscles and straightened in the seat. Relaxation pervaded him, though, like that which follows long sleep. He seemed detached from himself, an observer outside, emotionless. Yet he was totally awake. Every sensory detail stood forth, smells of his unwashed robe and body, mountain air coming sharp through the doorway, Varagan's sardonic Caesar visage, Raor with the box in her hand, the weight of the helmet, a fly that sat on the wall as if to remind him he was as mortal as it.

Varagan leaned back, crossed his legs, bridged his fingers, and said with weird courtesy, "Your name and origin, please."

"Stephen John Tamberly. Born in San Francisco, California, United States of America, June the twenty-third, 1937."

He answered fully and truthfully. He must. Or, rather, his memory, nerves, mouth must. The kyradex was the ultimate interrogator. He could not even feel the ghastliness of his condition. Deep underneath, something screamed, but his conscious mind had become a machine.

"And when were you recruited into the Patrol?"

"In 1968." It had happened too gradually for him to give an exact date. A colleague introduced him to some friends, interesting sorts who, he understood afterward, sounded him out; eventually he agreed to take certain tests, allegedly as part of a psychological research project; afterward the situation was revealed to him; he was invited to enlist, and accepted with infinite eagerness, as they had known he would. Well, he was on the rebound from divorce. The decision would have been more difficult if he'd had to lead a double life constantly. Regardless, he knew he would have, for it gave him worlds to explore that until then had been only writings, ruins, shards, and dead bones.

"What is your standing in the organization?"

"I'm not in enforcement or rescue or anything of that sort. I'm a field historian. At home I was an anthropologist, had done work among the modern Quechua, then went into the archaeology of the region. That made me a natural choice for the Conquest period. I would have liked better to study the pre-Columbian societies, but of course that was impossible; I'd have been too conspicuous."

"I see. How long is your Patrol career thus far?"

"About sixty years of lifespan." You could run up centuries, doubling around in time. A tremendous perquisite of membership was the longevity process of an era futureward of his own. To be sure, that brought the pain of watching people you loved grow old and die, never knowing what you knew. To escape that, as a general thing you phased out of their lives, let them believe you'd moved away, made contact with them dwindle gradually to nothing. For they must not notice how the years did not gnaw you down like them.

"Where and when did you depart on this latest mission of yours?"

"From California in 1968." He had maintained his old relationships longer than most agents did. His lifespan age might be ninety, his biological age thirty, but stress and sorrow told on a man, and in 1986 he could claim his calendrical age of fifty, though kinfolk often remarked how youthful he still looked. God knew there was grief aplenty in a Patrolman's days, along with the adventure. You witnessed too much.

"Hm," said Varagan. "We'll go into that in more detail. First describe your assignment. Just what were you doing last century in Cajamarca?"

The later name of the town, observed a distant part of Tamberly, while his automaton consciousness replied: "I told you, I'm a field historian, gathering data on the period of the Conquest." It was for more than the sake of science. How could the Patrol police the time lanes and maintain the reality of events unless it knew what those events were? Books were often misleading, and many a key happening was never chronicled. "The corps got me accredited—as Esteban Tanaquil, a Franciscan friar—accredited to Pizarro's expedition when he returned in 1530 from Spain to America." Before Waldseemüller bestowed that name. "I was simply to observe, recording as much as I was able unbeknownst." And do what heartbreakingly slight things he could to lighten, the tiniest bit, the brutality. "You must know, too, those years will loom large in history— futureward of my home century, pastward of yours—when the Resurgents call on their Andean heritage."

Varagan nodded. "Indeed," he said conversationally. "If matters had gone otherwise, why, already the twentieth century might be very different." He grinned. "Suppose, for example, the succession after Inca Huayna Capac had not been in dispute, Atahuallpa in a state of civil war with his rivals, when Pizarro arrived. That minuscule gang of Spanish adventurers could not possibly have overthrown the empire by themselves. The Conquest would have required more time, more resources. This would have affected the balance of power in Europe, where the Turks were pressing inward while the Reformation broke what scant unity Christendom had possessed."

"Is that your aim?" In a vague way Tamberly knew he should be furious, aghast, anything but apathetic. He barely had the curiosity to ask the question.

"Perhaps," Varagan taunted. "However, the men who found you were only scouts in advance of a much more modest enterprise, bringing Atahuallpa's ransom here. That would be quite upsetting in itself, of course." He laughed. "But it might preserve those priceless works of art. You were content to make holograms of them for people uptime."

"For all humankind," said Tamberly automatically.

"Well, for such of it as can be allowed to enjoy the fruits of time travel, under the watchful eye of the Patrol."

"Bring the treasure . . . here?" fumbled Tamberly. "Now?"

"Temporarily. We've camped where we are because it's a convenient base." Varagan scowled. "The Patrol is too vigilant in our original milieu. Arrogant swine!" Calm again: "As isolated as Machu Picchu is at present, it will not be noticeably affected by changes in the near past—for instance, by such a detail as Atahuallpa's ransom unaccountably disappearing one night. But your associates will be in full quest of you, Tamberly. They'll follow up every last clue they can find. Best we have that information at once, to forestall any moves of theirs."

I should be shaken to the roots of my soul. This utter, absolute recklessness—risking loops in the world lines, temporal vortices, destruction of the whole future—No, not risking. Deliberately bringing it about. But I cannot feel the horror. The thing that squats on my skull holds down my humanity.

Varagan leaned forward. "Therefore let us discuss your personal history," he said. "What do you consider your home? What family have you, friends, ties of any kind?"

The questions quickly became knife-sharp. Tamberly watched and listened while their skilled wielder cut from him detail after detail. When something especially interested Varagan, he pursued it to the end. Tamberly's second wife ought to be safe; she was also in the Patrol. His first wife was remarried, out of his life. But oh, God, his brother, and Bill's own wife, and he heard himself confess that his niece was like a daughter to him—

The doorway darkened. Luis Castelar bounded through.

His sword slashed. The guard there buckled, crumpled, fell and lay squirming. Blood spouted from his throat, its red like the shriek he could no longer sound forth.

Raor dropped the control box and snatched for her sidearm. Castelar reached her. His left fist smashed at her jaw. She staggered back, sagged, went to the floor and gaped up at him, stunned. His blade sang even as she dropped. Varagan was on his feet. Incredibly quick, he dodged a cut that would have laid him open. The room was too cramped for him to get past. Castelar stabbed. Varagan clutched his belly. Blood squirted between his fingers. He leaned against the wall and shouted.

Castelar wasted no time finishing him. The Spaniard ripped the helmet off Tamberly. It thudded to the floor. Wholeness of spirit broke like a sunbeam into the American.

"Get us away!" Castelar rasped. "The witch-horse outside—"

Tamberly reeled from his chair. His knees would barely hold him. Castelar's free arm gave support. They stumbled into the open. The timecycle waited. Tamberly crawled onto the front saddle, Castelar leaped to the rear. A man in black appeared in the courtyard gateway. He yelled and reached for his weapon.

Tamberly slapped the console.

11 May 2937 B.C.

Machu Picchu was gone. Wind surrounded him. Hundreds of feet below lay a river valley, lush with grass and groves. Ocean gleamed in the distance.

The cycle dropped. Air brawled. Tamberly's hands sought the gravity drive. The engine awoke. The fall stopped. He brought the vehicle to a smooth and silent landing.

He began to shake. Darkness went in rags before his eyes.

The reaction passed. He grew aware of Castelar standing on the ground beside him, and the Spaniard's sword point an inch from his throat.

"Get off that thing," Castelar said. "Move carefully, your arms up. You are no holy man. I think you may be a magician who should burn at the stake. We will find out."

3 November 1885

A hansom cab brought Manse Everard from Dalhousie & Roberts, Importers—which was also the Time Patrol's London base in this milieu—to the house on York Place. He mounted the stairs through a dense yellowish fog and turned the handle on a doorbell. A maidservant let him into a wainscoted anteroom. He gave her a card. She was back in a minute to say that Mrs. Tamberly would be pleased to receive him. He left his hat and overcoat on a rack and followed her. Interior heating failed to keep out all the dank chill, which made him for once glad to be dressed like a Victorian gentleman. Usually he found such clothes abominably uncomfortable. Otherwise this was, on the whole, a marvelous era to live in, if you had money, enjoyed robust health, and could pass for an Anglo-Saxon Protestant.

The parlor was a pleasant, gaslit room, lined with books and not overly cluttered with bric-a-brac. A coal fire burned low. Helen Tamberly stood close, as if in need of what cheer it offered. She was a small reddish-blond woman; the full dress subtly emphasized a figure that many doubtless envied. Her voice made the Queen's English musical. It wavered a little, though. "How do you do, Mr. Everard. Please be seated. Would you care for tea?"

"No, thanks, ma'm, unless you want some." He made no effort to dissemble his American accent. "Another man is due here shortly. Maybe after we've talked with him?"

"Certainly." She nodded dismissal to the maid, who left the door open behind her. Helen Tamberly went to close it. "I hope this doesn't shock Jenkins too badly," she said with a wan smile.

"I daresay she's grown used to somewhat unconventional ways around here," Everard responded in an effort to match her self-possession.

"Well, we try not to be too outré. People tolerate a certain amount of eccentricity. If our front were upper class, rather than well-to-do bourgeois, we could get away with anything; but then we'd be too much in the public eye." She stepped across the carpet to stand before him, fists clenched at her sides. "Enough of that," she said desperately. "You're from the Patrol. An Unattached agent, am I right? It's about Stephen. Must be. Tell me."

Without fear of eavesdroppers, he continued in the English language, which might sound gentler in her ears than Temporal. "Yes. Now we don't yet know anything for sure. He's—missing. Failed to report in. I suppose you remember that was to have been in Lima late in 1535, several months after Pizarro founded it. We have an outpost there. Discreet inquiries turned up the fact that the friar Esteban Tanaquil vanished mysteriously two years before, in Cajamarca. Vanished, mind you, not died in some accident or affray or whatever." Bleakly: "Nothing as simple as that."

"But he could be alive?" she cried.

"We may hope. I can't promise more than that the Patrol will try its damnedest—uh, pardon me."

She gave a broken laugh. "That's all right. If you're from Stephen's milieu, everybody's careless with speech, true?"

"Well, he and I were both born and raised in the USA, middle twentieth century. That's why I've been asked to lead this investigation. A background shared with your husband just might give me some useful insight."

"You were asked," she murmured. "Nobody gives orders to an Unattached agent, nobody less than a Danellian."

"That's not quite correct," he said awkwardly. Sometimes his status—assigned to no particular milieu, but free to go anywhere and anywhen there was need and act on his own judgment—embarrassed him. He was by nature unpretentious, a meat-and-potatoes kind of man.

"Good of you to agree," she said, and blinked hard against tears. "Do please be seated. Smoke if you wish. Are you quite sure you wouldn't care for tea and biscuits or perhaps a spot of brandy?"

"Maybe later, thanks. But I will avail myself of my pipe." He waited till she sat down by the hearth to take the armchair opposite, which must be Steve Tamberly's. The fire quivered blue between them.

"I've been in on a few cases like this in the past—my lifeline past, that is," he began cautiously. "It's desirable to start by learning as much as possible about the person concerned. That means talking with those close to him or her. So I've come a tad early today, hoping we could get acquainted. An agent who's been on the spot will be along in a while to tell us what he discovered. I assumed you wouldn't mind."

"Oh, no." She drew breath. "But tell me, please. I've always had difficulty understanding, even when I think in Temporal. My father was a physics don, and it's hard to set aside the strict logic of cause and effect he drilled into me. Stephen . . . encountered trouble somehow, in sixteenth-century Perú. Maybe the Patrol can save him, maybe it can't. Whatever, though, whatever the result is . . . the Patrol will know. There'll be a report in the files. Can't you go at once and read it? Or, or skip ahead in time and ask your future self? Why must we go through *this?*"

Upbringing or no, she must be hideously shaken to raise such a question, she who had also been trained at that academy back in the Oligocene period—back before there was any human history for its existence to upset. Everard didn't think the less of her. Rather, it made him appreciate the courage that maintained calmness. And, after all, her work did not expose her to the paradoxes and hazards of mutable time. Nor had Tamberly experienced them—he had been a straightforward, if disguised, observer—till suddenly they laid hold on him.

"You know that's forbidden." He kept his tone soft. "Causal loops can too easily turn into temporal vortices. Annulment of the whole effort would be the least of the disasters we'd risk. And it'd be futile, anyway. Those records, those memories could be of something that never happened. Just think how our actions would be influenced by what we believed was foreknowledge. No, we've got to go through with our jobs in as nearly causational a way as we possibly can, in order to *make* our successes or failures real."

For reality is conditional. It is like a wave pattern on a sea. Let the waves—the probability-waves of ultimate underlying quantum chaos—change their rhythm, and abruptly that tracery of ripples and foam-swirls will be gone, transformed into another. Already in the twentieth century, physicists had a dim glimmering of this. But not until time travel came to be did the fact of it stab into human lives.

If you have gone into the past, you have made it your present. You have the same free will as always. You have laid no special constraints on yourself. Inevitably, you influence what happens.

Ordinarily the effects are slight. It's as if the space-time continuum were like a mesh of tough rubber bands, restoring its configuration after it's felt some disturbing force. Indeed, ordinarily you are a part of that past. There really was a man who traveled with Pizarro and called himself Brother Tanaquil. That was "always" true, and the fact that he wasn't born in that century, but long afterward, is incidental. If he does minor anachronistic things, they don't matter; they may excite comment, but memory of them will die out. It's a philosophical question whether or not reality keeps flickering through such insignificant changes.

Some acts, though, do make a difference. What if a lunatic went back to the fifth century and provided Attila the Hun with machine guns? That kind of thing is so obvious it's fairly easy to guard against. But subtler changes— The Bolshevik Revolution of 1917 came near failing. Only the energy and genius of Lenin pulled it through. What if you traveled to the nineteenth century and quietly, harmlessly prevented Lenin's parents from ever meeting each other? Whatever else the Russian Empire later became, it would not be the Soviet Union, and the consequences of that would pervade all history afterward. You, pastward of the change, would still be there; but returning futureward, you'd find a totally different world, a world in which you yourself were probably never born. You'd exist, but as an effect without a cause, thrown up into existence by that anarchy which is at its foundation.

When the first time machine had been built, the Danellians appeared, the superhumans who inhabit the remote future. They ordained the rules of time traffic and established the Patrol to enforce these. Like other police, we mostly assist people on their lawful occasions; we get them out of tight spots when we can; we give what help and kindness we dare to the victims of history. But always our basic mission is to protect and preserve that history, because it is what shall finally bring forth the glorious Danellians.

"I'm sorry," Helen Tamberly said. "That was idiotic of me. But I've been . . . so worried. Stephen was only supposed to be gone three days. Six years for him, three days for me. He wanted that much time merely to reaccustom himself to this milieu. He meant to wander about incognito, getting back into Victorian habits, so he wouldn't absent-mindedly do something that would surprise the servants or our local friends. It's been a week!" She bit her lip. "Forgive me. I'm still babbling, am I not?"

"Far from it." Everard took forth pipe and tobacco pouch. He wanted that small comfort in the face of this anguish. "Loving couples like you make a bachelor like me feel wistful. But let's get down to business. Best for us both. You're native to England of this century, aren't you?"

She nodded. "Born in Cambridge, 1856. I was orphaned at seventeen, left with modest independent means, studied classics, became rather a bluestocking, eventually was recruited into the Patrol. Stephen and I met at the Academy. In spite of the age difference—which doesn't matter for us, thank God—we . . . hit it off, and married after we graduated. He didn't think I would like his birthtime." She grimaced. "I visited it, and he was right. For his part, he felt—feels happy here and now. His persona is that of an American employee of the import firm. When I go off to my own work, or bring some home with me, well, it is unusual for a woman to have scholarly interests, but not extraordinary. Marie Sklodowska—Madame Curie—will enroll in the Sorbonne just a few years hence."

"And people in this milieu are better at minding their own affairs than they are in mine." Everard occupied himself with tamping his briar full. "Uh, I daresay you two do more things together than is common for man and wife these days."

"Oh, yes." Her eagerness was pathetic to hear. "Beginning with our holidays, in this era and that. We fell quite in love with archaic Japan, and have been back several times." Everard concluded that that was a country isolated enough, with a population small and unsophisticated enough, illiterate, that the Patrol allowed occasional visits by blatant outsiders. "We've taken up handicrafts; pottery, for example; that ashtray beside you is his work—" Her voice died away.

Hastily, he queried onward. "Your field is ancient Greece?" The man who met him at the base hadn't been sure.

"The Ionian colonies, chiefly in the seventh and sixth centuries before Christ." She sighed. "It's ironic that there the Patrol cannot admit me, a Nordic woman." She tried to rally. "But as I said, we've seen much else that is wonderful." Suitably outfitted, carefully guided. "No, I mustn't complain." The stoicism cracked. "If Stephen—if you do bring him back—do you think he can be persuaded to settle down and do research in place, like me?"

Everard's match cast a loud *scrit* across the silence that followed. He rolled smoke over his tongue and cradled the rough wood in his hand. "Don't count on it," he said. "Besides, good field historians are scarce. Good people of every kind are. You may not be fully aware of how undermanned we are in the corps. Your sort make it possible for his sort to operate. And mine. Normally we came home safe."

Patrol work was anything but bravado and derring-do. It depended on exact knowledge. Agents like Steve collected most of that on the spot, but they too required the patient labor of those like Helen, who collated the reports. Thus, observers in Ionia brought back immensely more information than those chronicles and relics that survived into the nineteenth century had ever contained; but they could not do her job, which was to put it all together, interpret, arrange, and prepare briefings for the next expeditions.

"Someday he must find something safer." She blushed. "I refuse to start a family until he does."

"Oh, I'm sure he'll move into an administrative post in due course," Everard answered. *If we can save him.* "He'll have gotten far too much experience for us to let him go on grubbing around. Instead, he'll direct the efforts of newer people. Um, that may well require his assuming a Spanish colonial persona for a few decades. It'd be easiest if you could join him."

"What an adventure! I should adapt. We didn't plan on remaining Victorians forever."

"And you've ruled out twentieth-century America. Hm, what about his ties there?"

"He comes from an old California family. It has distant Peruvian connections. A great-grandfather of his was a sea captain who married a young lady in Lima and brought her home with him. Perhaps that helped interest him in early Perú. I suppose you know he became an anthropologist, later practiced archaeology down there. He has a married brother in San Francisco. His own first marriage ended in divorce, shortly before he enlisted in the Patrol. That was—will be—in 1968. Subsequently he resigned his professorship and told everyone he had a grant from a learned institution, which would enable him to do independent research. This explains his frequent prolonged absences. He does still keep bachelor quarters, so as to remain in touch with kin and friends, and has no plans at present to phase out of their lives. At last he must, and knows it, but—" She smiled. "He has talked about seeing his favorite niece get married and have a baby. He says he wants to enjoy being a granduncle."

Everard ignored the scrambled tenses. It was inevitable when you spoke any language but Temporal. "Favorite niece, eh?" he murmured. "That kind of person is often useful, apt to know a lot and tell it freely without getting suspicious. What do you know about her?"

"Her name is Wanda, and she was born in 1965. The last several mentions of her that Stephen made to me, she was, m-m, a student of biology at a place called Stanford University. As a matter of fact, he scheduled his departure on this last mission from California rather than London so he could first see his relatives there in, oh, yes, 1986."

"I had better interview her."

A knock sounded on the door. "Come in," the woman called.

The maid entered. "There is a person who asks to see you, missus," she announced. "Mr. Basscase, he says is his name." With frosty disapproval: "A gentleman of color."

"That's the other agent," Everard muttered to his hostess. "Earlier than I expected."

"Send him in," she directed.

Julio Vasquez did indeed look out of place: short, stocky, bronze of skin, black of hair, with wide features and arched nose. He was almost pure native Andean, though born in the twenty-second century, Everard knew. Still, this neighborhood had doubtless grown somewhat accustomed to exotic visitors.

Not only was London the center of a planet-wide empire, York Place divided Baker Street.

Helen Tamberly received the newcomer graciously, and now she did send for tea. The Patrol had cured her of any Victorian racism. Necessarily, the language became Temporal, for she had no Spanish (or Quechua!) and English was not important enough in Vasquez's life, either before or after he joined the Patrol, for him to acquire more than some stock phrases.

"I have learned very little," he said. "It was an especially difficult undertaking, the more so on such short notice. To the Spaniards I was merely another Indian. How could I approach one, let alone make inquiries of him? I could have been flogged for insolence, or killed out of hand."

"The Conquistadores were a bunch of bas—of hellhounds, all right," Everard remarked. "As I recall, after Atahuallpa's ransom was in, Pizarro didn't let him go. No, he put him before a kangaroo court on a bunch of trumped-up charges and sentenced him to death. To be burned alive, wasn't it?"

"It was commuted to strangling when he accepted baptism," Vasquez said, "and a number of the Spanish, including Pizarro himself, felt guilty about the matter afterward. They had been afraid Atahuallpa, set free, would stir up a revolt against them. Their later puppet Inca, Manco, did." He paused. "Yes, the Conquest was ghastly, slaughters, lootings, enslavements. But, my friends, you were taught history in anglophone schools, and Spain was for centuries England's rival. Propaganda from that conflict has endured. The truth is that the Spaniards, Inquisition and all, were no worse than anyone else of that era, and better than many. Some, such as Cortés himself, and even Torquemada, tried to get a measure of justice for the natives. It is worth remembering that those populations survived throughout most of Latin America, on ancestral soil, whereas the English, with their yanqui and Canadian successors, made a nearly clean sweep."

"Touché," said Everard wryly.

"Please," Helen Tamberly whispered.

"My apologies, señora." Vasquez gave her a bow from his chair. "I did not mean to tantalize you, only to explain why I could find out very little. Apparently the friar and a soldier went into the house where the hoard was kept one night. When they did not reappear by dawn, the guards grew nervous and opened the door. They were not inside. Every door had been watched. Sensational rumors flew. What I heard was through the Indios, and I could not query them either. Remember, I was a stranger among them, and they hardly ever traveled away from home. The upheaval in progress allowed me to concoct a story accounting for my presence in the city, but it would not have withstood examination, had anyone grown interested in me."

Everard puffed hard on his pipe. "Hm," he said around it, "I gather that Tamberly, as the friar, had access to each new load of treasure, to pray over it or whatever. Actually, he took holograms of the artwork, for future people's information and enjoyment. But what about that soldier?"

Vasquez shrugged. "I heard his name, Luis Castelar, and that he was a cavalry officer who had distinguished himself in the campaign. Some said he might have plotted to steal the wealth, but others replied that that was unthinkable of so honorable a knight, not to mention good-hearted Fray Tanaquil. Pizarro interrogated the sentries at length but, I heard, satisfied himself about their honesty. After all, the hoard was still there. When I left, the general idea was that sorcerers had been at work. Hysteria was building rapidly. It could have hideous consequences."

"Which are *not* in the history we learned," Everard growled. "How critical is that exact piece of space-time?"

"The Conquest as a whole, certainly vital, a key part of world events. This one episode—who knows? We have not ceased to exist, in spite of being uptime of it."

"Which doesn't mean we can't cease," said Everard roughly. *We can have never been, ourselves and the whole world that begot us. It's a perishing more absolute than death.* "The Patrol shall concentrate everything it can spare on that span of days or weeks. And proceed with extreme caution," he added to Helen Tamberly. "What could have happened? Have you any clues, Agent Vasquez?"

"I may have a slender one," the other man told them. "I suspect that somebody with a time vehicle had in mind hijacking the ransom."

"Yeah, that's a fair guess. One of Tamberly's assignments was to keep an eye on developments and let the Patrol know of anything suspicious."

"How could he before he returned uptime?" the woman wondered aloud.

"He left recorded messages in what looked like ordinary rocks, but which emitted identifying Y-radiation," Everard explained. "The agreed-on spots were checked, but nothing was there except brief, routine reports on what he'd been experiencing."

"I was taken from my real mission for this investigation," Vasquez went on. "My work was a generation earlier, in the reign of Huayna Capac, father of Atahuallpa and Huáscar. We can't understand the Conquest without an understanding of the great and complex civilization that it destroyed." An imperium reaching from Ecuador deep into Chile, and from the Pacific seaboard to the headwaters of the Amazon. "And . . . it seems that strangers appeared at the court of that Inca in 1524, about a year before his death. They resembled Europeans and were taken to be such; the realm had heard rumors of men from afar. They left after a while, nobody knew where or how. But when I was called back uptime, I had begun to get intimations that they tried to persuade Huayna not to give Atahuallpa such power that he could rival Huáscar. They failed; the old man was stubborn. But that the attempt was made is significant, no?"

Everard whistled. "God, yes! Did you get any hint as to who those visitors might have been?"

"No. Nothing worthwhile. That entire milieu is exceptionally hard to penetrate." Vasquez made a crooked smile. "Having defended the Spaniards against the charge of having been monsters, by sixteenth-century standards, I must say that the Inca state was not a nation of peaceful innocents. It was aggressively expanding in every possible direction. And it was totalitarian; it regulated life down to the last detail. Not unkindly; if you conformed, you were provided for. But woe betide you if you did not. The very nobles lacked any freedom worth mentioning. Only the Inca, the god-king, had that. You can see the difficulties an outsider confronts, regardless of whether he belongs to the same race. In Caxamalca I said I had been sent to report on my district to the bureaucracy. Before Pizarro upset the reign, I could never have made that story stick. As it was, all I got to hear was second- and third-hand gossip."

Everard nodded. Like practically everything in history, the Spanish Conquest was neither entirely bad nor entirely good. Cortés at least put an end to the grisly massacre-sacrifices of the Aztecs, and Pizarro opened the way for a concept of individual dignity and worth. Both invaders had Indian allies, who joined them for excellent reasons.

Well, a Patrolman had no business moralizing. His duty was to preserve what *was*, from end to end of time, and to stand by his comrades.

"Let's talk about whatever we can think of that might conceivably be of help," he proposed. "Mrs. Tamberly, we will not abandon your husband to his fate. Maybe we can't rescue him, but we're sure going to give it our best try."

Jenkins brought in tea.

30 October 1986

Mr. Everard is a surprise. His letters and then his phone calls from New York were, well, polite and kind of intellectual. Here he is in person, a big bruiser with a dented nose. How old is he, forty? Hard to tell. I'm sure he's knocked around a lot.

No matter his looks. (They could be might sexy if things took that turn. Which they won't. Doubtless for the best, damn it.) He's soft-spoken, with the same old-fashioned quality as his communications had.

Shake hands. "Glad to meet you, Miss Tamberly," the deep voice says. "It's kind of you to come here." Downtown hotel, the lobby.

"Well, it concerns my one and only uncle, doesn't it?" I toss back.

He nods. "I'd like to speak with you at length. Uh, would it be forward of me if I offered to stand you a drink? Or dinner? I'll be putting you to a certain amount of trouble."

Caution. "Thanks, but let's see how it goes. Right now, frankly, I'm too keyed up. Could we just walk for a while?"

"Why not? A beautiful day, and I haven't been in Palo Alto in years. Maybe we can go to the university and stroll around?"

Gorgeous weather for sure, Indian summer before the rains start in earnest. If it lasts we'll have smog. Right now, clear blue overhead, sunlight spilling down like a waterfall. The eucalyptuses on campus will be all silvery and pale green and pungent. In spite of the situation (oh, what has become of Uncle Steve?) I can't keep excitement down. Me, with a real live detective.

Turn left in the street. "What do you want, Mr. Everard?"

"To interview you, exactly as I told you. I'd like to draw you out about Dr. Tamberly. Something you say might give an inkling."

Good of that foundation to care, to hire this man. Well, naturally, they have an investment in Uncle Steve. He's doing that research down in South America, that he's never talked much about. Must be one dynamite book he means to write. Reflect credit on the foundation. Help justify its tax exemption. No, I shouldn't think that. Cheap cynicism is for sophomores.

"Why me, though? I mean, my dad's his brother. He'd know a lot more."

"Maybe. I do intend to see him and his wife. But the information given me says you're a special favorite of your uncle's. I've got a hunch he's revealed things about himself to you—nothing big, nothing you imagine is very special—but things that might give some insight into his character, some clue as to where he went."

Swallow hard. Six months, now, with never so much as a postcard. "Have they no idea at the foundation?"

"You asked me before," Everard reminds. "He always was an independent operator. Made it a condition of accepting the funds. Yes, he was bound for the Andes, but we hardly know more than that. It's a huge territory. The police authorities of the several possible countries haven't been able to tell us a thing."

This is hard to say. Melodrama. But. "Do you suspect . . . foul play?"

"We don't know, Miss Tamberly. We hope not. Maybe he took too long a chance and— Anyway, my job's to try understanding him." He smiles. It creases his face. "My notion of how to do that is to start by understanding the people he feels close to."

"He always was, you know, reserved. Quite a private guy."

"With a soft spot for you, however. Mind if I ask you a few questions about yourself, for openers?"

"Go ahead. I don't guarantee to answer them all."

"Nothing too personal. Let's see. You're in your senior year at Stanford, right? What's your major?"

"Biology."

"That's about as broad a word as 'physics,' isn't it?"

He's no dummy. "Well, I'm mainly interested in evolutionary transitions. Probably I'll go into paleontology."

"You plan on grad school, then?"

"Oh, yes. A Ph.D.'s the union card if you want to do science."

"You look more athletic than academic, if I may say so."

"Tennis, backpacking, sure, I like it outdoors, and fossicking for fossils is a great way to get paid for being there." Impulse. "I've got a summer job lined up. Tourist guide in the Galápagos Islands. The Lost World if ever there was a Lost World." Suddenly my eyes sting and blur. "Uncle Steve arranged it for me. He has friends in Ecuador."

"Sounds terrific. How's your Spanish?"

"Pretty good. We, my family, used to vacation a lot in Mexico. I still go now and then, and I've traveled in South America."

—He's been remarkably easy to talk with. "Comfortable as an old shoe," Dad would say. We sat on a campus bench, we had a beer in the union, he did end up taking me to dinner. Nothing fancy, nothing romantic. But worth cutting those classes for. I've told him an awful lot.

Funny how little he's managed to tell about himself.

I realize that as he says good night outside my apartment building. "You've been most helpful, Miss Tamberly. Maybe more than you know. I'll get hold of your parents tomorrow. Then back to New York, I suppose. Here." He takes out his wallet, extracts a small white oblong. "My card. If anything else should come to your mind, please phone me at once, collect." Dead seriousness: "Or if anything happens that seems the least peculiar. Please. This might be a tad dangerous, this business."

Uncle Steve involved with the CIA, or what? Suddenly the evening doesn't feel mild. "Okay. Good night, Mr. Everard." I snatch the card and hurry through the door.

11 May 2937 B.C.

"When I saw they were off guard and close together," Castelar said, "I called on Sant'Iago in my mind, and sprang. My kick took the first in the throat and he went to the floor. I whirled about and gave the second the heel of my hand below the nose, an upward blow, *thus*." The movement was quick and savage. "He fell too. I retrieved my blade, made sure of them both, and came after you."

His tone was almost casual. Tamberly thought, in the daze dulling his brain, that the Exaltationists had made the common mistake of underestimating a man of a past era. This one was ignorant of nearly everything they knew, but his wits were fully equal to theirs. Thereon was laid a ferocity bred by centuries of war—not impersonal high-technological conflict but medieval combat, where you looked into your enemy's eyes and cut him down with your own hand.

"Were you not the least afraid of their . . . magic?" Tamberly mumbled.

Castelar shook his head. "I knew God was with me." He crossed himself, then sighed. "It was stupid of me to leave their guns behind. I will not fail like that again."

Despite the heat, Tamberly shivered.

He sat slumped in long grass beneath a noonday sun. Castelar stood above him, metal a-shine, hand on hilt, legs apart, like a colossus bestriding the world. The timecycle rested several yards off. Beyond, a stream flowed toward the sea, which was not visible here but which, he estimated from his glimpse aloft, lay twenty or thirty miles distant. Palm, chirimoya, and other vegetation told him they were "still" in tropical America. He had a vague recollection of chancing to give the temporal activator a harder thrust than the spatial.

Could he get up, make a break for it, beat the Spaniard to the machine and escape? Impossible. Were he in better shape, he would try. Like most field agents, he'd received training in martial arts. That might offset the other's cruder skills and greater strength. (Any cavalier spent his whole life in such physical activity that an Olympic champion would be flabby by comparison.) Now he was too weak, in body and mind alike. With the kyradex off his head, he had volition again. But it wasn't much use yet. He felt drained, sand in his synapses, lead in his eyelids, skull scooped hollow.

Castelar glowered downward. "Cease twisting words, sorcerer," he rapped. "It is for me to put you to the question."

Should I just keep mum and provoke him into killing me? Tamberly wondered in his weariness. *I imagine he'd apply torture first, seeking to force my cooperation. But afterward he'd be stranded, made harmless. . . . No. He'd be sure to monkey with the vehicle. That could easily bring about his destruction; but if it didn't, what else could happen? I must keep my death in reserve till I'm certain it's the only thing I have to offer.*

He lifted his gaze to the dark eagle visage and dragged forth: "I am no sorcerer. I merely have knowledge you don't, of various arts and devices. The Indios thought our musketeers commanded the lightning. It was simple gunpowder. A compass needle points north, but not by magic." *Though you don't understand the actual principle, do you?* "Likewise for weapons that stun without wounding, and for engines that overleap space and time."

Castelar nodded. "I had that feeling," he said slowly. "My captors whom I slew let words drop."

Lord, this is *a bright fellow! A genius, perhaps, in his fashion. Yes, I remember him remarking that besides his studies among the priests, he's enjoyed reading stories of Amadis—those fantastic romances that inflamed the imagination of his era—and another remark once showed a surprisingly sophisticated view of Islam.*

Castelar tautened. "Then tell me what this is about," he demanded. "What are you in truth, you who falsely claim ordainment?"

Tamberly groped through his mind. No barriers crossed it. The kyradex had wiped out his reflex against revealing that time travel and the Time Patrol existed. What remained was his duty.

Somehow he must get control of this horrible situation. Once he'd had a rest, let flesh and intelligence recover from the shocks they had suffered, he should have a pretty good chance of outwitting Castelar. No matter how quick on the uptake, the man would be overwhelmed by strangeness. At the moment, however, Tamberly was only half alive. And Castelar sensed the weakness and hammered shrewdly, pitilessly on it.

"Tell me! No dawdling, no sly roundabouts. Out with the truth!" The sword slid partly from its scabbard and snicked back.

"The tale is long and long, Don Luis—"

A boot caught Tamberly in the ribs. He rolled over and lay gasping. Pain went through him in waves. As if among thunders, he heard: "Come, now. Speak."

He forced himself back to a sitting position, hunched beneath implacability. "Yes, I masqueraded as a friar, but with no un-Christian intention." He coughed. "It was necessary. You see, there are evil men abroad who also have these engines. As it was, they sought to raid your treasury, and bore us two off—"

The interrogation went on. Had it been the Dominicans under whom Castelar studied, they who ran the Spanish Inquisition? Or had he simply learned how to deal with prisoners of war? At first Tamberly had a notion of concealing the time travel part. It slipped from him, or was jarred from him, and Castelar hounded it. Remarkable how swiftly he grasped the idea. None of the theory. Tamberly himself had just the ghostliest idea of that, which a science millennia beyond his people's was to create. The thought that space and time were united baffled Castelar, till he dismissed it with an oath and went on to practical questions. But he did come to realize that the machine could fly; could hover; could instantly be wherever and whenever else its pilot willed.

Perhaps his acceptance was natural. Educated men of the sixteenth century believed in miracles; it was Christian, Jewish, and Muslim dogma. They also lived in a world of revolutionary new discoveries, inventions, ideas. The Spanish, especially, were steeped in tales of chivalry and enchantment— would be, till Cervantes laughed that out of them. No scientist had told Castelar that travel into the past was physically impossible, no philosopher had listed the reasons why it was logically absurd. He met the simple fact.

Mutability, the danger of aborting an entire future, did seem to elude him. Or else he refused to let it curb him. "God will take care of the world," he stated, and went after knowledge of what he could do and how.

He readily imagined argosies faring between the ages, and it fired him. Not that he was much interested in the truly precious articles of that commerce: the origins of civilizations, the lost poems of Sappho, a performance by the greatest gamelan virtuoso who ever lived, three-dimensional pictures of art that would be melted down for a ransom. . . . He thought of rubies and slaves and, foremost, weapons. It was reasonable to him that kings of the future would seek to regulate that traffic and bandits seek to plunder it.

"So you were a spy for your lord, and his enemies were surprised to find us when they came as thieves in the night, but by God's grace we are free again," he said. "What next?"

The sun was low. Thirst raged in Tamberly's throat. His head felt ready to break open, his bones to fall apart. Blurred in his vision, Castelar squatted before him, tireless and terrible.

"Why, we . . . we should return . . . to my comrades in arms," Tamberly croaked. "They will reward you well and . . . bring you back to your proper place."

"Will they, now?" The grin was wolfish. "And what payment to me, at best? Nor am I sure you have spoken truth, Tanaquil. The single sure thing is that God has given this instrument into my hands, and I must use it for His glory and the honor of my nation."

Tamberly felt as if the words driven against him, hour after hour, had each been a fist. "What would you, then?"

Castelar stroked his beard. "I think first," he murmured, narrow-eyed, "yes, assuredly first, you shall teach me how to manage this steed." He bounced to his feet. "Up!"

He must well-nigh drag his prisoner to the timecycle.

I must lie, I must delay, at worst I must refuse and take my punishment. Tamberly couldn't. Exhaustion, pain, thirst, hunger betrayed him. He was physically incapable of resistance.

Castelar crouched over him, alert to every move, ready to pounce at the slightest suspicion; and Tamberly was too stupefied to deceive him.

Study the console between the steering bars. Press for the date. The machine recorded every shift it made through the continuum. Yes, they'd come far indeed into the past, the thirtieth century before Christ.

"Before Christ," Castelar breathed. "Why, of course, I can go to my Lord when he walked this earth and fall on my knees—"

At that instant of his ecstasy, a hale man might have given him a karate chop. Tamberly could merely sag across the saddles and reach for an activator. Castelar flung him aside like a sack of meal. He lay half conscious on the ground till the sword pricked him into creeping back up.

A map display. Location: near the coast of what would someday be southern Ecuador. At Castelar's behest, Tamberly made the whole world revolve in the screen. The Conquistador lingered a while over the Mediterranean. "Destroy the paynim," he murmured. "Regain the Holy Land."

With the help of the map unit, which could show a region at any scale desired, the space control was childishly simple to use. At least, it was if a coarse positioning sufficed. Castelar agreed shrewdly that he'd better not try such a stunt as appearing inside a locked treasure vault before he'd had plenty of practice. Time settings were as easy, once he learned the post-Arabic numerals. He did that in minutes.

Facile operation was necessary. A traveler might have to get out of somewhere or somewhen in a hell of a rush. Flying, on the antigravity drive, paradoxically required more skill. Castelar made Tamberly show him those controls, then get on behind him for a test flight. "If I fall, you do too," he reminded.

Tamberly wished they would. At first they wobbled, he nearly lost his seat, but soon Castelar was gleefully in charge. He experimented with a time jump, went back half a day. Abruptly the sun was high, and in the magnifying scanner screen he saw himself and the other a mile below in the valley. That shook him. Hastily, he sprang toward sunset. With the space jump, he shifted close to the now deserted ground. After hovering for a minute, he made a bumpy landing.

They got off. "Ah, praise God!" Castelar cried. "His wonders and mercies are without end."

"Please," Tamberly begged, "could we go to the river? I'm nigh dead of thirst."

"Presently you may drink," Castelar answered. "Here is neither food nor fire. Let us find a better place."

"Where?" Tamberly groaned.

"I have thought upon this," Castelar said. "Seeking your king, no, that would be to put myself in his power. He would reclaim this device that can mean so much to Christendom. Back to that night in Caxamalca? No, not at once. We could run afoul of the pirates. If not, then certainly my own great captain Pizarro—with due respect— It would be difficult. But if I come carrying invincible weapons, he will heed my counsel."

Amidst the inner murk bearing down on him, Tamberly remembered that the Indians of Perú were not fully subjugated when the Conquistadores fell into combat against each other.

"You tell me that you hail from some two thousand years after Our Lord," Castelar proceeded. "That age could be a good harbor for a while. You know your way about in it. At the same time, the marvels should not be too bewildering to me—if this invention was made long afterward, as you have said." Tamberly realized that he had no dream of automobiles, airplanes, skyscrapers, television. . . . He kept his tigerish wariness: "However, I would fain begin in a peaceful haven, a backwater where the surprises are few, and feel my way forward. Yes, if we can find one more person there, someone whose word I can compare with yours—" Explosively: "You heard. You must know. Speak!"

Light ran long and golden out of the west. Birds streamed home to roost in darkling trees. The river gleamed with water, water. Again Castelar used physical force. He was efficient about it.

Wanda . . . she'd be in the Galápagos in 1987, and God knew those islands were peaceful enough. . . . Exposing her to this danger did worse than break the Patrol's directive; the kyradex had broken that within Tamberly anyway. But she was as smart and resourceful, and almost as strong, as any man. She'd be loyal to her poor battered uncle. Her blond beauty would distract Castelar, while he grew incautious of a mere female. Between them, the Americans could find or make an opportunity. . . .

Afterward, often and often, the patrolman cursed himself. Yet it was not really himself that responded, by whimpers and jerks, to the urging of the warrior.

Maps and coordinates of the islands, which no man recorded in history would tread before 1535; some description of them; some explanation of what the girl did there (Castelar was amazed, until he remembered amazons in the medieval romances); something about her as a person; the likelihood that she would be surrounded by friends most of the time, but toward the end might well take occasion to hike off alone— Again it was the questions, the cunning carnivore mind, that hunted everything out into the open.

Dusk had fallen. Tropically rapid, it deepered toward night. Stars winked forth. A jaguar yowled.

"Ah, so." Castelar laughed, softly and joyously. "You have done well, Tanaquil. Not of your free will; nevertheless, you have earned surcease."

"Please, may I go drink?" Tamberly would have to crawl.

"As you wish. Abide here, though, so I can find you later. Otherwise I fear you will perish in this wilderness."

Dismay jagged through Tamberly. Roused, he sat straight in the grass. "What? We were leaving together!"

"No, no. I have scant trust in you yet, my friend. I will see what I can do for myself. Afterward—that is in the hands of God. Until I come fetch you, farewell."

Sky-glow sheened on helmet and corselet. The knight of Spain strode to the time machine. He mounted it. Luminous, the controls yielded to his fingers. "Sant'Iago and at them!" rang aloud. He lifted several yards into the air. There followed a puff, and he was gone.

12 May 2937 B.C.

Tamberly woke at sunrise. The riverside was wet beneath him. Reeds rustled in a low wind, water purled and clucked. Smells of growth filled his nostrils.

His entire body hurt. Hunger clawed at him. But his head was clear, healed of the kyradex confusion and the torments that had followed. He could think again, be a man again. He climbed stiffly to his feet and stood for a span inhaling coolness.

The sky reached pale blue, empty save for a flight of crows that cawed past and disappeared. Castelar had not returned. Maybe he'd allow extra time. Seeing himself from above had perturbed him. Maybe he wouldn't return. He could meet death, off in the future, or could decide he didn't give a damn about the false friar.

No telling. What I can do is try to nail down that he never does find me. I can try to stay free.

Tamberly began walking. He was weak, but if he husbanded his energy, following the river, he should reach the sea. Chances were there'd be a settlement at the estuary. Humans had long since crossed over from Asia to America. They'd be primitive, but likely hospitable. With the skills he possessed, he could become important among them.

After that— Already he had an idea.

22 July 1435

He lets go of me. I drop a few inches to the ground, lose my footing, fall. Bounce up again. Scramble back from him. Stop. Stare.

Still in the saddle, he smiles. Through the blood racketing in my ears, I hear: "Be not afraid, señorita. I beg your pardon for this rough treatment, but saw no other way. Now, alone, we can talk."

Alone! Look around. We're close to water, a bay, see those outlines against the sky, got to be Academy Bay near Darwin Station, only what became of the station? Of the road to Puerto Ayora? Matazarno bushes, Palo Santo trees, grass in clumps, cactus between, sparse. Empty, empty. Ashes of a campfire. Jesus Christ! The giant shell, gnawed bones of a tortoise! This man's killed a Galápagos tortoise!

"Please do not flee," he says. "I would simply have to overtake you. Believe me, your honor is safe. More safe than it would be anywhere else. For we are quite by ourselves in these islands, like Adam and Eve before the Fall."

Throat dry, tongue thick, "Who are you? What is this?"

He gets off his machine. Sweeps me a courtly bow. "Don Luis Ildefonso Castelar y Moreno, from Barracota in Castile, lately with the captain Francisco Pizarro in Perú, at your service, my lady."

He's crazy, or I am, or the whole world is. Again I wonder if I'm dreaming, hit my head, caught a fever, delirious. Sure doesn't feel that way. Those are plants I know. They stay put. The sun's shifted overhead and the air's less warm, but the smells baked out of the earth, they're like always. A grasshopper chirrs. A blue heron flaps by. Could this be for *real?*

"Sit down," he says. "You are taken aback. Would you like a drink of water?" As if to soothe me: "I fetch it from elsewhere. This is a desolate country. But you are welcome to all you want."

I nod, do as he suggests. He picks a container off the ground, brings it in reach of me, steps off at once. Not to alarm the little girl. It's a bucket, pink, cracked at the top, usable but scarcely worth keeping. He must have scrounged it from wherever it got tossed out. Even in those shacky little houses in the village, plastic's cheap.

Plastic.

Final touch. Practical joke. 'Tain't funny, God. Got to laugh anyway. Whoop. Howl.

"Be calm, señorita. I tell you, while you behave wisely you have nothing to fear. I will protect you."

That pig! I'm no ultrafeminist, but when a kidnapper starts patronizing me, too much. The laughter rattles down to silence. Rise. Brace muscles. They shiver a bit.

Somehow, regardless, I am no longer afraid. Coldly furious. At the same time, more aware than ever before. He stands in front of me as sharp as if a lightning flash lit him up. Not a big man; thin; but remember that strength of his. Hispanic features, all right, of the pure European kind, tanned practically black. Not in costume. Those clothes are faded, mended, grubby; vegetable dyes. Unwashed, like himself. Smell powerful but he doesn't really stink, it's an outdoor kind of odor. The ridged helmet, sweeping down to guard his neck, and the cuirass are tarnished. I see scratches in the steel. From battle? Sword hung at his left hip. Sheath at the right meant for a knife. It being gone, he must have butchered the tortoise and cut a skewer for roasting it with the sword. Firewood he could break off these parched branches. Yonder, a fire drill he made. Sinew for cord. He's been here a while.

Whisper: "Where is here?"

"Another island of the same archipelago. You know it as Santa Cruz. That is five hundred years hence. Today is one hundred years before the discovery."

Breathe slow and deep. Heart, take it easy. I've read my share of science fiction. Time travel. Only, a Spanish Conquistador!

"*When* are you from?"

"I told you. About a century in the future. I fared with the brothers Pizarro and we overthrew the pagan king of Perú."

"No. I shouldn't understand you." Wrong, Wanda. I remember. Uncle Steve told me once. If I met a sixteenth-century Englishman, I'd have a devil of a time. Spelling didn't change (won't change) too much, but pronunciation did. Spanish is a more stable language.

Uncle Steve!

Cool it. Speak steadily. Can't quite. Look this man in the eyes, at least. "You mentioned my kinsman just before you . . . laid violent hands on me."

He sounds exasperated. "I did no more than was necessary. Yes, if you are indeed Wanda Tamberly, I know your father's brother." He peers like a cat at a mouse hole. "The name he used among us was Esteban Tanaquil."

Uncle Steve a time traveler too? I can't help it, dizziness rushes through me.

I shake myself free of it. Don Luis Et Cetera sees I'm bewildered. Or else he knew I'd be. I think he wants to push things along, keep me off balance. Says, "I warned you he is in danger. That is true. He is my hostage, left in a wilderness where starvation will soon take him off, unless wild beasts do so first. It is for you to earn his ransom."

22 May 1987

Blink. We're there. Like a blow to the solar plexus. I almost fall off. Grab his waist. Face burrows into roughness of his cloak.

Calm, lassie. He told you to expect this . . . transition. He's awed. Hasty in the wind, *"Ave Maria gratiae plena—"* It's cold up here in heaven. No moon, but stars everywhere. Riding lights of a plane, blink, blink, blink.

The Peninsula tremendous, a sprawled galaxy, half a mile underneath us. White, yellow, red, green, blue, shining blood-flow of cars, from San Jose to San Francisco. Hulks of black to the left where the hills rise. Shimmering darkness to the right, the Bay, fire-streaked by the bridges. Towns glimpsed, clusters of sparks, on the far shore. About ten o'clock of a Friday evening.

How often have I seen this before? From airliners. A space-time bike hanging aloft, me in the buddy seat behind a man born almost five centuries ago, that's something else.

He masters himself. The sheer lion courage of him—except a lion wouldn't charge headlong into the unknown, the way those guys did after Columbus showed them half a world to plunder. "Is this the realm of Morgana la Hada?" he breathes.

"No, it's where I live, those are lamps you see, lamps in the streets and houses and . . . on the wagons. They move by themselves, the wagons, without horses. Yonder goes a flying vessel. But it can't skip from place to place and year to year like this one."

A superwoman wouldn't babble facts. She'd feed him a line, mislead him, use his ignorance to trap him somehow. Yeah, "somehow," that's the catch. I'm just me, and he's a superman, or pretty close to it. Natural selection, back in his day. If you weren't physically tough, you didn't live to have kids. And a peasant could be stupid, might even do better if he was, but not a military officer who didn't have a Pentagon to plan his moves for him. Also, those hours of questioning on Santa Cruz Island (which I, Wanda May Tamberly, am the first woman ever to walk on) have beaten me down. He never laid a hand on me, but he kept at it and kept at it. Eroded the resistance out of me. My main thought right now is that I'd better cooperate. Otherwise he could too easily make some blunder that'd kill us both and leave Uncle Steve stranded.

"I have thought the saints might dwell in such a blaze of glory," Luis murmurs. The cities he knew went blackout after dark. You needed a lantern to find your way. If it was a fine city, it put stepping stones down the middle of the sidewalkless streets, to keep you above the horse droppings and garbage.

He turns tactical. "Can we descend unseen?"

"If you're careful. Go slowly as I guide you." I recognize the Stanford campus, a mostly unlighted patch. Lean forward against him, left hand holding onto the cloak. These are well-designed seats; my knees will keep me in place. That's a mighty long drop, though. Reach right arm past his side. Point. "Toward there."

The machine tilts forward. We slant down. My nose fills with the scents of him. I've already noticed: pungent rather than sour, yes, very macho.

Got to admire him. A hero, on his own terms. Can't stop a sneaking wish that he'll get away with his desperate caper.

Whoa, girl. That's a pitfall. You've heard about kidnapped people, even tortured people, developing sympathy with their captors. Don't you be a Patty Hearst.

Still, damn it, what Luis has done is fantastic. Brains as well as bravery. Think back. Try, while we chase through the air, try to get straight in your mind what he told you, what you saw, what you figured out.

Hard to. He admitted a lot of confusion himself. Mainly he hews to his faith in the Trinity and the warlike saints. He'll succeed, dedicating his victories to them, and become greater than the Holy Roman Emperor; or he'll die in the attempt and go to Paradise, all sins forgiven because what he did was in the cause of Christendom. Catholic Christendom.

Time travel for real. Some kind of *guarda del tiempo*, and Uncle Steve works for it. (Oh, Uncle Steve, while we laughed and chatted and went on family picnics and watched TV and played chess or tennis, this was behind your eyes.) Some kind of bandits or pirates also running loose through history, and isn't that a terrifying thought? Luis escaped from them, has this machine, has me, for his wild purposes.

How he got at me—wrung the basic information out of Uncle Steve. I'm afraid to imagine how, though he claims he didn't do any permanent damage. Flitted to the Galápagos, established camp before the islands were discovered. Made cautious reconnaissance trips into the twentieth century, 1987 to be exact. He knew I'd be around then, and I was the one person he had any hope of . . . using.

The campsite's in the arboretum behind Darwin Station. He could safely leave the machine there for a few hours at a stretch, especially in the early morning or late afternoon and at night. Walk into town or around the area, minus his armor. Clothes look funny, but he's careful to approach only working-class locals, and they're used to crazy tourists. Wheedle some, browbeat some, maybe bribe some. I got the impression he stole money. Ruthless. Anyhow, a few shrewd inquiries, at well-spaced intervals. Found out things about this era. Found out things about me. Once he knew I'd gone off on terminal leave, and roughly where, he could hover too high for us to see, watch through that magnifying screen he showed me, wait for an opportunity, swoop. And here we are.

He *will* do these things, come September. This is Memorial Day weekend. He wanted me to bring him to my home at a time when nobody would disturb us. Mainly me. (What's it like, meeting yourself in the living flesh?) I'm with Dad and Mom and Suzy in San Francisco. Tomorrow we're bound for Yosemite. Won't be back till Monday evening.

Him and me in my apartment. The other three units are vacant, I know, students also away for the holiday.

Well, I dare hope he'll continue "respecting my honor." He did make that nasty crack about me dressing like a man *o una puta*. Thank—well, be glad I had the wit to get up indignant and tell him this is respectable ladies' garb where I come from. He apologized, sort of. Said I was a white woman, in spite of being a heretic. Indian women's feelings didn't count, of course.

What will he do next? What does he want of me? I don't know. Probably he isn't sure either, yet. If I got the same chance he's got, how would I use it? It's a godlike power. Hard to stay sensible with those controls between your hands.

"Turn right. Slowly, now."

We've flown above University Avenue, across Middlefield, and yonder's the Plaza; my street's that-a-way. Yep. "Halt." We stop. I look past his shoulder at the square building, ten feet below us and twenty ahead. The windows glimmer blind.

"I have rooms in that upper story."

"Have you space for the chariot?"

Gulp. "Well, yes, in the largest chamber. A few feet"—how many, damn it?—"about three feet behind those panes at the very corner." I'm guessing the Spanish foot of his day is not too different from the English foot of mine.

Evidently not. He leans forward, peers, gauges. My pulse gallops. Sweat prickles my skin. He means to make a quantum jump through space (no, not really through space. Around it?) and appear in my living room. What if we come out in the middle of something?

Oh, he's experimented, in his Galápagos retreat. The nerve that that took! He's made discoveries. He tried to explain them to me. As near as I can follow it, put in twentieth-century words, you pass directly from one set of space-time coordinates to another. Maybe it's through a "wormhole"—vague recollection of articles in *Scientific American, Science News, Analog*—and for a moment your dimensions equal zero; then as you expand into your destination volume, you displace whatever matter is there. Air molecules, obviously. Luis found out that if a small solid object is in the way, it gets pushed aside. A big object, and the machine, with you aboard, settles beside it, off the exact spot you punched for. Probably mutual displacement. Action equals reaction. Agreed, Sir Isaac?

There must be limits. Suppose he gets it badly wrong and we end up in the wall. Splintering studs, nails shoved through my guts, stucco and plaster like cannonballs, and a ten- or twelve-foot drop to the ground on this heavy thing.

"Saint James be with us," he says. I feel his motions. Whoops!

We're here, inches above the floor. He sets us down. We're here.

Street glow dim through the windows. Get off. Knees weak. Start. Stop—his grip on my arm like jaws. "Halt," he commands.

"I only want to give us better light."

"I will make quite sure of that, my lady." He comes along. When I flick the switch and everything turns bright, he gasps. His fingers close bruisingly hard. "Ow!" He lets go and stares around him.

Must have seen electric bulbs on Santa Cruz. But Puerto Ayora's a poor little village, and I don't suppose he peeped into the station personnel's quarters. Try to look at this through his eyes. Difficult. I take it all for granted. How much can he actually *see*, as alien as it is to him?

Bike fills most of the rug. Crowds my desk, the sofa, the entertainment cabinet and bookshelf. It knocked two chairs over. Fourth wall, door open on the short hall. Bathroom and broom closet to the left, bedroom and clothes closet to the right, kitchen at the end, those doors closed. Cubbyholes. And I'll bet nobody less than a merchant prince lived like this in the sixteenth century.

What immediately astounds him: "So many books? You cannot be a cleric."

Why, I doubt if I have a hundred, texts included. And Gutenberg was before Columbus, wasn't he?

"How poorly bound they are." That seems to renew his confidence. I suppose books were still scarce and expensive. And no paperbacks.

He shakes his head at a couple of magazines; the covers must seem downright garish. Harshness again. "You will show me these lodgings."

I do, explaining things as best I can. He has glimpsed (will glimpse) faucets and flush toilets in Puerto Ayora. "How I wish for a bath," I sigh. Give me a hot shower and clean clothes, you can keep your Paradise, Don Luis.

"Presently, if you like. However, it shall be in my sight, like all else you do."

"What? Even the, uh, even that?"

He's embarrassed but determined. "I regret this, my lady, and will keep my face averted, save that I must see enough to be certain you make ready no trick. For I believe yours to be a valiant soul, and you have mysteries and devices that I do not fathom at your beck."

Ha. If only I did keep a .45 under my lingerie. At that, I've a bit of trouble convincing him the upright vacuum cleaner isn't a gun. He makes me lug it into the living room and demonstrate. A grin turns him human. "Give me a charwoman," he says. "She doesn't howl like a mad wolf."

We leave it where it is and return down the hall. In the kitchen-dinette, he admires the pilot-lighted gas range. Tell him, "I need a sandwich—food—and a beer. What about you? Tepid water and half-cooked tortoise for days."

"Do you offer me hospitality?" He sounds amazed.

"Call it that."

He ponders. "No. My thanks, but I cannot in conscience eat your salt."

Funny how touching that is. "Old-fashioned, aren't you? If I remember rightly, the Borgias were in business in your time. Or was that earlier? Well, let us agree we're opponents who've sat down to negotiate."

He inclines his head, takes off his helmet, and sets it on the counter. "My lady is most gracious."

A snack will do me a lot of good. And maybe disarm him. I am an attractive wench when I choose to be. Learn as much as possible. Keep alert. And beneath the tension—damn it, this is flat-out fascinating.

He watches me start the coffee maker. He's interested when I open the fridge, startled when I pop the tops on a couple of brews. I take a sip from the first and hand it to him. "Not poisoned, you see. Take a chair." He settles himself at the table. I get busy with bread and cheese and stuff.

"A curious drink," he says. Surely they had beer in his time, but doubtless it was quite different from ours.

"I have wine, if you'd rather."

"No, I must not dull my senses."

Beer in California wouldn't get a cat tiddly. Too bad.

"Tell me more about yourself, Lady Wanda."

"If you'll do likewise for me, Don Luis."

I serve us. We talk. What a life he's led! He finds mine just as remarkable. Well, I am a woman. By his lights, I should have devoted my efforts to breeding, housekeeping, and prayers. Unless I was Queen Isabella— Rein it in. Make him underestimate you.

That requires technique. I'm not used to flapping my lashes and cheering a man on to describe how wonderful he is. Can do it when called for, though.

One way to keep a date from deteriorating into a wrestling match. Never date that kind twice. Give me a guy who considers himself my equal.

Luis isn't the swinish sort either. He's keeping his promise, absolutely polite. Unyielding, but polite. A killer, a racist, a fanatic; a man of his word, fearless, ready to die for king or comrade; Charlemagne dreams, tender little memories of his mother, poor and proud in Spain. Kind of humorless, but a flaming romantic.

Glance at my watch. Close to midnight. Good Lord, have we sat here that long?

"What do you mean to do, Don Luis?"

"Obtain weapons of your country."

Level voice. Smile on lips. Sees my shock. "Are you surprised, my lady? What else could I seek? I would not abide in this place. From above, it may resemble the gates of Heaven, but I think down on earth, those engines rushing and roaring demonic in their thousands must make it more akin to Hell. Foreign folk, foreign language, foreign ways. Heresy and shamelessness rampant, no? Forgive me. I believe you are chaste, in spite of those garments. But are you not an infidel? Clearly, you defy God's law concerning the proper status of women." He shakes his head. "No, I will return to that age which is mine and my country's. Return well armed."

Appalled: "How?"

He tugs his beard. "I have given thought to this. A wagon of your kind would be of small use or none where there are neither roads nor fuel for it. Moreover, it would at best be a clumsy steed, set beside my gallant Florio—or the chariot I have captured. However, you must have firearms as far beyond our muskets and cannon as those are beyond the spears and bows of the Indios. Hand-held, yes, that would be best."

"But, but I haven't any weapons. I can't get any."

"You know what they are like and where they are kept. In military arsenals, for example. I will have much to ask you in the days to come. Thereafter, why, I have the means to pass unseen by bolts and bars, and carry off what I wish."

True. Chances are he'll succeed. He'll have me, first for briefing, later for guide. No way do I get out of that, unless I'm heroic and make him kill me. Which would leave him free to try elsewhere, and Uncle Steve forsaken wherever-whenever it is.

"How—how will you—use those guns?"

Solemn: "In the end, marshal the armies of the Emperor and lead them to victory. Hurl back the Turks. Uproot the Lutheran sedition in the North that I've heard of. Humble the French and English. The final Crusade." Draws breath. "First, I should assure the conquest of the New World and my own power within it. Not that I am more greedy for fame than others. But God has appointed me to this."

My mind spins through an insanity of what would follow from the least of his projects. "But everything around us now, it'll never have been! I'll never have been born!"

He crosses himself. "That is as God wills. However, if you give faithful service, I can take you back with me and see to your well-being."

Yeah. Well-being à la sixteenth-century Spanish female. If I exist. My parents wouldn't have, would they? I've no idea. I'm simply convinced Luis is juggling forces beyond his imagining, or mine, or anybody's except maybe that Time Guard—like a child playing on a snowfield ripe for an avalanche—

The Time Guard! That Everard man last year. Asking about Uncle Steve, why? Because Stephen Tamberly didn't really work for a scientific foundation. He worked for the Time Guard.

Their job has got to include heading off disasters. Everard gave me his card. Phone number on it. Where'd I put that bit of cardboard? Tonight the universe is balanced on it.

"I should begin by learning what did happen in Perú after I . . . left it," Luis is saying. "Then I can plan how to amend the tale. Tell me."

Shudder. Shake off the sense of nightmare. Think what to *do*. "I can't. How should I know? It was more than four hundred years ago." Solid, sinewy, sweaty, a ghost from that vanished past sits across from me, behind soiled plates, coffee cups, and beer cans.

Eruption in my head.

Hold voice low. Look downward. Demure. "We have history books, of course. And libraries that everyone may enter. I'll go find out."

He chuckles. "You are bold, my lady. However, you shall not leave these rooms, nor be out of my sight, until I am certain of my mastery of things. When I venture forth—to look about, or sleep, or for whatever reason—I will return to the same minute as I departed. Avoid the middle of the floor."

Time machine appears in the same space as me. Boom! No, likelier it'd be jarred aside a few inches. I'd be thrown against the wall. Could break bones, uselessly.

"Well, I c-can talk to somebody who knows the history. We have . . . devices . . . for sending speech through wires, across miles. There's one in the main room."

"And how shall I tell whom you speak with or what you say in your English tongue? Most assuredly, you shall lay no hand on that engine." He doesn't know what a phone looks like, but I couldn't begin to use mine before he realized.

The hostility drops. Earnest: "My lady, I pray you, understand that I bear no ill will. I do what I must. Those are my friends yonder, my country, my Church. Have you the wisdom—the compassion—to accept that? I know you are learned. Do you have any book of your own that may help? Remember, whatever happens, I am going ahead with my sacred mission. You can make the course of it less terrible for those whom you love."

Excitement ebbs away with hope. I feel how tired I am. An ache in every cell of me. Cooperate in this. Maybe afterward he'll let me sleep. What dreams may come couldn't possibly be as bad as my wakefulness.

The encyclopedia. Birthday present from Suzy a couple of years ago, my sister, who's doomed if Spain will have conquered Europe, the Near East, and both the Americas.

Ice-thrill. I remember! I dropped Everard's card in a desk drawer, upper left where I keep miscellany. Phone right above, beside the typewriter.

"Señorita, you tremble."

"Haven't I reason to?" Rise. "Come." The cold wind through me whistles the exhaustion out. "I do have a book or two that have information."

He follows directly behind. His presence is a shadow over me, a shadow with weight.

At the desk, "Hold! What do you want from that drawer!"

I never was a good liar. Can keep my face turned away, and a wobble in my voice is to be expected. "You see how many the volumes are. I must consult my record of them, to locate the chronicle. Watch. No hidden arquebus." Whip it open before he grabs my wrist. Stand passive, let him paw through, satisfy himself. The card skips amongst the clutter. Like my pulse.

"I beg your pardon, my lady. Give me no occasion to suspect you, and I will give you no roughness."

Flip the card right side up. Make that look accidental. Read again: Manson Everard, midtown Manhattan address, the phone number, the phone number. Cram that into my mind. Scratch about. What can I palm off as a sort of library catalogue? Ah, my auto insurance policy. Had it out for a look after that fender-bender months ago—no, last month, April—and haven't—hadn't—gotten around to putting it back in the safe deposit. Make a show of studying it. "Ah, here we are."

Okay, now I know how to call for help. Opportunity to do it is lacking. Stay watchful.

Sidle past the time bike to the bookshelf. Luis treads close against me. *Payn to Polka*. Take it out, page through. He looks across my shoulder. Exclaims when he recognizes *Peru*. He's literate. Not in English, though.

Translate. Early history. Pizarro's journey to Túmbez, the awful hardships, his eventual return to Spain in search of backing, "Yes, yes, I have heard, how often I have heard." To Panama in 1530, Túmbez in 1531, "I was with him."

Fighting. A small detachment makes an epic trek over the mountains. Entry into Cajamarca, capture of the Inca, his ransom. "And then, and then?" Judicial murder of Atahuallpa. "Oh, bad. Well, no doubt my captain decided it was necessary." March to Cuzco. Almagro's expedition to Chile. Pizarro founds Lima. Manco, his puppet Inca, escapes, raises the people against the invaders. Cuzco besieged from early February 1536 till Almagro comes back and relieves it in April 1537; meanwhile, desperate valor on both sides, throughout the country. Right after the hard-won Spanish victory, Indians still waging guerrilla warfare, the Pizarro brothers and Almagro fall out with each other. Pitched battle in 1538, Almagro defeated and executed. His half-caste son and friends embittered; conspire; assassinate Francisco Pizarro in Lima, 26 June 1541. "No! Body of Christ, this shall not happen!" Charles V has sent a new governor, who now takes over, beats the Almagro faction, and beheads the young man. "Horrible, horrible. Christian against Christian. No, it is clear, we require a strong man to take leadership at the earliest moment of misfortune."

Luis draws his sword. What the hell? Alarmed, I drop the volume, back off past the machine toward my desk. He falls on his knees. Lifts the sword by the blade, makes it a cross. Tears run down the leather cheeks, into the midnight beard. "Almighty God, holy Mother of God," sob, "be with your servant."

A chance? No time to think.

Grab the upright vacuum cleaner. Swing it on high. He hears, turns on his knees, crouches to bound up. A heavy, awkward club. Give it everything my arms and shoulders have got. Across the bike, crash the motor end onto his bare head.

He sags. Blood flows like crazy, neon-light red. Lacerated scalp. Have I knocked him out? Don't stop to check. Let the vac clatter down on top of him. Leap to the phone.

Buzz-zz. The number? I'd better have it right. Punch-punch-punch—Luis groans. He hauls himself to all fours. Punch-punch.

Ring.

Ring. Ring. Luis takes hold of a shelf, clambers his way to a stance.

The remembered voice. "Hello. This is Manse Everard's answering machine."

Oh, God, no!

Luis shakes his head, wipes the blood from his eyes. It's smeared, it drips, impossibly much, impossibly brilliant.

"I'm sorry I can't come to the phone. If you wish to leave a message, I'll get back to you soon's may be."

Luis stands slumped, his arms dangle, but he glares at me. "So," he mumbles. "Treachery."

"You may begin talking when you hear the beep. Thank you."

He stoops, takes up his sword, advances. Unevenly, inexorably.

Scream, "Wanda Tamberly. Palo Alto. Time traveler." What's the date, what the hell's the date? "Friday night before Memorial Day. Help!"

The sword point is at my throat. "Drop that thing," he snarls. I do. He's got me backed against the desk. "I should kill you for this. Perhaps I will."

Or forget his scruples about my virtue and—

And at least I left a clue for Everard. Didn't I?

Whoosh. The second machine above the first, its riders flattening themselves below the ceiling.

Luis yells. Scuttles backward, onto the driver's saddle of his. Sword in hand. Other hand dances on the controls. Everard's hampered. I see a gun in his fist. But whoosh. Luis is gone.

Everard sets down.

Whirling, keening, darkening. I never passed out before. If I can just sit for a minute.

23 May 1987

She came in from the hallway wearing a bathrobe over her pajamas. Its snugness brought forth a lithe figure, its blueness the hue of her eyes. Sunlight through the west window made gold of her hair.

She blinked. "Oh, my. Afternoon," she murmured. "How long have I slept?"

Everard had risen from the sofa where he'd sat with one of her books. "About fourteen hours, I guess," he said. "You needed it. Welcome back."

She stared around. There was no timecycle, nor any bloodstains. "After my partner tucked you in bed, she and I fetched supplies and cleaned up the mess as best we could," Everard explained. "She took off. No point in cluttering your place. A guard was necessary, of course, as a precaution. Better check around at your convenience and make sure everything is in order. Wouldn't do for your earlier self to return and find traces of the ruckus. You didn't, after all."

Wanda sighed. "No, never a hint."

"We've got to prevent paradoxes like that. The situation is tangled enough as is." *And dangerous,* Everard thought. *More than deadly dangerous. I should hearten her.* "Hey, I'll bet you're starved."

He liked the way she laughed. "Could eat the proverbial horse with a side of French fries, and apple pie for dessert."

"Well, I took the liberty of laying in some groceries, and could use lunch myself, if you don't mind my joining you."

"Mind? Try not to!"

In the kitchen he urged that she be seated while he put the meal together. "I'm a pretty competent man with a steak and a salad. You've been through the meat grinder. Most people would be in a daze."

"Thanks." She accepted. For a minute, only the sounds of him at work broke the silence. Then, her look steady upon him, she said, "You belong to the Time Guard, don't you?"

"Huh?" He glanced about. "Yes. In English, it's usually the Time Patrol." He paused. "Outsiders aren't supposed to know that time travel goes on. We can't tell them unless authorized, and that's just when circumstances warrant. Clearly they do in this case; you've crashed into the fact. And I have authority to make the decision. I'll level with you, Miss Tamberly."

"Great. How did you find me? When I got your answering machine, I was in despair."

"You're new to the concept. Think. After I'd played your message, what'd you expect me to do but mount an expedition? We hovered outside the window, saw that man threatening you, hopped inside. Unfortunately, I was too crowded to get a shot at him before he vamoosed."

"Why didn't you jump back in time?"

"And save you some unpleasant hours? Sorry. I'll tell you later about the hazards of changing the past."

She frowned. "I know a bit already."

"Hm, I suppose you do. Look, we needn't discuss this till you feel recovered. Take a couple of days and get over the shock."

She lifted her head pridefully. "Thanks, but no need. I'm unhurt, hungry, and eaten alive by curiosity. Concern, too. My uncle—No, really, please, I'd much rather not wait."

"Wow, you're a tough cookie. Okay. Let's start by you telling me your experiences. Take it slow. I'll interrupt you a lot with questions. The Patrol needs to know everything. Needs it more than you're aware."

"And the world is?" She shivered, swallowed, clenched fingers on the tabletop edge, launched into her story. They were halfway through their meal before he had exhausted it of detail.

Starkly, he said, "Yes, this is very bad. Be a lot worse if you hadn't proved so courageous and resourceful, Miss Tamberly."

She flushed. "Please, I'm Wanda."

He forced a smile. "All right, I'm Manse. Spent my boyhood in Middle America of the nineteen-twenties and thirties. The manners they installed have stuck. But if you prefer first names, that's fine by me."

She gave him a long look. "Yes, you would stay a polite country boy, wouldn't you? Roving through history, you'd miss out on the social changes in your homeland."

Intelligent, he thought. *And beautiful, in a strong-boned fashion.*

Anxiety touched her. "What about my uncle?"

He winced. "I'm sorry. The Don told you nothing more than that he left Steve Tamberly on the same continent but in the far past. No location, no date."

"You have—time to search for him."

He shook his head. "I wish we did, but we don't. We could use up thousands of man-years. And we haven't got them. The Patrol's stretched too thin. We're barely enough to carry out our normal missions and try to cope with emergencies like this. Only so many man-years available, you see, because sooner or later every agent is bound to die or be disabled. Here events have gotten out of hand. We'll need every resource we can spare to set matters right—if we can."

"Might Luis go back for him?"

"Maybe. I suspect not. He'll have more important things in mind. Hide out till his injury heals, and then—" Everard stared past her. "A hard, smart, unmerciful, reckless man, loose on a machine. He could appear anywhere, anywhen. The harm he can do is unlimited."

"Uncle Steve—"

"He might be able to help himself. I'm not sure how, but he may hit on a plan, if he survives. He's bright and strong. I see now why you've been his favorite relative."

She dabbed at a tear. "Damn it, I will not bawl! Maybe later—maybe later we'll find a clue. Meanwhile, m-my steak's getting cold." She attacked it as if it were an enemy.

He resumed his own eating. In an odd way, the silence between them changed from strained to companionable. After a while she asked quietly, "How about telling me the whole truth?"

"An outline of it," he agreed. "That alone will take a couple of hours."

—In the end she sat wide-eyed on the sofa while he paced before her, to and fro. His fist hammered his palm. "A Ragnarok situation," he said. "But not hopeless. Wanda, whatever has become or will become of Stephen Tamberly, he did not live in vain. Through Castelar, he passed two names on to you, 'Exaltationists' and 'Machu Picchu.' Not that I imagine Castelar would have done it if you hadn't had the wits—under those conditions, at that—to lead him on, get him to tell what he knew."

"That was very little," she demurred.

"A bomb can be small too, till it explodes. Look, the Exaltationists—I'll tell you more in due course, but briefly, they're a gang of desperados from the rather far future. Outlaws in their milieu; snatched several vehicles and escaped into space-time tracklessness. We've had to cope with results of their doings before now—'before now' in terms of my life, that is—but they've always avoided capture. Well, you've told me they were in Machu Picchu. We know the natives didn't abandon that city entirely till the last resistance to the Spaniards was crushed. So from the descriptions you got out of Castelar, the date the Exaltationists were there must be soon after. That's a sufficient lead for our scouts to locate the scene exactly.

"An agent of ours had 'already' reported outsiders active in the court of the Inca, some years before Pizarro arrived. It seems they tried and failed to head off an apportionment of power that led to civil war and paved the way for that corporal's guard of invaders. In the light of what you've told me, I'm sure they were the Exaltationists, attempting to change history. When it didn't work, they decided they'd at least hijack Atahuallpa's ransom. That'd be disruptive enough, and could well enable them to do still more mischief."

"Why?" she whispered.

"Why, to abort the whole future. Make themselves overlords, first in America, eventually throughout the world. There'd never have been a you or a me, a United States, a Danellian destiny, a Time Patrol . . . unless they organized one of their own to protect the misshapen history they brought into being. Not that I think they could long have stayed in charge. Selfishness like that generally turns on itself. Battles through time, a chaos of changes—I wonder how much flux the space-time fabric could survive."

She whitened, then whistled. "Ye gods, Manse!"

He stopped his prowling, leaned over, touched her below the chin to bring her face upward toward his, and asked with a crooked smile. "How does it feel knowing you may have saved the universe?"

15 April 1610

The spacecraft was black, lest they on Earth see a star pass over them, swift before sunrise or after sunset, and know they were watched. Nevertheless a broad one-way transparency filled it with light. It was orbiting dayside when Everard arrived, and the planet stretched vast, blue swirled with white around the ruddinesses that were continents.

His cycle appeared in the receiver bay and he jumped off without pausing to love the sight as he had done often and often. The gravitor put full weight under his feet. He hastened to the pilot deck. Three agents whom he knew, though centuries sundered their births, awaited him.

"We believe we've acquired the moment," said Umfanduma immediately. "Here's the playback."

Another vessel, of those that between them kept Machu Picchu under surveillance, had taken the data. This was the command ship. Everard had come as soon as messages transmitted through space and relayed through time reached him. The image was from minutes earlier. At ultramagnification after light had crossed atmosphere, it was blurry. Yet when Everard froze its motion and peered closer, he saw metal shine on the head and torso of a man. That one and another were getting to their feet beside a timecycle, on a platform where the view swept from end to end of the great dead city, on to the mountains around. Dark-clad people crowded near.

He nodded. "Got to be," he said. "We don't know just when Castelar will make his break for freedom, but I'd guess it as within the next two or three hours. What we want to do is hit the Exaltationists right afterward."

Not before, because that did not happen. We dare not undermine even this forbidden pattern of events. The enemy dares do anything. That is why we must destroy him.

Umfanduma frowned. "Tricky," she said. "They always keep a machine aloft, well equipped with detectors. I'm sure they're prepared to flee at an instant's notice."

"Uh-huh. However, their scooters are too few to carry them all at once. They'd have to ferry. Or else, likelier, abandon those who aren't so lucky as to be right by the transportation. We won't need many of our own. Let's get organized."

In the span that followed, the ships filled with armed vehicles and their riders. Tight-beamed communications flickered back and forth. Everard developed his plan, gave out his assignments.

Thereafter he must stand by, try to keep his nerves quiet, abide the word. He found it helpful to think about Wanda Tamberly.

"Now!"

He leaped to the saddle. Gunner Tetsuo Motonobu was already in place. Everard's fingers flew over the console.

They hung aloft in enormous azure. A condor wheeled afar. The mountainscape spread beneath, a majestic labyrinth, intensely green save where snow flashed on peaks or gorges plunged shadowful. Machu Picchu was mightiness in stone. What would the civilization that created it have done, had fate allowed it to live?

Again Everard could not pause to wonder. The Exaltationist sentry hovered yards off. He saw the man clearly in thin air and candent sunlight, astounded but fierce, snatching for a sidearm. Motonobu fired his energy gun. Lightning flared, thunder crashed. The man dropped charred from his mount and fell as Lucifer fell. Smoke trailed him. The vehicle wavered out of control.

We'll take care of it later. Down!

Everard didn't overjump the space between. He wanted an overview. As he power-dived, wind roared around an invisible force screen. The buildings swelled in his vision.

His fellow Patrolmen were raking them with fire. Bolts flew hell-colored. When Everard got there, the battle was over.

—Evening yellowed the western sky. Night rose from the valleys to lap ever higher around the walls of Machu Picchu. It had grown chilly and hushed.

Everard left the house he had used for interrogation. Two agents stood outside. "Round up the rest of the squad, bring out the prisoners, prepare to return to base," he said wearily.

"Have you learned something, sir?" asked Motonobu.

Everard shrugged. "Something. The intelligence staff will get more out of them, of course, though I doubt it'll prove of much use. I did find one who's willing to cooperate in return for a promise of comfortable surroundings on the exile planet. Trouble is, he doesn't know what I wish he did."

"Where-when those that got away have gone?"

Everard nodded. "The ringleader, name of Merau Varagan, took a bad sword wound when Castelar fought free. A couple of his men were about to whisk him off to a destination he alone knew to tell them, for medical care. So they were in a position to scram with him when we showed up. Three more managed it too."

He straightened. "Ah," he said, "we succeeded as well as could be looked for. The bulk of the gang are dead or under arrest. The few who escaped must have scattered randomly. They may never find each other. The conspiracy's broken."

Motonobu's tone was wistful. "If only we could have come earlier, arranged a proper trap. We'd have bagged the lot."

"We couldn't because we didn't," said Everard sharply. "We are the law, remember?"

"Yes, sir. What I also remember is that crazy Spaniard and the havoc he may yet make. How're we going to track him down . . . before—it's too late?"

Everard made no reply, but turned toward the esplanade where the vehicles were parked. To the east he saw the Gate of the Sun on its ridge, etched black against heaven.

24 May 1987

Wanda let him in when he knocked on her door. "Hi!" she exclaimed breathlessly. "How are you? How'd things go?"

"They went," he said.

She took both his hands. Her voice softened. "I've been so worried about you, Manse."

That felt almighty good to hear. "Oh, I take care of my hide. The operation, well, we nabbed most of the bandits without loss to ourselves. Machu Picchu is clean once more." *Was clean. Was left in its loneliness for another three centuries. Now tourists halloo everywhere. But a Patrolman shouldn't pass judgments. He needs to be case-hardened, if he's to work in the history of humankind.*

"Marvelous!" Impulsively, she hugged him. He hugged back. They retreated in a slight, shared confusion.

"If you'd come ten minutes ago, you wouldn't've found me," she said. "I couldn't sit and do nothing. Went for a long, long walk."

Dismayed, he snapped, "I told you not to leave this place! You aren't safe. We've planted an instrument here that'll warn of any intruder, but we can't trail around after you. Damnation, girl, Castelar's still at large."

She wrinkled her nose at him. "Better I should climb these walls? Why would he chase after me again?"

"You were his single twentieth-century contact. You could possibly give us a lead to him. Or so he may fear."

She grew serious. "As a matter of fact, I can."

"Huh? What do you mean?"

She tugged his hand. How warm hers was. "C'mon, relax, let me fetch us a beer, and we'll talk. That hike I took cleared my head. I started thinking back, reliving the whole business, except free of terror and, and unfamiliarity. And, yes, I believe I can tell you what point Luis is bound to make for."

He stood where he was. His pulse slugged. "How?"

The blue eyes searched him. "I did get to know the man," she said low. "Not what you'd call intimately, but the relationship sure was intense while it lasted. He isn't a monster. By our standards he's cruel, but he's a son of his era. Ambitious and greedy—and in his heart a knight errant. I searched my memory, minute by minute. Kind of stood outside and watched the two of us. And I saw how he reacted when he learned the Indians would rebel and besiege Francisco Pizarro's brothers in Cuzco, and the troubles that would follow. If he appears as if by miracle and raises the siege, that'll put him straightaway in command of the whole shebang. But over and above any such calculations, Manse, he has got to be there. His honor calls him."

6 February 1536 [Julian calendar]

In the upland dawn, the imperial city burned. Fire arrows and rocks wrapped in blazing oil-soaked cotton flew like meteors. Thatch and wood kindled. Stone walls enclosed furnaces. Flames howled high, sparks showered, smoke roiled thick on the wind. Soot dulled the rivers where they met. Through the noise, conchs lowed, throats shrieked. In their tens of thousands, the Indios seethed around Cuzco. They were a brown tide, out of which tossed chieftainly banners, feather crests, copper-edged axes and spears. They surged against the thin Spanish lines, smote, struggled, recoiled in blood and turmoil, billowed again forward.

Castelar arrived above a citadel that brooded north of the combat. He glimpsed its massiveness filled with natives. For an instant he wanted to swoop down, kill and kill and kill. But no, yonder was where his comrades fought. Sword in right hand, left on the helm board, he rushed through the air to their deliverance.

What matter if he had failed to bring guns from the future? His blade was sharp, his arm strong, and the archangel of war winged over his bare head. Nonetheless he kept wholly alert. Foes might lurk in this sky or snap forth out of nowhere. Let him be ready to jump through time, evade pursuit, return to strike swiftly again and again, as a wolf slashes at an elk.

He swept above a central square, where a great building raged with conflagration. Horsemen trotted down a street. Their steel flashed, their pennons streamed. They were bound on a sally, out into the enemy horde.

Castelar's decision sprang into being. He would veer off, wait a few minutes, let them become engaged, and then smite. With such an avenging eagle on their side, the Spanish would know God had heard him, and hew a road through foemen smitten with panic.

Some saw him pass over. He glimpsed upturned faces, heard cries. There followed a thunder of gallop, a deep-toned "Sant'Iago and at them!"

He crossed the southern bounds of the city, banked, swung about for his onslaught. Now that he knew this machine, how splendidly it responded to him—his horse of the wind, that he would ride into liberated Jerusalem—and at last, at last, into the presence of the Saviour on earth?

Ya-a-a!

Alongside him, another flyer, two men upon it. His fingers stabbed for the controls. Agony seared. "Mother of God, have mercy!" His steed was slain. It toppled through emptiness. At least he would die in battle. Though the forces of Satan had prevailed against him, they would not against the gates of Heaven that stood wide for Christ's soldier.

His soul whirled from him, away into night.

24 May 1987

"The ambush worked almost perfectly," Carlos Navarro reported to Everard. "When we spotted him from space, we activated the electromagnetic generator and jumped to his vicinity. The field it projected induced voltages that caused his machine to give him a severe electric shock. Disabled it, too, scrambled the electronics. But you know this. We gave him a stun shot to make sure and plucked him out of the air before he hit the ground. Meanwhile the cargo carrier appeared, scooped up the crippled vehicle, and made off. Everything was complete in less than two minutes. I suppose a number of men glimpsed us, but it would have been fleetingly, and in the general confusion of battle."

"Good work," said Everard. He leaned back in his shabby old armchair. His New York apartment surrounded them, comfortable with souvenirs—Bronze Age helmet and spears above the bar, polar bear rug from Viking Age Greenland on the floor, stuff such as would not cause outsiders to wonder much but did hold memories for him.

He hadn't gone on the mission. No reason thus to waste an Unattached agent's lifespan. There had been no danger, except that Castelar would be too quick and get away. The electric gimmick prevented that.

"As a matter of fact," he said, "your operation is part of history." He gestured at the volume of Prescott on an end table beside him. "I've been reading that. The Spanish chronicles describe apparitions of the Virgin above the burning hall of Viracocha, where the cathedral was later built, and of Saint James on the battlefield, inspiring the troops. That's generally taken to be a pious legend, or an account of hysterical illusions, but—ah, well. How's the prisoner?"

"When I left him, he was resting under sedation," Navarro replied. "His burns will heal without scars. What will they do with him?"

"That depends on a number of things." Everard took his pipe from the ashtray where he had laid it and coaxed it back to life. "High on the list is Stephen Tamberly. You know about him?"

"Yes." Navarro scowled. "Unfortunately, though unavoidably, the current surge through the vehicle wiped the molecular record of where and when it's traveled. Castelar's gotten a preliminary kyradex quiz—we knew you'd want to know—and doesn't recall the place and date he left Tamberly at, merely that it was thousands of years ago and near the Pacific coast of South America. He knew he could retrieve the exact data if he wanted to, and rather doubted he would. Therefore he didn't bother memorizing the coordinates."

Everard sighed. "I was afraid of that. Poor Wanda."

"Sir?"

"Never mind." Everard consoled himself with smoke. "You may leave. Go out on the town and enjoy yourself."

"Wouldn't you like to come along?" Navarro asked diffidently.

Everard shook his head. "I'll sit tight for a while. It's barely possible that Tamberly found some way to get rescued. If so, he was brought first to one of our bases for debriefing, and inquiry has shown I'm involved in his case, and I'll be informed. Naturally, that couldn't be before we wind up this job otherwise. Maybe I'll get a call soon."

"I see. Thank you. Good-bye."

Navarro departed. Everard settled back down. Dusk seeped into the room, but he didn't turn on the lights. He wanted just to sit thinking, and quietly hoping.

18 August 2930 B.C

Where the river met the sea, the village clustered its houses of clay. Only two dugout canoes lay drawn up on the shore, for fishers were out on this calm day. Most women were likewise gone, cultivating small patches of gourd, squash, potato, and cotton at the edge of the mangrove swamp. Smoke lifted slow from the communal fire that an old person always tended. Other women and aged men had tasks to do in their homes, while small children took care of smaller. Folk wore brief skirts of twisted fiber, ornaments of shell, teeth, feathers. They laughed and chattered.

The Vesselmaker sat cross-legged in the doorway of his dwelling. Today he did not shape pots and bowls or bake them hard. Instead, he stared into space and kept silence. He often did, since he learned the speech of men and began his wondrous labors. It must be respected. He was kindly, but these fits came upon him. Perhaps he planned a beautiful new piece of work, or perhaps he communed with spirits. Certainly he was a special being, with his great height, pale skin and hair and eyes, enormous whiskers. A cape decked him against the sun, which he found harsher than common folk did. Inside the house, his woman ground wild seeds in her mortar. Their two living infants slept.

Shouts arose. The field tillers swarmed into sight. People in the village hurried to see what this meant. The Vesselmaker rose and followed them.

Along the riverbank came a stranger striding. Visitors were frequent, mainly bringing trade goods, but nobody had seen this man before. He looked much like anyone else, though heavier muscled. His garb was noticeably different. Something hard and shiny rested in a sheath on his hip.

Where could he be from? Surely hunters would days ago have noticed a newcomer making his way down the valley. The women squealed when he hailed them. The old men gestured them back and offered seemly greeting.

The Vesselmaker arrived.

For a long while Tamberly and the explorer stood gaze upon gaze. *He's of the local race.* Odd how calm the knowledge was in him, now when at last time had brought him to the goal of his yearnings. *Would be. Best not to raise extra questions, even in the heads of simple Stone Agers. How'd he plan to explain that sidearm?*

The explorer nodded. "I half expected this," he said in slow Temporal. "Do you understand me?"

The language had rusted in Tamberly. However— "I do. Welcome. You're what I've waited for these past . . . seven years, I think."

"I am Guillem Cisneros. Thirtieth-century born, but with the Universarium of Halla." —in a milieu after time travel had been achieved and could therefore be done openly.

"And I, Stephen Tamberly, twentieth century, field historian for the Patrol."

Cisneros laughed. "A handshake is appropriate."

The villagers watched in dumbstruck awe.

"You were marooned here?" Cisneros asked redundantly.

"Yes. The Patrol must be told. Take me to a base."

"Certainly. I hid my vehicle about ten kilometers upstream." Cisneros hesitated. "My object was to pose as a wanderer stay for a time, try to solve an archaeological mystery. I suspect you are the answer to it."

"I am," Tamberly said. "When I realized I was trapped unless help should come, I remembered the Valdivia ware."

The most ancient ceramics known in the western hemisphere, as of his home period. Almost a duplicate of the contemporaneous Jomon pottery in archaic Japan. The conventional explanation was that a fishing boat was blown across the Pacific, and the crew found refuge where they landed and taught the art to the natives. It didn't make much sense. More than eight thousand nautical miles to survive; and those men just happened to possess a set of intricate skills which in their society were the province of women. "So I provided it, and waited for somebody from the future to come looking."

He hadn't entirely violated the law for which the Patrol existed. It was necessarily flexible. Under the circumstances, his return was important.

"You were ingenious," Cisneros said. "How was your life here?"

"They're sweet people," Tamberly answered.

It will hurt, saying farewell to Aruna and the little ones. If I were a saint, I'd never have accepted her father's offer of her to me. Those seven years grew very long, and I didn't know if they would ever end. My family will miss me, but I'll leave them with such mana *that she'll soon get a new husband—a strong provider, probably Ulamamo—and they'll live as well and gladly as any of their tribe. Which in its humble fashion is better than a lot of human beings live much farther up in time.*

He could not quite shed doubts and guilt, and knew he never would, but joy awakened. *I'm going home.*

25 May 1987

Soft light. Fine china, silverware, glass. I don't know if Ernie's is the top restaurant in San Francisco—matter of taste, that—but it's sure in the top ten. Except Manse has said he'd like to take me back to the nineteen-seventies, before the owners of the Mingei-Ya retired.

He raises his sherry. "To the future," he says.

I do the same. "And the past." Clink. Magnificent stuff.

"We can talk now." When he smiles, his face kind of creases and isn't homely at all. "I'm sorry we couldn't earlier, aside from my calling to let you know your uncle's okay and invite you to dinner, but I've been hopping around like a flea on a griddle, tying up loose ends in this case."

Tease him. "Couldn't you have done it and then ducked back several hours to let me off the hook?"

He goes serious. Oh, a lot of unspoken sorrow in his voice. "No. That would have cut things too close. We're allowed our pleasure jaunts in the Patrol, but not when they'd tangle events."

"Aw, Manse, I was kidding." Reach across the linen, pat his hand. "I'm getting a great meal out of this, am I not?" And a slinky dress on me, and my hair brushed just so.

"You've earned it," he says, more relieved than a big tough guy who's rambled from end to end of space-time reality ought to be.

Enough of this, for the time being. Too much to ask. "What about Uncle Steve? You told me how he released himself, but not where he is."

Manse chuckles. "That's hardly relevant, is it? A debriefing center somewhere and somewhen. He'll spend a long furlough with his wife in London before returning to duty. I'm sure he'll visit you and the rest of his kin. Be patient."

"And . . . afterward?"

"Well, we do have to terminate matters in a way that leaves the time structure intact. We'll put Fray Esteban Tanaquil and Don Luis Castelar in that treasure house in Cajamarca, 1533, a minute or two after the Exaltationists bore them away. They'll exit on foot, and that will be that."

Frown. "Uh, you mentioned before that the guards got worried, looked inside, and found nobody. It caused a nasty sensation. Can you change that?"

He beams. "Smart lady! Excellent question. Yes, in such cases, when the past has been deformed, the Patrol does annul the events that flow from it. We restore the 'original' history, so to speak. As nearly as possible, anyhow."

Concern, oddly hurtful. "Luis, though. After what he's been through."

Manse takes a sip, twirls his glass between his fingers, stares into the amber it holds. "We considered inviting him to enroll, but his values are incompatible with ours. He will receive secrecy conditioning. It's harmless in itself, but makes a person unable to reveal anything about time travel. If he tries, and he will, his throat squeezes shut and his tongue locks on him. He'll soon stop trying."

Shake my head. "For him, terrible."

Manse stays calm. He's like a mountain, small shy flowers scattered around, but underneath them, that rock mass. "Would you rather we killed him, or wiped his memories and left him mindless? In spite of the woe he gave us, we bear no grudge."

"He does!"

"Uh-huh. He doesn't attack your uncle in the treasury, because Fray Tanaquil opens the door at once and tells the sentries that he's done. However, it wouldn't be wise keeping Fray Tanaquil around. In the morning he wanders off, as if to take a stroll while he meditates, and nobody sees him again. The soldiers miss him, he was such a nice fellow, and search, and fail, and decide at last that he came to grief in some unknown way. Don Luis tells them he knows nothing." Manse sighs. "We'll have to write off the holography project. Well, maybe someone can go to those objects when they were in their rightful places. We'll plant new agents to monitor the rest of Pizarro's career. Your uncle will get a different assignment. He may well elect to go into administration, as his wife wishes he would."

I take a gently molten swallow from my glass. "What will—what became of Luis?"

He looks at me closely. "You do care about him, don't you?"

Heat in my cheeks. "Not in any, you know, romantic way. I wouldn't have him off the Christmas tree. But he's a person I've *known*."

He smiles afresh. "I see. Well, that's another thing I've been looking into this day. We keep tabs on Don Luis Castelar for the remainder of his life, just in case.

"He adapts fast. Continues as an officer of Pizarro's, distinguishes himself at Cuzco and in the fight against Almagro." With what inward-bitten grimness. "Finally, when the country is divvied up among the conquerors, he becomes a large landowner. By the way, he's one of those few Spaniards who tried to get a reasonably square deal for the Indians. Later, when his wife has died, he takes holy orders and ends as a monk. He's had children by her, whose descendants flourish. Among them is a woman who marries a sea captain from North America. Yes, Wanda, the man you had that runaround with is your ancestor."

Whew!

Recover after a minute. "Time travel indeed." All the ages open to wandering. We ought to study our menus. But.

Be still, my heart, or whatever that foolish phrase is. I lean forward. Somehow I'm not afraid, not when he's looking at me like that. Only, my words stumble, while little cold lightnings run along my backbone. "Wh-wh-what about me, Manse? I know the secret too."

"Ah, yes," he says. How gently. "Typical of you, I think, that first you asked about the others. Well, you have your role to play out. We'll return you to your Galápagos island, dressed in the same clothes as then, a few minutes afterward. You'll rejoin your friends, finish your jaunt, fly from Baltra to that madhouse known as Guayaquil International Airport, and so home to California."

And then? Then?

"What happens next is for you to decide," he goes on. "You can take the conditioning. Not that we don't trust you, but the rule is firm. I repeat, it's painless and does no harm, and since I'm positive you'd never willingly betray us, it should make no noticeable difference. You can proceed with your twentieth-century life. Whenever you and your Uncle Steve get together privately, you'll be able to talk freely with him."

Stiffen the sinews, summon up the blood. "Have I got any other choice?"

"Sure. You can become a time traveler yourself. You'd be a valuable recruit."

Unbelievable. Me? And yet I expected this. And yet. "I, I, I wonder how good a policewoman I'd make."

"Probably not very," I hear across the radiance. "You're too independent. But the Patrol's responsible for prehistoric as well as historic eras. That requires a knowledge of the environment, which requires field scientists. How'd you like to do your paleontology with living animals?"

Okay, okay, I disgrace myself. I jump to my feet and violate the peace of Ernie's with a war-whoop. Manse laughs.

Mammoths and cave bears and dodos, oh, my!